ARISTOPHANES

II

LCL 488

"ARISTOPHANES"

CLOUDS · WASPS
PEACE

EDITED AND TRANSLATED BY

JEFFREY HENDERSON

HARVARD UNIVERSITY PRESS
CAMBRIDGE, MASSACHUSETTS
LONDON, ENGLAND
1998

Library of Congress Cataloging-in-Publication Data

Aristophanes.
[Works.   English & Greek.   1998]
Aristophanes / edited and translated by Jeffrey Henderson.
p.   cm.—(Loeb classical library ; 488)
Includes bibliographical references and index.
ISBN 0-674-99537-6 (v.2)
1. Aristophanes—Translations into English.   2. Greek drama
(Comedy)—Translations into English.   I. Henderson, Jeffrey.
II. Title.   III. Series.
PA3877.A1H46   1998
882'.01—dc21   97-24063

CONTENTS

CLOUDS

INTRODUCTORY NOTE

Clouds was first produced at the Dionysia of 423, placing third and last behind Cratinus' first-place *Wine Flask* (*Pytine*) and Ameipsias' *Connus*. This defeat angered Aristophanes, for in the following year he called *Clouds* his best play and abused the spectators for rejecting it (*Wasps* 1037-47). At some point he began to revise the play for a second production, but for some reason he never completed the revision;[1] internal evidence suggests that he abandoned it sometime between 419 and 416.[2] The revised text was nevertheless put into circulation (at what time is unclear). Although ancient editors had both the original festival version and the incomplete revision at their disposal, only the revision has survived.

Lack of evidence about the first version of *Clouds* makes it impossible to determine how much Aristophanes

---

[1] This is confirmed by the retention of such highly topical passages as the parabatic epirrhemes at 574 ff. and 607 ff. and by signs of incompleteness like the absence of a choral song after line 888.

[2] In particular, lines 551-59 allude to at least three plays attacking Hyperbolus that were produced after Eupolis' *Maricas* (Lenaea 421), and no such play was produced in 420; Hyperbolus was ostracized, never to return to Athens, in 416.

3

altered in the process of revision.[3] Definitely new is the parabasis speech (518-62) discussing the defeat of the original play and hoping for success with the new version. In other respects we must rely mainly on the testimony of an anonymous ancient scholar who wrote, "this play is the same as the first, but has been revised in details, as though the poet wanted to produce it again but for whatever reason did not after all do so. To take the play as a whole, correction, which has occurred in almost every part ‹. . .›. Some parts have been removed, while others have been woven in and altered both in the arrangement and in the alternation of speaking parts. Some parts as they stand belong entirely to the revised version: thus the chorus' parabasis [518–62] has been replaced, and where Better Argument speaks to Worse, and finally where Socrates' school is burned." (Hyp. I Dover)

Clouds explores the growth of untraditional forms of scientific inquiry and of new techniques in the education of young men, particularly rhetorical training, and depicts these as useless, immoral, atheistic, and therefore dangerous to Athens. At the center of the play is the philosopher Socrates, portrayed as the arch-sophist who runs an educational cult located in a "Thinkery," where young men could pay to learn the latest scientific lore and rhetorical skills in order to achieve fame, power, and wealth. The Thinkery houses two Arguments: the Better, an old gentleman who represents traditional customs, beliefs, and virtues, and the Worse, a young dandy who advocates the techniques of unscrupulous self-promotion and the desir-

---

[3] The few remaining fragments of the original play (*PCG* 392-401) are uninformative.

ability of selfish hedonism. Drawn to the Thinkery is the forgetful old rustic Strepsiades, who has run up huge debts as a result of his son Phidippides' passion for horses and who wants to learn how to evade them. When Strepsiades proves unable to learn the new techniques himself, he insists that Phidippides enroll in the Thinkery. Strepsiades' wish comes true in that Phidippides emerges from the Thinkery as a skilled sophist, easily able to evade debts by dishonest arguments. At the same time, however, he has become so arrogant and amoral that he beats Strepsiades and convinces him that it is just to do so. But when he proposes to beat his mother as well, Strepsiades realizes that he has made a terrible mistake and takes vengeance on Socrates by burning the Thinkery to the ground. Above the action float the Chorus of Clouds: in their protean whimsicality they seem appropriate goddesses for Socrates, but they gradually reveal themselves to be a wishing-mirror for people in love with wickedness, luring them to a well-deserved punishment.

Aristophanes' portrait of Socrates as the arch-sophist, atheist, and corrupter of the young is at variance with the portraits later drawn by philosophical writers like Plato and Xenophon; in *Apology,* Plato tries to show the inaccuracy and unfairness of the popular image of Socrates, fueled by comedies like *Clouds,* that played what he considered the decisive role in Socrates' condemnation on capital charges in 399 (*Ap.* 18b-c). In the absence of unbiased information about Socrates, however, we must accept *Clouds* as a valid expression of what public opinion believed, or might be expected to believe, about him in the Athens of 423-*c.* 416.

ARISTOPHANES

Text

Six papyri preserve fragments of *Clouds*.[4] There are
over 130 medieval MSS, which divide into two main fami-
lies, with RV on one side and the later MSS, designated by
the siglum *n*, on the other. In this edition *n* is represented
by EKNΘ; other MSS are cited only for significant read-
ings.[5]

Sigla

Π1	*PBerol.* 13225+13226 (V), lines 177-270, 936-73
Π2	*PBerol.* 13219 (V/VI), lines 946-1015
Π3	*PStrasb.* inv. 621 (V-VII), lines 1372-85, 1407-28
R	Ravennas 429 (*c.* 950)
V	Venetus Marcianus 474 (*c.* 1300)
S	readings found in the Suda
E	Estensis gr. 127 = *a* U.5.10 (XIV-XV in.)
K	Ambrosianus C222 inf. (XIII-XIV)
N	Neapolitanus 184 = II F 27 (XV)
Θ	Laurentianus *conv. soppr.* 140 (XIV)
A	Parisinus Regius 2712 (XIV)
a	the archetype of RV*n*
n	the consensus of EKNΘ

[4] Three of these are not cited in the notes: *POxy.* 1371 (V)
preserves parts of lines 1-11, 38-48; *PLaurent.* 3.318 (IV) of lines
1-7; and *PSI* 1171 (III) of lines 577-635.

[5] See further Dover's *Clouds,* pp. xcix-cxxv, and "Explorations
in the History of the Text of Aristophanes," in *The Greeks and
Their Legacy* (Oxford 1988) 223-65.

6

b	one or more *n* MSS unaffected by Thoman or Triclinian recensions
x	one or more *n* MSS containing Triclinian and later conjectures

Annotated Editions

F. H. M. Blaydes (Halle 1890)
T. Kock (Leipzig 1894^2)
J. van Leeuwen (Leiden 1899)
W. J. M. Starkie (London 1911), with English translation.
B. B. Rogers (London 1916), with English translation.
K. J. Dover (Oxford 1968).
A. H. Sommerstein (Warminster 1982), with English translation.

ΤΑ ΤΟΥ ΔΡΑΜΑΤΟΣ ΠΡΟΣΩΠΑ

ΣΤΡΕΨΙΑΔΗΣ *πατήρ*
ΦΕΙΔΙΠΠΙΔΗΣ *υἱός*
ΟΙΚΕΤΗΣ *Στρεψιάδου*
ΜΑΘΗΤΑΙ *Σωκράτους,*
  δύο
ΣΩΚΡΑΤΗΣ
ΚΡΕΙΤΤΩΝ ΛΟΓΟΣ
ΗΤΤΩΝ ΛΟΓΟΣ
ΧΡΗΣΤΗΣ Α
ΧΡΗΣΤΗΣ Β

ΧΟΡΟΣ Νεφελῶν

ΚΩΦΑ ΠΡΟΣΩΠΑ
ΜΑΘΗΤΑΙ *Σωκράτους*
ΚΛΗΤΗΡ *τοῦ προτέρου*
  χρήστου
ΧΑΝΘΙΑΣ *οἰκέτης*
  Στρεψιάδου
ΟΙΚΕΤΑΙ *Στρεψιάδου*

8

DRAMATIS PERSONAE

STREPSIADES
PHIDIPPIDES, his son
SLAVE of Strepsiades
PUPILS of Socrates, two
SOCRATES
BETTER ARGUMENT
WORSE ARGUMENT
FIRST CREDITOR
SECOND CREDITOR

CHORUS of Clouds

SILENT CHARACTERS
PUPILS of Socrates
WITNESS, with First
   Creditor
XANTHIAS, slave of
   Strepsiades
SLAVES of Strepsiades

ΝΕΦΕΛΑΙ

ΣΤΡΕΨΙΑΔΗΣ

ἰοὺ ἰού.
ὦ Ζεῦ βασιλεῦ, τὸ χρῆμα τῶν νυκτῶν ὅσον.
ἀπέραντον. οὐδέποθ᾽ ἡμέρα γενήσεται;
καὶ μὴν πάλαι γ᾽ ἀλεκτρυόνος ἤκουσ᾽ ἐγώ.
5 οἱ δ᾽ οἰκέται ῥέγκουσιν. ἀλλ᾽ οὐκ ἂν πρὸ τοῦ.
ἀπόλοιο δῆτ᾽, ὦ πόλεμε, πολλῶν οὕνεκα,
ὅτ᾽ οὐδὲ κολάσ᾽ ἔξεστί μοι τοὺς οἰκέτας.[1]
ἀλλ᾽ οὐδ᾽ ὁ χρηστὸς οὑτοσὶ νεανίας
ἐγείρεται τῆς νυκτός, ἀλλὰ πέρδεται
10 ἐν πέντε σισύραις ἐγκεκορδυλημένος.
ἀλλ᾽ εἰ δοκεῖ, ῥέγκωμεν ἐγκεκαλυμμένοι.
ἀλλ᾽ οὐ δύναμαι δείλαιος εὕδειν δακνόμενος
ὑπὸ τῆς δαπάνης καὶ τῆς φάτνης καὶ τῶν χρεῶν
διὰ τουτονὶ τὸν υἱόν. ὁ δὲ κόμην ἔχων
15 ἱππάζεταί τε καὶ ξυνωρικεύεται
ὀνειροπολεῖ θ᾽ ἵππους. ἐγὼ δ᾽ ἀπόλλυμαι
ὁρῶν ἄγουσαν τὴν σελήνην εἰκάδας·[2]

---

[1] For fear they might desert to the enemy.
[2] I.e., more than twenty days (in the month) old.

CLOUDS

The stage building contains two doors. One represents Strepsiades' house and has a statue of Hermes outside; the other represents Socrates' Thinkery and has a large cup outside.

STREPSIADES and PHIDIPPIDES lie sleeping. Strepsiades sits up restlessly.

STREPSIADES

Oh dear, oh dear! Lord Zeus, what a stretch of nighttime! Interminable. Will it never be day? I did hear a cock crow quite a while back, but the slaves are snoring. They wouldn't in the old days. Damn you, War, for my many worries, when I can't even punish my slaves![1] And this fine young man here won't rouse himself before daybreak either, but farts away wrapped up in five woollen coverlets. All right then, let's all get under the covers and snore! No use, I can't get to sleep, poor soul; I'm being eaten alive by my bills and stable fees and debts, on account of this son of mine. He wears his hair long and rides horses and races chariots, and he even dreams about horses, while I go to pieces as I watch the moon in her twenties,[2] because my interest payment looms just ahead. Boy!

Enter SLAVE.

οἱ γὰρ τόκοι χωροῦσιν. ἅπτε παῖ λύχνον
κἄκφερε τὸ γραμματεῖον, ἵν' ἀναγνῶ λαβὼν
20 ὁπόσοις ὀφείλω καὶ λογίσωμαι τοὺς τόκους.
φέρ' ἴδω, τί ὀφείλω; δώδεκα μνᾶς Πασίᾳ.
τοῦ δώδεκα μνᾶς Πασίᾳ; τί ἐχρησάμην;
ὅτ' ἐπριάμην τὸν κοππατίαν. οἴμοι τάλας,
εἴθ' ἐξεκόπην πρότερον τὸν ὀφθαλμὸν λίθῳ.

ΦΕΙΔΙΠΠΙΔΗΣ

25 Φίλων, ἀδικεῖς. ἔλαυνε τὸν σαυτοῦ δρόμον.

ΣΤΡΕΨΙΑΔΗΣ

τοῦτ' ἐστὶ τουτὶ τὸ κακὸν ὅ μ' ἀπολώλεκεν·
ὀνειροπολεῖ γὰρ καὶ καθεύδων ἱππικήν.

ΦΕΙΔΙΠΠΙΔΗΣ

πόσους δρόμους ἐλᾷ τὰ πολεμιστήρια;

ΣΤΡΕΨΙΑΔΗΣ

ἐμὲ μὲν σὺ πολλοὺς τὸν πατέρ' ἐλαύνεις δρόμους.
30 ἀτὰρ τί χρέος ἔβα με μετὰ τὸν Πασίαν;
τρεῖς μναῖ διφρίσκου καὶ τροχοῖν Ἀμυνίᾳ.

ΦΕΙΔΙΠΠΙΔΗΣ

ἄπαγε τὸν ἵππον ἐξαλίσας οἴκαδε.

ΣΤΡΕΨΙΑΔΗΣ

ἀλλ' ὦ μέλ' ἐξήλικας ἐμέ γ' ἐκ τῶν ἐμῶν,
ὅτε καὶ δίκας ὤφληκα χἄτεροι τόκου
ἐνεχυράσεσθαί φασιν.

31 Ἀμυνίᾳ] Ἀμεινίᾳ V fort. recte

Light a lamp, and bring me my ledger book, so I can count
my creditors and reckon the interest. Let's see, what do I
owe? Twelve minas to Pasias.[3] What were the twelve minas
to Pasias for? What did I use it for? When I bought that
branded hack. Oh me oh my! I wish I'd had my eye
knocked out with a stone first.

PHIDIPPIDES

Philon, you're cheating! Drive in your own lane!

STREPSIADES

That's it, that's the bane that's done me in; even in his sleep
he dreams of riding.

PHIDIPPIDES

How many laps will the war chariots be driving?

STREPSIADES

It's a good many laps you're driving me, your father. But
what arrears overtook me after Pasias? Three minas to
Amynias[4] for a small seat and a pair of wheels.

PHIDIPPIDES

Give the horse a good roll and take him home.

STREPSIADES

Actually, dear boy, it's me you've been rolling, right off my
property. Now I'm on the losing side of lawsuits, and others
threaten to have my goods seized in lieu of their interest.

[3] No contemporary with this name is attested.

[4] Probably the son of Pronapes of Prasiae, an envoy to Thessaly in 423/2, criticized for shirking duty (692), pretentiousness, and perhaps for being a Spartan sympathizer, cf. *Wasps* 74 etc., Cratinus 227, Eupolis 222.

ΦΕΙΔΙΠΠΙΔΗΣ

35   ἐτεόν, ὦ πάτερ,
τί δυσκολαίνεις καὶ στρέφει τὴν νύχθ᾽ ὅλην;

ΣΤΡΕΨΙΑΔΗΣ
δάκνει μέ τις δήμαρχος ἐκ τῶν στρωμάτων.

ΦΕΙΔΙΠΠΙΔΗΣ
ἔασον ὦ δαιμόνιε καταδαρθεῖν τί με.

ΣΤΡΕΨΙΑΔΗΣ
σὺ δ᾽ οὖν κάθευδε. τὰ δὲ χρέα ταῦτ᾽ ἴσθ᾽ ὅτι
40 εἰς τὴν κεφαλὴν ἅπαντα τὴν σὴν τρέψεται.
φεῦ. εἴθ᾽ ὤφελ᾽ ἡ προμνήστρι᾽ ἀπολέσθαι κακῶς
ἥτις με γῆμ᾽ ἐπῆρε τὴν σὴν μητέρα.
ἐμοὶ γὰρ ἦν ἄγροικος ἥδιστος βίος,
εὐρωτιῶν, ἀκόρητος, εἰκῇ κείμενος,
45 βρύων μελίτταις καὶ προβάτοις καὶ στεμφύλοις.
ἔπειτ᾽ ἔγημα Μεγακλέους τοῦ Μεγακλέους
ἀδελφιδῆν ἄγροικος ὢν ἐξ ἄστεως,
σεμνήν, τρυφῶσαν, ἐγκεκοισυρωμένην.
ταύτην ὅτ᾽ ἐγάμουν, συγκατεκλινόμην ἐγὼ
50 ὄζων τρυγός, τρασιᾶς, ἐρίων, περιουσίας,
ἡ δ᾽ αὖ μύρου, κρόκου, καταγλωττισμάτων,
δαπάνης, λαφυγμοῦ, Κωλιάδος, Γενετυλλίδος.
οὐ μὴν ἐρῶ γ᾽ ὡς ἀργὸς ἦν, ἀλλ᾽ ἐσπάθα,
ἐγὼ δ᾽ ἂν αὐτῇ θοἰμάτιον δεικνὺς τοδὶ
55 πρόφασιν ἔφασκον· ὦ γύναι, λίαν σπαθᾷς.

ΟΙΚΕΤΗΣ
ἔλαιον ἡμῖν οὐκ ἔνεστ᾽ ἐν τῷ λύχνῳ.

PHIDIPPIDES

(*awakening*) Really, father, why do you grouse and toss all night long?

STREPSIADES

There's a bailiff in the bedclothes biting me.

PHIDIPPIDES

For heaven's sake, let me catch a little sleep.

STREPSIADES

All right then, sleep! But bear in mind, all these debts will end up on your head. Ah, I wish she'd died a terrible death, that matchmaker who talked me into marrying your mother! Mine was a very pleasant country life, moldy, unswept, aimlessly leisured, abounding in honey bees, sheep, and olive cakes. Then I married the niece of Megacles son of Megacles, I a rustic, she from town, haughty, spoiled, thoroughly Coesyrized.[5] When I married her I climbed into bed smelling of new wine, figs, fleeces, and abundance; and she of perfume, saffron, tongue kisses, extravagance, gluttony, Colias and Genetyllis.[6] But still, I won't say she was lazy; she used plenty of thread when she wove. I used to show her this cloak of mine as proof and say, "Woman, you go too heavy on the thread!"

SLAVE

We've got no oil in the lamp.

[5] Megacles and his exotic mother, Coisyra, typified the aristocracy.

[6] Colias was the name of an Attic promontory where women held festivals for Aphrodite and the Genetyllides, goddesses of procreation.

ΣΤΡΕΨΙΑΔΗΣ

οἴμοι. τί γάρ μοι τὸν πότην ἧπτες λύχνον;
δεῦρ᾽ ἔλθ᾽ ἵνα κλάῃς.

ΟΙΚΕΤΗΣ
διὰ τί δῆτα κλαύσομαι;

ΣΤΡΕΨΙΑΔΗΣ
ὅτι τῶν παχειῶν ἐνετίθεις θρυαλλίδων.
60 μετὰ ταῦθ᾽, ὅπως νῷν ἐγένεθ᾽ υἱὸς οὑτοσί,
ἐμοί τε δὴ καὶ τῇ γυναικὶ τἀγαθῇ,
περὶ τοὐνόματος δὴ ᾽ντεῦθεν ἐλοιδορούμεθα.
ἡ μὲν γὰρ ἵππον προσετίθει πρὸς τοὔνομα,
Ξάνθιππον ἢ Χαίριππον ἢ Καλλιππίδην,
65 ἐγὼ δὲ τοῦ πάππου ᾽τιθέμην Φειδωνίδην.
τέως μὲν οὖν ἐκρινόμεθ᾽· εἶτα τῷ χρόνῳ
κοινῇ ξυνέβημεν κἀθέμεθα Φειδιππίδην.
τοῦτον τὸν υἱὸν λαμβάνουσ᾽ ἐκορίζετο·
"ὅταν σὺ μέγας ὢν ἅρμ᾽ ἐλαύνῃς πρὸς πόλιν,
70 ὥσπερ Μεγακλέης, ξυστίδ᾽ ἔχων—" ἐγὼ δ᾽ ἔφην·
"ὅταν μὲν οὖν τὰς αἶγας ἐκ τοῦ φελλέως,
ὥσπερ ὁ πατήρ σου, διφθέραν ἐνημμένος—".
ἀλλ᾽ οὐκ ἐπείθετο τοῖς ἐμοῖς οὐδὲν λόγοις,
ἀλλ᾽ ἵππερόν μου κατέχεεν τῶν χρημάτων.
75 νῦν οὖν ὅλην τὴν νύκτα φροντίζων ὁδοῦ
μίαν ηὗρον ἀτραπὸν δαιμονίως ὑπερφυᾶ,
ἣν ἢν ἀναπείσω τουτονί, σωθήσομαι.
ἀλλ᾽ ἐξεγεῖραι πρῶτον αὐτὸν βούλομαι.

64 Χαίριππον V: Χάριππον n: Κάλλιπον R

STREPSIADES

Damn it, why did you light me the thirsty lamp? Come here and take your beating.

SLAVE

Why should I get a beating, then?

STREPSIADES

Because you put in one of the thick wicks!

The SLAVE runs inside.

After that, when this son was born to us, I mean to me and my high-class wife, we started to bicker over his name. She was for adding *hippos* to the name,[7] Xanthippus or Chaerippus or Callippides, while I was for calling him Phidonides after his grandfather.[8] So for a while we argued, until finally we compromised and called him Phidippides. She used to pick up this boy and coo at him, "When you're grown you'll drive a chariot to the Acropolis,[9] like Megacles, and don a saffron robe." And I would say, "No, you'll drive the goats from the Rocky Bottom, like your father, and wear a leather jacket." But he wouldn't listen to anything I said; instead he's infected my estate with the galloping trots. So now I've spent the whole night thinking of a way out, and I've found a singular shortcut, devilishly marvellous. If I can talk this boy into it, I'll be saved. But first I need to wake him up. Now how might I

[7] Because *hippos* (horse) would sound aristocratic and because she wanted her son to become a horseman.

[8] The grandfather's name was Phidon (cf. 134), which means "thrifty."

[9] That is, in the Panathenaic procession.

πῶς δῆτ᾽ ἂν ἥδιστ᾽ αὐτὸν ἐπεγείραιμι; πῶς;
Φειδιππίδη, Φειδιππίδιον.

ΦΕΙΔΙΠΠΙΔΗΣ

80 τί, ὦ πάτερ;

ΣΤΡΕΨΙΑΔΗΣ

κύσον με καὶ τὴν χεῖρα δὸς τὴν δεξιάν.

ΦΕΙΔΙΠΠΙΔΗΣ

ἰδού. τί ἐστιν;

ΣΤΡΕΨΙΑΔΗΣ

εἰπέ μοι, φιλεῖς ἐμέ;

ΦΕΙΔΙΠΠΙΔΗΣ

νὴ τὸν Ποσειδῶ τουτονὶ τὸν ἵππιον.

ΣΤΡΕΨΙΑΔΗΣ

μή μοι γε τοῦτον μηδαμῶς τὸν ἵππιον·
85 οὗτος γὰρ ὁ θεὸς αἴτιός μοι τῶν κακῶν.
ἀλλ᾽ εἴπερ ἐκ τῆς καρδίας μ᾽ ὄντως φιλεῖς,
ὦ παῖ, πιθοῦ.

ΦΕΙΔΙΠΠΙΔΗΣ

τί οὖν πίθωμαι δῆτά σοι;

ΣΤΡΕΨΙΑΔΗΣ

ἔκτρεψον ὡς τάχιστα τοὺς σαυτοῦ τρόπους
καὶ μάνθαν᾽ ἐλθὼν ἂν ἐγὼ παραινέσω.

ΦΕΙΔΙΠΠΙΔΗΣ

λέγε δή, τί κελεύεις;

get him up in the nicest way? Hmm. Phidippides! Phidippidarling!

PHIDIPPIDES

What, father?

STREPSIADES

Kiss me and give me your right hand.

PHIDIPPIDES

There. What's up?

STREPSIADES

Tell me, do you love me?

PHIDIPPIDES

Yes, by Poseidon here, the Lord of Horses.

STREPSIADES

Don't give me any of your Lord of Horses! That god's responsible for my troubles. But if you really love me with all your heart, my son, do as I say.

PHIDIPPIDES

Do what as you say?

STREPSIADES

Reverse your way of life as soon as possible, and go learn what I'm going to recommend.

PHIDIPPIDES

All right, tell me what you're asking me to learn.

ΣΤΡΕΨΙΑΔΗΣ
καί τι πείσει;

ΦΕΙΔΙΠΠΙΔΗΣ

90   πείσομαι,
νὴ τὸν Διόνυσον.

ΣΤΡΕΨΙΑΔΗΣ
δεῦρό νυν ἀπόβλεπε.
ὁρᾷς τὸ θύριον τοῦτο καὶ τοἰκίδιον;

ΦΕΙΔΙΠΠΙΔΗΣ
ὁρῶ. τί οὖν τοῦτ᾽ ἐστὶν ἐτεόν, ὦ πάτερ;

ΣΤΡΕΨΙΑΔΗΣ
ψυχῶν σοφῶν τοῦτ᾽ ἐστὶ φροντιστήριον.
95 ἐνταῦθ᾽ ἐνοικοῦσ᾽ ἄνδρες οἳ τὸν οὐρανὸν
λέγοντες ἀναπείθουσιν ὡς ἔστιν πνιγεύς,
κἄστιν περὶ ἡμᾶς οὗτος, ἡμεῖς δ᾽ ἄνθρακες.
οὗτοι διδάσκουσ᾽, ἀργύριον ἤν τις διδῷ,
λέγοντα νικᾶν καὶ δίκαια κἄδικα.

ΦΕΙΔΙΠΠΙΔΗΣ
εἰσὶν δὲ τίνες;

ΣΤΡΕΨΙΑΔΗΣ
100   οὐκ οἶδ᾽ ἀκριβῶς τοὔνομα.
μεριμνοφροντισταὶ καλοί τε κἀγαθοί.

ΦΕΙΔΙΠΠΙΔΗΣ
αἰβοῖ, πονηροί γ᾽, οἶδα. τοὺς ἀλαζόνας,
τοὺς ὠχριῶντας, τοὺς ἀνυποδήτους λέγεις,
ὧν ὁ κακοδαίμων Σωκράτης καὶ Χαιρεφῶν.

20

STREPSIADES

And you will obey?

PHIDIPPIDES

I will obey, by Dionysus.

STREPSIADES

All right, look over there. Do you see that little door and that little house?

PHIDIPPIDES

I see it. So, what exactly is it, father?

STREPSIADES

That is a Thinkery for sage souls. Some gentlemen live there who argue convincingly that the sky is a barbeque lid, and that it surrounds us, and that we're the coals. These people train you, if you give them money, to win any argument whether it's right or wrong.

PHIDIPPIDES

And who are they?

STREPSIADES

I don't know the term exactly. Thoughtful cogitators, fine and genteel people.

PHIDIPPIDES

Yuk! That scum. I know them: you mean the charlatans, the pasty-faced, the unshod, like that miserable Socrates, and Chaerephon.[10]

---

[10] Chaerephon, ridiculed in comedy for his thin, sallow appearance, was the long-time friend of Socrates who, according to Plato's *Apology,* asked the Delphic oracle whether anyone was wiser than Socrates.

ΣΤΡΕΨΙΑΔΗΣ

105 ἦ ἤ, σιώπα. μηδὲν εἴπῃς νήπιον.
ἀλλ' εἴ τι κήδει τῶν πατρῴων ἀλφίτων,
τούτων γενοῦ μοι, σχασάμενος τὴν ἱππικήν.

ΦΕΙΔΙΠΠΙΔΗΣ

οὐκ ἂν μὰ τὸν Διόνυσον εἰ δοίης γέ μοι
τοὺς φασιανοὺς οὓς τρέφει Λεωγόρας.

ΣΤΡΕΨΙΑΔΗΣ

110 ἴθ', ἀντιβολῶ σ', ὦ φίλτατ' ἀνθρώπων ἐμοί,
ἐλθὼν διδάσκου.

ΦΕΙΔΙΠΠΙΔΗΣ

καὶ τί σοι μαθήσομαι;

ΣΤΡΕΨΙΑΔΗΣ

εἶναι παρ' αὐτοῖς φασὶν ἄμφω τὼ λόγω,
τὸν κρείττον', ὅστις ἐστί, καὶ τὸν ἥττονα.
τούτοιν τὸν ἕτερον τοῖν λόγοιν, τὸν ἥττονα,
115 νικᾶν λέγοντά φασι τἀδικώτερα.
ἢν οὖν μάθῃς μοι τὸν ἄδικον τοῦτον λόγον,
ἃ νῦν ὀφείλω διὰ σέ, τούτων τῶν χρεῶν
οὐκ ἂν ἀποδοίην οὐδ' ἂν ὀβολὸν οὐδενί.

ΦΕΙΔΙΠΠΙΔΗΣ

οὐκ ἂν πιθοίμην· οὐ γὰρ ἂν τλαίην ἰδεῖν
120 τοὺς ἱππέας τὸ χρῶμα διακεκναισμένος.

ΣΤΡΕΨΙΑΔΗΣ

οὐκ ἄρα μὰ τὴν Δήμητρα τῶν γ' ἐμῶν ἔδει
οὔτ' αὐτὸς οὔθ' ὁ ζύγιος οὔθ' ὁ σαμφόρας,

STREPSIADES

Hey, hey! Be quiet, don't say anything so childish! Now, if you care at all about your father's daily bread, cut out the riding and please become one of them.

PHIDIPPIDES

No way, by Dionysus, not even if you gave me those fancy pheasants that Leogoras[11] breeds.

STREPSIADES

Come on, I'm begging you, dearest of all to me, go and be trained.

PHIDIPPIDES

And what am I supposed to learn?

STREPSIADES

I'm told they have both Arguments there, the Better, whatever that may be, and the Worse. And one of these Arguments, the Worse, I'm told, can plead the unjust side of a case and win. So, if you learn this Unjust Argument for me, then I wouldn't have to pay anyone even a penny of these debts that I now owe on your account.

PHIDIPPIDES

I won't do it: I wouldn't dare face the Knights with all the tan scraped off me.

STREPSIADES

Then, by Demeter, you'll be eating none of my food, you or your yoke horse or your branded nag. I'll throw you the

[11] Father of the orator Andocides, wealthy and aristocratic, later denounced, though not prosecuted, in the scandal of the herms and mysteries in 415.

ἀλλ' ἐξελῶ σ' εἰς κόρακας ἐκ τῆς οἰκίας.

ΦΕΙΔΙΠΠΙΔΗΣ

ἀλλ' οὐ περιόψεταί μ' ὁ θεῖος Μεγακλέης
125 ἄνιππον. ἀλλ' εἴσειμι, σοῦ δ' οὐ φροντιῶ.

ΣΤΡΕΨΙΑΔΗΣ

ἀλλ' οὐδ' ἐγὼ μέντοι πεσών γε κείσομαι,
ἀλλ' εὐξάμενος τοῖσιν θεοῖς διδάξομαι
αὐτὸς βαδίζων εἰς τὸ φροντιστήριον.
πῶς οὖν γέρων ὢν κἀπιλήσμων καὶ βραδὺς
130 λόγων ἀκριβῶν σκινδαλάμους μαθήσομαι;
ἰτητέον. τί ταῦτ' ἔχων στραγγεύομαι
ἀλλ' οὐχὶ κόπτω τὴν θύραν; παῖ, παιδίον.

ΜΑΘΗΤΗΣ

βάλλ' εἰς κόρακας. τίς ἐσθ' ὁ κόψας τὴν θύραν;

ΣΤΡΕΨΙΑΔΗΣ

Φείδωνος υἱὸς Στρεψιάδης Κικυννόθεν.

ΜΑΘΗΤΗΣ

135 ἀμαθής γε νὴ Δί', ὅστις οὑτωσὶ σφόδρα
ἀπεριμερίμνως τὴν θύραν λελάκτικας
καὶ φροντίδ' ἐξήμβλωκας ἐξηυρημένην.

ΣΤΡΕΨΙΑΔΗΣ

σύγγνωθί μοι· τηλοῦ γὰρ οἰκῶ τῶν ἀγρῶν.
ἀλλ' εἰπέ μοι τὸ πρᾶγμα τοὐξημβλωμένον.

ΜΑΘΗΤΗΣ

140 ἀλλ' οὐ θέμις πλὴν τοῖς μαθηταῖσιν λέγειν.

hell out of the house!

PHIDIPPIDES

Well, my uncle Megacles won't stand by and see me go horseless. I'm going inside and paying you no mind!

PHIDIPPIDES goes into the house.

STREPSIADES

And I won't take this fall lying down; I'll say a prayer to the gods and go to the Thinkery to be trained myself. But then again, how is an old man like me, forgetful and dense, to learn the hairsplitting of precise arguments? I've got to go. Why do I keep hanging back like this? Why not just knock on the door? Boy, boyo!

PUPIL

(*within*) Buzz off to blazes! (*opening the door*) Who's been pounding on the door?

STREPSIADES

Strepsiades, son of Phidon, from Cicynna.[12]

PUPIL

A dunce, damn it, the way you kick at the door so very inconsiderately, and abort a newfound idea.

STREPSIADES

Forgive me; I live way out in the country. But tell me about the matter that's been aborted.

PUPIL

It's sacrilege to tell anyone but the pupils.

---

[12] A small, rural, and seldom attested deme.

ΣΤΡΕΨΙΑΔΗΣ

λέγε νυν ἐμοὶ θαρρῶν· ἐγὼ γὰρ οὑτοσὶ
ἥκω μαθητὴς εἰς τὸ φροντιστήριον.

ΜΑΘΗΤΗΣ

λέξω, νομίσαι δὲ ταῦτα χρὴ μυστήρια.
ἀνήρετ᾽ ἄρτι Χαιρεφῶντα Σωκράτης
145 ψύλλαν ὁπόσους ἅλλοιτο τοὺς αὑτῆς πόδας.
δακοῦσα γὰρ τοῦ Χαιρεφῶντος τὴν ὀφρῦν
ἐπὶ τὴν κεφαλὴν τὴν Σωκράτους ἀφήλατο.

ΣΤΡΕΨΙΑΔΗΣ

πῶς δῆτα διεμέτρησε;

ΜΑΘΗΤΗΣ

δεξιώτατα.
κηρὸν διατήξας, εἶτα τὴν ψύλλαν λαβὼν
150 ἐνέβαψεν εἰς τὸν κηρὸν αὐτῆς τὼ πόδε,
κᾆτα ψυχείσῃ περιέφυσαν Περσικαί.
ταύτας ὑπολύσας ἀνεμέτρει τὸ χωρίον.

ΣΤΡΕΨΙΑΔΗΣ

ὦ Ζεῦ βασιλεῦ, τῆς λεπτότητος τῶν φρενῶν.

ΜΑΘΗΤΗΣ

τί δῆτ᾽ ἄν, ἕτερον εἰ πύθοιο Σωκράτους
φρόντισμα;

ΣΤΡΕΨΙΑΔΗΣ

155 ποῖον; ἀντιβολῶ, κάτειπέ μοι.

ΜΑΘΗΤΗΣ

ἀνήρετ᾽ αὐτὸν Χαιρεφῶν ὁ Σφήττιος

STREPSIADES

Well, don't worry about telling *me:* I've come to the Thinkery to be a pupil myself.

PUPIL

I'll tell you, but you've got to consider these matters holy secrets.[13] Just now Socrates asked Chaerephon how many of its own feet a flea can jump, because one had bitten Chaerephon's eyebrow and jumped off onto Socrates' head.

STREPSIADES

And how did he measure it off?

PUPIL

Very cleverly. He melted some wax, then picked up the flea and dipped both its feet in the wax, and then when the wax cooled the flea had Persian slippers stuck to it. He took these off and went about measuring the distance.

STREPSIADES

Lord Zeus, what subtlety of mind!

PUPIL

Then I wonder what you'd say if you heard another idea Socrates had?

STREPSIADES

What idea? Do tell me.

PUPIL

Chaerephon of Sphettus[14] asked him where he stood in

---

[13] Aristophanes intends to portray the Thinkery as a private mystery cult with novel gods (252 n.).

[14] Chaerephon's deme is not attested elsewhere, and Sphettus may simply be a pun on *sphex* "wasp."

27

ὁπότερα τὴν γνώμην ἔχοι, τὰς ἐμπίδας
κατὰ τὸ στόμ᾽ ᾄδειν ἢ κατὰ τοὐρροπύγιον.

ΣΤΡΕΨΙΑΔΗΣ
τί δῆτ᾽ ἐκεῖνος εἶπε περὶ τῆς ἐμπίδος;

ΜΑΘΗΤΗΣ
160 ἔφασκεν εἶναι τοὔντερον τῆς ἐμπίδος
στενόν, διὰ λεπτοῦ δ᾽ ὄντος αὐτοῦ τὴν πνοὴν
βίᾳ βαδίζειν εὐθὺ τοὐρροπυγίου·
ἔπειτα κοῖλον πρὸς στενῷ προσκείμενον
τὸν πρωκτὸν ἠχεῖν ὑπὸ βίας τοῦ πνεύματος.

ΣΤΡΕΨΙΑΔΗΣ
165 σάλπιγξ ὁ πρωκτός ἐστιν ἄρα τῶν ἐμπίδων.
ὦ τρισμακάριος τοῦ διεντερεύματος.
ἦ ῥᾳδίως φεύγων ἂν ἀποφύγοι δίκην
ὅστις δίοιδε τοὔντερον τῆς ἐμπίδος.

ΜΑΘΗΤΗΣ
πρῴην δέ γε γνώμην μεγάλην ἀφῃρέθη
ὑπ᾽ ἀσκαλαβώτου.

ΣΤΡΕΨΙΑΔΗΣ
170   τίνα τρόπον; κάτειπέ μοι.

ΜΑΘΗΤΗΣ
ζητοῦντος αὐτοῦ τῆς σελήνης τὰς ὁδοὺς
καὶ τὰς περιφοράς, εἶτ᾽ ἄνω κεχηνότος
ἀπὸ τῆς ὀροφῆς νύκτωρ γαλεώτης κατέχεσεν.

ΣΤΡΕΨΙΑΔΗΣ
ἤσθην γαλεώτῃ καταχέσαντι Σωκράτους.

28

regard to the question, whether gnats hum via the mouth
or via the rump.

STREPSIADES

So what did Socrates say about the gnat?

PUPIL

He said that the gnat's gut is narrow, and that the air travels
violently through this small space on its way to the rump,
and then the arsehole, being an orifice attached to a narrow
tube, resounds from the force of the wind.

STREPSIADES

So the gnat's arsehole turns out to be a bugle. Thrice happy
man, for such penetrating enterology! As a defendant he'd
certainly be able to escape conviction, since he knows the
gnat's gut inside out.

PUPIL

Yes, and just recently he had a great idea snatched away by
a lizard.

STREPSIADES

How was that? Tell me.

PUPIL

He was investigating the moon's paths and revolutions, and
as he was looking upwards with his mouth open, from the
roof in darkness a gecko shat on him.

STREPSIADES

I like that, a gecko shitting on Socrates!

ΜΑΘΗΤΗΣ

175 ἐχθὲς δέ γ᾽ ἡμῖν δεῖπνον οὐκ ἦν ἑσπέρας.

ΣΤΡΕΨΙΑΔΗΣ

εἶέν. τί οὖν πρὸς τἄλφιτ᾽ ἐπαλαμήσατο;

ΜΑΘΗΤΗΣ

κατὰ τῆς τραπέζης καταπάσας λεπτὴν τέφραν,
κάμψας ὀβελίσκον, εἶτα διαβήτην λαβὼν
ἐκ τῆς παλαίστρας θοἰμάτιον ὑφείλετο.

ΣΤΡΕΨΙΑΔΗΣ

180 τί δῆτ᾽ ἐκεῖνον τὸν Θαλῆν θαυμάζομεν;
ἄνοιγ᾽ ἄνοιγ᾽ ἀνύσας τὸ φροντιστήριον
καὶ δεῖξον ὡς τάχιστά μοι τὸν Σωκράτη.
μαθητιῶ γάρ. ἀλλ᾽ ἄνοιγε τὴν θύραν.
ὦ Ἡράκλεις, ταυτὶ ποδαπὰ τὰ θηρία;

ΜΑΘΗΤΗΣ

185 τί ἐθαύμασας; τῷ σοι δοκοῦσιν εἰκέναι;

ΣΤΡΕΨΙΑΔΗΣ

τοῖς ἐκ Πύλου ληφθεῖσι, τοῖς Λακωνικοῖς.
ἀτὰρ τί ποτ᾽ εἰς τὴν γῆν βλέπουσιν οὑτοί;

ΜΑΘΗΤΗΣ

ζητοῦσιν οὗτοι τὰ κατὰ γῆς.

---

15 At first Socrates seems to have been performing a scientific demonstration, but then turns out to have robbed a passive homosexual of his clothing; the joke turns on the double meaning of *diabetes* "compass" and "one who spreads his legs."

PUPIL

Yes, and last night we had no dinner to eat.

STREPSIADES

Aha. So how did he finagle your eats?

PUPIL

Over the table he sprinkled a fine layer of ash and bent a skewer, then he picked up a faggot from the wrestling school and swiped his jacket.[15]

STREPSIADES

Then why do we marvel at the great Thales?[16] Hurry and open up the Thinkery, and show me this Socrates as soon as possible. I yearn to learn! Come on, open up the door!

The eccyclema is rolled out, revealing other Pupils and an assortment of devices.

Heracles, what sort of critters are these?

PUPIL

Why are you taken aback? What do they look like to you?

STREPSIADES

Like the Spartan prisoners from Pylos.[17] But those there, why on earth are they peering at the ground?

PUPIL

They're investigating what's beneath the ground.

[16] The early sixth-century founder of the Milesian school of philosophy.

[17] 292 Spartan soldiers captured in the late summer of 425 and imprisoned at Athens since then (Thucydides 4.38-41).

ΣΤΡΕΨΙΑΔΗΣ

βολβοὺς ἄρα

ζητοῦσι. μή νυν τουτό γ᾽ ἔτι φροντίζετε·
190 ἐγὼ γὰρ οἶδ᾽ ἵν᾽ εἰσὶ μεγάλοι καὶ καλοί.
τί γὰρ οἴδε δρῶσιν οἱ σφόδρ᾽ ἐγκεκυφότες;

ΜΑΘΗΤΗΣ

οὗτοι δ᾽ ἐρεβοδιφῶσιν ὑπὸ τὸν Τάρταρον.

ΣΤΡΕΨΙΑΔΗΣ

τί δῆθ᾽ ὁ πρωκτὸς εἰς τὸν οὐρανὸν βλέπει;

ΜΑΘΗΤΗΣ

αὐτὸς καθ᾽ αὑτὸν ἀστρονομεῖν διδάσκεται.
195 ἀλλ᾽ εἴσιθ᾽, ἵνα μὴ ᾽κεῖνος ὑμῖν ἐπιτύχῃ.

ΣΤΡΕΨΙΑΔΗΣ

μήπω γε μήπω γ᾽, ἀλλ᾽ ἐπιμεινάντων, ἵνα
αὐτοῖσι κοινώσω τι πραγμάτιον ἐμόν.

ΜΑΘΗΤΗΣ

ἀλλ᾽ οὐχ οἷόν τ᾽ αὐτοῖσι πρὸς τὸν ἀέρα
ἔξω διατρίβειν πολὺν ἄγαν ἐστὶν χρόνον.

ΣΤΡΕΨΙΑΔΗΣ

200 πρὸς τῶν θεῶν, τί γὰρ τάδ᾽ ἐστίν; εἰπέ μοι.

ΜΑΘΗΤΗΣ

ἀστρονομία μὲν αὑτηί.

ΣΤΡΕΨΙΑΔΗΣ

τουτὶ δὲ τί;

195 ὑμῖν Σ^R: ἡμῖν a

32

STREPSIADES

Oh, it's bulbs they're trying to find! *(to the other pupils)*
You can stop worrying about that; I know where there are
nice big ones. *(to Pupil)* And these here, what are they
doing all bent over?

PUPIL

They're scrutinizing the murkiness below Tartarus.

STREPSIADES

Then why the arsehole peering at the sky?

PUPIL

Learning astronomy on its own. *(to the Pupils)* Well, inside
with you; he mustn't find you out here.

STREPSIADES

Not yet, not yet! Let them stay awhile; I want to share with
them a small problem of my own.

PUPIL

No, they're not at liberty to spend very much time outside
in the open air.

The other Pupils go inside.

STREPSIADES

(pointing at the instruments) What in god's name are these,
then? Tell me.

PUPIL

This one here is for astronomy.

STREPSIADES

And this one?

ΜΑΘΗΤΗΣ

γεωμετρία.

ΣΤΡΕΨΙΑΔΗΣ

τοῦτ' οὖν τί ἐστι χρήσιμον;

ΜΑΘΗΤΗΣ

γῆν ἀναμετρεῖσθαι.

ΣΤΡΕΨΙΑΔΗΣ

πότερα τὴν κληρουχικήν;

ΜΑΘΗΤΗΣ

οὔκ, ἀλλὰ τὴν σύμπασαν.

ΣΤΡΕΨΙΑΔΗΣ

ἀστεῖον λέγεις·

205 τὸ γὰρ σόφισμα δημοτικὸν καὶ χρήσιμον.

ΜΑΘΗΤΗΣ

αὕτη δέ σοι γῆς περίοδος πάσης. ὁρᾷς;
αἵδε μὲν Ἀθῆναι.

ΣΤΡΕΨΙΑΔΗΣ

τί σὺ λέγεις; οὐ πείθομαι,
ἐπεὶ δικαστὰς οὐχ ὁρῶ καθημένους.

ΜΑΘΗΤΗΣ

ὡς τοῦτ' ἀληθῶς Ἀττικὸν τὸ χωρίον.

ΣΤΡΕΨΙΑΔΗΣ

210 καὶ ποῦ Κικυννῆς εἰσίν, οὑμοὶ δημόται;

ΜΑΘΗΤΗΣ

ἐνταῦθ' ἔνεισιν. ἡ δέ γ' Εὔβοι', ὡς ὁρᾷς,
ἡδὶ παρατέταται μακρὰ πόρρω πάνυ.

PUPIL

Geometry.

STREPSIADES

So what's that good for?

PUPIL

For measuring land.

STREPSIADES

You mean land for settlers?

PUPIL

No, land in general.

STREPSIADES

Talk about sophisticated! That device is democratic, and useful too.

PUPIL

And look, this is a map of the entire world. See? That's Athens right here.

STREPSIADES

What do you mean? I don't believe it; I don't see any juries in session.

PUPIL

Anyway, this really is the territory of Attica.

STREPSIADES

Then where are the Cicynnians, my fellow demesmen?

PUPIL

They're over here. And Euboea, as you can see, is laid out here, over a very long stretch.

ΣΤΡΕΨΙΑΔΗΣ

οἶδ᾿· ὑπὸ γὰρ ἡμῶν παρετάθη καὶ Περικλέους.
ἀλλ᾿ ἡ Λακεδαίμων ποῦ ᾿στίν;

ΜΑΘΗΤΗΣ

ὅπου ᾿στίν; αὑτηί.

ΣΤΡΕΨΙΑΔΗΣ

215 ὡς ἐγγὺς ἡμῶν. τοῦτο μεταφροντίζετε,
ταύτην ἀφ᾿ ἡμῶν ἀπαγαγεῖν πόρρω πάνυ.

ΜΑΘΗΤΗΣ

ἀλλ᾿ οὐχ οἷόν τε.

ΣΤΡΕΨΙΑΔΗΣ

νὴ Δί᾿, οἰμώξεσθ᾿ ἄρα.
φέρε τίς γὰρ οὗτος οὑπὶ τῆς κρεμάθρας ἀνήρ;

ΜΑΘΗΤΗΣ

αὐτός.

ΣΤΡΕΨΙΑΔΗΣ

τίς αὐτός;

ΜΑΘΗΤΗΣ

Σωκράτης.

ΣΤΡΕΨΙΑΔΗΣ

ὦ Σωκράτης.

220 ἴθ᾿ οὗτος ἀναβόησον αὐτόν μοι μέγα.

215 μεταφροντίζετε Bentley: μέγα φροντίζετε S: πάνυ
φροντίζετε a

STREPSIADES

I know; we laid it out ourselves, with Pericles.[18] But where's Sparta?

PUPIL

Let me see; right here.

STREPSIADES

So close to us! Do change your minds and move it very far away from us.

PUPIL

That's impossible.

STREPSIADES

By Zeus, you'll be sorry if you don't!

SOCRATES appears overhead, suspended in a basket.

Hey, who's that man in the basket?[19]

PUPIL

Himself.

STREPSIADES

Whose self?

PUPIL

Socrates.

STREPSIADES

Ah, Socrates! Come on, you, call up to him for me, loudly!

[18] Pericles had invaded Euboea to suppress a revolt in 446 (Thucydides 1.114).

[19] In Plato's *Apology* 19b Socrates recalls this image as having contributed to popular prejudice against him.

ARISTOPHANES

ΜΑΘΗΤΗΣ

αὐτὸς μὲν οὖν σὺ κάλεσον· οὐ γάρ μοι σχολή.

ΣΤΡΕΨΙΑΔΗΣ

ὦ Σώκρατες.
ὦ Σωκρατίδιον.

ΣΩΚΡΑΤΗΣ

τί με καλεῖς, ὦ 'φήμερε;

ΣΤΡΕΨΙΑΔΗΣ

πρῶτον μὲν ὅτι δρᾷς, ἀντιβολῶ, κάτειπέ μοι.

ΣΩΚΡΑΤΗΣ

225 ἀεροβατῶ καὶ περιφρονῶ τὸν ἥλιον.

ΣΤΡΕΨΙΑΔΗΣ

ἔπειτ' ἀπὸ ταρροῦ τοὺς θεοὺς ὑπερφρονεῖς,
ἀλλ' οὐκ ἀπὸ τῆς γῆς, εἴπερ;

ΣΩΚΡΑΤΗΣ

οὐ γὰρ ἄν ποτε
ἐξηῦρον ὀρθῶς τὰ μετέωρα πράγματα
εἰ μὴ κρεμάσας τὸ νόημα καὶ τὴν φροντίδα,
230 λεπτὴν καταμείξας εἰς τὸν ὅμοιον ἀέρα.
εἰ δ' ὢν χαμαὶ τἄνω κάτωθεν ἐσκόπουν,
οὐκ ἄν ποθ' ηὗρον· οὐ γὰρ ἀλλ' ἡ γῆ βίᾳ
ἕλκει πρὸς αὑτὴν τὴν ἰκμάδα τῆς φροντίδος.
πάσχει δὲ ταὐτὸ τοῦτο καὶ τὰ κάρδαμα.

ΣΤΡΕΨΙΑΔΗΣ

235 πῶς φής;
ἡ φροντὶς ἕλκει τὴν ἰκμάδ' εἰς τὰ κάρδαμα;

PUPIL

No, you call him yourself; I haven't got the time.

Exit PUPIL.

STREPSIADES

Oh Socrates! Socratikins!

SOCRATES

Why do you summon me, o creature of a day?

STREPSIADES

Well, first of all tell me, please, what you're up to.

SOCRATES

I tread the air and scrutinize the sun.

STREPSIADES

So you look down on the gods from a basket? Why not do it from the ground, if that's what you're doing?

SOCRATES

Why, for accurate discoveries about meteorological phenomena I had to suspend my mind, to commingle my rarefied thought with its kindred air. If I had been on the ground and from down there contemplated what's up here, I would have made no discoveries at all: the earth, you see, simply must forcibly draw to itself the moisture of thought. The very same thing happens to watercress.

STREPSIADES

How's that? The mind draws moisture into watercress?

---

226 ὑπερφρ-] περιφρ- V
235 πῶς Π1: τί a

39

ἴθι νυν κατάβηθ', ὦ Σωκρατίδιον, ὡς ἐμέ,
ἵνα με διδάξῃς ὧνπερ ἕνεκ' ἐλήλυθα.

ΣΩΚΡΑΤΗΣ

ἦλθες δὲ κατὰ τί;

ΣΤΡΕΨΙΑΔΗΣ

βουλόμενος μαθεῖν λέγειν·
240 ὑπὸ γὰρ τόκων χρήστων τε δυσκολωτάτων
ἄγομαι, φέρομαι, τὰ χρήματ' ἐνεχυράζομαι.

ΣΩΚΡΑΤΗΣ

πόθεν δ' ὑπόχρεως σαυτὸν ἔλαθες γενόμενος;

ΣΤΡΕΨΙΑΔΗΣ

νόσος μ' ἐπέτριψεν ἱππική, δεινὴ φαγεῖν.
ἀλλά με δίδαξον τὸν ἕτερον τοῖν σοῖν λόγοιν,
245 τὸν μηδὲν ἀποδιδόντα. μισθὸν δ' ὅντιν' ἂν
πράττῃ μ', ὀμοῦμαί σοι καταθήσειν τοὺς θεούς.

ΣΩΚΡΑΤΗΣ

ποίους θεοὺς ὀμεῖ σύ; πρῶτον γὰρ θεοὶ
ἡμῖν νόμισμ' οὐκ ἔστι.

ΣΤΡΕΨΙΑΔΗΣ

τῷ γὰρ ὄμνυτε;
σιδαρέοισιν, ὥσπερ ἐν Βυζαντίῳ;

ΣΩΚΡΑΤΗΣ

250 βούλει τὰ θεῖα πράγματ' εἰδέναι σαφῶς
ἅττ' ἐστὶν ὀρθῶς;

ΣΤΡΕΨΙΑΔΗΣ

νὴ Δί', εἴπερ ἐστί γε.

Come down here to me, Socratikins, so you can teach me
what I've come to learn.

SOCRATES

(*descending to the ground*) And why have you come?

STREPSIADES

Anxious to learn public speaking. You see, I'm being har-
ried and plundered by debts and cantankerous creditors,
and having my property foreclosed.

SOCRATES

And how did you become indebted without noticing it?

STREPSIADES

A galloping consumption has destroyed me with its terrible
voracity. Now: teach me one of your two Arguments, the
one that repays no debts. Whatever fee you may charge,
I'll swear to you by the gods to pay in cash.

SOCRATES

What do you mean, you'll swear by the gods? First of all,
gods aren't legal tender here.

STREPSIADES

So, what do you swear by? Iron coins, as in Byzantium?

SOCRATES

Would you like to know the truth about matters divine,
what they really are?

STREPSIADES

I certainly would, if it's actually possible.

ΣΩΚΡΑΤΗΣ

καὶ συγγενέσθαι ταῖς Νεφέλαισιν εἰς λόγους,
ταῖς ἡμετέραισι δαίμοσιν;

ΣΤΡΕΨΙΑΔΗΣ

μάλιστά γε.

ΣΩΚΡΑΤΗΣ

κάθιζε τοίνυν ἐπὶ τὸν ἱερὸν σκίμποδα.

ΣΤΡΕΨΙΑΔΗΣ

ἰδού, κάθημαι.

ΣΩΚΡΑΤΗΣ

255   τουτονὶ τοίνυν λαβὲ
τὸν στέφανον.

ΣΤΡΕΨΙΑΔΗΣ

ἐπὶ τί στέφανον; οἴμοι, Σώκρατες,
ὥσπερ με τὸν Ἀθάμανθ᾽ ὅπως μὴ θύσετε.

ΣΩΚΡΑΤΗΣ

οὔκ, ἀλλὰ ταῦτα πάντα τοὺς τελουμένους
ἡμεῖς ποιοῦμεν.

ΣΤΡΕΨΙΑΔΗΣ

εἶτα δὴ τί κερδανῶ;

ΣΩΚΡΑΤΗΣ

260   λέγειν γενήσει τρῖμμα, κρόταλον, παιπάλη.
ἀλλ᾽ ἔχ᾽ ἀτρεμεί.

258 ταῦτα πάντα RVNΘ: πάντα ταῦτα EK: πάντας ταῦτα
Reiske

CLOUDS

SOCRATES
And to have converse with the Clouds, our own deities?[20]

STREPSIADES
Yes, very much.

SOCRATES
Then sit down upon the sacred sofa.

STREPSIADES
All right, I'm sitting.

SOCRATES
Now take hold of this, the wreath.

STREPSIADES
What's the wreath for? Dear me, Socrates, mind you don't sacrifice me, like Athamas![21]

SOCRATES
I won't. All this is our procedure for initiands.

STREPSIADES
And what's in it for me?

SOCRATES
At speaking you'll become a smoothie, a castanet, the flower of orators. Now don't move. (*Socrates sprinkles flour on Strepsiades*)

[20] Lines 252-274 parody the initiation rites and prayers characteristic of private mystery cults, e.g. those of the Orphics and Pythagoreans.

[21] In Sophocles' lost play *Athamas* the hero sits, wreathed, on Zeus' altar, about to be sacrificed for wronging his wife Nephele ("cloud").

ARISTOPHANES

ΣΤΡΕΨΙΑΔΗΣ

μὰ τὸν Δί' οὐ ψεύσει γέ με·
καταπαττόμενος γὰρ παιπάλη γενήσομαι;

ΣΩΚΡΑΤΗΣ

εὐφημεῖν χρὴ τὸν πρεσβύτην καὶ τῆς εὐχῆς ἐπακού-
ειν.

ὦ δέσποτ' ἄναξ, ἀμέτρητ' Ἀήρ, ὃς ἔχεις τὴν γῆν
μετέωρον,

265 λαμπρός τ' Αἰθήρ, σεμναί τε θεαὶ Νεφέλαι βροντη-
σικέραυνοι,

ἄρθητε, φάνητ', ὦ δέσποιναι, τῷ φροντιστῇ μετέωροι.

ΣΤΡΕΨΙΑΔΗΣ

μήπω, μήπω γε, πρὶν ἂν τουτὶ πτύξωμαι, μὴ κατα-
βρεχθῶ.

τὸ δὲ μηδὲ κυνῆν οἴκοθεν ἐλθεῖν ἐμὲ τὸν κακοδαί-
μον' ἔχοντα.

ΣΩΚΡΑΤΗΣ

ἔλθετε δῆτ', ὦ πολυτίμητοι Νεφέλαι, τῷδ' εἰς ἐπίδει-
ξιν·

270 εἴτ' ἐπ' Ὀλύμπου κορυφαῖς ἱεραῖς χιονοβλήτοισι
κάθησθε,

εἴτ' Ὠκεανοῦ πατρὸς ἐν κήποις ἱερὸν χορὸν ἵστατε
Νύμφαις,

εἴτ' ἄρα Νείλου προχοαῖς ὑδάτων χρυσέαις ἀρύ-
τεσθε πρόχοισιν,

ἢ Μαιῶτιν λίμνην ἔχετ' ἢ σκόπελον νιφόεντα
Μίμαντος·

44

CLOUDS

STREPSIADES

By Zeus, you won't trick me! You mean getting dredged is how I'll become flour?

SOCRATES

The old man must keep silence and listen to the prayer. O Lord and Master, measureless Air, who hold the earth aloft, and you, shining Empyrean, and ye Clouds, awesome goddesses of thunder and lightning, arise, appear aloft, o Mistresses, to the thinker!

STREPSIADES

(*covering himself with his cloak*) Not yet, not until I get this over me, so I don't get soaked. To think I left home, poor fool, without even a cap!

SOCRATES

Come then, illustrious Clouds, in an exhibition for this man, whether you now sit on Olympus' holy snow-struck peaks, or start up a holy dance for the Nymphs in father Ocean's gardens, or whether again at the Nile's mouths you scoop its waters in golden pitchers, or inhabit Lake Maeotis or the snowy steeps of Mimas: hear my prayer,

ὑπακούσατε δεξάμεναι θυσίαν καὶ τοῖς ἱεροῖσι
    χαρεῖσαι.

(στρ) ἀέναοι Νεφέλαι,
    ἀρθῶμεν φανεραὶ δροσερὰν φύσιν εὐάγητον
    πατρὸς ἀπ' Ὠκεανοῦ βαρυαχέος
        ὑψηλῶν ὀρέων κορυφὰς ἔπι
280   δενδροκόμους, ἵνα
    τηλεφανεῖς σκοπιὰς ἀφορώμεθα
    καρπούς τ' ἀρδομέναν ἱερὰν χθόνα
    καὶ ποταμῶν ζαθέων κελαδήματα
    καὶ πόντον κελάδοντα βαρύβρομον·
285   ὄμμα γὰρ αἰθέρος ἀκάματον σελαγεῖται
    μαρμαρέαισιν αὐγαῖς.
    ἀλλ' ἀποσεισάμεναι νέφος ὄμβριον
    ἀθανάτας ἰδέας ἐπιδώμεθα
290   τηλεσκόπῳ ὄμματι γαῖαν.

ὦ μέγα σεμναὶ Νεφέλαι, φανερῶς ἠκούσατέ μου
    καλέσαντος.
ἤσθου φωνῆς ἅμα καὶ βροντῆς μυκησαμένης
    θεοσέπτου;

καὶ σέβομαί γ', ὦ πολυτίμητοι, καὶ βούλομαι ἀντ-
    αποπαρδεῖν
πρὸς τὰς βροντάς· οὕτως αὐτὰς τετραμαίνω καὶ πε-
    φόβημαι.

CLOUDS

accept my sacrifice and enjoy these holy rites.

CHORUS

(*from afar*)

> Clouds everlasting,
> let us arise, revealing our dewy bright form,
> from deep roaring father Ocean
> onto high mountain peaks
> with tresses of trees, whence
> to behold heights of distant vantage,
> and holy earth whose crops we water,
> and divine rivers' rushing,
> and the sea crashing with deep thunder.
> For heaven's tireless eye is ablaze
> with gleaming rays.
> So let us shake off the rainy haze
> from our deathless shape and survey
> the land, with telescopic eye.

SOCRATES

Most stately Clouds, you have clearly heard my summons.
(*to Strepsiades*) Did you mark their voice and, in concert,
the bellowing thunder that prompts holy reverence?

STREPSIADES

I do revere you, illustrious ones, and I'm ready to answer
those thunderclaps with a fart; that's how much I fear and

295 κεἰ θέμις ἐστίν, νυνί γ' ἤδη, κεἰ μὴ θέμις ἐστί, χε-
σείω.

ΣΩΚΡΑΤΗΣ

οὐ μὴ σκώψει μηδὲ ποιήσεις ἅπερ οἱ τρυγο-
δαίμονες οὗτοι,
ἀλλ' εὐφήμει· μέγα γάρ τι θεῶν κινεῖται σμῆνος
ἀοιδαῖς.

ΧΟΡΟΣ

(ἀντ) παρθένοι ὀμβροφόροι,
300 ἔλθωμεν λιπαρὰν χθόνα Παλλάδος, εὔανδρον γᾶν
Κέκροπος ὀψόμεναι πολυήρατον·
οὗ σέβας ἀρρήτων ἱερῶν, ἵνα
μυστοδόκος δόμος
ἐν τελεταῖς ἁγίαις ἀναδείκνυται·
305 οὐρανίοις τε θεοῖς δωρήματα,
ναοί θ' ὑψερεφεῖς καὶ ἀγάλματα,
καὶ πρόσοδοι μακάρων ἱερώταται
εὐστέφανοί τε θεῶν θυσίαι θαλίαι τε
310 παντοδαπαῖσιν ὥραις,
ἦρί τ' ἐπερχομένῳ Βρομία χάρις
εὐκελάδων τε χορῶν ἐρεθίσματα
καὶ μοῦσα βαρύβρομος αὐλῶν.

ΣΤΡΕΨΙΑΔΗΣ

πρὸς τοῦ Διός, ἀντιβολῶ σε, φράσον, τίνες εἰσ', ὦ
Σώκρατες, αὗται
315 αἱ φθεγξάμεναι τοῦτο τὸ σεμνόν; μῶν ἡρῷναί τινές
εἰσιν;

tremble at them. And right now, if it's sanctioned, and even if it isn't, I need to shit!

SOCRATES

Don't be scurrilous and act like those hapless comedians! Now keep silence, for a great swarm of gods is on the move, in song.

CHORUS

(*closer*)

Rainbearing maidens,
let us visit the gleaming land of Pallas, to see the
    ravishing country
of Cecrops with its fine men,
where ineffable rites are celebrated, where
the temple that receives initiates
is thrown open during the pure mystic festival;[22]
and where there are offerings to the heavenly host,
temples with lofty roofs and statues,
most holy processions for the Blessed Ones,
well-garlanded victims for the gods, and feasts
in all seasons;
and with spring comes the grace of Bromius,[23]
the rivalry of melodious choruses
and the deep toned music of pipes.

STREPSIADES

By Zeus, I beg you, tell me who they are, Socrates, these females who intoned that awesome song? They're not lady heroes of some sort, are they?

---

[22] The Eleusinian Mysteries.
[23] "The Noisy," a poetic title for Dionysus; the festival envisioned here is the City Dionysia with its dramas.

ΣΩΚΡΑΤΗΣ

ἥκιστ', ἀλλ' οὐράνιαι Νεφέλαι, μεγάλαι θεαὶ ἀνδρά-
σιν ἀργοῖς,
αἵπερ γνώμην καὶ διάλεξιν καὶ νοῦν ἡμῖν παρέχου-
σιν
καὶ τερατείαν καὶ περίλεξιν καὶ κροῦσιν καὶ κατά-
ληψιν.

ΣΤΡΕΨΙΑΔΗΣ

ταῦτ' ἄρ' ἀκούσασ' αὐτῶν τὸ φθέγμ' ἡ ψυχή μου
πεπότηται
320 καὶ λεπτολογεῖν ἤδη ζητεῖ καὶ περὶ καπνοῦ στενο-
λεσχεῖν
καὶ γνωμιδίῳ γνώμην νύξασ' ἑτέρῳ λόγῳ ἀντι-
λογῆσαι·
ὥστ' εἴ πως ἐστίν, ἰδεῖν αὐτὰς ἤδη φανερῶς ἐπι-
θυμῶ.

ΣΩΚΡΑΤΗΣ

βλέπε νυν δευρὶ πρὸς τὴν Πάρνηθ'· ἤδη γὰρ ὁρῶ
κατιούσας
ἡσυχῇ αὐτάς.

ΣΤΡΕΨΙΑΔΗΣ

φέρε ποῦ; δεῖξον.

ΣΩΚΡΑΤΗΣ

χωροῦσ' αὗται πάνυ πολλαὶ
διὰ τῶν κοίλων καὶ τῶν δασέων, αὗται πλάγιαι.

SOCRATES

Not at all; they're heavenly Clouds, great goddesses for idle gentlemen, who provide us with judgment and dialectic and intelligence, fantasy and circumlocution and verbal thrust and parry.

STREPSIADES

So that's why my soul has taken flight at the sound of their voice, and now seeks to split hairs, prattle narrowly about smoke, and meet argument with counterargument, puncturing a point with a pointlet. So if at all possible, I want to see them now in person.

SOCRATES

Then look over here, toward Mount Parnes, because now I see them quietly descending.

STREPSIADES

Where? Come on, show me!

The CHORUS *files along the wings toward the orchestra.*

SOCRATES

They're on the march, quite a lot of them, through the hollows and thickets—there, to the side.

ΣΤΡΕΨΙΑΔΗΣ

325   τί τὸ χρῆμα;
ὡς οὐ καθορῶ.

ΣΩΚΡΑΤΗΣ
παρὰ τὴν εἴσοδον.

ΣΤΡΕΨΙΑΔΗΣ
        ἤδη νυνὶ μόλις οὕτως.

ΣΩΚΡΑΤΗΣ
νῦν γέ τοι ἤδη καθορᾷς αὐτάς, εἰ μὴ λημᾷς
κολοκύνταις.

ΣΤΡΕΨΙΑΔΗΣ
νὴ Δί᾽ ἔγωγ᾽. ὦ πολυτίμητοι· πάντα γὰρ ἤδη
κατέχουσιν.

ΣΩΚΡΑΤΗΣ
ταύτας μέντοι σὺ θεὰς οὔσας οὐκ ᾔδησθ᾽ οὐδ᾽
ἐνόμιζες;

ΣΤΡΕΨΙΑΔΗΣ
330 μὰ Δί᾽, ἀλλ᾽ ὁμίχλην καὶ δρόσον αὐτὰς ἡγούμην
καὶ καπνὸν εἶναι.

ΣΩΚΡΑΤΗΣ
οὐ γὰρ μὰ Δί᾽ οἶσθ᾽ ὁτιὴ πλείστους αὗται βόσκουσι
σοφιστάς,
Θουριομάντεις, ἰατροτέχνας, σφραγιδονυχαργοκο-
μήτας·
κυκλίων τε χορῶν ᾀσματοκάμπτας, ἄνδρας μετεωρο-
φένακας,

STREPSIADES

What's going on? I don't see them.

SOCRATES

In the wings!

STREPSIADES

Yes, now I can almost see them.

SOCRATES

By now you must see them, unless you've got styes like pumpkins!

STREPSIADES

Yes, now I see them. Heaven be praised, they're permeating everything!

SOCRATES

And you didn't realize that they're goddesses, or believe it?

STREPSIADES

God no; I thought they were mist and dew and smoke.

SOCRATES

You didn't because you're unaware that they nourish a great many sophists, diviners from Thurii,[24] medical experts, long-haired idlers with onyx signet rings, and tune bending composers of dithyrambic choruses, men of highflown pretension, whom they maintain as do-nothings,

---

[24] The Athenian colony in southern Italy founded in 444/3. Aristophanes probably alludes to the seer Lampon, appointed by Pericles to conduct the official foundation ceremonies and still a prominent figure at Athens (Thucydides 5.19, 24).

---

326 παρὰ] πρὸς VE^{pc}N
329 ἤδησθ' Hirschig: ἤδεις a

οὐδὲν δρῶντας βόσκουσ᾽ ἀργούς, ὅτι ταύτας μουσο-
ποιοῦσιν.

ΣΤΡΕΨΙΑΔΗΣ

335 ταῦτ᾽ ἄρ᾽ ἐποίουν "ὑγρᾶν Νεφελᾶν στρεπταίγλαν
δάϊον ὁρμάν",
"πλοκάμους θ᾽ ἑκατογκεφάλα Τυφῶ", "πρημαινού-
σας τε θυέλλας",
εἶτ᾽ "ἀερίας διεράς", "γαμψούς τ᾽ οἰωνοὺς ἀερονηχεῖς",
"ὄμβρους θ᾽ ὑδάτων δροσερᾶν νεφελᾶν"· εἶτ᾽ ἀντ᾽
αὐτῶν κατέπινον
κεστρᾶν τεμάχη μεγαλᾶν ἀγαθᾶν κρέα τ᾽ ὀρνίθεια
κιχηλᾶν.

ΣΩΚΡΑΤΗΣ

διὰ μέντοι τάσδ᾽. οὐχὶ δικαίως;

ΣΤΡΕΨΙΑΔΗΣ

340   λέξον δή μοι, τί παθοῦσαι,
εἴπερ νεφέλαι γ᾽ εἰσὶν ἀληθῶς, θνηταῖς εἴξασι γυ-
ναιξίν;
οὐ γὰρ ἐκεῖναί γ᾽ εἰσὶ τοιαῦται.

ΣΩΚΡΑΤΗΣ

                         φέρε, ποῖαι γάρ τινές εἰσιν;

ΣΤΡΕΨΙΑΔΗΣ

οὐκ οἶδα σαφῶς· εἴξασιν δ᾽ οὖν ἐρίοισιν πεπταμέ-
νοισιν,
κοὐχὶ γυναιξίν, μὰ Δί᾽, οὐδ᾽ ὁτιοῦν· αὗται δὲ ῥῖνας
ἔχουσιν.

because they compose music about these Clouds.[25]

STREPSIADES

So that's why they compose verses like "dire downdraft of humid clouds zigzaggedly braceleted," and "locks of hundred-headed Typhus," and "blasting squalls," and then "airy scudders crooked of talon, birds swimming on high," and "rain of waters from dewy clouds." Then, as their reward, they get to gulp down nice big mullet fillets and avian thrush cutlets![26]

SOCRATES

Certainly, thanks to these Clouds. Isn't that fair?

STREPSIADES

So tell me, if these really are Clouds, how is it that they look like mortal women? (*pointing skyward*) Because those clouds aren't like that.

SOCRATES

Well, what do they look like?

STREPSIADES

I don't know exactly, but they look like fleeces spread out, not like women, no, surely not in any way. And these Clouds have noses!

---

[25] Comic poets ridiculed dithyrambists for verbosity and for overworking metaphors from flight; cf. *Peace* 828 ff., *Birds* 1372 ff.

[26] I.e., at the banquet provided by the producer of a dithyrambic chorus.

ΣΩΚΡΑΤΗΣ

ἀπόκριναί νυν ἅττ᾽ ἂν ἔρωμαι.

ΣΤΡΕΨΙΑΔΗΣ

345   λέγε νυν ταχέως ὅτι βούλει.

ΣΩΚΡΑΤΗΣ

ἤδη ποτ᾽ ἀναβλέψας εἶδες νεφέλην κενταύρῳ ὁμοίαν
ἢ παρδάλει ἢ λύκῳ ἢ ταύρῳ;

ΣΤΡΕΨΙΑΔΗΣ

νὴ Δί᾽ ἔγωγ᾽. εἶτα τί τοῦτο;

ΣΩΚΡΑΤΗΣ

γίγνονται πάνθ᾽ ὅτι βούλονται· κᾆτ᾽ ἢν μὲν ἴδωσι
    κομήτην
ἄγριόν τινα τῶν λασίων τούτων, οἱόνπερ τὸν Ξενο-
    φάντου,
350 σκώπτουσαι τὴν μανίαν αὐτοῦ κενταύροις ἤκασαν
    αὐτάς.

ΣΤΡΕΨΙΑΔΗΣ

τί γὰρ ἢν ἅρπαγα τῶν δημοσίων κατίδωσι Σίμωνα,
τί δρῶσιν;

ΣΩΚΡΑΤΗΣ

ἀποφαίνουσαι τὴν φύσιν αὐτοῦ λύκοι ἐξαίφνης
ἐγένοντο.

ΣΤΡΕΨΙΑΔΗΣ

ταῦτ᾽ ἄρα, ταῦτα Κλεώνυμον αὗται τὸν ῥίψασπιν
χθὲς ἰδοῦσαι,

CLOUDS

SOCRATES

Now answer some questions for me.

STREPSIADES

Ask away, whatever you like.

SOCRATES

Have you ever looked up and seen a cloud resembling a centaur, or a leopard, or a wolf, or a bull?

STREPSIADES

Certainly I have. So what?

SOCRATES

Clouds turn into anything they want. Thus, if they see a savage with long hair, one of these furry types, like the son of Xenophantus,[27] they mock his obsession by making themselves look like centaurs.

STREPSIADES

And what if they look down and see a predator of public funds like Simon,[28] what do they do?

SOCRATES

To expose his nature they immediately turn into wolves.

STREPSIADES

That must be why, when the other day they caught sight of

[27] Identified in the scholia as Hieronymus, a tragic and dithyrambic poet. His "obsession" would be pederasty.

[28] Called an embezzler also by Eupolis (fr. 235), and a perjurer at 399 below.

ὅτι δειλότατον τοῦτον ἑώρων, ἔλαφοι διὰ τοῦτ᾽
ἐγένοντο.

ΣΩΚΡΑΤΗΣ

355 καὶ νῦν γ᾽ ὅτι Κλεισθένη εἶδον, ὁρᾷς, διὰ τοῦτ᾽
ἐγένοντο γυναῖκες.

ΣΤΡΕΨΙΑΔΗΣ

χαίρετε τοίνυν, ὦ δέσποιναι· καὶ νῦν, εἴπερ τινὶ κἄλλῳ,
οὐρανομήκη ῥήξατε κἀμοὶ φωνήν, ὦ παμβασίλειαι.

ΔΚΟΡΤΦΑΙΑ

χαῖρ᾽, ὦ πρεσβῦτα παλαιογενές, θηρατὰ λόγων
φιλομούσων.
σύ τε, λεπτοτάτων λήρων ἱερεῦ, φράζε πρὸς ἡμᾶς
ὅτι χρῄζεις·

360 οὐ γὰρ ἂν ἄλλῳ γ᾽ ὑπακούσαιμεν τῶν νῦν μετεωρο-
σοφιστῶν
πλὴν ἢ Προδίκῳ, τῷ μὲν σοφίας καὶ γνώμης
οὕνεκα, σοὶ δὲ
ὅτι βρενθύει τ᾽ ἐν ταῖσιν ὁδοῖς καὶ τὠφθαλμὼ
παραβάλλεις
κἀνυπόδητος κακὰ πόλλ᾽ ἀνέχει κἀφ᾽ ἡμῖν σεμνο-
προσωπεῖς.

ΣΤΡΕΨΙΑΔΗΣ

ὦ Γῆ, τοῦ φθέγματος, ὡς ἱερὸν καὶ σεμνὸν καὶ
τερατῶδες.

ΣΩΚΡΑΤΗΣ

365 αὗται γάρ τοι μόναι εἰσὶ θεαί, τἄλλα δὲ πάντ᾽ ἐστὶ
φλύαρος.

Cleonymus the shield thrower, they knew him for a great coward, and turned into deer!

SOCRATES

And today, because they've seen Cleisthenes—see him?—that's why they've turned into women![29]

STREPSIADES

Then hail, Mistresses! And now, almighty Queens, if you've ever so favored another man, break forth for me too a sound that spans the sky!

CHORUS LEADER

Hail, oldster born long ago, stalker of erudite arguments, and you too, priest of subtlest hogwash, tell us what you desire; for we would pay no attention to any other contemporary sophist of celestial studies except for Prodicus,[30] for his wisdom and intelligence, and you, because you strut like a popinjay through the streets and cast your eyes sideways and, unshod, endure many woes and wear a haughty expression for our sake.

STREPSIADES

Mother Earth, what a voice! How holy and august and marvelous!

SOCRATES

That's because they are the only true goddesses; all the rest are rubbish.

[29] Cleonymus was an obese politician who probably lost his shield in the Athenian retreat at Delium the previous year (Thucydides 4.96). Cleisthenes was a beardless man frequently ridiculed for effeminacy.

[30] Prodicus of Ceos, a contemporary of Socrates, pursued interests ranging from natural science to semantics and ethics, and enjoyed a reputation comparable to Einstein's today.

ΣΤΡΕΨΙΑΔΗΣ

ὁ Ζεὺς δ᾽ ὑμῖν, φέρε, πρὸς τῆς Γῆς, Οὐλύμπιος οὐ
θεός ἐστιν;

ΣΩΚΡΑΤΗΣ

ποῖος Ζεύς; οὐ μὴ ληρήσεις. οὐδ᾽ ἐστὶ Ζεύς.

ΣΤΡΕΨΙΑΔΗΣ

τί λέγεις σύ;
ἀλλὰ τίς ὕει; τουτὶ γὰρ ἔμοιγ᾽ ἀπόφηναι πρῶτον
ἁπάντων.

ΣΩΚΡΑΤΗΣ

αὗται δήπου· μεγάλοις δέ σ᾽ ἐγὼ σημείοις αὐτὸ
διδάξω.
370 φέρε, ποῦ γὰρ πώποτ᾽ ἄνευ νεφελῶν ὕοντ᾽ ἤδη τε-
θέασαι;
καίτοι χρῆν αἰθρίας ὕειν αὐτόν, ταύτας δ᾽
ἀποδημεῖν.

ΣΤΡΕΨΙΑΔΗΣ

νὴ τὸν Ἀπόλλω, τοῦτό γέ τοι τῷ νυνὶ λόγῳ εὖ
προσέφυσας.
καίτοι πρότερον τὸν Δί᾽ ἀληθῶς ᾤμην διὰ κοσκίνου
οὐρεῖν.
ἀλλ᾽ ὅστις ὁ βροντῶν ἐστι φράσον, τοῦθ᾽ ὅ με
ποιεῖ τετραμαίνειν.

ΣΩΚΡΑΤΗΣ

αὗται βροντῶσι κυλινδόμεναι.

CLOUDS

STREPSIADES

Come now, by Earth, doesn't Olympian Zeus count as a god with you people?

SOCRATES

What do you mean, Zeus? Do stop driveling. Zeus doesn't even exist!

STREPSIADES

What are you talking about? Then who makes it rain? Answer me that one, first of all.

SOCRATES

These do, of course! And I'll teach you how, with grand proofs. Now then: where have you ever yet seen rain without Clouds? Though according to you, Zeus should make rain himself on a clear day, when the Clouds are out of town.

STREPSIADES

By Apollo, you've nicely spliced that point with what you were saying a moment ago. And imagine, before now I thought that rain is Zeus pissing through a sieve! But tell me who does the thundering that makes me tremble.

SOCRATES

These do the thundering, by rolling around.

ΣΤΡΕΨΙΑΔΗΣ

375   τῷ τρόπῳ, ὦ πάντα σὺ τολμῶν;

ΣΩΚΡΑΤΗΣ

ὅταν ἐμπλησθῶσ' ὕδατος πολλοῦ κἀναγκασθῶσι
    φέρεσθαι
κατακριμνάμεναι πλήρεις ὄμβρου δι' ἀνάγκην, εἶτα
    βαρεῖαι
εἰς ἀλλήλας ἐμπίπτουσαι ῥήγνυνται καὶ
    παταγοῦσιν.

ΣΤΡΕΨΙΑΔΗΣ

ὁ δ' ἀναγκάζων ἐστὶ τίς αὐτάς—οὐχ ὁ Ζεύς;
    —ὥστε φέρεσθαι;

ΣΩΚΡΑΤΗΣ

ἥκιστ', ἀλλ' αἰθέριος δῖνος.

ΣΤΡΕΨΙΑΔΗΣ

380   Δῖνος; τουτί μ' ἐλελήθει,
ὁ Ζεὺς οὐκ ὤν, ἀλλ' ἀντ' αὐτοῦ Δῖνος νυνὶ βασι-
    λεύων.
ἀτὰρ οὐδέν πω περὶ τοῦ πατάγου καὶ τῆς βροντῆς
    μ' ἐδίδαξας.

ΣΩΚΡΑΤΗΣ

οὐκ ἤκουσάς μου τὰς νεφέλας ὕδατος μεστὰς ὅτι
    φημὶ
ἐμπιπτούσας εἰς ἀλλήλας παταγεῖν διὰ τὴν πυκνό-
    τητα;

STREPSIADES

In what way, you daredevil?

SOCRATES

When they fill up with lots of water and are forced to drift, by natural compulsion sagging down with rain, then run into one other, and become sodden, they explode and crash.

STREPSIADES

But who is it that forces them to drift? Doesn't Zeus?

SOCRATES

Not at all; it's cosmic whirl.[31]

STREPSIADES

Whirl? That's a new one on me, that Zeus is gone and Whirl now rules in his place. But you still haven't taught me anything about the thunder's crash.

SOCRATES

Didn't you hear me? I repeat: when the clouds are full of water and run into one another, they crash because of their density.

[31] The rotation of the universe was widely recognized in the fifth century, and *dinos* "whirl" was a fundamental element of atomic theory, e.g. Democritus B167. In everyday usage *dinos* meant a kind of cup; the joke at 1473 suggests that such a cup stood outside the Thinkery instead of the usual statue of Hermes (1478 n.).

ΣΤΡΕΨΙΑΔΗΣ

φέρε, τουτὶ τῷ χρὴ πιστεύειν;

ΣΩΚΡΑΤΗΣ

385   ἀπὸ σαυτοῦ 'γώ σε διδάξω.
ἤδη ζωμοῦ Παναθηναίοις ἐμπλησθεὶς εἶτ᾿ ἐταράχθης
τὴν γαστέρα καὶ κλόνος ἐξαίφνης αὐτὴν διεκορκο-
ρύγησεν;

ΣΤΡΕΨΙΑΔΗΣ

νὴ τὸν Ἀπόλλω, καὶ δεινὰ ποιεῖ γ᾿ εὐθύς μοι καὶ
τετάρακται,
χὤσπερ βροντὴ τὸ ζωμίδιον παταγεῖ καὶ δεινὰ
κέκραγεν,
390 ἀτρέμας πρῶτον, παππὰξ παππάξ, κἄπειτ᾿ ἐπάγει
παπαπαππάξ·
χὤταν χέζω, κομιδῇ βροντᾷ, παπαπαππάξ, ὥσπερ
ἐκεῖναι.

ΣΩΚΡΑΤΗΣ

σκέψαι τοίνυν ἀπὸ γαστριδίου τυννουτουὶ οἷα
πέπορδας·
τὸν δ᾿ ἀέρα τόνδ᾿ ὄντ᾿ ἀπέραντον πῶς οὐκ εἰκὸς
μέγα βροντᾶν;

ΣΤΡΕΨΙΑΔΗΣ

ταῦτ᾿ ἄρα καὶ τὠνόματ᾿ ἀλλήλοιν, "βροντὴ" καὶ
"πορδή", ὁμοίω.
395 ἀλλ᾿ ὁ κεραυνὸς πόθεν αὖ φέρεται λάμπων πυρί,
τοῦτο δίδαξον,

STREPSIADES

Come now, why should anyone believe that?

SOCRATES

I'll teach you from your own person. Have you ever gorged yourself with soup at the Panathenaea and then had an upset stomach, and a sudden turmoil sets it all arumble?

STREPSIADES

By Apollo I have! It does carry on terribly and shake me up, and like thunder that bit of soup crashes and roars terribly, gently at first, *pappax pappax,* and then stepping up the pace, *papapappax,* and when I shit it absolutely thunders, *papapappax,* just like those Clouds!

SOCRATES

Now then, consider what farts you let off from such a little tummy; isn't it natural that this sky, being limitless, should thunder mightily?

STREPSIADES

So that's why the words are similar, *bronte* "thunder" and *porde* "fart"! But now explain this: where does the lightning bolt come from, blazing with fire, that incinerates us

καὶ καταφρύγει βάλλων ἡμᾶς, τοὺς δὲ ζῶντας περι-
φλεύει.
τοῦτον γὰρ δὴ φανερῶς ὁ Ζεὺς ἵησ᾽ ἐπὶ τοὺς ἐπιόρ-
κους.

ΣΩΚΡΑΤΗΣ

καὶ πῶς, ὦ μῶρε σὺ καὶ Κρονίων ὄζων καὶ βεκκεσέ-
ληνε,
εἴπερ βάλλει τοὺς ἐπιόρκους, δῆτ᾽ οὐχὶ Σίμων᾽
ἐνέπρησεν
400 οὐδὲ Κλεώνυμον οὐδὲ Θέωρον; καίτοι σφόδρα γ᾽
εἶσ᾽ ἐπίορκοι.
ἀλλὰ τὸν αὑτοῦ γε νεὼν βάλλει καὶ Σούνιον, ἄκρον
Ἀθηνέων,
καὶ τὰς δρῦς τὰς μεγάλας, τί μαθών; οὐ γὰρ δὴ
δρῦς γ᾽ ἐπιορκεῖ.

ΣΤΡΕΨΙΑΔΗΣ

οὐκ οἶδ᾽· ἀτὰρ εὖ σὺ λέγειν φαίνει. τί γάρ ἐστιν
δῆθ᾽ ὁ κεραυνός;

ΣΩΚΡΑΤΗΣ

ὅταν εἰς ταύτας ἄνεμος ξηρὸς μετεωρισθεὶς κατα-
κλεισθῇ,
405 ἔνδοθεν αὐτὰς ὥσπερ κύστιν φυσᾷ, κἄπειθ᾽ ὑπ᾽
ἀνάγκης
ῥήξας αὐτὰς ἔξω φέρεται σοβαρὸς διὰ τὴν πυκνό-
τητα,
ὑπὸ τοῦ ῥοίβδου καὶ τῆς ῥύμης αὐτὸς ἑαυτὸν κατα-
κάων.

on contact and badly burns the survivors? It's quite obvious that Zeus hurls it against perjurers.

SOCRATES

How's that, you moron redolent of the Cronia,[32] you moon-calf! If he really strikes perjurers, then why hasn't he burned up Simon or Cleonymus or Theorus, since they're paramount perjurers? On the other hand, he strikes his own temple, and Sunium headland of Athens, and the great oaks.[33] What's his point? An oak tree certainly doesn't perjure itself!

STREPSIADES

I don't know; but you seem to have a good argument. Very well, what is the thunderbolt, then?

SOCRATES

When a dry wind rises skyward and gets locked up in these Clouds, it blows them up from within like a bladder, and then by natural compulsion it bursts them and is borne out in a whoosh by dint of compression, burning itself up with the friction and velocity.

---

[32] A festival celebrating Zeus' father Cronus, who symbolized a bygone age.

[33] Oak trees were considered sacred to Zeus.

---

[401] Ἀθηνέων Porson (cf. Hom. γ 278): Ἀθηναίων vel Ἀθηνῶν a

ΣΤΡΕΨΙΑΔΗΣ

νὴ Δί ἐγὼ γοῦν ἀτεχνῶς ἔπαθον τουτί ποτε Δια-
σίοισιν.
ὀπτῶν γαστέρα τοῖς συγγενέσιν κᾆτ᾽ οὐκ ἔσχων
ἀμελήσας,
410 ἡ δ᾽ ἄρ᾽ ἐφυσᾶτ᾽, εἶτ᾽ ἐξαίφνης διαλακήσασα πρὸς
αὐτὼ
τὠφθαλμώ μου προσετίλησεν καὶ κατέκαυσεν τὸ
πρόσωπον.

ΚΟΡΥΦΑΙΑ

ὦ τῆς μεγάλης ἐπιθυμήσας σοφίας ἄνθρωπε παρ᾽
ἡμῶν,
ὡς εὐδαίμων ἐν Ἀθηναίοις καὶ τοῖς Ἕλλησι γενήσει
εἰ μνήμων εἶ καὶ φροντιστὴς καὶ τὸ ταλαίπωρον
ἔνεστιν
415 ἐν τῇ ψυχῇ καὶ μὴ κάμνεις μήθ᾽ ἑστὼς μήτε
βαδίζων
μήτε ῥιγῶν ἄχθει λίαν μήτ᾽ ἀριστᾶν ἐπιθυμεῖς
οἴνου τ᾽ ἀπέχει καὶ γυμνασίων καὶ τῶν ἄλλων
ἀνοήτων
καὶ βέλτιστον τοῦτο νομίζεις, ὅπερ εἰκὸς δεξιὸν
ἄνδρα,
νικᾶν πράττων καὶ βουλεύων καὶ τῇ γλώττῃ πολε-
μίζων.

ΣΤΡΕΨΙΑΔΗΣ

420 ἀλλ᾽ εἵνεκα γε ψυχῆς στερρᾶς δυσκολοκοίτου τε
μερίμνης

CLOUDS

STREPSIADES

By Zeus, exactly the same thing happened to me one time at the Diasia,[34] when I was cooking a haggis for my relatives and forgot to make a slit. So it bloated up, then suddenly it exploded, spattering gore in my eyes and burning my face.

CHORUS LEADER

Ah, creature who yearn for grand wisdom from us, how blessed you will become among the Athenians and all Greeks, if you're retentive and a cogitator, if endurance abides in your soul, if you don't tire out either standing or walking, if you're not too annoyed by the cold or too keen on having breakfast, if you stay away from wine and gymnasiums and all other follies, and if, as befits a clever man, you consider absolute excellence to be victory in action, in counsel, and in tongue warfare.

STREPSIADES

Well, if it has to do with a rigorous soul, and restless anxiety,

---

[34] An important festival of Zeus and an occasion for family banquets.

412–17 adaptavit Diogenes Laertius 2.27
417 οἴνου a: ὕπνου Et. Mag.

καὶ φειδωλοῦ καὶ τρυσιβίου γαστρὸς καὶ θυμβρεπι-
   δείπνου,
ἀμέλει, θαρρῶν εἵνεκα τούτων ἐπιχαλκεύειν παρ-
   έχοιμ' ἄν.

ΣΩΚΡΑΤΗΣ

ἄλλο τι δῆτ' οὐ νομιεῖς ἤδη θεὸν οὐδένα πλὴν ἅπερ
   ἡμεῖς,
τὸ Χάος τουτὶ καὶ τὰς Νεφέλας καὶ τὴν Γλῶτταν,
   τρία ταυτί;

ΣΤΡΕΨΙΑΔΗΣ

425   οὐδ' ἂν διαλεχθείην γ' ἀτεχνῶς τοῖς ἄλλοις οὐδ' ἂν
   ἀπαντῶν,
οὐδ' ἂν θύσαιμ' οὐδ' ἂν σπείσαιμ' οὐδ' ἐπιθείην
   λιβανωτόν.

ΚΟΡΥΦΑΙΑ

λέγε νυν ἡμῖν ὅτι σοι δρῶμεν θαρρῶν, ὡς οὐκ
   ἀτυχήσεις
ἡμᾶς τιμῶν καὶ θαυμάζων καὶ ζητῶν δεξιὸς εἶναι.

ΣΤΡΕΨΙΑΔΗΣ

ὦ δέσποιναι, δέομαι τοίνυν ὑμῶν τουτὶ πάνυ μικρόν,
430   τῶν Ἑλλήνων εἶναί με λέγειν ἑκατὸν σταδίοισιν
   ἄριστον.

ΚΟΡΥΦΑΙΑ

ἀλλ' ἔσται σοι τοῦτο παρ' ἡμῶν, ὥστε τὸ λοιπόν γ'
   ἀπὸ τουδὶ
ἐν τῷ δήμῳ γνώμας οὐδεὶς νικήσει πλείονας ἢ σύ.

and a belly that's stingy, poorly nourished, and able to make a meal out of herbs, never fear: on these counts I'd dauntlessly present myself for hammering into shape.

SOCRATES
Then I take it you will now believe in no god but those we believe in: this Void, and the Clouds, and the Tongue, and only these three?

STREPSIADES
I wouldn't speak a word to the other gods even if I met them in the street; and I won't sacrifice to them, or pour them libations, or offer them incense.

CHORUS LEADER
Then tell us frankly what we can do for you, because nothing bad will happen to you if you honor and respect us and seek to be smart.

STREPSIADES
Well then, Mistresses, I ask of you this very small favor: that among the Greeks I be by a hundred miles the very best speaker.

CHORUS LEADER
Done! You will get that from us, so that from this moment on, no one will carry more motions in the assembly than you.

ΣΤΡΕΨΙΑΔΗΣ

μή μοι γε λέγειν γνώμας μεγάλας· οὐ γὰρ τούτων
  ἐπιθυμῶ,
ἀλλ' ὅσ' ἐμαυτῷ στρεψοδικῆσαι καὶ τοὺς χρήστας
  διολισθεῖν.

ΚΟΡΥΦΑΙΑ

435 τεύξει τοίνυν ὧν ἱμείρεις· οὐ γὰρ μεγάλων ἐπιθυμεῖς.
ἀλλὰ σεαυτὸν παράδος θαρρῶν τοῖς ἡμετέροις προ-
  πόλοισιν.

ΣΤΡΕΨΙΑΔΗΣ

δράσω ταῦθ' ὑμῖν πιστεύσας· ἡ γὰρ ἀνάγκη με πιέζει
διὰ τοὺς ἵππους τοὺς κοππατίας καὶ τὸν γάμον ὅς
  μ' ἐπέτριψεν.
νῦν οὖν ἀτεχνῶς ὅτι βούλονται
440   τουτὶ τό γ' ἐμὸν σῶμ' αὐτοῖσιν
    παρέχω τύπτειν, πεινῆν, διψῆν,
    αὐχμεῖν, ῥιγῶν, ἀσκὸν δείρειν,
    εἴπερ τὰ χρέα διαφευξοῦμαι
    τοῖς τ' ἀνθρώποις εἶναι δόξω
445   θρασύς, εὔγλωττος, τολμηρός, ἴτης,
    βδελυρός, ψευδῶν συγκολλητής,
    εὑρησιεπής, περίτριμμα δικῶν,
    κύρβις, κρόταλον, κίναδος, τρύμη,
    μάσθλης, εἴρων, γλοιός, ἀλαζών,
450   κέντρων, μιαρός, στρόφις, ἀργαλέος,
    ματιολοιχός.
    ταῦτ' εἴ με καλοῦσ' ἀπαντῶντες,

72

CLOUDS

STREPSIADES

No speaking on important motions for me, please! That's not what I desire, only twisting lawsuits to my own advantage and giving my creditors the slip.

CHORUS LEADER

Then you shall get what you crave, for it is nothing grand that you desire. Now be resolute and commit yourself to our agents here.

STREPSIADES

That I will do, taking you at your word, for necessity bears down on me on account of those branded horses and the marriage that's screwed me.

So now I wholeheartedly turn this body of mine over
    to them
to do with as they please, for beating, starving,
    parching,
soiling, freezing, flaying into a wineskin,
if that's how I'll escape my debts
and win the world's admiration
as pushy, glib, nervy, reckless,
a disgusting fib-fabricator,
a coiner of legalese, a lawcourt smoothie,
a *corpus juris,* a castanet, a fox, a loophole,
a slicker, a double-talker, a slippery character, a fraud,
a cudgel magnet, a pariah, a twister, a pest,
a trifle licker.
If I'm called all this to my face,
they may do whatever they like with me

δρώντων ἀτεχνῶς ὅτι χρῄζουσιν·
κεὶ βούλονται,
455 νὴ τὴν Δήμητρ' ἔκ μου χορδὴν
τοῖς φροντισταῖς παραθέντων.

ΧΟΡΟΣ

λῆμα μὲν πάρεστι τῷδέ γ'
οὐκ ἄτολμον ἀλλ' ἕτοιμον.
ἴσθι δ' ὡς
460 ταῦτα μαθὼν παρ' ἐμοῦ κλέος οὐρανόμηκες
ἐν βροτοῖσιν ἕξεις.

ΣΤΡΕΨΙΑΔΗΣ

τί πείσομαι;

ΧΟΡΟΣ

τὸν πάντα χρόνον μετ' ἐμοῦ
465 ζηλωτότατον βίον ἀνθρώπων διάξεις.

ΣΤΡΕΨΙΑΔΗΣ

ἆρά γε τοῦτ' ἂν ἐγώ ποτ' ὄψομαι;

ΧΟΡΟΣ

ὥστε γέ σου
πολλοὺς ἐπὶ ταῖσι θύραις ἀεὶ καθῆσθαι,
470 βουλομένους ἀνακοινοῦσθαί τε καὶ εἰς λόγον ἐλθεῖν
πράγματα κἀντιγραφὰς πολλῶν ταλάντων,
475 ἄξια σῇ φρενὶ συμβουλευσομένους μετὰ σοῦ.

ΚΟΡΥΦΑΙΑ

ἀλλ' ἐγχείρει τὸν πρεσβύτην ὅτιπερ μέλλεις
προδιδάσκειν

unconditionally;
and if they want,
by Demeter let them turn me into sausage
and serve it to the thinkers!

CHORUS

This one's got a spirit
that's not gutless but ready to go!
Listen,
when you've learned all this from me, sky-high glory
you'll have among mortals.

STREPSIADES

What's in store for me?

CHORUS

With us, you will live for all the rest of your days
the most enviable life in the world.

STREPSIADES

So I'm really likely to see that someday?

CHORUS

Really!
Multitudes will constantly be camped at your door,
wanting to meet with you and discuss
legal problems and claims involving vast sums,
aiming to consult about matters worth your
    intelligence.

CHORUS LEADER

Now try your hand at starting the old man on whatever

καὶ διακίνει τὸν νοῦν αὐτοῦ καὶ τῆς γνώμης
   ἀποπειρῶ.

ΣΩΚΡΑΤΗΣ

ἄγε δή, κάτειπέ μοι σὺ τὸν σαυτοῦ τρόπον,
ἵν' αὐτὸν εἰδὼς ὅστις ἐστὶ μηχανὰς
480 ἤδη 'πὶ τούτοις πρὸς σὲ καινὰς προσφέρω.

ΣΤΡΕΨΙΑΔΗΣ

τί δέ; τειχομαχεῖν μοι διανοεῖ, πρὸς τῶν θεῶν;

ΣΩΚΡΑΤΗΣ

οὔκ, ἀλλὰ βραχέα σου πυθέσθαι βούλομαι,
εἰ μνημονικὸς εἶ.

ΣΤΡΕΨΙΑΔΗΣ

       δύο τρόπω, νὴ τὸν Δία.
ἢν μέν γ' ὀφείληταί τι μοι, μνήμων πάνυ,
485 ἐὰν δ' ὀφείλω σχέτλιος, ἐπιλήσμων πάνυ.

ΣΩΚΡΑΤΗΣ

ἔνεστι δῆτά σοι λέγειν ἐν τῇ φύσει;

ΣΤΡΕΨΙΑΔΗΣ

λέγειν μὲν οὐκ ἔνεστ', ἀποστερεῖν δ' ἔνι.

ΣΩΚΡΑΤΗΣ

πῶς οὖν δυνήσει μανθάνειν;

ΣΤΡΕΨΙΑΔΗΣ

        ἀμέλει, καλῶς.

ΣΩΚΡΑΤΗΣ

ἄγε νυν ὅπως, ὅταν τι προβάλωμαι σοφὸν
490 περὶ τῶν μετεώρων, εὐθέως ὑφαρπάσει.

lessons you intend to give him; agitate his mind and test his intelligence.

SOCRATES
Now then, describe for me your own characteristics; when I know what they are, on that basis I can apply to you the latest plans of attack.

STREPSIADES
How's that? Are you thinking of besieging me? Good heavens!

SOCRATES
No, I just want to ask you a few questions. For instance, do you have a good memory?

STREPSIADES
Yes and no, by Zeus: if I'm owed something, it's good, but if I'm the hapless debtor, it's bad.

SOCRATES
Well, is there eloquence in your nature?

STREPSIADES
Eloquence, no; fraudulence, yes.

SOCRATES
Then how will you manage to learn?

STREPSIADES
Don't worry, I'll do fine.

SOCRATES
Very well, whatever sage bit of cosmology I toss you, try to snap it up at once.

ΣΤΡΕΨΙΑΔΗΣ

τί δαί; κυνηδὸν τὴν σοφίαν σιτήσομαι;

ΣΩΚΡΑΤΗΣ

ἄνθρωπος ἀμαθὴς οὑτοσὶ καὶ βάρβαρος.
δέδοικά σ᾽, ὦ πρεσβῦτα, μὴ πληγῶν δέει.
φέρ᾽ ἴδω, τί δρᾷς ἤν τίς σε τύπτῃ;

ΣΤΡΕΨΙΑΔΗΣ

                         τύπτομαι,

495 κἄπειτ᾽ ἐπισχὼν ὀλίγον ἐπιμαρτύρομαι·
εἶτ᾽ αὖθις ἀκαρῆ διαλιπὼν δικάζομαι.

ΣΩΚΡΑΤΗΣ

ἴθι νυν κατάθου θοἰμάτιον.

ΣΤΡΕΨΙΑΔΗΣ

                ἠδίκηκά τι;

ΣΩΚΡΑΤΗΣ

οὔκ, ἀλλὰ γυμνοὺς εἰσιέναι νομίζεται.

ΣΤΡΕΨΙΑΔΗΣ

ἀλλ᾽ οὐχὶ φωράσων ἔγωγ᾽ εἰσέρχομαι.

ΣΩΚΡΑΤΗΣ

κατάθου. τί ληρεῖς;

ΣΤΡΕΨΙΑΔΗΣ

500   εἰπὲ δή νυν μοι τοδί·
ἢν ἐπιμελὴς ὦ καὶ προθύμως μανθάνω,
τῷ τῶν μαθητῶν ἐμφερὴς γενήσομαι;

CLOUDS

STREPSIADES

What? Will I be consuming my sagacity like a dog?

SOCRATES

This fellow's ignorant and barbaric! Old man, I fear you'll need a whipping. Let's see, what would you do if someone hit you?

STREPSIADES

I get hit; I wait a bit and summon witnesses; after another little while I go to court.

SOCRATES

Come on, lay down your cloak.

STREPSIADES

Have I done something wrong?

SOCRATES

No, it's our custom to go inside undressed.

STREPSIADES

But I'm not looking for stolen goods in there.

SOCRATES

Lay it down! What's this jabbering?

STREPSIADES

(*disrobing*) All right then, tell me this: if I'm attentive and study hard, which of your students will I come to resemble?

ΣΩΚΡΑΤΗΣ

οὐδὲν διοίσεις Χαιρεφῶντος τὴν φύσιν.

ΣΤΡΕΨΙΑΔΗΣ

οἴμοι κακοδαίμων, ἡμιθνὴς γενήσομαι.

ΣΩΚΡΑΤΗΣ

505   οὐ μὴ λαλήσεις, ἀλλ' ἀκολουθήσεις ἐμοὶ
ἀνύσας τι δευρὶ θᾶττον.

ΣΤΡΕΨΙΑΔΗΣ

                εἰς τὼ χεῖρέ νυν
δός μοι μελιτοῦτταν πρότερον, ὡς δέδοικ' ἐγὼ
εἴσω καταβαίνων ὥσπερ εἰς Τροφωνίου.

ΣΩΚΡΑΤΗΣ

χώρει. τί κυπτάζεις ἔχων περὶ τὴν θύραν;

ΚΟΡΥΦΑΙΑ

510   ἀλλ' ἴθι χαίρων τῆς ἀνδρείας
οὕνεκα ταύτης.

ΧΟΡΟΣ

εὐτυχία γένοιτο τἀν-
    θρώπῳ, ὅτι προήκων
εἰς βαθὺ τῆς ἡλικίας
515   νεωτέροις τὴν φύσιν αὑ-
    τοῦ πράγμασιν χρωτίζεται
    καὶ σοφίαν ἐπασκεῖ.

SOCRATES
In your nature you'll be indistinguishable from Chaerephon.

STREPSIADES
Heavens no, I'm going to be a zombie!

SOCRATES
Stop jabbering. Hurry up and follow me inside here, on the double!

STREPSIADES
Put a honey cake into my hands first, because I'm scared to go down inside there, as if into the cave of Trophonius.[35]

SOCRATES
Get going! Why are you skulking around the doorway?

STREPSIADES and SOCRATES go into the Thinkery.

CHORUS LEADER
Go, and good luck to you, thanks
to this show of courage.

CHORUS
May good fortune befall
the fellow, for though advancing
to the twilight of his life,
he colors his nature
with newfangled notions
and cultivates sagacity.

[35] The subterranean oracular shrine of the hero Trophonius at Lebadeia (in Boeotia) contained sacred snakes, which visitors placated with honey cakes.

ΚΟΡΥΦΑΙΑ

ὦ θεώμενοι, κατερῶ πρὸς ὑμᾶς ἐλευθέρως
τἀληθῆ, νὴ τὸν Διόνυσον τὸν ἐκθρέψαντά με.
520 οὕτω νικήσαιμί τ' ἐγὼ καὶ νομιζοίμην σοφὸς
ὡς ὑμᾶς ἡγούμενος εἶναι θεατὰς δεξιοὺς
καὶ ταύτην σοφώτατ' ἔχειν τῶν ἐμῶν κωμῳδιῶν
πρώτους ἠξίωσ' ἀναγεῦσ' ὑμᾶς, ἣ παρέσχε μοι
ἔργον πλεῖστον· εἶτ' ἀνεχώρουν ὑπ' ἀνδρῶν φορτικῶν
525 ἡττηθεὶς οὐκ ἄξιος ὤν. ταῦτ' οὖν ὑμῖν μέμφομαι
τοῖς σοφοῖς, ὧν οὕνεκ' ἐγὼ ταῦτ' ἐπραγματευόμην.
ἀλλ' οὐδ' ὡς ὑμῶν ποθ' ἑκὼν προδώσω τοὺς δεξιούς.
ἐξ ὅτου γὰρ ἐνθάδ' ὑπ' ἀνδρῶν, οὓς ἡδὺ καὶ λέγειν,
ὁ σώφρων τε χὠ καταπύγων ἄριστ' ἠκουσάτην,
530 κἀγώ, παρθένος γὰρ ἔτ' ἦ κοὐκ ἐξῆν πώ μοι τεκεῖν,
ἐξέθηκα, παῖς δ' ἑτέρα τις λαβοῦσ' ἀνείλετο,
ὑμεῖς δ' ἐξεθρέψατε γενναίως κἀπαιδεύσατε,
ἐκ τούτου μοι πιστὰ παρ' ὑμῶν γνώμης ἔσθ' ὅρκια.
νῦν οὖν Ἠλέκτραν κατ' ἐκείνην ἥδ' ἡ κωμῳδία
535 ζητοῦσ' ἦλθ', ἥν που 'πιτύχῃ θεαταῖς οὕτω σοφοῖς.
γνώσεται γάρ, ἤνπερ ἴδῃ, τἀδελφοῦ τὸν βόστρυχον.
ὡς δὲ σώφρων ἐστὶ φύσει σκέψασθ', ἥτις πρῶτα μὲν
οὐδὲν ἦλθε ῥαψαμένη σκύτινον καθειμένον
ἐρυθρὸν ἐξ ἄκρου, παχύ, τοῖς παιδίοις ἵν' ᾖ γέλως·

527 ὑμῶν] ὑμᾶς A
528 οὓς Blaydes: οἷς a

82

CHORUS LEADER

Spectators, I will speak the truth to you frankly, so help me Dionysus, the god who reared me. So may I win the prize and be thought sage, I took you for intelligent theatergoers and this for the most sophisticated of my comedies; that is why I thought you deserved to be the first to savor it, a play that cost me very hard work. Then I lost the contest, defeated by vulgar men, though I didn't deserve to. For that I blame you sophisticated ones, for whose sake I was doing all that work. Even so, I will never deliberately betray the intelligent among you. For since the time when in this place my Virtuous Boy and my Buggered Boy[36] were very highly spoken of by certain gentlemen whom it is a pleasure even to mention; and when I, being a maiden still unmarried and not yet allowed to be a mother, exposed my child and another maiden took it up,[37] and you nobly raised and educated it—since that time I have held sworn pledges of a favorable verdict from you. So now this new comedy of mine, like the legendary Electra, has come on a quest, hoping somewhere to find similarly intelligent spectators: for she will recognize the lock of her brother's hair if she sees it.[38] Look how naturally decent she is: first of all, she hasn't come with any dangling leather stitched to her, red at the tip and thick, to make the children laugh; nor does

[36] Characters in Aristophanes' first play, *Banqueters*, which was produced by Callistratus in 427, probably at the Lenaea, and won second prize.

[37] I.e., another man produced the play.

[38] An allusion to the scene in Aeschylus' *Libation Bearers* (164-200) where Elektra comes to the tomb of her father Agamemnon and there recognizes a lock of her long lost brother's hair.

540 οὐδ' ἔσκωψεν τοὺς φαλακρούς, οὐδὲ κόρδαχ'
  εἵλκυσεν·
οὐδὲ πρεσβύτης ὁ λέγων τἄπη τῇ βακτηρία
τύπτει τὸν παρόντ', ἀφανίζων πονηρὰ σκώμματα·
οὐδ' εἰσῆξε δᾷδας ἔχουσ' οὐδ' "ἰοὺ ἰού" βοᾷ·
ἀλλ' αὑτῇ καὶ τοῖς ἔπεσιν πιστεύουσ' ἐλήλυθεν.

545 κἀγὼ μὲν τοιοῦτος ἀνὴρ ὢν ποιητὴς οὐ κομῶ,
οὐδ' ὑμᾶς ζητῶ 'ξαπατᾶν δὶς καὶ τρὶς ταῦτ' εἰσάγων,
ἀλλ' ἀεὶ καινὰς ἰδέας εἰσφέρων σοφίζομαι
οὐδὲν ἀλλήλαισιν ὁμοίας καὶ πάσας δεξιάς·
ὃς μέγιστον ὄντα Κλέων' ἔπαισ' εἰς τὴν γαστέρα

550 κοὐκ ἐτόλμησ' αὖθις ἐπεμπηδῆσ' αὐτῷ κειμένῳ.
οὗτοι δ', ὡς ἅπαξ παρέδωκεν λαβὴν Ὑπέρβολος,
τοῦτον δείλαιον κολετρῶσ' ἀεὶ καὶ τὴν μητέρα.
Εὔπολις μὲν τὸν Μαρικᾶν πρώτιστον παρείλκυσεν
ἐκστρέψας τοὺς ἡμετέρους Ἱππέας κακὸς κακῶς,

555 προσθεὶς αὐτῷ γραῦν μεθύσην τοῦ κόρδακος
  οὕνεχ', ἣν
Φρύνιχος πάλαι πεποίηχ', ἣν τὸ κῆτος ἤσθιεν.
εἶθ' Ἕρμιππος αὖθις ἐποίησεν εἰς Ὑπέρβολον,
ἄλλοι τ' ἤδη πάντες ἐρείδουσιν εἰς Ὑπέρβολον,
τὰς εἰκοὺς τῶν ἐγχέλεων τὰς ἐμὰς μιμούμενοι.

560 ὅστις οὖν τούτοισι γελᾷ, τοῖς ἐμοῖς μὴ χαιρέτω.

---

39 A lewd dance associated with drunks and comedians.
40 I.e. in *Knights* of 424; cf. 581 ff.
41 Cleon's successor as the leading politician in Athens; ostracized probably in 416.

she mock bald men, nor dance a *kordax*;[39] nor does an old man, while speaking his lines, cover up bad jokes by beating the interlocutor with his stick; nor does she dash onstage brandishing torches, nor yell "ow ow." On the contrary, she has come relying only on herself and her script. And I myself, being a poet of the same kind, do not act like a bigwig, nor try to fool you by presenting the same material two or three times; rather I have the skill to present novel forms of comedy every time out, none of them like the others and all of them ingenious. I'm the one who hit Cleon in the belly when he was at the height of his power,[40] but I wasn't so brazen as to jump on him again when he was down. Not so these others: from the moment Hyperbolus[41] lowered his guard, they have been stomping the wretch without letup, and his mother too.[42] First of all Eupolis[43] dragged his *Maricas* before you, hacking over our *Knights,* hack that he is, and tacking onto it a drunken crone for the sake of the *kordax,* the same crone that Phrynichus[44] long ago put onstage, the one the sea monster wanted to eat. Then Hermippus[45] again attacked Hyperbolus in a play, and now all the others[46] are launching into Hyperbolus, copying my own similes about the eels.[47] And so whoever finds their plays funny, may he not enjoy mine;

[42] As would Aristophanes himself: *Thesm.* 839 ff.

[43] Eupolis, a close contemporary of Aristophanes and regarded in antiquity as his chief rival, produced his first play in 429 and died *c.* 411. His *Maricas* was produced at the Lenaea of 421.

[44] Phrynichus made his debut in 429 and was still competing in 405.

[45] Hermippus, who had been competing since the 430's, attacked Hyperbolus in *Breadsellers,* produced in 420 or 419.

[46] E.g. Plato in *Hyperbolus.*   [47] Cf. *Knights* 864-867.

ἢν δ᾽ ἐμοὶ καὶ τοῖσιν ἐμοῖς εὐφραίνησθ᾽ εὑρήμασιν,
εἰς τὰς ὥρας τὰς ἑτέρας εὖ φρονεῖν δοκήσετε.

ΧΟΡΟΣ

(στρ) ὑψιμέδοντα μὲν θεῶν
Ζῆνα τύραννον εἰς χορὸν
565 πρῶτα μέγαν κικλήσκω·
τόν τε μεγασθενῆ τριαίνης ταμίαν,
γῆς τε καὶ ἁλμυρᾶς θαλάσ-
σης ἄγριον μοχλευτήν·
καὶ μεγαλώνυμον ἡμέτερον πατέρ᾽
570 Αἰθέρα σεμνότατον, βιοθρέμμονα πάντων·
τόν θ᾽ ἱππονώμαν, ὃς ὑπερ-
λάμπροις ἀκτῖσιν κατέχει
γῆς πέδον, μέγας ἐν θεοῖς
ἐν θνητοῖσί τε δαίμων.

ΚΟΡΥΦΑΙΑ

575 ὦ σοφώτατοι θεαταί, δεῦρο τὸν νοῦν προσέχετε·
ἠδικημέναι γὰρ ὑμῖν μεμφόμεσθ᾽ ἐναντίον.
πλεῖστα γὰρ θεῶν ἁπάντων ὠφελούσαις τὴν πόλιν
δαιμόνων ἡμῖν μόναις οὐ θύετ᾽ οὐδὲ σπένδετε,
αἵτινες τηροῦμεν ὑμᾶς. ἢν γὰρ ᾖ τις ἔξοδος
580 μηδενὶ ξὺν νῷ, τότ᾽ ἢ βροντῶμεν ἢ ψακάζομεν.
εἶτα τὸν θεοῖσιν ἐχθρὸν βυρσοδέψην Παφλαγόνα
ἡνίχ᾽ ᾑρεῖσθε στρατηγόν, τὰς ὀφρῦς ξυνήγομεν
κἀποιοῦμεν δεινά, βροντὴ δ᾽ ἐρράγη δι᾽ ἀστραπῆς.
ἡ σελήνη δ᾽ ἐξέλειπεν τὰς ὁδούς, ὁ δ᾽ ἥλιος
585 τὴν θρυαλλίδ᾽ εἰς ἑαυτὸν εὐθέως ξυνελκύσας

but if you take pleasure in me and my creations, you will
be respected in ages to come for your good sense.

CHORUS

High guardian of the gods,
Zeus the great chieftain,
I invite first to my dance;
and the hugely strong Keeper of the Trident,
wild upheaver
of land and salty sea;[48]
and our own father of glorious name,
most august Empyrean,[49] nourisher of all life;
and the Charioteer, who
covers the plain of earth
with dazzling rays, a mighty deity
among gods and mortals.

CHORUS LEADER

Most sage spectators, give us your attention, for we are
going to reproach you with the wrong you have done us.
Of all the gods we do the most good for your city, but we
are the only deities to whom you make no offerings or
libations, the very ones who watch over you! Whenever
there is a senseless expedition, we thunder and rain.[50] Fur-
thermore, when you were about to elect as general the
godforsaken tanner Paphlagon,[51] we furrowed our brows
and carried on dreadfully: thunder crashed amid lightning
bolts, the moon deserted her orbit, and the sun forthwith

---

[48] I.e. Poseidon.

[49] *Aether,* a scientific entity; cf. 265.

[50] Signs of ill omen.   [51] I.e. Cleon (cf. *Knights*); the elec-
tion was held in March of 424/3.

οὐ φανεῖν ἔφασκεν ὑμῖν εἰ στρατηγήσοι Κλέων.
ἀλλ' ὅμως εἵλεσθε τοῦτον· φασὶ γὰρ δυσβουλίαν
τῇδε τῇ πόλει προσεῖναι, ταῦτα μέντοι τοὺς θεούς,
ἅττ' ἂν ὑμεῖς ἐξαμάρτητ', ἐπὶ τὸ βέλτιον τρέπειν.
590 ὡς δὲ καὶ τοῦτο ξυνοίσει, ῥᾳδίως διδάξομεν.
ἢν Κλέωνα τὸν λάρον δώρων ἑλόντες καὶ κλοπῆς
εἶτα φιμώσητε τούτου τῷ ξύλῳ τὸν αὐχένα,
αὖθις εἰς τἀρχαῖον ὑμῖν, εἴ τι κἀξημάρτετε,
ἐπὶ τὸ βέλτιον τὸ πρᾶγμα τῇ πόλει ξυνοίσεται.

ΧΟΡΟΣ

(ἀντ) ἀμφί μοι αὖτε Φοῖβ' ἄναξ
596 Δήλιε, Κυνθίαν ἔχων
ὑψικέρατα πέτραν·
ἤ τ' Ἐφέσου μάκαιρα πάγχρυσον ἔχεις
οἶκον, ἐν ᾧ κόραι σε Λυ—
600 δῶν μεγάλως σέβουσιν·
ἤ τ' ἐπιχώριος ἡμετέρα θεὸς
αἰγίδος ἡνίοχος, πολιοῦχος Ἀθάνα·
Παρνασσίαν θ' ὃς κατέχων
πέτραν σὺν πεύκαις σελαγεῖ
605 Βάκχαις Δελφίσιν ἐμπρέπων
κωμαστὴς Διόνυσος.

ΚΟΡΤΦΑΙΑ

ἡνίχ' ἡμεῖς δεῦρ' ἀφορμᾶσθαι παρεσκευάσμεθα,
ἡ Σελήνη ξυντυχοῦσ' ἡμῖν ἐπέστειλεν φράσαι
πρῶτα μὲν χαίρειν Ἀθηναίοισι καὶ τοῖς ξυμμάχοις·

withdrew his wick and refused to shine for you if Cleon became general.[52] But you elected him anyway! They say that bad policymaking afflicts this city, but also that whatever mistakes you make the gods convert into successes. And we will easily teach you how even this mistake can benefit you. If you convict that vulture Cleon of bribery and theft, then clamp his neck in the pillory, your situation will be as it was before, and everything will turn out better for the city, in spite of your mistake.

CHORUS

Join me as well, Phoebus, Lord
of Delos, who dwell on Cynthus'
sheer escarpment of rock;[53]
and you, blest Maiden, who dwell at Ephesus
in the golden house, where Lydian maidens
greatly revere you;[54]
and our own native goddess,
wielder of the aegis, guardian of the city;
and he who haunts Parnassus' rock
and glows in the light of pine torches,
eminent among Delphic bacchants,
the reveller Dionysus.

CHORUS LEADER

When we were ready to set forth on our trip here, the Moon happened to run into us and told us first to say hello[55] to the Athenians and their allies, but then she ex-

[52] In 424/3 there was a lunar eclipse on 29 October and a solar eclipse on 21 March. [53] I.e. Apollo.
[54] I.e. Artemis. [55] Perhaps a jab at Cleon, whom Eupolis mocked for using the epistolary greeting *chairein* in an official dispatch to the Athenians after his victory at Pylos in 424 (fr. 331).

610 εἶτα θυμαίνειν ἔφασκε. δεινὰ γὰρ πεπονθέναι
ὠφελοῦσ' ὑμᾶς ἅπαντας οὐ λόγοις ἀλλ' ἐμφανῶς·
πρῶτα μὲν τοῦ μηνὸς εἰς δᾷδ' οὐκ ἔλαττον ἢ
   δραχμήν,
ὥστε καὶ λέγειν ἅπαντας ἐξιόντας ἑσπέρας
"μὴ πρίῃ, παῖ, δᾷδ', ἐπειδὴ φῶς Σεληναίης καλόν."
615 ἄλλα τ' εὖ δρᾶν φησίν, ὑμᾶς δ' οὐκ ἄγειν τὰς ἡμέρας
οὐδὲν ὀρθῶς, ἀλλ' ἄνω τε καὶ κάτω κυδοιδοπᾶν,
ὥστ' ἀπειλεῖν φησὶν αὐτῇ τοὺς θεοὺς ἑκάστοτε,
ἡνίκ' ἂν ψευσθῶσι δείπνου κἀπίωσιν οἴκαδε
τῆς ἑορτῆς μὴ τυχόντες κατὰ λόγον τῶν ἡμερῶν.
620 κᾆθ' ὅταν θύειν δέῃ, στρεβλοῦτε καὶ δικάζετε,
πολλάκις δ' ἡμῶν ἀγόντων τῶν θεῶν ἀπαστίαν,
ἡνίκ' ἂν πενθῶμεν ἢ τὸν Μέμνον' ἢ Σαρπηδόνα,
σπένδεθ' ὑμεῖς καὶ γελᾶτ'· ἀνθ' ὧν λαχὼν Ὑπέρβολος
τῆτες ἱερομνημονεῖν κἄπειθ' ὑφ' ἡμῶν τῶν θεῶν
625 τὸν στέφανον ἀφῃρέθη· μᾶλλον γὰρ οὕτως εἴσεται
κατὰ σελήνην ὡς ἄγειν χρὴ τοῦ βίου τὰς ἡμέρας.

ΣΩΚΡΑΤΗΣ

μὰ τὴν Ἀναπνοήν, μὰ τὸ Χάος, μὰ τὸν Ἀέρα,
οὐκ εἶδον οὕτως ἄνδρ' ἄγροικον οὐδαμοῦ
οὐδ' ἄπορον οὐδὲ σκαιὸν οὐδ' ἐπιλήσμονα,
630 ὅστις σκαλαθυρμάτι' ἄττα μικρὰ μανθάνων
ταῦτ' ἐπιλέλησται πρὶν μαθεῖν. ὅμως γε μὴν
αὐτὸν καλῶ θύραζε δεῦρο πρὸς τὸ φῶς.

pressed her annoyance at the awful way she has been treated, after helping you all not with mere talk but with plain action. First of all, she saves you at least a drachma per month in torches, so that when you go out in the evening you all say, "Don't buy a torch, boy; the Moon's shining nicely." She says that though she does you other favors too, you don't keep track of your dates correctly, but scramble them topsy-turvy, so that the gods scold her, she says, every time they're misled about a dinner and go home having missed the festival that was specified in the calendar. Furthermore, when a sacrifice is scheduled, you're busy armtwisting witnesses and rendering verdicts; and time and again, when we gods are holding a fast in mourning for Memnon or Sarpedon,[56] you're pouring libations and laughing. As a result Hyperbolus, allotted this year to be Holy Recorder, was stripped of his chaplet by us gods.[57] That way he will better understand that the days of his life should be reckoned by the Moon.

Enter SOCRATES from the Thinkery.

SOCRATES

By Respiration, by Void, by Air, I've never seen a man so rustic anywhere, so inept, brainless, and forgetful, the sort who tries to learn a few dinky snippets and then forgets them before he's learned them. All the same I'll call him

---

[56] Memnon, son of Dawn, and Sarpedon, son of Zeus, were killed at Troy.

[57] Holders of this office represented Athens at the Amphictyonic Council at Delphi; perhaps the wind had blown off Hyperbolus' chaplet during an official ceremony.

ποῦ Στρεψιάδης; ἔξει τὸν ἀσκάντην λαβών;

ΣΤΡΕΨΙΑΔΗΣ

ἀλλ᾽ οὐκ ἐῶσί μ᾽ ἐξενεγκεῖν οἱ κόρεις.

ΣΩΚΡΑΤΗΣ

ἀνύσας τι κατάθου καὶ πρόσεχε τὸν νοῦν.

ΣΤΡΕΨΙΑΔΗΣ

635   ἰδού.

ΣΩΚΡΑΤΗΣ

ἄγε δή, τί βούλει πρῶτα νυνὶ μανθάνειν
ὧν οὐκ ἐδιδάχθης πώποτ᾽ οὐδέν; εἰπέ μοι.
πότερον περὶ μέτρων ἢ ῥυθμῶν ἢ περὶ ἐπῶν;

ΣΤΡΕΨΙΑΔΗΣ

περὶ τῶν μέτρων ἔγωγ᾽· ἔναγχος γάρ ποτε
640 ὑπ᾽ ἀλφιταμοιβοῦ παρεκόπην διχοινίκῳ.

ΣΩΚΡΑΤΗΣ

οὐ τοῦτ᾽ ἐρωτῶ σ᾽, ἀλλ᾽ ὅ τι κάλλιστον μέτρον
ἡγεῖ, πότερον τὸ τρίμετρον ἢ τὸ τετράμετρον;

ΣΤΡΕΨΙΑΔΗΣ

ἐγὼ μὲν οὐδὲν πρότερον ἡμιέκτεω.

ΣΩΚΡΑΤΗΣ

οὐδὲν λέγεις, ὤνθρωπε.

ΣΤΡΕΨΙΑΔΗΣ

                    περίδου νυν ἐμοὶ
645 εἰ μὴ τετράμετρόν ἐστιν ἡμιέκτεως.

638 ἢ ῥυθμῶν ἢ περὶ ἐπῶν Hermann: ἢ περὶ ἐπῶν ἢ
ῥυθμῶν a

outside here into the light. Where's Strepsiades? Will you pick up your bed and come out?

STREPSIADES
I can't; the bedbugs won't let me bring it out!

Enter STREPSIADES.

SOCRATES
Hurry up and put it down, and pay attention.

STREPSIADES
There you are.

SOCRATES
Very well then, what would you begin learning now, of the subjects you were never taught anything about? Tell me, would it be measures, or rhythms, or words?

STREPSIADES
I'll take the measures: the other day a corn dealer shorted me two quarts.

SOCRATES
That's not what I'm asking you; I'm asking what you consider to be the most beautiful measure, the three-measure or the four-measure?

STREPSIADES
I say nothing beats the gallon.

SOCRATES
You're making no sense, man!

STREPSIADES
Bet me then, that a gallon isn't a four-measure.

ΣΩΚΡΑΤΗΣ

εἰς κόρακας. ὡς ἄγροικος εἶ καὶ δυσμαθής.
ταχύ γ᾽ ἂν δύναιο μανθάνειν περὶ ῥυθμῶν.

ΣΤΡΕΨΙΑΔΗΣ

τί δέ μ᾽ ὠφελήσουσ᾽ οἱ ῥυθμοὶ πρὸς τἄλφιτα;

ΣΩΚΡΑΤΗΣ

πρῶτον μὲν εἶναι κομψὸν ἐν συνουσίᾳ,
650 ἐπαΐειν θ᾽ ὁποῖός ἐστι τῶν ῥυθμῶν
κατ᾽ ἐνόπλιον, χὠποῖος αὖ κατὰ δάκτυλον.

ΣΤΡΕΨΙΑΔΗΣ

κατὰ δάκτυλον; νὴ τὸν Δί᾽, ἀλλ᾽ οἶδ᾽.

ΣΩΚΡΑΤΗΣ

εἰπὲ δή.

ΣΤΡΕΨΙΑΔΗΣ

τίς ἄλλος ἀντὶ τουτουὶ τοῦ δακτύλου;
πρὸ τοῦ μέν, ἔτ᾽ ἐμοῦ παιδὸς ὄντος, οὑτοσί.

ΣΩΚΡΑΤΗΣ

ἀγρεῖος εἶ καὶ σκαιός.

ΣΤΡΕΨΙΑΔΗΣ

655 οὐ γὰρ ὦζυρὲ
τούτων ἐπιθυμῶ μανθάνειν οὐδέν.

ΣΩΚΡΑΤΗΣ

τί δαί;

ΣΤΡΕΨΙΑΔΗΣ

ἐκεῖν᾽ ἐκεῖνο, τὸν ἀδικώτατον λόγον.

SOCRATES

To hell with you! You're a stupid clod. No doubt you'd soon learn about rhythms!

STREPSIADES

But how will these rhythms help me get my daily bread?

SOCRATES

To begin with, by making you smart in society, and enabling you to recognize which rhythms are shaped for marches, say, and which by the finger.[58]

STREPSIADES

By the finger? That one I know, by Zeus.

SOCRATES

Well, tell me then.

STREPSIADES

What could it be but this finger here? (*raising his middle finger to Socrates*) In the old days, when I was a boy, it was this one.

SOCRATES

You're a brainless lout!

STREPSIADES

The fact is, poor fellow, I don't care to learn any of this stuff.

SOCRATES

What *do* you want then?

STREPSIADES

That one, that, that Very Worst Argument!

[58] I.e. the dactylic meter.

---

653 del. Dover

ΣΩΚΡΑΤΗΣ

ἀλλ᾽ ἕτερα δεῖ σε πρότερα τούτου μανθάνειν,
τῶν τετραπόδων ἅττ᾽ ἐστὶν ὀρθῶς ἄρρενα.

ΣΤΡΕΨΙΑΔΗΣ

660 ἀλλ᾽ οἶδ᾽ ἔγωγε τἄρρεν᾽, εἰ μὴ μαίνομαι·
κριός, τράγος, ταῦρος, κύων, ἀλεκτρυών.

ΣΩΚΡΑΤΗΣ

ὁρᾷς ἃ πάσχεις; τήν τε θήλειαν καλεῖς
ἀλεκτρυόνα κατὰ ταὐτὸ καὶ τὸν ἄρρενα.

ΣΤΡΕΨΙΑΔΗΣ

πῶς δή, φέρε;

ΣΩΚΡΑΤΗΣ

πῶς; ἀλεκτρυὼν κἀλεκτρυών.

ΣΤΡΕΨΙΑΔΗΣ

665 νὴ τὸν Ποσειδῶ. νῦν δὲ πῶς με χρὴ καλεῖν;

ΣΩΚΡΑΤΗΣ

ἀλεκτρύαιναν, τὸν δ᾽ ἕτερον ἀλέκτορα.

ΣΤΡΕΨΙΑΔΗΣ

ἀλεκτρύαιναν; εὖ γε νὴ τὸν Ἀέρα·
ὥστ᾽ ἀντὶ τούτου τοῦ διδάγματος μόνου
διαλφιτώσω σου κύκλῳ τὴν κάρδοπον.

ΣΩΚΡΑΤΗΣ

670 ἰδοὺ μάλ᾽ αὖθις, τοῦθ᾽ ἕτερον. τὴν κάρδοπον
ἄρρενα καλεῖς θήλειαν οὖσαν.

CLOUDS

SOCRATES
But there are other things you must learn before that; say, which of the quadrupeds are strictly speaking masculine.[59]

STREPSIADES
I certainly know the masculine ones, if I'm not daft: ram, billy goat, bull, dog, fowl.

SOCRATES
Do you see your mistake? You use the same word to refer both to the female fowl and the male.

STREPSIADES
How's that, I'd like to know?

SOCRATES
How? Fowl and fowl.

STREPSIADES
That's right, by Poseidon. Now just how am I supposed to refer to them?

SOCRATES
"Fowless," and the other is "fowl."

STREPSIADES
Fowless? By Air, that's good. So good that for this lesson alone I'll fill up your mortar all around with groats.

SOCRATES
There, you did it again; this is another example. You refer to a masculine mortar, though it's a feminine noun.

[59] The following passage parodies sophistic (e.g. Prodicus') prescriptions for grammatically more precise usage, in this case, more consistent marking of the gender of nouns.

ΣΤΡΕΨΙΑΔΗΣ

τῷ τρόπῳ;

ἄρρενα καλῶ 'γὼ κάρδοπον;

ΣΩΚΡΑΤΗΣ

μάλιστά γε,

ὥσπερ γε καὶ Κλεώνυμον.

ΣΤΡΕΨΙΑΔΗΣ

πῶς δή; φράσον.

ΣΩΚΡΑΤΗΣ

ταὐτὸν δύναταί σοι κάρδοπος Κλεωνύμῳ.

ΣΤΡΕΨΙΑΔΗΣ

675 ἀλλ' ὦ 'γάθ', οὐδ' ἦν κάρδοπος Κλεωνύμῳ,
ἀλλ' ἐν θυείᾳ στρογγύλῃ γ' ἀνεμάττετο.
ἀτὰρ τὸ λοιπὸν πῶς με χρὴ καλεῖν;

ΣΩΚΡΑΤΗΣ

ὅπως;

τὴν καρδόπην, ὥσπερ καλεῖς τὴν Σωστράτην.

ΣΤΡΕΨΙΑΔΗΣ

τὴν καρδόπην θήλειαν;

ΣΩΚΡΑΤΗΣ

ὀρθῶς γὰρ λέγεις.

ΣΤΡΕΨΙΑΔΗΣ

680 ἐκεῖνο δύναμαι· καρδόπη, Κλεωνύμη.

ΣΩΚΡΑΤΗΣ

ἔτι δέ γε περὶ τῶν ὀνομάτων μαθεῖν σε δεῖ,
ἅττ' ἄρρεν' ἐστίν, ἅττα δ' αὐτῶν θήλεα.

STREPSIADES
How so? Do I refer to "mortar" as masculine?

SOCRATES
Absolutely, just like "Cleonymus."

STREPSIADES
How's that? Tell me.

SOCRATES
For you, "mortar" and "Cleonymus" are formally equivalent.

STREPSIADES
But dear fellow, Cleonymus never had a mortar; a round can was where *his* kneading was done! Anyway, how should I say it from now on?

SOCRATES
How? "Morté," just as you say Sostraté.

STREPSIADES
"Morté" is feminine?

SOCRATES
That's correct.

STREPSIADES
I can handle that: morté, Cleonymé.

SOCRATES
But you still must learn about names, which of them are masculine and which feminine.

---

680 δύναμαι West: δ' ἦν ἄν a

ΣΤΡΕΨΙΑΔΗΣ

ἀλλ᾽ οἶδ᾽ ἔγωγ᾽ ἃ θῆλέ᾽ ἐστίν.

ΣΩΚΡΑΤΗΣ

εἰπὲ δή.

ΣΤΡΕΨΙΑΔΗΣ

Λύσιλλα, Φίλιννα, Κλειταγόρα, Δημητρία.

ΣΩΚΡΑΤΗΣ

ἄρρενα δὲ ποῖα τῶν ὀνομάτων;

ΣΤΡΕΨΙΑΔΗΣ

685
                  μυρία.

Φιλόξενος, Μελησίας, Ἀμυνίας.

ΣΩΚΡΑΤΗΣ

ἀλλ᾽ ὦ πόνηρε, ταῦτά γ᾽ ἔστ᾽ οὐκ ἄρρενα.

ΣΤΡΕΨΙΑΔΗΣ

οὐκ ἄρρεν᾽ ὑμῖν ἐστίν;

ΣΩΚΡΑΤΗΣ

               οὐδαμῶς γ᾽, ἐπεὶ

πῶς γ᾽ ἂν καλέσειας ἐντυχὼν Ἀμυνίᾳ;

ΣΤΡΕΨΙΑΔΗΣ

690
ὅπως ἄν; ὡδί· δεῦρο δεῦρ᾽, Ἀμυνία.

ΣΩΚΡΑΤΗΣ

ὁρᾷς; γυναῖκα τὴν Ἀμυνίαν καλεῖς.

ΣΤΡΕΨΙΑΔΗΣ

οὔκουν δικαίως, ἥτις οὐ στρατεύεται;

STREPSIADES

But I know which are feminine.

SOCRATES

Tell me then.

STREPSIADES

Lysilla, Philinna, Cleitagora, Demetria.

SOCRATES

And which are masculine?

STREPSIADES

Zillions: Philoxenus, Melesias, Amynias.

SOCRATES

But those aren't masculine, you nitwit!

STREPSIADES

You people don't think they're masculine?

SOCRATES

Not at all. Look, how would you address Amynias if you happened to see him?

STREPSIADES

How? This way: "Over here, over here, Amynia!"[60]

SOCRATES

See? You're calling Amynias a woman.

STREPSIADES

Isn't that appropriate, since she doesn't go out to battle?

[60] *-ia*, the vocative ending of Greek masculine names in *-ias*, is formally like a feminine.

---

686 Ἀμυνίας] Ἀμεινίας V fort. recte

ἀτὰρ τί ταῦθ᾽ ἃ πάντες ἴσμεν μανθάνω;

ΣΩΚΡΑΤΗΣ

οὐδὲν μὰ Δί᾽, ἀλλὰ κατακλινεὶς δευρί—

ΣΤΡΕΨΙΑΔΗΣ

τί δρῶ;

ΣΩΚΡΑΤΗΣ

695 ἐκφρόντισόν τι τῶν σεαυτοῦ πραγμάτων.

ΣΤΡΕΨΙΑΔΗΣ

μὴ δῆθ᾽, ἱκετεύω, 'νταῦθά γ᾽, ἀλλ᾽ εἴπερ γε χρή,
χαμαί μ᾽ ἔασον αὐτὰ ταῦτ᾽ ἐκφροντίσαι.

ΣΩΚΡΑΤΗΣ

οὐκ ἔστι παρὰ ταῦτ᾽ ἄλλα.

ΣΤΡΕΨΙΑΔΗΣ

κακοδαίμων ἐγώ.
οἵαν δίκην τοῖς κόρεσι δώσω τήμερον.

ΧΟΡΟΣ

(στρ) φρόντιζε δὴ καὶ διάθρει
701 πάντα τρόπον τε σαυτὸν
στρόβει πυκνώσας. ταχὺς δ᾽, ὅταν εἰς ἄπορον
πέσῃς, ἐπ᾽ ἄλλο πήδα
705 νόημα φρενός· ὕπνος δ᾽ ἀπέ-
στω γλυκύθυμος ὀμμάτων.

ΣΤΡΕΨΙΑΔΗΣ

ἀτταταῖ ἀτταταῖ.

706 post hunc versum lacunam suspicat Σᴱ ad 700 et 804

But what's the point of my learning these things? We all
know them.

SOCRATES
No point at all, by god. (*indicating the bed*) Just lie down
here.

STREPSIADES
And do what?

SOCRATES
Think out one of your own problems.

STREPSIADES
Oh please, I beg you, not there! If I really must, let me do
my thinking on the ground instead.

SOCRATES
There's only one way to do this.

STREPSIADES
Heavens me, I'm going to pay the bedbugs dearly today!

Exit SOCRATES.

CHORUS
Now think and contemplate,
twirl yourself every way
and concentrate; and whenever you hit a dead end,
quickly jump to another
line of thought; and let sweet-spirited sleep
be remote from your eyes.

STREPSIADES
Ouch! Ouch!

ΧΟΡΟΣ

τί πάσχεις; τί κάμνεις;

ΣΤΡΕΨΙΑΔΗΣ

ἀπόλλυμαι δείλαιος. ἐκ τοῦ σκίμποδος
710 δάκνουσί μ' ἐξέρποντες οἱ Κορίνθιοι,
καὶ τὰς πλευρὰς δαρδάπτουσιν
καὶ τὴν ψυχὴν ἐκπίνουσιν
καὶ τοὺς ὄρχεις ἐξέλκουσιν
καὶ τὸν πρωκτὸν διορύττουσιν,
715 καί μ' ἀπολοῦσιν.

ΧΟΡΟΣ

μή νυν βαρέως ἄλγει λίαν.

ΣΤΡΕΨΙΑΔΗΣ

καὶ πῶς; ὅτε μου
φροῦδα τὰ χρήματα, φροῦδη χροιά,
φροῦδη ψυχή, φροῦδη δ' ἐμβάς,
720 καὶ πρὸς τούτοις ἔτι τοῖσι κακοῖς
φρουρᾶς ᾄδων
ὀλίγου φροῦδος γεγένημαι.

ΣΩΚΡΑΤΗΣ

οὗτος τί ποιεῖς; οὐχὶ φροντίζεις;

ΣΤΡΕΨΙΑΔΗΣ

ἐγώ;
νὴ τὸν Ποσειδῶ.

ΣΩΚΡΑΤΗΣ

καὶ τί δῆτ' ἐφρόντισας;

CLOUDS

CHORUS

What's the matter? What's the trouble?

STREPSIADES

Calamity! I'm undone! Some Cootie-rinthians are crawling
out of this pallet and biting me!
    They're chomping my flanks,
    draining my lifeblood,
    yanking my balls,
    poking my arsehole
    and altogether killing me!

CHORUS

Well, don't make such a fuss about it.

STREPSIADES

Just what do you suggest?
Gone is my money, gone my suntan,
gone my lifeblood, gone my shoes;[61]
    and to top off these misfortunes,
    I whistle in the dark,
    and I'm all but gone myself!

Enter SOCRATES.

SOCRATES

Hey, what are you up to? Aren't you thinking?

STREPSIADES

Me? Yes I am, by Poseidon.

SOCRATES

And what have you thought of?

---

[61] In tragic style, reminiscent of Euripides' *Hecuba* 159-61.

ΣΤΡΕΨΙΑΔΗΣ

725 ὑπὸ τῶν κόρεων εἴ μου τι περιλειφθήσεται.

ΣΩΚΡΑΤΗΣ

ἀπολεῖ κάκιστ'.

ΣΤΡΕΨΙΑΔΗΣ

ἀλλ' ὦ 'γάθ' ἀπόλωλ' ἀρτίως.

ΚΟΡΥΘΑΙΑ

οὐ μαλθακιστέ' ἀλλὰ περικαλυπτέα.
ἐξευρετέος γὰρ νοῦς ἀποστερητικὸς
κἀπαιόλημ'.

ΣΤΡΕΨΙΑΔΗΣ

οἴμοι τίς ἂν δῆτ' ἐπιβάλοι

730 ἐξ ἀρνακίδων γνώμην ἀποστερητρίδα;

ΣΩΚΡΑΤΗΣ

φέρε νυν ἀθρήσω πρῶτον, ὅτι δρᾷ, τουτονί.
οὗτος, καθεύδεις;

ΣΤΡΕΨΙΑΔΗΣ

μὰ τὸν Ἀπόλλω 'γὼ μὲν οὔ.

ΣΩΚΡΑΤΗΣ

ἔχεις τι;

ΣΤΡΕΨΙΑΔΗΣ

μὰ Δί' οὐ δῆτ' ἔγωγ'.

ΣΩΚΡΑΤΗΣ

οὐδὲν πάνυ;

STREPSIADES

Whether the bedbugs will leave anything of me behind.

SOCRATES

Oh go to hell!

STREPSIADES

But I'm already there, dear fellow!

Exit SOCRATES.

CHORUS LEADER

You mustn't soften; cover your head, for you have to discover a fraudacious scheme and a swindle.

STREPSIADES

Damn, if only someone would lay a fraudulent plan on me, to go with these coverlets!

Enter SOCRATES.

SOCRATES

Now then, I'll begin by observing what this one's up to. You there, are you asleep?

STREPSIADES

By Apollo, I'm *not*.

SOCRATES

Have you come up with anything?

STREPSIADES

I certainly haven't.

SOCRATES

Nothing at all?

ΣΤΡΕΨΙΑΔΗΣ

οὐδέν γε πλὴν ἢ τὸ πέος ἐν τῇ δεξιᾷ.

ΣΩΚΡΑΤΗΣ

735   οὐκ ἐγκαλυψάμενος ταχέως τι φροντιεῖς;

ΣΤΡΕΨΙΑΔΗΣ

περὶ τοῦ; σὺ γάρ μοι τοῦτο φράσον, ὦ Σώκρατες.

ΣΩΚΡΑΤΗΣ

αὐτὸς ὅτι βούλει πρῶτος ἐξευρὼν λέγε.

ΣΤΡΕΨΙΑΔΗΣ

ἀκήκοας μυριάκις ἁγὼ βούλομαι,
περὶ τῶν τόκων, ὅπως ἂν ἀποδῶ μηδενί.

ΣΩΚΡΑΤΗΣ

740   ἴθι νυν καλύπτου, καὶ σχάσας τὴν φροντίδα
λεπτὴν κατὰ μικρὸν περιφρόνει τὰ πράγματα
ὀρθῶς διαιρῶν καὶ σκοπῶν.

ΣΤΡΕΨΙΑΔΗΣ
                              οἴμοι τάλας.

ΣΩΚΡΑΤΗΣ

ἔχ᾽ ἀτρέμα· κἂν ἀπορῇς τι τῶν νοημάτων,
ἀφεὶς ἄπελθε, κᾆτα τῇ γνώμῃ πάλιν
745   κίνησον αὖθις αὐτὸ καὶ ζυγώθρισον.

ΣΤΡΕΨΙΑΔΗΣ

ὦ Σωκρατίδιον φίλτατον.

ΣΩΚΡΑΤΗΣ
                        τί, ὦ γέρον;

STREPSIADES

Not a thing, except my cock in my right hand.

SOCRATES

Please cover up and think of something, quick.

STREPSIADES

But what? You tell me that, Socrates.

SOCRATES

First tell me in your own words what you want to discover.

STREPSIADES

You've heard a million times what I want: my interest payments, a way to avoid paying them to anyone.

SOCRATES

Go on then, cover up; now cut loose your thinking and refine it; examine the problem piece by piece, correctly sorting and investigating.

STREPSIADES

Ouch, oh my!

SOCRATES

Hold still; and if you hit a dead end with one of your ideas, toss it aside and abandon it, then later try putting it in play again with your mind and weigh it up.

STREPSIADES

Socratikins, my darling!

SOCRATES

What, old man?

ΣΤΡΕΨΙΑΔΗΣ

ἔχω τόκου γνώμην ἀποστερητικήν.

ΣΩΚΡΑΤΗΣ

ἐπίδειξον αὐτήν.

ΣΤΡΕΨΙΑΔΗΣ

εἰπὲ δή νυν μοι—

ΣΩΚΡΑΤΗΣ

τὸ τί;

ΣΤΡΕΨΙΑΔΗΣ

γυναῖκα φαρμακίδ᾽ εἰ πριάμενος Θετταλὴν
750 καθέλοιμι νύκτωρ τὴν σελήνην, εἶτα δὴ
αὐτὴν καθείρξαιμ᾽ εἰς λοφεῖον στρογγύλον
ὥσπερ κάτροπτον, κᾆτα τηροίην ἔχων.

ΣΩΚΡΑΤΗΣ

τί δῆτα τοῦτ᾽ ἂν ὠφελήσειέν σ᾽;

ΣΤΡΕΨΙΑΔΗΣ

ὅτι
εἰ μηκέτ᾽ ἀνατέλλοι σελήνη μηδαμοῦ,
οὐκ ἂν ἀποδοίην τοὺς τόκους.

ΣΩΚΡΑΤΗΣ

755 ὁτιὴ τί δή;

ΣΤΡΕΨΙΑΔΗΣ

ὁτιὴ κατὰ μῆνα τἀργύριον δανείζεται.

ΣΩΚΡΑΤΗΣ

εὖ γ᾽. ἀλλ᾽ ἕτερον αὖ σοι προβαλῶ τι δεξιόν.

STREPSIADES

I've got a fraudacious scheme for dodging interest!

SOCRATES

Present it.

STREPSIADES

Now then, tell me...

SOCRATES

What?

STREPSIADES

Suppose I bought a Thessalian witch and had her pull down the moon at night, and then locked it up in a round case, like a mirror, and then stood guard over it.

SOCRATES

And how would that help you?

STREPSIADES

How? If the moon never again rose anywhere, I'd never pay my interest.

SOCRATES

And why not?

STREPSIADES

Because money is loaned out by the month!

SOCRATES

That's good! Now let me toss you something else that's

εἴ σοι γράφοιτο πεντετάλαντός τις δίκη,
ὅπως ἂν αὐτὴν ἀφανίσειας εἰπέ μοι.

ΣΤΡΕΨΙΑΔΗΣ

760 ὅπως; ὅπως; οὐκ οἶδ'. ἀτὰρ ζητητέον.

ΣΩΚΡΑΤΗΣ

μή νυν περὶ σαυτὸν εἶλλε τὴν γνώμην ἀεί,
ἀλλ' ἀποχάλα τὴν φροντίδ' εἰς τὸν ἀέρα
λινόδετον ὥσπερ μηλολόνθην τοῦ ποδός.

ΣΤΡΕΨΙΑΔΗΣ

ηὕρηκ' ἀφάνισιν τῆς δίκης σοφωτάτην,
ὥστ' αὐτὸν ὁμολογεῖν σέ μοι.

ΣΩΚΡΑΤΗΣ

765   ποίαν τινά;

ΣΤΡΕΨΙΑΔΗΣ

ἤδη παρὰ τοῖσι φαρμακοπώλαις τὴν λίθον
ταύτην ἑόρακας, τὴν καλήν, τὴν διαφανῆ,
ἀφ' ἧς τὸ πῦρ ἅπτουσι;

ΣΩΚΡΑΤΗΣ

τὴν ὕαλον λέγεις;

ΣΤΡΕΨΙΑΔΗΣ

ἔγωγε. φέρε, τί δῆτ' ἄν, εἰ ταύτην λαβών,
770 ὁπότε γράφοιτο τὴν δίκην ὁ γραμματεύς,
ἀπωτέρω στὰς ὧδε πρὸς τὸν ἥλιον
τὰ γράμματ' ἐκτήξαιμι τῆς ἐμῆς δίκης;

ΣΩΚΡΑΤΗΣ

σοφῶς γε νὴ τὰς Χάριτας.

challenging. If a lawsuit were filed against you for five
talents, how would you get it dismissed? Tell me.

STREPSIADES
How? How? Don't know. I've got to think.

SOCRATES
Now don't keep winding yourself up in your thoughts;
rather, unreel your mind into the air, like a beetle leashed
by its leg with a thread.

STREPSIADES
I've found a brilliant dismissal of that lawsuit; even you'll
have to agree.

SOCRATES
What sort of dismissal?

STREPSIADES
Have you ever seen that stone at pharmacies, the nice
transparent one, that they light fires with?

SOCRATES
You mean glass?

STREPSIADES
That's it. OK, what if I got that, and when the clerk was
entering the lawsuit, if I stood away a bit, like this, with my
back to the sun, couldn't I melt away the record of my case?

SOCRATES
By the Graces, that's ingenious!

ΣΤΡΕΨΙΑΔΗΣ

οἴμ', ὡς ἥδομαι
ὅτι πεντετάλαντος διαγέγραπταί μοι δίκη.

ΣΩΚΡΑΤΗΣ

ἄγε δὴ ταχέως τουτὶ ξυνάρπασον.

ΣΤΡΕΨΙΑΔΗΣ

775   τὸ τί;

ΣΩΚΡΑΤΗΣ

ὅπως ἀποστρέψαις ἂν ἀντιδικῶν δίκην,
μέλλων ὀφλήσειν, μὴ παρόντων μαρτύρων.

ΣΤΡΕΨΙΑΔΗΣ

φαυλότατα καὶ ῥᾷστ'.

ΣΩΚΡΑΤΗΣ

εἰπὲ δή.

ΣΤΡΕΨΙΑΔΗΣ

καὶ δὴ λέγω.
εἰ πρόσθεν ἔτι μιᾶς ἐνεστώσης δίκης
780 πρὶν τὴν ἐμὴν καλεῖσθ' ἀπαγξαίμην τρέχων.

ΣΩΚΡΑΤΗΣ

οὐδὲν λέγεις.

ΣΤΡΕΨΙΑΔΗΣ

νὴ τοὺς θεοὺς ἔγωγ', ἐπεὶ
οὐδεὶς κατ' ἐμοῦ τεθνεῶτος εἰσάξει δίκην.

ΣΩΚΡΑΤΗΣ

ὑθλεῖς. ἄπερρ'. οὐκ ἂν διδαξαίμην σ' ἔτι.

STREPSIADES

Gosh, how good I feel! I've had a five-talent lawsuit ex-
punged!

SOCRATES

Come on then, quickly snap up this one.

STREPSIADES

What is it?

SOCRATES

See if you can present a counterargument that rebuts a
lawsuit you were about to lose for lack of witnesses.

STREPSIADES

That's very simple and very easy.

SOCRATES

Tell me.

STREPSIADES

Here goes then. When only one case was left on the docket
before mine was called, I could run off and hang myself!

SOCRATES

You're making no sense.

STREPSIADES

Heavens above, I am too making sense: nobody's about to
bring a lawsuit against me if I'm dead!

SOCRATES

You're blathering. Get lost! I'm not going to be your
teacher any longer.

ΣΤΡΕΨΙΑΔΗΣ

ὁτιὴ τί; ναί, πρὸς τῶν θεῶν, ὦ Σώκρατες.

ΣΩΚΡΑΤΗΣ

785 ἀλλ᾽ εὐθὺς ἐπιλήθει σύ γ᾽ ἅττ᾽ ἂν καὶ μάθῃς.
ἐπεὶ τί νυνὶ πρῶτον ἐδιδάχθης; λέγε.

ΣΤΡΕΨΙΑΔΗΣ

φέρ᾽ ἴδω, τί μέντοι πρῶτον ἦν; τί πρῶτον ἦν;
τίς ἦν ἐν ᾗ ματτόμεθα μέντοι τἄλφιτα;
οἴμοι, τίς ἦν;

ΣΩΚΡΑΤΗΣ

οὐκ εἰς κόρακας ἀποφθερεῖ,
790 ἐπιλησμότατον καὶ σκαιότατον γερόντιον;

ΣΤΡΕΨΙΑΔΗΣ

οἴμοι. τί οὖν δῆθ᾽ ὁ κακοδαίμων πείσομαι;
ἀπὸ γὰρ ὀλοῦμαι μὴ μαθὼν γλωττοστροφεῖν.
ἀλλ᾽ ὦ Νεφέλαι, χρηστόν τι συμβουλεύσατε.

ΚΟΡΥΦΑΙΑ

ἡμεῖς μέν, ὦ πρεσβῦτα, συμβουλεύομεν,
795 εἴ σοι τις υἱός ἐστιν ἐκτεθραμμένος,
πέμπειν ἐκεῖνον ἀντὶ σαυτοῦ μανθάνειν.

ΣΤΡΕΨΙΑΔΗΣ

ἀλλ᾽ ἔστ᾽ ἔμοιγ᾽ υἱὸς καλός τε κἀγαθός·
ἀλλ᾽ οὐκ ἐθέλει γὰρ μανθάνειν, τί ἐγὼ πάθω;

ΚΟΡΥΦΑΙΑ

σὺ δ᾽ ἐπιτρέπεις;

STREPSIADES

Why not? In heaven's name, please, Socrates!

SOCRATES

But you immediately forget anything you've learned. Look, what was your first lesson just now? Speak up.

STREPSIADES

Let me see, whatever was first? What was first? What was it that we knead groats in? Damn me, what was it?

SOCRATES

To hell and be damned with you, you oblivious, moronic old coot! (*he turns his back on Strepsiades*)

STREPSIADES

Dear me, I'm out of luck; what's going to happen to me now? I'm a goner if I don't learn tongue twisting. You Clouds, please give me some good advice.

CHORUS LEADER

What we advise, old man, is that if you have a grown-up son, send him to school in your place.

STREPSIADES

Why, I do have a son, a fine gentleman, but he refuses to go to school, so what can I do?

CHORUS LEADER

And you give in to him?

ΣΤΡΕΨΙΑΔΗΣ

εὐσωματεῖ γὰρ καὶ σφριγᾷ,
800 κᾆστ᾽ ἐκ γυναικῶν εὐπτέρων καὶ Κοισύρας.
ἀτὰρ μέτειμί γ᾽ αὐτόν· ἢν δὲ μὴ θέλῃ,
οὐκ ἔσθ᾽ ὅπως οὐκ ἐξελῶ ᾽κ τῆς οἰκίας.
ἀλλ᾽ ἐπανάμεινόν μ᾽ ὀλίγον εἰσελθὼν χρόνον.

ΧΟΡΟΣ

(ἀντ) ἆρ᾽ αἰσθάνει πλεῖστα δι᾽ ἡ-
805 μᾶς ἀγάθ᾽ αὐτίχ᾽ ἕξων
μόνας θεῶν; ὡς ἕτοιμος ὅδ᾽ ἐστὶν ἅπαν-
τα δρᾶν ὅσ᾽ ἂν κελεύῃς.
σὺ δ᾽ ἀνδρὸς ἐκπεπληγμένου
καὶ φανερῶς ἐπηρμένου
810 γνοὺς ἀπολάψεις ὅτι πλεῖστον δύνασαι
ταχέως· φιλεῖ γάρ πως τὰ τοι-
αῦθ᾽ ἑτέρᾳ τρέπεσθαι.

ΣΤΡΕΨΙΑΔΗΣ

οὔτοι μὰ τὴν Ὁμίχλην ἔτ᾽ ἐνταυθοῖ μενεῖς,
815 ἀλλ᾽ ἔσθι᾽ ἐλθὼν τοὺς Μεγακλέους κίονας.

ΦΕΙΔΙΠΠΙΔΗΣ

ὦ δαιμόνιε, τί χρῆμα πάσχεις, ὦ πάτερ;
οὐκ εὖ φρονεῖς, μὰ τὸν Δία τὸν Ὀλύμπιον.

ΣΤΡΕΨΙΑΔΗΣ

ἰδού γ᾽ ἰδοὺ Δί᾽ Ὀλύμπιον. τῆς μωρίας·
τὸν Δία νομίζειν ὄντα τηλικουτονί.

810 ἀπολάψεις a: ἀπολέψεις v.l. Σᴱ S

STREPSIADES

Look, he's well built and hard bodied, and the scion of
Coesyra and her high flown line. But I'll go fetch him; and
if he refuses, I'll throw him out of the house for sure. (*to
Socrates*) Go inside and wait for me a little while.

CHORUS

(*to Strepsiades as he enters his house*)
　　Are you aware that soon
　　you will get a great many rewards
　　from us of the gods alone? For this man is ready
　　to do whatever you command.
(*to Socrates as he enters the Thinkery*)
　　And you, recognizing a man infatuated
　　and visibly keyed up,
　　will doubtless lap up as much as you can—
　　but quickly, for this sort of business has a way
　　of taking unexpected turns.

Enter STREPSIADES *and* PHIDIPPIDES.

STREPSIADES

By Fog, you're not going to stay in this house a moment
longer! Go and feed off Megacles' colonnade!

PHIDIPPIDES

Good heavens, father, what's gotten into you? By Olympian
Zeus, you're mentally ill.

STREPSIADES

Get a load of that! Olympian Zeus. What stupidity, believing in Zeus at your age!

ΦΕΙΔΙΠΠΙΔΗΣ

τί δὲ τοῦτ᾽ ἐγέλασας ἐτεόν;

ΣΤΡΕΨΙΑΔΗΣ

820   ἐνθυμούμενος
ὅτι παιδάριον εἶ καὶ φρονεῖς ἀρχαϊκά.
ὅμως γε μὴν πρόσελθ᾽, ἵν᾽ εἰδῇς πλείονα,
καί σοι φράσω τι πρᾶγμ᾽ ὃ μαθὼν ἀνὴρ ἔσει.
ὅπως δὲ τοῦτο μὴ διδάξεις μηδένα.

ΦΕΙΔΙΠΠΙΔΗΣ

ἰδού. τί ἐστιν;

ΣΤΡΕΨΙΑΔΗΣ

825   ὤμοσας νυνὶ Δία.

ΦΕΙΔΙΠΠΙΔΗΣ

ἔγωγ᾽.

ΣΤΡΕΨΙΑΔΗΣ

ὁρᾷς οὖν ὡς ἀγαθὸν τὸ μανθάνειν;
οὐκ ἔστιν, ὦ Φειδιππίδη, Ζεύς.

ΦΕΙΔΙΠΠΙΔΗΣ

ἀλλὰ τίς;

ΣΤΡΕΨΙΑΔΗΣ

Δῖνος βασιλεύει τὸν Δί᾽ ἐξεληλακώς.

ΦΕΙΔΙΠΠΙΔΗΣ

αἰβοῖ· τί ληρεῖς;

ΣΤΡΕΨΙΑΔΗΣ

ἴσθι τοῦθ᾽ οὕτως ἔχον.

PHIDIPPIDES

And what's so funny about that?

STREPSIADES

Just marveling that a child like you has such old fashioned ideas. All the same, come over here if you want to broaden your knowledge, and I'll tell you a secret that'll make a man of you when you've learned it. But see that you don't share this lesson with anyone else.

PHIDIPPIDES

All right. What is it?

STREPSIADES

You swore just now by Zeus.

PHIDIPPIDES

I did.

STREPSIADES

Now do you see the high value of education? Phidippides, Zeus does not exist.

PHIDIPPIDES

Then who does?

STREPSIADES

Whirl is king, having kicked out Zeus.

PHIDIPPIDES

Psh, what's this drivel?

STREPSIADES

Believe me, that's how it is.

ΦΕΙΔΙΠΠΙΔΗΣ

τίς φησι ταῦτα;

ΣΤΡΕΨΙΑΔΗΣ

830   Σωκράτης ὁ Μήλιος
καὶ Χαιρεφῶν, ὃς οἶδε τὰ ψυλλῶν ἴχνη.

ΦΕΙΔΙΠΠΙΔΗΣ

σὺ δ᾽ εἰς τοσοῦτον τῶν μανιῶν ἐλήλυθας
ὥστ᾽ ἀνδράσιν πείθει χολῶσιν;

ΣΤΡΕΨΙΑΔΗΣ

                εὐστόμει
καὶ μηδὲν εἴπῃς φλαῦρον ἄνδρας δεξιοὺς
835 καὶ νοῦν ἔχοντας, ὧν ὑπὸ τῆς φειδωλίας
ἀπεκείρατ᾽ οὐδεὶς πώποτ᾽ οὐδ᾽ ἠλείψατο
οὐδ᾽ εἰς βαλανεῖον ἦλθε λουσόμενος· σὺ δὲ
ὥσπερ τεθνεῶτος καταλόει μου τὸν βίον.
ἀλλ᾽ ὡς τάχιστ᾽ ἐλθὼν ὑπὲρ ἐμοῦ μάνθανε.

ΦΕΙΔΙΠΠΙΔΗΣ

840 τί δ᾽ ἂν παρ᾽ ἐκείνων καὶ μάθοι χρηστόν τις ἄν;

ΣΤΡΕΨΙΑΔΗΣ

ἄληθες; ὅσαπέρ ἐστιν ἀνθρώποις σοφά.
γνώσει δὲ σαυτὸν ὡς ἀμαθὴς εἶ καὶ παχύς.
ἀλλ᾽ ἐπανάμεινόν μ᾽ ὀλίγον ἐνταυθοῖ χρόνον.

ΦΕΙΔΙΠΠΙΔΗΣ

οἴμοι· τί δράσω παραφρονοῦντος τοῦ πατρός;

PHIDIPPIDES

Who says so?

STREPSIADES

The Melian Socrates,[62] and Chaerephon, connoisseur of
flea footsteps.

PHIDIPPIDES

Are you so far gone in your insanity that you trust those
bilious quacks?

STREPSIADES

Watch your mouth, and don't say anything disrespectful
about sage and intelligent men, men so frugal that not one
of them has ever cut his hair or anointed himself or gone
to the bath house to wash; whereas you have been washing
me out of house and home as if I were already dead! Now
get a move on and take my place at school.

PHIDIPPIDES

But what's even worth learning from people like that?

STREPSIADES

Are you serious? Whatever wisdom human beings have!
And you'll find out how ignorant and thick you really are.
Just wait right here a moment.

STREPSIADES enters the Thinkery.

PHIDIPPIDES

Oh dear, what should I do? My father's off his rocker.

[62] Strepsiades confuses Socrates with Diagoras of Melos,
author of a sophistic proof of the nonexistence of the gods, who
was outlawed by the Athenian Assembly around the time Aristo-
phanes was revising *Clouds*.

845 πότερον παρανοίας αὐτὸν εἰσαγαγὼν ἕλω,
ἢ τοῖς σοροπηγοῖς τὴν μανίαν αὐτοῦ φράσω;

ΣΤΡΕΨΙΑΔΗΣ

φέρ' ἴδω, σὺ τοῦτον τίνα νομίζεις; εἰπέ μοι.

ΦΕΙΔΙΠΠΙΔΗΣ

ἀλεκτρυόνα.

ΣΤΡΕΨΙΑΔΗΣ

καλῶς γε. ταυτηνὶ δὲ τί;

ΦΕΙΔΙΠΠΙΔΗΣ

ἀλεκτρυόν'.

ΣΤΡΕΨΙΑΔΗΣ

ἄμφω ταὐτό; καταγέλαστος εἶ.
850 μή νυν τὸ λοιπόν, ἀλλὰ τήνδε μὲν καλεῖν
ἀλεκτρύαιναν, τουτονὶ δ' ἀλέκτορα.

ΦΕΙΔΙΠΠΙΔΗΣ

ἀλεκτρύαιναν; ταῦτ' ἔμαθες τὰ δεξιὰ
εἴσω παρελθὼν ἄρτι παρὰ τοὺς γηγενεῖς;

ΣΤΡΕΨΙΑΔΗΣ

χἀτερά γε πόλλ'· ἀλλ' ὅ τι μάθοιμ' ἑκάστοτε
855 ἐπελανθανόμην ἂν εὐθὺς ὑπὸ πλήθους ἐτῶν.

ΦΕΙΔΙΠΠΙΔΗΣ

διὰ ταῦτα δὴ καὶ θοἰμάτιον ἀπώλεσας;

ΣΤΡΕΨΙΑΔΗΣ

ἀλλ' οὐκ ἀπολώλεκ', ἀλλὰ καταπεφρόντικα.

Should I take him to court and have him certified insane,
or report his madness to the coffin makers?

Reenter STREPSIADES *with a Slave carrying a pair of fowls.*

STREPSIADES
All right, look: what do you call this? Speak up.

PHIDIPPIDES
A fowl.

STREPSIADES
Good. And this?

PHIDIPPIDES
A fowl.

STREPSIADES
The same for both? You make me laugh! You'd better stop
doing that; call this one here a fowl, this one here a fowless.

PHIDIPPIDES
Fowless? Is this the kind of ingenuity you've learned in
your recent sojourn with that scum of the earth?

STREPSIADES
That and lots more. But every lesson I learned I forgot
right away because I'm too old.

PHIDIPPIDES
I guess that's also why you've lost your cloak.

STREPSIADES
It's not lost, merely sublimated.

ΦΕΙΔΙΠΠΙΔΗΣ

τὰς δ' ἐμβάδας ποῖ τέτροφας, ὦ 'νόητε σύ;

ΣΤΡΕΨΙΑΔΗΣ

ὥσπερ Περικλέης, εἰς τὸ δέον ἀπώλεσα.
860 ἀλλ' ἴθι, βάδιζ', ἴωμεν. εἶτα τῷ πατρὶ
πιθόμενος ἐξάμαρτε. κἀγώ τοι ποτὲ
οἶδ' ἑξέτει σοι τραυλίσαντι πιθόμενος.
ὃν πρῶτον ὀβολὸν ἔλαβον ἡλιαστικόν,
τούτου 'πριάμην σοι Διασίοις ἁμαξίδα.

ΦΕΙΔΙΠΠΙΔΗΣ

865 ἦ μὴν σὺ τούτοις τῷ χρόνῳ ποτ' ἀχθέσει.

ΣΤΡΕΨΙΑΔΗΣ

εὖ γ' ὅτι ἐπείσθης. δεῦρο δεῦρ' ὦ Σώκρατες,
ἔξελθ'· ἄγω γάρ σοι τὸν υἱὸν τουτονὶ
ἄκοντ' ἀναπείσας.

ΣΩΚΡΑΤΗΣ

νηπύτιος γάρ ἐστ' ἔτι
καὶ τῶν κρεμαστῶν οὐ τρίβων τῶν ἐνθάδε.

ΦΕΙΔΙΠΠΙΔΗΣ

870 αὐτὸς τρίβων εἴης ἄν, εἰ κρέμαιό γε.

ΣΤΡΕΨΙΑΔΗΣ

οὐκ εἰς κόρακας; καταρᾷ σὺ τῷ διδασκάλῳ;

PHIDIPPIDES

And what have you done with your shoes, you idiot?

STREPSIADES

As Pericles put it, "I've expended them as required."[63] But come on, get moving, let's go. Be bad if only to humor your father. I know I've done the same for you, remember? When you were a lisping six-year-old, the very first obol of jury pay I earned I spent on a toy cart for you at the Diasia.[64]

PHIDIPPIDES

You'll live to regret this, just mark my words!

STREPSIADES

Good for you, you listened to me! Come out here, come out, Socrates! I've brought this son of mine; I persuaded him against his wishes.

Enter SOCRATES.

SOCRATES

But this one's still a baby, and doesn't know the ropes in a place like this.

PHIDIPPIDES

You learn the ropes: go and hang yourself!

STREPSIADES

Damn you, how dare you curse your teacher?

[63] Pericles' public explanation of a suspicious expenditure of ten talents during the Euboean campaign of 445; cf. Plutarch, *Pericles* 23.

[64] See 408 n.

ΣΩΚΡΑΤΗΣ

ἰδοὺ κρέμαι· ὡς ἠλίθιον ἐφθέγξατο
καὶ τοῖσι χείλεσιν διερρυηκόσιν.
πῶς ἂν μάθοι ποθ᾽ οὗτος ἀπόφευξιν δίκης
875 ἢ κλῆσιν ἢ χαύνωσιν ἀναπειστηρίαν;
καίτοι ταλάντου τοῦτ᾽ ἔμαθεν Ὑπέρβολος.

ΣΤΡΕΨΙΑΔΗΣ

ἀμέλει δίδασκε. θυμόσοφός ἐστιν φύσει.
εὐθύς γε τοι παιδάριον ὂν τυννουτονὶ
ἔπλαττεν ἔνδον οἰκίας ναῦς τ᾽ ἔγλυφεν
880 ἁμαξίδας τε συκίνας ἠργάζετο
κἀκ τῶν σιδίων βατράχους ἐποίει, πῶς δοκεῖς;
ὅπως δ᾽ ἐκείνω τὼ λόγω μαθήσεται,
τὸν κρείττον᾽, ὅστις ἐστί, καὶ τὸν ἥττονα,
ὃς τἄδικα λέγων ἀνατρέπει τὸν κρείττονα·
885 ἐὰν δὲ μή, τὸν γοῦν ἄδικον πάσῃ τέχνῃ.

ΣΩΚΡΑΤΗΣ

αὐτὸς μαθήσεται παρ᾽ αὐτοῖν τοῖν λόγοιν·
ἐγὼ δ᾽ ἀπέσομαι.

ΣΤΡΕΨΙΑΔΗΣ

τοῦτό νυν μέμνησ᾽, ὅπως
πρὸς πάντα τὰ δίκαι᾽ ἀντιλέγειν δυνήσεται.

Ο ΚΡΕΙΤΤΩΝ ΛΟΓΟΣ

χώρει δευρί· δεῖξον σαυτὸν
890 τοῖσι θεαταῖς καίπερ θρασὺς ὤν.

880 συκίνας Naber: σκυτίνας a

128

SOCRATES

You hear how he said "wopes"? How babyish, with his lips all slack! How could this one ever learn courtroom defence, or summonsing, or effective bamboozling? But then again, Hyperbolus managed to learn them, for a very high fee.

STREPSIADES

Never mind, just teach him. He's a born philosopher at heart. Why, when he was still a tyke this high, he could make clay houses at home, and carve boats, and fashion figwood carts, and he'd make frogs out of pomegranates as pretty as you please. Just see that he learns that pair of Arguments, the Better, whatever that may be, and the Worse, the one that pleads what's wrong and overturns the Better. And if not both, by all means teach him at least the Worse!

SOCRATES

He'll be taught by the Arguments themselves; I'll be elsewhere.

STREPSIADES

Just remember this: see that he's able to counter all just claims!

Exit SOCRATES; enter BETTER ARGUMENT.

BETTER ARGUMENT

Come out here, exhibit yourself to the spectators, though you need no encouragement to show off.

Enter WORSE ARGUMENT.

Ο ΗΤΤΩΝ ΛΟΓΟΣ
ἴθ᾽ ὅποι χρῄζεις· πολὺ γὰρ μᾶλλόν σ᾽
ἐν τοῖς πολλοῖσι λέγων ἀπολῶ.

Ο ΚΡΕΙΤΤΩΝ ΛΟΓΟΣ
ἀπολεῖς σύ; τίς ὤν;

Ο ΗΤΤΩΝ ΛΟΓΟΣ
λόγος.

Ο ΚΡΕΙΤΤΩΝ ΛΟΓΟΣ
ἥττων γ᾽ ὤν.

Ο ΗΤΤΩΝ ΛΟΓΟΣ
ἀλλά σε νικῶ τὸν ἐμοῦ κρείττω
φάσκοντ᾽ εἶναι.

Ο ΚΡΕΙΤΤΩΝ ΛΟΓΟΣ
895   τί σοφὸν ποιῶν;

Ο ΗΤΤΩΝ ΛΟΓΟΣ
γνώμας καινὰς ἐξευρίσκων.

Ο ΚΡΕΙΤΤΩΝ ΛΟΓΟΣ
ταῦτα γὰρ ἀνθεῖ διὰ τουτουσὶ
τοὺς ἀνοήτους.

Ο ΗΤΤΩΝ ΛΟΓΟΣ
οὔκ, ἀλλὰ σοφούς.

Ο ΚΡΕΙΤΤΩΝ ΛΟΓΟΣ
ἀπολῶ σε κακῶς.

Ο ΗΤΤΩΝ ΛΟΓΟΣ
εἰπέ, τί ποιῶν;

CLOUDS

WORSE ARGUMENT
You go wherever you like: speaking before a crowd I'll destroy you much more effectively.

BETTER ARGUMENT
You destroy me? Who do you think you are?

WORSE ARGUMENT
An Argument.

BETTER ARGUMENT
Yes, but a Worse one.

WORSE ARGUMENT
But I'll defeat you despite your claim to be Better than me.

BETTER ARGUMENT
With what smart maneuver?

WORSE ARGUMENT
By inventing novel ideas.

BETTER ARGUMENT
That's certainly in vogue, thanks to these idiots (*indicating the spectators*).

WORSE ARGUMENT
Not idiots; they're smart.

BETTER ARGUMENT
I'll utterly destroy you.

WORSE ARGUMENT
How will you do that, pray tell?

Ο ΚΡΕΙΤΤΩΝ ΛΟΓΟΣ

900 τὰ δίκαια λέγων.

Ο ΗΤΤΩΝ ΛΟΓΟΣ

ἀλλ᾽ ἀνατρέψω ταῦτ᾽ ἀντιλέγων·
οὐδὲ γὰρ εἶναι πάνυ φημὶ Δίκην.

Ο ΚΡΕΙΤΤΩΝ ΛΟΓΟΣ

οὐκ εἶναι φής;

Ο ΗΤΤΩΝ ΛΟΓΟΣ

φέρε γάρ, ποῦ ᾽στίν;

Ο ΚΡΕΙΤΤΩΝ ΛΟΓΟΣ

παρὰ τοῖσι θεοῖς.

Ο ΗΤΤΩΝ ΛΟΓΟΣ

πῶς δῆτα Δίκης οὔσης ὁ Ζεὺς
905 οὐκ ἀπόλωλεν τὸν πατέρ᾽ αὑτοῦ
δήσας;

Ο ΚΡΕΙΤΤΩΝ ΛΟΓΟΣ

αἰβοῖ, τουτὶ καὶ δὴ
χωρεῖ τὸ κακόν. δότε μοι λεκάνην.

Ο ΗΤΤΩΝ ΛΟΓΟΣ

τυφογέρων εἶ κἀνάρμοστος.

Ο ΚΡΕΙΤΤΩΝ ΛΟΓΟΣ

καταπύγων εἶ κἀναίσχυντος.

Ο ΗΤΤΩΝ ΛΟΓΟΣ

ῥόδα μ᾽ εἴρηκας.

BETTER ARGUMENT

By pleading a just case.

WORSE ARGUMENT

But I'll upend it in rebuttal, for I flatly deny the existence of justice.

BETTER ARGUMENT

You deny its existence?

WORSE ARGUMENT

Well then, where is it?

BETTER ARGUMENT

With the gods.

WORSE ARGUMENT

If that's where justice is, then how come Zeus hasn't been destroyed for chaining up his own father?

BETTER ARGUMENT

Yuk, this vileness is going too far. Give me a puke pan!

WORSE ARGUMENT

You're an outmoded old blowhard.

BETTER ARGUMENT

You're a shameless faggot!

WORSE ARGUMENT

A rosy compliment!

Ο ΚΡΕΙΤΤΩΝ ΛΟΓΟΣ

910   καὶ βωμολόχος.

Ο ΗΤΤΩΝ ΛΟΓΟΣ

κρίνεσι στεφανοῖς.

Ο ΚΡΕΙΤΤΩΝ ΛΟΓΟΣ

καὶ πατραλοίας.

Ο ΗΤΤΩΝ ΛΟΓΟΣ

χρυσῷ πάττων μ' οὐ γιγνώσκεις.

Ο ΚΡΕΙΤΤΩΝ ΛΟΓΟΣ

οὐ δῆτα πρὸ τοῦ γ', ἀλλὰ μολύβδῳ.

Ο ΗΤΤΩΝ ΛΟΓΟΣ

νῦν δέ γε κόσμος τοῦτ' ἐστὶν ἐμοί.

Ο ΚΡΕΙΤΤΩΝ ΛΟΓΟΣ

θρασὺς εἶ πολλοῦ.

Ο ΗΤΤΩΝ ΛΟΓΟΣ

915   σὺ δέ γ' ἀρχαῖος.

Ο ΚΡΕΙΤΤΩΝ ΛΟΓΟΣ

διὰ σὲ δὲ φοιτᾶν
οὐδεὶς ἐθέλει τῶν μειρακίων.
καὶ γνωσθήσει ποτ' Ἀθηναίοις
οἷα διδάσκεις τοὺς ἀνοήτους.

Ο ΗΤΤΩΝ ΛΟΓΟΣ

αὐχμεῖς αἰσχρῶς.

Ο ΚΡΕΙΤΤΩΝ ΛΟΓΟΣ

920   σὺ δέ γ' εὖ πράττεις.

BETTER ARGUMENT

And a clown!

WORSE ARGUMENT

A lily crown!

BETTER ARGUMENT

And a parricide!

WORSE ARGUMENT

You don't realize that you're sprinkling me with gold.

BETTER ARGUMENT

In the old days these words weren't gold but lead.

WORSE ARGUMENT

Nowadays I regard them as a badge of honor.

BETTER ARGUMENT

You're pretty brazen.

WORSE ARGUMENT

And you're pretty antique.

BETTER ARGUMENT

It's your fault that none of the younger generation wants to go to school, and one day the Athenians will realize what sort of education you've been giving the idiots!

WORSE ARGUMENT

You're disgustingly seedy.

BETTER ARGUMENT

And you're prospering, though you used to go begging,

καίτοι πρότερόν γ᾽ ἐπτώχευες,
Τήλεφος εἶναι Μυσὸς φάσκων
ἐκ πηριδίου
γνώμας τρώγων Πανδελετείους.

Ο ΗΤΤΩΝ ΛΟΓΟΣ

ὤμοι σοφίας—

Ο ΚΡΕΙΤΤΩΝ ΛΟΓΟΣ

925 ὤμοι μανίας—

Ο ΗΤΤΩΝ ΛΟΓΟΣ

ἧς ἐμνήσθης.

Ο ΚΡΕΙΤΤΩΝ ΛΟΓΟΣ

τῆς σῆς πόλεως θ᾽
ἥτις σε τρέφει
λυμαινόμενον τοῖς μειρακίοις.

Ο ΗΤΤΩΝ ΛΟΓΟΣ

οὐχὶ διδάξεις τοῦτον Κρόνος ὤν.

Ο ΚΡΕΙΤΤΩΝ ΛΟΓΟΣ

930 εἴπερ γ᾽ αὐτὸν σωθῆναι χρὴ
καὶ μὴ λαλιὰν μόνον ἀσκῆσαι.

Ο ΗΤΤΩΝ ΛΟΓΟΣ

δεῦρ᾽ ἴθι, τοῦτον δ᾽ ἔα μαίνεσθαι.

Ο ΚΡΕΙΤΤΩΝ ΛΟΓΟΣ

κλαύσει, τὴν χεῖρ᾽ ἢν ἐπιβάλλῃς.

ΚΟΡΥΦΑΙΑ

παύσασθε μάχης καὶ λοιδορίας.

claiming to be the Mysian Telephus and living on Pendeletean *bon mots* from a little bag.[65]

WORSE ARGUMENT
My, the cleverness—

BETTER ARGUMENT
My, the craziness—

WORSE ARGUMENT
—of your allusion!

BETTER ARGUMENT
—of you, and of the polis that supports you while you defile its younger generation!

WORSE ARGUMENT
You won't be this boy's teacher, Cronus[66] that you are!

BETTER ARGUMENT
Oh yes I will, if he's to be kept safe and not coached exclusively in drivel.

WORSE ARGUMENT
(*to Phidippides*) Come this way and let him rave on.

BETTER ARGUMENT
You'll be sorry if you lay a hand on him!

CHORUS LEADER
Stop your scrapping and name calling. Rather make a pres-

---

[65] The hero of Euripides' *Telephus* (extensively parodied in *Acharnians*) disguised himself as a beggar to plead his own case. Pendeletus, mentioned elsewhere only in Cratinus' *Cheirons* (fr. 260, *ante* 429), is said by the scholiast to have been a politician and a predatory prosecutor.

[66] See 398 n.

935 ἀλλ᾽ ἐπίδειξαι σύ τε τοὺς προτέρους
ἅττ᾽ ἐδίδασκες, σύ τε τὴν καινὴν
παίδευσιν, ὅπως ἂν ἀκούσας σφῷν
ἀντιλεγόντοιν κρίνας φοιτᾷ.

Ο ΚΡΕΙΤΤΩΝ ΛΟΓΟΣ
δρᾶν ταῦτ᾽ ἐθέλω.

Ο ΗΤΤΩΝ ΛΟΓΟΣ
κἄγωγ᾽ ἐθέλω.

ΚΟΡΥΦΑΙΑ
940 φέρε δή, πότερος λέξει πρότερος;

Ο ΗΤΤΩΝ ΛΟΓΟΣ
τούτῳ δώσω·
κᾆτ᾽ ἐκ τούτων ὧν ἂν λέξῃ
ῥηματίοισιν καινοῖς αὐτὸν
καὶ διανοίαις κατατοξεύσω,
945 τὸ τελευταῖον δ᾽, ἢν ἀναγρύζῃ,
τὸ πρόσωπον ἅπαν καὶ τὠφθαλμὼ
κεντούμενος ὥσπερ ὑπ᾽ ἀνθρηνῶν
ὑπὸ τῶν γνωμῶν ἀπολεῖται.

ΧΟΡΟΣ
(στρ) νῦν δείξετον τὼ πισύνω
950 τοῖς περιδεξίοισιν
λόγοισι καὶ φροντίσι καὶ
γνωμοτύποις μερίμναις
ὁπότερος αὐτοῖν ἀμεί-
νων λέγων φανήσεται.

138

entation: you describe how you used to teach our fore-
bears, and you, the new education. That way the boy will
hear both sides of the case and go to the school of his
choice.

BETTER ARGUMENT

I'm willing to do that.

WORSE ARGUMENT

So am I.

CHORUS LEADER

Excellent. Who will speak first?

WORSE ARGUMENT

I'll give him openers; and then, whatever arguments he's
made, I'll shoot him down with novel phraselets and con-
ceptions; and in the end, if he so much as mutters, he'll get
his whole face and both eyes stung by debating points like
hornets, and so perish.

CHORUS

Now these two will demonstrate—
relying on superior dexterity
in argument, and intellectuality,
and maxim-minting ingenuity,
—which of them, by what he says,
will reveal himself the better man.

---

954 φανήσεται] γενήσεται V

νῦν γὰρ ἅπας ἐνθάδε κίν-
955 δυνος ἀνεῖται σοφίας,
ἧς πέρι τοῖς ἐμοῖς φίλοις
ἐστὶν ἀγὼν μέγιστος.

ΚΟΡΥΦΑΙΑ

ἀλλ᾽ ὦ πολλοῖς τοὺς πρεσβυτέρους ἤθεσι χρηστοῖς
στεφανώσας,
960 ῥῆξον φωνὴν ᾗτινι χαίρεις καὶ τὴν σαυτοῦ φύσιν
εἰπέ.

Ο ΚΡΕΙΤΤΩΝ ΛΟΓΟΣ

λέξω τοίνυν τὴν ἀρχαίαν παιδείαν ὡς διέκειτο,
ὅτ᾽ ἐγὼ τὰ δίκαια λέγων ἤνθουν καὶ σωφροσύνη
'νενόμιστο.
πρῶτον μὲν ἔδει παιδὸς φωνὴν γρύξαντος μηδέν᾽
ἀκοῦσαι·
εἶτα βαδίζειν ἐν ταῖσιν ὁδοῖς εὐτάκτως εἰς κιθαρισ-
τοῦ
965 τοὺς κωμήτας γυμνοὺς ἀθρόους, κεἰ κριμνώδη
κατανείφοι.
εἶτ᾽ αὖ προμαθεῖν ᾆσμ᾽ ἐδίδασκεν τὼ μηρὼ μὴ
ξυνέχοντας,
ἢ "Παλλάδα περσέπολιν δεινάν" ἢ "τηλέπορόν τι
βόαμα",
ἐντειναμένους τὴν ἁρμονίαν ἣν οἱ πατέρες παρέδω-
καν.
969 εἰ δέ τις αὐτῶν βωμολοχεύσαιτ᾽ ἢ κάμψειέν τινα
καμπὴν

CLOUDS

For here and now
wisdom is wagered on one roll of the dice;
to control it is for my friends
the supreme showdown.

CHORUS LEADER
You crowned the older generation with many good traits
of character; now break out whatever speech is dear to your
heart and tell us your own nature.

BETTER ARGUMENT
Very well, I shall describe how the old education used to
operate in the days when I flourished by propounding
what's right, and when decency was accepted custom. The
first rule was that not a sound, not even a mutter, should
be heard from a boy. Furthermore, the boys of each neigh-
borhood had to walk through the streets to the music mas-
ter's all together and in good order, without coats even if
the snow was coming down like chaff. Then he would teach
them to memorize a song—while keeping their thighs
apart!—"Pallas, Dire City Sacker," or "A Cry Sounds From
Afar," and to tune their voices to the mode their fathers
handed down. And if any of them clowned around or
jazzed up the song with the sort of riff today's singers put

971　οἵας οἱ νῦν, τὰς κατὰ Φρῦνιν ταύτας τὰς δυσκολο-
　　　κάμπτους,
　　　ἐπετρίβετο τυπτόμενος πολλὰς ὡς τὰς Μούσας
　　　ἀφανίζων.
　　　ἐν παιδοτρίβου δὲ καθίζοντας τὸν μηρὸν ἔδει προ-
　　　βαλέσθαι
　　　τοὺς παῖδας, ὅπως τοῖς ἔξωθεν μηδὲν δείξειαν
　　　ἀπηνές·
975　εἶτ᾽ αὖ πάλιν αὖθις ἀνιστάμενον συμψῆσαι καὶ προ-
　　　νοεῖσθαι
　　　εἴδωλον τοῖσιν ἐρασταῖσιν τῆς ἥβης μὴ
　　　καταλείπειν.
　　　ἠλείψατο δ᾽ ἂν τοὐμφαλοῦ οὐδεὶς παῖς ὑπένερθεν
　　　τότ᾽ ἄν, ὥστε
　　　τοῖς αἰδοίοισι δρόσος καὶ χνοῦς ὥσπερ μήλοισιν
　　　ἐπήνθει.
　　　οὐδ᾽ ἂν μαλακὴν φυρασάμενος τὴν φωνὴν πρὸς τὸν
　　　ἐραστὴν
980　αὐτὸς ἑαυτὸν προαγωγεύων τοῖν ὀφθαλμοῖν ἐβάδιζεν.
　　　οὐδ᾽ ἀνελέσθαι δειπνοῦντ᾽ ἐξῆν κεφάλαιον τῆς
　　　ῥαφανῖδος,
　　　οὐδ᾽ ἄννηθον τῶν πρεσβυτέρων ἁρπάζειν οὐδὲ σέλι-
　　　νον,
　　　οὐδ᾽ ὀψοφαγεῖν οὐδὲ κιχλίζειν οὐδ᾽ ἴσχειν τὼ πόδ᾽
　　　ἐναλλάξ.

Ο ΗΤΤΩΝ ΛΟΓΟΣ

ἀρχαῖά γε καὶ Διπολιώδη καὶ τεττίγων ἀνάμεστα

in, these irritating riffles in the style of Phrynis,[67] he'd get a hiding, with plenty of lashes laid on for effacing the Muses. At the trainer's the boys had to cross their thighs when sitting, so they wouldn't reveal anything that would torment the onlookers; and when they stood up again, they had to smooth the sand and take care not to leave behind an image of their pubescence for their lovers to find. And in those days, no boy would oil himself below the navel, and so his privates bloomed with dewy down like apricots. Nor would he liquefy his voice to a simper for his lover and walk around pimping for himself with his eyes. At dinner he wasn't allowed to help himself to a head of radish, or to snatch his elders' dill or celery, or to eat the tasty tidbits, or giggle, or sit with his legs crossed.

WORSE ARGUMENT
How antiquated, how like the Dipolieia, how chock full of

---

[67] This citharode from Mantinea won the Panathenaic prize in 456/5 and was an important figure in the development of the new music of Aristophanes' day; cf. Pherecrates fr. 155.14 ff.

---

970 versum e S χ 296 intulit Brunck

καὶ Κηδείδου καὶ Βουφονίων.

Ο ΚΡΕΙΤΤΩΝ ΛΟΓΟΣ

985   ἀλλ᾽ οὖν ταῦτ᾽ ἐστὶν ἐκεῖνα
ἐξ ὧν ἄνδρας Μαραθωνομάχας ἡμὴ παίδευσις
    ἔθρεψεν.
σὺ δὲ τοὺς νῦν εὐθὺς ἐν ἱματίοισι διδάσκεις ἐντετυ-
    λίχθαι,
ὥστε μ᾽ ἀπάγχεσθ᾽ ὅταν ὀρχεῖσθαι Παναθηναίοις
    δέον αὐτοὺς
τὴν ἀσπίδα τῆς κωλῆς προέχων ἀμελῇ τις Τριτο-
    γενείης.
990 πρὸς ταῦτ᾽, ὦ μειράκιον, θαρρῶν ἐμὲ τὸν κρείττω
    λόγον αἱροῦ.
κἀπιστήσει μισεῖν ἀγορὰν καὶ βαλανείων ἀπέχεσθαι,
καὶ τοῖς αἰσχροῖς αἰσχύνεσθαι κἂν σκώπτῃ τίς σε
    φλέγεσθαι,
καὶ τῶν θάκων τοῖς πρεσβυτέροις ὑπανίστασθαι
    προσιοῦσιν,
καὶ μὴ περὶ τοὺς σαυτοῦ γονέας σκαιουργεῖν, ἄλλο
    τε μηδὲν
995 αἰσχρὸν ποιεῖν οὗ τῆς Αἰδοῦς μέλλεις τἄγαλμ᾽ ἀνα-
    πλήσειν,
μηδ᾽ εἰς ὀρχηστρίδος εἰσᾴττειν, ἵνα μὴ πρὸς ταῦτα
    κεχηνὼς
μήλῳ βληθεὶς ὑπὸ πορνιδίου τῆς εὐκλείας ἀπο-
    θραυσθῇς,

cicadas and Cedides and the slaughter of the ox![68]

BETTER ARGUMENT

But on precisely those foundations my education bred the
men who fought at Marathon, whereas you teach the men
of today to spend their lives muffled in cloaks; and so I
choke with rage when they're supposed to be dancing at
the Panathenaea[69] and one of them's holding his shield in
front of his haunch with no regard for Tritogeneia![70] Ac-
cordingly, my boy, boldly opt for me, the Better Argument,
and you will learn how to hate the agora and steer clear of
bath houses; to feel shame at what is shameful and flare at
anyone who mocks you; to offer your seats to your elders
when they approach; not to behave rudely towards your
own parents, or do anything else disgraceful that might
infect the image of Modesty; not to burst into a dancing
girl's house, lest while you're gaping after that sort of thing
you're struck by a little whore's apple and get your fair
name fractured; and never to talk back to your father, or

---

[68] The Dipolieia, with its ox sacrifice, honored Zeus Polieus;
Cedides (var. Cecides; cf. Cratinus fr. 168) was an early dithyram-
bist; for the cicadas see *Knights* 1331.

[69] In this martial dance (*pyrriche*), performed naked, the
shield was supposed to be held high and moved vigorously.

[70] A formal epithet of Athena.

---

985 Κηδ- Π2 S^V cf. *IG* I² 770: Κηκ- a
995 οὗ Henderson: ὅ τι a

μηδ' ἀντειπεῖν τῷ πατρὶ μηδὲν μηδ' Ἰαπετὸν
    καλέσαντα
μνησικακῆσαι τὴν ἡλικίαν ἐξ ἧς ἐνεοττοτροφήθης.

Ο ΗΤΤΩΝ ΛΟΓΟΣ

1000 εἰ ταῦτ', ὦ μειράκιον, πείσει τούτῳ, νὴ τὸν Διόνυσον
    τοῖς Ἱπποκράτους υἱέσιν εἴξεις καί σε καλοῦσι βλι-
    τομάμμαν.

Ο ΚΡΕΙΤΤΩΝ ΛΟΓΟΣ

ἀλλ' οὖν λιπαρός γε καὶ εὐανθὴς ἐν γυμνασίοις δια-
    τρίψεις,
οὐ στωμύλλων κατὰ τὴν ἀγορὰν τριβολεκτράπελ',
    οἷάπερ οἱ νῦν,
οὐδ' ἑλκόμενος περὶ πραγματίου γλισχραντιλο-
    γεξεπιτρίπτου,
1005 ἀλλ' εἰς Ἀκαδήμειαν κατιὼν ὑπὸ ταῖς μορίαις ἀπο-
    θρέξει
στεφανωσάμενος καλάμῳ λευκῷ μετὰ σώφρονος
    ἡλικιώτου,
σμίλακος ὄζων καὶ ἀπραγμοσύνης καὶ λεύκης φυλ-
    λοβολούσης,
ἦρος ἐν ὥρᾳ, χαίρων ὁπόταν πλάτανος πτελέᾳ ψιθυ-
    ρίζῃ.
ἢν ταῦτα ποιῇς ἁγὼ φράζω
1010 καὶ πρὸς τούτοις προσέχῃς τὸν νοῦν
    ἕξεις ἀεὶ
στῆθος λιπαρόν, χροιὰν λαμπράν,
ὤμους μεγάλους, γλῶτταν βαιάν,

146

by calling him Iapetus[71] speak scornfully of his years, many of which he spent on your fledging.

WORSE ARGUMENT

My boy, if you listen to his advice, by Dionysus you'll be just like Hippocrates' sons,[72] and people will call you a clodhopper.

BETTER ARGUMENT

No, you'll be hale and glistening and pass your days in gymnasia, not in the agora chattering about the thorny subjects currently in vogue, or being dragged into court about some trifling, obstinatious, disputatious, ruinatious case. No, down to the Academy[73] you shall go, and under the sacred olive trees you shall crown yourself with white reed and have a race with a decent boy your own age, fragrant with woodbine and carefree content, and the catkins flung by the poplar tree, luxuriating in spring's hour, when the plane tree whispers to the elm.

> If you follow my recommendations,
> and keep them ever in mind,
> you will always have a rippling chest, radiant skin,
> broad shoulders, a wee tongue,

[71] The brother of Cronus, cf. 398 n.

[72] Hippocrates, nephew of Pericles, was killed at Delium in 424; his three sons (Demophon, Pericles, and Telesippus) are ridiculed elsewhere in comedy as being swinish and uneducated.

[73] A public park with sporting facilities, and later the site of Plato's school.

πυγὴν μεγάλην, πόσθην μικράν·
1015 ἢν δ' ἅπερ οἱ νῦν ἐπιτηδεύῃς,
πρῶτα μὲν ἕξεις
στῆθος λεπτόν, χροιὰν ὠχράν,
ὤμους μικρούς, γλῶτταν μεγάλην,
πυγὴν μικράν, ψήφισμα μακρόν·
1020 καί σ' ἀναπείσει τὸ μὲν αἰσχρὸν ἅπαν
καλὸν ἡγεῖσθαι, τὸ καλὸν δ' αἰσχρόν,
καὶ πρὸς τούτοις τῆς Ἀντιμάχου
καταπυγοσύνης ἀναπλήσει.

ΧΟΡΟΣ

(ἀντ) ὦ καλλίπυργον σοφίαν
1025 κλεινοτάτην ἐπασκῶν,
ὡς ἡδύ σου τοῖσι λόγοις
σῶφρον ἔπεστιν ἄνθος.
εὐδαίμονές γ' ἦσαν ἀρ' οἱ
ζῶντες ἐπὶ Κρόνου τότε.
1030 πρὸς τάδε σ', ὦ κομψοπρεπῆ μοῦσαν ἔχων,
δεῖ σε λέγειν τι καινόν, ὡς
ηὐδοκίμηκεν ἀνήρ.

ΚΟΡΥΦΑΙΑ

δεινῶν δέ σοι βουλευμάτων ἔοικε δεῖν πρὸς αὐτόν,
1035 εἴπερ τὸν ἄνδρ' ὑπερβαλεῖ καὶ μὴ γέλωτ' ὀφλήσεις.

1017–18 στῆθος . . . χροιὰν . . . ὤμους Bücheler: χροιὰν
. . . ὤμους . . . στῆθος a
1019 κωλὴν μεγάλην post μικρὰν del. Austin
1029 ἐπὶ Κρόνου τότε Zimmermann: τότ' ἐπὶ τῶν προ-
τέρων a

a grand rump and a petite dick.
But if you adopt current practices,
you'll start by having
a puny chest, pasty skin,
narrow shoulders, a grand tongue,
a wee rump and a lengthy edict. And he will
    persuade you
to consider all that's foul fair,
and fair foul,
and furthermore he'll infect you
with Antimachus' faggotry.[74]

CHORUS

Ah, you who practice wisdom
towering and preeminent,
how sweet upon your words
is decency's flower!
The people living
in that age of Cronus[75] really were fortunate.
(*to Worse Argument*)
To rebut this, you with your speciously stylish muse
will have to make a truly original speech,
since your opponent has distinguished himself.

CHORUS LEADER

Apparently you'll need some impressive schemes to
counter him, if you mean to overthrow your man and avoid
humiliation.

---

[74] According to the scholiast, not the Antimachus of *Acharnians* 1150 ff.; correctly, if this is a man of Phidippides' generation.
[75] See 398 n.

Ο ΗΤΤΩΝ ΛΟΓΟΣ

καὶ μὴν πάλαι 'γὼ 'πνιγόμην τὰ σπλάγχνα κἀπεθύ-
μουν
ἅπαντα ταῦτ' ἐναντίαις γνώμαισι συνταράξαι.
ἐγὼ γὰρ ἥττων μὲν λόγος δι' αὐτὸ τοῦτ' ἐκλήθην
ἐν τοῖσι φροντισταῖσιν, ὅτι πρώτιστος ἐπενόησα
1040 τοῖσιν νόμοις καὶ ταῖς δίκαις τἀναντί' ἀντιλέξαι.
καὶ τοῦτο πλεῖν ἢ μυρίων ἔστ' ἄξιον στατήρων,
αἱρούμενον τοὺς ἥττονας λόγους ἔπειτα νικᾶν.
σκέψαι δὲ τὴν παίδευσιν ᾗ πέποιθεν, ὡς ἐλέγξω,
ὅστις σε θερμῷ φησὶ λοῦσθαι πρῶτον οὐκ ἐάσειν.
1045 καίτοι τίνα γνώμην ἔχων ψέγεις τὰ θερμὰ λουτρά;

Ο ΚΡΕΙΤΤΩΝ ΛΟΓΟΣ

ὁτιὴ κάκιστόν ἐστι καὶ δειλὸν ποιεῖ τὸν ἄνδρα.

Ο ΗΤΤΩΝ ΛΟΓΟΣ

ἐπίσχες· εὐθὺς γάρ σε μέσον ἔχω λαβὼν ἄφυκτον.
καί μοι φράσον· τῶν τοῦ Διὸς παίδων τίν' ἄνδρ'
ἄριστον
ψυχὴν νομίζεις, εἰπέ, καὶ πλείστους πόνους πονῆσαι;

Ο ΚΡΕΙΤΤΩΝ ΛΟΓΟΣ

1050 ἐγὼ μὲν οὐδέν' Ἡρακλέους βελτίον' ἄνδρα κρίνω.

Ο ΗΤΤΩΝ ΛΟΓΟΣ

ποῦ ψυχρὰ δῆτα πώποτ' εἶδες Ἡράκλεια λουτρά;
καίτοι τίς ἀνδρειότερος ἦν;

Ο ΚΡΕΙΤΤΩΝ ΛΟΓΟΣ

ταῦτ' ἐστί, ταῦτ', ἐκεῖνα

WORSE ARGUMENT

Actually, I've had a cramp in my guts for quite a while now, longing to trash all of his arguments with considered refutations. For this very reason I've earned the name Worse Argument in intellectual circles, because I pioneered the idea of arguing what's contrary to established principles of justice. (*to Phidippides*) And it'll repay you more money than you can count, this ability to adopt the worse arguments and yet win. Observe how I cross examine the education he believes in. First, he forbids you to bathe in hot water. (*to Better Argument*) Now what's your reason for scorning hot baths?

BETTER ARGUMENT

Because they're utterly bad and turn a man into a coward.

WORSE ARGUMENT

Stop right there! I've already got you in an unbreakable hammerlock. Pray tell me which of Zeus' sons you consider the heartiest he-man and the doer of the doughtiest deeds? Speak up.

BETTER ARGUMENT

In my opinion, no hero outclasses Heracles.

WORSE ARGUMENT

But where have you ever seen Heraclean *cold* baths?[76] And yet who was ever manlier?

BETTER ARGUMENT

That there, that's just the sort of thing the teenagers spend

---

[76] Hot springs were associated with Heracles.

ἃ τῶν νεανίσκων ἀεὶ δι' ἡμέρας λαλούντων
πλῆρες τὸ βαλανεῖον ποιεῖ, κενὰς δὲ τὰς
παλαίστρας.

Ο ΗΤΤΩΝ ΛΟΓΟΣ

1055 εἶτ' ἐν ἀγορᾷ τὴν διατριβὴν ψέγεις, ἐγὼ δ' ἐπαινῶ.
εἰ γὰρ πονηρὸν ἦν, Ὅμηρος οὐδέποτ' ἂν ἐποίει
τὸν Νέστορ' ἀγορητὴν ἄν, οὐδὲ τοὺς σοφοὺς ἅπαντας.
ἄνειμι δῆτ' ἐντεῦθεν εἰς τὴν γλῶτταν, ἣν ὁδὶ μὲν
οὔ φησι χρῆναι τοὺς νέους ἀσκεῖν, ἐγὼ δέ φημι.
1060 καὶ σωφρονεῖν αὖ φησὶ χρῆναι, δύο κακὼ μεγίστω.
ἐπεὶ σὺ διὰ τὸ σωφρονεῖν τῷ πώποτ' εἶδες ἤδη
ἀγαθόν τι γενόμενον; φράσον, καί μ' ἐξέλεγξον εἰπών.

Ο ΚΡΕΙΤΤΩΝ ΛΟΓΟΣ

πολλοῖς. ὁ γοῦν Πηλεὺς ἔλαβε διὰ τοῦτο τὴν μάχαι-
ραν.

Ο ΗΤΤΩΝ ΛΟΓΟΣ

μάχαιραν; ἀστεῖόν γε κέρδος ἔλαβεν ὁ κακοδαίμων.
1065 Ὑπέρβολος δ' οὐκ τῶν λύχνων πλεῖν ἢ τάλαντα
πολλὰ
εἴληφε διὰ πονηρίαν, ἀλλ' οὐ μὰ Δί' οὐ μάχαιραν.

Ο ΚΡΕΙΤΤΩΝ ΛΟΓΟΣ

καὶ τὴν Θέτιν γ' ἔγημε διὰ τὸ σωφρονεῖν ὁ Πηλεύς.

Ο ΗΤΤΩΝ ΛΟΓΟΣ

κᾆτ' ἀπολιποῦσά γ' αὐτὸν ᾤχετ'· οὐ γὰρ ἦν
ὑβριστὴς
οὐδ' ἡδὺς ἐν τοῖς στρώμασιν τὴν νύκτα παννυχίζειν·

day after day chattering about, that fills up the bath house and empties the wrestling schools!

WORSE ARGUMENT

Then you scorn time spent in the agora, while I encourage it. If it were something bad, Homer would never have called Nestor, and every other sagacious person, "man of the agora."[77] That brings me to the question of the tongue, which according to my opponent young men should not exercise. I say they should. And again, he says they should be decent. That makes two very bad principles. Have you ever seen anyone get anything good by being decent?

BETTER ARGUMENT

Lots of people. Peleus, for one, got his knife that way.[78]

WORSE ARGUMENT

A knife? What a civilized reward the poor sucker got! Now Hyperbolus, the man from the lamp market, has made a vast amount of money by being a rascal, but never a knife, no indeed!

BETTER ARGUMENT

And Peleus got to marry Thetis by being decent.

WORSE ARGUMENT

And then she up and deserted him because he wasn't a roughneck, and no fun to spend the night with between

---

[77] In the Homeric poems agora meant not "market" or "downtown" (as in Aristophanes' day) but "place of assembly."

[78] Acastus' wife propositioned Achilles' father Peleus; when he refused her she accused him of attempted rape. Acastus abandoned him to the animals in the forest, but the gods gave him a knife to defend himself.

1070 γυνὴ δὲ σιναμωρουμένη χαίρει. σὺ δ᾽ εἶ Κρόνιππος.
σκέψαι γάρ, ὦ μειράκιον, ἐν τῷ σωφρονεῖν ἅπαντα
ἄνεστιν, ἡδονῶν θ᾽ ὅσων μέλλεις ἀποστερεῖσθαι·
παίδων, γυναικῶν, κοττάβων, ὄψων, πότων, καχασ-
  μῶν.
καίτοι τί σοι ζῆν ἄξιον, τούτων ἐὰν στερηθῇς;
1075 εἰέν. πάρειμ᾽ ἐντεῦθεν εἰς τὰς τῆς φύσεως ἀνάγκας.
ἥμαρτες, ἠράσθης, ἐμοίχευσάς τι, κᾆτ᾽ ἐλήφθης.
ἀπόλωλας· ἀδύνατος γὰρ εἶ λέγειν. ἐμοὶ δ᾽ ὁμιλῶν
χρῶ τῇ φύσει, σκίρτα, γέλα, νόμιζε μηδὲν αἰσχρόν.
μοιχὸς γὰρ ἢν τύχῃς ἁλούς, τάδ᾽ ἀντερεῖς πρὸς
  αὐτόν,
1080 ὡς οὐδὲν ἠδίκηκας· εἶτ᾽ εἰς τὸν Δί᾽ ἐπανενεγκεῖν,
κἀκεῖνος ὡς ἥττων ἔρωτός ἐστι καὶ γυναικῶν·
καίτοι σὺ θνητὸς ὢν θεοῦ πῶς μεῖζον ἂν δύναιο;

Ο ΚΡΕΙΤΤΩΝ ΛΟΓΟΣ

τί δ᾽ ἢν ῥαφανιδωθῇ πιθόμενός σοι τέφρᾳ τε τιλθῇ;
ἕξει τινὰ γνώμην λέγειν τὸ μὴ εὐρύπρωκτος εἶναι;

Ο ΗΤΤΩΝ ΛΟΓΟΣ

1085 ἢν δ᾽ εὐρύπρωκτος ᾖ, τί πείσεται κακόν;

Ο ΚΡΕΙΤΤΩΝ ΛΟΓΟΣ

τί μὲν οὖν ἂν ἔτι μεῖζον πάθοι τούτου ποτέ;

Ο ΗΤΤΩΝ ΛΟΓΟΣ

τί δῆτ᾽ ἐρεῖς, ἢν τοῦτο νικηθῇς ἐμοῦ;

Ο ΚΡΕΙΤΤΩΝ ΛΟΓΟΣ

σιγήσομαι. τί δ᾽ ἄλλο;

154

the sheets. A woman enjoys being lewdly used. But you're just a king-sized Cronus.[79] My boy, do consider everything that decency entails, and all the pleasures you stand to lose: boys, women, dice, fine food and drink, laughs. If you're deprived of all this, what's the point of living? Now then, I'll proceed to the necessities of nature. Say you slip up, fall in love, engage in a little adultery, and then get caught. You're done for because you're unable to argue. But if you follow me, go ahead and indulge your nature, romp, laugh, think nothing shameful. If you happen to get caught *in flagrante,* tell him this: that you've done nothing wrong. Then pass the buck to Zeus, on the grounds that even he is worsted by lust for women, so how can you, a mere mortal, be stronger than a god?

BETTER ARGUMENT

But say he listens to you and then gets violated with a radish and depilated with hot ash?[80] What line of argument will he have on hand to avoid becoming wide-arsed?

WORSE ARGUMENT

And if he does become wide-arsed, what's the harm in that?

BETTER ARGUMENT

You mean, what harm could ever be worse than that?

WORSE ARGUMENT

All right, what will you say if I defeat you on this point?

BETTER ARGUMENT

I'll shut up; what else could I do?

[79] See 398 n.
[80] A form of vengeance legally available to cuckolded men.

Ο ΗΤΤΩΝ ΛΟΓΟΣ
φέρε δή μοι φράσον,
συνηγοροῦσιν ἐκ τίνων;

Ο ΚΡΕΙΤΤΩΝ ΛΟΓΟΣ
ἐξ εὐρυπρώκτων.

Ο ΗΤΤΩΝ ΛΟΓΟΣ
1090   πείθομαι.
τί δαί; τραγῳδοῦσ᾽ ἐκ τίνων;

Ο ΚΡΕΙΤΤΩΝ ΛΟΓΟΣ
ἐξ εὐρυπρώκτων.

Ο ΗΤΤΩΝ ΛΟΓΟΣ
εὖ λέγεις.
δημηγοροῦσι δ᾽ ἐκ τίνων;

Ο ΚΡΕΙΤΤΩΝ ΛΟΓΟΣ
ἐξ εὐρυπρώκτων.

Ο ΗΤΤΩΝ ΛΟΓΟΣ
ἆρα δῆτ᾽
1095 ἔγνωκας ὡς οὐδὲν λέγεις;
καὶ τῶν θεατῶν ὁπότεροι
πλείους σκόπει.

Ο ΚΡΕΙΤΤΩΝ ΛΟΓΟΣ
καὶ δὴ σκοπῶ.

Ο ΗΤΤΩΝ ΛΟΓΟΣ
τί δῆθ᾽ ὁρᾷς;

WORSE ARGUMENT

Very well, tell me: what group do prosecutors come from?

BETTER ARGUMENT

From the wide-arsed.

WORSE ARGUMENT

I agree. And what about tragedians?

BETTER ARGUMENT

From the wide-arsed.

WORSE ARGUMENT

Correct. And politicians?

BETTER ARGUMENT

From the wide-arsed.

WORSE ARGUMENT

Now do you see that you have no case? Just look and see which make up the majority of the spectators.

BETTER ARGUMENT

I certainly will.

WORSE ARGUMENT

Well, what do you see?

Ο ΚΡΕΙΤΤΩΝ ΛΟΓΟΣ

πολὺ πλείονας, νὴ τοὺς θεούς,
τοὺς εὐρυπρώκτους. τουτονὶ
γοῦν οἶδ᾽ ἐγὼ κἀκεινονὶ
1100 καὶ τὸν κομήτην τουτονί.

Ο ΗΤΤΩΝ ΛΟΓΟΣ

τί δῆτ᾽ ἐρεῖς;

Ο ΚΡΕΙΤΤΩΝ ΛΟΓΟΣ

ἡττήμεθ᾽. ὦ κινούμενοι,
πρὸς τῶν θεῶν δέξασθέ μου
θοἰμάτιον, ὡς
ἐξαυτομολῶ πρὸς ὑμᾶς.

Ο ΗΤΤΩΝ ΛΟΓΟΣ

1105 τί δῆτα; πότερα τοῦτον ἀπάγεσθαι λαβὼν
βούλει τὸν υἱόν, ἢ διδάσκω σοι λέγειν;

ΣΤΡΕΨΙΑΔΗΣ

δίδασκε καὶ κόλαζε καὶ μέμνησ᾽ ὅπως
εὖ μοι στομώσεις αὐτόν, ἐπὶ μὲν θάτερα
οἷον δικιδίοις, τὴν δ᾽ ἑτέραν αὐτοῦ γνάθον
1110 στόμωσον οἵαν εἰς τὰ μείζω πράγματα.

Ο ΗΤΤΩΝ ΛΟΓΟΣ

ἀμέλει, κομιεῖ τοῦτον σοφιστὴν δεξιόν.

ΦΕΙΔΙΠΠΙΔΗΣ

ὠχρὸν μὲν οὖν οἶμαί γε καὶ κακοδαίμονα.

ΧΟΡΟΣ

χωρεῖτέ νυν. οἶμαι δὲ σοὶ

CLOUDS

BETTER ARGUMENT
Gods above, the great majority are wide-arsed! I can vouch
for this one here, anyway, and that one there, and this one
here, with the long hair.

WORSE ARGUMENT
Well, what have you got to say?

BETTER ARGUMENT
Uncle! You buggers, for heaven's sake take my cloak; I'm
deserting to your side!

BETTER ARGUMENT dashes into the Thinkery.

WORSE ARGUMENT
Your move: do you want to take this son of yours home, or
shall I teach him oratory for you?

STREPSIADES
Teach him and discipline him, and remember to give him
a sharp edge for me; whet one side of his mug for small-fry
lawsuits, and the other side for meatier business.

WORSE ARGUMENT
Don't worry, you'll take home a handy sophist.

PHIDIPPIDES
Not to say pasty and ill-starred, if you ask me.

CHORUS
Off with you, then.

WORSE ARGUMENT takes PHIDIPPIDES into the Thinkery.

1105–6 et 1111 Socrati dant a

ταῦτα μεταμελήσειν.

ΚΟΡΥΦΑΙΑ

1115 τοὺς κριτὰς ἃ κερδανοῦσιν, ἤν τι τόνδε τὸν χορὸν
ὠφελῶσ᾽ ἐκ τῶν δικαίων, βουλόμεσθ᾽ ἡμεῖς φράσαι.
πρῶτα μὲν γάρ, ἢν νεᾶν βούλησθ᾽ ἐν ὥρᾳ τοὺς
ἀγρούς,
ὕσομεν πρώτοισιν ὑμῖν, τοῖσι δ᾽ ἄλλοις ὕστερον.
εἶτα τὸν καρπόν τε καὶ τὰς ἀμπέλους φυλάξομεν,
1120 ὥστε μήτ᾽ αὐχμὸν πιέζειν μήτ᾽ ἄγαν ἐπομβρίαν.
ἢν δ᾽ ἀτιμάσῃ τις ἡμᾶς θνητὸς ὢν οὔσας θεάς,
προσεχέτω τὸν νοῦν πρὸς ἡμῶν οἷα πείσεται κακά,
λαμβάνων οὔτ᾽ οἶνον οὔτ᾽ ἄλλ᾽ οὐδὲν ἐκ τοῦ χωρίου.
ἡνίκ᾽ ἂν γὰρ αἵ τ᾽ ἐλαῖαι βλαστάνωσ᾽ αἵ τ᾽
ἄμπελοι,
1125 ἀποκεκόψονται· τοιαύταις σφενδόναις παιήσομεν.
ἢν δὲ πλινθεύοντ᾽ ἴδωμεν, ὕσομεν καὶ τοῦ τέγους
τὸν κέραμον αὐτοῦ χαλάζαις στρογγύλαις συν-
τρίψομεν.
κἂν γαμῇ ποτ᾽ αὐτὸς ἢ τῶν ξυγγενῶν ἢ τῶν φίλων,
ὕσομεν τὴν νύκτα πᾶσαν, ὥστ᾽ ἴσως βουλήσεται
1130 κἂν ἐν Αἰγύπτῳ τυχεῖν ὢν μᾶλλον ἢ κρῖναι κακῶς.

ΣΤΡΕΨΙΑΔΗΣ

πέμπτη, τετράς, τρίτη· μετὰ ταύτην δευτέρα·
εἶθ᾽ ἣν ἐγὼ μάλιστα πασῶν ἡμερῶν
δέδοικα καὶ πέφρικα καὶ βδελύττομαι,

---

¹¹¹⁶ ἡμεῖς RV: ὑμεῖς K: ὑμῖν ΕΘ: ἡμῖν N
¹¹¹⁹ τε καὶ τὰς Coraes: τεκούσας τὰς N: τεκούσας cett.

(*to Strepsiades*)
  As for you, I think you'll come to regret this.

STREPSIADES enters his own house.

CHORUS LEADER

We want to announce what the judges stand to gain if they do the right thing and give this Chorus their support. One, if you want to plow your fields in season, we'll rain on you first and everyone else later. Two, we'll guard your crops and vines against attack either by drought or too much drenching. But any mortal who would slight our honor as goddesses should bear in mind what punishments he'll suffer from us: he'll get no wine or anything else from his land, for when his olives and vines start to sprout, we'll let fly at them so hard that they'll be sheared off. And if we spot him making bricks, we'll start raining and pulverize his roof tiles with a salvo of hailstones. And when he or any of his relatives or friends has a wedding, we'll rain all night long, so that maybe he'll wish he'd wound up in Egypt instead of miscasting his vote.

Enter STREPSIADES.

STREPSIADES

Day five, day four, day three, after that day two, then the day that above all days intimidates me, that gives me the shivers and scares the crap out of me, because the next day

εὐθὺς μετὰ ταύτην ἔσθ᾽ ἕνη τε καὶ νέα.
1135 πᾶς γάρ τις ὀμνύς, οἷς ὀφείλων τυγχάνω,
θείς μοι πρυτανεῖ᾽ ἀπολεῖν μέ φησι κἀξολεῖν.
κἀμοῦ μέτριά τε καὶ δίκαι᾽ αἰτουμένου,
"ὦ δαιμόνιε, τὸ μέν τι νυνὶ μὴ λάβῃς,
τὸ δ᾽ ἀναβαλοῦ μοι, τὸ δ᾽ ἄφες", οὔ φασίν ποτε
1140 οὕτως ἀπολήψεσθ᾽, ἀλλὰ λοιδοροῦσί με
ὡς ἄδικός εἰμι, καὶ δικάσεσθαί φασί μοι.
νῦν οὖν δικαζέσθων. ὀλίγον γάρ μοι μέλει,
εἴπερ μεμάθηκεν εὖ λέγειν Φειδιππίδης.
τάχα δ᾽ εἴσομαι κόψας τὸ φροντιστήριον.
παῖ, ἠμί, παῖ, παῖ.

ΣΩΚΡΑΤΗΣ

1145   Στρεψιάδην ἀσπάζομαι.

ΣΤΡΕΨΙΑΔΗΣ

κἄγωγέ σ᾽. ἀλλὰ τουτονὶ πρῶτον λαβέ.
χρὴ γὰρ ἐπιθαυμάζειν τι τὸν διδάσκαλον.
καί μοι τὸν υἱόν, εἰ μεμάθηκε τὸν λόγον
ἐκεῖνον, εἴφ᾽, ὃν ἀρτίως εἰσήγαγες.

ΣΩΚΡΑΤΗΣ

μεμάθηκεν.

ΣΤΡΕΨΙΑΔΗΣ

1150   εὖ γ᾽, ὦ παμβασίλει᾽ Ἀπαιόλη.

ΣΩΚΡΑΤΗΣ

ὥστ᾽ ἀποφύγοις ἂν ἥντιν᾽ ἂν βούλῃ δίκην.

is the Old and New Day,[81] when every single one of my creditors has vowed to file a lawsuit against me, ruin me, and wipe me out. I've requested fair and reasonable terms: "Look, don't be unreasonable and insist on getting this one right now; please postpone that one; forgive that one." But they say they'll never be paid on those terms, and instead they yell at me for being dishonest and promise to sue me. All right, now let them sue! I couldn't care less, if Phidippides has really learned effective oratory. I'll soon find out if I knock at the Thinkery. Boy! I say, boy!

SOCRATES answers the door.

SOCRATES
Hello, Strepsiades.

STREPSIADES
The same to you. (*giving him a purse*) But first, take this here, since one should show the teacher some appreciation. And about my son, tell me, has he learned the Argument that you brought on stage just now?

SOCRATES
He has.

STREPSIADES
Well done, Omnipotent Boondoggle!

SOCRATES
So you can beat whatever lawsuit you like.

[81] The last day of the month, felt to bridge the old and the new month.

163

ΣΤΡΕΨΙΑΔΗΣ

κεἰ μάρτυρες παρῆσαν ὅτ' ἐδανειζόμην;

ΣΩΚΡΑΤΗΣ

πολλῷ γε μᾶλλον, κἂν παρῶσι χίλιοι.

ΣΤΡΕΨΙΑΔΗΣ

βοάσομαι τἄρα τὰν ὑπέρτονον
1155 βοάν. ἰώ, κλάετ' ὦ 'βολοστάται,
αὐτοί τε καὶ τἀρχαῖα καὶ τόκοι τόκων.
οὐδὲν γὰρ ἄν με φλαῦρον ἐργάσαισθ' ἔτι,
οἷος ἐμοὶ τρέφεται
τοῖσδ' ἐνὶ δώμασι παῖς
1160 ἀμφήκει γλώττῃ λάμπων,
πρόβολος ἐμός, σωτὴρ δόμοις, ἐχθροῖς βλάβη,
λυσανίας πατρῴων μεγάλων κακῶν·
ὃν κάλεσον τρέχων ἔνδοθεν ὡς ἐμέ.
1165 ὦ τέκνον, ὦ παῖ, ἔξελθ' οἴκων,
ἄιε σοῦ πατρός.

ΣΩΚΡΑΤΗΣ

ὅδ' ἐκεῖνος ἀνήρ.

ΣΤΡΕΨΙΑΔΗΣ

ὦ φίλος, ὦ φίλος.

ΣΩΚΡΑΤΗΣ

ἄπιθι λαβών.

STREPSIADES

Even if witnesses were present when I borrowed the money?

SOCRATES

Even if a thousand show up; the more the merrier.

STREPSIADES

Then I'll shout a fortissimo shout!
Hah! Mourn, you moneylenders,
you and your principal and the interest on your
    interest!
No longer can you do me any harm,
with a boy like mine
being reared in these halls,
his double-edged tongue gleaming,
my fortress, savior of my domicile, bane of my
    enemies,
his father's rescuer from heavy woes!
Run inside and tell him to come out to me.

SOCRATES enters the Thinkery.

My child, my boy, come out of the house;
to your father lend an ear!

Enter SOCRATES *with* PHIDIPPIDES.

SOCRATES

Here is the very man.

STREPSIADES

Dear, dear boy!

SOCRATES

Take him and go.

ΣΤΡΕΨΙΑΔΗΣ

1170 ἰὼ ἰώ, τέκνον.
ἰοὺ ἰού.
ὡς ἥδομαί σου πρῶτα τὴν χροιὰν ἰδών.
νῦν μέν γ᾽ ἰδεῖν εἶ πρῶτον ἐξαρνητικὸς
κἀντιλογικός, καὶ τοῦτο τοὐπιχώριον
ἀτεχνῶς ἐπανθεῖ, τὸ "τί λέγεις σύ;" καὶ δοκεῖν
1175 ἀδικοῦντ᾽ ἀδικεῖσθαι, καὶ κακουργοῦντ᾽, οἶδ᾽ ὅτι.
ἐπὶ τοῦ προσώπου τ᾽ ἐστὶν Ἀττικὸν βλέπος.
νῦν οὖν ὅπως σώσεις μ᾽, ἐπεὶ κἀπώλεσας.

ΦΕΙΔΙΠΠΙΔΗΣ

φοβεῖ δὲ δὴ τί;

ΣΤΡΕΨΙΑΔΗΣ
        τὴν ἕνην τε καὶ νέαν.

ΦΕΙΔΙΠΠΙΔΗΣ

ἕνη γάρ ἐστι καὶ νέα τις ἡμέρα;

ΣΤΡΕΨΙΑΔΗΣ

1180 εἰς ἥν γε θήσειν τὰ πρυτανεῖά φασί μοι.

ΦΕΙΔΙΠΠΙΔΗΣ

ἀπολοῦσ᾽ ἄρ᾽ αὔθ᾽ οἱ θέντες. οὐ γάρ ἐσθ᾽ ὅπως
μί᾽ ἡμέρα γένοιτ᾽ ἂν ἡμέραι δύο.

ΣΤΡΕΨΙΑΔΗΣ

οὐκ ἂν γένοιτο;

ΦΕΙΔΙΠΠΙΔΗΣ
        πῶς γάρ, εἰ μή περ γ᾽ ἅμα
αὐτὴ γένοιτ᾽ ἂν γραῦς τε καὶ νέα γυνή.

CLOUDS

SOCRATES goes in.

STREPSIADES

Oho, son! Ta da! Good gracious, how it tickles me right away to see your color! Now it's clear at first glance that you're repudiative and contradictive, and that national trait of ours simply blooms on your face, that "What are you talking about?" look, that innocent look when you're guilty, even of a serious crime, oh don't I know it! Yes, you've got that Athenian expression all over you! Now then, it's up to you to save me, since you ruined me.

PHIDIPPIDES

And just what are you afraid of?

STREPSIADES

The Old and New Day.

PHIDIPPIDES

You mean there's a day that's old and also new?

STREPSIADES

The very day they promise to file their suits against me!

PHIDIPPIDES

Then the filers will lose, because there's no way a single day can become two days.

STREPSIADES

It can't?

PHIDIPPIDES

How could it? Unless it's possible that the same woman can simultaneously be a crone and a girl.

ΣΤΡΕΨΙΑΔΗΣ

καὶ μὴν νενόμισταί γ'.

ΦΕΙΔΙΠΠΙΔΗΣ

1185   οὐ γὰρ οἶμαι τὸν νόμον
ἴσασιν ὀρθῶς ὅτι νοεῖ.

ΣΤΡΕΨΙΑΔΗΣ

νοεῖ δὲ τί;

ΦΕΙΔΙΠΠΙΔΗΣ

ὁ Σόλων ὁ παλαιὸς ἦν φιλόδημος τὴν φύσιν.

ΣΤΡΕΨΙΑΔΗΣ

τουτὶ μὲν οὐδέν πω πρὸς ἕνην τε καὶ νέαν.

ΦΕΙΔΙΠΠΙΔΗΣ

ἐκεῖνος οὖν τὴν κλῆσιν εἰς δύ' ἡμέρας
1190   ἔθηκεν, εἴς γε τὴν ἕνην τε καὶ νέαν,
ἵν' αἱ θέσεις γίγνοιντο τῇ νουμηνίᾳ.

ΣΤΡΕΨΙΑΔΗΣ

ἵνα δὴ τί τὴν ἕνην προσέθηκεν;

ΦΕΙΔΙΠΠΙΔΗΣ

ἵν', ὦ μέλε,
παρόντες οἱ φεύγοντες ἡμέρᾳ μιᾷ
πρότερον ἀπαλλάττοινθ' ἑκόντες· εἰ δὲ μή,
1195   ἕωθεν ὑπανιῷντο τῇ νουμηνίᾳ.

ΣΤΡΕΨΙΑΔΗΣ

πῶς οὐ δέχονται δῆτα τῇ νουμηνίᾳ
ἀρχαὶ τὰ πρυτανεῖ', ἀλλ' ἕνῃ τε καὶ νέᾳ;

STREPSIADES

But that's the custom.

PHIDIPPIDES

I think it's because they don't correctly understand the point of the law.

STREPSIADES

And what is the point?

PHIDIPPIDES

Our venerable Solon[82] was by nature a lover of the people.

STREPSIADES

So far this has nothing to do with Old and New Day.

PHIDIPPIDES

Well, Solon established the summons on two days, the Old Day and the New Day, so that filings would occur on the day of the new moon.

STREPSIADES

And why did he establish Old Day as well?

PHIDIPPIDES

Well sir, that way defendants could appear a day early and settle out of court, and if they didn't, they'd be in for it on New Moon Morning.

STREPSIADES

Then why don't the magistrates accept the sureties on New Moon Day, but only on Old and New Day?

---

[82] Archon in 594/3 and credited with inventing the traditional Athenian law code.

ΦΕΙΔΙΠΠΙΔΗΣ

ὅπερ οἱ προτένθαι γὰρ δοκοῦσί μοι παθεῖν·
ὅπως τάχιστα τὰ πρυτανεῖ ὑφελοίατο,
1200 διὰ τοῦτο προυτένθευσαν ἡμέρᾳ μιᾷ.

ΣΤΡΕΨΙΑΔΗΣ

εὖ γ'. ὦ κακοδαίμονες, τί κάθησθ' ἀβέλτεροι,
ἡμέτερα κέρδη τῶν σοφῶν, ὄντες λίθοι,
ἀριθμός, πρόβατ' ἄλλως, ἀμφορῆς νενησμένοι;
ὥστ' εἰς ἐμαυτὸν καὶ τὸν υἱὸν τουτονὶ
1205 ἐπ' εὐτυχίαισιν ᾀστέον μοὐγκώμιον.

"μάκαρ ὦ Στρεψίαδες
αὐτός τ' ἔφυς, ὡς σοφός,
χοῖον τὸν υἱὸν τρέφεις,"
φήσουσι δή μ' οἱ φίλοι
χοἱ δημόται
1210 ζηλοῦντες ἡνίκ' ἂν σὺ νι-
κᾷς λέγων τὰς δίκας.
ἀλλ' εἰσάγων σε βούλομαι
πρῶτον ἑστιᾶσαι.

ΧΡΗΣΤΗΣ Α΄

εἶτ' ἄνδρα τῶν αὑτοῦ τι χρὴ προϊέναι;
1215 οὐδέποτέ γ', ἀλλὰ κρεῖττον εὐθὺς ἦν τότε
ἀπερυθριᾶσαι μᾶλλον ἢ σχεῖν πράγματα,
ὅτε τῶν ἐμαυτοῦ γ' ἕνεκα νυνὶ χρημάτων
ἕλκω σε κλητεύσοντα, καὶ γενήσομαι
ἐχθρὸς ἔτι πρὸς τούτοισιν ἀνδρὶ δημότῃ.

PHIDIPPIDES

I think they're under the same compulsion as the food inspectors before a festival: to embezzle the sureties as soon as possible, they start tasting a day early.

STREPSIADES

Well done! (*to the spectators*) You pitiful saps, why are you sitting there brainless, pure money in the bank for us intellectuals? You're stones, ciphers, mere sheep, a bunch of empty jars! I've simply got to sing an encomium for me and this son of mine to celebrate our success.

> "Happy Strepsiades,
> you yourself were born sage,
> and what a son you're rearing!"
> That's what my friends will say to me,
> and my neighbors too,
> in envy, when you win my lawsuits
> with your oratory.
> But first I want to take you home
> and throw you a dinner party.

STREPSIADES and PHIDIPPIDES go into their house. Enter FIRST CREDITOR with Witness.

FIRST CREDITOR

So is a man supposed to throw away a piece of his own estate? No, never! An unblushing refusal right at the start would have been better than this hassle. Here I am dragging you along to witness a summons over my money, and on top of that I'll be making an enemy of a man from my

1220 ἀτὰρ οὐδέποτέ γε τὴν πατρίδα καταισχυνῶ
ζῶν, ἀλλὰ καλοῦμαι Στρεψιάδην—

ΣΤΡΕΨΙΑΔΗΣ
τίς οὑτοσί;

ΧΡΗΣΤΗΣ Α´
—εἰς τὴν ἔνην τε καὶ νέαν.

ΣΤΡΕΨΙΑΔΗΣ
μαρτύρομαι
ὅτι εἰς δύ᾽ εἶπεν ἡμέρας. τοῦ χρήματος;

ΧΡΗΣΤΗΣ Α´
τῶν δώδεκα μνῶν, ἃς ἔλαβες ὠνούμενος
τὸν ψαρὸν ἵππον.

ΣΤΡΕΨΙΑΔΗΣ
1225 ἵππον; οὐκ ἀκούετε;
ὃν πάντες ὑμεῖς ἴστε μισοῦνθ᾽ ἱππικήν.

ΧΡΗΣΤΗΣ Α´
καὶ νὴ Δί᾽ ἀποδώσειν γ᾽ ἐπώμνυς τοὺς θεούς.

ΣΤΡΕΨΙΑΔΗΣ
μὰ τὸν Δί᾽ οὐ γάρ πω τότ᾽ ἐξηπίστατο
Φειδιππίδης μοι τὸν ἀκατάβλητον λόγον.

ΧΡΗΣΤΗΣ Α´
1230 νῦν δὲ διὰ τοῦτ᾽ ἔξαρνος εἶναι διανοεῖ;

ΣΤΡΕΨΙΑΔΗΣ
τί γὰρ ἄλλ᾽ ἂν ἀπολαύσαιμι τοῦ μαθήματος;

own neighborhood. But as long as I live I'll never disgrace my country! I hereby summon Strepsiades—

STREPSIADES

(*coming outside*) Who's that?

FIRST CREDITOR

—to appear on Old and New Day.

STREPSIADES

(*to the spectators*) I call you to witness that he specified two days. (*to First Creditor*) What's the problem?

FIRST CREDITOR

The twelve minas that you borrowed to buy the charcoal stallion.

STREPSIADES

Horse? Listen to that! You all know that I can't stand anything to do with horses!

FIRST CREDITOR

By Zeus, you also swore by the gods that you'd repay me.

STREPSIADES

I won't, by Zeus; back then, my Phidippides hadn't yet learned the irrefutable Argument.

FIRST CREDITOR

And for that reason you now intend to deny the debt?

STREPSIADES

Well, what other return will I get on his tuition?

ΧΡΗΣΤΗΣ Α΄

καὶ ταῦτ' ἐθελήσεις ἀπομόσαι μοι τοὺς θεοὺς
ἵν' ἂν κελεύσω 'γώ σε;

ΣΤΡΕΨΙΑΔΗΣ

τοὺς ποίους θεούς;

ΧΡΗΣΤΗΣ Α΄

τὸν Δία, τὸν Ἑρμῆν, τὸν Ποσειδῶ.

ΣΤΡΕΨΙΑΔΗΣ

νὴ Δία,

1235   κἂν προσκαταθείην γ', ὥστ' ὀμόσαι, τριώβολον.

ΧΡΗΣΤΗΣ Α΄

ἀπόλοιο τοίνυν ἕνεκ' ἀναιδείας ἔτι.

ΣΤΡΕΨΙΑΔΗΣ

ἁλσὶν διασμηχθεὶς ὄναιτ' ἂν οὑτοσί.

ΧΡΗΣΤΗΣ Α΄

οἴμ' ὡς καταγελᾷς.

ΣΤΡΕΨΙΑΔΗΣ

ἐξ χοᾶς χωρήσεται.

ΧΡΗΣΤΗΣ Α΄

οὗτοι μὰ τὸν Δία τὸν μέγαν καὶ τοὺς θεοὺς
ἐμοῦ καταπροΐξει.

ΣΤΡΕΨΙΑΔΗΣ

θαυμασίως ἥσθην θεοῖς,

1240   καὶ Ζεὺς γελοῖος ὀμνύμενος τοῖς εἰδόσιν.

FIRST CREDITOR

And you'll be willing to forswear it by the gods, wherever I prescribe?

STREPSIADES

What sort of gods?

FIRST CREDITOR

Zeus, Hermes, Poseidon.

STREPSIADES

Certainly Zeus! I'd even put down an extra three obols to swear by him!

FIRST CREDITOR

Then I hope your shamelessness ruins you yet!

STREPSIADES

(*patting the First Creditor's belly*) This here would do nicely with a brine treatment.[83]

FIRST CREDITOR

Good god, you're making fun of me!

STREPSIADES

It'll hold ten liters.

FIRST CREDITOR

So help me mighty Zeus, so help me all the gods, you won't get away with treating me this way!

STREPSIADES

"Gods!" That's wonderfully amusing. Swearing by Zeus is a joke among the cognoscenti.

[83] I.e. as a preliminary to tanning, to make a wineskin.

ΧΡΗΣΤΗΣ Α´

ἦ μὴν σὺ τούτων τῷ χρόνῳ δώσεις δίκην.
ἀλλ᾽ εἴτ᾽ ἀποδώσεις μοι τὰ χρήματ᾽ εἴτε μή,
ἀπόπεμψον ἀποκρινάμενος.

ΣΤΡΕΨΙΑΔΗΣ

ἔχε νυν ἥσυχος·
1245 ἐγὼ γὰρ αὐτίκ᾽ ἀποκρινοῦμαί σοι σαφῶς.

ΧΡΗΣΤΗΣ Α´

τί σοι δοκεῖ δράσειν; ἀποδώσειν σοι δοκεῖ;

ΣΤΡΕΨΙΑΔΗΣ

ποῦ ᾽σθ᾽ οὗτος ἀπαιτῶν με τἀργύριον; λέγε,
τουτὶ τί ἐστι;

ΧΡΗΣΤΗΣ Α´

τοῦθ᾽ ὅ τι ἐστί; κάρδοπος.

ΣΤΡΕΨΙΑΔΗΣ

ἔπειτ᾽ ἀπαιτεῖς ἀργύριον τοιοῦτος ὤν;
1250 οὐκ ἂν ἀποδοίην οὐδ᾽ ἂν ὀβολὸν οὐδενὶ
ὅστις καλέσειε "κάρδοπον" τὴν καρδόπην.

ΧΡΗΣΤΗΣ Α´

οὐκ ἄρ᾽ ἀποδώσεις;

ΣΤΡΕΨΙΑΔΗΣ

οὐχ ὅσον γ᾽ ἔμ᾽ εἰδέναι.
οὔκουν ἀνύσας τι θᾶττον ἀπολιταργιεῖς
ἀπὸ τῆς θύρας;

FIRST CREDITOR

Mark my words, the time will come when you'll get your just deserts for this. But for now, just tell me before I go whether you intend to repay me or not.

STREPSIADES

Just hold still; I'll be right back with a straight answer for you.

STREPSIADES goes into his house.

FIRST CREDITOR

(*to the Witness*)What do you think he'll do? Do you think he'll pay?

STREPSIADES returns with a mortar.

STREPSIADES

Where's the guy who's demanding the money from me? Tell me, what's this?

FIRST CREDITOR

That? A mortar.

STREPSIADES

And you're demanding money, after an answer like that? I wouldn't repay a single penny to anyone who calls a morté a mortar.

FIRST CREDITOR

I take it you won't pay.

STREPSIADES

Not as far as I know. Now take a hike, and make it snappy too, away from my door.

ΧΡΗΣΤΗΣ Α´

ἄπειμι· καὶ τοῦτ᾽ ἴσθ᾽, ὅτι
1255 θήσω πρυτανεῖ, ἢ μηκέτι ζῴην ἐγώ.

ΣΤΡΕΨΙΑΔΗΣ

προσαποβαλεῖς ἄρ᾽ αὐτὰ πρὸς ταῖς δώδεκα.
καίτοι σε τοῦτό γ᾽ οὐχὶ βούλομαι παθεῖν
ὁτιὴ ᾽κάλεσας εὐηθικῶς "τὴν κάρδοπον".

ΧΡΗΣΤΗΣ Β´

ἰώ μοι μοι.

ΣΤΡΕΨΙΑΔΗΣ

ἔα·
1260 τίς οὑτοσί ποτ᾽ ἔσθ᾽ ὁ θρηνῶν; οὔ τι που
τῶν Καρκίνου τις δαιμόνων ἐφθέγξατο;

ΧΡΗΣΤΗΣ Β´

τί δ᾽, ὅστις εἰμί, τοῦτο βούλεσθ᾽ εἰδέναι;
ἀνὴρ κακοδαίμων.

ΣΤΡΕΨΙΑΔΗΣ

κατὰ σεαυτόν νυν τρέπου.

ΧΡΗΣΤΗΣ Β´

ὦ σκληρὲ δαῖμον· ὦ τύχαι θραυσάντυγες
1265 ἵππων ἐμῶν· ὦ Παλλάς, ὥς μ᾽ ἀπώλεσας.

ΣΤΡΕΨΙΑΔΗΣ

τί δαί σε Τληνπόλεμός ποτ᾽ εἴργασται κακόν;

---

84 A tragic dramatist who won at least one first prize (Dionysia

FIRST CREDITOR

I'm going. But be aware that I'll be depositing sureties if it's the last thing I do!

STREPSIADES

Then you'll be throwing that away on top of the twelve minas. Still, I don't want that to happen to you just because you were simple enough to say "mortar."

Exit FIRST CREDITOR *with* Witness. *Enter* SECOND CREDI-TOR.

SECOND CREDITOR

Oh me, oh my!

STREPSIADES

Eh? Who can this be, beating his breast? Could it possibly be one of Carcinus' deities that made that sound?[84]

SECOND CREDITOR

Who am I? Why do you want to know? A man ill-fated.

STREPSIADES

Then keep it to yourself.

SECOND CREDITOR

O cruel deity, o mischance that unhorsed my chariot rail! O Pallas, how you have ruined me![85]

STREPSIADES

And what harm has Tlempolemus ever done you?

446), served as a general in 431, and had three sons who were famous dancers; one of them, Xenocles, also wrote tragedies.

[85] These lines parody Alcmena's speech in the tragedy *Licymnius* by Carcinus' son, Xenocles; Tlempolemus had killed her half-brother.

ΧΡΗΣΤΗΣ Β΄

μὴ σκῶπτέ μ᾽, ὦ τᾶν, ἀλλά μοι τὰ χρήματα
τὸν υἱὸν ἀποδοῦναι κέλευσον ἅλαβεν,
ἄλλως τε μέντοι καὶ κακῶς πεπραγότι.

ΣΤΡΕΨΙΑΔΗΣ

τὰ ποῖα ταῦτα χρήμαθ᾽;

ΧΡΗΣΤΗΣ Β΄

ἁδανείσατο.

1270

ΣΤΡΕΨΙΑΔΗΣ

κακῶς ἄρ᾽ ὄντως εἶχες, ὥς γ᾽ ἐμοὶ δοκεῖς.

ΧΡΗΣΤΗΣ Β΄

ἵππους γ᾽ ἐλαύνων ἐξέπεσον νὴ τοὺς θεούς.

ΣΤΡΕΨΙΑΔΗΣ

τί δῆτα ληρεῖς ὥσπερ ἀπ᾽ ὄνου καταπεσών;

ΧΡΗΣΤΗΣ Β΄

ληρῶ, τὰ χρήματ᾽ ἀπολαβεῖν εἰ βούλομαι;

ΣΤΡΕΨΙΑΔΗΣ

οὐκ ἔσθ᾽ ὅπως σύ γ᾽ αὐτὸς ὑγιαίνεις.

ΧΡΗΣΤΗΣ Β΄

τί δαί;

1275

ΣΤΡΕΨΙΑΔΗΣ

τὸν ἐγκέφαλον ὥσπερ σεσεῖσθαί μοι δοκεῖς.

ΧΡΗΣΤΗΣ Β΄

σὺ δὲ νὴ τὸν Ἑρμῆν προσκεκλήσεσθαί γ᾽ ἐμοί,
εἰ μὴ ᾽ποδώσεις τἀργύριον.

SECOND CREDITOR

Don't mock me, sir; just tell your son to pay back the money he borrowed, especially now that I'm in a bad way.

STREPSIADES

What money is that?

SECOND CREDITOR

What he borrowed!

STREPSIADES

Then you really are in a bad way, it seems to me.

SECOND CREDITOR

Yes, by heaven, I was driving a chariot and fell off.

STREPSIADES

The way you're jabbering, I'd say you fell off your rocker!

SECOND CREDITOR

Me jabber, just wanting to get my money back?

STREPSIADES

There's no way you'll ever regain your sanity.

SECOND CREDITOR

How so?

STREPSIADES

In my opinion, there's something wrong with your brain.

SECOND CREDITOR

And in my opinion, by Hermes, you're going to get a summons from me if you don't repay my money.

ΣΤΡΕΨΙΑΔΗΣ

κάτειπέ νυν·
πότερα νομίζεις καινὸν ἀεὶ τὸν Δία
1280 ὕειν ὕδωρ ἑκάστοτ', ἢ τὸν ἥλιον
ἕλκειν κάτωθεν ταὐτὸ τοῦθ' ὕδωρ πάλιν;

ΧΡΗΣΤΗΣ Β'
οὐκ οἶδ' ἔγωγ' ὁπότερον, οὐδέ μοι μέλει.

ΣΤΡΕΨΙΑΔΗΣ
πῶς οὖν ἀπολαβεῖν τἀργύριον δίκαιος εἶ,
εἰ μηδὲν οἶσθα τῶν μετεώρων πραγμάτων;

ΧΡΗΣΤΗΣ Β'
1285 ἀλλ' εἰ σπανίζεις τἀργυρίου μοι τὸν τόκον
ἀπόδοτε.

ΣΤΡΕΨΙΑΔΗΣ
τοῦτο δ' ἔσθ', ὁ τόκος, τί θηρίον;

ΧΡΗΣΤΗΣ Β'
τί δ' ἄλλο γ' ἢ κατὰ μῆνα καὶ καθ' ἡμέραν
πλέον πλέον τἀργύριον ἀεὶ γίγνεται
ὑπορρέοντος τοῦ χρόνου;

ΣΤΡΕΨΙΑΔΗΣ
καλῶς λέγεις.
1290 τί δῆτα; τὴν θάλατταν ἔσθ' ὅτι πλείονα
νυνὶ νομίζεις ἢ πρὸ τοῦ;

ΧΡΗΣΤΗΣ Β'
μὰ Δί', ἀλλ' ἴσην.
οὐ γὰρ δίκαιον πλείον' εἶναι.

CLOUDS

STREPSIADES

So tell me, do you think that Zeus rains new water every time, or that the sun draws up from below the very same water again?

SECOND CREDITOR

I don't know and I don't care!

STREPSIADES

Then how can you justifiably ask for your money back, knowing nothing of meteorology?

SECOND CREDITOR

Look, if you're short, at least pay me the interest on my money.

STREPSIADES

This "interest," what sort of beast is it?

SECOND CREDITOR

None other than the tendency of a given sum of money to grow ever bigger and bigger, day by day and month by month, as time flows by.

STREPSIADES

Well said. Now then, the sea: do you think it's any bigger now than it used to be?

SECOND CREDITOR

Certainly not; it's the same. It's against the rules for it to be bigger.

ΣΤΡΕΨΙΑΔΗΣ

κᾷτα πῶς
αὕτη μέν, ὦ κακόδαιμον, οὐδὲν γίγνεται
ἐπιρρεόντων τῶν ποταμῶν πλείων, σὺ δὲ
1295 ζητεῖς ποιῆσαι τἀργύριον πλέον τὸ σόν;
οὐκ ἀποδιώξει σαυτὸν ἀπὸ τῆς οἰκίας;
φέρε μοι τὸ κέντρον.

ΧΡΗΣΤΗΣ Β΄
ταῦτ᾽ ἐγὼ μαρτύρομαι.

ΣΤΡΕΨΙΑΔΗΣ
ὕπαγε. τί μέλλεις; οὐκ ἐλᾷς, ὦ σαμφόρα;

ΧΡΗΣΤΗΣ Β΄
ταῦτ᾽ οὐχ ὕβρις δῆτ᾽ ἐστίν;

ΣΤΡΕΨΙΑΔΗΣ
ἄξεις; ἐπιαλῶ
1300 κεντῶν ὑπὸ τὸν πρωκτόν σε τὸν σειραφόρον.
φεύγεις; ἔμελλόν σ᾽ ἄρα κινήσειν ἐγὼ
αὐτοῖς τροχοῖς τοῖς σοῖσι καὶ ξυνωρίσιν.

ΧΟΡΟΣ
(στρ) οἷον τὸ πραγμάτων ἐρᾶν φλαύρων· ὁ γὰρ
γέρων ὅδ᾽ ἐρασθεὶς
1305 ἀποστερῆσαι βούλεται
τὰ χρήμαθ᾽ ἁδανείσατο.
κοὐκ ἔσθ᾽ ὅπως οὐ τήμερον
λήψεταί τι πρᾶγμ᾽ ὃ τοῦ-
τον ποιήσει τὸν σοφι-

STREPSIADES

Then what about this, you sadsack: if the sea grows no bigger even though rivers flow into it, where do you get off looking to make your money grow bigger? So prosecute yourself right off my property! Boy, fetch me my goad!

SECOND CREDITOR

(*to the spectators*) Be my witnesses to this!

STREPSIADES

Giddyup! Quit stalling! Get going, you branded nag!

SECOND CREDITOR

This is a clear case of assault!

STREPSIADES

Move out! I'm going to grab you and shove this goad up your thoroughbred arsehole! Running off, eh? I knew I'd get you to move, for all your wheels and teams of steeds.

SECOND CREDITOR runs off. STREPSIADES goes into house.

CHORUS

How momentous it is to lust for villainous business,
like this old man: in the grip of this lust,
he wants to avoid repaying
the money he borrowed.

And today for sure,
he'll lay hold of some business
that will make this sophist suddenly

στὴν ⟨ἀπάντων⟩ ὧν πανουργεῖν ἤρξατ᾽ ἐξ-
1310 αἴφνης †τι κακὸν λαβεῖν†.

(ἀντ) οἶμαι γὰρ αὐτὸν αὐτίχ᾽ εὑρήσειν ὅπερ
πάλαι ποτ᾽ ἐπῄτει,
εἶναι τὸν υἱὸν δεινόν οἱ
γνώμας ἐναντίας λέγειν
1315 τοῖσιν δικαίοις, ὥστε νι–
κᾶν ἅπαντας, οἷσπερ ἂν
ξυγγένηται, κἂν λέγῃ
παμπόνηρ᾽. ἴσως δ᾽ ἴσως βουλήσεται
1320 κἄφωνον αὐτὸν εἶναι.

ΣΤΡΕΨΙΑΔΗΣ

ἰοὺ ἰού.
ὦ γείτονες καὶ ξυγγενεῖς καὶ δημόται,
ἀμυνάθετέ μοι τυπτομένῳ πάσῃ τέχνῃ.
οἴμοι κακοδαίμων τῆς κεφαλῆς καὶ τῆς γνάθου.
ὦ μιαρέ, τύπτεις τὸν πατέρα;

ΦΕΙΔΙΠΠΙΔΗΣ

1325   φήμ᾽, ὦ πάτερ.

ΣΤΡΕΨΙΑΔΗΣ

ὁρᾶθ᾽ ὁμολογοῦνθ᾽ ὅτι με τύπτει;

ΦΕΙΔΙΠΠΙΔΗΣ

                        καὶ μάλα.

1309 ⟨ἀπάντων⟩ Austin   1310 †τι κακὸν λαβεῖν† e.g.
ἄποινα τεῖσαι Henderson, ἀποστραφῆναι Sommerstein

⟨pay dearly for⟩
all the wrongful activities he undertook.

For I think he'll soon find
what he's long been asking for,
a son grown formidable
at arguing views counter
to what's right, so that
he can beat anyone he may meet,
even if he argues what's totally bad.
But maybe, just maybe,
his father will wish
his son were mute.

STREPSIADES runs from the house, pursued by PHIDIP-PIDES.

STREPSIADES

Help! Help! Neighbors, kinsmen, fellow demesmen, rescue me any way you can! I'm being beaten! Oh dear, my unlucky head! My jaw! (*to Phidippides*) You scum, you'd beat your father?

PHIDIPPIDES

That's right, father.

STREPSIADES

See, he admits beating me!

PHIDIPPIDES

Sure I do.

1312 ἐπῄτει Hermann: ἐπεζήτει RV: ἐζήτει cett.

ΣΤΡΕΨΙΑΔΗΣ

ὦ μιαρὲ καὶ πατραλοῖα καὶ τοιχωρύχε.

ΦΕΙΔΙΠΠΙΔΗΣ

αὖθίς με ταὐτὰ ταῦτα καὶ πλείω λέγε.
ἆρ᾽ οἶσθ᾽ ὅτι χαίρω πόλλ᾽ ἀκούων καὶ κακά;

ΣΤΡΕΨΙΑΔΗΣ

ὦ λακκόπρωκτε.

ΦΕΙΔΙΠΠΙΔΗΣ

1330   πάττε πολλοῖς τοῖς ῥόδοις.

ΣΤΡΕΨΙΑΔΗΣ

τὸν πατέρα τύπτεις;

ΦΕΙΔΙΠΠΙΔΗΣ

            κἀποφανῶ γε νὴ Δία
ὡς ἐν δίκῃ σ᾽ ἔτυπτον.

ΣΤΡΕΨΙΑΔΗΣ

            ὦ μιαρώτατε,
καὶ πῶς γένοιτ᾽ ἂν πατέρα τύπτειν ἐν δίκῃ;

ΦΕΙΔΙΠΠΙΔΗΣ

ἔγωγ᾽ ἀποδείξω καί σε νικήσω λέγων.

ΣΤΡΕΨΙΑΔΗΣ

τουτὶ σὺ νικήσεις;

ΦΕΙΔΙΠΠΙΔΗΣ

1335   πολύ γε καὶ ῥᾳδίως.
ἑλοῦ δ᾽ ὁπότερον τοῖν λόγοιν βούλει λέγειν.

STREPSIADES

You scum, you parricide, you criminal!

PHIDIPPIDES

Call me those very names again, and worse. Do you know
I enjoy being called lots of bad names?

STREPSIADES

You giant arsehole!

PHIDIPPIDES

Strew me with lots of roses!

STREPSIADES

You're beating your father?

PHIDIPPIDES

God yes, and I'll prove that I was right to beat you.

STREPSIADES

Scum of the earth! Just how could it be right to beat a
father?

PHIDIPPIDES

I'll demonstrate, and I'll win the argument too.

STREPSIADES

You'll win that argument?

PHIDIPPIDES

Completely, with no sweat. Just choose which of the two
arguments you want to defend.

ΣΤΡΕΨΙΑΔΗΣ

ποίοιν λόγοιν;

ΦΕΙΔΙΠΠΙΔΗΣ

τὸν κρείττον᾽ ἢ τὸν ἥττονα.

ΣΤΡΕΨΙΑΔΗΣ

ἐδιδαξάμην μέντοι σε νὴ Δί᾽, ὦ μέλε,
τοῖσιν δικαίοις ἀντιλέγειν, εἰ ταῦτά γε
1340 μέλλεις ἀναπείσειν, ὡς δίκαιον καὶ καλὸν
τὸν πατέρα τύπτεσθ᾽ ἐστὶν ὑπὸ τῶν υἱέων.

ΦΕΙΔΙΠΠΙΔΗΣ

ἀλλ᾽ οἶμαι μέντοι σ᾽ ἀναπείσειν, ὥστε γε
οὐδ᾽ αὐτὸς ἀκροασάμενος οὐδὲν ἀντερεῖς.

ΣΤΡΕΨΙΑΔΗΣ

καὶ μὴν ὅ τι καὶ λέξεις ἀκοῦσαι βούλομαι.

ΧΟΡΟΣ

(στρ) σὸν ἔργον, ὦ πρεσβῦτα, φροντίζειν ὅπῃ
1346   τὸν ἄνδρα κρατήσεις,
        ὡς οὗτος, εἰ μή τῳ 'πεποίθειν, οὐκ ἂν ἦν
        οὕτως ἀκόλαστος.
        ἀλλ᾽ ἔσθ᾽ ὅτῳ θρασύνεται· δῆλόν ⟨γε τοι⟩
1350   τὸ λῆμα τὸ τἀνδρός.

ΚΟΡΥΦΑΙΑ

ἀλλ᾽ ἐξ ὅτου τὸ πρῶτον ἤρξαθ᾽ ἡ μάχη γενέσθαι
ἤδη λέγειν χρὴ πρὸς χορόν· πάντως δὲ τοῦτο
        δράσεις.

STREPSIADES

What do you mean, two arguments?

PHIDIPPIDES

The Better or the Worse.

STREPSIADES

By god I truly have had you taught to speak against what's right, my boy, if you can carry this proposal, that it's right and good for a father to be beaten by his sons.

PHIDIPPIDES

But I think I can carry it. When you've heard me out, not even you will have anything to say in rebuttal.

STREPSIADES

All right then, I'd like to hear your side of the argument.

CHORUS

Your task, old man, is to figure a way
to master your opponent,
for if he had nothing up his sleeve
he wouldn't have been so sassy.
Yes, there's something that feeds his mettle; certainly
the man's boldness is plain.

CHORUS LEADER

But now you're supposed to tell the Chorus how this quarrel originally started, though you'll do that anyway.

ARISTOPHANES

ΣΤΡΕΨΙΑΔΗΣ

καὶ μὴν ὅθεν γε πρῶτον ἠρξάμεσθα λοιδορεῖσθαι
ἐγὼ φράσω. ἐπειδὴ γὰρ εἰστιώμεθ', ὥσπερ ἴστε,
πρῶτον μὲν αὐτὸν τὴν λύραν λαβόντ' ἐγὼ 'κέλευσα
ᾆσαι Σιμωνίδου μέλος, τὸν Κριόν, ὡς ἐπέχθη.
ὁ δ' εὐθέως ἀρχαῖον εἶν' ἔφασκε τὸ κιθαρίζειν
ᾄδειν τε πίνονθ', ὡσπερεὶ κάχρυς γυναῖκ' ἀλοῦσαν.

ΦΕΙΔΙΠΠΙΔΗΣ

οὐ γὰρ τότ' εὐθὺς χρῆν σ' ἀράττεσθαί τε καὶ
    πατεῖσθαι,
ᾄδειν κελεύονθ', ὡσπερεὶ τέττιγας ἑστιῶντα;

ΣΤΡΕΨΙΑΔΗΣ

τοιαῦτα μέντοι καὶ τότ' ἔλεγεν ἔνδον, οἷάπερ νῦν,
καὶ τὸν Σιμωνίδην ἔφασκ' εἶναι κακὸν ποιητήν.
κἀγὼ μόλις μέν, ἀλλ' ὅμως, ἠνεσχόμην τὸ πρῶτον.
ἔπειτα δ' ἐκέλευσ' αὐτὸν ἀλλὰ μυρρίνην λαβόντα
τῶν Αἰσχύλου λέξαι τί μοι. κᾆθ' οὗτος εὐθὺς εἶπεν·
"ἐγὼ γὰρ Αἰσχύλον νομίζω πρῶτον ἐν ποιηταῖς—
ψόφου πλέων, ἀξύστατον, στόμφακα, κρημνοποιόν."
κἀνταῦθα πῶς οἴεσθέ μου τὴν καρδίαν ὀρεχθεῖν;
ὅμως δὲ τὸν θυμὸν δακὼν ἔφην· "σὺ δ' ἀλλὰ τούτων
λέξον τι τῶν νεωτέρων, ἅττ' ἐστὶ τὰ σοφὰ ταῦτα."
ὁ δ' εὐθὺς ᾖγ' Εὐριπίδου ῥῆσίν τιν', ὡς ἐκίνει
ἀδελφός, ὦ 'λεξίκακε, τὴν ὁμομητρίαν ἀδελφήν.

1355
1360
1365
1370

---

¹³⁷¹ ᾖγ' Borthwick: ᾖσ(εν) a

---

⁸⁶ Simonides of Ceos (c. 556-468) composed this victory ode

STREPSIADES

I will indeed tell you how our name-calling first started.
You'll recall that we were having a feast. First of all I asked
him to pick up his lyre and sing a song by Simonides, the
one about how Ram got shorn,[86] and he right away said it
was old fashioned to play the lyre and sing at a drinking
party, like a woman hulling barley.

PHIDIPPIDES

Why, right then and there you should have been pounded
and stomped—asking me sing, as if you were throwing a
feast for cicadas!

STREPSIADES

That's just the kind of thing he kept saying there in the
house, what he's saying now. And he said that Simonides
was a bad poet! I only just put up with it, but I did put up
with it, at first. Then I asked him if he would at least take
a myrtle sprig[87] and sing me something from the works of
Aeschylus. And he right away said, "In my opinion, Aeschy-
lus is chief among poets—chiefly full of noise, incoherent,
a windbag, a maker of lofty locutions." Can you imagine
how that jolted my heart? But I bit back my anger and said,
"All right then, recite something from these modern poets,
that brainy stuff, whatever it is." And he right away tossed
off some speech by Euripides about how a brother, god
save me, was screwing his sister by the same mother![88] I

(fr. 507 Campbell) around the turn of the fifth century for a wres-
tler who had defeated Crius of Aegina (the name means "Ram")
at the Nemean games.   [87] The custom at symposia when a
singer did not accompany himself on the lyre.

   [88] An allusion probably to Macareus and Canace in the tragedy
Aeolus.

κἀγὼ οὐκέτ᾽ ἐξηνεσχόμην, ἀλλ᾽ εὐθέως ἀράττω
πολλοῖς κακοῖς καἰσχροῖσι. κᾆτ᾽ ἐντεῦθεν, οἷον εἰκός,
1375 ἔπος πρὸς ἔπος ἠρειδόμεσθ᾽· εἶθ᾽ οὗτος ἐπαναπηδᾷ,
κἄπειτ᾽ ἔφλα με κἀσπόδει κἄπνιγε κἀπέτριβεν.

ΦΕΙΔΙΠΠΙΔΗΣ

οὔκουν δικαίως, ὅστις οὐκ Εὐριπίδην ἐπαινεῖς,
σοφώτατον;

ΣΤΡΕΨΙΑΔΗΣ

σοφώτατον γ᾽ ἐκεῖνον, ὦ—τί σ᾽ εἴπω;
ἀλλ᾽ αὖθις αὖ τυπτήσομαι.

ΦΕΙΔΙΠΠΙΔΗΣ

νὴ τὸν Δί᾽, ἐν δίκῃ γ᾽ ἄν.

ΣΤΡΕΨΙΑΔΗΣ

1380 καὶ πῶς δικαίως; ὅστις ὦ ᾽ναίσχυντέ σ᾽ ἐξέθρεψα
αἰσθανόμενός σου πάντα τραυλίζοντος, ὅτι νοοίης.
εἰ μέν γε βρῦν εἴποις, ἐγὼ γνοὺς ἂν πιεῖν ἐπέσχον·
μαμμᾶν δ᾽ ἂν αἰτήσαντος, ἧκόν σοι φέρων ἂν ἄρτον·
κακκᾶν δ᾽ ἂν οὐκ ἔφθης φράσας, κἀγὼ λαβὼν θύραζε
1385 ἐξέφερον ἂν καὶ προυσχόμην σε. σὺ δέ με νῦν
ἀπάγχων,
βοῶντα καὶ κεκραγόθ᾽ ὅτι
χεζητιῴην, οὐκ ἔτλης
ἔξω ᾽ξενεγκεῖν, ὦ μιαρέ,
θύραζέ μ᾽, ἀλλὰ πνιγόμενος
1390 αὐτοῦ ᾽ποίησα κακκᾶν.

1376 κἀπέτριβεν Π3 n S: κἀπέθλιβεν RV

couldn't put up with it any longer, but right away started pelting him with lots of nasty, dirty words. And from that point on, as you might expect, we laid into each other word for word. Then he jumps up at me, and starts to bash me and thump me and throttle me and crush me!

PHIDIPPIDES

And didn't you have it coming, for refusing to praise Euripides, a genius?

STREPSIADES

Oh, that one's certainly a genius, you, oh what'll I call you? No, I'll only get beaten all over again.

PHIDIPPIDES

Zeus yes, and you'd deserve it!

STREPSIADES

Just how would I deserve it? I'm the one who raised you, you brazen ingrate, the one who listened to all your baby talk and knew what you meant. If you said "dwik," I would know to get you a drink. When you asked for "babba," I'd be there with bread. And before you even finished saying "poopie," I'd pick you up, take you outside, and hold you at arm's length. But when you were choking me just now, and I was bellowing and screaming that I had to shit, you balked at taking *me* outside, you scum, but you kept choking me until I made poopie right there!

ΧΟΡΟΣ

(ἀντ) οἶμαί γε τῶν νεωτέρων τὰς καρδίας
πηδᾶν ὅ τι λέξει.
εἰ γὰρ τοιαῦτά γ᾿ οὗτος ἐξειργασμένος
λαλῶν ἀναπείσει,
1395 τὸ δέρμα τῶν γεραιτέρων λάβοιμεν ἂν
ἀλλ᾿ οὐδ᾿ ἐρεβίνθου.

ΚΟΡΥΦΑΙΑ

σὸν ἔργον, ὦ καινῶν ἐπῶν κινητὰ καὶ μοχλευτά,
πειθώ τινα ζητεῖν, ὅπως δόξεις λέγειν δίκαια.

ΦΕΙΔΙΠΠΙΔΗΣ

ὡς ἡδὺ καινοῖς πράγμασιν καὶ δεξιοῖς ὁμιλεῖν
1400 καὶ τῶν καθεστώτων νόμων ὑπερφρονεῖν δύνασθαι.
ἐγὼ γὰρ ὅτε μὲν ἱππικῇ τὸν νοῦν μόνῃ προσεῖχον,
οὐδ᾿ ἂν τρί᾿ εἰπεῖν ῥήμαθ᾿ οἷός τ᾿ ἦν πρὶν
ἐξαμαρτεῖν·
νυνὶ δ᾿, ἐπειδή μ᾿ οὑτοσὶ τούτων ἔπαυσεν αὐτός,
γνώμαις δὲ λεπταῖς καὶ λόγοις ξύνειμι καὶ μερίμ-
ναις,
1405 οἶμαι διδάξειν ὡς δίκαιον τὸν πατέρα κολάζειν.

ΣΤΡΕΨΙΑΔΗΣ

ἵππευε τοίνυν νὴ Δί᾿, ὡς ἔμοιγε κρεῖττόν ἐστιν
ἵππων τρέφειν τέθριππον ἢ τυπτόμενον ἐπιτριβῆναι.

ΦΕΙΔΙΠΠΙΔΗΣ

ἐκεῖσε δ᾿ ὅθεν ἀπέσχισάς με τοῦ λόγου μέτειμι,
καὶ πρῶτ᾿ ἐρήσομαί σε τουτί· παῖδά μ᾿ ὄντ᾿ ἔτυπτες;

CLOUDS

CHORUS

I'm sure the hearts of the young
are throbbing to hear his reply.
If he can practice that sort of behavior,
and then win approval by glib talk,
we'd value the oldsters' hides
at nary a fig.

CHORUS LEADER

The floor is yours, you instigator and engineer of novel discourse. Find a way to talk us into thinking what you say is right.

PHIDIPPIDES

How agreeable is intimacy with novel and clever activities, and the power to scorn established customs! Back when I had a one-track mind for horse racing, I couldn't get three words out before I stumbled over them. But now that my adversary himself has made me give all that up, and I'm at home with subtle ideas, arguments, and contemplations, I'm sure I can demonstrate that it's right to spank one's father.

STREPSIADES

Back to the cavalry then, by Zeus! I'd much rather support a four-horse team than get beaten to a pulp.

PHIDIPPIDES

I'll pursue my argument from the point where you cut me off, and first ask you this: did you beat me when I was a boy?

ΣΤΡΕΨΙΑΔΗΣ

ἔγωγέ σ᾽, εὐνοῶν τε καὶ κηδόμενος.

ΦΕΙΔΙΠΠΙΔΗΣ

1410   εἰπὲ δή μοι,
οὐ κἀμὲ σοὶ δίκαιόν ἐστιν εὐνοεῖν ὁμοίως
τύπτειν τ᾽, ἐπειδήπερ γε τοῦτ᾽ ἔστ᾽ εὐνοεῖν, τὸ τύπτειν;
πῶς γὰρ τὸ μὲν σὸν σῶμα χρὴ πληγῶν ἀθῷον εἶναι,
τοὐμὸν δὲ μή; καὶ μὴν ἔφυν ἐλεύθερός γε κἀγώ.
1415 "κλάουσι παῖδες, πατέρα δ᾽ οὐ κλάειν δοκεῖς;"
φήσεις νομίζεσθαι σὺ παιδὸς τοῦτο τοὔργον εἶναι·
ἐγὼ δέ γ᾽ ἀντείποιμ᾽ ἂν ὡς δὶς παῖδες οἱ γέροντες.
εἰκός τε μᾶλλον τοὺς γέροντας ἢ νέους τι κλάειν,
ὅσῳπερ ἐξαμαρτάνειν ἧττον δίκαιον αὐτούς.

ΣΤΡΕΨΙΑΔΗΣ

1420 ἀλλ᾽ οὐδαμοῦ νομίζεται τὸν πατέρα τοῦτο πάσχειν.

ΦΕΙΔΙΠΠΙΔΗΣ

οὔκουν ἀνὴρ ὁ τὸν νόμον θεὶς τοῦτον ἦν τὸ πρῶτον,
ὥσπερ σὺ κἀγώ, καὶ λέγων ἔπειθε τοὺς παλαιούς;
ἧττόν τι δῆτ᾽ ἔξεστι κἀμοὶ καινὸν αὖ τὸ λοιπὸν
θεῖναι νόμον τοῖς υἱέσιν, τοὺς πατέρας ἀντιτύπτειν;
1425 ὅσας δὲ πληγὰς εἴχομεν πρὶν τὸν νόμον τεθῆναι,
ἀφίεμεν, καὶ δίδομεν αὐτοῖς προῖκα συγκεκόφθαι.
σκέψαι δὲ τοὺς ἀλεκτρυόνας καὶ τἄλλα τὰ βοτὰ ταυτί,
ὡς τοὺς πατέρας ἀμύνεται· καίτοι τί διαφέρουσιν
ἡμῶν ἐκεῖνοι, πλήν γ᾽ ὅτι ψηφίσματ᾽ οὐ γράφουσιν;

ΣΤΡΕΨΙΑΔΗΣ

1430 τί δῆτ᾽, ἐπειδὴ τοὺς ἀλεκτρυόνας ἅπαντα μιμεῖ,

STREPSIADES

Yes indeed, out of good will and concern.

PHIDIPPIDES

Then tell me, if administering beatings is an expression of good will, isn't it right that I show you good will in the same way, with a beating? How is it fair that your body should be immune from blows, but not mine? "The children wail; you think the father shouldn't?"[89] You'll reply that this treatment of children is customary; but I'd counter that old men have become children again. And it makes better sense for old men to wail than young ones, in that their misbehavior is less appropriate.

STREPSIADES

But nowhere is it the law that a father be treated this way.

PHIDIPPIDES

Well, wasn't it a man like you and me who originally proposed this law and persuaded the ancients to adopt it? If so, am I any less free to establish in my turn a new law for the sons of tomorrow, that they should beat their fathers back? We award amnesty to fathers for all the blows we got before the law took effect, and we waive compensation for our beatings. Consider how roosters and other such creatures stand up to their fathers. After all, how do they differ from us, except that they don't legislate?

STREPSIADES

If you're going to ape roosters in every respect, then why

[89] Adapting Euripides, *Alcestis* 691 (Pheres to his son Admetus, who had asked him to die in his stead): "You like the daylight; you think your father doesn't?"

οὐκ ἐσθίεις καὶ τὴν κόπρον κἀπὶ ξύλου καθεύδεις;

ΦΕΙΔΙΠΠΙΔΗΣ

οὐ ταὐτόν, ὦ τᾶν, ἐστίν, οὐδ᾽ ἂν Σωκράτει δοκοίη.

ΣΤΡΕΨΙΑΔΗΣ

πρὸς ταῦτα μὴ τύπτ᾽· εἰ δὲ μή, σαυτόν ποτ᾽ αἰτιάσει.

ΦΕΙΔΙΠΠΙΔΗΣ

καὶ πῶς;

ΣΤΡΕΨΙΑΔΗΣ

ἐπεὶ σὲ μὲν δίκαιός εἰμ᾽ ἐγὼ κολάζειν,
σὺ δ᾽, ἢν γένηταί σοι, τὸν υἱόν.

ΦΕΙΔΙΠΠΙΔΗΣ

1435   ἢν δὲ μὴ γένηται,
μάτην ἐμοὶ κεκλαύσεται, σὺ δ᾽ ἐγχανὼν τεθνήξεις.

ΣΤΡΕΨΙΑΔΗΣ

ἐμοὶ μέν, ὦνδρες ἥλικες, δοκεῖ λέγειν δίκαια,
κἄμοιγε συγχωρεῖν δοκεῖ τούτοισι τἀπιεικῆ·
κλάειν γὰρ ἡμᾶς εἰκός ἐστ᾽, ἢν μὴ δίκαια δρῶμεν.

ΦΕΙΔΙΠΠΙΔΗΣ

σκέψαι δὲ χἀτέραν ἔτι γνώμην.

ΣΤΡΕΨΙΑΔΗΣ

1440   ἀπὸ γὰρ ὀλοῦμαι.

ΦΕΙΔΙΠΠΙΔΗΣ

καὶ μὴν ἴσως γ᾽ οὐκ ἀχθέσει παθὼν ἃ νῦν πέπονθας.

ΣΤΡΕΨΙΑΔΗΣ

πῶς δή; δίδαξον γὰρ τί μ᾽ ἐκ τούτων ἐπωφελήσεις.

don't you peck dung too, and sleep on a perch?

PHIDIPPIDES
That's different, sir, as Socrates would agree.

STREPSIADES
In that case don't beat me; if you do, you'll kick yourself one day.

PHEDIPPIDES
Why is that?

STREPSIADES
Because I'm within my rights to spank you, and you to spank your son, if you have one.

PHIDIPPIDES
But if I don't have one, I'll have wailed for nothing and you'll go to your grave laughing at me!

STREPSIADES
In my opinion, you gentlemen of my own age out there, his argument is right, and we should concede that these youngsters have made a valid point. It's only fitting that we should wail if we misbehave.

PHIDIPPIDES
Now consider yet another proposition.

STREPSIADES
No, it'll be the death of me!

PHIDIPPIDES
Not at all; you may even be less annoyed about what just happened to you.

STREPSIADES
How so? Explain what further benefit you can bring me out of all this!

ARISTOPHANES

ΦΕΙΔΙΠΠΙΔΗΣ

τὴν μητέρ' ὥσπερ καὶ σὲ τυπτήσω.

ΣΤΡΕΨΙΑΔΗΣ

τί φῄς, τί φῂς σύ;
τοῦθ' ἕτερον αὖ μεῖζον κακόν.

ΦΕΙΔΙΠΠΙΔΗΣ

τί δ' ἢν ἔχων τὸν ἥττω

1445 λόγον σε νικήσω λέγων
τὴν μητέρ' ὡς τύπτειν χρεών;

ΣΤΡΕΨΙΑΔΗΣ

τί δ' ἄλλο γ' ἤ, ταῦτ' ἢν ποιῇς,
οὐδέν σε κωλύσει σεαυ-
τὸν ἐμβαλεῖν
εἰς τὸ βάραθρον
1450 μετὰ Σωκράτους
καὶ τὸν λόγον τὸν ἥττω;

ταυτὶ δι' ὑμᾶς, ὦ Νεφέλαι, πέπονθ' ἐγώ,
ὑμῖν ἀναθεὶς ἅπαντα τἀμὰ πράγματα.

ΚΟΡΥΦΑΙΑ

αὐτὸς μὲν οὖν σαυτῷ σὺ τούτων αἴτιος,
1455 στρέψας σεαυτὸν εἰς πονηρὰ πράγματα.

ΣΤΡΕΨΙΑΔΗΣ

τί δῆτα ταῦτ' οὔ μοι τότ' ἠγορεύετε,
ἀλλ' ἄνδρ' ἄγροικον καὶ γέροντ' ἐπήρατε;

CLOUDS

PHIDIPPIDES

I'll beat mother as I beat you.

STREPSIADES

What's that? What did you say? That's different, a far greater crime!

PHIDIPPIDES

And what if I use the Worse Argument to defeat you on the resolution, it's right to beat one's mother?

STREPSIADES

Just this: if you do, nothing will save you from jumping into the Pit[90] along with Socrates and the Worse Argument. Clouds, it's your fault this has happened to me! I trusted you with all my affairs.

CHORUS LEADER

No, you've only yourself to blame, since you took the twisted path that leads to evildoing.

STREPSIADES

Then why didn't you tell me that at the start, instead of leading an old bumpkin on?

[90] Where criminals were executed.

ΚΟΡΥΦΑΙΑ

ἡμεῖς ποιοῦμεν ταῦθ᾽ ἑκάστοθ᾽, ὅντιν᾽ ἂν
γνῶμεν πονηρῶν ὄντ᾽ ἐραστὴν πραγμάτων,
1460 ἕως ἂν αὐτὸν ἐμβάλωμεν εἰς κακόν,
ὅπως ἂν εἰδῇ τοὺς θεοὺς δεδοικέναι.

ΣΤΡΕΨΙΑΔΗΣ

ὤμοι, πονηρά γ᾽, ὦ Νεφέλαι, δίκαια δέ·
οὐ γάρ με χρῆν τὰ χρήμαθ᾽ ἁδανεισάμην
ἀποστερεῖν. νῦν οὖν ὅπως, ὦ φίλτατε,
1465 τὸν Χαιρεφῶντα τὸν μιαρὸν καὶ Σωκράτη
ἀπολεῖς μετ᾽ ἐμοῦ 'λθών, οἵ σὲ κἄμ᾽ ἐξηπάτων.

ΦΕΙΔΙΠΠΙΔΗΣ

ἀλλ᾽ οὐκ ἂν ἀδικήσαιμι τοὺς διδασκάλους.

ΣΤΡΕΨΙΑΔΗΣ

ναὶ ναί, καταιδέσθητι πατρῷον Δία.

ΦΕΙΔΙΠΠΙΔΗΣ

ἰδού γε Δία πατρῷον. ὡς ἀρχαῖος εἶ.
Ζεὺς γάρ τις ἐστίν;

ΣΤΡΕΨΙΑΔΗΣ
ἐστίν.

ΦΕΙΔΙΠΠΙΔΗΣ
1470   οὐκ ἔστ᾽, οὐκ, ἐπεὶ
Δῖνος βασιλεύει, τὸν Δί᾽ ἐξεληλακώς.

ΣΤΡΕΨΙΑΔΗΣ

οὐκ ἐξελήλακ᾽, ἀλλ᾽ ἐγὼ τοῦτ᾽ ᾠόμην
διὰ τουτονὶ τὸν δῖνον. ὤμοι δείλαιος,

CHORUS LEADER

We do the same thing every time to anyone we catch lusting for shady dealings: we plunge him into calamity until he learns respect for the gods.

STREPSIADES

Ah, Clouds, a lesson hard but just! I shouldn't have tried to get out of repaying the money I borrowed. Now, dear son, what say you come with me and help me destroy that scum Chaerephon and Socrates for cheating you and me both?

PHIDIPPIDES

But I couldn't do my teachers any harm.

STREPSIADES

Oh yes you should: to Zeus of the Fathers tender your respect!

PHIDIPPIDES

Listen to him, "Zeus of the Fathers"! How antiquated! Do you think there's a Zeus?

STREPSIADES

I do.

PHIDIPPIDES

There isn't, no, because Whirl is king, having kicked out Zeus.

STREPSIADES

He hasn't kicked him out. I thought he had, because of this Whirligig.[91] What a poor sap I was to treat you, a mere

---

[91] See 380 n.

ὅτε καὶ σὲ χυτρεοῦν ὄντα θεὸν ἡγησάμην.

ΦΕΙΔΙΠΠΙΔΗΣ

1475 ἐνταῦθα σαυτῷ παραφρόνει καὶ φληνάφα.

ΣΤΡΕΨΙΑΔΗΣ

οἴμοι παρανοίας. ὡς ἐμαινόμην ἄρα
ὅτ᾽ ἐξέβαλον καὶ τοὺς θεοὺς διὰ Σωκράτη.
ἀλλ᾽ ὦ φίλ᾽ Ἑρμῆ, μηδαμῶς θύμαινέ μοι,
μηδέ μ᾽ ἐπιτρίψῃς, ἀλλὰ συγγνώμην ἔχε
1480 ἐμοῦ παρανοήσαντος ἀδολεσχίᾳ.
καί μοι γενοῦ ξύμβουλος, εἴτ᾽ αὐτοὺς γραφὴν
διωκάθω γραψάμενος, εἴθ᾽ ὅτι σοι δοκεῖ.
ὀρθῶς παραινεῖς οὐκ ἐῶν δικορραφεῖν
ἀλλ᾽ ὡς τάχιστ᾽ ἐμπιμπράναι τὴν οἰκίαν
1485 τῶν ἀδολεσχῶν. δεῦρο δεῦρ᾽, ὦ Ξανθία,
κλίμακα λαβὼν ἔξελθε καὶ σμινύην φέρων,
κἄπειτ᾽ ἐπαναβὰς ἐπὶ τὸ φροντιστήριον
τὸ τέγος κατάσκαπτ᾽, εἰ φιλεῖς τὸν δεσπότην,
ἕως ἂν αὐτοῖς ἐμβάλῃς τὴν οἰκίαν.
1490 ἐμοὶ δὲ δᾷδ᾽ ἐνεγκάτω τις ἡμμένην.
κἀγώ τιν᾽ αὐτῶν τήμερον δοῦναι δίκην
ἐμοὶ ποιήσω, κεἰ σφόδρ᾽ εἴσ᾽ ἀλαζόνες.

ΜΑΘΗΤΗΣ Α΄

ἰοὺ ἰού.

ΣΤΡΕΨΙΑΔΗΣ

σὸν ἔργον, ὦ δᾷς, ἱέναι πολλὴν φλόγα.

piece of pottery, like a god!

PHIDIPPIDES
Stay here and rant and rave to yourself.

PHIDIPPIDES goes inside.

STREPSIADES
Dear me, what lunacy! I must have been insane when I rejected the gods for Socrates. Well, Hermes old friend,[92] don't be angry with me or bring me some disaster, but forgive me for taking leave of my senses because of their idle talk. You be my counsellor: should I slap them with an indictment and pursue them in court? Or whatever you think best. (*putting his ear closer to Hermes*) That's good advice: I shouldn't cobble up lawsuits but rather burn down the idle talkers' house as quick as I can. Xanthias, come out here; bring a ladder and a hatchet with you. Now if you love your master, climb up onto the Thinkery and demolish the roof, until you bring the house down on them. Now somebody fetch me a lighted torch; I'll make someone in there pay dearly for what they've done to me, even if they *are* big-time blowhards!

Xanthias, a Slave, and STREPSIADES climb on to the roof of the Thinkery.

FIRST PUPIL
(*inside*) Help! Help!

STREPSIADES
Go on, torch, launch lots of fire!

[92] Images of Hermes stood in the street outside houses.

ΜΑΘΗΤΗΣ Α′

ἄνθρωπε, τί ποιεῖς;

ΣΤΡΕΨΙΑΔΗΣ

1495 ὅτι ποιῶ; τί δ᾽ ἄλλο γ᾽ ἢ
διαλεπτολογοῦμαι ταῖς δοκοῖς τῆς οἰκίας;

ΜΑΘΗΤΗΣ Β′

οἴμοι· τίς ἡμῶν πυρπολεῖ τὴν οἰκίαν;

ΣΤΡΕΨΙΑΔΗΣ

ἐκεῖνος οὗπερ θοἰμάτιον εἰλήφατε.

ΜΑΘΗΤΗΣ Β′

ἀπολεῖς, ἀπολεῖς.

ΣΤΡΕΨΙΑΔΗΣ

τοῦτ᾽ αὐτὸ γὰρ καὶ βούλομαι,
1500 ἢν ἡ σμινύη μοι μὴ προδῷ τὰς ἐλπίδας
ἢ ᾽γὼ πρότερόν πως ἐκτραχηλισθῶ πεσών.

ΣΩΚΡΑΤΗΣ

οὗτος, τί ποιεῖς ἐτεόν, οὑπὶ τοῦ τέγους;

ΣΤΡΕΨΙΑΔΗΣ

ἀεροβατῶ καὶ περιφρονῶ τὸν ἥλιον.

ΣΩΚΡΑΤΗΣ

οἴμοι τάλας δείλαιος, ἀποπνιγήσομαι.

ΜΑΘΗΤΗΣ Β′

1505 ἐγὼ δὲ κακοδαίμων γε κατακαυθήσομαι.

1504 Chaerephonti dant *b*
1505 Chaerephonti dant ΚΝΘ

PUPILS rush out.

FIRST PUPIL
What are you doing, man?

STREPSIADES
What am I doing? What do you think? I'm mincing words
with the rafters of your house!

SECOND PUPIL
(*at a window*) Me oh my, who's torching our house?

STREPSIADES
It's me, whose cloak you stole!

SECOND PUPIL
You'll kill us, kill us!

STREPSIADES
That's precisely my intention, if this hatchet doesn't betray
my hopes or I fall first and break my neck!

SOCRATES rushes outside.

SOCRATES
You there, you on the roof, what do you think you're doing?

STREPSIADES
I tread the air and scrutinize the sun!

SOCRATES
Ah, poor me, I'm going to choke to death!

SECOND PUPIL
And my wretched fate is to be burned up!

*SECOND PUPIL jumps to the stage as STREPSIADES and
Xanthias descend from the roof.*

ARISTOPHANES

ΣΤΡΕΨΙΑΔΗΣ

τί γὰρ μαθόντες τοὺς θεοὺς ὑβρίζετε
καὶ τῆς σελήνης ἐσκοπεῖσθε τὴν ἕδραν;
δίωκε, παῖε, βάλλε, πολλῶν οὕνεκα,
μάλιστα δ᾽ εἰδὼς τοὺς θεοὺς ὡς ἠδίκουν.

ΚΟΡΥΦΑΙΑ

1510 ἡγεῖσθ᾽ ἔξω· κεχόρευται γὰρ
μετρίως τό γε τήμερον ἡμῖν.

CLOUDS

STREPSIADES

Then what was the idea of outraging the gods and peering at the backside of the Moon? Chase them! Hit them! Stone them! They've got it coming many times over, but most of all for wronging the gods.

SOCRATES and PUPILS flee, pursued by STREPSIADES and Xanthias.

CHORUS

Lead the dancers on their way:
we've done enough performing for today.

WASPS

INTRODUCTORY NOTE

Wasps was produced by Aristophanes himself[1] at the Lenaea of 422 and placed second; Philonides placed first with *The Preview (Proagon)* and Leucon third with *Ambassadors*. It is likely, however, that Aristophanes also wrote *The Preview:* ancient citations from it are ascribed to Aristophanes, never to Philonides, who produced at least two other plays for Aristophanes (*Amphiaraus* in 414 and *Frogs* in 405). Perhaps Aristophanes' failure with *Clouds* at the previous year's Dionysia inclined him against producing there in 422, so that he entered two plays at the Lenaea; there may even have been a rule preventing last-place finishers at the Dionysia from producing there in the following year.[2]

Wasps satirizes Athenian jurors and criticizes their staunch devotion to demagogic politicians. As in *Knights*, the chief demagogue is Cleon, who is again harshly caricatured, this time as a malevolent watchdog. Cleon had recently recovered from a political eclipse: after the Athe-

[1] Cf. lines 1017-22.

[2] As has been argued from a statement by Eratosthenes about the comic poet Plato: "He was successful so long as he produced comedies for other poets, but when he first produced his own play *Staff Bearers* he placed fourth and was shunted back to the Lenaean contest" (*POxy.* 2737.44 = Plato test. 7 K-A).

nian defeat at Delium in late 424 and the subsequent loss
of Amphipolis, public opinion had turned against his ag-
gressive war policies, so that he was not reelected to the
board of generals; and in spring 423 the Athenians voted,
against his advice, in favor of a one-year truce with Sparta.
But then Scione and Mende revolted from Athens, provok-
ing a resurgence of anti-Spartan sentiment in Athens and
reviving Cleon's political fortunes; in *Wasps* he is portrayed
as planning judicial revenge against Laches, one of the
proposers of the truce. But the focus in *Wasps* is not so
much on Cleon personally as on how he and other dema-
gogues could (allegedly) manipulate the jury courts, a cen-
tral Athenian institution, for their own purposes: to attack
political opponents, shake down the rich, and pocket the
money that rightfully belonged to the people. As in *Clouds,*
the play's satirical themes are exemplified by a conflict be-
tween an uncouth father and his sophisticated son, though
this time the characterizations are more spacious and the
son has a larger role.

Lovecleon (*Philocleon*), a fierce member of the gen-
eration that defeated the Persians and built the Athenian
empire, has surrendered control of his estate to his ele-
gant, well-to-do son, Loathecleon (*Bdelycleon*), and now
spends his time sitting on juries. His fellow jurors, repre-
sented by the waspish Chorus, are members of the same
generation, but they, unlike Lovecleon, must rely solely on
their jury pay to support themselves and their families.
Loathecleon regards his father's passion for the hard life of
a juror as sheer madness. After fruitlessly trying several
cures, Loathecleon and his slaves barricade Lovecleon in
the house. But in the face of determined escape attempts
and a battle with the Chorus, who regard Loathecleon as

an enemy of the people, Loathecleon offers to debate his father on the virtues of jury service, winner take all.

In his (quite rational) defence, Lovecleon stresses the juror's power and independence, the importance of the juror's pay to the older generation, and the pleasure taken by poor, elderly jurors in lording it over, and especially in convicting, rich young defendants. In his rebuttal, Loathecleon demonstrates that the jurors are actually slaves of men like Cleon, that the defendants they convict are the real benefactors of Athens, and that the jurors' pay is a mere pittance; Lovecleon and his friends, whose toil made Athens unprecedentedly prosperous, deserve to live a life of luxury, but as it is, the politicians, who contribute nothing to Athens, reap all the rewards. Loathecleon offers to provide just such a life of luxury for his father, if he will abandon the courts and stay at home; if he likes, he can even set up his own lawcourt in the courtyard. The Chorus is won over, and Lovecleon has no choice but to obey his son.

Aristophanes now exploits the parallelism between Lovecleon's position in the city (enthrallment by the vulgar Cleon) and his status in his own household (dependence on his cultivated son) in order to consider what might happen if men like Loathecleon were to win the allegiance of Cleon's followers and introduce them to the finer things of life. At first, the plan goes well. Lovecleon is allowed to judge a case involving two household dogs: Demadogue (Cleon) prosecutes Grabes (Laches) for the theft of some Sicilian cheese.[3] Thanks to Loathecleon's intervention, Grabes is acquitted on the grounds that he is a good dog

[3] See 240 n.

who works hard for the people and stole only for their good, while Demadogue is well fed for doing nothing. Then in the parabasis Aristophanes claims, much like Loathecleon, that his efforts to expose Cleon and his ilk have always aimed to help the people; and the Chorus recapitulates the contributions of the older generation and vows henceforth to reward only those who make similar contributions.

Now Loathecleon invites his father to an elegant banquet and coaches him in the appropriate etiquette. But the banquet is a disaster: Lovecleon becomes drunk and disorderly, insulting the guests, abducting the girl piper, and assaulting every ordinary citizen he meets on his way home. To make matters worse, he rudely rejects every attempt by his victims and his son to settle out of court. Loathecleon can only look on helplessly. Clearly the vulgarity, selfishness, and aggression that Lovecleon displayed as a juror have not been lost but only let loose on society at large. Apparently Loathecleon's suggestion—that the ordinary folk who fight for Athens should be allowed to enjoy the fruits of their valor, but leave the details of government to wiser heads—works better in theory than in practice, at least in the case of the incorrigible Lovecleon.

Text

One papyrus preserves fragments of *Wasps*.[4] There are twelve medieval MSS that represent four independent witnesses: RVΓ and *j*, the archetype of the *recentiores*

---

[4] *POxy.* 1374 (V), containing parts of some 150 lines from 443-878.

Vp2HLVv17B (which derive from Triclinian editions) and
Vp3C (which do not). In *Wasps* any two of these witnesses
may agree in error against the other two, showing that the
medieval transmission of the play was open, though V pre-
serves more true readings alone than any of the other
three.

Sigla

R   Ravennas 429 (*c.* 950)
S   readings found in the Suda
V   Venetus Marcianus 474 (XI/XII)
Γ   Laurentianus 31.15 (*c.* 1325)
Vp3   Vaticanus Palatinus 128 (XV)
C   Parisinus gr. 2717 (XV/XVI)
Vp2   Vaticanus Palatinus 67 (XV)
H   Hauniensis 1980 (XV)
L   Holkhamensis 88 (XV[in])
Vv17   Vaticanus gr. 2181 (XIV[ex])
B   Parisinus Regius 2715 (XIV[ex])
a   the archetype of RVΓ*j*
j   the hyparchetype of Vp3CVp2HLVv17B

Annotated Editions

F. H. M. Blaydes (Halle 1893)
W. J. M. Starkie (London 1897)
J. van Leeuwen (Leiden 1909)
B. B. Rogers (London 1915), with English translation.
D. M. MacDowell (Oxford 1971)
A. H. Sommerstein (Warminster 1983), with English trans-
    lation.
G. Mastromarco (Turin 1983), with Italian translation.
G. Paduano (Milan 1990)

ΤΑ ΤΟΥ ΔΡΑΜΑΤΟΣ ΠΡΟΣΩΠΑ

ΣΩΣΙΑΣ οἰκέτης
  Βδελυκλέωνος
ΧΑΝΘΙΑΣ οἰκέτης
  Βδελυκλέωνος
ΒΔΕΛΥΚΛΕΩΝ υἱός
ΦΙΛΟΚΛΕΩΝ πατήρ
ΠΑΙΣ υἱὸς τοῦ
  κορυφαίου
ΚΥΩΝ Κυδαθηναιεύς
ΑΝΗΡ ὑπὸ Φιλοκλέωνος
  ὑβριζόμενος
ΜΥΡΤΙΑ ἀρτόπωλις
ΚΑΤΗΓΟΡΟΣ Φιλοκλέωνος

ΧΟΡΟΣ γερόντων
  δικαστῶν

ΚΩΦΑ ΠΡΟΣΩΠΑ
ΟΝΟΣ Βδελυκλέωνος
ΠΑΙΔΕΣ υἱοὶ τοῦ χοροῦ
ΟΙΚΕΤΑΙ τοῦ
  Βδελυκλέωνος
ΛΑΒΗΣ Αἰξωνεύς, κύων
ΣΚΕΥΗ ἐκ τοῦ ἱπνοῦ
ΚΥΝΙΔΙΑ τοῦ Λάβητος
ΔΑΡΔΑΝΙΣ αὐλητρίς
ΑΝΔΡΕΣ ὑπὸ
  Φιλοκλέωνος
  ὑβριζόμενοι
ΧΑΙΡΕΦΩΝ
ΚΛΗΤΗΡ τοῦ κατηγόρου
ΥΙΟΙ ΚΑΡΚΙΝΟΥ
  ὀρχησταί, τρεῖς
ΚΑΡΚΙΝΟΣ

DRAMATIS PERSONAE

SOSIAS, slave of Loathecleon

XANTHIAS, slave of Loathecleon

LOATHECLEON, a wealthy young man

LOVECLEON, his father

BOY, the Chorus Leader's son

DEMADOGUE, watchdog of Cydathenaeum

VICTIM of Lovecleon

MYRTIA, a breadwoman

ACCUSER of Lovecleon

CHORUS of old jurymen (imagined as wasps)

SILENT CHARACTERS

DONKEY of Loathecleon

BOYS, sons of the Chorus members

SLAVES of Loathecleon

GRABES, a dog of Aexone

KITCHEN UTENSILS

PUPPIES of Grabes

DARDANIS, a girl piper

VICTIMS of Lovecleon

CHAEREPHON

WITNESS for the Accuser

SONS OF CARCINUS, three dancers

CARCINUS

NOTE. Loathecleon and Lovecleon translate the fictional Greek names Bdelycleon and Philocleon.

221

ΣΦΗΚΕΣ

Οὗτος, τί πάσχεις, ὦ κακόδαιμον Ξανθία;

ΞΑΝΘΙΑΣ

φυλακὴν καταλύειν νυκτερινὴν διδάσκομαι.

ΣΩΣΙΑΣ

κακὸν ἄρα ταῖς πλευραῖς τι προὐφείλεις μέγα.
ἆρ᾽ οἶσθά γ᾽ οἷον κνώδαλον φυλάττομεν;

ΞΑΝΘΙΑΣ

5 οἶδ᾽, ἀλλ᾽ ἐπιθυμῶ σμικρὸν ἀπομερμηρίσαι.

ΣΩΣΙΑΣ

σὺ δ᾽ οὖν παρακινδύνευ᾽, ἐπεὶ καὐτοῦ γ᾽ ἐμοῦ
κατὰ τοῖν κόραιν ἤδη τι καταχεῖται γλυκύ.

ΞΑΝΘΙΑΣ

ἀλλ᾽ ἦ παραφρονεῖς ἐτεὸν ἢ κορυβαντιᾷς;

---

[1] The Corybants were Asiatic divinities whose worship featured frantic dancing.

WASPS

*The stage building represents the house of LOVECLEON
and LOATHECLEON, who is asleep on the roof. Netting
covers the entire house, and the slaves SOSIAS and XAN-
THIAS guard the door.*

SOSIAS

Hey Xanthias, you damned jinx, what's the matter with
you?

XANTHIAS

(*waking up*) I'm learning how to relieve the night watch.

SOSIAS

Then your ribs will have a bad grudge against you. Don't
you realize what a monster we've got in our custody?

XANTHIAS

Certainly; that's why I want to absent me from solicitude
awhile.

SOSIAS

Take your own chances then. Why should I care? Some-
thing pleasant is beginning to drop over my eyeballs too.
(*he snoozes, then begins to thrash about*)

XANTHIAS

Whoa there, are you losing your mind, or having a cory-
bantic fit?[1]

ΣΩΣΙΑΣ

οὔκ, ἀλλ᾽ ὕπνος μ᾽ ἔχει τις ἐκ Σαβαζίου.

ΞΑΝΘΙΑΣ

10 τὸν αὐτὸν ἄρ᾽ ἐμοὶ βουκολεῖς Σαβάζιον.
κἀμοὶ γὰρ ἀρτίως ἐπεστρατεύσατο
Μῆδός τις ἐπὶ τὰ βλέφαρα νυστακτὴς ὕπνος.
καὶ δῆτ᾽ ὄναρ θαυμαστὸν εἶδον ἀρτίως.

ΣΩΣΙΑΣ

κἄγωγ᾽ ἀληθῶς οἷον οὐδεπώποτε.

ἀτὰρ σὺ λέξον πρότερος.

ΞΑΝΘΙΑΣ

15 ἐδόκουν αἰετὸν
καταπτάμενον εἰς τὴν ἀγορὰν μέγαν πάνυ
ἀναρπάσαντα τοῖς ὄνυξιν ἀσπίδα
φέρειν ἐπίχαλκον ἀνεκὰς εἰς τὸν οὐρανόν,
κἄπειτα ταύτην ἀποβαλεῖν Κλεώνυμον.

ΣΩΣΙΑΣ

20 οὐδὲν ἄρα γρίφου διαφέρει Κλεώνυμος.

ΞΑΝΘΙΑΣ

πῶς δή;

ΣΩΣΙΑΣ

προερεῖ τις τοῖσι συμπόταις, λέγων
ὅτι "ταὐτὸν ἐν γῇ τ᾽ ἀπέβαλεν κἀν οὐρανῷ
κἀν τῇ θαλάττῃ θηρίον τὴν ἀσπίδα."

WASPS

SOSIAS
No, Sabazius[2] has put me under a sleepy spell.

XANTHIAS
So you're bowing your head to Sabazius just like me. A moment ago a snoozy slumber invaded my eyelids too, like a platoon of Persians. And I just had an amazing dream.

SOSIAS
Me too—no lie—like none I've ever had. But you tell yours first.

XANTHIAS
I saw a great big eagle swoop down into the market and snatch up a bronzed shield in its talons and take it right up to the sky, and then it became Cleonymus and lost its shield!

SOSIAS
Cleonymus does make a fine riddle at that.

XANTHIAS
How so?

SOSIAS
A man could challenge his fellow drinkers by asking, "what beast sheds its shield on land, in the air, and at sea?"

---

[2] A Phrygian god associated with Dionysus and popular with women and slaves.

---

10 Σαβάζιον a: σὺ δαίμονα Herwerden

ΞΑΝΘΙΑΣ

οἴμοι, τί δῆτά μοι κακὸν γενήσεται
ἰδόντι τοιοῦτον ἐνύπνιον;

ΣΩΣΙΑΣ

25   μὴ φροντίσῃς·
οὐδὲν γὰρ ἔσται δεινόν, οὐ μὰ τοὺς θεούς.

ΞΑΝΘΙΑΣ

δεινόν γέ πού 'στ' ἄνθρωπος ἀποβαλὼν ὅπλα.
ἀτὰρ σὺ τὸ σὸν αὖ λέξον.

ΣΩΣΙΑΣ

                    ἀλλ' ἔστιν μέγα.
περὶ τῆς πόλεως γάρ ἐστι τοῦ σκάφους ὅλου.

ΞΑΝΘΙΑΣ

30 λέγε νυν ἀνύσας τι τὴν τρόπιν τοῦ πράγματος.

ΣΩΣΙΑΣ

ἔδοξέ μοι περὶ πρῶτον ὕπνον ἐν τῇ Πυκνὶ
ἐκκλησιάζειν πρόβατα συγκαθήμενα,
βακτηρίας ἔχοντα καὶ τριβώνια.
κἄπειτα τούτοις τοῖσι προβάτοις μοὐδόκει
35 δημηγορεῖν φάλλαινα πανδοκεύτρια,
ἔχουσα φωνὴν ἐμπεπρημένης ὑός.

ΞΑΝΘΙΑΣ

αἰβοῖ.

ΣΩΣΙΑΣ

    τί ἐστι;

WASPS

XANTHIAS

Uh oh, what sort of bad luck is coming my way, having a dream like that?

SOSIAS

Don't worry, nothing awful's going to happen, god forbid.

XANTHIAS

Still, there's something awful about a man shedding his gear. But tell me your dream now.

SOSIAS

Oh, it's momentous, it's about the whole ship of state.

XANTHIAS

Hurry up then, tell me the hull story!

SOSIAS

Just as I was nodding off, I dreamed that sheep were meeting in Assembly on the Pnyx,[3] wearing cheap jackets and carrying walking sticks; then a ravening dragon started haranguing these sheep with a voice like a scalded pig.

XANTHIAS

Yuk!

SOSIAS

What is it?

---

[3] See *Knights* 42 n.

ΞΑΝΘΙΑΣ

παῦε παῦε, μὴ λέγε·
ὄζει κάκιστον τοὐνύπνιον βύρσης σαπρᾶς.

ΣΩΣΙΑΣ

εἶθ᾽ ἡ μιαρὰ φάλλαιν᾽ ἔχουσα τρυτάνην
ἵστη βόειον δημόν.

ΞΑΝΘΙΑΣ

40   οἴμοι δείλαιος·
τὸν δῆμον ἡμῶν βούλεται διιστάναι.

ΣΩΣΙΑΣ

ἐδόκει δέ μοι Θέωρος αὐτῆς πλησίον
χαμαὶ καθῆσθαι τὴν κεφαλὴν κόρακος ἔχων.
εἶτ᾽ Ἀλκιβιάδης εἶπε πρός με τραυλίσας·
45 "ὁλᾷς; Θέωλος τὴν κεφαλὴν κόλακος ἔχει."

ΞΑΝΘΙΑΣ

ὀρθῶς γε τοῦτ᾽ Ἀλκιβιάδης ἐτραύλισεν.

ΣΩΣΙΑΣ

οὔκουν ἐκεῖν᾽ ἀλλόκοτον, ὁ Θέωρος κόραξ
γιγνόμενος;

ΞΑΝΘΙΑΣ

        ἥκιστ᾽, ἀλλ᾽ ἄριστον.

ΣΩΣΙΑΣ

                    πῶς;

ΞΑΝΘΙΑΣ

                        ὅπως;
ἄνθρωπος ὢν εἶτ᾽ ἐγένετ᾽ ἐξαίφνης κόραξ·

WASPS

XANTHIAS

Stop talking, stop! Your dream reeks horribly of rotten hides.[4]

SOSIAS

Then this sickening dragon was holding a pair of scales and weighing *pea pulse*.

XANTHIAS

Good heavens, he means to divide our *people!*

SOSIAS

And I dreamed that Theorus was squatting on the ground beside the dragon, with the head of a plover. Then Alcibiades said to me in his baby lisp, "Wookit! Theowus has the head of a gwoveller!"

XANTHIAS

Alcibiades was wight about that!

SOSIAS

Well, isn't it eerie, Theorus turning into a plover?

XANTHIAS

Not at all; it's a very good sign.

SOSIAS

How so?

XANTHIAS

Look: first a man, then suddenly a plover; isn't it plain as

---

[4] Identifying the dragon as Cleon, portrayed as a tanner in *Knights*. Theorus is often mentioned as a crony of Cleon's. Alcibiades, nephew of Pericles, was now about 30 and just beginning his notorious political career.

ARISTOPHANES

50 οὔκουν ἐναργὲς τοῦτο συμβαλεῖν, ὅτι
ἀρθεὶς ἀφ᾽ ἡμῶν ἐς κόρακας οἰχήσεται;

ΣΩΣΙΑΣ

εἶτ᾽ οὐκ ἐγὼ δοὺς δύ᾽ ὀβολὼ μισθώσομαι
οὕτως ὑποκρινόμενον σοφῶς ὀνείρατα;

ΞΑΝΘΙΑΣ

φέρε νυν, κατείπω τοῖς θεαταῖς τὸν λόγον,
55 ὀλίγ᾽ ἄτθ᾽ ὑπειπὼν πρῶτον αὐτοῖσιν ταδί,
μηδὲν παρ᾽ ἡμῶν προσδοκᾶν λίαν μέγα,
μηδ᾽ αὖ γέλωτα Μεγαρόθεν κεκλεμμένον.
ἡμῖν γὰρ οὐκ ἔστ᾽ οὔτε κάρυ᾽ ἐκ φορμίδος
δούλω διαρριπτοῦντε τοῖς θεωμένοις,
60 οὔθ᾽ Ἡρακλῆς τὸ δεῖπνον ἐξαπατώμενος,
οὐδ᾽ αὖθις ἀνασελγαινόμενος Εὐριπίδης·
οὐδ᾽ εἰ Κλέων γ᾽ ἔλαμψε τῆς τύχης χάριν,
αὖθις τὸν αὐτὸν ἄνδρα μυττωτεύσομεν.
ἀλλ᾽ ἔστιν ἡμῖν λογίδιον γνώμην ἔχον,
65 ὑμῶν μὲν αὐτῶν οὐχὶ δεξιώτερον,
κωμῳδίας δὲ φορτικῆς σοφώτερον·
ἔστιν γὰρ ἡμῖν δεσπότης ἐκεινοσὶ
ἄνω καθεύδων, ὁ μέγας, οὑπὶ τοῦ τέγους.
οὗτος φυλάττειν τὸν πατέρ᾽ ἐπέταξε νῷν,
70 ἔνδον καθείρξας, ἵνα θύραζε μὴ 'ξίῃ.
νόσον γὰρ ὁ πατὴρ ἀλλόκοτον αὐτοῦ νοσεῖ,
ἣν οὐδ᾽ ἂν εἷς γνοίη ποτ᾽ οὐδὲ ξυμβάλοι,
εἰ μὴ πύθοιθ᾽ ἡμῶν· ἐπεὶ τοπάζετε.
Ἀμυνίας μὲν ὁ Προνάπους φήσ᾽ οὑτοσὶ

day that Theorus is up and leaving us and going to the
vultures?

SOSIAS

Say, why don't I put you on a two obol salary, since you
interpret dreams so cleverly?

XANTHIAS

All right then, it's time I let the audience in on the plot.
But first I'll give them the following short preface. Don't
expect anything terribly grand, or conversely, any jokes
swiped from Megara. We've got no pair of slaves broad-
casting basketfuls of nuts to the spectators, no Heracles
cheated of his dinner, no Euripides once again taking out-
rageous abuse, and even if Cleon had the pure luck to
shine,[5] we won't make mincemeat out of the same man
twice.[6] No, ours is a simple plot with a point, no brainier
than you are yourselves, but more artistic than lowbrow
comedy. Very well then: that's our master up there, the big
man asleep on the roof. He's put his father under house
arrest and posted us as sentries to prevent his escape. His
father, you see, suffers from a bizarre sickness, which no
one here will be able to recognize or diagnose unless we
tell you. Go ahead then, take a guess. Pronapes' son

[5] Perhaps referring to the recent revolt of Scione, which oc-
curred only days after the Athenians, on the advice of Laches (240
n.), had made a truce with Sparta against Cleon's advice; Cleon
then passed a motion to besiege and punish Scione (Thucydides
4.118-22).

[6] A reference to the attack on Cleon in *Knights*.

εἶναι φιλόκυβον αὐτόν.

ΣΩΣΙΑΣ

75   ἀλλ' οὐδὲν λέγει,
μὰ Δί', ἀλλ' ἀφ' αὑτοῦ τὴν νόσον τεκμαίρεται.

ΞΑΝΘΙΑΣ

οὔκ, ἀλλὰ "φιλο-" μέν ἐστιν ἀρχὴ τοῦ κακοῦ.
ὁδὶ δέ φησι Σωσίας πρὸς Δερκύλον
εἶναι φιλοπότην αὐτόν.

ΣΩΣΙΑΣ

              οὐδαμῶς γ', ἐπεὶ
80 αὕτη γε χρηστῶν ἐστιν ἀνδρῶν ἡ νόσος.

ΞΑΝΘΙΑΣ

Νικόστρατος δ' αὖ φησιν ὁ Σκαμβωνίδης
εἶναι φιλοθύτην αὐτὸν ἢ φιλόξενον.

ΣΩΣΙΑΣ

μὰ τὸν κύν', ὦ Νικόστρατ', οὐ φιλόξενος,
ἐπεὶ καταπύγων ἐστὶν ὅ γε Φιλόξενος.

ΞΑΝΘΙΑΣ

85 ἄλλως φλυαρεῖτ'· οὐ γὰρ ἐξευρήσετε.
εἰ δὴ 'πιθυμεῖτ' εἰδέναι, σιγᾶτέ νυν·
φράσω γὰρ ἤδη τὴν νόσον τοῦ δεσπότου.
φιληλιαστής ἐστιν ὡς οὐδεὶς ἀνήρ·
ἐρᾷ τε τούτου τοῦ δικάζειν, καὶ στένει
90 ἢν μὴ 'πὶ τοῦ πρώτου καθίζηται ξύλου.
ὕπνου δ' ὁρᾷ τῆς νυκτὸς οὐδὲ πασπάλην·
ἢν δ' οὖν καταμύσῃ κἂν ἄχνην, ὅμως ἐκεῖ

Amynias here says he's addicted to gambling.

SOSIAS

Wrong! He's using his own symptoms to guess the disease.

XANTHIAS

He's wrong, but the affliction does begin with "addicted to." Now Sosias here is telling Dercylus that he's addicted to drink.[7]

SOSIAS

Not at all: that disease afflicts only gentlemen.

XANTHIAS

Nicostratus of Scambonidae[8] has a different guess, that he's addicted to holding sacrifices or entertaining guests.

SOSIAS

Doggonit no, Nicostratus, not a philoxenist; Philoxenus is a faggot.

XANTHIAS

You're getting nowhere with all this hot air; you'll never find the answer. If you really want to know, then be quiet. I'm going to tell you what the master's sickness is: addiction to jury service, and the world's worst case! That's his passion, judging, and he groans if he can't sit on the front bench. At night he gets no sleep, not a wink, and even if he does nod off for the merest instant, his mind's still over

---

[7] Neither man is identifiable.

[8] A perennially successful commander and an associate of Nicias.

ὁ νοῦς πέτεται τὴν νύκτα περὶ τὴν κλεψύδραν.
ὑπὸ τοῦ δὲ τὴν ψῆφόν γ᾽ ἔχειν εἰωθέναι
95 τοὺς τρεῖς ξυνέχων τῶν δακτύλων ἀνίσταται,
ὥσπερ λιβανωτὸν ἐπιτιθεὶς νουμηνίᾳ.
καὶ νὴ Δί᾽ ἢν ἴδῃ γέ που γεγραμμένον
υἱὸν Πυριλάμπους ἐν θύρᾳ Δῆμον καλόν,
ἰὼν παρέγραψε πλησίον "κημὸς καλός".
100 τὸν ἀλεκτρυόνα δ᾽, ὃς ᾖδ᾽ ἀφ᾽ ἑσπέρας, ἔφη
ὄψ᾽ ἐξεγείρειν αὐτὸν ἀναπεπεισμένον,
παρὰ τῶν ὑπευθύνων ἔχοντα χρήματα·
εὐθὺς δ᾽ ἀπὸ δορπηστοῦ κέκραγεν ἐμβάδας,
κᾆπειτ᾽ ἐκεῖσ᾽ ἐλθὼν προκαθεύδει πρῲ πάνυ,
105 ὥσπερ λεπὰς προσεχόμενος τῷ κίονι.
ὑπὸ δυσκολίας δ᾽ ἅπασι τιμῶν τὴν μακρὰν
ὥσπερ μέλιττ᾽ ἢ βομβυλιὸς εἰσέρχεται
ὑπὸ τοῖς ὄνυξι κηρὸν ἀναπεπλασμένος.
ψήφων δὲ δείσας μὴ δεηθείη ποτέ,
110 ἵν᾽ ἔχοι δικάζειν, αἰγιαλὸν ἔνδον τρέφει.
τοιαῦτ᾽ ἀλύει· νουθετούμενος δ᾽ ἀεὶ
μᾶλλον δικάζει. τοῦτον οὖν φυλάττομεν
μοχλοῖσιν ἐνδήσαντες, ὡς ἂν μὴ 'ξίῃ.
ὁ γὰρ υἱὸς αὐτοῦ τὴν νόσον βαρέως φέρει.
115 καὶ πρῶτα μὲν λόγοισι παραμυθούμενος
ἀνέπειθεν αὐτὸν μὴ φορεῖν τριβώνιον
μηδ᾽ ἐξιέναι θύραζ᾽· ὁ δ᾽ οὐκ ἐπείθετο.
εἶτ᾽ αὐτὸν ἀπέλου κἀκάθαιρ᾽· ὁ δ᾽ οὐ μάλα.
μετὰ τοῦτ᾽ ἐκορυβάντιζ᾽· ὁ δ᾽ αὐτῷ τυμπάνῳ
120 ᾄξας ἐδίκαζεν εἰς τὸ Καινὸν ἐμπεσών.

there fluttering around the water clock all night long.[9] He's
so used to holding a voting pebble that he gets out of bed
with his first three fingers pressed together, like somebody
offering incense at the new moon. By heaven, if he sees
"Pyrilampes' son Demos is cute"[10] written on a doorway,
he goes and writes next to it "the ballot box is cute." When
the cock started crowing just after bedtime, he claimed it
had been bribed by the magistrates under audit to wake
him up too late. Right after dinner he calls for his sandals
and goes out to stand watch before the courthouse, cling-
ing to the post like a barnacle. From sheer nastiness he
scratches a long penalty line for all convicts, and comes
home with his nails caked with wax like a honeybee or a
bumblebee. He was so scared he'd run out of voting peb-
bles that he keeps a whole beach in the house. That's how
crazy he is, and the more you reason with him, the more
cases he hears. So we've shut him in behind bars, and we
watch so he doesn't escape. That's because his son's taking
his sickness very hard. At first he tried soothing words to
persuade him not to wear a flimsy cloak and leave the
house, but he wouldn't listen. Next he tried immersion and
exorcism, but he didn't yield. Then he joined him up with
the Corybants, but he burst into Common Court, tom-tom
and all, and started hearing cases. Well, the son was getting

[9] A device used to time courtroom speeches.

[10] Pyrilampes was a friend of Pericles and the stepfather of
Plato; for the formula see *Acharnians* 144 n.

ὅτε δῆτα ταύταις ταῖς τελεταῖς οὐκ ὠφέλει,
διέπλευσεν εἰς Αἴγιναν· εἶτα ξυλλαβὼν
νύκτωρ κατέκλινεν αὐτὸν εἰς Ἀσκληπιοῦ·
ὁ δ᾽ ἀνεφάνη κνεφαῖος ἐπὶ τῇ κιγκλίδι.
125 ἐντεῦθεν οὐκέτ᾽ αὐτὸν ἐξεφρίομεν·
ὁ δ᾽ ἐξεδίδρασκε διά τε τῶν ὑδορροῶν
καὶ τῶν ὀπῶν· ἡμεῖς δ᾽ ὅσ᾽ ἦν τετρημένα
ἐνεβύσαμεν ῥακίοισι κἀπακτώσαμεν·
ὁ δ᾽ ὡσπερεὶ κολοιὸς αὑτῷ παττάλους
130 ἐνέκρουεν εἰς τὸν τοῖχον, εἶτ᾽ ἐξήλλετο·
ἡμεῖς δὲ τὴν αὐλὴν ἅπασαν δικτύοις
καταπετάσαντες ἐν κύκλῳ φυλάττομεν.
ἔστιν δ᾽ ὄνομα τῷ μὲν γέροντι Φιλοκλέων,
ναὶ μὰ Δία, τῷ δ᾽ υἱεῖ γε τωδὶ Βδελυκλέων,
135 ἔχων τρόπους φρυαγμοσεμνάκους τινάς.

BΔΕΛΤΚΛΕΩΝ
ὦ Ξανθία καὶ Σωσία, καθεύδετε;

ΞΑΝΘΙΑΣ
οἴμοι.

ΣΩΣΙΑΣ
τί ἐστι;

ΞΑΝΘΙΑΣ
Βδελυκλέων ἀνίσταται.

BΔΕΛΤΚΛΕΩΝ
οὐ περιδραμεῖται σφῷν ταχέως δεῦρ᾽ ἅτερος;
ὁ γὰρ πατὴρ εἰς τὸν ἰπνὸν ἐξελήλυθεν,

236

nowhere with these rituals, so he took his father by boat to
Aegina and bedded him down for a night in Asclepius'
temple.[11] But before daybreak next morning, there he was
at the courtroom gate. After that we stopped letting him
out altogether. But he kept escaping through the gutters
and the chinks. We stuffed every single gap with plugs and
sealed them up. But he hammered pegs into the wall and
hopped up and away like a pet crow. We countered by
draping the whole courtyard with netting and standing
guard all around the house. The old man has a name, Love-
cleon—I swear!—and his son's named Loathecleon, a chap
with some high-horsical traits.

LOATHECLEON

Xanthias! Sosias! Are you asleep?

XANTHIAS

Uh oh.

SOSIAS

What?

XANTHIAS

Loathecleon's getting up.

LOATHECLEON

One or the other of you two, run around here on the
double! Father's got into the kitchen. He's on all fours,

---

[11] Asclepius was a healing god.

140   *καὶ μυσπολεῖ τι καταδεδυκώς. ἀλλ' ἄθρει*
κατὰ τῆς πυέλου τὸ τρῆμ' ὅπως μὴ 'κδύσεται.
σὺ δὲ τῇ θύρᾳ πρόσκεισο.

ΞΑΝΘΙΑΣ
         ταῦτ', ὦ δέσποτα.

ΒΔΕΛΤΚΛΕΩΝ
ἄναξ Πόσειδον, τί ποτ' ἄρ' ἡ κάπνη ψοφεῖ;
οὗτος, τίς εἶ σύ;

ΦΙΛΟΚΛΕΩΝ
      καπνὸς ἔγωγ' ἐξέρχομαι.

ΒΔΕΛΤΚΛΕΩΝ
καπνός; φέρ' ἴδω, ξύλου τίνος σύ;

ΦΙΛΟΚΛΕΩΝ
145   *συκίνου.*

ΒΔΕΛΤΚΛΕΩΝ
νὴ τὸν Δί', ὅσπερ γ' ἐστὶ δριμύτατος καπνῶν.
ἀτὰρ οὐκέτ' ἐρρήσεις γε; ποῦ 'σθ' ἡ τηλία;
δύου πάλιν. φέρ', ἐπαναθῶ σοι καὶ ξύλον.
ἐνταῦθά νυν ζήτει τιν' ἄλλην μηχανήν.
150 *ἀτὰρ ἄθλιός γ' εἴμ' ὡς ἕτερος οὐδεὶς ἀνήρ,*
ὅστις πατρὸς νυνὶ Καπνίου κεκλήσομαι.

ΦΙΛΟΚΛΕΩΝ
παῖ.

scurrying about like a mouse. Keep an eye on the sink drain
so he doesn't slip out that way. And you cover the door!

Exit SOSIAS behind the house.

XANTHIAS
Right, sir.

LOATHECLEON
God almighty, what's all that racket in the chimney? You in
there! Who are you?

LOVECLEON appears.

LOVECLEON
Me? I'm smoke coming out.

LOATHECLEON
Smoke? All right then, smoke from what kind of wood?

LOVECLEON
Impeach wood.[12]

LOATHECLEON
Of course! That's the most irritating kind of smoke. But no
more evaporation for you. Where's the chimney cover? Get
back in there! Here, let me put a log on top for good
measure. There now, think up some other scheme. Really,
no one else has the trouble I have! I'm all set to be called
the son of Old Smoky!

LOVECLEON
Open up, boy!

[12] "Figwood" (*sykinos*) puns on "malicious prosecutor" (*syko-phantes*).

239

ARISTOPHANES

ΞΑΝΘΙΑΣ

ΞΑΝΘΙΑΣ

τὴν θύραν ὠθεῖ.

ΒΔΕΛΤΚΛΕΩΝ

πίεζέ νυν σφόδρα,
εὖ κἀνδρικῶς· κἀγὼ γὰρ ἐνταυθ᾽ ἔρχομαι.
καὶ τῆς κατάκλῃδος ἐπιμελοῦ καὶ τοῦ μοχλοῦ,
155 φύλαττέ θ᾽ ὅπως μὴ τὴν βάλανον ἐκτρώξεται.

ΦΙΛΟΚΛΕΩΝ

τί δράσετ᾽; οὐκ ἐκφρήσετ᾽, ὦ μιαρώτατοι,
δικάσοντά μ᾽, ἀλλ᾽ ἐκφεύξεται Δρακοντίδης;

ΞΑΝΘΙΑΣ

σὺ δὲ τοῦτο βαρέως ἂν φέροις;

ΦΙΛΟΚΛΕΩΝ

ὁ γὰρ θεὸς
μαντευομένῳ μοὔχρησεν ἐν Δελφοῖς ποτε,
160 ὅταν τις ἐκφύγῃ μ᾽, ἀποσκλῆναι τότε.

ΞΑΝΘΙΑΣ

Ἄπολλον ἀποτρόπαιε, τοῦ μαντεύματος.

ΦΙΛΟΚΛΕΩΝ

ἴθ᾽, ἀντιβολῶ σ᾽, ἔκφρες με, μὴ διαρραγῶ.

ΞΑΝΘΙΑΣ

μὰ τὸν Ποσειδῶ, Φιλοκλέων, οὐδέποτέ γε.

ΦΙΛΟΚΛΕΩΝ

διατρώξομαι τοίνυν ὀδὰξ τὸ δίκτυον.

WASPS

XANTHIAS
He's pushing on the door!

LOATHECLEON
Then lean into it good and hard! I'm coming down there too. And mind the lock and the bar; make sure he doesn't munch the nut right off the bolt!

LOVECLEON
What are you doing? Let me out, you utter scum, I've got a case to hear! Do you want Dracontides[13] to get off scot free?

XANTHIAS
That would upset you?

LOVECLEON
Yes! I once consulted the Delphic oracle, and the god foretold that the moment I ever acquitted anyone, I'd dry up and blow away!

XANTHIAS
Apollo save us, what a prophecy!

LOVECLEON
Come on, I beg you, let me out, or I'll explode!

XANTHIAS
By god, Lovecleon, you'll never get out!

LOVECLEON
Then I'll gnaw through this netting with my teeth!

[13] Several men with this name ("Serpentine") are known in this period.

ΞΑΝΘΙΑΣ

ἀλλ' οὐκ ἔχεις ὀδόντας.

ΦΙΛΟΚΛΕΩΝ

165
οἴμοι δείλαιος.
πῶς ἄν σ' ἀποκτείναιμι; πῶς; δότε μοι ξίφος
ὅπως τάχιστ', ἢ πινάκιον τιμητικόν.

ΒΔΕΛΤΚΛΕΩΝ

ἄνθρωπος οὗτος μέγα τι δρασείει κακόν.

ΦΙΛΟΚΛΕΩΝ

μὰ τὸν Δί' οὐ δῆτ', ἀλλ' ἀποδόσθαι βούλομαι
170
τὸν ὄνον ἄγων αὐτοῖσι τοῖς κανθηλίοις·
νουμηνία γάρ ἐστιν.

ΒΔΕΛΤΚΛΕΩΝ

οὔκουν κἂν ἐγὼ
αὐτὸν ἀποδοίμην δῆτ' ἄν;

ΦΙΛΟΚΛΕΩΝ

οὐχ ὥσπερ γ' ἐγώ.

ΒΔΕΛΤΚΛΕΩΝ

μὰ Δί', ἀλλ' ἄμεινον.

ΦΙΛΟΚΛΕΩΝ

ἀλλὰ τὸν ὄνον ἔξαγε.

ΞΑΝΘΙΑΣ

οἴαν πρόφασιν καθῆκεν, ὡς εἰρωνικῶς,
ἵν' αὐτὸν ἐκπέμψειας.

XANTHIAS

You haven't any teeth!

LOVECLEON

Heaven save me, how can I kill you? How? Quick, give me a sword, or better yet, a penalty tablet!

LOATHECLEON

The man's set to commit some awful crime!

LOVECLEON

Not at all, I swear to god! I just want to take the donkey and its panniers out and sell them. It's market day.

LOATHECLEON

Surely I could do that, couldn't I?

LOVECLEON

Not the way I would.

LOATHECLEON

That's right, I'd do it better.

LOVECLEON

All right, let the donkey out.

XANTHIAS

What an excuse he tried to hook you with to let him out. Pretty sly.

ΒΔΕΛΤΚΛΕΩΝ

175   ἀλλ' οὐκ ἔσπασεν

ταύτῃ γ'· ἐγὼ γὰρ ᾐσθόμην τεχνωμένου.

ἀλλ' εἰσιών μοι τὸν ὄνον ἐξάγειν δοκῶ,

ὅπως ἂν ὁ γέρων μηδὲ παρακύψῃ πάλιν.

κάνθων, τί κλάεις; ὅτι πεπράσει τήμερον;

180 βάδιζε θᾶττον. τί στένεις, εἰ μὴ φέρεις

'Οδυσσέα τιν';

ΞΑΝΘΙΑΣ

            ἀλλὰ ναὶ μὰ Δία φέρει

κάτω γε τουτονί τιν' ὑποδεδυκότα.

ΒΔΕΛΤΚΛΕΩΝ

ποῖον; φέρ' ἴδωμαι.

ΞΑΝΘΙΑΣ

           τουτονί.

ΒΔΕΛΤΚΛΕΩΝ

              τουτὶ τί ἦν;

τίς εἶ ποτ', ὦνθρωπ', ἐτεόν;

ΦΙΛΟΚΛΕΩΝ

                Οὖτις, νὴ Δία.

ΒΔΕΛΤΚΛΕΩΝ

Οὖτις σύ; ποδαπός;

ΦΙΛΟΚΛΕΩΝ

185   'Ίθακος 'Αποδρασιππίδου.

ΒΔΕΛΤΚΛΕΩΝ

Οὖτις μὰ τὸν Δί' οὖτι χαιρήσων γε σύ.

LOATHECLEON

But he didn't catch me with that one; I'm on to his tricks.
But I think I'll go in and get the donkey myself. I don't want
the old man so much as peeping out again. (*goes in and
fetches the donkey*) Why all the braying, Jenny? Don't want
to be sold today? Get along there. Why are you fussing?
Unless you've got Odysseus or somebody under there.[14]

XANTHIAS

Wait a minute. Good lord, somebody *is* curled up under
here, look!

LOATHECLEON

What? Let me have a look.

XANTHIAS

There he is.

LOATHECLEON

What's this? Who might you be, my good man? Well?

LOVECLEON

Noman. Honestly.

LOATHECLEON

You're Noman? From where?

LOVECLEON

Ithaca. Son of Escapides.

LOATHECLEON

Well, you're one Noman who'll be enjoying no manner of

14 For the parody that follows see Homer, *Odyssey* 9.424 ff.

ὕφελκε θᾶττον αὐτόν. ὦ μιαρώτατος,
ἵν' ὑποδέδυκεν· ὥστ' ἔμοιγ' ἰνδάλλεται
ὁμοιότατος κλητῆρος εἶναι πωλίῳ.

ΦΙΛΟΚΛΕΩΝ

190 εἰ μή μ' ἐάσεθ' ἥσυχον, μαχούμεθα.

ΒΔΕΛΤΚΛΕΩΝ

περὶ τοῦ μαχεῖ νῷν δῆτα;

ΦΙΛΟΚΛΕΩΝ

περὶ ὄνου σκιᾶς.

ΒΔΕΛΤΚΛΕΩΝ

πονηρὸς εἶ πόρρω τέχνης καὶ παράβολος.

ΦΙΛΟΚΛΕΩΝ

ἐγὼ πονηρός; οὐ μὰ Δί', ἀλλ' οὐκ οἶσθα σὺ
νῦν μ' ὄντ' ἄριστον; ἀλλ' ἴσως, ὅταν φάγῃς
195 ὑπογάστριον γέροντος ἡλιαστικοῦ.

ΒΔΕΛΤΚΛΕΩΝ

ὤθει τὸν ὄνον καὶ σαυτὸν εἰς τὴν οἰκίαν.

ΦΙΛΟΚΛΕΩΝ

ὦ ξυνδικασταὶ καὶ Κλέων, ἀμύνατε.

ΒΔΕΛΤΚΛΕΩΝ

ἔνδον κέκραχθι τῆς θύρας κεκλημένης.
ὤθει σὺ πολλοὺς τῶν λίθων πρὸς τὴν θύραν,
200 καὶ τὴν βάλανον ἔμβαλλε πάλιν εἰς τὸν μοχλόν,
καὶ τὴν δόκον προσθεὶς τὸν ὅλμον τὸν μέγαν
ἀνύσας τι προσκύλισον.

success. Quick, drag him out from under there. The skunk, look what he's crawled under! If you ask me, he's just like a burro-crat's hack!

LOVECLEON

Leave me alone or we'll soon be fighting.

LOATHECLEON

Fighting about what?

LOVECLEON

The donkey's shadow![15]

LOATHECLEON

You're a master crook and rotten to the core.

LOVECLEON

Me rotten? Certainly not! I'll have you know I'm perfectly fine. Maybe you'll find that out when you sink your teeth into a slab of tough old juryman.

LOATHECLEON

You and the donkey giddyup into the house.

LOVECLEON

(*hustled into the house*) Fellow jurors! Cleon! Help!

LOATHECLEON

Do your yelling inside; the door's locked. You there, pile up lots of stones against the door, and shoot that bolt back into its slot, and reinforce it with that plank, and roll the big millstone against it, and make it snappy!

[15] Proverbial for something not worth fighting about.

ΞΑΝΘΙΑΣ

οἴμοι δείλαιος·
πόθεν ποτ᾽ ἐμπέπτωκέ μοι τὸ βωλίον;

ΒΔΕΛΤΚΛΕΩΝ

ἴσως ἄνωθεν μῦς ἐνέβαλέ σοί ποθεν.

ΞΑΝΘΙΑΣ

205 μῦς; οὐ μὰ Δί᾽, ἀλλ᾽ ὑποδυόμενός τις οὑτοσὶ
ὑπὸ τῶν κεραμίδων ἡλιαστὴς ὀροφίας.

ΒΔΕΛΤΚΛΕΩΝ

οἴμοι κακοδαίμων· στροῦθος ἀνὴρ γίγνεται·
ἐκπτήσεται. ποῦ ποῦ ᾽στί μοι τὸ δίκτυον;
σοῦ, σοῦ, πάλιν, σοῦ. νὴ Δί᾽ ἦ μοι κρεῖττον ἦν
210 τηρεῖν Σκιώνην ἀντὶ τούτου τοῦ πατρός.

ΞΑΝΘΙΑΣ

ἄγε νυν, ἐπειδὴ τουτονὶ σεσοβήκαμεν,
κοὐκ ἔσθ᾽ ὅπως διαδὺς ἂν ἡμᾶς ἔτι λάθοι,
τί οὐκ ἀπεκοιμήθημεν ὅσον ὅσον στίλην;

ΒΔΕΛΤΚΛΕΩΝ

ἀλλ᾽, ὦ πόνηρ᾽, ἥξουσιν ὀλίγον ὕστερον
215 οἱ ξυνδικασταὶ παρακαλοῦντες τουτονὶ
τὸν πατέρα.

ΞΑΝΘΙΑΣ

τί λέγεις; ἀλλὰ νῦν γ᾽ ὄρθρος βαθύς.

ΒΔΕΛΤΚΛΕΩΝ

νὴ τὸν Δί᾽, ὀψέ γ᾽ ἆρ᾽ ἀνεστήκασι νῦν.
ὡς ἀπὸ μέσων νυκτῶν γε παρακαλοῦσ᾽ ἀεί,

248

WASPS

XANTHIAS

Dammit, where did that dirtball fall down on me from?

LOATHECLEON

Maybe a mouse knocked it loose on you from somewhere
up above.

XANTHIAS

A mouse? Certainly not. What's scuttling up there under
the tiles is a roof juror!

LOATHECLEON

Oh my god, the man's turning into a sparrow! He's going
to fly his way out! Where's my net? Where is it? Shoo! Shoo!
Go back, shoo! I swear, I'd be better off blockading
Scione[16] than this father of mine.

XANTHIAS

Well now, we've shooed him back and there's no way he
can sneak past us, so why don't we take a break for just a
teeny bit of shuteye?

LOATHECLEON

You sorry fool, the other jurors will be here to pick up my
father any minute now!

XANTHIAS

What are you talking about? It's hardly dawn.

LOATHECLEON

Then they've got up late today. Just after midnight's when

16 See 62 n.

λύχνους ἔχοντες καὶ μινυρίζοντες μέλη
220 ἀρχαιομελισιδωνοφρυνιχήρατα,
οἷς ἐκκαλοῦνται τοῦτον.

ΞΑΝΘΙΑΣ

οὐκοῦν, ἢν δέῃ,
ἤδη ποτ' αὐτοὺς τοῖς λίθοις βαλλήσομεν.

ΒΔΕΛΥΚΛΕΩΝ

ἀλλ', ὦ πόνηρε, τὸ γένος ἤν τις ὀργίσῃ
τὸ τῶν γερόντων, ἔσθ' ὅμοιον σφηκιᾷ.
225 ἔχουσι γὰρ καὶ κέντρον ἐκ τῆς ὀσφύος
ὀξύτατον, ᾧ κεντοῦσι, καὶ κεκραγότες
πηδῶσι καὶ βάλλουσιν ὥσπερ φέψαλοι.

ΞΑΝΘΙΑΣ

μὴ φροντίσῃς· ἐὰν ἐγὼ λίθους ἔχω,
πολλῶν δικαστῶν σφηκιὰν διασκεδῶ.

ΚΟΡΥΦΑΙΟΣ

230 χώρει, πρόβαιν' ἐρρωμένως. ὦ Κωμία, βραδύνεις.
μὰ τὸν Δί' οὐ μέντοι πρὸ τοῦ γ', ἀλλ' ἦσθ' ἱμὰς
    κύνειος·
νυνὶ δὲ κρείττων ἐστί σου Χαρινάδης βαδίζειν.
ὦ Στρυμόδωρε Κονθυλεῦ, βέλτιστε συνδικαστῶν,
Εὐεργίδης ἆρ' ἐστί που 'νταῦθ', ἢ Χάβης ὁ Φλυεύς;
235 πάρεσθ' ὃ δὴ λοιπόν γ' ἔτ' ἐστίν, ἀππαπαῖ παπαιάξ,

234 Χάβης RV: Χάρης j

250

they usually pick him up, toting torches and warbling sweet old Sidon Songs by Phrynichus;[17] that's how they call him out.

XANTHIAS

Well, if need be we'll pelt them with stones without further ado.

LOATHECLEON

You sorry fool, whoever riles that tribe of oldsters riles a wasps' nest. They've even got stingers, extremely sharp, sticking out from their rumps, that they stab with, and they leap and attack, crackling like sparks.

XANTHIAS

Don't you worry, if I've got stones I can scatter a big nestful of jurors.

XANTHIAS and LOATHECLEON sit down and are soon asleep. Enter the CHORUS, accompanied by BOYS.

CHORUS LEADER

Get along, press on hardy. Comias,[18] you're lagging. By god, you didn't use to; you were sturdy as a dog leash, but now Charinades can outwalk you. You there, Strymodorus of Conthyle, my excellent brother juror, do you see Euergides anywhere, or Chabes of Phlya? I'm afraid what's here is—oh my!—all that's left of that youthful time, when we

---

[17] A tragedian of the Persian War period famous for his lyrics; the "Sidon Songs" were from his *Phoenician Women* (produced between 478 and 473).

[18] The names given to several members of the chorus seem to be generic.

251

ἥβης ἐκείνης, ἡνίκ' ἐν Βυζαντίῳ ξυνῆμεν
φρουροῦντ' ἐγώ τε καὶ σύ· κᾆτα περιπατοῦντε νύκτωρ
τῆς ἀρτοπώλιδος λαθόντ' ἐκλέψαμεν τὸν ὅλμον·
κᾆθ' ἥψομεν τοῦ κορκόρου κατασχίσαντες αὐτόν.

240 ἀλλ' ἐγκονῶμεν, ὦνδρες, ὡς ἔσται Λάχητι νυνί·
σίμβλον δέ φασι χρημάτων ἔχειν ἅπαντες αὐτόν.
χθὲς οὖν Κλέων ὁ κηδεμὼν ἡμῖν ἐφεῖτ' ἐν ὥρᾳ
ἥκειν ἔχοντας ἡμερῶν ὀργὴν τριῶν πονηρὰν
ἐπ' αὐτόν, ὡς κολωμένους ὧν ἠδίκησεν. ἀλλὰ

245 σπεύσωμεν, ὦνδρες ἥλικες, πρὶν ἡμέραν γενέσθαι.
χωρῶμεν, ἅμα τε τῷ λύχνῳ πάντη διασκοπῶμεν,
μή που λίθος τις ἐμποδὼν ἡμᾶς κακόν τι δράσῃ.

ΠΑΙΣ

ὤ.
τὸν πηλόν, ὦ πάτερ πάτερ, τουτονὶ φύλαξαι.

ΚΟΡΥΦΑΙΟΣ

κάρφος χαμᾶθέν νυν λαβὼν τὸν λύχνον πρόβυσον.

ΠΑΙΣ

250 οὔκ, ἀλλὰ τῳδί μοι δοκῶ τὸν λύχνον προβύσειν.

ΚΟΡΥΦΑΙΟΣ

τί δὴ μαθὼν τῷ δακτύλῳ τὴν θρυαλλίδ' ὠθεῖς,
καὶ ταῦτα τοῦ 'λαίου σπανίζοντος, ὦ 'νόητε;

---

[19] Captured from the Persians 56 years earlier.

[20] Laches of Aexone was a successful general and political ally
of Nicias (and the title character of Plato's dialogue), who the
previous year had sponsored a one-year treaty with Sparta. Later

shared guard duty at Byzantium,[19] you and I. Remember how we went rambling at night and pinched the bread-woman's kneading bowl, and how we split it up for firewood, and boiled some pimpernel porridge? Anyway, let's get a move on, lads; Laches is going to get it today![20] Everybody says he's stuffed his hive with money. That's why yesterday our patron Cleon ordered us to report for duty in good time, with three days' rations of rotten rage against that bloke, to punish him for his crimes. Anyway, let's hurry up, old colleagues, before it gets to be daybreak. Let's move out, and take care to search in all directions with our lamps in case there's a stone underfoot somewhere waiting to hurt someone.

BOY

Whoa! Father, father, mind the mud there!

CHORUS LEADER

Then pick up a twig and trim the lamp.

BOY

(*holding up a finger*) No, I think I'll use this to trim the lamp.

CHORUS LEADER

Who taught you to shove the wick around with your finger, you idiot, especially when oil's scarce? Of course it's not

in this play (835-43, 891-1002) there is a mock prosecution of Laches by Cleon for misconduct in Laches' Sicilian campaign of 427-5: this may reprise an actual trial or deposition from the generalship (which would have occurred in 425), or else Aristophanes may be imagining a trial in response to recent threats by Cleon against Laches, in which the Sicilian business would have been brought up.

οὐ γὰρ δάκνει σ᾽, ὅταν δέῃ τίμιον πρίασθαι.

ΠΑΙΣ

εἰ νὴ Δί᾽ αὖθις κονδύλοις νουθετήσεθ᾽ ἡμᾶς,
255 ἀποσβέσαντες τοὺς λύχνους ἄπιμεν οἴκαδ᾽ αὐτοί.
κἄπειτ᾽ ἴσως ἐν τῷ σκότῳ τουτουὶ στερηθεὶς
τὸν πηλὸν ὥσπερ ἀτταγᾶς τυρβάσεις βαδίζων.

ΚΟΡΥΦΑΙΟΣ

ἦ μὴν ἐγώ σου χἀτέρους μείζονας κολάζω.
ἀλλ᾽ οὑτοσί μοι βόρβορος φαίνεται πατοῦντι.
260 κοὐκ ἔσθ᾽ ὅπως οὐχ ἡμερῶν τεττάρων τὸ πλεῖστον
ὕδωρ ἀναγκαίως ἔχει τὸν θεὸν ποιῆσαι.
ἔπεισι γοῦν τοῖσιν λύχνοις οὑτοὶ μύκητες·
φιλεῖ δ᾽, ὅταν τοῦτ᾽ ᾖ, ποιεῖν ὑετὸν μάλιστα.
δεῖται δὲ καὶ τῶν καρπίμων ἅττα μή 'στι πρῷα
265 ὕδωρ γενέσθαι κἀπιπνεῦσαι βόρειον αὐτοῖς.
τί χρῆμ᾽ ἄρ᾽ οὐκ τῆς οἰκίας τῆσδε συνδικαστὴς
πέπονθεν, ὡς οὐ φαίνεται δεῦρο πρὸς τὸ πλῆθος;
οὐ μὴν πρὸ τοῦ γ᾽ ἐφολκὸς ἦν, ἀλλὰ πρῶτος ἡμῶν
ἡγεῖτ᾽ ἂν ᾄδων Φρυνίχου· καὶ γάρ ἐστιν ἀνὴρ
270 φιλῳδός. ἀλλά μοι δοκεῖ στάντας ἐνθάδ᾽, ὦνδρες,
ᾄδοντας αὐτὸν ἐκκαλεῖν, ἤν τί πως ἀκούσας
τοῦ 'μοῦ μέλους ὑφ᾽ ἡδονῆς ἑρπύσῃ θύραζε.

ΧΟΡΟΣ

(στρ) τί ποτ᾽ οὐ πρὸ θυρῶν φαίνετ᾽ ἄρ᾽ ἡμῖν
ὁ γέρων οὐδ᾽ ὑπακούει;
μῶν ἀπολώλεκε τὰς
275 ἐμβάδας; ἢ προσέκοψ᾽ ἐν

you that feels the bite when prices are high!

BOY

Use your fists to teach me that lesson one more time, and I promise you we'll put out the lamps and go home by ourselves! Maybe without this lamp you'll stumble around in the dark, churning up the mud like a marsh snipe!

CHORUS LEADER

I warn you, I dish out punishment to people bigger than you! Hold on, this looks like mud I'm stepping in. No question the god's bound to make water within four days at the outside. Anyway, there's mold on these lamps, and that's when he's most fond of making rain. Well, the crops that aren't up yet could certainly use a rainfall, and then the breath of the north wind. (*stopping before Lovecleon's house*) What's the matter with our brother juror from this house, not showing up to join the crew? He's never been tardy before. In fact he always leads us on our way with something from Phrynichus; the man's an avid singer. Well, gentlemen, I think we should pause here and sing him out of the house. Maybe when he hears my song he'll be happy to hobble outside.

CHORUS

Why does the old man not appear to us
at his door or answer our call?
Maybe he couldn't find his shoes?

τῷ σκότῳ τὸν δάκτυλόν που,
εἶτ᾽ ἐφλέγμηνεν αὐτοῦ
τὸ σφυρὸν γέροντος ὄντος;
καὶ τάχ᾽ ἂν βουβωνιῴη.
ἦ μὴν πολὺ δριμύτατός γ᾽ ἦν τῶν παρ᾽ ἡμῖν,
καὶ μόνος οὐκ ἀνεπείθετ᾽,
ἀλλ᾽ ὁπότ᾽ ἀντιβολοίη
τις, κάτω κύπτων ἂν οὕτω
280   "λίθον ἕψεις" ἔλεγεν.

(ἀντ)   τάχα δ᾽ ἂν διὰ τὸν χθιζινὸν ἄνθρω-
πον, ὃς ἡμᾶς διέδυ ⟨πως⟩
ἐξαπατῶν καὶ λέγων
ὡς φιλαθήναιος ἦν καὶ
τἀν Σάμῳ πρῶτος κατείποι,
διὰ τοῦτ᾽ ὀδυνηθεὶς
εἶτ᾽ ἴσως κεῖται πυρέττων.
285   ἔστι γὰρ τοιοῦτος ἀνήρ.
ἀλλ᾽, ὦγάθ᾽, ἀνίστασο, μηδ᾽ οὕτω σεαυτὸν
ἔσθιε, μηδ᾽ ἀγανάκτει.
καὶ γὰρ ἀνὴρ παχὺς ἥκει
τῶν προδόντων τἀπὶ Θρᾴκης·
ὃν ὅπως ἐγχυτριεῖς.

KORYΦAIOΣ
290   ὕπαγ᾽, ὦ παῖ, ὕπαγε.

281 διέδυ (Bentley) ⟨πως⟩ Dindorf: διεδύετ᾽ a

256

Or stubbed his toe on something in the dark
and got a swollen ankle, an oldster like him,
and maybe even a lump in his groin?
I tell you, he was by far the fiercest of us all,
and the only one who couldn't be sweet-talked;
no, when anyone begged for mercy
he'd put his head down like this and say,
"you're trying to cook a stone."

Maybe it was yesterday's case,
the guy who somehow slipped through our fingers
by fooling us into believing
that he's a friend to Athens
and the first to tell us what was going on at Samos;[21]
maybe he got sore about that
and took to his bed with a fever.
That's the sort of man he is!
But do get up, dear fellow! Don't
eat your heart out and feed your vexation.
There's a plump one on the docket today,
one of those who betrayed the Thracian front.[22]
See that you pot him!

CHORUS LEADER

Move along, boy, move along.

[21] The Samian revolt of 440; the scholia identify the informant
as one Carystion, who was rewarded with citizenship.
[22] Perhaps Laches; see 240 n.

ΠΑΙΣ

(στρ) ἐθελήσεις τί μοι οὖν, ὦ
πάτερ, ἤν σού τι δεηθῶ;

ΚΟΡΥΦΑΙΟΣ

πάνυ γ', ὦ παιδίον. ἀλλ' εἰ-
πέ, τί βούλει με πρίασθαι
295 καλόν; οἶμαι δέ σ' ἐρεῖν ἀσ-
τραγάλους δήπουθεν, ὦ παῖ.

ΠΑΙΣ

μὰ Δί', ἀλλ' ἰσχάδας, ὦ πα-
πία· ἥδιον γάρ—

ΚΟΡΥΦΑΙΟΣ

οὐκ ἂν
μὰ Δί', εἰ κρέμαισθέ γ' ὑμεῖς.

ΠΑΙΣ

μὰ Δί' οὔ τἄρα προπέμψω σε τὸ λοιπόν.

ΚΟΡΥΦΑΙΟΣ

300 ἀπὸ γὰρ τοῦδέ με τοῦ μισθαρίου
τρίτον αὐτὸν ἔχειν ἄλ-
φιτα δεῖ καὶ ξύλα κὤψον·
σὺ δὲ σῦκά μ' αἰτεῖς.

ΠΑΙΣ

(ἀντ) ἄγε νυν, ὦ πάτερ, ἢν μὴ
τὸ δικαστήριον ἄρχων
305 καθίσῃ νῦν, πόθεν ὠνη-
σόμεθ' ἄριστον; ἔχεις ἐλ-

WASPS

BOY

Will you give me something then,
father, if I ask you for it?

CHORUS LEADER

Of course, my lad. Just tell me
what nice thing you want me to buy.
I'm pretty sure you're going to say
knucklebone dice, my boy.

BOY

God no. Figs, daddy!
It's nicer—

CHORUS LEADER

Absolutely not,
not even if you hang yourselves!

BOY

Then I'll stop guiding you altogether.

CHORUS LEADER

Look, out of this tiny pittance
I've got to get barley meal,
firewood, and dinner for the three of us,
and you ask me for figs!

BOY

Tell me then, father,
if the archon doesn't call the court
into session today, how
can we buy lunch?

πίδα χρηστήν τινα νῷν ἢ
πόρον Ἑλλὰς ἱερόν;

ΚΟΡΥΦΑΙΟΣ

ἀπαπαῖ φεῦ.

310   μὰ Δί᾽ οὐκ ἔγωγε νῷν οἶδ᾽
ὁπόθεν γε δεῖπνον ἔσται.

ΠΑΙΣ

τί με δῆτ᾽, ὦ μελέα μῆτερ, ἔτικτες;

ΚΟΡΥΦΑΙΟΣ

ἵν᾽ ἐμοὶ πράγματα βόσκειν παρέχῃς.

ΠΑΙΣ

ἀνόνητον ἄρ᾽ ὦ θυ-
λάκιόν σ᾽ εἶχον ἄγαλμα.

315   ἐέ.
πάρα νῷν στενάζειν.

ΦΙΛΟΚΛΕΩΝ

φίλοι, τήκομαι μὲν
πάλαι διὰ τῆς ὀπῆς
ὑμῶν ἐπακούων.
ἀλλ᾽, οὐ γὰρ οἷός τ᾽ εἴμ᾽
ᾄδειν, τί ποιήσω;
τηροῦμαι δ᾽ ὑπὸ τῶνδ᾽, ἐπεὶ
320   βούλομαί γε πάλαι μεθ᾽ ὑ-
μῶν ἐλθὼν ἐπὶ τοὺς καδίσ-
κους κακόν τι ποιῆσαι.
ἀλλ᾽, ὦ Ζεῦ μεγαβρόντα,

Do you have any firm hope for us,
any "holy way to Helle"?[23]

CHORUS LEADER

Alas and ah me!
I surely don't know
where our dinner's coming from.

BOY

Why then, miserable mother, did you bear me?

CHORUS LEADER

So that I'd have the problem of feeding you!

BOY

Ah shopping bag, it seems you've been
a useless ornament to carry!
Boo hoo.
All we can do is bawl.

LOVECLEON

(*from a window*)
Friends, I've been pining
all this time, listening to you
through this chink.
But since I can't sing,
what am I to do?
These men are watching me because
I'm ever ready to go with you
to the voting urns and cause some pain.
Ah, great thundering Zeus,

[23] Pindar fr. 189.

ἤ με ποίησον καπνὸν ἐξαίφνης
325   ἢ Προξενίδην ἢ τὸν Σέλλου
τοῦτον τὸν ψευδαμάμαξυν.
τόλμησον, ἄναξ, χαρίσασθαί μοι,
πάθος οἰκτίρας· ἤ με κεραυνῷ
διατινθαλέῳ σπόδισον ταχέως,
330   κἄπειτ᾽ ἀνελών μ᾽ ἀποφυσήσας
εἰς ὀξάλμην ἔμβαλε θερμήν·
ἢ δῆτα λίθον με ποίησον, ἐφ᾽ οὗ
τὰς χοιρίνας ἀριθμοῦσιν.

ΧΟΡΟΣ

(στρ) τίς γάρ ἐσθ᾽ ὁ ταῦτά σ᾽ εἴργων
κἀποκλῄων τῇ θύρᾳ; λέ-
335   ξον· πρὸς εὔνους γὰρ φράσεις.

ΦΙΛΟΚΛΕΩΝ

οὑμὸς υἱός. ἀλλὰ μὴ βοᾶτε· καὶ γὰρ τυγχάνει
οὑτοσὶ πρόσθεν καθεύδων. ἀλλ᾽ ὕφεσθε τοῦ τόνου.

ΧΟΡΟΣ

τοῦ δ᾽ ἔφεξιν, ὦ μάταιε, ταῦτα δρᾶν σε βούλεται;
τίνα πρόφασιν ἔχων;

ΦΙΛΟΚΛΕΩΝ

340   οὐκ ἐᾷ μ᾽, ὦνδρες, δικάζειν οὐδὲ δρᾶν οὐδὲν κακόν·
ἀλλά μ᾽ εὐωχεῖν ἕτοιμός ἐστ᾽, ἐγὼ δ᾽ οὐ βούλομαι.

turn me right now into hot air,
like Proxenides[24] or the son of Bluster[25] here,
that climbing vine.
Deign, Lord, to do me a favor,
in pity at my plight: either bake me
with a boiling thunderbolt,
then hoist me aloft, blow off the ashes
and toss me into hot salsa;
or else turn me to stone,
the one they count the votes on!

CHORUS

Just who is it that shuts you in this way
behind locked doors?
You can tell us: we're on your side.

LOVECLEON

My son. No, don't shout: that's him there, sleeping in front
of the house. So tone it down.

CHORUS

On what pretext does he want to treat you this way,
you incompetent?
What's his excuse?

LOVECLEON

Gentlemen, he won't let me hear cases or do any harm.
Instead, he wants to wine and dine me, though that's not
what I want.

[24] Ridiculed as a boaster also in *Birds* 1126.
[25] Both Aeschines (cf. 459, 1243) and Amynias (cf. 74-6, 1267)
are thus called.

ΧΟΡΟΣ

τοῦτ᾽ ἐτόλμησ᾽ ὁ μιαρὸς χα-
νεῖν, ὁ Δημολογοκλέων,
ὅτι λέγεις τι περὶ τῶν νε-
ῶν ἀληθές; οὐ γὰρ ἄν ποθ᾽
οὗτος ἀνὴρ τοῦτ᾽ ἐτόλμη-
σεν λέγειν, εἰ
345 μὴ ξυνωμότης τις ἦν.

ΚΟΡΥΦΑΙΟΣ

ἀλλ᾽ ἐκ τούτων ὥρα τινά σοι ζητεῖν καινὴν ἐπίνοιαν,
ἥτις σε λάθρα τἀνδρὸς τουδὶ καταβῆναι δεῦρο
ποιήσει.

ΦΙΛΟΚΛΕΩΝ

τίς ἂν οὖν εἴη; ζητεῖθ᾽ ὑμεῖς, ὡς πᾶν ἂν ἔγωγε
ποιοίην·
οὕτω κιττῶ διὰ τῶν σανίδων μετὰ χοιρίνης περιελ-
θεῖν.

ΚΟΡΥΦΑΙΟΣ

350 ἔστιν ὀπὴ δῆθ᾽ ἥντιν᾽ ἂν ἔνδοθεν οἷός τ᾽ εἴης
διορύξαι,
εἶτ᾽ ἐκδῦναι ῥάκεσιν κρυφθεὶς ὥσπερ πολύμητις
Ὀδυσσεύς;

ΦΙΛΟΚΛΕΩΝ

πάντα πέφρακται κοὐκ ἔστιν ὀπῆς οὐδ᾽ εἰ σέρφῳ
διαδῦναι.
ἀλλ᾽ ἄλλο τι δεῖ ζητεῖν ὑμᾶς· ὀπίαν δ᾽ οὐκ ἔστι
γενέσθαι.

WASPS

CHORUS
Has the slimy fellow the gall,
this Demagogocleon, to mouth off that way,
because you voiced an awkward truth
about the fleet?[26] This man
would never have dared
to say that unless
he were some sort of conspirator!

CHORUS LEADER
Well, under the circumstances it's time you came up with
a fresh idea for getting down here behind this man's back.

LOVECLEON
What could it be? You come up with one; I'm ready to do
anything. That's how much I crave to stroll among the
docket boards with my voting shell.

CHORUS LEADER
Then is there a chink that you could excavate from inside
and then slip out disguised in rags, like wily Odysseus?

LOVECLEON
Everything's sealed up; there isn't enough of a chink for
even a gnat to slip through. You've got to think of some-
thing else; I can't turn myself into runny whey.

---

26 Or, with the alternative accentuation, "about the younger
generation."

---

343 νέων Bentley

ARISTOPHANES

ΚΟΡΥΦΑΙΟΣ

μέμνησαι δῆθ᾽ ὅτ᾽ ἐπὶ στρατιᾶς κλέψας ποτὲ τοὺς
ὀβελίσκους
355 ἵεις σαυτὸν κατὰ τοῦ τείχους ταχέως, ὅτε Νάξος ἑάλω;

ΦΙΛΟΚΛΕΩΝ

οἶδ᾽· ἀλλὰ τί τοῦτ᾽; οὐδὲν γὰρ τοῦτ᾽ ἔστιν ἐκείνῳ
προσόμοιον.
ἥβων γάρ, κἀδυνάμην κλέπτειν, ἴσχυόν τ᾽ αὐτὸς
ἐμαυτοῦ,
κοὐδείς μ᾽ ἐφύλαττ᾽, ἀλλ᾽ ἐξῆν μοι
φεύγειν ἀδεῶς. νῦν δὲ ξὺν ὅπλοις
360 ἄνδρες ὁπλῖται διαταξάμενοι
κατὰ τὰς διόδους σκοπιωροῦνται,
τὼ δὲ δύ᾽ αὐτῶν ἐπὶ ταῖσι θύραις
ὥσπερ με γαλῆν κρέα κλέψασαν
τηροῦσιν ἔχοντ᾽ ὀβελίσκους.

ΧΟΡΟΣ

(ἀντ) ἀλλὰ καὶ νῦν ἐκπόριζε
365 μηχανὴν ὅπως τάχισθ᾽· ἕ-
ως γάρ, ὦ μελίττιον.

ΦΙΛΟΚΛΕΩΝ

διατραγεῖν τοίνυν κράτιστόν ἐστί μοι τὸ δίκτυον.
ἡ δέ μοι Δίκτυννα συγγνώμην ἔχοι τοῦ δικτύου.

ΧΟΡΟΣ

ταῦτα μὲν πρὸς ἀνδρός ἐστ᾽ ἄνοντος ἐς σωτηρίαν.
370 ἀλλ᾽ ἔπαγε τὴν γνάθον.

266

CHORUS LEADER

OK, do you remember when we were on campaign one time and you stole the skewers and launched yourself down from the battlement in a flash, when Naxos was taken?[27]

LOVECLEON

Yes; but so what? This is an entirely different situation. I was young then, I could get away with things, I could count on my strength, and nobody was watching me, so I could escape carefree. But now soldiers in arms are drawn up for battle and patrol the passes, two of them at the door holding skewers and watching me like a cat who's stolen some meat.

CHORUS

Well, you'd better come up
with a plan this time too, as quick as you can;
it's daybreak, little honeybee.

LOVECLEON

Then my best course is to gnaw through the netting, and may Dictynna of the Nets forgive me if I've nettled her!

CHORUS

Now you're talking like a man headed for salvation!
Get that jaw working!

---

[27] Around 470 (Thucydides 1.98.4).

ΦΙΛΟΚΛΕΩΝ

διατέτρωκται τοῦτό γ'. ἀλλὰ μὴ βοᾶτε μηδαμῶς,
ἀλλὰ τηρώμεσθ' ὅπως μὴ Βδελυκλέων αἰσθήσεται.

ΧΟΡΟΣ

μηδέν, ὦ τᾶν, δέδιθι, μηδέν·
  ὡς ἐγὼ τοῦτόν γ', ἐὰν γρύ-
  ξῃ τι, ποιήσω δακεῖν τὴν
375 καρδίαν καὶ τὸν περὶ ψυ-
  χῆς δρόμον δραμεῖν, ἵν' εἰδῇ
  μὴ πατεῖν τὰ
  ταῖν θεαῖν ψηφίσματα.

ΚΟΡΥΦΑΙΟΣ

ἀλλ' ἐξάψας διὰ τῆς θυρίδος τὸ καλῴδιον εἶτα καθίμα
380 δήσας σαυτὸν καὶ τὴν ψυχὴν ἐμπλησάμενος
  Διοπείθους.

ΦΙΛΟΚΛΕΩΝ

ἄγε νυν, ἢν αἰσθομένω τούτω ζητῆτόν μ' ἐσκαλα-
  μᾶσθαι
κἀνασπαστὸν ποιεῖν εἴσω, τί ποιήσετε; φράζετε νυνί.

ΚΟΡΥΦΑΙΟΣ

ἀμυνούμέν σοι τὸν πρινώδη θυμὸν ἅπαντες καλέ-
  σαντες
ὥστ' οὐ δυνατόν σ' εἴργειν ἔσται· τοιαῦτα ποιήσο-
  μεν ἡμεῖς.

ΦΙΛΟΚΛΕΩΝ

385 δράσω τοίνυν ὑμῖν πίσυνος. καὶ μανθάνετ', ἤν τι
  πάθω 'γώ,

268

LOVECLEON

There, it's cut through. But absolutely no cheering; let's see
that we don't alert Loathecleon.

CHORUS

Never fear, old boy, never fear:
if he makes a peep I'll have him
eating his heart out
and running for dear life,
so he'll know better
than to wipe his feet
on the Two Goddesses'[28] legislation!

CHORUS LEADER

Now lash that cord to the window frame, tie it around you
and let yourself down, and fill your spirit with Diopeithes!

LOVECLEON

Say, what if these two catch on and try to get me reeled up
and hauled in, then what will you do? Tell me right now.

CHORUS LEADER

We'll all summon up our hardwood spirit and defend you.
The things we'll do, there will be no containing you!

LOVECLEON

All right, then I'll do it, on your say-so. And listen, if any-

---

[28] Demeter and Kore, the principal deities of the Eleusinian
Mysteries. Diopeithes was a fanatical harrier of atheists.

---

378 ταῖν θεαῖν] τῶν θεῶν R

ARISTOPHANES

ἀνελόντες καὶ κατακλαύσαντες θεῖναί μ' ὑπὸ τοῖσι
    δρυφάκτοις.

ΚΟΡΥΦΑΙΟΣ
οὐδὲν πείσει· μηδὲν δείσῃς. ἀλλ', ὦ βέλτιστε, καθίει
σαυτὸν θαρρῶν κἀπευξάμενος τοῖσι πατρῴοισι
    θεοῖσιν.

ΦΙΛΟΚΛΕΩΝ
ὦ Λύκε δέσποτα, γείτων ἥρως, σὺ γὰρ οἷσπερ ἐγὼ
    κεχάρησαι,
390 τοῖς δακρύοισιν τῶν φευγόντων ἀεὶ καὶ τοῖς ὀλοφυρ-
    μοῖς·
ᾤκησας γοῦν ἐπίτηδες ἰὼν ἐνταῦθ' ἵνα ταῦτ' ἀκροῷο,
κἀβουλήθης μόνος ἡρώων παρὰ τὸν κλάοντα καθῆ-
    σθαι,
ἐλέησον καὶ σῶσον νυνὶ τὸν σαυτοῦ πλησιόχωρον,
κοὐ μή ποτέ σου παρὰ τὰς κάννας οὐρήσω μηδ'
    ἀποπάρδω.

ΒΔΕΛΥΚΛΕΩΝ
οὗτος, ἐγείρου.

ΞΑΝΘΙΑΣ
        τί τὸ πρᾶγμ';

ΒΔΕΛΥΚΛΕΩΝ
395   ὥσπερ φωνή μέ τις ἐγκεκύκλωται.
μῶν ὁ γέρων πῃ διαδύεται αὖ;

thing happens to me, gather me up, give me a funeral, and bury me under the court railings.

CHORUS LEADER

Never fear, nothing will happen to you. Now let yourself down intrepidly, with a prayer to your ancestral gods, there's a good fellow.

LOVECLEON

Lord Lycus,[29] my nextdoor hero—for you enjoy the same things I do, the tears and wailings of each day's defendants, and of course chose to live where you could best hear them, the only hero eager to seat himself next to a weeper—now pity and rescue your very own neighbor, and I vow never to piss or fart on your fence!

LOATHECLEON

Hey! Wake up!

XANTHIAS

What's going on?

LOATHECLEON

A sound of voices seems to encircle me. The old man isn't trying somehow to slip by us again, is he?

---

[29] An Athenian hero whose shrine was next to a lawcourt.

ARISTOPHANES

ΞΑΝΘΙΑΣ

μὰ Δί᾽ οὐ δῆτ᾽, ἀλλὰ καθιμᾷ
αὐτὸν δήσας.

ΒΔΕΛΥΚΛΕΩΝ

ὦ μιαρώτατε, τί ποιεῖς; οὐ μὴ καταβήσει.
ἀνάβαιν᾽ ἀνύσας κατὰ τὴν ἑτέραν καὶ ταῖσιν φυλ-
λάσι παῖε,
ἤν πως ἀνακρούσηται πρύμναν πληγεὶς ταῖς εἰρε-
σιώναις.

ΦΙΛΟΚΛΕΩΝ

400 οὐ ξυλλήψεσθ᾽, ὁπόσοισι δίκαι τῆτες μέλλουσιν
ἔσεσθαι,
ὦ Σμικυθίων καὶ Τεισιάδη καὶ Χρήμων καὶ Φερέ-
δειπνε;
πότε δ᾽, εἰ μὴ νῦν, ἐπαρήξετέ μοι, πρίν μ᾽ εἴσω
μᾶλλον ἄγεσθαι;

ΧΟΡΟΣ

(στρ) εἰπέ μοι, τί μέλλομεν κινεῖν ἐκείνην τὴν χολήν,
ἥνπερ ἡνίκ᾽ ἄν τις ἡμῶν ὀργίσῃ τὴν σφηκιάν;
405 νῦν ἐκεῖνο νῦν ἐκεῖνο
τοὐξύθυμον, ᾧ κολαζόμεσθα, κέντρον
ἐντατέον ὀξέως.
ἀλλὰ θαἰμάτια λαβόντες ὡς τάχιστα, παιδία,
θεῖτε καὶ βοᾶτε, καὶ Κλέωνι ταῦτ᾽ ἀγγέλλετε,

---

407 ἐντατέον ὀξέως Jones: ἐντέτατ᾽ ὀξύ a

XANTHIAS

(*looking upward*) No indeed, but he's letting himself down on a rope!

LOATHECLEON

What are you doing, you scum of the earth? Don't you come down here! (*to Xanthias*) Go up the other way, quick, and hit him with those branches. Maybe he'll back water if he's swatted with the harvest wreath.[30]

LOVECLEON

All you prosecutors out there with cases coming up this year, won't you lend me a hand? Smicythion! Teisiades! Chremon! Pheredeipnus![31] Help me now or never, before I'm dragged inside!

CHORUS

Tell me, why are we waiting to launch the wrath
we feel when anyone vexes our nest?
Out now, out now
with that sharp-tempered stinger that we use to
   punish,
and brace it sharply.
Now grab your cloaks as quick as you can, lads,
and run and shout, report this to Cleon,
and tell him to come

---

[30] Hung on house doors during the autumn Pyanopsia festival for Apollo and left there during the year.

[31] The first two names are unidentifiable; the last two are comic distortions ("Needy" and "Dinner Getter").

410 καὶ κελεύετ' αὐτὸν ἥκειν
　　ὡς ἐπ' ἄνδρα μισόπολιν
　　ὄντα κἀπολούμενον, ὅτι
　　τόνδε λόγον εἰσφέρει,
　　μὴ δικάζειν δίκας.

ΒΔΕΛΤΚΛΕΩΝ

415 ὦγαθοί, τὸ πρᾶγμ' ἀκούσατ', ἀλλὰ μὴ κεκράγατε.

ΚΟΡΥΦΑΙΟΣ

νὴ Δί', εἰς τὸν οὐρανόν γ'.

ΒΔΕΛΤΚΛΕΩΝ

　　　　　　　ὡς τόνδ' ἐγὼ οὐ μεθήσομαι.

ΧΟΡΟΣ

ταῦτα δῆτ' οὐ δεινὰ καὶ τυραννίς ἐστιν ἐμφανής;
ὦ πόλις καὶ Θεώρου θεοισεχθρία,
κεἴ τις ἄλλος προέστηκεν ἡμῶν κόλαξ.

ΞΑΝΘΙΑΣ

420 Ἡράκλεις, καὶ κέντρ' ἔχουσιν. οὐχ ὁρᾷς, ὦ δέσποτα;

ΒΔΕΛΤΚΛΕΩΝ

οἷς γ' ἀπώλεσαν Φίλιππον ἐν δίκῃ τὸν Γοργίου.

ΚΟΡΥΦΑΙΟΣ

καὶ σέ γ' αὐτοῖς ἐξολοῦμεν. ἀλλ' ἅπας ἐπίστρεφε
δεῦρο κἀξείρας τὸ κέντρον εἶτ' ἐπ' αὐτὸν ἵεσο,
ξυσταλείς, εὔτακτος, ὀργῆς καὶ μένους ἐμπλήμενος,
425 ὡς ἂν εὖ εἰδῇ τὸ λοιπὸν σμῆνος οἷον ὤργισεν.

and confront a man who hates his country
and who'll be destroyed
for proposing the idea
that lawsuits be abolished!

LOATHECLEON
Gentlemen, consider the facts, but without screaming!

CHORUS LEADER
I'll scream, by god, and to high heaven!

LOATHECLEON
I assure you I won't release him.

CHORUS
Isn't this terrible? Isn't this bare-faced tyranny?
Oh my country, oh my god-forsaken Theorus,
oh any other bootlicker who stands up for us!

XANTHIAS
Holy Heracles, they've really got stingers! Look, master!

LOATHECLEON
The very ones they used to destroy Gorgias' son Philip-
pus,[32] and rightly.

CHORUS LEADER
And we'll destroy you as well with them! Now every man
wheel this way, draw stingers and charge him, with ranks
closed, in good order, full of rage and spirit, so he'll never
forget what a swarm he's angered.

[32] Philippus may be not literally the son but a disciple of Gor-
gias, the Sicilian rhetorician who visited Athens in 427; see *Birds*
1694-1705, fr. 118.

ΞΑΝΘΙΑΣ

τοῦτο μέντοι δεινὸν ἤδη, νὴ Δί', εἰ μαχούμεθα.
ὡς ἔγωγ' αὐτῶν ὁρῶν δέδοικα τὰς ἐγκεντρίδας.

ΧΟΡΟΣ

ἀλλ' ἀφίει τὸν ἄνδρ'· εἰ δὲ μή, φήμ' ἐγὼ
τὰς χελώνας μακαριεῖν σε τοῦ δέρματος.

ΦΙΛΟΚΛΕΩΝ

430 εἶά νυν, ὦ ξυνδικασταί, σφῆκες ὀξυκάρδιοι,
οἱ μὲν εἰς τὸν πρωκτὸν αὐτῶν εἰσπέτεσθ' ὠργισ-
μένοι,
οἱ δὲ τὠφθαλμὼ κύκλῳ κεντεῖτε καὶ τοὺς δακτύλους.

ΒΔΕΛΤΚΛΕΩΝ

ὦ Μίδα καὶ Φρύξ, βοήθει δεῦρο, καὶ Μασυντία,
καὶ λάβεσθε τουτουὶ καὶ μὴ μεθῆσθε μηδενί·
435 εἰ δὲ μή, 'ν πέδαις παχείαις οὐδὲν ἀριστήσετε,
ὡς ἐγὼ πολλῶν ἀκούσας οἶδα θρίων τὸν ψόφον.

ΚΟΡΥΦΑΙΟΣ

εἰ δὲ μὴ τοῦτον μεθήσεις, ἔν τί σοι παγήσεται.

ΦΙΛΟΚΛΕΩΝ

ὦ Κέκροψ ἥρως ἄναξ, τὰ πρὸς ποδῶν Δρακοντίδη,
περιορᾷς οὕτω μ' ὑπ' ἀνδρῶν βαρβάρων χειρού-
μενον,
440 οὓς ἐγὼ 'δίδαξα κλάειν τέτταρ' εἰ τὴν χοίνικα;

WASPS

XANTHIAS
My god, this is really terrible, if we're in for a fight. I'm scared just looking at their stingers.

CHORUS LEADER
Now let the man go. If you don't, I do declare you'll envy turtles their shells!

LOVECLEON
At 'em then, fellow jurors, sharp-hearted wasps! Division One get riled up and dive-bomb his arse! Division Two stab all around his eyes, and his fingers too!

LOATHECLEON
(*calling into the house*) Midas! Phrygian! Help me here! You too, Jaws!

Enter Slaves.

Hold on to him and don't turn him over to anybody. Otherwise, it's thick leg irons for you and no lunch. I recognize the rustle of fig leaves[33] when I hear it.

LOATHECLEON and XANTHIAS enter the house.

CHORUS LEADER
Let him go, or you'll get something stuck into you!

LOVECLEON
Lord Hero Cecrops, Dracontides below the waist, will you simply look on when I'm being manhandled this way by barbarians, the very ones I myself taught how to cry at four tears to the quart?

[33] I.e. empty bluster.

ΚΟΡΥΦΑΙΟΣ

εἶτα δῆτ᾽ οὐ πόλλ᾽ ἔνεστι δεινὰ τῷ γήρᾳ κακά;
δηλαδή· καὶ νῦν γε τούτω τὸν παλαιὸν δεσπότην
πρὸς βίαν χειροῦσιν, οὐδὲν τῶν πάλαι μεμνημένοι
διφθερῶν κἀξωμίδων, ἃς οὗτος αὐτοῖς ἠμπόλα,
445 καὶ κυνᾶς· καὶ τοὺς πόδας χειμῶνος ὄντος ὠφέλει,
ὥστε μὴ ῥιγῶν γ᾽ ἑκάστοτ᾽· ἀλλὰ τούτοις γ᾽ οὐκ ἔνι
οὐδὲν ὀφθαλμοῖσιν αἰδὼς τῶν παλαιῶν ἐμβάδων.

ΦΙΛΟΚΛΕΩΝ

οὐκ ἀφήσεις οὐδὲ νυνί μ᾽, ὦ κάκιστον θηρίον,
οὐδ᾽ ἀναμνησθεὶς ὅθ᾽ εὑρὼν τοὺς βότρυς κλέπτοντά σε
450 προσαγαγὼν πρὸς τὴν ἐλάαν ἐξέδειρ᾽ εὖ κἀνδρικῶς,
ὥστε σε ζηλωτὸν εἶναι; σὺ δ᾽ ἀχάριστος ἦσθ᾽ ἄρα.
ἀλλ᾽ ἄνες με καὶ σὺ καὶ σύ, πρὶν τὸν υἱὸν ἐκδραμεῖν.

ΚΟΡΥΦΑΙΟΣ

ἀλλὰ τούτων μὲν τάχ᾽ ἡμῖν δώσετον καλὴν δίκην,
οὐκέτ᾽ ἐς μακράν, ἵν᾽ εἰδῆθ᾽ οἷός ἐστ᾽ ἀνδρῶν τρόπος
455 ὀξυθύμων καὶ δικαίων καὶ βλεπόντων κάρδαμα.

ΒΔΕΛΥΚΛΕΩΝ

παῖε, παῖ᾽, ὦ Ξανθία, τοὺς σφῆκας ἀπὸ τῆς οἰκίας.

ΞΑΝΘΙΑΣ

ἀλλὰ δρῶ τοῦτ᾽. ἀλλὰ καὶ σὺ τῦφε πολλῷ τῷ καπνῷ.

ΒΔΕΛΥΚΛΕΩΝ

οὐχὶ σοῦσθ᾽; οὐκ ἐς κόρακας; οὐκ ἄπιτε; παῖε τῷ
ξύλῳ.

CHORUS LEADER

So doesn't old age truly hold evils in abundance? Obviously
it does: these two forcibly manhandle their former master,
completely forgetting all the jackets and tunics he used to
buy them, and the caps, and how in wintertime he saw to
their feet so they wouldn't always be frozen. But in their
eyes there's no respect at all for their former footwear.

LOVECLEON

You still won't let me go, you vile animal? Even when you
recall the time I caught you stealing grapes, marched you
to the olive tree, and did a right manly job flaying you raw,
so that everyone envied you? But you were apparently
ungrateful. Come on you two, let me go, before my son
darts out.

CHORUS LEADER

Ah, but this will soon cost you both dearly. It won't be long
now before you know the character of men who are sharp-
spirited and righteous, and look mustard at you.

The Chorus attacks. Enter LOATHECLEON *with a smoke-
pot and* XANTHIAS *with a stick.*

LOATHECLEON

Xanthias, beat the wasps, beat them away from the house!

XANTHIAS

That's what I'm doing! But you help too: blow lots of smoke
on them!

LOATHECLEON

Shoo! Get the hell away! Go! Lay on with your stick!

ΞΑΝΘΙΑΣ

καὶ σὺ προσθεὶς Αἰσχίνην ἔντυφε τὸν Σελλαρτίου.

ΒΔΕΛΥΚΛΕΩΝ

460 ἆρ᾽ ἐμέλλομέν ποθ᾽ ὑμᾶς ἀποσοβήσειν τῷ χρόνῳ.

ΦΙΛΟΚΛΕΩΝ

(ἀντ) ἀλλὰ μὰ Δί᾽ οὐ ῥᾳδίως οὕτως ἂν αὐτοὺς διέφυγες,
εἴπερ ἔτυχον τῶν μελῶν τῶν Φιλοκλέους βεβρωκότες.

ΧΟΡΟΣ

ἆρα δῆτ᾽ οὐκ αὐτὰ δῆλα
τοῖς πένησιν, ἡ τυραννὶς ὡς λάθρᾳ γ᾽ ἐ-
465 λάμβαν᾽ ὑπιοῦσά με,
εἰ σύ γ᾽, ὦ πόνῳ πόνηρε καὶ Κομηταμυνία,
τῶν νόμων ἡμᾶς ἀπείργεις ὧν ἔθηκεν ἡ πόλις,
οὔτε τιν᾽ ἔχων πρόφασιν
οὔτε λόγον εὐτράπελον,
470 αὐτὸς ἄρχων μόνος;

ΒΔΕΛΥΚΛΕΩΝ

ἔσθ᾽ ὅπως ἄνευ μάχης καὶ τῆς κατοξείας βοῆς
ἐς λόγους ἔλθοιμεν ἀλλήλοισι καὶ διαλλαγάς;

ΧΟΡΟΣ

σοὶ λόγους, ὦ μισόδημε καὶ μοναρχίας ἐραστὰ
475 καὶ ξυνὼν Βρασίδᾳ καὶ φορῶν κράσπεδα

---

34 Nephew of Aeschylus and a tragic poet (victorious over
Sophocles' *Oedipus the King*), nicknamed "son of Briny" for his
harsh and bitter style.

XANTHIAS

And you, suffocate them with a billow of Aeschines, son of
Hotair!

The Chorus retreats.

LOATHECLEON

I knew we'd eventually shoo you away.

LOVECLEON

But you wouldn't have escaped them so easily if they'd
been munching on Philocles' songs.[34]

CHORUS

Don't the poor folk see it plainly,
how tyranny has sneaked up on me
from behind and tried to jump me,
now that you, you troublesome troublemaker, you
    long-haired Amynias,
debar us from our country's established legal rights,
without making any excuse
or dextrous argument,
but autocratically?

LOATHECLEON

Might we enter into discussion and compromise without
this fighting and shrill screaming?

CHORUS

Discussion with you, you enemy of the people, you
    lover of monarchy,
you buddy of Brasidas,[35] with the woollen fringes on

---

[35] The leading Spartan general of this period, currently active
on the Thracian front (cf. 288).

281

ARISTOPHANES

στεμμάτων τήν θ᾽ ὑπήνην ἄκουρον τρέφων;

νὴ Δί᾽ ἢ μοι κρεῖττον ἐκστῆναι τὸ παράπαν τοῦ πα-
τρὸς
μᾶλλον ἢ κακοῖς τοσούτοις ναυμαχεῖν ὁσημέραι.

ΚΟΡΥΦΑΙΟΣ
480   οὐδὲ μὴν οὐδ᾽ ἐν σελίνῳ σοὐστὶν οὐδ᾽ ἐν πηγάνῳ·
τοῦτο γὰρ παρεμβαλοῦμεν τῶν τριχοινίκων ἐπῶν.
ἀλλὰ νῦν μὲν οὐδὲν ἀλγεῖς, ἀλλ᾽ ὅταν ξυνήγορος
ταὐτὰ ταῦτά σου καταντλῇ καὶ ξυνωμότην καλῇ.

ΒΔΕΛΤΚΛΕΩΝ
ἆρ᾽ ἄν, ὦ πρὸς τῶν θεῶν, ὑμεῖς ἀπαλλαχθεῖτέ μου;
485   ἢ δέδοκται καὶ δέρεσθαι καὶ δέρειν δι᾽ ἡμέρας;

ΧΟΡΟΣ
οὐδέποτέ γ᾽, οὔχ, ἕως ἄν τί μου λοιπὸν ᾖ—
ὅστις ἡμῶν ἐπὶ τυραννίδ᾽ ἐξεστάλης.

ΒΔΕΛΤΚΛΕΩΝ
ὡς ἅπανθ᾽ ὑμῖν τυραννίς ἐστι καὶ ξυνωμόται,
ἤν τε μεῖζον ἤν τ᾽ ἔλαττον πρᾶγμά τις κατηγορῇ.
490   ἧς ἐγὼ οὐκ ἤκουσα τοὔνομ᾽ οὐδὲ πεντήκοντ᾽ ἐτῶν·
νῦν δὲ πολλῷ τοῦ ταρίχους ἐστὶν ἀξιωτέρα,
ὥστε καὶ δὴ τοὔνομ᾽ αὐτῆς ἐν ἀγορᾷ κυλίνδεται.
ἢν μὲν ὠνῆταί τις ὀρφῶς, μεμβράδας δὲ μὴ ᾽θέλῃ,
εὐθέως εἴρηχ᾽ ὁ πωλῶν πλησίον τὰς μεμβράδας·

483 -την Cobet et Hirschig: -τας fere codd.
488 ὑμῖν] ἡμῖν R Vp3

282

your clothes and the untrimmed beard on your
face?

LOATHECLEON

I swear I'd do better to write my father off altogether,
instead of battling day after day in such a sea of troubles.

CHORUS LEADER

Hah! You haven't even got past the soup course yet, or the
salad either—we'll toss that in from our stock of ten gallon
metaphors. No, your present pain is nothing. Just wait till
a prosecutor dumps these very charges over your head and
calls you a conspirator!

LOATHECLEON

Heavens above, I do wish you'd get off my back! Or is it
now decreed that we're to spend the whole day skinning
each other alive?

CHORUS

No, never, not while there's any breath left in my
body,
with a man who plans to be our tyrant!

LOATHECLEON

How you see tyranny and conspirators everywhere, as soon
as anyone voices a criticism large or small! I hadn't even
heard of the word being used for at least fifty years,[36] but
nowadays it's cheaper than sardines. Look how it's bandied
about in the marketplace. If someone buys perch but
doesn't want sprats, the sprat seller next door pipes right

[36] Fifty-seven, to be exact, since Xerxes' attempt to install the
Pisistratids (Herodotus 7.6, 8.52). The last Athenian tyrant was
Hippas, exiled in 510.

495 "οὗτος ὀψωνεῖν ἔοιχ᾽ ἄνθρωπος ἐπὶ τυραννίδι."
ἦν δὲ γήτειον προσαιτῇ ταῖς ἀφύαις ἥδυσμά τι,
ἡ λαχανόπωλις παραβλέψασά φησι θάτέρῳ·
"εἰπέ μοι· γήτειον αἰτεῖς· πότερον ἐπὶ τυραννίδι;
ἢ νομίζεις τὰς Ἀθήνας σοὶ φέρειν ἡδύσματα;"

ΞΑΝΘΙΑΣ

500 κἀμέ γ᾽ ἡ πόρνη χθὲς εἰσελθόντα τῆς μεσημβρίας,
ὅτι κελητίσαι 'κέλευον, ὀξυθυμηθεῖσά μοι
ἤρετ᾽ εἰ τὴν Ἱππίου καθίσταμαι τυραννίδα.

ΒΔΕΛΥΚΛΕΩΝ

ταῦτα γὰρ τούτοις ἀκούειν ἡδέ᾽, εἰ καὶ νῦν ἐγώ,
τὸν πατέρ᾽ ὅτι βούλομαι τούτων ἀπαλλαχθέντα τῶν
505 ὀρθροφοιτοσυκοφαντοδικοταλαιπώρων τρόπων
ζῆν βίον γενναῖον ὥσπερ Μόρυχος, αἰτίαν ἔχω
ταῦτα δρᾶν ξυνωμότης ὢν καὶ φρονῶν τυραννικά.

ΦΙΛΟΚΛΕΩΝ

νὴ Δί᾽, ἐν δίκῃ γ᾽· ἐγὼ γὰρ οὐδ᾽ ἂν ὀρνίθων γάλα
ἀντὶ τοῦ βίου λάβοιμ᾽ ἂν οὗ με νῦν ἀποστερεῖς.
510 οὐδὲ χαίρω βατίσιν οὐδ᾽ ἐγχέλεσιν, ἀλλ᾽ ἥδιον ἂν
δικίδιον σμικρὸν φάγοιμ᾽ ἂν ἐν λοπάδι πεπνιγμένον.

ΒΔΕΛΥΚΛΕΩΝ

νὴ Δί᾽, εἰθίσθης γὰρ ἥδεσθαι τοιούτοις πράγμασιν.
ἀλλ᾽ ἐὰν σιγῶν ἀνάσχῃ καὶ μάθῃς ἁγὼ λέγω,
ἀναδιδάξειν οἴομαί σ᾽ ὡς πάντα ταῦθ᾽ ἁμαρτάνεις.

ΦΙΛΟΚΛΕΩΝ

ἐξαμαρτάνω δικάζων;

up and says, "This guy buys fish like a would-be tyrant."
And if he asks for a free onion to spice his sardines a bit,
the vegetable lady gives him the fish eye and says, "Say, are
you asking for an onion because you want to be tyrant? Or
maybe you think Athens grows spices as her tribute to
you?"

XANTHIAS

My slut got sharp-tempered with me too, when I went to
her place yesterday noon. I told her to ride me, and she
asked if I was jockeying for a tyranny à la Hippias!

LOATHECLEON

Yes, these people enjoy hearing talk like that, if my present
case is any indication. Just because I want my father to
quit his dawn-wandering, nuisance-suing, jury-serving,
trouble-seeking habits and live a genteel life like Mory-
chus, for my efforts I get called a conspirator with tyranny
in mind.

LOVECLEON

Yes, and rightly so! For pigeons' milk I wouldn't trade the
living you'd take away from me now. Skate and eels don't
tempt me either. I'd much rather sit down to a nice little
lawsuit baked *en casserole*.

LOATHECLEON

Sure, because you're addicted to that kind of fun. But if
you'll hold your tongue and open your mind to what I have
to say, I think I'll enlighten you about the total error of your
ways.

LOVECLEON

Jurying is an error?

ΒΔΕΛΤΚΛΕΩΝ

515   καταγελώμενος μὲν οὖν
οὐκ ἐπαΐεις ὑπ' ἀνδρῶν, οὓς σὺ μόνον οὐ
 προσκυνεῖς.
ἀλλὰ δουλεύων λέληθας.

ΦΙΛΟΚΛΕΩΝ

      παῦε δουλείαν λέγων—
ὅστις ἄρχω τῶν ἀπάντων.

ΒΔΕΛΤΚΛΕΩΝ

      οὐ σύ γ', ἀλλ' ὑπηρετεῖς
οἰόμενος ἄρχειν· ἐπεὶ δίδαξον ἡμᾶς, ὦ πάτερ,
520 ἥτις ἡ τιμή 'στί σοι καρπουμένῳ τὴν Ἑλλάδα.

ΦΙΛΟΚΛΕΩΝ

πάνυ γε· καὶ τούτοισί γ' ἐπιτρέψαι 'θέλω.

ΒΔΕΛΤΚΛΕΩΝ

         καὶ μὴν ἐγώ.
ἄφετέ νυν ἅπαντες αὐτόν.

ΦΙΛΟΚΛΕΩΝ

      καὶ ξίφος γέ μοι δότε·
ἢν γὰρ ἡττηθῶ λέγων σου, περιπεσοῦμαι τῷ ξίφει.

ΒΔΕΛΤΚΛΕΩΝ

εἰπέ μοι, τί δ', ἤν—τὸ δεῖνα—τῇ διαίτῃ μὴ 'μμένῃς;

ΦΙΛΟΚΛΕΩΝ

525 μηδέποτε πίοιμ' ἄκρατον μισθὸν ἀγαθοῦ δαίμονος.

LOATHECLEON

What's more, you don't realize that you're the laughing-stock of men you all but grovel to. You're unaware that you've been enslaved.

LOVECLEON

Stop talking about slavery. I'm master of everyone!

LOATHECLEON

Not you. You're just a slave who thinks he's a master. No? Then describe for us, father, what profit you get from reaping the fruits of Greece.

LOVECLEON

By all means, and I want these men to be our arbitrators.

LOATHECLEON

So do I. Let him go, everyone.

The Slaves go back into the house.

LOVECLEON

And give me a sword. If I lose the debate to you, I'm going to fall on it!

LOATHECLEON

Tell me, what if you fail to—what's the term?—abide by the arbitration?

LOVECLEON

Then never again will I toast the Good Spirit with unmixed jury pay!

ARISTOPHANES

(στρ) νῦν δὴ τὸν ἐκ θἠμετέρου
γυμνασίου λέγειν τι δεῖ
καινόν, ὅπως φανήσει—

ΒΔΕΛΤΚΛΕΩΝ

ἐνεγκάτω μοι δεῦρο τὴν κίστην τις ὡς τάχιστα.
530 ἀτὰρ φανεῖ ποῖός τις ὤν, εἰ ταῦτα παρακελεύει;

ΧΟΡΟΣ

—μὴ κατὰ τὸν νεανίαν
τόνδε λέγειν. ὁρᾷς γὰρ ὡς
σοι μέγας ἐστ᾽ ἀγὼν ⟨νῦν⟩
535 καὶ περὶ τῶν ἁπάντων.
εἰ γάρ, ὃ μὴ γένοιθ᾽, οὗ-
τος σε λέγων κρατήσει—

ΒΔΕΛΤΚΛΕΩΝ

καὶ μὴν ὅσ᾽ ἂν λέξῃ γ᾽ ἁπλῶς μνημόσυνα
γράψομαι ᾽γώ.

ΦΙΛΟΚΛΕΩΝ

τί γὰρ φαθ᾽ ὑμεῖς, ἢν ὁδί με τῷ λόγῳ κρατήσῃ;

ΧΟΡΟΣ

540 —οὐκέτι πρεσβυτῶν ὄχλος
χρήσιμός ἐστ᾽ οὐδ᾽ ἀκαρῆ·
σκωπτόμενοι δ᾽ ἐν ταῖς ὁδοῖς
θαλλοφόροι καλούμεθ᾽, ἀντ-

536-7 εἰ γάρ Sommerstein: εἴπερ a
σε λέγων κρατήσει Blaydes: ἐθέλει κρατῆσαι a

WASPS

CHORUS

Now the chap from *our* school
must argue a novel case.
See that you turn out—

LOATHECLEON

Someone bring me out my writing case right away. Now
then, what kind of man will he show himself to be, if that's
what you're telling him to do?

CHORUS

—to top this youngster in debate!
For you can see that you face a great contest now,
where everything's at stake.
Because if, god forbid,
this man does beat you in debate—

LOATHECLEON

That I shall, and I'm going to jot down every single point
he makes.

LOVECLEON

What were you saying will happen if he beats me in debate?

CHORUS

—then the elderly crowd
are no damn good anymore.
They'll mock us
all over town
and call us olive bearers,[37]

[37] A function performed by very old men in the Panathenaic
parade.

545   ωμοσιῶν κελύφη.

ΚΟΡΥΦΑΙΟΣ

ἀλλ᾽, ὦ περὶ τῆς πάσης μέλλων βασιλείας ἀντι-
    λογήσειν
τῆς ἡμετέρας, νυνὶ θαρρῶν πᾶσαν γλῶτταν βασάνιζε.

ΦΙΛΟΚΛΕΩΝ

καὶ μὴν εὐθύς γ᾽ ἀπὸ βαλβίδων περὶ τῆς ἀρχῆς
    ἀποδείξω
τῆς ἡμετέρας ὡς οὐδεμιᾶς ἥττων ἐστὶν βασιλείας.
550   τί γὰρ εὔδαιμον καὶ μακαριστὸν μᾶλλον νῦν ἐστι
    δικαστοῦ,
ἢ τρυφερώτερον ἢ δεινότερον ζῷον, καὶ ταῦτα γέρον-
    τος;
ὃν πρῶτα μὲν ἕρποντ᾽ ἐξ εὐνῆς τηροῦσ᾽ ἐπὶ τοῖσι
    δρυφάκτοις
ἄνδρες μεγάλοι καὶ τετραπήχεις· κἄπειτ᾽ εὐθὺς
    προσιόντι
ἐμβάλλει μοι τὴν χεῖρ᾽ ἁπαλὴν τῶν δημοσίων
    κεκλοφυῖαν.
555   ἱκετεύουσίν θ᾽ ὑποκύπτοντες τὴν φωνὴν οἰκτροχοοῦν-
    τες·
"οἴκτιρόν μ᾽, ὦ πάτερ, αἰτοῦμαί σ᾽, εἰ καὐτὸς
    πώποθ᾽ ὑφείλου
ἀρχὴν ἄρξας ἢ ᾽πὶ στρατιᾶς τοῖς ξυσσίτοις ἀγο-
    ράζων."
ὃς ἔμ᾽ οὐδ᾽ ἂν ζῶντ᾽ ᾔδειν, εἰ μὴ διὰ τὴν προτέραν
    ἀπόφευξιν.

mere shells of affidavits!

CHORUS LEADER

So I call on you, who are to make the case for our whole
dominion, to take courage now and throw your whole
tongue into the task!

LOVECLEON

I will indeed, and right out of the gate I'll demonstrate that
our sovereignty is as strong as any king's. What living thing
is there today more fortunate and felicitated than a juror,
more coddled or commanding, oldster though he is? To
begin with, I crawl out of bed to find big men, six-footers,
watching for me at the court railings. As soon as I ap-
proach, one of them gives me his soft hand, fresh from
stealing public money. They beg and grovel, pitifully pour-
ing out their pleas: "Pity me, father, I beg you! Maybe one
time you too pocketed something when holding office or
procuring field rations for your messmates." He wouldn't
even have known I exist if I hadn't gone easy on him last
time.

ΒΔΕΛΥΚΛΕΩΝ

τουτὶ περὶ τῶν ἀντιβολούντων ἔστω τὸ μνημόσυνόν
μοι.

ΦΙΛΟΚΛΕΩΝ

560 εἶτ᾽ εἰσελθὼν ἀντιβοληθεὶς καὶ τὴν ὀργὴν ἀπομορ-
χθεὶς
ἔνδον τούτων ὧν ἂν φάσκω πάντων οὐδὲν πεποίηκα,
ἀλλ᾽ ἀκροῶμαι πάσας φωνὰς ἱέντων εἰς ἀπόφευξιν.
φέρ᾽ ἴδω, τί γὰρ οὐκ ἔστιν ἀκοῦσαι θώπευμ᾽ ἐν-
ταῦθα δικαστῇ;
οἱ μέν γ᾽ ἀποκλάονται πενίαν αὑτῶν, καὶ προστιθέα-
σιν
565 κακὰ πρὸς τοῖς οὖσιν, ἕως ἄν πως ἀνισώσῃ τοῖσιν
ἐμοῖσιν·
οἱ δὲ λέγουσιν μύθους ἡμῖν, οἱ δ᾽ Αἰσώπου τι γέλοιον·
οἱ δὲ σκώπτουσ᾽, ἵν᾽ ἐγὼ γελάσω καὶ τὸν θυμὸν
καταθῶμαι.
κἂν μὴ τούτοις ἀναπειθώμεσθα, τὰ παιδάρι᾽ εὐθὺς
ἀνέλκει
τὰς θηλείας καὶ τοὺς υἱεῖς τῆς χειρός, ἐγὼ δ᾽
ἀκροῶμαι,
570 τὰ δὲ συγκύψανθ᾽ ἅμα βληχᾶται, κᾆπειθ᾽ ὁ πατὴρ
ὑπὲρ αὐτῶν
ὥσπερ θεὸν ἀντιβολεῖ με τρέμων τῆς εὐθύνης ἀπο-
λῦσαι·
"εἰ μὲν χαίρεις ἀρνὸς φωνῇ, παιδὸς φωνὴν
ἐλεήσαις·"

LOATHECLEON

Let me make a note of that: *suppliants.*

LOVECLEON

Then after I've been supplicated and had my anger wiped away, I go inside and act on none of those promises I made. I just listen to them spouting every sort of alibi. Tell me, is there any brand of wheedling I don't hear in court? Some of them bewail their poverty and go on exaggerating their troubles until they somehow seem as bad as my own. Others tell us stories, others something funny from Aesop.[38] Others crack jokes to make me laugh and put away my anger. And if none of this persuades us, he starts dragging his kids up there by the hand, daughters and sons, and I listen while they cringe and bleat in chorus, and then their father implores me for their sake, trembling as if I were a god, to let him off in his audit: "If you enjoy the bleat of the lamb, please pity the cry of the kid!" And if I enjoy a

[38] The foremost author of animal fables, who lived in the early sixth century.

565 ἄν πως Platnauer: ἀνιὼν V: ἂν cett.
ἀνισώσῃ V: ἰσώσῃ cett.

293

εἰ δ' αὖ τοῖς χοιριδίοις χαίρω, θυγατρὸς φωνῇ με
πιθέσθαι.

χἠμεῖς αὐτῷ τότε τῆς ὀργῆς ὀλίγον τὸν κόλλοπ'
ἀνεῖμεν.

575 ἆρ' οὐ μεγάλη τοῦτ' ἔστ' ἀρχὴ καὶ τοῦ πλούτου
καταχήνη;

ΒΔΕΛΤΚΛΕΩΝ

δεύτερον αὖ σου τουτὶ γράφομαι, τὴν τοῦ πλούτου
καταχήνην.

καὶ τἀγαθά μοι μέμνησ' ἄχεις φάσκων τῆς Ἑλλά-
δος ἄρχειν.

ΦΙΛΟΚΛΕΩΝ

παίδων τοίνυν δοκιμαζομένων αἰδοῖα πάρεστι
θεᾶσθαι.

κἂν Οἴαγρος εἰσέλθῃ φεύγων, οὐκ ἀποφεύγει πρὶν
ἂν ἡμῖν

580 ἐκ τῆς Νιόβης εἴπῃ ῥῆσιν τὴν καλλίστην ἀπολέξας.
κἂν αὐλητής γε δίκην νικᾷ, ταύτης ἡμῖν ἐπίχειρα
ἐν φορβειᾷ τοῖσι δικασταῖς ἔξοδον ηὔλησ' ἀπιοῦσιν.
κἂν ἀποθνῄσκων ὁ πατήρ τῳ δῷ καταλείπων παῖδ'
ἐπίκληρον,

κλάειν ἡμεῖς μακρὰ τὴν κεφαλὴν εἰπόντες τῇ διαθήκῃ

585 καὶ τῇ κόγχῃ τῇ πάνυ σεμνῶς τοῖς σημείοισιν
ἐπούσῃ,

ἔδομεν ταύτην ὅστις ἂν ἡμᾶς ἀντιβολήσας ἀναπείσῃ.

καὶ ταῦτ' ἀνυπεύθυνοι δρῶμεν· τῶν δ' ἄλλων
οὐδεμί' ἀρχή.

bit of pork, I'm supposed to heed the cry of his daughter. And then we wind down the pitch of our anger a little. Isn't this high authority, and derision of wealth?

LOATHECLEON

I'll make a note of that too: *derision of wealth*. Now please mention the benefits you get from your alleged rule over Greece.

LOVECLEON

Well, when boys are being examined for deme registration, we get to look at their privates. And if Oeagrus[39] comes to court as a defendant, he won't get off till he chooses the best speech from *Niobe*[40] and recites it for us. And if a piper wins his case, the price he pays the jurors is to put on his harness and pipe us an exit tune as we leave. And if a dying father bequeaths his heiress daughter to someone, we tell that last will and testament to go soak its head, and the same to the clasp sitting so pretty over its seals, and we award that girl to whoever talks us into it. And for doing all this we can't be called to account, something no other office holders can claim.

---

[39] Evidently a tragic actor, unattested elsewhere.
[40] Both Aeschylus and Sophocles wrote plays with this title.

ΒΔΕΛΥΚΛΕΩΝ

τουτὶ γάρ τοί σε μόνον τούτων ὧν εἴρηκας μακαρίζω.
τῆς δ' ἐπικλήρου τὴν διαθήκην ἀδικεῖς ἀνακογχυ-
λιάζων.

ΦΙΛΟΚΛΕΩΝ

590 ἔτι δ' ἡ βουλὴ χὠ δῆμος, ὅταν κρῖναι μέγα πρᾶγμ'
     ἀπορήσῃ,
     ἐψήφισται τοὺς ἀδικοῦντας τοῖσι δικασταῖς παρα-
     δοῦναι·
     εἶτ' Εὔαθλος χὠ μέγας οὗτος Κολακώνυμος, ἀσπι-
     δαποβλής,
     οὐχὶ προδώσειν ἡμᾶς φασιν, περὶ τοῦ πλήθους δὲ
     μαχεῖσθαι.
     κἂν τῷ δήμῳ γνώμην οὐδεὶς πώποτ' ἐνίκησεν, ἐὰν μὴ
595 εἴπῃ τὰ δικαστήρι' ἀφεῖναι πρώτιστα μίαν δικάσαν-
     τας.
     αὐτὸς δὲ Κλέων ὁ κεκραξιδάμας μόνον ἡμᾶς οὐ
     περιτρώγει,
     ἀλλὰ φυλάττει διὰ χειρὸς ἔχων καὶ τὰς μυίας
     ἀπαμύνει·
     σὺ δὲ τὸν πατέρ' οὐδ' ὁτιοῦν τούτων τὸν σαυτοῦ
     πώποτ' ἔδρασας.
     ἀλλὰ Θέωρος—καίτοὐστὶν ἀνὴρ Εὐφημίου οὐδὲν
     ἐλάττων—
600 τὸν σπόγγον ἔχων ἐκ τῆς λεκάνης τἀμβάδι' ἡμῶν
     περικωνεῖ.

LOATHECLEON

Yes, that's the only thing you've said that I congratulate you on. But it's wrong of you to unclasp the heiress' endowments.

LOVECLEON

Furthermore, when the Council and People are stumped about how to decide an important case, they vote to hand over the wrongdoers to the jurors. Then Euathlus and Toadyonymus here, the weighty shield-shedder,[41] swear that they'll never betray us, that they'll fight for the masses. And no one ever carries a motion before the People unless he's proposed to adjourn the courts after the very first case tried. And even Cleon, the scream champion, takes no bites out of us! No, he puts his arm around us and swats away the flies. You've never done anything of the kind for your own father! But Theorus—and he's every bit the bigshot Euphemius is[42]—takes the sponge right from his pail

---

[41] I.e. Cleonymus. Euathlus, son of Cephisodemus, was a zealous prosecutor (see *Acharnians* 703ff.).

[42] Unknown.

---

588 σε μόνον Reiske: σεμνόν· a

σκέψαι μ' ἀπὸ τῶν ἀγαθῶν οἵων ἀποκλήεις καὶ
   κατερύκεις,
ἣν δουλείαν οὖσαν ἔφασκες καὶ ὑπηρεσίαν
   ἀποδείξειν.

ΒΔΕΛΤΚΛΕΩΝ

ἔμπλησο λέγων· πάντως γάρ τοι παύσει ποτέ, κἀνα-
   φανήσει
πρωκτὸς λουτροῦ περιγιγνόμενος, τῆς ἀρχῆς τῆς
   περισέμνου.

ΦΙΛΟΚΛΕΩΝ

605   ὃ δέ γ' ἥδιστον τούτων ἐστὶν πάντων, οὗ 'γὼ 'πελε-
   λήσμην,
ὅταν οἴκαδ' ἴω τὸν μισθὸν ἔχων, κἄπειθ' ἥκονθ'
   ἅμα πάντες
ἀσπάζωνται διὰ τἀργύριον, καὶ πρῶτα μὲν ἡ
   θυγάτηρ με
ἀπονίζῃ καὶ τὼ πόδ' ἀλείφῃ καὶ προσκύψασα φιλήσῃ
καὶ παππίζουσ' ἅμα τῇ γλώττῃ τὸ τριώβολον ἐκ-
   καλαμᾶται,
610   καὶ τὸ γύναιόν μ' ὑποθωπεῦσαν φυστὴν μᾶζαν
   προσενέγκῃ,
κἄπειτα καθεζομένη παρ' ἐμοὶ προσαναγκάζῃ·
   "φάγε τουτί,
ἔντραγε τουτί." τούτοισιν ἐγὼ γάνυμαι· κοὐ μή με
   δεήσῃ
εἰς σὲ βλέψαι καὶ τὸν ταμίαν, ὁπότ' ἄριστον παρα-
   θήσει

and starts shining my shoes. Look what kind of advantages you're locking me out of and holding me back from, the ones you said you'd demonstrate were really slavery and drudgery!

LOATHECLEON

Have your fill of talking; you're bound to stop eventually, and when you do you'll stand revealed as an arsehole that can't be washed clean with that grand authority of yours.

LOVECLEON

But the nicest part of all, which slipped my mind, is when I come home with my pay. That's when everyone gives me a warm welcome at the door because of the money. First my daughter washes me and oils my feet and bends down to kiss me, calling me "daddy" while she tries to fish out the three obol piece with her tongue. And the little woman fusses over me and brings me a puff pastry, and then sits by and coaxes me, "Eat this, eat this up!" I love all that, and I don't have to look to you and your steward to see when he'll get around to serving my lunch with his usual curses

ARISTOPHANES

κατarasάμενος καὶ τονθορύσας· ἀλλ᾽ ἢν μή μοι
ταχὺ μάξῃ,
615 τάδε κέκτημαι πρόβλημα κακῶν, "σκευὴν βελέων
ἀλεωρήν".
κἂν οἶνόν μοι μὴ ᾽γχῇς σὺ πιεῖν, τὸν ὄνον τόνδ᾽
ἐσκεκόμισμαι
οἴνου μεστόν, κᾆτ᾽ ἐγχέομαι κλίνας· οὗτος δὲ κεχηνὼς
βρωμησάμενος τοῦ σοῦ δίνου μέγα καὶ στράτιον
κατέπαρδεν.
ἆρ᾽ οὐ μεγάλην ἀρχὴν ἄρχω καὶ τοῦ Διὸς οὐδὲν
ἐλάττω,
620 ὅστις ἀκούω ταῦθ᾽ ἅπερ ὁ Ζεύς;
ἢν γοῦν ἡμεῖς θορυβήσωμεν,
πᾶς τίς φησιν τῶν παριόντων·
"οἷον βροντᾷ τὸ δικαστήριον,
ὦ Ζεῦ βασιλεῦ."
625 κἂν ἀστράψω, ποππύζουσιν
κἀγκεχόδασίν μ᾽ οἱ πλουτοῦντες
καὶ πάνυ σεμνοί.
καὶ σὺ δέδοικάς με μάλιστ᾽ αὐτός·
νὴ τὴν Δήμητρα, δέδοικας. ἐγὼ δ᾽
630 ἀπολοίμην εἰ σὲ δέδοικα.

ΧΟΡΟΣ
(ἀντ) οὐπώποθ᾽ οὕτω καθαρῶς
οὐδενὸς ἠκούσαμεν οὐ-
δὲ ξυνετῶς λέγοντος.

and grumbles. And if he isn't quick about kneading my pastry, I've got this pay to shield me from troubles, a "bulwark against missiles." And if you won't pour me a drink of wine, I fill this donkey-eared flask with wine on my way home, tip it up, and pour myself a drink. It opens wide and brays a great big soldierly fart at that goblet of yours. So don't I wield great authority, as great as Zeus'? I'm even spoken of in the same way as Zeus. For instance, if we're in an uproar, every passerby says, "Zeus Almighty, the jury's really thundering!" And if I look lightning, the fat cats and the VIPs say a prayer and shit in their pants. And you're very much afraid of me yourself. Oh yes, by Demeter, you're afraid. But I'll be damned if I'm afraid of you!

CHORUS
Never have we heard anyone
speak with such clarity
and intelligence!

ΦΙΛΟΚΛΕΩΝ

οὔκ, ἀλλ᾽ ἐρήμας ᾤεθ᾽ οὕτω ῥᾳδίως τρυγήσειν·
635 καλῶς γὰρ ᾔδειν ὡς ἐγὼ ταύτῃ κράτιστός εἰμι.

ΧΟΡΟΣ

ὡς δ᾽ ἐπὶ πάντ᾽ ἐλήλυθεν
κοὐδὲν παρῆλθεν, ὥστ᾽ ἔγωγ᾽
  ηὐξανόμην ἀκούων,
κἀν μακάρων δικάζειν
640 αὐτὸς ἔδοξα νήσοις,
ἡδόμενος λέγοντι.

ΦΙΛΟΚΛΕΩΝ

ὥσθ᾽ οὗτος ἤδη σκορδινᾶται κἄστιν οὐκ ἐν αὑτοῦ.
ἦ μὴν ἐγώ σε τήμερον σκύτη βλέπειν ποιήσω.

ΧΟΡΟΣ

δεῖ δέ σε παντοίας πλέκειν
645 εἰς ἀπόφευξιν παλάμας·
  τὴν γὰρ ἐμὴν ὀργὴν πεπᾶ-
    ναι χαλεπὸν ⟨νεανίᾳ⟩
  μὴ πρὸς ἐμοῦ λέγοντι.

ΚΟΡΥΦΑΙΟΣ

πρὸς ταῦτα μύλην ἀγαθὴν ὥρα ζητεῖν σοι καὶ νεό-
  κοπτον,
ἢν μή τι λέγῃς, ἥτις δυνατὴ τὸν ἐμὸν θυμὸν
  κατερεῖξαι.

ΒΔΕΛΥΚΛΕΩΝ

650 χαλεπὸν μὲν καὶ δεινῆς γνώμης καὶ μείζονος ἢ 'πὶ
  τρυγῳδοῖς

302

LOVECLEON

No you haven't; he just thought he'd be picking unwatched vines and getting off easy that way. He knew very well that I'm the boss in this business!

CHORUS

And how he's explored every avenue,
and left nothing out! I for one
swelled with pride as I listened,
and I saw myself judging
in the Islands of the Blessed,
basking in the sound of his voice.

LOVECLEON

Yes, he's fidgeting now! Now he's off his stride! Yes indeed, I'll have you looking whipped today!

CHORUS

You'll have to weave
every wile in the book
to win acquittal,
because it's hard ‹for a youth›
to soften my anger
if I don't like what I hear.

CHORUS LEADER

So unless you've got something sensible to say, it's time you went looking for a good millstone with new treads that's hard enough to grind down my temper.

LOATHECLEON

It's a hard task, and one requiring formidable intellect be-

---

636 δ' ἐπὶ πάντ' ἐλ- Bentley: δὲ πάντ' ἐπελ- a
646 ‹νεανίᾳ› Porson

ἰάσασθαι νόσον ἀρχαίαν ἐν τῇ πόλει ἐντετοκυῖαν.
ἀτάρ, ὦ πάτερ ἡμέτερε Κρονίδη—

ΦΙΛΟΚΛΕΩΝ

παῦσαι καὶ μὴ πατέριζε.
εἰ μὴ γάρ, ὅπως δουλεύω 'γώ, τουτὶ ταχέως με
διδάξεις,
οὐκ ἔστιν ὅπως οὐχὶ τεθνήσει, κἂν χρῇ σπλάγχνων
μ' ἀπέχεσθαι.

ΒΔΕΛΥΚΛΕΩΝ

655 ἀκρόασαί νυν, ὦ παππίδιον, χαλάσας ὀλίγον τὸ
μέτωπον.
καὶ πρῶτον μὲν λόγισαι φαύλως, μὴ ψήφοις ἀλλ'
ἀπὸ χειρός,
τὸν φόρον ἡμῖν ἀπὸ τῶν πόλεων συλλήβδην τὸν
προσιόντα,
κἄξω τούτου τὰ τέλη χωρὶς καὶ τὰς πολλὰς ἑκατοστάς,
πρυτανεῖα, μέταλλ', ἀγοράς, λιμένας, μισθώσεις,
δημιόπρατα·
660 τούτων πλήρωμα τάλαντ' ἐγγὺς δισχίλια γίγνεται
ἡμῖν.
ἀπὸ τούτου νυν κατάθες μισθὸν τοῖσι δικασταῖς ἐνι-
αυτοῦ,
ἐξ χιλιάσιν—"κοὔπω πλείους ἐν τῇ χώρᾳ κατένασθεν".
γίγνεται ἡμῖν ἑκατὸν δήπου καὶ πεντήκοντα τάλαντα.

ΦΙΛΟΚΛΕΩΝ

οὐδ' ἡ δεκάτη τῶν προσιόντων ἡμῖν ἄρ' ἐγίγνεθ' ὁ
μισθός.

yond the scope of comedians, to heal an inveterate sickness
endemic to the city. But here goes. Our father, son of
Cronus—

LOVECLEON

Stop that; don't be "fathering" me! The topic was how I'm
a slave, and if you don't explain that to me right now, you'll
surely meet your death, even if I'd be barred from
sacrificial meat![43]

LOATHECLEON

Then listen, pop, and relax your frown a bit. First of all,
calculate roughly, not with counters but on your fingers,
how much tribute we receive altogether from the allied
cities. Then make a separate count of the taxes and the
many one percents, court dues, mines, markets, harbors,
rents, proceeds from confiscations. Our total income from
all this is nearly 2000 talents. Now set aside the annual
payment to the jurors, all six thousand of them, "for never
yet have more dwelt in this land." We get, I reckon, a sum
of 150 talents.

LOVECLEON

So the pay we've been getting doesn't even amount to a
tenth of the revenue!

[43] I.e. polluted as a homicide.

ARISTOPHANES

μὰ Δί᾽ οὐ μέντοι.

ΦΙΛΟΚΛΕΩΝ

665   καὶ ποῖ τρέπεται δὴ ᾽πειτα τὰ χρήματα τἄλλα;

ΒΔΕΛΤΚΛΕΩΝ

ἐς τούτους τοὺς "οὐχὶ προδώσω τὸν Ἀθηναίων κολο-
       συρτόν,
ἀλλὰ μαχοῦμαι περὶ τοῦ πλήθους ἀεί". σὺ γάρ, ὦ
       πάτερ, αὐτοὺς
ἄρχειν αἱρεῖ σαυτοῦ τούτοις τοῖς ῥηματίοις περι-
       πεφθείς.
κᾆθ᾽ οὗτοι μὲν δωροδοκοῦσιν κατὰ πεντήκοντα
       τάλαντα
670   ἀπὸ τῶν πόλεων ἐπαπειλοῦντες τοιαυτὶ κἀναφοβοῦν-
       τες·
"δώσετε τὸν φόρον, ἢ βροντήσας τὴν πόλιν ὑμῶν
       ἀνατρέψω."
σὺ δὲ τῆς ἀρχῆς ἀγαπᾷς τῆς σῆς τοὺς ἀργελόφους
       περιτρώγων.
οἱ δὲ ξύμμαχοι, ὡς ᾔσθηνται τὸν μὲν σύρφακα τὸν
       ἄλλον
ἐκ κηθαρίου λαγαριζόμενον καὶ τραγαλίζοντα τὸ
       μηδέν,
675   σὲ μὲν ἡγοῦνται Κόννου ψῆφον, τούτοισι δὲ δωρο-
       φοροῦσιν
ὕρχας, οἶνον, δάπιδας, τυρόν, μέλι, σήσαμα,
       προσκεφάλαια,

306

LOATHECLEON

It certainly doesn't.

LOVECLEON

In that case, where is the rest of the money routed?

LOATHECLEON

To the "I won't betray the Athenian rabble and I'll fight for the masses" bunch! You choose them to rule you, father, because you've been buttered up by these slogans. And then they extort fifty talent bribes from the allied cities by terrifying them with threats like this: "You'll hand over the tribute, or I'll upend your city with my thundering!" While you're content to gnaw the rinds of your own empire. The allies have caught on that you and the rest of the riffraff are starving on what you get from the ballot funnel and splurging on nothing, so they figure you for the Simple Simon vote, while they bring presents for these guys: jugged fish, wine, coverlets, cheese, honey, sesame, lounge

ARISTOPHANES

φιάλας, χλανίδας, στεφάνους, ὅρμους, ἐκπώματα,
πλουθυγιείαν.
σοὶ δ', ὧν ἄρχεις "πολλὰ μὲν ἐν γῇ, πολλὰ δ' ἐφ'
ὑγρᾷ πιτυλεύσας",
οὐδεὶς οὐδὲ σκορόδου κεφαλὴν τοῖς ἑψητοῖσι δίδωσιν.

680 μὰ Δί', ἀλλὰ παρ' Εὐχαρίδου καὐτὸς τρεῖς ἄγλιθας
μετέπεμψα.
ἀλλ' αὐτήν μοι τὴν δουλείαν οὐκ ἀποφαίνων
ἀποκναίεις.

οὐ γὰρ μεγάλη δουλεία 'στὶν τούτους μὲν ἅπαντας
ἐν ἀρχαῖς
αὑτούς τ' εἶναι καὶ τοὺς κόλακας τοὺς τούτων
μισθοφοροῦντας;
σοὶ δ' ἤν τις δῷ τοὺς τρεῖς ὀβολούς, ἀγαπᾷς, οὓς
αὐτὸς ἐλαύνων
685 καὶ πεζομαχῶν καὶ πολιορκῶν ἐκτήσω πολλὰ
πονήσας.
καὶ πρὸς τούτοις ἐπιταττόμενος φοιτᾷς, ὃ μάλιστά
μ' ἀπάγχει,
ὅταν εἰσελθὸν μειράκιόν σοι κατάπυγον, Χαιρέου
υἱός,
ὡδὶ διαβάς, διακινηθεὶς τῷ σώματι καὶ τρυφερανθείς,
ἥκειν εἴπῃ πρῲ κἀν ὥρᾳ δικάσονθ'· "ὡς ὅστις ἂν ὑμῶν
690 ὕστερος ἔλθῃ τοῦ σημείου, τὸ τριώβολον οὐ
κομιεῖται."

pillows, chalices, capes, crowns, necklaces, tumblers, healthy wealthiness! And for you? You rule them, having "tirelessly tramped the land and rowed the waves," but not one of them gives you a head of garlic for your chowder.

LOVECLEON

They certainly don't! I had to send for three cloves from Eucharides'[44] grocery myself. But you're rubbing me the wrong way by not spelling out my alleged slavery.

LOATHECLEON

How's this for sheer slavery? All these guys, along with their flunkies, hold office and draw salaries, while you're content if someone gives you those three obols, the ones you earned by your own hard work, rowing and soldiering and laying siege. What's more, you march to their tune. It really lifts my gorge when in comes some young faggot, Chaereas' son,[45] spreading his legs like this, all dandied up and waggling his arse, and he tells you to show up bright and early for jury duty and don't be late, "because any of you who misses the signal won't get his three obols." But

44 Unknown.
45 Both father and son are unknown.

αὐτὸς δὲ φέρει τὸ συνηγορικὸν δραχμήν, κἂν
    ὕστερος ἔλθῃ·
καὶ κοινωνῶν τῶν ἀρχόντων ἑτέρῳ τινὶ τῶν μεθ᾽
    ἑαυτοῦ,
ἤν τίς τι διδῷ τῶν φευγόντων, ξυνθέντε τὸ πρᾶγμα
    δύ᾽ ὄντε
ἐσπουδάκατον, κᾆθ᾽ ὡς πρίονθ᾽ ὁ μὲν ἕλκει, ὁ δ᾽
    ἀντενέδωκεν·
695 σὺ δὲ χασκάζεις τὸν κωλακρέτην, τὸ δὲ πραττόμε-
    νόν σε λέληθεν.

ΦΙΛΟΚΛΕΩΝ

ταυτί με ποιοῦσ᾽; οἴμοι, τί λέγεις; ὥς μου τὸν θῖνα
    ταράττεις,
καὶ τὸν νοῦν μου προσάγεις μᾶλλον, κοὐκ οἶδ᾽ ὅ τι
    χρῆμά με ποιεῖς.

ΒΔΕΛΥΚΛΕΩΝ

σκέψαι τοίνυν ὡς ἐξόν σοι πλουτεῖν καὶ τοῖσιν
    ἅπασιν
ὑπὸ τῶν ἀεὶ δημιζόντων οὐκ οἶδ᾽ ὅπῃ ἐγκεκύκλησαι,
700 ὅστις πόλεων ἄρχων πλείστων ἀπὸ τοῦ Πόντου
    μέχρι Σαρδοῦς
οὐκ ἀπολαύεις πλὴν τοῦθ᾽ ὃ φέρεις ἀκαρῆ· καὶ τοῦτ᾽
    ἐρίῳ σοι
ἐνστάζουσιν κατὰ μικρὸν ἀεὶ τοῦ ζῆν ἕνεχ᾽ ὥσπερ
    ἔλαιον.
βούλονται γάρ σε πένητ᾽ εἶναι, καὶ τοῦθ᾽ ὧν εἵνεκ᾽
    ἐρῶ σοι·

he gets his prosecutor's pay, six obols, even if he does come late. And any bribe a defendant might offer he splits with one of his fellow office holders, the two of them teaming up on the case and keeping a straight face, then going to work like a couple of sawyers, one pulling while the other pushes. But you're so busy panting after the paymaster that you don't see what's going on.

LOVECLEON
Is that how they treat me? Heavens me, what are you saying? You're shaking me to my very depths, pulling me closer to your viewpoint, doing I don't know what to me!

LOATHECLEON
Then consider this: you could be rich, and everyone else too, but somehow or other these populists have got you boxed in. You, master of a multitude of cities from the Black Sea to Sardinia, enjoy absolutely no reward, except for this jury pay, and they drip that into you like droplets of oil from a tuft of wool, always a little at a time, just enough to keep you alive. Because they want to keep you poor, and I'll tell you the reason: so you'll recognize your

ARISTOPHANES

ἵνα γιγνώσκῃς τὸν τιθασευτήν, κᾆθ᾽ ὅταν οὗτός γ᾽
   ἐπισίξῃ
705 ἐπὶ τῶν ἐχθρῶν τιν᾽ ἐπιρρύξας, ἀγρίως αὐτοῖς ἐπι-
   πηδᾷς.
εἰ γὰρ ἐβούλοντο βίον πορίσαι τῷ δήμῳ, ῥᾴδιον ἦν
   ἄν.
εἰσίν γε πόλεις χίλιαι αἳ νῦν τὸν φόρον ἡμῖν ἀπά-
   γουσιν·
τούτων εἴκοσιν ἄνδρας βόσκειν εἴ τις προσέταξεν
   ἑκάστῃ,
δύο μυριάδ᾽ ἂν τῶν δημοτικῶν ἔζων ἐν πᾶσι λαγῴοις
710 καὶ στεφάνοισιν παντοδαποῖσιν καὶ πυῷ καὶ πυριάτῃ,
ἄξια τῆς γῆς ἀπολαύοντες καὶ τοῦ ᾽ν Μαραθῶνι
   τροπαίου.
νῦν δ᾽ ὥσπερ ἐλαολόγοι χωρεῖθ᾽ ἅμα τῷ τὸν μισθὸν
   ἔχοντι.

ΦΙΛΟΚΛΕΩΝ

οἴμοι, τί ποθ᾽ ὥσπερ νάρκη μου κατὰ τῆς χειρὸς
   καταχεῖται;
καὶ τὸ ξίφος οὐ δύναμαι κατέχειν, ἀλλ᾽ ἤδη μαλθα-
   κός εἰμι.

ΒΔΕΛΥΚΛΕΩΝ

715 ἀλλ᾽ ὁπόταν μὲν δείσωσ᾽ αὐτοί, τὴν Εὔβοιαν διδόασιν
ὑμῖν, καὶ σῖτον ὑφίστανται κατὰ πεντήκοντα μεδί-
   μνους
πορεῖν. ἔδοσαν δ᾽ οὐπώποτέ σοι· πλὴν πρώην
   πέντε μεδίμνους,

trainer, and whenever he whistles at you to attack one of
his enemies, you'll leap on that man like a savage. If they
wanted to provide a living for the people, it would be easy.
A thousand cities there are that now pay us tribute. If
someone ordered each one to support twenty men, then
twenty thousand loyal proles would be rolling in hare meat,
every kind of garland, beestings and eggnog, living it up as
befits their country and their trophy at Marathon. As it is,
you traipse around for your employer like olive pickers!

LOVECLEON

Heavens me, what can it be that's creeping over my hand
like a paralysis? I can't even hold my sword; I've gone limp.

LOATHECLEON

But whenever they're scared themselves, they promise you
Euboea and get set to supply you with fifty-bushel rations
of grain. But they never give it to you, not counting yester-
day when you got five bushels, but only after narrowly

καὶ ταῦτα μόλις ξενίας φεύγων, ἔλαβες κατὰ χοί-
νικα κριθῶν.
ὧν εἵνεκ᾽ ἐγώ σ᾽ ἀπέκλῃον ἀεὶ
720 βόσκειν ἐθέλων καὶ μὴ τούτους
ἐγχάσκειν σοι στομφάζοντας.
καὶ νῦν ἀτεχνῶς ἐθέλω παρέχειν
ὅ τι βούλει σοι,
πλὴν κωλακρέτου γάλα πίνειν.

ΚΟΡΥΦΑΙΟΣ

725 ἦ που σοφὸς ἦν ὅστις ἔφασκεν· "πρὶν ἂν ἀμφοῖν
μῦθον ἀκούσῃς,
οὐκ ἂν δικάσαις." σὺ γὰρ οὖν νῦν μοι νικᾶν πολλῷ
δεδόκησαι·
ὥστ᾽ ἤδη τὴν ὀργὴν χαλάσας τοὺς σκίπωνας κατα-
βάλλω.
ἀλλ᾽, ὦ τῆς ἡλικίας ἡμῖν τῆς αὐτῆς συνθιασῶτα,

ΧΟΡΟΣ

(στρ) πιθοῦ πιθοῦ λόγοισι, μηδ᾽ ἄφρων γένῃ
730 μηδ᾽ ἀτενὴς ἄγαν ἀτεράμων τ᾽ ἀνήρ.
εἴθ᾽ ὤφελέν μοι κηδεμὼν ἢ ξυγγενὴς
εἶναί τις ὅστις τοιαῦτ᾽ ἐνουθέτει.
σοὶ δὲ νῦν τις θεῶν
παρὼν ἐμφανὴς
ξυλλαμβάνει τοῦ πράγματος, καὶ δῆλός ἐστιν εὖ
ποιῶν·
735 σὺ δὲ παρὼν δέχου.

escaping a challenge to your citizenship, and then it was barley in one quart installments. Which is why I kept you locked up: I wanted to feed you and I didn't want these blowhards to make a chump of you. And now I want to provide you with absolutely anything you want, except paymaster's milk to drink.

CHORUS LEADER

"Don't judge till you've heard both sides of the story": whoever said that was pretty wise. Because in this case you've won my vote hands down. I've slackened my anger and now throw in the towel. Wherefore, brother of our age and order,

CHORUS

listen, listen to his words, and don't be stupid,
or too unyielding and tough a man.
I wish I had some kinsman or relative
to give me that kind of criticism.
Now some god
has shown up before your very eyes
to help with your problem, and he's clearly doing you
    good.
You show up too, and accept his help.

ΒΔΕΛΤΚΛΕΩΝ

καὶ μὴν θρέψω γ᾽ αὐτὸν παρέχων
ὅσα πρεσβύτῃ ξύμφορα, χόνδρον
λείχειν, χλαῖναν μαλακήν, σισύραν,
πόρνην, ἥτις τὸ πέος τρίψει
740   καὶ τὴν ὀσφῦν.
ἀλλ᾽ ὅτι σιγᾷ κοὐδὲν γρύζει,
τοῦτ᾽ οὐ δύναταί με προσέσθαι.

ΧΟΡΟΣ

(ἀντ)   νενουθέτηκεν αὐτὸν ἐς τὰ πράγμαθ᾽, οἷς
τότ᾽ ἐπεμαίνετ᾽. ἔγνωκε γὰρ ἀρτίως,
745   λογίζεταί τ᾽ ἐκεῖνα πάνθ᾽ ἁμαρτίας
ἃ σοῦ κελεύοντος οὐκ ἐπείθετο.
νῦν δ᾽ ἴσως τοῖσι σοῖς
λόγοις πείθεται,
καὶ σωφρονεῖ μέντοι μεθιστὰς ἐς τὸ λοιπὸν τὸν τρόπον
πειθόμενός τέ σοι.

ΦΙΛΟΚΛΕΩΝ

750   ἰώ μοί μοι.

ΒΔΕΛΤΚΛΕΩΝ

οὗτος, τί βοᾷς;

ΦΙΛΟΚΛΕΩΝ

μή μοι τούτων μηδὲν ὑπισχνοῦ.
κείνων ἔραμαι, κεῖθι γενοίμαν,
ἵν᾽ ὁ κῆρύξ φησι· "τίς ἀψήφι-
στος; ἀνιστάσθω."
κἀπισταίην ἐπὶ τοῖς κημοῖς

316

LOATHECLEON

That's right, and I'll support him by providing
whatever a senior citizen needs: gruel to lick up,
a cozy cloak, an overcoat,
a whore to massage his cock
and his tailbone.
But I can't help being displeased
that he's silent and won't so much as grunt.

CHORUS

He's been criticizing himself for the activities
he was crazy about before. For he's just now seen the
    light,
and understands that he was wrong
not to listen to your past warnings.
Maybe now he's listening
to your arguments
and really being sensible, changing his ways from
    now on,
and listening to you.

LOVECLEON

What misery!

LOATHECLEON

Here, why are you bellowing?

LOVECLEON

Don't promise me any of your promises!
What I yearn for is over there. There is where I want
    to be,
where the herald says,
"Whoever hasn't voted please stand!"
Yes, I long to stand at the ballot box,

755   ψηφιζομένων ὁ τελευταῖος.
      "σπεῦδ᾽, ὦ ψυχή." —ποῦ μοι ψυχή;—
      "πάρες, ὦ σκιερά—". μὰ τὸν Ἡρακλέα,
      μή νυν ἔτ᾽ ἐγὼ 'ν τοῖσι δικασταῖς
      κλέπτοντα Κλέωνα λάβοιμι.

ΒΔΕΛΤΚΛΕΩΝ

760   ἴθ᾽, ὦ πάτερ, πρὸς τῶν θεῶν ἐμοὶ πιθοῦ.

ΦΙΛΟΚΛΕΩΝ

τί σοι πίθωμαι; λέγ᾽ ὅ τι βούλει πλὴν ἑνός.

ΒΔΕΛΤΚΛΕΩΝ

ποίου; φέρ᾽ ἴδω.

ΦΙΛΟΚΛΕΩΝ

            τοῦ μὴ δικάζειν. τοῦτο δὲ
Ἅιδης διακρινεῖ πρότερον ἢ 'γὼ πείσομαι.

ΒΔΕΛΤΚΛΕΩΝ

σὺ δ᾽ οὖν, ἐπειδὴ τοῦτο κεχάρηκας ποιῶν,
765   ἐκεῖσε μὲν μηκέτι βάδιζ᾽, ἀλλ᾽ ἐνθάδε
      αὐτοῦ μένων δίκαζε τοῖσιν οἰκέταις.

ΦΙΛΟΚΛΕΩΝ

περὶ τοῦ; τί ληρεῖς;

ΒΔΕΛΤΚΛΕΩΝ

           ταῦθ᾽ ἅπερ ἐκεῖ πράττεται.
ὅτι τὴν θύραν ἀνέῳξεν ἡ σηκὶς λάθρᾳ,
ταύτης ἐπιβολὴν ψηφιεῖ μίαν μόνην·
770   πάντως δὲ κἀκεῖ ταῦτ᾽ ἔδρας ἑκάστοτε.
      καὶ ταῦτα μὲν νῦν εὐλόγως, ἢν ἐξέχῃ

the last of the voters!
Onward, my soul! Where are you, soul?
Let me pass, you shadowy—![46] Great Heracles,
if you're telling the truth, I'd better not be on a jury
that convicts Cleon of theft!

LOATHECLEON

Please, father, for gods' sake listen to me.

LOVECLEON

What would you have me do? Just name it, except for one thing.

LOATHECLEON

What thing, tell me?

LOVECLEON

To stop being a juror. Before I do that for you, death will decide between us!

LOATHECLEON

All right, since that's what you enjoy doing, just stop going to court. Stay here instead, and judge the household slaves.

LOVECLEON

On what charge? What's this nonsense?

LOATHECLEON

You'll be doing exactly what's done at court. Say the maid opens the door without permission. Vote her a single stiff penalty—anyway, it's what you used to do regularly at court. And now you'll do this judging in a reasonable way,

---

[46] From Euripides' *Bellerophon;* the full line (fr. 308) is, "Let me pass, you shadowy foliage, let me cross the watery dells; I am eager to see the heaven above."

εἴλη κατ' ὄρθρον, ἡλιάσει πρὸς ἥλιον·
ἐὰν δὲ νείφῃ, πρὸς τὸ πῦρ καθήμενος·
ὕοντος εἴσει· κἂν ἔγρῃ μεσημβρινός,
775   οὐδείς σ' ἀποκλῄσει θεσμοθέτης τῇ κιγκλίδι.

ΦΙΛΟΚΛΕΩΝ

τουτί μ' ἀρέσκει.

ΒΔΕΛΤΚΛΕΩΝ

                    πρὸς δὲ τούτοις γ', ἢν δίκην
λέγῃ μακράν τις, οὐχὶ πεινῶν ἀναμενεῖς
δάκνων σεαυτὸν καὶ τὸν ἀπολογούμενον.

ΦΙΛΟΚΛΕΩΝ

πῶς οὖν διαγιγνώσκειν καλῶς δυνήσομαι
780   ὥσπερ πρότερον τὰ πράγματ' ἔτι μασώμενος;

ΒΔΕΛΤΚΛΕΩΝ

πολλῷ γ' ἄμεινον· καὶ λέγεται γὰρ τουτογί,
ὡς οἱ δικασταὶ ψευδομένων τῶν μαρτύρων
μόλις τὸ πρᾶγμ' ἔγνωσαν ἀναμασώμενοι.

ΦΙΛΟΚΛΕΩΝ

ἀνά τοί με πείθεις. ἀλλ' ἐκεῖν' οὔπω λέγεις,
τὸν μισθὸν ὁπόθεν λήψομαι.

ΒΔΕΛΤΚΛΕΩΝ

                    παρ' ἐμοῦ.

ΦΙΛΟΚΛΕΩΝ

785   καλῶς,
ὁτιὴ κατ' ἐμαυτὸν κοὐ μεθ' ἑτέρου λήψομαι.

320

out in the sun if it's warm at dawn; if it's snowing, then sitting by the fire; if it starts to rain, going indoors. And if you sleep till noon, no magistrate will close the gate on you.

LOVECLEON

That I like.

LOATHECLEON

And that's not all. If someone's making a long speech, you needn't sit there hungry, gnashing your teeth and the defendant too.

LOVECLEON

But then how will I decide cases with my usual competence if I'm still chewing my food?

LOATHECLEON

A lot more competently! People do say that when witnesses lie, the jurors get to the meat of the matter by chewing it over.

LOVECLEON

You know, you're winning me over. But there's one issue you still haven't addressed: where will I get my pay?

LOATHECLEON

From me.

LOVECLEON

Good! Then I'll be getting paid individually and not with

---

[772] κατ᾽ ὀρθὸν v.l. Σ^Γ Callistratus

αἴσχιστα γάρ τοί μ' ἠργάσατο Λυσίστρατος
ὁ σκωπτόλης. δραχμὴν μετ' ἐμοῦ πρῴην λαβὼν
ἐλθὼν διεκερματίζετ' ἐν τοῖς ἰχθύσιν,
790 κἄπειτ' ἐνέθηκε τρεῖς λοπίδας μοι κεστρέων,
κἀγὼ 'νέκαψ'· ὀβολοὺς γὰρ ᾠόμην λαβεῖν.
κᾆτα βδελυχθεὶς ὀσφρόμενος ἐξέπτυσα·
κᾆθ' εἷλκον αὐτόν.

BΔΕΛΤΚΛΕΩΝ
ὁ δὲ τί πρὸς ταῦτ' εἶφ';

ΦΙΛΟΚΛΕΩΝ
ὅ τι;
ἀλεκτρυόνος μ' ἔφασκε κοιλίαν ἔχειν.
795 "ταχὺ γοῦν καθέψεις τἀργύριον," ἦ δ' ὃς λέγων.

BΔΕΛΤΚΛΕΩΝ
ὁρᾷς ὅσον καὶ τοῦτο δῆτα κερδανεῖς.

ΦΙΛΟΚΛΕΩΝ
οὐ πάνυ τι μικρόν. ἀλλ' ὅπερ μέλλεις ποίει.

BΔΕΛΤΚΛΕΩΝ
ἀνάμενέ νυν· ἐγὼ δὲ ταῦθ' ἥξω φέρων.

ΦΙΛΟΚΛΕΩΝ
ὅρα τὸ χρῆμα, τὰ λόγι' ὡς περαίνεται.
800 ἠκηκόειν γὰρ ὡς Ἀθηναῖοί ποτε
δικάσοιεν ἐπὶ ταῖς οἰκίαισι τὰς δίκας,
κἀν τοῖς προθύροις ἐνοικοδομήσει πᾶς ἀνὴρ
αὑτῷ δικαστηρίδιον μικρὸν πάνυ,

a partner.[47] You know, that joker Lysistratus played a very dirty trick on me the other day. We got our drachma and he went to get it changed in the fish market. Then he handed me three mullet scales, which I popped into my mouth, thinking they were obols. Then I smelled them and retched and spat them out. Then I grabbed hold of him.

LOATHECLEON
And what did he have to say for himself?

LOVECLEON
Get this: he said I had the guts of a rooster. "Anyway," says he, "you decoct your money pretty fast!"

LOATHECLEON
You see what a great advantage you'll have there, too.

LOVECLEON
Not too bad! Very well, proceed with your plan.

LOATHECLEON
Then wait here. I'll be right back with the things we need.

LOATHECLEON goes inside.

LOVECLEON
Lo and behold, the prophecies come true. I'd heard that some day the Athenians would judge cases in their very houses, and that every man would build himself an itty bitty lawcourt in his yard; they'd be on doorsteps every-

---

[47] Jury pay was distributed in drachmas, which each pair of jurors would have to change into obols on their own. Lysistratus of Cholargus is often mentioned as a penurious wit and jokester.

ὥσπερ Ἑκατεῖον πανταχοῦ πρὸ τῶν θυρῶν.

ΒΔΕΛΤΚΛΕΩΝ

805 ἰδού. τί ἔτ᾽ ἐρεῖς; ὡς ἅπαντ᾽ ἐγὼ φέρω,
ὅσαπέρ γ᾽ ἔφασκον κἄτι πολλῷ πλείονα.
ἀμὶς μέν, ἢν οὐρητιάσῃς, αὑτηὶ
παρὰ σοὶ κρεμήσετ᾽ ἐγγὺς ἐπὶ τοῦ παττάλου.

ΦΙΛΟΚΛΕΩΝ

σοφόν γε τουτὶ καὶ γέροντι πρόσφορον
810 ἐξηῦρες ἀτεχνῶς φάρμακον στραγγουρίας.

ΒΔΕΛΤΚΛΕΩΝ

καὶ πῦρ γε τουτί· καὶ προσέστηκεν φακῆ
ῥοφεῖν, ἐὰν δέῃ τι.

ΦΙΛΟΚΛΕΩΝ

τοῦτ᾽ αὖ δεξιόν.
κἂν γὰρ πυρέττω, τόν γε μισθὸν λήψομαι·
αὐτοῦ μένων γὰρ τὴν φακῆν ῥοφήσομαι.
815 ἀτὰρ τί τὸν ὄρνιν ὡς ἔμ᾽ ἐξηνέγκατε;

ΒΔΕΛΤΚΛΕΩΝ

ἵνα γ᾽, ἢν καθεύδῃς ἀπολογουμένου τινός,
ᾄδων ἄνωθεν ἐξεγείρῃ σ᾽ οὑτοσί.

ΦΙΛΟΚΛΕΩΝ

ἓν ἔτι ποθῶ, τὰ δ᾽ ἄλλ᾽ ἀρέσκει μοι.

ΒΔΕΛΤΚΛΕΩΝ

τὸ τί;

---

[48] A deity of roads and traveling, whose image, like that of

where, like shrines for Hecate.[48]

LOATHECLEON and slaves enter with courtroom para-phernalia.

LOATHECLEON
Just look! Now what have you got to say? I've brought everything I said I would, and lots more. For one thing, this chamberpot here will be hanging by that peg, right beside you in case you need to piss.

LOVECLEON
That's ingenious of you; you've really thought of the perfect antidote to an old man's incontinence.

LOATHECLEON
And here's some fire, and right next to it some lentil soup to slurp, any time you want.

LOVECLEON
That's handy too. Even if I have a cold, I'll still get my pay, because I'll stay right here and slurp the soup. But why have you brought me out the rooster?

LOATHECLEON
Why, if you fall asleep while a defendant is speaking, this rooster up here will crow you awake.

LOVECLEON
Everything's to my liking, except one thing I'm still missing.

LOATHECLEON
Namely?

Apollo Agyieus (875), was placed before many an Athenian doorway.

325

ARISTOPHANES

ΦΙΛΟΚΛΕΩΝ

θήρῳον εἴ πως ἐκκομίσαις τὸ τοῦ Λύκου.

ΒΔΕΛΤΚΛΕΩΝ

820 πάρεστι τουτί, καὐτὸς ἄναξ οὑτοσί.

ΦΙΛΟΚΛΕΩΝ

ὦ δέσποθ᾽ ἥρως, ὡς χαλεπὸν ἄρ᾽ ἦν σ᾽ ἰδεῖν.

ΒΔΕΛΤΚΛΕΩΝ

οἷόσπερ ἡμῖν φαίνεται Κλεώνυμος.

ΦΙΛΟΚΛΕΩΝ

οὔκουν ἔχει γ᾽ οὐδ᾽ αὐτὸς ἥρως ὢν ὅπλα.

ΒΔΕΛΤΚΛΕΩΝ

εἰ θᾶττον ἐκαθίζου σύ, θᾶττον ἂν δίκην
ἐκάλουν.

ΦΙΛΟΚΛΕΩΝ

825   κάλει νυν, ὡς κάθημ᾽ ἐγὼ πάλαι.

ΒΔΕΛΤΚΛΕΩΝ

φέρε νυν, τίν᾽ αὐτῷ πρῶτον εἰσαγάγω δίκην;
τί τις κακὸν δέδρακε τῶν ἐν τῇ οἰκίᾳ;
ἡ Θρᾷττα προσκαύσασα πρώην τὴν χύτραν—

ΦΙΛΟΚΛΕΩΝ

ἐπίσχες, οὗτος· ὡς ὀλίγου μ᾽ ἀπώλεσας.
830 ἄνευ δρυφάκτου τὴν δίκην μέλλεις καλεῖν,
ὃ πρῶτον ἡμῖν τῶν ἱερῶν ἐφαίνετο;

ΒΔΕΛΤΚΛΕΩΝ

μὰ τὸν Δί᾽ οὐ πάρεστιν.

LOVECLEON

Is there any way you could supply the shrine of Lycus?

LOATHECLEON

(*pointing to the stage altar*) There's this. (*motioning one of the slaves on to the altar*) And here's the hero himself!

LOVECLEON

(*getting up to look closer*) Lord Hero, I couldn't see you there.

LOATHECLEON

He's about as hard to see as Cleonymus!

LOVECLEON

Well, I admit that even though he's a hero, he's got no equipment either.[49]

LOATHECLEON

The sooner you take your seat, the sooner I can call a case.

LOVECLEON

(*taking his seat*) Call away; I've been sitting here patiently.

LOATHECLEON

Let me see now, what case will I bring him first? Has any of the household staff misbehaved? The Thracian girl, who scorched the pot yesterday—

LOVECLEON

Hold on there, you just about killed me! Do you mean to call the case without court railings, the first of the holy objects to meet our eyes?

LOATHECLEON

Oh god, there aren't any!

[49] I.e., the slave wears no phallus, as Cleonymus had lost his weapons.

327

ΦΙΛΟΚΛΕΩΝ

ἀλλ' ἐγὼ δραμὼν
αὐτὸς κομιοῦμαι τό γε παραυτίκ' ἔνδοθεν.

ΒΔΕΛΤΚΛΕΩΝ

τί ποτε τὸ χρῆμ'; ὡς δεινὸν ἡ φιλοχωρία.

ΞΑΝΘΙΑΣ

835 βάλλ' ἐς κόρακας. τοιουτονὶ τρέφειν κύνα.

ΒΔΕΛΤΚΛΕΩΝ

τί δ' ἐστὶν ἐτεόν;

ΞΑΝΘΙΑΣ

οὐ γὰρ ὁ Λάβης ἀρτίως,
ὁ κύων, παράξας εἰς τὸν ἱπνὸν ἁρπάσας
τροφαλίδα τυροῦ Σικελικὴν κατεδήδοκεν;

ΒΔΕΛΤΚΛΕΩΝ

τοῦτ' ἆρα πρῶτον τἀδίκημα τῷ πατρὶ
840 εἰσακτέον μοι. σὺ δὲ κατηγόρει παρών.

ΞΑΝΘΙΑΣ

μὰ Δί' οὐκ ἔγωγ', ἀλλ' ἅτερός φησιν κύων
κατηγορήσειν, ἤν τις εἰσάγῃ γραφήν.

ΒΔΕΛΤΚΛΕΩΝ

ἴθι νυν, ἄγ' αὐτὼ δεῦρο.

ΞΑΝΘΙΑΣ

ταῦτα χρὴ ποιεῖν.

---

[50] The name "Labes" (*labein* "snatch") puns on the name of
Laches; see 24 n.

LOVECLEON

Well, I'll run into the house myself and get something that'll serve.

LOVECLEON goes into the house.

LOATHECLEON

What's the big problem? Love of place is such a powerful thing!

XANTHIAS runs out of the house, shouting over his shoulder.

XANTHIAS

To hell with him! Imagine keeping a dog like that!

LOATHECLEON

What's the matter here?

XANTHIAS

As if that dog Grabes[50] didn't dart into the kitchen just now and gobble up a wheel of Sicilian cheese!

LOATHECLEON

All right then, this should be the first crime brought before my father. You stay and prosecute.

XANTHIAS

No sir, not me. The other dog says he'll be the prosecutor if any case is brought.

LOATHECLEON

Very well, go bring the two of them out here.

XANTHIAS

Consider it done.

ΒΔΕΛΤΚΛΕΩΝ

τουτὶ τί ἐστι;

ΦΙΛΟΚΛΕΩΝ

χοιροκομεῖον Ἑστίας.

ΒΔΕΛΤΚΛΕΩΝ

εἶθ' ἱεροσυλήσας φέρεις;

ΦΙΛΟΚΛΕΩΝ

845   οὔκ, ἀλλ' ἵνα
ἀφ' Ἑστίας ἀρχόμενος ἐπιτρίψω τινά.
ἀλλ' εἴσαγ' ἀνύσας, ὡς ἐγὼ τιμᾶν βλέπω.

ΒΔΕΛΤΚΛΕΩΝ

φέρε νυν, ἐνέγκω τὰς σανίδας καὶ τὰς γραφάς.

ΦΙΛΟΚΛΕΩΝ

οἴμοι, διατρίβεις κἀπολεῖς τριψημερῶν.
850 ἐγὼ δ' ἀλοκίζειν ἐδεόμην τὸ χωρίον.

ΒΔΕΛΤΚΛΕΩΝ

ἰδού.

ΦΙΛΟΚΛΕΩΝ

κάλει νυν.

ΒΔΕΛΤΚΛΕΩΝ

ταῦτα δή.

WASPS

XANTHIAS goes inside as LOVECLEON comes out with part of a fence.

LOATHECLEON

What's that?

LOVECLEON

Hestia's pigpen.[51]

LOATHECLEON

So you've committed sacrilege to get that?

LOVECLEON

Not at all. I'm beginning with Hestia, since I'm about to slaughter someone. So hurry up and call the case: I'm in a punitive mood.

LOATHECLEON

All right then, let me fetch the dockets and indictments.

LOVECLEON

Good grief, you'll be the death of me, procrastinating and wasting the whole day! (*holding up a penalty tablet*) I've been itching to plow up this plot.

LOATHECLEON

Here you are.

LOVECLEON

Then call the case!

LOATHECLEON

All right.

[51] The goddess to whom domestic sacrifice was offered, and with whose name all sacrifices, prayers, and oaths began.

ARISTOPHANES

ΦΙΛΟΚΛΕΩΝ

τίς οὑτοσὶ

ὁ πρῶτός ἐστιν;

ΒΔΕΛΥΚΛΕΩΝ

ἐς κόρακας. ὡς ἄχθομαι,

ὁτιὴ 'πελαθόμην τοὺς καδίσκους ἐκφέρειν.

ΦΙΛΟΚΛΕΩΝ

οὗτος σύ, ποῖ θεῖς;

ΒΔΕΛΥΚΛΕΩΝ

ἐπὶ καδίσκους.

ΦΙΛΟΚΛΕΩΝ

μηδαμῶς·

855 ἐγὼ γὰρ εἶχον τούσδε τοὺς ἀρυστίχους.

ΒΔΕΛΥΚΛΕΩΝ

κάλλιστα τοίνυν. πάντα γὰρ πάρεστι νῷν
ὅσων δεόμεθα—πλήν γε δὴ τῆς κλεψύδρας.

ΦΙΛΟΚΛΕΩΝ

ἡδὶ δὲ δὴ τίς ἐστιν; οὐχὶ κλεψύδρα;

ΒΔΕΛΥΚΛΕΩΝ

εὖ γ᾽ ἐκπορίζεις αὐτὰ κἀπιχωρίως.
860 ἀλλ᾽ ὡς τάχιστα πῦρ τις ἐξενεγκάτω
καὶ μυρρίνας καὶ τὸν λιβανωτὸν ἔνδοθεν,
ὅπως ἂν εὐξώμεσθα πρῶτα τοῖς θεοῖς.

ΧΟΡΟΣ

καὶ μὴν ἡμεῖς ἐπὶ ταῖς σπονδαῖς
καὶ ταῖς εὐχαῖς

WASPS

LOVECLEON

Who's this first one here?

LOATHECLEON

Oh hell! How annoying, I've forgotten to bring out the voting urns.

LOVECLEON

Hey you, where are you running off to?

LOATHECLEON

To get the urns.

LOVECLEON

Don't bother, I've already got these soup ladles.

LOATHECLEON

They'll do just fine. So now we've got everything we need—everything except a water clock!

LOVECLEON

(*pointing to the chamberpot*) And what's this here if it isn't a water clock?

LOATHECLEON

You've truly got the native Athenian's resourcefulness. On the double now, somebody fetch fire and myrtle wreaths and the incense from the house, so that we can begin by praying to the gods.

CHORUS

And to celebrate your truce
and your prayers

865   φήμην ἀγαθὴν ἕξομεν ὑμῖν,
        ὅτι γενναίως ἐκ τοῦ πολέμου
        καὶ τοῦ νείκους ξυνέβητον.

ΒΔΕΛΥΚΛΕΩΝ

εὐφημία μὲν πρῶτα νῦν ὑπαρχέτω.

ΚΟΡΥΦΑΙΟΣ

ὦ Φοῖβ' Ἄπολλον Πύθι', ἐπ' ἀγαθῇ τύχῃ

ΧΟΡΟΣ

(στρ)   τὸ πρᾶγμ', ὃ μηχανᾶται
871   ἔμπροσθεν οὗτος τῶν θυρῶν,
        ἄπασιν ἡμῖν ἁρμόσαι
        παυσαμένοις πλάνων.
        ἰήιε Παιάν.

ΒΔΕΛΥΚΛΕΩΝ

875   ὦ δέσποτ' ἄναξ γεῖτον Ἀγυιεῦ, τοῦ 'μοῦ προθύρου
        προπύλαιε,
        δέξαι τελετὴν καινήν, ὦναξ, ἣν τῷ πατρὶ καινοτο-
        μοῦμεν.
        παῦσόν τ' αὐτοῦ τουτὶ τὸ λίαν στρυφνὸν καὶ πρίνι-
        νον ἦθος,
        ἀντὶ σιραίου μέλιτος σμικρὸν τῷ θυμιδίῳ παραμείξας.
880   ἤδη δ' εἶναι τοῖς ἀνθρώποις
        ἤπιον αὐτόν, τοὺς φεύγοντάς τ'
        ἐλεεῖν μᾶλλον τῶν γραψαμένων,
        κἀπιδακρύειν ἀντιβολούντων,

865 ἕξομεν Rᵃᶜ V: λέξομεν Rᵖᶜ Γ j

we shall sing you a propitious song,
because like gentlemen
you've settled your warfare and strife.

LOATHECLEON
First let there be respectful silence now.

CHORUS LEADER
Pythian Phoebus Apollo, bless with fair fortune

CHORUS
the experiment this man has devised
right on his doorstep,
and may it work for us too,
when our roving is over.
Hail, Paean!

LOATHECLEON
Sidewalk Apollo,[52] Lord, Master, and Neighbor,
    Forefront of My Forecourt,
accept a new rite, Lord, which we're launching for
    my father.
Purge him of this excessively harsh and hardhearted
    disposition,
infusing his dear little heart, like syrup, with a bit of
    honey.
Let him now treat people
gently, and have more pity
for the defendants than the prosecutors,
and shed a tear when people beseech him,

---

[52] See 804 n.

---

875 προπύλαιε Bentley: πρὸς πύλας a

ARISTOPHANES

καὶ παυσάμενον τῆς δυσκολίας
ἀπὸ τῆς ὀργῆς
τὴν ἀκαλήφην ἀφελέσθαι.

KOPYΦAIOΣ

885 ξυνευχόμεσθα ⟨ταῦτά⟩ σοι κἀπᾴδομεν
νέαισιν ἀρχαῖς εἵνεκα τῶν προλελεγμένων.

KOPYΦAIOΣ

(ἀντ) εὖνοι γάρ ἐσμεν ἐξ οὗ
τὸν δῆμον ᾐσθόμεσθά σου
φιλοῦντος ὡς οὐδεὶς ἀνὴρ
890 τῶν γε νεωτέρων.

BΔEΛTKΛEΩN

εἴ τις θύρασιν ἡλιαστής, εἰσίτω·
ὡς ἡνίκ' ἂν λέγωσιν, οὐκ εἰσφρήσομεν.

ΦIΛOKΛEΩN

τίς ἆρ' ὁ φεύγων οὗτος; ὅσον ἁλώσεται.

BΔEΛTKΛEΩN

ἀκούετ' ἤδη τῆς γραφῆς. "ἐγράψατο
895 Κύων Κυδαθηναιεὺς Λάβητ' Αἰξωνέα
τὸν τυρὸν ἀδικεῖν ὅτι μόνος κατήσθιεν
τὸν Σικελικόν. τίμημα κλῳὸς σύκινος."

ΦIΛOKΛEΩN

θάνατος μὲν οὖν κύνειος, ἢν ἅπαξ ἁλῶ.

885 ⟨ταῦτά⟩ Dindorf: om. a
890 γε νεωτέρων Reisig cl. νεωτέρων vl. Σ^VΓ: γενναιοτέρων a:
συνετωτέρων vl. Σ^Γ

336

and put away his bad temper,
from his anger
drawing the sting.

CHORUS LEADER

We join you in these prayers and chime in with a song for
your new regime, on the strength of your pronouncements.

CHORUS

Yes, we have been on your side
since we sensed that you cherish the people
more than anyone else,
at least among the younger generation.

LOATHECLEON

If any juror is at the door, let him enter. We'll admit no one
once speeches have begun.

LOVECLEON

So who's this defendant? He's really going to get it!

LOATHECLEON

Now all hear the charge: "Demadogue, the watchdog of
Cydathenaeum,[53] indicts Grabes of Aexone of malefaction,
in that he devoured a Sicilian cheese all by himself. Pro-
posed penalty: a collar of impeach wood."[54]

LOVECLEON

No, he'll get death, a dog's death, if he takes this fall!

---

[53] Cleon's deme.
[54] See 145 n.

ARISTOPHANES

ΒΔΕΛΤΚΛΕΩΝ

καὶ μὴν ὁ φεύγων οὑτοσὶ Λάβης πάρα.

ΦΙΛΟΚΛΕΩΝ

900 ὦ μιαρὸς οὗτος. ὡς δὲ καὶ κλέπτον βλέπει.
οἷον σεσηρὼς ἐξαπατήσειν μ᾽ οἴεται.
ποῦ δ᾽ ὅ γε διώκων, ὁ Κυδαθηναιεὺς κύων;

ΚΤΩΝ

αὖ αὖ.

ΒΔΕΛΤΚΛΕΩΝ

πάρεστιν.

ΞΑΝΘΙΑΣ

ἕτερος οὗτος αὖ Λάβης,
ἀγαθός γ᾽ ὑλακτεῖν καὶ διαλείχειν τὰς χύτρας.

ΒΔΕΛΤΚΛΕΩΝ

905 σίγα, κάθιζε. σὺ δ᾽ ἀναβὰς κατηγόρει.

ΦΙΛΟΚΛΕΩΝ

φέρε νυν, ἅμα τήνδ᾽ ἐγχεάμενος κἀγὼ ῥοφῶ.

ΚΤΩΝ

τῆς μὲν γραφῆς ἠκούσαθ᾽ ἣν ἐγραψάμην,
ἄνδρες δικασταί, τουτονί. δεινότατα γὰρ
ἔργων δέδρακε κἀμὲ καὶ τὸ ῥυππαπαῖ.
910 ἀποδρὰς γὰρ ἐς τὴν γωνίαν τυρὸν πολὺν
κατεσικέλιζε κἀνέπλητ᾽ ἐν τῷ σκότῳ.

WASPS

LOATHECLEON

The aforesaid defendant is here present.

LOVECLEON

The dirty scum! He's got thief written all over him, too!
Look at him grin, thinking he'll fox me. But where's the
prosecutor, Demadogue of Cydathenaeum?

DEMADOGUE

Bow wow wow!

LOATHECLEON

He's present.

XANTHIAS

This one's just another Grabes, good at barking and licking
the bowls clean!

LOATHECLEON

Sit down and be quiet. You, take the stand and begin the
prosecution.

LOVECLEON

Well now, while that's going on I'll pour myself some soup
to slurp.

DEMADOGUE

Men of the jury, you have heard the indictment that I have
filed against this defendant. He has indeed perpetrated the
most shocking deeds both against me and against the
whole yo ho ho.[55] Sneaked off to a corner he did, sicilized
a big cheese, and bolted it down under cover of darkness.

---

[55] Athenian sailors, drawn mostly from the poorest classes,
strongly supported Cleon.

ARISTOPHANES

ΦΙΛΟΚΛΕΩΝ

νὴ τὸν Δί᾿, ἀλλὰ δῆλός ἐστ᾿· ἔμοιγέ τοι
τυροῦ κάκιστον ἀρτίως ἐνήρυγεν
ὁ βδελυρὸς οὗτος.

ΚΤΩΝ

κοὐ μετέδωκ᾿ αἰτοῦντί μοι.

915 καίτοι τίς ὑμᾶς εὖ ποιεῖν δυνήσεται,
ἢν μή τι κἀμοί τις προβάλλῃ, τῷ κυνί;

ΦΙΛΟΚΛΕΩΝ

οὐδὲν μετέδωκεν οὐδὲ τῷ κοινῷ γ᾿, ἐμοί.
θερμὸς γὰρ ἀνὴρ οὐδὲν ἧττον τῆς φακῆς.

ΒΔΕΛΥΚΛΕΩΝ

πρὸς τῶν θεῶν, μὴ προκαταγίγνωσκ᾿, ὦ πάτερ,
πρὶν ἄν γ᾿ ἀκούσῃς ἀμφοτέρων.

ΦΙΛΟΚΛΕΩΝ

920   ἀλλ᾿, ὦγαθέ,
τὸ πρᾶγμα φανερόν ἐστιν· αὐτὸ γὰρ βοᾷ.

ΚΤΩΝ

μή νυν ἀφῆτέ γ᾿ αὐτόν, ὡς ὄντ᾿ αὖ πολὺ
κυνῶν ἁπάντων ἄνδρα μονοφαγίστατον,
ὅστις περιπλεύσας τὴν θυείαν ἐν κύκλῳ
925 ἐκ τῶν πόλεων τὸ σκῖρον ἐξεδήδοκεν.

ΦΙΛΟΚΛΕΩΝ

ἐμοὶ δέ γ᾿ οὐκ ἔστ᾿ οὐδὲ τὴν ὑδρίαν πλάσαι.

ΚΤΩΝ

πρὸς ταῦτα τοῦτον κολάσατ᾿ (οὐ γὰρ ἄν ποτε

LOVECLEON

By god, he obviously did it! Just now he blew a horrible cheesy belch at me, the disgusting cur!

DEMADOGUE

And he didn't share any with me when I asked for some. Tell me, who will be able to give you a square deal unless a scrap or two gets thrown to me, your watchdog?

LOVECLEON

He didn't even share it with the public, that's me! The man's as hot as this soup.

LOATHECLEON

Good heavens, father, don't prejudge his guilt before you hear both sides.

LOVECLEON

But dear boy, it's an open and shut case. The facts bark for themselves!

DEMADOGUE

Just don't you let him off, because of all dogs he's far and away the most hoggish man. Sailed right around the platter he did, and ate the rind off the cities!

LOVECLEON

And me without enough plaster to patch my water pot!

DEMADOGUE

Under the circumstances you must punish him—as they

τρέφειν δύναιτ' ἂν μία λόχμη κλέπτα δύο),
ἵνα μὴ κεκλάγγω διὰ κενῆς ἄλλως ἐγώ·
930 ἐὰν δὲ μή, τὸ λοιπὸν οὐ κεκλάγξομαι.

ΦΙΛΟΚΛΕΩΝ

ἰοὺ ἰού.
ὅσας κατηγόρησε τὰς πανουργίας.
κλέπτον τὸ χρῆμα τἀνδρός. οὐ καὶ σοὶ δοκεῖ,
ὦλεκτρυών; νὴ τὸν Δί' ἐπιμύει γέ τοι.
935 ὁ θεσμοθέτης· ποῦ 'σθ' οὗτος; ἀμίδα μοι δότω.

ΒΔΕΛΥΚΛΕΩΝ

αὐτὸς καθελοῦ· τοὺς μάρτυρας γὰρ εἰσκαλῶ.
Λάβητι μάρτυρας παρεῖναι τρύβλιον,
δοίδυκα, τυρόκνηστιν, ἐσχάραν, χύτραν,
καὶ τἆλλα τὰ σκεύη τὰ προσκεκαυμένα.
940 ἀλλ' ἔτι σύ γ' οὐρεῖς καὶ καθίζεις οὐδέπω;

ΦΙΛΟΚΛΕΩΝ

τοῦτον δέ γ' οἶμ' ἐγὼ χεσεῖσθαι τήμερον.

ΒΔΕΛΥΚΛΕΩΝ

οὐκ αὖ σὺ παύσει χαλεπὸς ὢν καὶ δύσκολος,
καὶ ταῦτα τοῖς φεύγουσιν, ἀλλ' ὀδὰξ ἔχει;
ἀνάβαιν', ἀπολογοῦ. τί σεσιώπηκας; λέγε.

ΦΙΛΟΚΛΕΩΝ

945 ἀλλ' οὐκ ἔχειν οὗτός γ' ἔοικεν ὅ τι λέγῃ.

ΒΔΕΛΥΚΛΕΩΝ

οὔκ, ἀλλ' ἐκεῖνό μοι δοκεῖ πεπονθέναι,
ὅπερ ποτὲ φεύγων ἔπαθε καὶ Θουκυδίδης·

say, one copse can't support two robbers—so all my bark-
ing won't have been for nothing. Otherwise, I won't bark
next time.

LOVECLEON

Wowee! What a mass of misdeeds he's denounced! What a
thieving piece of work the man is! Don't you agree, Mr.
Rooster? By god he does, to judge by his wink. Mr. Chair-
man? Where is he? Chamberpot please!

LOATHECLEON

Get it yourself, I'm summoning the witnesses. (*calling into
the house*) Witnesses for Grabes please be present: Bowl,
Pestle, Cheesegrater, Brazier, Pot, and all other utensils
summoned to testi-fry.

Enter Utensils from the house.

Are you still pissing? Haven't you sat down yet?

LOVECLEON

No, but I think this one'll be shitting himself pretty soon!

LOATHECLEON

Won't you stop being hardhearted and ill tempered, and
toward defendants to boot? Must you chew on them? (*to
Grabes*) Take the stand and present your defence. Why
don't you say something? Speak up!

LOVECLEON

This one seems to have nothing to say for himself.

LOATHECLEON

No, I think the same thing's happened to him that once
happened to Thucydides when he was on trial: his jaws

ἀπόπληκτος ἐξαίφνης ἐγένετο τὰς γνάθους.
πάρεχ᾽ ἐκποδών· ἐγὼ γὰρ ἀπολογήσομαι.
950 χαλεπὸν μέν, ὦνδρες, ἐστὶ διαβεβλημένου
ὑπεραποκρίνεσθαι κυνός, λέξω δ᾽ ὅμως.
ἀγαθὸς γάρ ἐστι καὶ διώκει τοὺς λύκους.

ΦΙΛΟΚΛΕΩΝ

κλέπτης μὲν οὖν οὗτός γε καὶ ξυνωμότης.

ΒΔΕΛΥΚΛΕΩΝ

μὰ Δί᾽, ἀλλ᾽ ἄριστός ἐστι τῶν νυνὶ κυνῶν,
955 οἷός τε πολλοῖς προβατίοις ἐφεστάναι.

ΦΙΛΟΚΛΕΩΝ

τί οὖν ὄφελος, τὸν τυρὸν εἰ κατεσθίει;

ΒΔΕΛΥΚΛΕΩΝ

ὅ τι; σοῦ προμάχεται καὶ φυλάττει τὴν θύραν,
καὶ τἄλλ᾽ ἄριστός ἐστιν. εἰ δ᾽ ὑφείλετο,
σύγγνωθι· κιθαρίζειν γὰρ οὐκ ἐπίσταται.

ΦΙΛΟΚΛΕΩΝ

960 ἐγὼ δ᾽ ἐβουλόμην ἂν οὐδὲ γράμματα,
ἵνα μὴ κακουργῶν ἐνέγραφ᾽ ἡμῖν τὸν λόγον.

ΒΔΕΛΥΚΛΕΩΝ

ἄκουσον, ὦ δαιμόνιε, μου τῶν μαρτύρων.
ἀνάβηθι, τυρόκνηστι, καὶ λέξον μέγα·
σὺ γὰρ ταμιεύουσ᾽ ἔτυχες. ἀπόκριναι σαφῶς,
965 εἰ μὴ κατέκνησας τοῖς στρατιώταις ἄλαβες.
φησὶ κατακνῆσαι.

suddenly got paralyzed.[56] Move over for me; I'll present your defence. It is difficult, gentlemen of the jury, to speak on behalf of a slandered dog, but speak I shall. For he's a good dog, and he chases away the wolves.

LOVECLEON
No, he's a thief and a conspirator!

LOATHECLEON
On the contrary, he's top dog of his generation, able to control a multitude of sheep.

LOVECLEON
What good is that, if he eats the cheese?

LOATHECLEON
Why, he fights for you and guards your door, and he's an all-around top dog. If he did steal, pardon him. You see, he never learned how to play the lyre.

LOVECLEON
I wish he'd never learned reading and writing either; then he couldn't have submitted dishonest accounts to us.

LOATHECLEON
My dear sir, please listen to my witnesses. Take the stand, Cheesegrater, and speak up. Your position was Steward? Answer clearly about your consignment. Didn't you grate it out to the troops? He says he did.

---

[56] Thucydides, son of Melesias, had been Pericles' chief rival until he became tongue-tied at a trial; cf. *Acharnians* 703–12.

ARISTOPHANES

ΦΙΛΟΚΛΕΩΝ

νὴ Δί, ἀλλὰ ψεύδεται.

ΒΔΕΛΤΚΛΕΩΝ

ὦ δαιμόνι᾽, ἐλέει τοὺς ταλαιπωρουμένους.
οὗτος γὰρ ὁ Λάβης καὶ τραχήλι᾽ ἐσθίει
καὶ τὰς ἀκάνθας, κοὐδέποτ᾽ ἐν ταὐτῷ μένει.
970 ὁ δ᾽ ἕτερος οἷός ἐστιν. οἰκουρὸς μόνον·
αὐτοῦ μένων γάρ, ἅττ᾽ ἂν εἴσω τις φέρῃ,
τούτων μεταιτεῖ τὸ μέρος· εἰ δὲ μή, δάκνει.

ΦΙΛΟΚΛΕΩΝ

αἰβοῖ, τί τόδε ποτ᾽ ἔσθ᾽ ὅτῳ μαλάττομαι;
κακόν τι περιβαίνει με, κἀναπείθομαι.

ΒΔΕΛΤΚΛΕΩΝ

975 ἴθ᾽, ἀντιβολῶ σ᾽, οἰκτίρατ᾽ αὐτόν, ὦ πάτερ,
καὶ μὴ διαφθείρητε. ποῦ τὰ παιδία;
ἀναβαίνετ᾽, ὦ πόνηρα, καὶ κνυζούμενα
αἰτεῖτε κἀντιβολεῖτε καὶ δακρύετε.

ΦΙΛΟΚΛΕΩΝ

κατάβα, κατάβα, κατάβα, κατάβα.

ΒΔΕΛΤΚΛΕΩΝ

καταβήσομαι.

980 καίτοι τὸ "κατάβα" τοῦτο πολλοὺς δὴ πάνυ
ἐξηπάτηκεν. ἀτὰρ ὅμως καταβήσομαι.

ΦΙΛΟΚΛΕΩΝ

ἐς κόρακας. ὡς οὐκ ἀγαθόν ἐστι τὸ ῥοφεῖν.
ἐγὼ γὰρ ἀπεδάκρυσα νῦν γνώμην ἐμὴν

LOVECLEON

Sure, but he's lying.

LOATHECLEON

My dear sir, take pity on the careworn. Grabes here lives on a diet of giblets and bones, and he's never in the same place for long. And the other one—look what he is: a mere watchdog. He stays right here, and whatever's brought home he demands a share of, and if he doesn't get it, he bites.

LOVECLEON

Oh no! What can it be that's softening me? Something bad is closing in on me and changing my mind!

LOATHECLEON

Come on, father, I beg you, be merciful to him, don't destroy him! Where are his puppies?

Enter Grabes' Puppies.

Take the stand, you poor things. Whimper, beg, grovel, and weep!

LOVECLEON

Step down, step down, step down, step down!

LOATHECLEON

I'll step down, even though that outcry "step down" has fooled a great many people. Still, I'll step down.

LOVECLEON

Ah hell! It's not good, this slurping. I cried away my better

οὐδέν ποτέ γ᾽ ἀλλ᾽ ἢ τῆς φακῆς ἐμπλήμενος.

ΒΔΕΛΤΚΛΕΩΝ

οὔκουν ἀποφεύγει δῆτα;

ΦΙΛΟΚΛΕΩΝ

985   χαλεπὸν εἰδέναι.

ΒΔΕΛΤΚΛΕΩΝ

ἴθ᾽, ὦ πατρίδιον, ἐπὶ τὰ βελτίω τρέπου.
τηνδὶ λαβὼν τὴν ψῆφον ἐπὶ τὸν ὕστερον
μύσας παρᾶξον κἀπόλυσον, ὦ πάτερ.

ΦΙΛΟΚΛΕΩΝ

οὐ δῆτα· κιθαρίζειν γὰρ οὐκ ἐπίσταμαι.

ΒΔΕΛΤΚΛΕΩΝ

990 φέρε νύν σε τηδὶ τὴν ταχίστην περιάγω.

ΦΙΛΟΚΛΕΩΝ

ὅδ᾽ ἔσθ᾽ ὁ πρότερος;

ΒΔΕΛΤΚΛΕΩΝ

            οὗτος.

ΦΙΛΟΚΛΕΩΝ

               αὕτη ᾽ντευθενί.

ΒΔΕΛΤΚΛΕΩΝ

ἐξηπάτηται κἀπολέλυκεν οὐχ ἑκών.
φέρ᾽ ἐξεράσω.

ΦΙΛΟΚΛΕΩΝ

           πῶς ἄρ᾽ ἠγωνίσμεθα;

judgment, and all because I filled up on hot soup!

LOATHECLEON

He's not getting off, then?

LOVECLEON

It's hard to say.

LOATHECLEON

Come on, daddy, turn over a new leaf. Take this pebble, shut your eyes, rush over to the second urn, and acquit him, father.

LOVECLEON

Absolutely not! I never learned to play the lyre either.

LOATHECLEON

Come on then, let me usher you around this way, it's quickest.

LOVECLEON

This is the first urn?

LOATHECLEON

It is.

LOVECLEON

There she goes!

LOATHECLEON

(*to the audience*) He's fooled; he voted for acquittal unawares. (*to Lovecleon*) Let's do the count.

LOVECLEON

What's our verdict?

ARISTOPHANES

ΒΔΕΛΤΚΛΕΩΝ

δείξειν ἔοικεν. ἐκπέφευγας, ὦ Λάβης.
995 πάτερ πάτερ, τί πέπονθας; οἴμοι. ποῦ 'σθ' ὕδωρ;
ἔπαιρε σαυτόν.

ΦΙΛΟΚΛΕΩΝ

εἰπέ νυν ἐκεῖνό μοι·
ὄντως ἀπέφυγε;

ΒΔΕΛΤΚΛΕΩΝ

νὴ Δί.

ΦΙΛΟΚΛΕΩΝ

οὐδέν εἰμ' ἄρα.

ΒΔΕΛΤΚΛΕΩΝ

μὴ φροντίσῃς, ὦ δαιμόνι', ἀλλ' ἀνίστασο.

ΦΙΛΟΚΛΕΩΝ

πῶς οὖν ἐμαυτῷ τοῦτ' ἐγὼ ξυνείσομαι,
1000 φεύγοντ' ἀπολύσας ἄνδρα; τί ποτε πείσομαι;
ἀλλ', ὦ πολυτίμητοι θεοί, ξύγγνωτέ μοι·
ἄκων γὰρ αὔτ' ἔδρασα κοὐ τοῦ 'μοῦ τρόπου.

ΒΔΕΛΤΚΛΕΩΝ

καὶ μηδὲν ἀγανάκτει γ'. ἐγὼ γάρ σ', ὦ πάτερ,
θρέψω καλῶς, ἄγων μετ' ἐμαυτοῦ πανταχοῖ,
1005 ἐπὶ δεῖπνον, εἰς ξυμπόσιον, ἐπὶ θεωρίαν,
ὥσθ' ἡδέως διάγειν σε τὸν λοιπὸν χρόνον·
κοὐκ ἐγχανεῖταί σ' ἐξαπατῶν Ὑπέρβολος.
ἀλλ' εἰσίωμεν.

LOATHECLEON

I think it will soon be clear. Grabes, you're acquitted! (*as the courtroom parties depart*) Father, father, what's the matter? Dear me! Where's some water? Raise up!

LOVECLEON

Tell me one thing: did he really get off?

LOATHECLEON

He did indeed.

LOVECLEON

Then I'm done for!

LOATHECLEON

My dear father, don't think about it. Just stand up.

LOVECLEON

How am I going to live with this on my conscience, now that I've let a defendant off? Gods almighty, forgive me. I did it unintentionally, it was unlike me!

LOATHECLEON

Don't take it so hard. I'm going to take care of you in fine fashion, father, and take you with me everywhere, to dinner, to parties, to spectacles, so that you'll spend the rest of your days pleasantly; and no longer will Hyperbolus make a fool of you with his lies. Now let's go inside.

351

ΦΙΛΟΚΛΕΩΝ

ταῦτά νυν, εἴπερ δοκεῖ.

ΧΟΡΟΣ

ἀλλ᾽ ἴτε χαίροντες ὅποι βούλεσθ᾽.
ὑμεῖς δὲ τέως,
1010 ὦ μυριάδες ἀναρίθμητοι,
νῦν τὰ μέλλοντ᾽ εὖ λέγεσθαι
μὴ πέσῃ φαύλως χαμᾶζ᾽,
εὐλαβεῖσθε.
τοῦτο γὰρ σκαιῶν θεατῶν
ἐστι πάσχειν, κοὐ πρὸς ὑμῶν.

ΚΟΡΥΦΑΙΟΣ

1015 νῦν αὖτε, λεῴ, προσέχετε τὸν νοῦν, εἴπερ καθαρόν
τι φιλεῖτε.
μέμψασθαι γὰρ τοῖσι θεαταῖς ὁ ποιητὴς νῦν ἐπι-
θυμεῖ.
ἀδικεῖσθαι γάρ φησιν πρότερος πόλλ᾽ αὐτοὺς εὖ πε-
ποιηκώς·
τὰ μὲν οὐ φανερῶς ἀλλ᾽ ἐπικουρῶν κρύβδην
ἑτέροισι ποιηταῖς,
μιμησάμενος τὴν Εὐρυκλέους μαντείαν καὶ διάνοιαν,
1020 εἰς ἀλλοτρίας γαστέρας ἐνδὺς κωμῳδικὰ πολλὰ
χέασθαι,
μετὰ τοῦτο δὲ καὶ φανερῶς ἤδη κινδυνεύων καθ᾽
ἑαυτόν,
οὐκ ἀλλοτρίων ἀλλ᾽ οἰκείων μουσῶν στόμαθ᾽ ἡνιο-
χήσας.

WASPS

LOVECLEON

All right then, if you like.

LOATHECLEON and LOVECLEON go into the house.

CHORUS

Bon voyage, wherever you're going.
And you meanwhile,
you countless thousands,
take care that the good words to follow
don't simply fall to the ground;
that's what happens to stupid spectators,
and is hardly expected from you.

CHORUS LEADER

Now then, people, give me your attention, if you like frank talk. Our poet wants to chastise the audience today. He claims they've wronged him without provocation, even though he's treated them abundantly well, at first not openly but secretly, by helping other poets, taking his cue from the prophetic device of Eurycles:[57] slipping into other men's bellies and making lots of comic material pour out. After that, he took his chances openly on his own, holding the reins not of someone else's team of muses, but

---

[57] A seer-ventriloquist, cf. Plato, *Sophist* 252c, Plutarch, *Moralia* 414c.

ἀρθεὶς δὲ μέγας καὶ τιμηθεὶς ὡς οὐδεὶς πώποτ᾽ ἐν
    ὑμῖν,
οὐκ ἐκτελέσαι φησὶν ἐπαρθείς, οὐδ᾽ ὀγκῶσαι τὸ
    φρόνημα,
1025 οὐδὲ παλαίστρας περικωμάζειν πειρῶν· οὐδ᾽, εἴ τις
    ἐραστὴς
κωμῳδεῖσθαι παιδίχ᾽ ἑαυτοῦ μισῶν ἔσπευσε πρὸς
    αὑτόν,
οὐδενὶ πώποτέ φησι πιθέσθαι, γνώμην τιν᾽ ἔχων
    ἐπιεικῆ,
ἵνα τὰς μούσας αἷσιν χρῆται μὴ προαγωγοὺς
    ἀποφήνῃ·
οὐδ᾽, ὅτε πρῶτόν γ᾽ ἦρξε διδάσκειν, ἀνθρώποις
    φήσ᾽ ἐπιθέσθαι,
1030 ἀλλ᾽ Ἡρακλέους ὀργήν τιν᾽ ἔχων τοῖσι μεγίστοις
    ἐπιχειρεῖν,
θρασέως ξυστὰς εὐθὺς ἀπ᾽ ἀρχῆς αὐτῷ τῷ καρχα-
    ρόδοντι,
οὗ δεινόταται μὲν ἀπ᾽ ὀφθαλμῶν Κύννης ἀκτῖνες
    ἔλαμπον,
ἑκατὸν δὲ κύκλῳ κεφαλαὶ κολάκων οἰμωξομένων
    ἐλιχμῶντο
περὶ τὴν κεφαλήν, φωνὴν δ᾽ εἶχεν χαράδρας ὄλε-
    θρον τετοκυίας,
1035 φώκης δ᾽ ὀσμήν, Λαμίας δ᾽ ὄρχεις ἀπλύτους,
    πρωκτὸν δὲ καμήλου.
τοιοῦτον ἰδὼν τέρας οὔ φησι δείσας καταδωρο-
    δοκῆσαι,

his own. And when he was raised to greatness and honored among you as no one has ever been, he says he didn't end up getting above himself, his head didn't swell, and he didn't start cruising the wrestling schools looking for a pickup. And if a man in love pressed him to satirize a favorite of his, with whom he was angry, he says he never went along with any such request, on the highminded principle that he shouldn't turn the muses he employs into pimps. And when he first began to produce,[58] he says, he didn't attack ordinary people, but in the very spirit of Heracles he came to grips with the greatest monsters, boldly standing up right from the start to old Jagged Teeth himself,[59] whose eyes like the bitch Cynna's flashed terrible beams, and all around his pate licked a hundred heads of damned flatterers; he had the voice of a death dealing torrent, the smell of a seal, the unwashed balls of a Lamia,[60] and the arsehole of a camel. On seeing such an apparition, he says, he didn't get cold feet and take bribes

[58] With *Knights* at the Lenaea of 424.

[59] Cleon. Cynna was a notorious prostitute.

[60] An ogress, evidently hermaphroditic, who ate children; she appeared in plays by Crates and Euripides.

ἀλλ᾽ ὑπὲρ ὑμῶν ἔτι καὶ νυνὶ πολεμεῖ. φησίν τε μετ᾽
    αὐτοῦ
τοῖς ἠπιάλοις ἐπιχειρῆσαι πέρυσιν καὶ τοῖς πυρε-
    τοῖσιν,
οἳ τοὺς πατέρας τ᾽ ἦγχον νύκτωρ καὶ τοὺς πάππους
    ἀπέπνιγον,
1040 κατακλινόμενοί τ᾽ ἐπὶ ταῖς κοίταις ἐπὶ τοῖσιν
    ἀπράγμοσιν ὑμῶν
ἀντωμοσίας καὶ προσκλήσεις καὶ μαρτυρίας
    συνεκόλλων,
ὥστ᾽ ἀναπηδᾶν δειμαίνοντας πολλοὺς ὡς τὸν πολέ-
    μαρχον.
τοιόνδ᾽ εὑρόντες ἀλεξίκακον τῆς χώρας τῆσδε κα-
    θαρτὴν
πέρυσιν καταπρούδοτε καινοτάτας σπείραντ᾽ αὐτὸν
    διανοίας,
1045 ἃς ὑπὸ τοῦ μὴ γνῶναι καθαρῶς ὑμεῖς ἐποιήσατ᾽
    ἀναλδεῖς.
καίτοι σπένδων πόλλ᾽ ἐπὶ πολλοῖς ὄμνυσιν τὸν
    Διόνυσον
μὴ πώποτ᾽ ἀμείνον᾽ ἔπη τούτων κωμῳδικὰ μηδέν᾽
    ἀκοῦσαι.
τοῦτο μὲν οὖν ἐσθ᾽ ὑμῖν αἰσχρὸν τοῖς μὴ γνοῦσιν
    παραχρῆμα·
ὁ δὲ ποιητὴς οὐδὲν χείρων παρὰ τοῖσι σοφοῖς
    νενόμισται,
1050 εἰ παρελαύνων τοὺς ἀντιπάλους τὴν ἐπίνοιαν
    ξυνέτριψεν.

to betray you, but fought then as he fights now on your behalf. And he says that along with the monster he came to grips last year[61] with the shivers and fevers that by night choked fathers and strangled grandfathers, that climbed into the very beds of the peaceable citizens among you, comstructing affidavits, summonses, and depositions, so that many people jumped up in terror and ran to the pole-march.[62] Such a bulwark against evil, such a purifier of the land had you found, when last year you double-crossed him,[63] when he sowed a crop of brand-new ideas that you made fruitless by your failure to understand them clearly. And yet over and over again he swears solemnly by Diony-sus that no one ever heard any comic poetry better than that. So you're all disgraced for failing to appreciate it right away, though our poet is no worse off in the eyes of the sagacious if while overtaking his rivals with a novel concep-tion he took a spill.

---

61 I.e., at the Lenaia of 423, but the play has not been identified; *Merchant Ships* and *Farmers* are possible candidates.

62 The archon in charge of resident aliens; the implication is that professional informers ("sycophants") were typically non-Athenian.

63 By awarding third prize to *Clouds*.

1037 αὐτοῦ] αὐτὸν Bentley

ἀλλὰ τὸ λοιπὸν τῶν ποιητῶν,
ὦ δαιμόνιοι, τοὺς ζητοῦντας
καινόν τι λέγειν κἀξευρίσκειν
στέργετε μᾶλλον καὶ θεραπεύετε,
1055 καὶ τὰ νοήματα σῴζεσθ᾽ αὐτῶν,
ἐσβάλλετέ τ᾽ εἰς τὰς κιβωτοὺς
μετὰ τῶν μήλων.
κἂν ταῦτα ποιῆθ᾽, ὑμῖν δι᾽ ἔτους
τῶν ἱματίων
ὀζήσει δεξιότητος.

ΧΟΡΟΣ

(στρ) ὦ πάλαι ποτ᾽ ὄντες ἡμεῖς ἄλκιμοι μὲν ἐν χοροῖς,
1061 ἄλκιμοι δ᾽ ἐν μάχαις,
καὶ κατ᾽ αὐτὸ τοῦτο μόνον
ἄνδρες ἀλκιμώτατοι.
πρίν ποτ᾽ ἦν πρὶν ταῦτα, νῦν δ᾽
οἴχεται, κύκνου τε πολι-
1065 ώτεραι δὴ αἵδ᾽ ἐπανθοῦσιν τρίχες.
ἀλλὰ κἀκ τῶν λειψάνων δεῖ τῶνδε ῥώμην
νεανικὴν σχεῖν· ὡς ἐγὼ τοὐμὸν νομίζω
γῆρας εἶναι κρεῖττον ἢ πολλῶν κικίννους
1070 νεανιῶν καὶ σχῆμα κεὐρυπρωκτίαν.

ΚΟΡΥΦΑΙΟΣ

εἴ τις ὑμῶν, ὦ θεαταί, τὴν ἐμὴν ἰδὼν φύσιν
εἶτα θαυμάζει μ᾽ ὁρῶν μέσον διεσφηκωμένον,
ἥτις ἡμῶν ἐστιν ἡ 'πίνοια τῆς ἐγκεντρίδος,
ῥᾳδίως ἐγὼ διδάξω "κἂν ἄμουσος ᾖ τὸ πρίν".

But from now on, dear people,
cherish and foster more
the poets who seek to find something fresh to say;
save up their ideas
and put them in your hampers
with the potpourri.
If you do that, next year
your clothes will be fragrant
with the sweet scent of wit.

CHORUS

Ah, once upon a time we were valiant in choruses,
and valiant in battle,
and above all most valiant where *this* is concerned.[64]
But that's long, long ago,
all gone now, and these locks of mine
bloom whiter than a swan.
But even from these ruins we must
summon up youthful strength,
for I think that my
old age outdoes
the ringlets, the getups, and the wide-arsedness
of today's young men.

CHORUS LEADER

Spectators, if any of you has noticed our appearance and
sees our wasp waists, and wonders what's the point of our
stingers, I can easily edify him, "be he ever so unversed

---

[64] Indicating their phalli.

1075 ἐσμὲν ἡμεῖς, οἷς πρόσεστι τοῦτο τοὐρροπύγιον,
Ἀττικοὶ μόνοι δικαίως ἐγγενεῖς αὐτόχθονες,
ἀνδρικώτατον γένος καὶ πλεῖστα τήνδε τὴν πόλιν
ὠφελῆσαν ἐν μάχαισιν, ἡνίκ᾿ ἦλθ᾿ ὁ βάρβαρος,
τῷ καπνῷ τύφων ἅπασαν τὴν πόλιν καὶ πυρπολῶν,
1080 ἐξελεῖν ἡμῶν μενοινῶν πρὸς βίαν τἀνθρήνια.
εὐθέως γὰρ ἐκδραμόντες "ξὺν δορὶ ξὺν ἀσπίδι"
ἐμαχόμεσθ᾿ αὐτοῖσι, θυμὸν ὀξίνην πεπωκότες,
στὰς ἀνὴρ παρ᾿ ἄνδρ᾿, ὑπ᾿ ὀργῆς τὴν χελύνην ἐσθίων.
ὑπὸ δὲ τῶν τοξευμάτων οὐκ ἦν ἰδεῖν τὸν οὐρανόν.
1085 ἀλλ᾿ ὅμως ἐωσάμεσθα ξὺν θεοῖς πρὸς ἑσπέραν·
γλαῦξ γὰρ ἡμῶν πρὶν μάχεσθαι τὸν στρατὸν
διέπτατο.
εἶτα δ᾿ εἱπόμεσθα θυννάζοντες εἰς τοὺς θυλάκους,
οἱ δ᾿ ἔφευγον τὰς γνάθους καὶ τὰς ὀφρῦς κεντού-
μενοι,
ὥστε παρὰ τοῖς βαρβάροισι πανταχοῦ καὶ νῦν ἔτι
1090 μηδὲν Ἀττικοῦ καλεῖσθαι σφηκὸς ἀνδρικώτερον.

ΧΟΡΟΣ

(ἀντ) ἆρα δεινὸς ἦ τόθ᾿, ὥστε πάντας ἐμὲ δεδοικέναι,
καὶ κατεστρεψάμην
τοὺς ἐναντίους, πλέων ἐ-
κεῖσε ταῖς τριήρεσιν.
οὐ γὰρ ἦν ἡμῖν ὅπως
ῥῆσιν εὖ λέξειν ἐμέλλο-
1095 μεν τότ᾿ οὐδὲ συκοφαντήσειν τινὰ

before."[65] We who sport this kind of rump are the only truly indigenous native Athenians, a most virile breed and one that very substantially aided this city in battle, that time the barbarian came spewing smoke over all the city and incinerating it,[66] intent upon forcibly eradicating our hives. Right away we charged forth with spear, with shield, and we fought them, steeped in bitter spirits, each man standing beside the next, biting his lip with fury.[67] We couldn't see the sky for all the arrows overhead,[68] but still, with the gods' help, towards evening we pushed them back; for before the battle an owl had flown over our troops.[69] Then we pursued them, harpooning their baggy pants, and they kept running, stung in the jaws and the eyebrows. That's why to this day barbarians everywhere insist that there's nothing manlier than an Attic wasp.

CHORUS

Yes, I was awesome then, so everybody feared me,
    and I upended
my opponents when I sailed against them on my
        triremes.
No, in those days we didn't care
about getting ready to make a good speech
or to trump up a charge against someone,
but only about who would be

---

[65] From Euripides' *Stheneboea* (fr. 663).

[66] The Persians burned Athens in 480/79.

[67] This action refers to the battle of Marathon in 490.

[68] So Herodotus 7.226, of the battle of Thermopylae in 480.

[69] Athena's bird and so a good omen, especially for Athenians; Plutarch, *Themistocles* 12.1 assigns this omen to the battle of Salamis in 480.

φροντίς, ἀλλ᾽ ὅστις ἐρέτης ἔσοιτ᾽ ἄριστος.
τοιγαροῦν πολλὰς πόλεις Μήδων ἑλόντες
αἰτιώτατοι φέρεσθαι τὸν φόρον δεῦρ᾽
1100   ἐσμέν, ὃν κλέπτουσιν οἱ νεώτεροι.

ΚΟΡΥΦΑΙΟΣ

πολλαχοῦ σκοποῦντες ἡμᾶς εἰς ἅπανθ᾽ εὑρήσετε
τοὺς τρόπους καὶ τὴν δίαιταν σφηξὶν ἐμφερ-
εστάτους.
πρῶτα μὲν γὰρ οὐδὲν ἡμῶν ζῷον ἠρεθισμένον
1105   μᾶλλον ὀξύθυμόν ἐστιν οὐδὲ δυσκολώτερον.
εἶτα τἆλλ᾽ ὅμοια πάντα σφηξὶ μηχανώμεθα.
ξυλλεγέντες γὰρ καθ᾽ ἑσμοὺς ὥσπερ εἰς ἀνθρήνια
οἱ μὲν ἡμῶν οὗπερ ἄρχων, οἱ δὲ παρὰ τοὺς ἕνδεκα,
οἱ δ᾽ ἐν Ὠιδείῳ δικάζουσ᾽, ὧδε πρὸς τοῖς τειχίοις
1110   ξυμβεβυσμένοι πυκνόν, νεύοντες εἰς τὴν γῆν, μόλις
ὥσπερ οἱ σκώληκες ἐν τοῖς κυττάροις κινούμενοι.
ἔς τε τὴν ἄλλην δίαιτάν ἐσμεν εὐπορώτατοι·
πάντα γὰρ κεντοῦμεν ἄνδρα κἀκπορίζομεν βίον.
ἀλλὰ γὰρ κηφῆνες ἡμῖν εἰσιν ἐγκαθήμενοι
1115   οὐκ ἔχοντες κέντρον, οἳ μένοντες ἡμῶν τοῦ φόρου
τὸν γόνον κατεσθίουσιν οὐ ταλαιπωρούμενοι.
τοῦτο δ᾽ ἔστ᾽ ἄλγιστον ἡμῖν, ἤν τις ἀστράτευτος ὢν
ἐκροφῇ τὸν μισθὸν ἡμῶν, τῆσδε τῆς χώρας ὕπερ
μήτε κώπην μήτε λόγχην μήτε φλύκταιναν λαβών.
1120   ἀλλά μοι δοκεῖ τὸ λοιπὸν τῶν πολιτῶν ἔμβραχυ
ὅστις ἂν μὴ 'χῃ τὸ κέντρον μὴ φέρειν τριώβολον.

the best oarsman. That's why
we took many cities from the Medes
and are chiefly responsible
for the tribute's being brought to Athens,
for the younger generation to steal.

CHORUS LEADER

Looking at us from all sides, you'll find that in our character
and lifestyle we're in all respects most like wasps. First, no
creature is more sharp-tempered than we are when irri-
tated, or more cantankerous. Then again, we engineer
everything else just like wasps: we gather in swarms as if
into nests, some of us judging in the archon's court, some
before the Eleven, and some in the Odeum, packed in tight
against the walls like this, hunched toward the ground and
hardly moving, like grubs in their cells. We're very re-
sourceful at making a living, too: we sting everybody and
so provide our daily bread. But the problem is, there are
drones sitting among us who have no stingers, who stay at
home and feed off the fruits of the tribute without toiling
for it. And we're very nettled if some draft dodger gulps
down our pay, when in defence of this country he's never
raised an oar, a lance, or a blister. No, I think that from now
on any citizen, bar none, who doesn't have a stinger should
not be paid three obols.[70]

Enter LOVECLEON, LOATHECLEON, *and a Slave, who car-
ries a fine cloak and boots.*

[70] See 684 ff.

ΦΙΛΟΚΛΕΩΝ

οὔτοι ποτὲ ζῶν τοῦτον ἀποδυθήσομαι,
ἐπεὶ μόνος μ᾽ ἔσωσε παρατεταγμένον,
ὅθ᾽ ὁ βορέας ὁ μέγας ἐπεστρατεύσατο.

ΒΔΕΛΤΚΛΕΩΝ

1125   ἀγαθὸν ἔοικας οὐδὲν ἐπιθυμεῖν παθεῖν.

ΦΙΛΟΚΛΕΩΝ

μὰ τὸν Δί᾽, οὐ γὰρ οὐδαμῶς μοι ξύμφορον.
καὶ γὰρ πρότερον ἐπανθρακίδων ἐμπλήμενος
ἀπέδωκ᾽ ὀφείλων τῷ γναφεῖ τριώβολον.

ΒΔΕΛΤΚΛΕΩΝ

ἀλλ᾽ οὖν πεπειράσθω γ᾽, ἐπειδήπερ γ᾽ ἅπαξ
1130   ἐμοὶ σεαυτὸν παραδέδωκας εὖ ποιεῖν.

ΦΙΛΟΚΛΕΩΝ

τί οὖν κελεύεις δρᾶν με;

ΒΔΕΛΤΚΛΕΩΝ

τὸν τρίβων᾽ ἄφες,
τηνδὶ δὲ χλαῖναν ἀναβαλοῦ τριβωνικῶς.

ΦΙΛΟΚΛΕΩΝ

ἔπειτα παῖδας χρὴ φυτεύειν καὶ τρέφειν,
ὅθ᾽ οὑτοσί με νῦν ἀποπνῖξαι βούλεται;

ΒΔΕΛΤΚΛΕΩΝ

1135   ἔχ᾽, ἀναβαλοῦ τηνδὶ λαβών, καὶ μὴ λάλει.

ΦΙΛΟΚΛΕΩΝ

τουτὶ τὸ κακὸν τί ἐστι, πρὸς πάντων θεῶν;

LOVECLEON

No, I'll never take this off, not while I'm alive! It was my sole salvation when I was in the ranks, when the great north wind[71] made war on us.

LOATHECLEON

You don't seem to want anything nice done for you.

LOVECLEON

God no! It's never done me any good. Once before, when I'd gorged on sprats, I had to pay the cleaner three obols.

LOATHECLEON

Anyway, at least try it on. After all, you *have* put yourself in my hands for good treatment.

LOVECLEON

So, what do you want me to do?

LOATHECLEON

Take off this ratty jacket and nattily put on that cloak.

LOVECLEON

Why should we bear and rear children anyway, when now this one wants to smother me?

LOATHECLEON

Here, take this and put it on, and stop babbling.

LOVECLEON

What the hell is this, for heaven's sake?

[71] "North wind" is a surprise for "the great king" (of Persia); Lovecleon has been wearing his cloak for over 50 years.

ARISTOPHANES

ΒΔΕΛΤΚΛΕΩΝ

οἱ μὲν καλοῦσι Περσίδ᾽, οἱ δὲ καυνάκην.

ΦΙΛΟΚΛΕΩΝ

ἐγὼ δὲ σισύραν ᾠόμην Θυμαιτίδα.

ΒΔΕΛΤΚΛΕΩΝ

κοὐ θαῦμά γ᾽· ἐς Σάρδεις γὰρ οὐκ ἐλήλυθας.
ἔγνως γὰρ ἄν· νῦν δ᾽ οὐχὶ γιγνώσκεις.

ΦΙΛΟΚΛΕΩΝ

1140   ἐγὼ
μὰ τὸν Δί᾽ οὐ τοίνυν, ἀτὰρ δοκεῖ γέ μοι
ἐοικέναι μάλιστα Μορύχου σάγματι.

ΒΔΕΛΤΚΛΕΩΝ

οὔκ, ἀλλ᾽ ἐν Ἐκβατάνοισι ταῦθ᾽ ὑφαίνεται.

ΦΙΛΟΚΛΕΩΝ

ἐν Ἐκβατάνοισι γίγνεται κρόκης χόλιξ;

ΒΔΕΛΤΚΛΕΩΝ

1145 πόθεν, ὦγάθ᾽; ἀλλὰ τοῦτο τοῖσι βαρβάροις
ὑφαίνεται πολλαῖς δαπάναις. αὕτη γέ τοι
ἐρίων τάλαντον καταπέπωκε ῥᾳδίως.

ΦΙΛΟΚΛΕΩΝ

οὔκουν ἐριώλην δῆτ᾽ ἐχρῆν αὐτὴν καλεῖν
δικαιότερόν γ᾽ ἢ καυνάκην;

ΒΔΕΛΤΚΛΕΩΝ

                         ἔχ᾽, ὦγαθέ,
καὶ στῆθ᾽ ἀναμπισχόμενος.

LOATHECLEON

Some call it a Persian cloak, others a tasseled astrakhan.

LOVECLEON

I thought it was an overcoat from Thymaetidae.[72]

LOATHECLEON

No wonder; you've never been to Sardis.[73] Otherwise you'd have recognized it; as it is, you don't.

LOVECLEON

I admit I certainly don't. But it looks to me exactly like Morychus' knapsack.

LOATHECLEON

No it doesn't; these are woven in Ecbatana.[74]

LOVECLEON

In Ecbatana they make woollen sausages?

LOATHECLEON

Where do you get that notion, good sir? No, the natives weave these, at great expense. You know, this one easily sucked down a talent's worth of wool.

LOVECLEON

Then instead of an *astrakhan,* wouldn't it be better to call it a *woolpool?*

LOATHECLEON

Take it, good sir. And stand still while getting a change of clothes.

[72] A coastal deme not far north of Piraeus; *Etymologicum Magnum* 288.15 calls the inhabitants "most juridical," but the joke here is unclear.   [73] Former capital of Lydia.

[74] See *Acharnians* 64 n. Morychus was a noted gourmand.

ΦΙΛΟΚΛΕΩΝ

1150   οἴμοι δείλαιος.
ὡς θερμὸν ἡ μιαρά τί μου κατήρυγεν.

ΒΔΕΛΤΚΛΕΩΝ

οὐκ ἀναβαλεῖ;

ΦΙΛΟΚΛΕΩΝ

μὰ Δί᾽ οὐκ ἔγωγ᾽.

ΒΔΕΛΤΚΛΕΩΝ

                 ἀλλ᾽, ὦγαθέ—

ΦΙΛΟΚΛΕΩΝ

εἴπερ γ᾽ ἀνάγκη, κρίβανόν μ᾽ ἀμπίσχετε.

ΒΔΕΛΤΚΛΕΩΝ

φέρ᾽, ἀλλ᾽ ἐγώ σε περιβάλω. σὺ δ᾽ οὖν ἴθι.

ΦΙΛΟΚΛΕΩΝ

παράθου γε μέντοι καὶ κρεάγραν.

ΒΔΕΛΤΚΛΕΩΝ

1155   τιὴ τί δή;

ΦΙΛΟΚΛΕΩΝ

ἵν᾽ ἐξέλῃς με πρὶν διερρυηκέναι.

ΒΔΕΛΤΚΛΕΩΝ

ἄγε νυν, ὑπολύου τὰς καταράτους ἐμβάδας,
τασδὶ δ᾽ ἀνύσας ὑπόδυθι τὰς Λακωνικάς.

ΦΙΛΟΚΛΕΩΝ

ἐγὼ γὰρ ἂν τλαίην ὑποδύσασθαί ποτε
1160 ἐχθρῶν παρ᾽ ἀνδρῶν δυσμενῆ καττύματα;

WASPS

LOVECLEON

Good grief, what a hot belch the rotten thing blew at me!

LOATHECLEON

Please put it on.

LOVECLEON

I absolutely refuse.

LOATHECLEON

But good sir—

LOVECLEON

If this is compulsory, dress me in an oven instead.

LOATHECLEON

Very well, I'll dress you myself. (*to Slave*) You may go.

LOVECLEON

But at least put a meathook nearby.

LOATHECLEON

Why is that?

LOVECLEON

So you can pull me out before I fall apart.

LOATHECLEON

All right, please take off those accursed sandals. Hurry up and get into these spartans.[75]

LOVECLEON

How in the world could I bear to put on "hateful leathers from enemy lands"?

---

[75] Red boots with straps, worn only by men.

ARISTOPHANES

ΒΔΕΛΤΚΛΕΩΝ

ἔνθες ποτ᾽, ὦ τᾶν, κἀπόβαιν᾽ ἐρρωμένως
ἐς τὴν Λακωνικὴν ἀνύσας.

ΦΙΛΟΚΛΕΩΝ

ἀδικεῖς γέ με
εἰς τὴν πολεμίαν ἀποβιβάζων τὸν πόδα.

ΒΔΕΛΤΚΛΕΩΝ

φέρε, καὶ τὸν ἕτερον.

ΦΙΛΟΚΛΕΩΝ

μηδαμῶς τοῦτόν γ᾽, ἐπεὶ
πάνυ μισολάκων αὐτοῦ ᾽στιν εἷς τῶν δακτύλων.

ΒΔΕΛΤΚΛΕΩΝ

οὐκ ἔστι παρὰ ταῦτ᾽ ἄλλα.

ΦΙΛΟΚΛΕΩΝ

κακοδαίμων ἐγώ,
ὅστις ἐπὶ γήρᾳ χίμετλον οὐδὲν λήψομαι.

ΒΔΕΛΤΚΛΕΩΝ

ἄνυσόν ποθ᾽ ὑποδυσάμενος. εἶτα πλουσίως
ὡδὶ προβὰς τρυφερόν τι διασαλακώνισον.

ΦΙΛΟΚΛΕΩΝ

ἰδού. θεῶ τὸ σχῆμα, καὶ σκέψαι μ᾽ ὅτῳ
μάλιστ᾽ ἔοικα τὴν βάδισιν τῶν πλουσίων.

ΒΔΕΛΤΚΛΕΩΝ

ὅτῳ; δοθιῆνι σκόροδον ἠμφιεσμένῳ.

1165

1170

WASPS

LOATHECLEON

Put it in here any time now, sir. Push down firmly into that spartan, and hurry up.

LOVECLEON

It's a crime to make me set foot on enemy sole!

LOATHECLEON

There. Now the other.

LOVECLEON

Please, not this foot! One of its toes is very anti-Spartan.

LOATHECLEON

You have no choice.

LOVECLEON

Then I'm a goner, with not a single corn to look forward to in my old age!

LOATHECLEON

At least hurry up with the boots. Now step out as the wealthy do, like this, with a sort of voluptuous swagger.

LOVECLEON

All right. Watch my gait, and tell me which rich man walks most like it.

LOATHECLEON

Which one? Someone who's dressed a boil with garlic.

ΦΙΛΟΚΛΕΩΝ

καὶ μὴν προθυμοῦμαί γε σαυλοπρωκτιᾶν.

ΒΔΕΛΤΚΛΕΩΝ

ἄγε νυν, ἐπιστήσει λόγους σεμνοὺς λέγειν
1175 ἀνδρῶν παρόντων πολυμαθῶν καὶ δεξιῶν;

ΦΙΛΟΚΛΕΩΝ

ἔγωγε.

ΒΔΕΛΤΚΛΕΩΝ

τίνα δῆτ᾽ ἂν λέγοις;

ΦΙΛΟΚΛΕΩΝ

πολλοὺς πάνυ.
πρῶτον μὲν ὡς ἡ Λάμι᾽ ἁλοῦσ᾽ ἐπέρδετο,
ἔπειτα δ᾽ ὡς ὁ Καρδοπίων τὴν μητέρα—

ΒΔΕΛΤΚΛΕΩΝ

μὴ ᾽μοιγε μύθους, ἀλλὰ τῶν ἀνθρωπίνων,
1180 οἵους λέγομεν μάλιστα, τοὺς κατ᾽ οἰκίαν.

ΦΙΛΟΚΛΕΩΝ

ἐγᾦδα τοίνυν τῶν γε πάνυ κατ᾽ οἰκίαν
ἐκεῖνον ὡς "οὕτω ποτ᾽ ἦν μῦς καὶ γαλῆ—"

ΒΔΕΛΤΚΛΕΩΝ

ὦ σκαιὲ κἀπαίδευτε—Θεογένης ἔφη
τῷ κοπρολόγῳ, καὶ ταῦτα λοιδορούμενος·
1185 μῦς καὶ γαλᾶς μέλλεις λέγειν ἐν ἀνδράσιν;

ΦΙΛΟΚΛΕΩΝ

ποίους τινὰς δὲ χρὴ λέγειν;

LOVECLEON

I'm actually trying to do the hoochie-koochie.

LOATHECLEON

Now then, will you know how to recount impressive stories in the presence of very knowledgeable and intelligent gentlemen?

LOVECLEON

Sure I will.

LOATHECLEON

What story would you tell, then?

LOVECLEON

I've got lots of stories. First of all, how Lamia farted when captured. Then how Cardopion[76] got hold of his mother and—

LOATHECLEON

I don't want fairytales, I want stories with human interest, the sort we most often tell, the ones we tell at home.

LOVECLEON

Well, I know one that's very much about home, the one that goes, "Once there was a mouse and a cat"—

LOATHECLEON

You ignorant oaf—as Theogenes[77] said to the dung collector, and only while quarrelling. Do you intend to talk about mice and cats in the company of gentlemen?

LOVECLEON

What sort of stories *should* I tell?

---

[76] Unknown.　　[77] A shipowner and politician much satirized in comedy as greedy, boastful, dirty, and boorish.

ARISTOPHANES

ΒΔΕΛΥΚΛΕΩΝ

μεγαλοπρεπεῖς·
ὡς ξυνεθεώρεις Ἀνδροκλεῖ καὶ Κλεισθένει.

ΦΙΛΟΚΛΕΩΝ

ἐγὼ δὲ τεθεώρηκα πώποτ᾽ οὐδαμοῖ,
πλὴν εἰς Πάρον, καὶ ταῦτα δύ᾽ ὀβολὼ φέρων.

ΒΔΕΛΥΚΛΕΩΝ

1190 ἀλλ᾽ οὖν λέγειν χρή σ᾽ ὡς ἐμάχετό γ᾽ αὐτίκα
Ἐφουδίων παγκράτιον Ἀσκώνδᾳ καλῶς,
ἤδη γέρων ὢν καὶ πολιός, ἔχων δέ τοι
πλευρὰν βαθυτάτην καὶ χέρας καὶ λαγόνα καὶ
θώρακ᾽ ἄριστον.

ΦΙΛΟΚΛΕΩΝ

παῦε παῦ᾽, οὐδὲν λέγεις.
1195 πῶς ἂν μαχέσαιτο παγκράτιον θώρακ᾽ ἔχων;

ΒΔΕΛΥΚΛΕΩΝ

οὕτως διηγεῖσθαι νομίζουσ᾽ οἱ σοφοί.
ἀλλ᾽ ἕτερον εἰπέ μοι· παρ᾽ ἀνδράσι ξένοις
πίνων σεαυτοῦ ποῖον ἂν λέξαι δοκεῖς
ἐπὶ νεότητος ἔργον ἀνδρικώτατον;

ΦΙΛΟΚΛΕΩΝ

1200 ἐκεῖν᾽ ἐκεῖν᾽ ἀνδρειότατόν γε τῶν ἐμῶν,
ὅτ᾽ Ἐργασίωνος τὰς χάρακας ὑφειλόμην.

ΒΔΕΛΥΚΛΕΩΝ

ἀπολεῖς με. ποίας χάρακας; ἀλλ᾽ ὡς ἢ κάπρον

LOATHECLEON

Impressive ones, such as how you went on an official embassy with Androcles[78] and Cleisthenes.

LOVECLEON

I've never been on an embassy anywhere, except to Paros, and then I was paid only two obols.

LOATHECLEON

Well, in that case, you should at least tell about Ephudion's fine battle with Ascondas in the pancration,[79] when he was old and grey but had that deep chest, those hands and flanks, those magnificent arms.

LOVECLEON

Hold on now, that's nonsense! How could he have fought in a pancration armed?

LOATHECLEON

That's how sophisticated people typically tell stories. Now tell me something else: if you were drinking with unfamiliar people, what do you think you'd recount as the bravest exploit of your youth?

LOVECLEON

I know, I know! The bravest of my exploits: the time I swiped Ergasion's vine poles.

LOATHECLEON

You'll be the death of me! Vine poles? No, tell how you

---

[78] A demagogic politician who would be assassinated by oligarchs in 411.   [79] The Arcadian athlete Ephudion won the Olympic pancration (free-style wrestling) in 464 while in his prime; nothing is known about Ascondas.

ἐδιώκαθές ποτ᾽ ἢ λαγών, ἢ λαμπάδα
ἔδραμες, ἀνευρὼν ὅ τι νεανικώτατον.

ΦΙΛΟΚΛΕΩΝ

1205 ἐγᾦδα τοίνυν τό γε νεανικώτατον·
ὅτε τὸν δρομέα Φάυλλον ὢν βούπαις ἔτι
εἷλον διώκων λοιδορίας ψήφοιν δυοῖν.

ΒΔΕΛΤΚΛΕΩΝ

παῦ· ἀλλὰ δευρὶ κατακλινεὶς προσμάνθανε
ξυμποτικὸς εἶναι καὶ ξυνουσιαστικός.

ΦΙΛΟΚΛΕΩΝ

πῶς οὖν κατακλινῶ; φράζ᾽ ἀνύσας.

ΒΔΕΛΤΚΛΕΩΝ

1210   εὐσχημόνως.

ΦΙΛΟΚΛΕΩΝ

ὡδὶ κελεύεις κατακλινῆναι;

ΒΔΕΛΤΚΛΕΩΝ

                            μηδαμῶς.

ΦΙΛΟΚΛΕΩΝ

πῶς δαί;

ΒΔΕΛΤΚΛΕΩΝ

            τὰ γόνατ᾽ ἔκτεινε, καὶ γυμναστικῶς
ὑγρὸν χύτλασον σεαυτὸν ἐν τοῖς στρώμασιν.
ἔπειτ᾽ ἐπαίνεσόν τι τῶν χαλκωμάτων,
1215 ὀροφὴν θέασαι, κρεκάδι᾽ αὐλῆς θαύμασον.
ὕδωρ κατὰ χειρός· τὰς τραπέζας εἰσφέρειν·
δειπνοῦμεν· ἀπονενίμμεθ᾽· ἤδη σπένδομεν.

once hunted boar or hare, or ran a torch race. Recall something very lusty.

LOVECLEON

Well, I know what was the lustiest: when I was still a young bull and went after the runner Phayllus and beat him—in a lawsuit for defamation, by two votes.[80]

LOATHECLEON

Stop! Now come over here and recline, and learn how to be symposiastic and convivialistic.

LOVECLEON

How do I recline, then? Hurry up and tell me.

LOATHECLEON

Gracefully.

LOVECLEON

You're telling me to recline like this?

LOATHECLEON

Not at all.

LOVECLEON

Then how?

LOATHECLEON

Extend your legs and pour yourself out on the coverlets in a fluid, athletic way. Then praise one of the bronzes, gaze at the ceiling, admire the room's curtains. Water for our hands; serve the tables; now we're dining; now we've cleaned up; now it's time to pour the wine.

[80] A famous athlete from Croton in Sicily, who commanded a ship in the battle of Salamis in 480.

ARISTOPHANES

ΦΙΛΟΚΛΕΩΝ

πρὸς τῶν θεῶν, ἐνύπνιον ἑστιώμεθα;

ΒΔΕΛΤΚΛΕΩΝ

αὐλητρὶς ἐνεφύσησεν· οἱ δὲ συμπόται
1220 εἰσὶν Θέωρος, Αἰσχίνης, Φᾶνος, Κλέων,
ξένος τις ἕτερος πρὸς κεφαλῆς Ἀκέστορος.
τούτοις ξυνὼν τὰ σκόλι᾽ ὅπως δέξει καλῶς.

ΦΙΛΟΚΛΕΩΝ

ἄληθες; ὡς οὐδείς γε Διακρίων ἐγώ.

ΒΔΕΛΤΚΛΕΩΝ

ἐγὼ εἴσομαι. καὶ δὴ γάρ εἰμ᾽ ἐγὼ Κλέων,
1225 ᾄδω δὲ πρῶτος Ἁρμοδίου, δέξει δὲ σύ.
"οὐδεὶς πώποτ᾽ ἀνὴρ ἔγεντ᾽ Ἀθήναις—"

ΦΙΛΟΚΛΕΩΝ

"—οὐχ οὕτω γε πανοῦργος οὐδὲ κλέπτης."

ΒΔΕΛΤΚΛΕΩΝ

τουτὶ σὺ δράσεις; παραπολεῖ βοώμενος·
φήσει γὰρ ἐξολεῖν σε καὶ διαφθερεῖν
καὶ τῆσδε τῆς γῆς ἐξελᾶν.

ΦΙΛΟΚΛΕΩΝ

1230   ἐγὼ δέ γε,
ἐὰν ἀπειλῇ, νὴ Δί᾽ ἑτέραν ᾄσομαι.
"ὤνθρωφ᾽, οὗτος ὁ μαιόμενος τὸ μέγα κράτος,
1235 ἀντρέψεις ἔτι τὰν πόλιν· ἁ δ᾽ ἔχεται ῥοπᾶς."

1221 Ἀκέστορος legit Σ

378

LOVECLEON

Good heavens, are we dining on dream food?

LOATHECLEON

The girl piper has started to play. Your drinking companions are Theorus, Aeschines, Phanus, Cleon, and a second foreigner next to Acestor.[81] When in the company of men like these, be sure you take up the songs in fine fashion.

LOVECLEON

Oh really? I'll do it better than any Diacrian.[82]

LOATHECLEON

I'll find out. Suppose I'm Cleon, and I start singing the Harmodius Song, and you're going to take it up.
"Never was a man in Athens born . . ."

LOVECLEON

. . . so great a scoundrel, and such a thief!

LOATHECLEON

Is that what you're going to do? You'll be shouted to death! He'll vow to destroy you and annihilate you and hound you out of the country.

LOVECLEON

If he threatens me, by god I'll sing another one:
"You there, the fellow who seeks the high authority, you shall upend the city yet; it's poised to tilt."[83]

---

[81] A tragic dramatist ridiculed in comedy as a parasite with the nickname "Sacas" (implying Asian ancestry). With the variant read "and another foreigner next to you, Acestor's son" (not mentioned elsewhere), implying that Cleon is a foreigner, as in *Knights*.

[82] Diacris was a district in the foothills of Mt. Parnes in northern Attica.   [83] Adapted from Alcaeus' poem warning of the rise of the sixth-century tyrant Pittacus (fr. 141).

ΒΔΕΛΤΚΛΕΩΝ

τί δ', ὅταν Θέωρος πρὸς ποδῶν κατακείμενος
ᾄδῃ Κλέωνος λαβόμενος τῆς δεξιᾶς·
"Ἀδμήτου λόγον, ὦταῖρε, μαθὼν τοὺς ἀγαθοὺς
 φίλει—"
τούτῳ τί λέξεις σκόλιον;

ΦΙΛΟΚΛΕΩΝ

1240   ᾠδικῶς ἐγώ.
"οὐκ ἔστιν ἀλωπεκίζειν,
οὐδ' ἀμφοτέροισι γίγνεσθαι φίλον."

ΒΔΕΛΤΚΛΕΩΝ

μετὰ τοῦτον Αἰσχίνης ὁ Σέλλου δέξεται,
ἀνὴρ σοφὸς καὶ μουσικός, κᾆτ' ᾄσεται·
1245 "χρήματα καὶ βίον
Κλειταγόρᾳ τε κἀ-
μοὶ μετὰ Θετταλῶν—"

ΦΙΛΟΚΛΕΩΝ

"—πολλὰ δὴ διεκόμπασας σὺ κἀγώ."

ΒΔΕΛΤΚΛΕΩΝ

τουτὶ μὲν ἐπιεικῶς σύ γ' ἐξεπίστασαι.
1250 ὅπως δ' ἐπὶ δεῖπνον εἰς Φιλοκτήμονος ἴμεν.
παῖ παῖ· τὸ δεῖπνον, Χρυσέ, συσκεύαζε νῷν·
—ἵνα καὶ μεθυσθῶμεν διὰ χρόνου.

1245 βίον Tyrwhitt: βίαν a

LOATHECLEON

But what happens when Theorus, reclining at your feet,
grasps Cleon's right hand and sings:
"Remember, friend, the story of Admetus,
  and cherish the good people."[84]
What song will you cap that with?

LOVECLEON

I'll be lyrical:
"You cannot be foxy
  or befriend both sides."[85]

LOATHECLEON

After him, Aeschines the son of Hotair will take it up, a
sophisticated and cultured gentleman, and he'll sing:
"Money and substance
  for Clitagora and me
  midst the Thessalians . . ."[86]

LOVECLEON

. . . Yes, we did a lot of boasting, you and I!

LOATHECLEON

This part you seem to understand reasonably well. It's time
we were off to Philoctemon's[87] for dinner. (*calling into the
house*) Boy, boy! Pack dinner for the two of us, Chrysus, so
we can have a real booze-up at long last!

[84] The first line of a poem by Praxilla of Sicyon (fr. 3); Admetus' story was dramatized by Euripides in *Alcestis*.

[85] Source unknown.

[86] *Clitagora* was a popular drinking song, but nothing certain is known about it or its author.

[87] An attested name, but probably chosen here because it means "fond of possessions."

ARISTOPHANES

ΦΙΛΟΚΛΕΩΝ

μηδαμῶς.

κακὸν τὸ πίνειν. ἀπὸ γὰρ οἴνου γίγνεται
καὶ θυροκοπῆσαι καὶ πατάξαι καὶ βαλεῖν,
1255 κἄπειτ᾽ ἀποτίνειν ἀργύριον ἐκ κραιπάλης.

ΒΔΕΛΤΚΛΕΩΝ

οὔκ, ἢν ξυνῇς γ᾽ ἀνδράσι καλοῖς τε κἀγαθοῖς.
ἢ γὰρ παρῃτήσαντο τὸν πεπονθότα,
ἢ λόγον ἔλεξας αὐτὸς ἀστεῖόν τινα,
Αἰσωπικὸν γέλοιον ἢ Συβαριτικόν,
1260 ὧν ἔμαθες ἐν τῷ συμποσίῳ· κᾆτ᾽ ἐς γέλων
τὸ πρᾶγμ᾽ ἔτρεψας, ὥστ᾽ ἀφείς σ᾽ ἀποίχεται.

ΦΙΛΟΚΛΕΩΝ

μαθητέον γ᾽ ἄρ᾽ ἐστὶ πολλοὺς τῶν λόγων,
εἴπερ γ᾽ ἀποτείσω μηδέν, ἤν τι δρῶ κακόν.
ἄγε νυν, ἴωμεν· μηδὲν ἡμᾶς ἰσχέτω.

ΧΟΡΟΣ

(στρ) πολλάκις δὴ 'δοξ᾽ ἐμαυτῷ
1265 δεξιὸς πεφυκέναι καὶ
σκαιὸς οὐδεπώποτε,
ἀλλ᾽ Ἀμυνίας ὁ Σέλλου
μᾶλλον, οὐκ τῶν Κρωβύλου,
οὗτος ὅν γ᾽ ἐγώ ποτ᾽ εἶδον
ἀντὶ μήλου καὶ ῥοᾶς δειπ-
νοῦντα μετὰ Λεωγόρου· πει-

382

LOVECLEON

Oh no! Drinking's bad. Wine gets you doors broken in, assault and battery, then paying money for the damage while you're hung over.

LOATHECLEON

No, not if you're in the company of fine gentlemen. They'll beg the victim off, or else you yourself can tell him some witty story, something funny by Aesop or about Sybaris,[88] one of the stories you learned at the party, and then you've turned the whole thing into a joke, so he lets you off and goes on his merry way.

LOVECLEON

Sure, I'd better learn lots of those stories, if I'm to owe no damages when I do something bad.

Enter a Slave with two dinner baskets.

Come on now, let's go; let nothing stop us now!

Exit LOVECLEON, LOATHECLEON, and Slave.

CHORUS

I've very often thought that I
am naturally intelligent
and never ever stupid,
but Amynias son of Hotair,
he of the Hairbun family, is even more so.
He's the one I once saw
dining with Leogoras

---

[88] The destruction of this luxurious south Italian city by the neighboring Crotonians *c.* 510 inspired many tales about the ineptitude of its pampered inhabitants.

1270   νῆ γὰρ ἧπερ Ἀντιφῶν.

    ἀλλὰ πρεσβεύων γὰρ ἐς Φάρσαλον ᾤχετ᾽·

      εἶτ᾽ ἐκεῖ μόνος μόνοις

    τοῖς Πενέσταισι ξυνῆν τοῖς

      Θετταλῶν, αὐτὸς πενέστης

      ὢν ἐλάττων οὐδενός.

ΚΟΡΥΦΑΙΟΣ

1275   ὦ μακάρι᾽ Αὐτόμενες, ὥς σε μακαρίζομεν.

    παῖδας ἐφύτευσας ὅτι χειροτεχνικωτάτους·

    πρῶτα μὲν ἅπασι φίλον ἄνδρα τε σοφώτατον,

    τὸν κιθαραοιδότατον, ᾧ χάρις ἐφέσπετο·

    τὸν δ᾽ ὑποκριτὴν ἕτερον ἀργαλέον ὡς σοφόν·

1280   εἶτ᾽ Ἀριφράδην πολύ τι θυμοσοφικώτατον,

    ὅντινά ποτ᾽ ὤμοσε μαθόντα παρὰ μηδενὸς

    [ἀλλ᾽ ἀπὸ σοφῆς φύσεως αὐτόματον ἐκμαθεῖν]

    γλωττοποιεῖν εἰς τὰ πορνεῖ᾽ εἰσιόνθ᾽ ἑκάστοτε.

[ἀντ]

    εἰσί τινες οἵ μ᾽ ἔλεγον ὡς καταδιηλλάγην,

1285   ἡνίκα Κλέων μ᾽ ὑπετάραττεν ἐπικείμενος

    καί με κακίσας ἔκνισε, κᾆθ᾽, ὅτ᾽ ἀπεδειρόμην,

    οἱ ᾽κτὸς ἐγέλων μέγα κεκραγότα θεώμενοι,

    οὐδὲν ἄρ᾽ ἐμοῦ μέλον, ὅσον δὲ μόνον εἰδέναι

1282 del. Bothe
1283 post hunc versum lacunam indicavit Σ^{RVΓ}

---

89 The best candidates are the famous sophist and later oligarch, known for high living (cf. Xenophon, *Memorabilia* 1.6), or

instead of eating apple and pomegranate,
for he's as hungry as Antiphon.[89]
And he even went along on an embassy to Pharsalus,[90]
then spent his time there one on one
with the Thessalian Paupers,[91]
being himself a pauper
second to none.

CHORUS LEADER

Lucky Automenes,[92] we think you're so lucky! You've be-
gotten children as skillful as can be. First there's a man
universally loved and very talented, the outstanding lyre
player,[93] whom Charm herself attends. Then there's the
actor,[94] so awfully talented. And then there's Ariphrades,[95]
by far the most intrinsically talented, who, his father once
swore, needed no teacher to learn how to use his tongue
creatively whenever he enters a whorehouse.

< CHORUS >

CHORUS LEADER

There are some who said that I'd made peace, that time[96]
when Cleon laid into me and tried to shake me up some,
and did sting me with abuse. Furthermore, while I was
being skinned alive, the crowd outside kept laughing as
they watched him shouting hard, with no concern at all for

(more likely) Antiphon son of Lysonides, a wealthy man ridiculed
also in Cratinus' *Flask* of 423 (fr. 212).
   [90] A city in Thessaly.
   [91] As the serfs in that region were called.   [92] Unknown.
   [93] Arignotus, cf. *Knights* 1278.   [94] His name is unknown.
   [95] Brother of Arignotus; for his vice cf. *Knights* 1278ff.
   [96] After the performance of *Knights*.

ARISTOPHANES

σκωμμάτιον εἴ ποτέ τι θλιβόμενος ἐκβαλῶ.
1290 ταῦτα κατιδὼν ὑπό τι μικρὸν ἐπιθήκισα·
εἶτα νῦν ἐξηπάτησεν ἡ χάραξ τὴν ἄμπελον.

ΞΑΝΘΙΑΣ

ἰὼ χελῶναι μακάριαι τοῦ δέρματος
[καὶ τρισμακάριαι τοῦ 'πὶ ταῖς πλευραῖς]·
ὡς εὖ κατηρέψασθε καὶ νουβυστικῶς
1295 κεράμῳ τὸ νῶτον, ὥστε τὰς πλευρὰς στέγειν.
ἐγὼ δ' ἀπόλωλα στιζόμενος βακτηρίᾳ.

ΚΟΡΥΦΑΙΟΣ

τί δ' ἐστίν, ὦ παῖ; παῖδα γάρ, κἂν ᾖ γέρων,
καλεῖν δίκαιον ὅστις ἂν πληγὰς λάβῃ.

ΞΑΝΘΙΑΣ

οὐ γὰρ ὁ γέρων ἀτηρότατον ἄρ' ἦν κακὸν
1300 καὶ τῶν ξυνόντων πολὺ παροινικώτατος;
καίτοι παρῆν Ἵππυλλος, Ἀντιφῶν, Λύκων,
Λυσίστρατος, Θούφραστος, οἱ περὶ Φρύνιχον.
τούτων ἁπάντων ἦν ὑβριστότατος μακρῷ.
εὐθὺς γὰρ ὡς ἐνέπλητο πολλῶν κἀγαθῶν,
1305 ἀνήλατ', ἐσκίρτα, 'πεπόρδει, κατεγέλα,
ὥσπερ καχρύων ὀνίδιον εὐωχημένον·

1293 del. Dindorf

---

97 I.e., the attack in *Wasps* shows that Aristophanes has broken
his promise to mitigate his attacks on Cleon.   98 Unknown.

99 A socially prominent man frequently satirized in comedy for
high living, as were his wife and son, the handsome athlete Autoly-

me, save only to see if I would toss up some little joke when squeezed. I saw all this and pulled a little monkey business; and today the stake's played the vine for a fool.[97]

XANTHIAS runs in.

XANTHIAS

Ah tortoises, I envy you your shells! It was good and brainy of you to roof your backs with tile and so cover your sides. Me, I've been bruised within an inch of my life by a walking stick!

CHORUS LEADER

What is it, boy? Yes, it's fair to call anyone "boy" who takes a beating, even if he *is* an old man.

XANTHIAS

Why, see if the old man hasn't turned out to be an utter calamity, and far the most drunk and disorderly man at the party, even though Hippyllus[98] was there, and Antiphon, Lycon,[99] Lysistratus, Thuphrastus,[100] the Phrynichus[101] group. He was far and away the most outrageous of them all. As soon as he'd sated himself with lots of good food, he jumped up and started to prance about, fart, and make fun of people, like a little donkey living it up on barley. And he

cus (portrayed in Xenophon's *Symposium*).   [100] Unknown.

[101] Among several candidates are (1) the comic poet (cf. *Clouds* 566); (2) the oligarch of 411 (cf. *Frogs* 689); (3) the man implicated in the mutilation of the herms in 415, called "the ex-dancer" by Andocides (1.47); and, if this is not the same man, (4) a tragic actor or dancer mentioned in the scholia here, at *Clouds* 1091, and (as "son of Chorocles") *Birds* 750. (3) and/or (4) may be the tragic dancer mentioned in 1490, if this is not a reminiscence of the dead tragic poet (220 n.).

κἄτυπτε δή με νεανικῶς "παῖ παῖ" καλῶν.
εἶτ᾽ αὐτόν, ὡς εἶδ᾽, ἤκασεν Λυσίστρατος·
"ἔοικας, ὦ πρεσβῦτα, νεοπλούτῳ τρυγὶ
1310 κλητῆρί τ᾽ εἰς ἀχυρὸν ἀποδεδρακότι."
ὁ δ᾽ ἀνακραγὼν ἀντήκασ᾽ αὐτὸν πάρνοπι
τὰ θρῖα τοῦ τρίβωνος ἀποβεβληκότι,
Σθενέλῳ τε τὰ σκευάρια διακεκαρμένῳ.
οἱ δ᾽ ἀνεκρότησαν, πλήν γε Θουφράστου μόνου·
1315 οὗτος δὲ διεμύλλαινεν, ὡς δὴ δεξιός.
ὁ γέρων δὲ τὸν Θούφραστον ἤρετ᾽· "εἰπέ μοι,
ἐπὶ τῷ κομᾷς καὶ κομψὸς εἶναι προσποιεῖ,
κωμῳδολοιχῶν περὶ τὸν εὖ πράττοντ᾽ ἀεί;"
τοιαῦτα περιύβριζεν αὐτοὺς ἐν μέρει,
1320 σκώπτων ἀγροίκως καὶ προσέτι λόγους λέγων
ἀμαθέστατ᾽ οὐδὲν εἰκότας τῷ πράγματι.
ἔπειτ᾽, ἐπειδὴ 'μέθυεν, οἴκαδ᾽ ἔρχεται
τύπτων ἅπαντας, ἤν τις αὐτῷ ξυντύχῃ.
ὁδὶ δὲ καὶ δὴ σφαλλόμενος προσέρχεται.
1325 ἀλλ᾽ ἐκποδὼν ἄπειμι πρὶν πληγὰς λαβεῖν.

ΦΙΛΟΚΛΕΩΝ

ἄνεχε, πάρεχε.
κλαύσεταί τις τῶν ὄπισθεν
ἐπακολουθούντων ἐμοί.
οἷον, εἰ μὴ 'ρρήσεθ᾽, ὑμᾶς,
1330 ὦ πόνηροι, ταυτηὶ τῇ
δᾳδὶ φρυκτοὺς σκευάσω.

1309 τρυγὶ] Φρυγὶ Kock

388

gave me a right lusty beating, all the while yelling "boy, boy." Lysistratus took one look at him and made a comparison: "Old fellow, you're like a *nouveau riche* teenager, or an ass that's slipped away to a bran pile!" And he bellowed back with his own comparison of Lysistratus to a locust that's lost the wings off its cloak, or Sthenelus[102] shorn of his stage props. Everyone applauded, with the sole exception of Thuphrastus, who pursed his lips, as being intelligent. Then the old man asked Thuphrastus, "Say, why do you act the bigwig and pretend to be stylish, when you're only a clown sucking up to anyone who's doing well at the moment?" That's the way he insulted them, one after the other, mocking them like a yokel and also telling stories that were completely inappropriate to the situation. And after he gets drunk, he starts for home, hitting everyone who meets him. Look, here he comes, staggering drunk. I'm going to get out of his way before I start catching punches!

XANTHIAS runs into the house. LOVECLEON staggers in, one hand holding a torch and the other Dardanis. Lovecleon's VICTIMS follow.

LOVECLEON

Give way! Make way!
Some of those people back there following me
are going to be very sorry!
You scoundrels, if you don't scatter off,
oh how I'll make fried fish of you
with this torch!

[102] A tragic dramatist whose writing Aristotle considered uninspired, *Poetics* 1458a18-21.

ARISTOPHANES

ΑΝΗΡ

ἦ μὴν σὺ δώσεις αὔριον τούτων δίκην
ἡμῖν ἅπασιν, κεἰ σφόδρ' εἶ νεανίας.
ἀθρόοι γὰρ ἥξομέν σε προσκαλούμενοι.

ΦΙΛΟΚΛΕΩΝ

1335 ἰὴ ἰηῦ, "καλούμενοι".
ἀρχαῖά γ' ὑμῶν. ἆρά γ' ἴσθ'
ὡς οὐδ' ἀκούων ἀνέχομαι
δικῶν; ἰαιβοῖ αἰβοῖ.
τάδε μ' ἀρέσκει· βάλλε κημούς.
1340 οὐκ ἄπει; ποῦ 'στ'
ἡλιαστής; ἐκποδών.

ἀνάβαινε δεῦρο, χρυσομηλολόνθιον,
τῇ χειρὶ τουδὶ λαβομένη τοῦ σχοινίου.
ἔχου· φυλάττου δ', ὡς σαπρὸν τὸ σχοινίον·
ὅμως γε μέντοι τριβόμενον οὐκ ἄχθεται.
1345 ὁρᾷς ἐγώ σ' ὡς δεξιῶς ὑφειλόμην
μέλλουσαν ἤδη λεσβιεῖν τοὺς ξυμπότας·
ὧν εἵνεκ' ἀπόδος τῷ πέει τῳδὶ χάριν.
ἀλλ' οὐκ ἀποδώσεις οὐδ' ἐφιαλεῖς, οἶδ' ὅτι,
ἀλλ' ἐξαπατήσεις κἀγχανεῖ τούτῳ μέγα·
1350 πολλοῖς γὰρ ἤδη χἀτέροις αὔτ' ἠργάσω.
ἐὰν γένῃ δὲ μὴ κακὴ νυνὶ γυνή,
ἐγώ σ', ἐπειδὰν οὑμὸς υἱὸς ἀποθάνῃ,
λυσάμενος ἔξω παλλακήν, ὦ χοιρίον.
νῦν δ' οὐ κρατῶ 'γὼ τῶν ἐμαυτοῦ χρημάτων·

390

WASPS

VICTIM

You'll certainly have to answer for this tomorrow, to all of
us, even if you *are* a young blade. We'll all be here together,
with summonses.

LOVECLEON

Goodness me! Summonses!
How old-fashioned of you. Don't you know
that I can't even stand to hear
about lawsuits? Yuk, yuk!
This is what I like! Down with voting urns!
Get along! Where's
a juror, eh? Get out of here!

VICTIMS run away.

(*ascending the steps to his door*) Come up this way, my
little blonde cockchafer. (*offering his phallus*) Grab hold of
this rope here with your hand. Hang on, but be careful, the
rope's worn out; all the same, it doesn't mind being rubbed.
Did you see how handily I sneaked you away just when you
were supposed to start sucking the guests? For that you
owe my cock here a favor. But no, you won't pay up, you
won't come through, I know it. You'll trick me and stick
your tongue way out at it; you've done the same to lots of
other men. But if you don't act like a mean woman to me
now, I promise that, as soon as my son dies, I'll buy your
freedom and keep you as a concubine, my little pussy. As
it is, I don't control my own property. I'm young, and I'm

1335 ἰηῦ West, cf. *Pacem* 195: ἰεῦ a

1355 νέος γάρ εἰμι. καὶ φυλάττομαι σφόδρα·
τὸ γὰρ ὑίδιον τηρεῖ με, κἄστι δύσκολον
κἄλλως κυμινοπριστοκαρδαμογλύφον.
ταῦτ᾽ οὖν περί μου δέδοικε μὴ διαφθαρῶ·
πατὴρ γὰρ οὐδείς ἐστιν αὐτῷ πλὴν ἐμοῦ.
1360 ὁδὶ δὲ καὐτός. ἐπὶ σὲ κἄμ᾽ ἔοικε θεῖν.
ἀλλ᾽ ὡς τάχιστα στῆθι τάσδε τὰς δετὰς
λαβοῦσ᾽, ἵν᾽ αὐτὸν τωθάσω νεανικῶς,
οἵοις ποθ᾽ οὗτος ἐμὲ πρὸ τῶν μυστηρίων.

ΒΔΕΛΤΚΛΕΩΝ
ὦ οὗτος οὗτος, τυφεδανὲ καὶ χοιρόθλιψ,
1365 ποθεῖν ἐρᾶν τ᾽ ἔοικας ὡραίας σοροῦ.
οὔτοι καταπροίξει μὰ τὸν Ἀπόλλω τοῦτο δρῶν.

ΦΙΛΟΚΛΕΩΝ
ὡς ἡδέως φάγοις ἂν ἐξ ὄξους δίκην.

ΒΔΕΛΤΚΛΕΩΝ
οὐ δεινὰ τωθάζειν σε τὴν αὐλητρίδα
τῶν ξυμποτῶν κλέψαντα;

ΦΙΛΟΚΛΕΩΝ
                    ποίαν αὐλητρίδα;
1370 τί ταῦτα ληρεῖς ὥσπερ ἀπὸ τύμβου πεσών;

ΒΔΕΛΤΚΛΕΩΝ
νὴ τὸν Δί᾽, αὕτη πού ᾽στί σοί γ᾽ ἡ Δαρδανίς.

ΦΙΛΟΚΛΕΩΝ
οὔκ, ἀλλ᾽ ἐν ἀγορᾷ τοῖς θεοῖς δᾷς κάεται.

carefully guarded: my little son watches me. He's grouchy,
and on top of that he's a cress- and cumin-peeling skinflint.
You see, he's worried that I'll be spoiled; I'm the only father
he's got. But here he comes! He seems to be chasing after
you and me. Quick now, take this torch and stand still, so
I can play teenage tricks on him, the same tricks he played
on me when I stood for initiation.[103]

Enter LOATHECLEON.

LOATHECLEON

You there! Yes you, you psychotic pussy squeezer! You
seem to be fondly infatuated with a fresh—coffin! You
won't get away with this behavior, by Apollo you won't.

LOVECLEON

I can see you'd enjoy the taste of a good sour lawsuit!

LOATHECLEON

How dare you pull my leg, after stealing the girl piper from
the guests!

LOVECLEON

What girl piper? What's this you're raving about, like a man
who's taken leave of his—tomb?

LOATHECLEON

By god, this has got to be Dardanis you've got here!

LOVECLEON

No, it's a torch in the marketplace burning for the gods.

---

[103] Into the Eleusinian Mysteries, which featured ritual mock-
ery of initiates.

ΒΔΕΛΤΚΛΕΩΝ

δὰς ἥδε;

ΦΙΛΟΚΛΕΩΝ

δὰς δῆτ'. οὐχ ὁρᾷς ἐσχισμένην;

ΒΔΕΛΤΚΛΕΩΝ

τί δαὶ τὸ μέλαν τοῦτ' ἐστὶν αὐτῆς τοὐν μέσῳ;

ΦΙΛΟΚΛΕΩΝ

1375 ἡ πίττα δήπου καομένης ἐξέρχεται.

ΒΔΕΛΤΚΛΕΩΝ

ὁ δ' ὄπισθεν οὐχὶ πρωκτός ἐστιν οὑτοσί;

ΦΙΛΟΚΛΕΩΝ

ὄζος μὲν οὖν τῆς δᾳδὸς οὗτος ἐξέχει.

ΒΔΕΛΤΚΛΕΩΝ

τί λέγεις σύ; ποῖος ὄζος; οὐκ εἶ δεῦρο σύ;

ΦΙΛΟΚΛΕΩΝ

ἂ ἂ, τί μέλλεις δρᾶν;

ΒΔΕΛΤΚΛΕΩΝ

ἄγειν ταύτην λαβὼν

1380 ἀφελόμενός σε καὶ νομίσας εἶναι σαπρὸν
κοὐδὲν δύνασθαι δρᾶν.

ΦΙΛΟΚΛΕΩΝ

ἄκουσόν νυν ἐμοῦ.

Ὀλυμπίασιν, ἡνίκ' ἐθεώρουν ἐγώ,
Ἐφουδίων ἐμαχέσατ' Ἀσκώνδᾳ καλῶς
ἤδη γέρων ὤν· εἶτα τῇ πυγμῇ θενὼν

LOATHECLEON

This is a torch?

LOVECLEON

Yes, a torch. Don't you see its cleavage?

LOATHECLEON

And what's this dark patch in the middle?

LOVECLEON

That's easy: pitch coming out when it's hot.

LOATHECLEON

And behind here, isn't this an arsehole?

LOVECLEON

No, that's a knothole sticking out of the torch.

LOATHECLEON

What do you mean? Knothole! (*to Dardanis*) You get over here!

LOVECLEON

Hey, hey, what do you think you're doing?

LOATHECLEON

Grabbing her and taking her away from you, because I'm convinced that you're worn out and utterly unable to perform.

LOVECLEON

Listen to me now. When I was at Olympia on an embassy, Ephudion put up a fine fight against Ascondas, even as an old man. Then the older man hit the younger with his fist

1385 ὁ πρεσβύτερος κατέβαλε τὸν νεώτερον.
πρὸς ταῦτα τηροῦ μὴ λάβῃς ὑπώπια.

ΒΔΕΛΤΚΛΕΩΝ

νὴ τὸν Δί', ἐξέμαθές γε τὴν Ὀλυμπίαν.

ΑΡΤΟΠΩΛΙΣ

ἴθι μοι, παράστηθ', ἀντιβολῶ, πρὸς τῶν θεῶν.
ὁδὶ γὰρ ἀνήρ ἐστιν ὅς μ' ἀπώλεσεν
1390 τῇ δᾳδὶ παίων, κἀξέβαλεν ἐντευθενὶ
ἄρτους δέκ' ὀβολῶν κἀπιθήκην τέτταρας.

ΒΔΕΛΤΚΛΕΩΝ

ὁρᾷς ἃ δέδρακας; πράγματ' αὖ δεῖ καὶ δίκας
ἔχειν διὰ τὸν σὸν οἶνον.

ΦΙΛΟΚΛΕΩΝ

οὐδαμῶς γ', ἐπεὶ
λόγοι διαλλάξουσιν αὐτὰ δεξιοί·
1395 ὥστ' οἶδ' ὁτιὴ ταύτῃ διαλλαχθήσομαι.

ΑΡΤΟΠΩΛΙΣ

οὔτοι μὰ τὼ θεὼ καταπροίξει Μυρτίας
τῆς Ἀγκυλίωνος θυγατέρος καὶ Σωστράτης
οὕτω διαφθείρας ἐμοῦ τὰ φορτία.

ΦΙΛΟΚΛΕΩΝ

ἄκουσον, ὦ γύναι· λόγον σοι βούλομαι
λέξαι χαρίεντα.

and knocked him down. (*he knocks Loathecleon down*)
The moral: you should beware of getting a pair of black
eyes.

Dardanis runs off.

LOATHECLEON

By god, you've certainly learned the lesson about Olympia!

Enter MYRTIA *with an empty tray, and Chaerephon.*

MYRTIA

(*to Chaerephon*) Come here and stand by me; in the name
of the gods, please. That's the man who beat me with his
torch and demolished me, and who knocked ten obols'
worth of bread off here, plus four loaves more.

LOATHECLEON

See what you've done? Now we're sure to have trouble and
lawsuits, because of your drinking.

LOVECLEON

Not at all! Some adroit storytelling will settle things. I
know just how I'll settle things with this woman.

MYRTIA

No, by the Twin Gods,[104] you'll not sweet-talk Myrtia,
daughter of Ancylion and Sostrate,[105] after my stock's been
ruined like this!

LOVECLEON

Listen, madam; I'd like to tell you a charming story.

104 Demeter and Kore, a women's oath.
105 Myrtia insists on her citizen status; the names are ordinary.

ARISTOPHANES

ΑΡΤΟΠΩΛΙΣ

1400
μὰ Δία μὴ 'μοιγ', ὦ μέλε.

ΦΙΛΟΚΛΕΩΝ

Αἴσωπον ἀπὸ δείπνου βαδίζονθ' ἑσπέρας
θρασεῖα καὶ μεθύση τις ὑλάκτει κύων.
κἄπειτ' ἐκεῖνος εἶπεν· "ὦ κύον κύον,
εἰ νὴ Δί' ἀντὶ τῆς κακῆς γλώττης ποθὲν
1405
πυροὺς πρίαιο, σωφρονεῖν ἄν μοι δοκεῖς."

ΑΡΤΟΠΩΛΙΣ

καὶ καταγελᾷς μου; προσκαλοῦμαί σ', ὅστις εἶ,
πρὸς τοὺς ἀγορανόμους βλάβης τῶν φορτίων,
κλητῆρ' ἔχουσα Χαιρεφῶντα τουτονί.

ΦΙΛΟΚΛΕΩΝ

μὰ Δί', ἀλλ' ἄκουσον, ἤν τί σοι δόξω λέγειν.
1410
Λᾶσός ποτ' ἀντεδίδασκε καὶ Σιμωνίδης·
ἔπειθ' ὁ Λᾶσος εἶπεν· "ὀλίγον μοι μέλει."

ΑΡΤΟΠΩΛΙΣ

ἄληθες, οὗτος;

ΦΙΛΟΚΛΕΩΝ
καὶ σὺ δή μοι, Χαιρεφῶν,
γυναικὶ κλητεύεις ἐοικὼς θαψίνῃ

---

106 Lasus of Hermione was invited to Athens by the tyrant
Hipparchus between 527 and 514, where he may have helped to
establish the contests in dithyramb, his poetic specialty. Collec-

MYRTIA

Don't you tell it to *me,* sir.

LOVECLEON

When Aesop was walking home from dinner one evening, a bold and tipsy bitch started barking at him. And he said, "Bitch, bitch, if you'd trade that nasty tongue of yours for some flour, I think you'd be showing sense."

MYRTIA

Laughing at me too, are you? I'm summoning you, whatever your name is, to appear before the commissioners of the marketplace for ruining my stock, with Chaerephon here as my witness.

LOVECLEON

No! Just listen and see if you think I'm making sense. Once Lasus[106] and Simonides[107] were training rival choruses, and Lasus said, "I couldn't care less."

MYRTIA

So that's your attitude?

MYRTIA and Chaerephon walk off.

LOVECLEON

(*shouting after them*) Tell me Chaerephon, are you really acting as a summons witness for a woman? You look like a

tions of his witty sayings were still read in Roman times (cf. Athenaeus 8.338).

[107] Simonides of Ceus, one of the greatest Greek lyric poets, was, like Lasus, invited to Athens by Hipparchus; he boasted of 56 first prizes in dithyramb (*Epigrams* 27 Campbell), and his wise sayings were collected.

Ἰνοῖ κρεμαμένη πρὸς ποδῶν Εὐριπίδου;

ΒΔΕΛΤΚΛΕΩΝ

1415 ὁδί τις ἕτερος, ὡς ἔοικεν, ἔρχεται
καλούμενός σε· τόν γέ τοι κλητῆρ᾽ ἔχει.

ΚΑΤΗΓΟΡΟΣ

οἴμοι κακοδαίμων. προσκαλοῦμαί σ᾽, ὦ γέρον,
ὕβρεως.

ΒΔΕΛΤΚΛΕΩΝ

ὕβρεως; μὴ μὴ καλέσῃς, πρὸς τῶν θεῶν.
ἐγὼ γὰρ ὑπὲρ αὐτοῦ δίκην δίδωμί σοι,
1420 ἣν ἂν σὺ τάξῃς, καὶ χάριν προσείσομαι.

ΦΙΛΟΚΛΕΩΝ

ἐγὼ μὲν οὖν αὐτῷ διαλλαχθήσομαι
ἑκών· ὁμολογῶ γὰρ πατάξαι καὶ βαλεῖν.
ἀλλ᾽ ἐλθὲ δευρί. πότερον ἐπιτρέπεις ἐμοὶ
ὅ τι χρή μ᾽ ἀποτείσαντ᾽ ἀργύριον τοῦ πράγματος
1425 εἶναι φίλον τὸ λοιπόν, ἢ σύ μοι φράσεις;

ΚΑΤΗΓΟΡΟΣ

σὺ λέγε. δικῶν γὰρ οὐ δέομ᾽ οὐδὲ πραγμάτων.

ΦΙΛΟΚΛΕΩΝ

ἀνὴρ Συβαρίτης ἐξέπεσεν ἐξ ἅρματος,
καί πως κατεάγη τῆς κεφαλῆς μέγα σφόδρα·
ἐτύγχανεν γὰρ οὐ τρίβων ὢν ἱππικῆς.
1430 κἄπειτ᾽ ἐπιστὰς εἶπ᾽ ἀνὴρ αὐτῷ φίλος·
"ἔρδοι τις ἣν ἕκαστος εἰδείη τέχνην."

sallow Ino clutching the feet of Euripides![108]

LOATHECLEON

Here's someone else on his way to summon you; look, he's
got a witness with him.

Enter ACCUSER with Witness.

ACCUSER

(*clutching his head*) Oh, what a calamity! I summon you,
old man, for assault!

LOATHECLEON

Assault? Please, don't summon him for that; good heavens!
I'll compensate you on his behalf, whatever amount you
propose, and you will also have my gratitude.

LOVECLEON

No, I volunteer to settle with him. I admit I punched him
and pelted him. (*to Accuser*) Come over here. Will you let
me decide how much money I'll pay in this matter, and
then we'll be friends from now on, or will you make a
proposal?

ACCUSER

You say. I don't need any lawsuits and trouble.

LOVECLEON

A man from Sybaris[109] fell out of a chariot, and somehow
he got his head seriously injured. It happens he wasn't an
experienced driver. And then a friend of his stood over him
and said, "Let each practice the craft he knows." So why

---

[108] Substituting the tragedian for one of his characters, prob-
ably Ino's husband Athamas, whose second wife Ino had tricked
into killing her own children instead of Ino's. The point of Love-
cleon's allusion is elusive.   [109] See 1259 n.

οὕτω δὲ καὶ σὺ παράτρεχ᾽ εἰς τὰ Πιττάλου.

ΒΔΕΛΤΚΛΕΩΝ
ὅμοιά σοι καὶ ταῦτα τοῖς ἄλλοις τρόποις.

ΚΑΤΗΓΟΡΟΣ
ἀλλ᾽ οὖν σὺ μέμνησ᾽ αὐτὸς ἀπεκρίνατο.

ΦΙΛΟΚΛΕΩΝ
1435   ἄκουε, μὴ φεῦγ᾽. ἐν Συβάρει γυνή ποτε
κατέαξ᾽ ἐχῖνον.

ΚΑΤΗΓΟΡΟΣ
ταῦτ᾽ ἐγὼ μαρτύρομαι.

ΦΙΛΟΚΛΕΩΝ
οὑχῖνος οὖν ἔχων τιν᾽ ἐπεμαρτύρατο.
εἶθ᾽ ἡ Συβαρῖτις εἶπεν· "εἰ ναὶ τὰν Κόραν
τὴν μαρτυρίαν ταύτην ἐάσας ἐν τάχει
1440   ἐπίδεσμον ἐπρίω, νοῦν ἂν εἶχες πλείονα."

ΚΑΤΗΓΟΡΟΣ
ὕβριζ᾽, ἕως ἂν τὴν δίκην ἄρχων καλῇ.

ΒΔΕΛΤΚΛΕΩΝ
οὗτοι μὰ τὴν Δήμητρ᾽ ἔτ᾽ ἐνταυθοῖ μενεῖς,
ἀλλ᾽ ἀράμενος οἴσω σε—

ΦΙΛΟΚΛΕΩΝ
τί ποιεῖς;

ΒΔΕΛΤΚΛΕΩΝ
ὅ τι ποιῶ;
εἴσω φέρω σ᾽ ἐντεῦθεν· εἰ δὲ μή, τάχα
κλητῆρες ἐπιλείψουσι τοὺς καλουμένους.

don't you do the same and run off to Pittalus' clinic!

LOATHECLEON

You know, this is just like the rest of your behavior.

ACCUSER

In that case, see that you remember his reply.

LOVECLEON

Listen, don't run away! Once upon a time in Sybaris, a woman broke her pot.

ACCUSER

Witness, take note!

LOVECLEON

So this pot told its companion to be a witness. Then the Sybarite woman said, "By Kore, if you'd let this witness business go and bought a bandage right away, you'd have been smarter!"

ACCUSER

Go on, be outrageous—until the magistrate calls your case!

LOATHECLEON

By Demeter, you'll not stay out here any longer; I'm going to pick you up and carry you—

LOVECLEON

What are you doing?

LOATHECLEON

What am I doing? I'm carrying you into the house. If I don't, the people who want to summon you will run out of witnesses!

ARISTOPHANES

1445 Αἴσωπον οἱ Δελφοί ποτ'—

ΒΔΕΛΤΚΛΕΩΝ

ὀλίγον μοι μέλει.

ΦΙΛΟΚΛΕΩΝ

—φιάλην ἐπῃτιῶντο κλέψαι τοῦ θεοῦ.
ὁ δ' ἔλεξεν αὐτοῖς ὡς ὁ κάνθαρός ποτε—

ΒΔΕΛΤΚΛΕΩΝ

οἴμ', ὡς ἀπολεῖς με τοῖσι σοῖσι κανθάροις.

ΧΟΡΟΣ

(στρ) ζηλῶ γε τῆς εὐτυχίας
τὸν πρέσβυν, οἷ μετέστη
1451 ξηρῶν τρόπων καὶ βιοτῆς.
ἕτερα δὲ νῦν ἀντιμαθὼν
ἦ μέγα τι μεταπεσεῖται
ἐπὶ τὸ τρυφῶν καὶ μαλακόν.
1455 τάχα δ' ἂν ἴσως οὐκ ἐθέλοι·
τὸ γὰρ ἀποστῆναι χαλεπὸν
φύσεως, ἣν ἔχοι τις ἀεί.
καίτοι πολλοὶ ταῦτ' ἔπαθον·
ξυνόντες γνώμαις ἑτέρων
1460 μετεβάλοντο τοὺς τρόπους.

(ἀντ) πολλοῦ δ' ἐπαίνου παρ' ἐμοὶ

---

[110] A well-known Aesopic fable (3 Perry, Schol. *Peace* 130)

LOVECLEON

One time the Delphians accused Aesop—

LOATHECLEON

I'm not interested!

LOVECLEON

—of stealing a bowl from the god. He told them how once upon a time the beetle—[110]

LOATHECLEON

Damn it, you'll be the death of me with these beetles of yours!

LOVECLEON and LOATHCLEON go into the house.

CHORUS

I do envy the old man
his luck; what a turn-around
from his arid habits and lifestyle!
Now he's learned different ways,
and he'll make a really great change
to a life of delicate luxury.
But maybe he'll not want that;
it's hard for anyone to depart
from his normal and natural character.
Yet many have had this experience;
when exposed to others' ideas,
they have changed their habits.

With high praise from me

whose moral was that a determined victim, no matter how power-less, can have his revenge; for the legend of Aesop's death at Delphi see the *Life of Aesop* 124-42 Perry.

καὶ τοῖσιν εὖ φρονοῦσιν
τυχὼν ἄπεισιν διὰ τὴν
1465   φιλοπατρίαν καὶ σοφίαν
ὁ παῖς ὁ Φιλοκλέωνος.
οὐδενὶ γὰρ οὕτως ἀγανῷ
ξυνεγενόμην, οὐδὲ τρόποις
ἐπεμάνην οὐδ᾽ ἐξεχύθην.
1470   τί γὰρ ἐκεῖνος ἀντιλέγων
οὐ κρείττων ἦν, βουλόμενος
τὸν φύσαντα σεμνοτέροις
κατακοσμῆσαι πράγμασιν;

ΞΑΝΘΙΑΣ

νὴ τὸν Διόνυσον, ἀπορά γ᾽ ἡμῖν πράγματα
1475 δαίμων τις εἰσκεκύκληκεν εἰς τὴν οἰκίαν.
ὁ γὰρ γέρων, ὡς ἔπιε διὰ πολλοῦ χρόνου
ἤκουσέ τ᾽ αὐλοῦ, περιχαρὴς τῷ πράγματι
ὀρχούμενος τῆς νυκτὸς οὐδὲν παύεται
τἀρχαῖ᾽ ἐκεῖν᾽ οἷς Θέσπις ἠγωνίζετο·
1480 καὶ τοὺς τραγῳδούς φησιν ἀποδείξειν Κρόνους
τοὺς νῦν διορχησάμενος ὀλίγον ὕστερον.

ΦΙΛΟΚΛΕΩΝ

τίς ἐπ᾽ αὐλείοισι θύραις θάσσει;

ΞΑΝΘΙΑΣ

τουτὶ καὶ δὴ χωρεῖ τὸ κακόν.

and from others with good sense,
he'll go his way, thanks to
filial love and understanding,
this son of Lovecleon.
So kind a man I've never
met, nor with anyone's behavior
have I been so ecstatic and melted away.
For where in his rebuttals
was he not superior, in his wish
to adorn his begetter
with more dignified pursuits?

XANTHIAS comes out of the house.

XANTHIAS
By Dionysus, some god has set our house awhirl with some
baffling business! Since the old man hadn't had a drink or
heard the pipes for so long, he's overjoyed with the whole
business, and all night he hasn't stopped dancing those old
dances that Thespis used in his competitions.[111] And he
says that pretty soon he'll take on the modern tragic danc-
ers and show them up as old Cronuses.

LOVECLEON appears at the door.

LOVECLEON
Who couches at the outer gates?

XANTHIAS
There he is, here comes the trouble!

---

[111] The earliest known tragic poet, for whom a victory is at-
tested in 534.

ΦΙΛΟΚΛΕΩΝ

κλῆθρα χαλάσθω τάδε. καὶ δὴ γὰρ
1485 σχήματος ἀρχὴ—

ΞΑΝΘΙΑΣ

μᾶλλον δέ γ᾽ ἴσως μανίας ἀρχή.

ΦΙΛΟΚΛΕΩΝ

—πλευρὰν λυγίσαντος ὑπὸ ῥώμης.
οἷον μυκτὴρ μυκᾶται καὶ
σφόνδυλος ἀχεῖ.

ΞΑΝΘΙΑΣ

πῖθ᾽ ἑλλέβορον.

ΦΙΛΟΚΛΕΩΝ

1490 πτήσσει Φρύνιχος ὥς τις ἀλέκτωρ—

ΞΑΝΘΙΑΣ

τάχα βαλλήσει.

ΦΙΛΟΚΛΕΩΝ

—σκέλος οὐρανίαν ἐκλακτίζων.
πρωκτὸς χάσκει· —

ΞΑΝΘΙΑΣ

κατὰ σαυτὸν ὅρα.

ΦΙΛΟΚΛΕΩΝ

—νῦν γὰρ ἐν ἄρθροις τοῖς ἡμετέροις
1495 στρέφεται χαλαρὰ κοτυληδών.
οὐκ εὖ;

1487 ῥώμης] ῥύμης Lobeck

408

WASPS

LOVECLEON
Let these gates be unbolted! Look here,
the opening steps—

XANTHIAS
Maybe more like the onset of madness!

LOVECLEON
—where you bend the torso vigorously.
How the snout snorts, and
the spine cracks!

XANTHIAS
Drink hellebore![112]

LOVECLEON
Phrynichus crouches like a rooster—

XANTHIAS
Soon you'll be pelted![113]

LOVECLEON
—kicking his legs sky high!
The arsehole splits—

XANTHIAS
Watch yourself there!

LOVECLEON
—because now my hip joints
roll smoothly in their sockets!
Wasn't that good?

[112] A plant used to make a purgative thought to relieve some mental disorders.
[113] I.e. with stones by passersby, a common way to treat madmen.

ΞΑΝΘΙΑΣ

μὰ Δί᾽ οὐ δῆτ᾽, ἀλλὰ μανικὰ πράγματα.

ΦΙΛΟΚΛΕΩΝ

φέρε νυν, ἀνείπω κἀνταγωνιστὰς καλῶ.
εἴ τις τραγῳδός φησιν ὀρχεῖσθαι καλῶς,
ἐμοὶ διορχησόμενος ἐνθάδ᾽ εἰσίτω.
φησίν τις, ἢ οὐδείς;

ΞΑΝΘΙΑΣ

1500   εἷς γ᾽ ἐκεινοσὶ μόνος.

ΦΙΛΟΚΛΕΩΝ

τίς ὁ κακοδαίμων ἐστίν;

ΞΑΝΘΙΑΣ

                    υἱὸς Καρκίνου
ὁ μέσατος.

ΦΙΛΟΚΛΕΩΝ

          ἀλλ᾽ οὗτός γε καταποθήσεται·
ἀπολῶ γὰρ αὐτὸν ἐμμελείᾳ κονδύλου.
ἐν τῷ ῥυθμῷ γὰρ οὐδέν ἐστ᾽.

ΞΑΝΘΙΑΣ

                    ἀλλ᾽, ὦζυρέ,
1505   ἕτερος τραγῳδὸς Καρκινίτης ἔρχεται,
ἀδελφὸς αὐτοῦ.

---

114 The name Carcinus (for whom see *Clouds* 1220 n.) means
"crab." It is not clear whether the actual sons of Carcinus (Xeno-
timus, Xenarchus, and Xenocles) performed in this scene, but in

XANTHIAS

It certainly was not; it's crazy business!

LOVECLEON

Come now, let me make an announcement: I challenge all comers! Any tragic performer who claims to be a good dancer, come right up here and dance against me! Anyone out there care to try? No one?

XANTHIAS

Only that one over there.

A Son of Carcinus, costumed as a crab, enters the orchestra.[114]

LOVECLEON

Who *is* the unfortunate person?

XANTHIAS

A son of Carcinus, the midmost one.[115]

LOVECLEON

Him? He'll be eaten alive! I'll demolish him with a *pas de fist!* Rhythmically, he's nothing at all.

XANTHIAS

You sorry fool, here's another Carcinite tragedian coming, this one's brother![116]

Enter a second Son of Carcinus.

the following year Aristophanes' chorus does warn the spectators never to dance with Carcinus' sons (*Peace* 781-86), perhaps an allusion to trouble with their performance in *Wasps*.

[115] The middle son, Xenarchus.
[116] The eldest son, Xenotimus.

411

ΦΙΛΟΚΛΕΩΝ

νὴ Δί᾽ ὠψώνηκ᾽ ἄρα.

ΞΑΝΘΙΑΣ

μὰ τὸν Δί᾽ οὐδέν γ᾽ ἄλλο πλὴν τρεῖς καρκίνους.
προσέρχεται γὰρ ἕτερος αὖ τῶν Καρκίνου.

ΦΙΛΟΚΛΕΩΝ

τουτὶ τί ἦν τὸ προσέρπον; ὀξὶς ἢ φάλαγξ;

ΞΑΝΘΙΑΣ

1510 ὁ πινοτήρης οὗτός ἐστι τοῦ γένους,
ὁ σμικρότατος, ὃς τὴν τραγῳδίαν ποιεῖ.

ΦΙΛΟΚΛΕΩΝ

ὦ Καρκίν᾽, ὦ μακάριε τῆς εὐπαιδίας,
ὅσον τὸ πλῆθος κατέπεσεν τῶν ὀρχίλων.
ἀτὰρ καταβατέον γ᾽ ἐπ᾽ αὐτούς μοι· σὺ δὲ
1515 ἅλμην κύκα τούτοισιν, ἢν ἐγὼ κρατῶ.

ΚΟΡΥΦΑΙΟΣ

φέρε νυν, ἡμεῖς αὐτοῖς ὀλίγον ξυγχωρήσωμεν ἅπαν-
τες,
ἵν᾽ ἐφ᾽ ἡσυχίας ἡμῶν πρόσθεν βεμβικίζωσιν ἑ-
αυτούς.

1507 τρεῖς Badham: γε a
1514 μοι· σὺ δὲ Hermann: μ᾽ ὠζυρέ a

---

117 *Oxis* (properly "vinegar cruet") referred to some venom-
ous, and evidently crablike, creature, cf. Iamblichus, *Protrepticus*
21θ.

LOVECLEON

Then by god, I've got myself a tasty meal!

XANTHIAS

No you haven't; you've got nothing but three crabs, because here comes yet another son of Carcinus!

Enter a third Son of Carcinus.

LOVECLEON

What's this thing crawling towards us? A scorpion[117] or a spider?

XANTHIAS

He's the pea crab of the family, the tiniest one, who writes tragedy.[118]

LOVECLEON

Ah Carcinus, congratulations on your fine offspring! What a flock of wagtails has alighted! Well, I must go down to compete with them; you be stirring up the broth for them, in case I win.

LOVECLEON descends into the orchestra; XANTHIAS goes into the house.

CHORUS LEADER

Come then, let's all give them a bit of room, so that they can spin themselves around before us without interference.

---

[118] The youngest son, Xenocles, who defeated Euripides' *Trojan Women* in 415 and also had a political career (cf. *Women at the Thesmophoria* 440-42).

413

ΧΟΡΟΣ

ἄγ᾽, ὦ μεγαλώνυμα τέκνα
τοῦ θαλασσίοιο,
1520 πηδᾶτε παρὰ ψάμαθον
καὶ θῖν᾽ ἁλὸς ἀτρυγέτοιο,
καρίδων ἀδελφοί·
ταχὺν πόδα κυκλοσοβεῖτε,
καὶ τὸ Φρυνίχειον
1525 ἐκλακτισάτω τις, ὅπως
ἰδόντες ἄνω σκέλος ὤ-
ζωσιν οἱ θεαταί.

στρόβει· παράβαινε κύκλῳ καὶ γάστρισον σεαυτόν·
1530 ῥῖπτε σκέλος οὐράνιον· βέμβικες ἐγγενέσθων.
καὐτὸς γὰρ ὁ ποντομέδων ἄναξ πατὴρ προσέρπει
ἡσθεὶς ἐπὶ τοῖσιν ἑαυτοῦ παισί, τοῖς τριόρχοις.
1535 ἀλλ᾽ ἐξάγετ᾽, εἴ τι φιλεῖτ᾽, ὀρχούμενοι θύραζε
ἡμᾶς ταχύ· τοῦτο γὰρ οὐδείς πω πάρος δέδρακεν,
ὀρχούμενος ὅστις ἀπήλλαξεν χορὸν τρυγῳδῶν.

CHORUS

Up, you renowned children
of Sir Salty,[119]
jump along the sand
and the shore of the barren sea,
brethren of shrimps;
whirl a swift foot all around,
and someone kick out
the Phrynichus caper,
so that seeing the foot in the air
the audience will cry ooh!

Whirl! Sidle around and slap your belly;
throw a leg sky high; pirouettes included please!

CARCINUS enters the orchestra.

Because the Lord and Master of the Deep scuttles
    hither himself,
delighted with his very own children, the triple
    duckers!
Now lead us out of here dancing, if you please,
and quickly; for no one has ever done this before,
to take a comic chorus off in dance.

[119] Carcinus had shared command of an Athenian fleet in 431.

PEACE

INTRODUCTORY NOTE

Peace was produced by Aristophanes at the Dionysia of 421 and won the second prize; Eupolis was first with *Flatterers* and Leucon third with *The Phratry*. In *Peace*, as in *Acharnians*, a farmer-hero renounces the war and reaps the blessings of peace, but this time the hero does not face an outraged majority, for the end of the war was actually in sight: less than a fortnight after the production the Athenians and the Peloponnesians would ratify the Peace of Nicias.[1]

Negotiations had begun the previous summer after the battle of Amphipolis, where an Athenian expeditionary force commanded by Cleon was defeated by the Spartan Brasidas, and both commanders were killed. Thus were removed, as Aristophanes puts it in *Peace*, the two pestles with which War had been pounding the Greeks. Cleon had persuaded the Athenians to reject Spartan offers of peace after their success at Pylos in 425, and to abandon the truce that followed their defeat at Delium in 424; and Brasidas' energetic campaigning during the past two years had weakened the Athenians' strategically vital position in northern Greece. Now the Athenians inclined toward Nicias' view that negotiation of favorable terms was more

---

[1] For the process and terms see Thucydides 5.14-24.

prudent than further attempts to win the war outright, and that there was real danger of general allied revolt. The Spartans, for their part, were still hobbled by the Athenians' retention of the 292 hostages from Pylos, and they faced dangers close to home: a potential helot revolt, and a possible alliance between Athens and Argos, whose 30-year treaty with Sparta would soon expire.

But even at the time of the Dionysia peace was hardly a foregone conclusion. The negotiations had dragged on all winter; Sparta's two most powerful allies, Corinth and Thebes, were uncooperative, and in the end refused to sign; and there was still opposition in Athens from Cleon-style politicians like Hyperbolus—so much so that as spring approached the Spartans asked their allies to prepare for an invasion of Attica, "so that the Athenians would take their proposals more seriously" (Thucydides 5.17.2). In the event, the fifty-year Peace of Nicias would last barely six.

The obstacles faced by the hero of *Peace* reflect the difficulty of the negotiations, and despite the play's generally confident and celebratory mood, there is clear apprehension that the peace effort could yet fail: the danger came not only from obstructionists at home and abroad, but also from supporters inclined to celebrate prematurely (like the Chorus, 301-39). The play's import is that peace is attainable, but only if all Greeks make a final, concerted effort to secure it.

The hero Trygaeus ("Vintager"), sick of war and determined to ask Zeus in person why he wants to destroy Greece, flies to heaven on a dung beetle, parodying Bellerophon's ride on the winged horse Pegasus in Euripides' tragedy. There Trygaeus learns from Hermes that the gods have moved away, leaving humanity at the mercy of the

cruel ogre War, who has hidden Peace in a deep cave. War intends to pound the Greeks in a great mortar, but since Cleon and Brasidas are now in the underworld, his minion Hubbub cannot find a pestle. When War goes inside to make a new pestle, Trygaeus seizes this opportunity to excavate Peace, who is represented by a statue. He wins the allegiance of Hermes and calls on all Greeks to assist him. But when not everyone pulls properly or in the right direction, all are ordered to stop pulling except the country folk, who complete the job on their own.

When Trygaeus asks why Peace has been away so long, Hermes on her behalf gives an account of the war's origins and subsequent course, fixing blame on all the combatants (including the allies) but identifying Pericles and Cleon as the principal culprits, and stressing that the country folk alone are innocent, though they have suffered the most harm. Hermes' account invites comparison with Dicae-opolis' in *Acharnians*, but differs greatly in its emphases, its panhellenic scope, and its more abundant detail, some of which seems to have been unfamiliar to many of the spectators (cf. 615-16).

After the parabasis (739-818), in which Aristophanes again boasts of his courage in attacking Cleon, it remains to establish a permanent abode for Peace, and to illustrate the rewards enjoyed by Trygaeus and his helpers. Trygaeus performs a sacrificial ritual and prays to Peace as a goddess, suggesting the establishment of a new cult.[2] Peace's two attendants, the attractive girls Opora ("Cornucopia") and Theoria ("Holiday"), represent the blessings that have re-

[2] An actual cult of Peace was not established at Athens until 374, to celebrate a treaty with Sparta.

turned with Peace: sexual enjoyment, agricultural fertility, and a carefree life in the country. Theoria is given to the Council, while Opora will become Trygaeus' bride.

Not everyone welcomes the advent of Peace. While conducting the sacrifice and preparing his wedding feast, Trygaeus is interrupted by the seer Hierocles, whose oracles warn against any pact with Sparta, and an assortment of arms dealers. But these are mocked and sent away hungry, while newly prosperous makers of farm equipment are invited to the wedding. The joyous finale is reminiscent of the end of *Acharnians*, but with greater emphasis on the return to the countryside and the panhellenic benefits of peace.

Peace, in tune with the mood of its time, is tamer and less biting than Aristophanes' previous plays: its visionary and rather genial hero does not face a hostile chorus or a dangerous opponent, and its satire lacks the usual cynicism and pugnacity. But in other respects the play is vintage Aristophanes. Trygaeus' ride on the dung beetle is spectacular, and the statue of Peace a striking novelty, though perhaps not an entirely successful idea: rival comic poets ridiculed it, and Aristophanes did not repeat the experiment.[3] *Peace* contains much impressive choral writing and virtuoso adaptations of other poetic genres, and its imagery is especially rich: a contrapuntal association of war and urban politics with excrement and urine, dishonesty, poor food, sterile discipline, confinement and deprivation; and peace with the sights and smells of bounteous fields, good food and wine, productive labor, wholesome sexuality, and

[3] Eupolis 62, Plato Com. 86; in *Wealth* 1191 ff. the god Wealth is installed off stage.

the honest freedoms of country life. There is a high degree of spectator participation: the audience partakes of Trygaeus' feast, Theoria is handed over to the actual Councilmen, and there is frequent allusion to all the various categories of spectators, including the Ionian allies. The identity of the Chorus is remarkably fluid: collectively it is the generic comic chorus or a chorus of country folk, but during the excavation scenes it breaks up into the various groups engaged in the work, choreographically mirroring a Greek world at cross purposes. Finally, *Peace* is especially notable for a panhellenic ideology quite at odds with contemporary Greek practice.

Text

Four papyri preserve fragments of some 160 lines of *Peace*. There are nine independent medieval MSS, only two of which (RV) preserve the complete text. The others, which descend from a lost MS lacking lines 948-1011 (y), divide into two families: the first (*x*) comprises Γ (containing only about half the play), *p* (the hyparchetype of Vp2CH), and a lost MS which furnished some corrections in V; and the second the Triclinian recension(s) represented by LVv17 and B (which also contains readings from lost MSS related to Γ). The Florentine scholar Piero Vettori (Petrus Victorius, 1499-1585) inserted lines 948-1011 into his copy of the Aldine *editio princeps* (Venice, 1498) from a lost MS related to R.

Sigla

Π1	*PBerol.* 21223 (VI), lines 141–52, 175, 178-87, 194–200[4]
Π2	*PSI* 720 (III), lines 721-827
Π3	*PVindob.G.* 29354 (V), lines 609–19, 655–67[5]
Π4	*POxy.* 1373 (V), lines 1326–34
R	Ravennas 429 (*c.* 950)
V	Venetus Marcianus 474 (*c.* 1300)
S	readings found in the Suda
	all the following MSS omit lines 948–1011
Γ	Laurentianus 31.15 (*c.* 1325), omits lines 1–377, 491–547, 838-892, 1127–89, 1301–end
Vp2	Vaticanus Palatinus gr. 67 (XV)
C	Parisinus Regius 2717 (XV/XVI)
H	Hauniensis 1980 (XV)
L	Holkhamensis 1980 (1400-1430), originally lacked lines 1228–end
Vv17	Vaticanus Graecus 2181 (XIVex), omits lines 1228–end
B	Parisinus Regius 2715 (XV), omits lines 1301–end
z	the archetype of RV*y*
y	the consensus of *xt*
x	the consensus of Γ*p*
p	the hyparchetype of Vp2CH
t	the hyparchetype of LVv17B

---

[4] See H. Maehler, *ArchPF* 30 (1984) 17-18.

[5] See A. Carlini, ed., *Papiri letterari greci* (Pisa, 1978) 135-39 (#17).

Annotated Editions

F. H. M. Blaydes (Halle 1883)

H. van Herwerden (Leiden 1897)

P. Mazon (Paris 1904)

H. Sharpley (London 1905)

J. van Leeuwen (Leiden 1906)

B. B. Rogers (London 1913), with English translation.

M. Platnauer (Oxford 1964)

A. H. Sommerstein (Warminster 1985), with English translation.

ΤΟΥ ΔΡΑΜΑΤΟΣ ΠΡΟΣΩΠΑ

ΟΙΚΕΤΗΣ Α Τρυγαίου
ΟΙΚΕΤΗΣ Β Τρυγαίου
ΤΡΥΓΑΙΟΣ Ἀθμονεύς
ΘΥΓΑΤΗΡ Τρυγαίου

ΕΡΜΗΣ

ΠΟΛΕΜΟΣ
ΚΥΔΟΙΜΟΣ, θεράπων
    Πολέμου
ΙΕΡΟΚΛΗΣ
ΔΡΕΠΑΝΟΥΡΓΟΣ
ΚΑΠΗΛΟΣ ΟΠΛΩΝ
ΠΑΙΔΙΟΝ Α, υἱὸς
    Λαμάχου
ΠΑΙΔΙΟΝ Β, υἱὸς
    Κλεωνύμου

ΧΟΡΟΣ

kwfa proswpa
ΘΥΓΑΤΕΡΕΣ Τρυγαίου
ΕΙΡΗΝΗ, ἄγαλμα
ΟΠΩΡΑ, ἀκόλουθος
    Εἰρήνης
ΘΕΩΡΙΑ, ἀκόλουθος
    Εἰρήνης
ΟΙΚΕΤΑΙ Τρυγαίου
ΚΕΡΑΜΕΥΣ
ΚΡΑΝΟΠΟΙΟΣ
ΔΟΡΥΞΟΣ

426

DRAMATIS PERSONAE

FIRST SLAVE of Trygaeus
SECOND SLAVE of Trygaeus
TRYGAEUS of Athmonum
DAUGHTER of Trygaeus

HERMES

WAR
HUBBUB, servant of War
HIEROCLES
SICKLE MAKER
ARMS DEALER
FIRST BOY, son of
   Lamachus
SECOND BOY, son of
   Cleonymus

CHORUS

SILENT CHARACTERS
DAUGHTERS of Trygaeus
PEACE, a statue
CORNUCOPIA, attendant
   of Peace
HOLIDAY, attendant of
   Peace
SLAVES of Trygaeus
POTTER
HELMET MAKER
SPEAR MAKER

ΕΙΡΗΝΗ

ΟΙΚΕΤΗΣ Α´

αἶρ᾽ αἶρε μᾶζαν ὡς τάχιστα κανθάρῳ.

ΟΙΚΕΤΗΣ Β´

ἰδού. δὸς αὐτῷ, τῷ κάκιστ᾽ ἀπολουμένῳ·
καὶ μήποτ᾽ αὐτῆς μᾶζαν ἡδίω φάγοι.

ΟΙΚΕΤΗΣ Α´

δὸς μᾶζαν ἑτέραν, ἐξ ὀνίδων πεπλασμένην.

ΟΙΚΕΤΗΣ Β´

5   ἰδοὺ μάλ᾽ αὖθις. ποῦ γὰρ ἦν νυνδὴ 'φερες;
οὐ κατέφαγεν;

ΟΙΚΕΤΗΣ Α´

        μὰ τὸν Δί᾽, ἀλλ᾽ ἐξαρπάσας
ὅλην ἐνέκαψε περικυλίσας τοῖν ποδοῖν.
ἀλλ᾽ ὡς τάχιστα τρῖβε πολλὰς καὶ πυκνάς.

---

[1] "Beetle" (*kantharos*) could initially be taken to refer to the comic poet Cantharus, the probable victor at the previous year's Dionysia.

428

PEACE

*The central door of the stage building represents a cavern,
and two flanking doors represent respectively the house
of* TRYGAEUS *and the palace of Zeus.* SECOND SLAVE *is
kneading cakes from a tub of dung as* FIRST SLAVE *hurries
out of the house.*

FIRST SLAVE
Hand me a cake for beetle, quick quick![1]

SECOND SLAVE
Here. (*First Slave rushes back inside*) Give it to the god-
damned thing! And I hope it never eats a tastier cake than
that one.

FIRST SLAVE
(*returning*) Give me another cake, shaped from donkey
dung.

SECOND SLAVE
Here, have another. But what happened to the one you
served just now? It can't have eaten it!

FIRST SLAVE
Oh no; it only grabbed it, trundled it with its feet, and
scoffed it whole! So knead lots of them as fast as you can,
and keep them coming! (*goes inside*)

ΟΙΚΕΤΗΣ Β΄

ἄνδρες κοπρολόγοι, προσλάβεσθε πρὸς θεῶν,
10 εἰ μή με βούλεσθ᾽ ἀποπνιγέντα περιδεῖν.

ΟΙΚΕΤΗΣ Α΄

ἑτέραν ἑτέραν δός, παιδὸς ἡταιρηκότος·
τετριμμένης γάρ φησιν ἐπιθυμεῖν.

ΟΙΚΕΤΗΣ Β΄

ἰδού.
ἑνὸς μέν, ὦνδρες, ἀπολελύσθαι μοι δοκῶ·
οὐδεὶς γὰρ ἂν φαίη με μάττοντ᾽ ἐσθίειν.

ΟΙΚΕΤΗΣ Α΄

15 αἰβοῖ· φέρ᾽ ἄλλην χἀτέραν μοι χἀτέραν,
καὶ τρῖβ᾽ ‹ἔθ᾽› ἑτέρας.

ΟΙΚΕΤΗΣ Β΄

μὰ τὸν Ἀπόλλω ᾽γὼ μὲν οὔ·
οὐ γὰρ ἔθ᾽ οἷός τ᾽ εἴμ᾽ ὑπερέχειν τῆς ἀντλίας.

ΟΙΚΕΤΗΣ Α΄

αὐτὴν ἄρ᾽ οἴσω συλλαβὼν τὴν ἀντλίαν.

ΟΙΚΕΤΗΣ Β΄

νὴ τὸν Δί᾽ ἐς κόρακάς γε, καὶ σαυτόν γε πρός.
20 ὑμῶν δέ γ᾽ εἴ τις οἶδέ μοι κατειπάτω
πόθεν ἂν πριαίμην ῥῖνα μὴ τετρημένην.
οὐδὲν γὰρ ἔργον ἦν ἄρ᾽ ἀθλιώτερον
ἢ κανθάρῳ μάττοντα παρέχειν ἐσθίειν.
ὗς μὲν γάρ, ὥσπερ ἂν χέσῃ τις, ἢ κύων
25 φαύλως ἐρείδει τοῦθ᾽· ὁ δ᾽ ὑπὸ φρονήματος

430

SECOND SLAVE

(*to the spectators*) You dung collectors, for god's sake lend
a hand, unless you want to watch me suffocate!

FIRST SLAVE

(*returning*) Another one, give me another one, from a boy
whore; it says it hankers for a well pounded one.

SECOND SLAVE

Here. (*to the spectators, as First Slave goes inside*) There's
one charge, gentlemen, that I think I'm clear of: no one
will accuse me of tasting what I'm kneading.

FIRST SLAVE

(*returning*) Yuk! Give me another, and another, and an-
other, and keep kneading still more!

SECOND SLAVE

No, by Apollo, I won't! I can't keep up with the bilge any
longer!

FIRST SLAVE

Very well, I'll pick up the whole bilge hold and take it
inside. (*takes the tub inside*)

SECOND SLAVE

By heaven, you can take it to hell, and yourself with it! (*to
the spectators*) If any of you knows where I can buy an
unperforated nose, please tell me! Because there's no job
more wretched than kneading food to serve to a beetle. A
pig or a dog will simply gobble up any shit that falls, but

βρενθύεταί τε καὶ φαγεῖν οὐκ ἀξιοῖ,
ἢν μὴ παραθῶ τρίψας δι᾿ ἡμέρας ὅλης
ὥσπερ γυναικὶ γογγύλην μεμαγμένην.
ἀλλ᾿ εἰ πέπαυται τῆς ἐδωδῆς σκέψομαι
30 τῃδὶ παροίξας τῆς θύρας, ἵνα μή μ᾿ ἴδῃ.
ἔρειδε, μὴ παύσαιο μηδέποτ᾿ ἐσθίων
τέως ἕως σαυτὸν λάθῃς διαρραγείς.
οἷον δὲ κύψας ὁ κατάρατος ἐσθίει,
ὥσπερ παλαιστής, παραβαλὼν τοὺς γομφίους,
35 καὶ ταῦτα τὴν κεφαλήν τε καὶ τὼ χεῖρέ πως
ὡδὶ περιάγων, ὥσπερ οἱ τὰ σχοινία
τὰ παχέα συμβάλλοντες εἰς τὰς ὁλκάδας.

ΟΙΚΕΤΗΣ Α΄
μιαρὸν τὸ χρῆμα καὶ κάκοσμον καὶ βορόν,
χὥτου ποτ᾿ ἐστὶ δαιμόνων ἡ προσβολὴ
40 οὐκ οἶδ᾿. Ἀφροδίτης μὲν γὰρ οὔ μοι φαίνεται,
οὐ μὴν Χαρίτων γε.

ΟΙΚΕΤΗΣ Β΄
τοῦ γάρ ἐστ᾿;

ΟΙΚΕΤΗΣ Α΄
οὐκ ἔσθ᾿ ὅπως
τοῦτ᾿ ἔστι τὸ τέρας οὐ Διὸς καταιβάτου.

ΟΙΚΕΤΗΣ Β΄
οὐκοῦν ἂν ἤδη τῶν θεατῶν τις λέγοι
νεανίας δοκησίσοφος· "τόδε πρᾶγμα τί;
45 ὁ κάνθαρος δὲ πρὸς τί;"

this conceited thing puts on airs and won't deign to eat anything that I don't spend the whole day mashing and serve kneaded into a ball, as for a lady. I'll look and see if it's done with its dinner, opening the door just this far, so it won't spot me. (*looking in*) Go on, gobble away! Don't ever stop eating, not till you surprise yourself by bursting apart! (*closing the door*) The way that devil eats! Crouching like a wrestler, moving its grinders back and forth, and all the while going like this, swivelling its head and hands like the men who plait thick ropes for barges.

FIRST SLAVE

(*coming from the house*) That thing is filthy, smelly, and voracious, a visitation from I don't know what divinity. Apparently not from Aphrodite, or the Graces either.

SECOND SLAVE

Then who's it from?

FIRST SLAVE

I can't but think this prodigy's from Zeus of the Thunder Crap.

SECOND SLAVE

Well, by now some young smart aleck in the audience may be saying, "What's going on? What's the point of the beetle?"

ARISTOPHANES

ΟΙΚΕΤΗΣ Α'

κᾆτ' αὐτῷ γ' ἀνὴρ
Ἰωνικός τίς φησι παρακαθήμενος·
"δοκέω μέν, ἐς Κλέωνα τοῦτ' αἰνίσσεται,
ὡς κεῖνος ἀναιδέως τὴν σπατίλην ἐσθίει."
ἀλλ' εἰσιὼν τῷ κανθάρῳ δώσω πιεῖν.

ΟΙΚΕΤΗΣ Β'

50 ἐγὼ δὲ τὸν λόγον γε τοῖσι παιδίοις
καὶ τοῖσιν ἀνδρίοισι καὶ τοῖς ἀνδράσιν
καὶ τοῖς ὑπερτάτοισιν ἀνδράσιν φράσω
καὶ τοῖς ὑπερηνορέουσιν ἔτι τούτοις μάλα.
ὁ δεσπότης μου μαίνεται καινὸν τρόπον,
55 οὐχ ὅνπερ ὑμεῖς, ἀλλ' ἕτερον καινὸν πάνυ.
δι' ἡμέρας γὰρ εἰς τὸν οὐρανὸν βλέπων
ὡδὶ κεχηνὼς λοιδορεῖται τῷ Διὶ
καί φησιν· "ὦ Ζεῦ, τί ποτε βουλεύει ποιεῖν;
κατάθου τὸ κόρημα· μὴ 'κκόρει τὴν Ἑλλάδα."
60 ἔα ἔα·
σιγήσαθ', ὡς φωνῆς ἀκούειν μοι δοκῶ.

ΤΡΥΓΑΙΟΣ

ὦ Ζεῦ, τί δρασείεις ποθ' ἡμῶν τὸν λεών;
λήσεις σεαυτὸν τὰς πόλεις ἐκκοκκίσας.

ΟΙΚΕΤΗΣ Β'

τοῦτ' ἔστι τουτὶ τὸ κακὸν αὔθ' οὑγὼ 'λεγον·

---

48 ἀναιδέως τὴν] ἐν Ἀίδεω van Leeuwen
52 ὑπερτάτοισιν B: ὑπὲρ τούτοισιν cett. S

434

PEACE

FIRST SLAVE

Yes, and then the guy sitting next to him, some Ionian, says, "In my view it's an allusion to Cleon, because he shamelessly eats loose shit."[2] But I'm going inside to give the beetle a drink.

Exit FIRST SLAVE.

SECOND SLAVE

And I'm going to explain the plot to the children, to the teenagers, to the men, to the high and mighty gentlemen, and above all to these supermen here. My master's mad in a novel way; not the way you all are, but another, quite novel way. All day long he gazes at the sky, with his mouth open like this, railing at Zeus. "Zeus," he says, "what on earth do you plan to do? Lay down your broom; don't sweep Greece away!" What's that? Be quiet; I think I hear a voice.

TRYGAEUS[3]

(*within*) Zeus! What on earth are you trying to do to our people? Before you know it you'll have pitted and pulped our cities!

SECOND SLAVE

There, that's exactly the business I was talking about;

---

[2] Cleon, though killed the previous summer in the battle at Amphipolis (Thucydides 5.6-11), earns continued abuse as having been the principal advocate of the war now ending.

[3] A fictive name meaning "vintager" and suggesting *trygoidia* (wine song), a word for comedy.

435

65 τὸ γὰρ παράδειγμα τῶν μανιῶν ἀκούετε·
ἃ δ' εἶπε πρῶτον ἡνίκ' ἤρχεθ' ἡ χολὴ
πεύσεσθ'. ἔφασκε γὰρ πρὸς αὑτὸν ἂν ταδί·
"πῶς ἄν ποτ' ἀφικοίμην ἂν εὐθὺ τοῦ Διός;"
ἔπειτα λεπτὰ κλιμάκια ποιούμενος,
70 πρὸς ταῦτ' ἀνηρριχᾶτ' ἂν εἰς τὸν οὐρανόν,
ἕως ξυνετρίβη τῆς κεφαλῆς καταρρυείς.
ἐχθὲς δὲ μετὰ ταῦτ' ἐκφθαρεὶς οὐκ οἶδ' ὅποι
εἰσήγαγ' Αἰτναῖον μέγιστον κάνθαρον,
κἄπειτα τοῦτον ἱπποκομεῖν μ' ἠνάγκασεν,
75 καὐτὸς καταψῶν αὐτὸν ὥσπερ πωλίον·
"ὦ Πηγάσιόν μοι," φησί, "γενναῖον πτερόν,
ὅπως πετήσει μ' εὐθὺ τοῦ Διὸς λαβών."
ἀλλ' ὅ τι ποιεῖ τηδὶ διακύψας ὄψομαι.
οἴμοι τάλας· ἴτε δεῦρο δεῦρ', ὦ γείτονες·
80 ὁ δεσπότης γάρ μου μετέωρος αἴρεται
ἱππηδὸν εἰς τὸν ἀέρ' ἐπὶ τοῦ κανθάρου.

ΤΡΥΓΑΙΟΣ
ἥσυχος ἥσυχος, ἠρέμα, κάνθων·
μή μοι σοβαρὸς χώρει λίαν
εὐθὺς ἀπ' ἀρχῆς, ῥώμῃ πίσυνος,
85 πρὶν ἂν ἰδίῃς καὶ διαλύσῃς
ἄρθρων ἶνας πτερύγων ῥύμῃ.
καὶ μὴ πνεῖ μοι κακόν, ἀντιβολῶ σ'·
εἰ δὲ ποιήσεις τοῦτο, κατ' οἴκους
αὐτοῦ μεῖνον τοὺς ἡμετέρους.

you're hearing the typical symptom of his delusions. I'll tell you what he said when the bile first came over him; this is what he kept muttering to himself: "How on earth can I get right to Zeus?" Then he'd have light scaling ladders made and try to scramble up to heaven that way, till he tumbled off and bashed his head. Then yesterday he went out, the devil only knows where, and brought home a huge Etna beetle,[4] and then he forced me to be its groom, while he gentles it like a young colt and says, "My little Pegasus, my thoroughbred wings,[5] you must pick me up and fly me straight to Zeus." Now I'll peek inside here and see what he's doing. Oh my god! Come here, neighbors, come here! My master's up off the ground, soaring into the air on beetle-back!

TRYGAEUS flies above the stage on the mechane.

TRYGAEUS

Whoa, whoa, easy does it, dobbin,
don't get too frisky on me
in pride of your power, right out of the gate,
not till you raise a sweat and loosen up
your leg muscles by dint of wingpower.
And don't blow bad breath at me, I beg you;
if that's your intention, you can stay
right here in our house.

[4] Reputedly man-sized (Plato com. fr. 36), Etna beetles had pulled the Pygmies' chariot in a play by Epicharmus (fr. 76 Kaibel).

[5] Euripides, *Bellerophon* fr. 306, signalling the parody to come (see Introduction).

ΟΙΚΕΤΗΣ Β΄

90   ὦ δέσποτ᾽ ἄναξ, ὡς παραπαίεις.

ΤΡΥΓΑΙΟΣ

σῖγα σῖγα.

ΟΙΚΕΤΗΣ Β΄

ποῖ δῆτ᾽ ἄλλως μετεωροκοπεῖς;

ΤΡΥΓΑΙΟΣ

ὑπὲρ Ἑλλήνων πάντων πέτομαι
τόλμημα νέον παλαμησάμενος.

ΟΙΚΕΤΗΣ Β΄

95   τί πέτει; τί μάτην οὐχ ὑγιαίνεις;

ΤΡΥΓΑΙΟΣ

εὐφημεῖν χρὴ καὶ μὴ φλαῦρον
μηδὲν γρύζειν, ἀλλ᾽ ὀλολύζειν·
τοῖς τ᾽ ἀνθρώποισι φράσον σιγᾶν,
τούς τε κοπρῶνας καὶ τὰς λαύρας
100   καιναῖς πλίνθοισιν ἀποικοδομεῖν
καὶ τοὺς πρωκτοὺς ἐπικλῄειν.

ΟΙΚΕΤΗΣ Β΄

οὐκ ἔσθ᾽ ὅπως σιγήσομ᾽, ἢν μή μοι φράσῃς
ὅποι πέτεσθαι διανοεῖ.

ΤΡΥΓΑΙΟΣ

            τί δ᾽ ἄλλο γ᾽ ἢ
ὡς τὸν Δί᾽ εἰς τὸν οὐρανόν;

ΟΙΚΕΤΗΣ Β΄

            τίνα νοῦν ἔχων;

SECOND SLAVE
Ah master, lord, you're so deranged!

TRYGAEUS
Be quiet, be quiet!

SECOND SLAVE
Well why are you vainly beating the air?

TRYGAEUS
I'm flying for the sake of all Greeks,
trying my hand at a novel adventure.

SECOND SLAVE
Why do you fly? Why act crazy for nothing?

TRYGAEUS
You must speak auspiciously and make
no foolish noise, but raise a cheer;
and bid mankind be quiet,
and wall off with fresh bricks
the privies and alleyways,
and lock up their arseholes!

SECOND SLAVE
There's no way I'll be quiet unless you tell me where you
mean to fly.

TRYGAEUS
Where else but to Zeus in heaven?

SECOND SLAVE
The point being?

ΤΡΥΓΑΙΟΣ

105 ἐρησόμενος ἐκεῖνον Ἑλλήνων πέρι
ἁπαξαπάντων ὅ τι ποιεῖν βουλεύεται.

ΟΙΚΕΤΗΣ Β'

ἐὰν δὲ μή σοι καταγορεύσῃ;

ΤΡΥΓΑΙΟΣ
γράψομαι
Μήδοισιν αὐτὸν προδιδόναι τὴν Ἑλλάδα.

ΟΙΚΕΤΗΣ Β'

μὰ τὸν Διόνυσον οὐδέποτε ζῶντός γ' ἐμοῦ.

ΤΡΥΓΑΙΟΣ
110 οὐκ ἔστι παρὰ ταῦτ' ἄλλ'.

ΟΙΚΕΤΗΣ Β'
ἰοὺ ἰοὺ ἰού·
ὦ παιδί', ὁ πατὴρ ἀπολιπὼν ἀπέρχεται
ὑμᾶς ἐρήμους εἰς τὸν οὐρανὸν λάθρᾳ.
ἀλλ' ἀντιβολεῖτε τὸν πατέρ', ὦ κακοδαίμονα.

ΠΑΙΔΙΟΝ
ὦ πάτερ, ὦ πάτερ, ἆρ' ἔτυμός γε
115 δώμασιν ἡμετέροις φάτις ἥκει,
ὡς σὺ μετ' ὀρνίθων προλιπὼν ἐμὲ
ἐς κόρακας βαδιεῖ μεταμώνιος;
ἔστι τι τῶνδ' ἐτύμως; εἴπ', ὦ πάτερ, εἴ τι φιλεῖς με.

TRYGAEUS

To ask him about the Greeks, all of them, what he's trying
to do with them.

SECOND SLAVE

And if he doesn't tell you?

TRYGAEUS

I'll indict him for betraying Greece to the Medes![6]

SECOND SLAVE

So help me Dionysus, not while I'm alive!

TRYGAEUS

There's no other way.

SECOND SLAVE

My oh my oh my! (*calling into the house*) Children, your
father's gone to heaven on the sly and left you all alone!

Trygaeus' DAUGHTERS come out of the house.

Come plead with your father, you poor things!

DAUGHTER[7]

Ah father, father, is it really true,
the tale that has come to our house,
that to be with the birds you have left me,
and, riding the wind, mean to go to the buzzards?
Is any of this true? Tell me, father, if you love me at all.

[6] Panhellenic war, by weakening all Greeks, invites a new invasion by the Persians (colloquial "Medes" recalls the earlier invasions).

[7] The duet parodies Euripides' *Aeolus*, whose hero married his children to one another, and the following dialogue the *Bellerophon*.

441

ARISTOPHANES

ΤΡΥΓΑΙΟΣ

δοξάσαι ἔστι, κόραι· τὸ δ᾽ ἐτήτυμον, ἄχθομαι ὑμῖν,
120 ἡνίκ᾽ ἂν αἰτίζητ᾽ ἄρτον πάππαν με καλοῦσαι,
ἔνδον δ᾽ ἀργυρίου μηδὲ ψακὰς ᾖ πάνυ πάμπαν.
ἢν δ᾽ ἐγὼ εὖ πράξας ἔλθω πάλιν, ἕξετ᾽ ἐν ὥρᾳ
κολλύραν μεγάλην καὶ κόνδυλον ὄψον ἐπ᾽ αὐτῇ.

ΠΑΙΔΙΟΝ

καὶ τίς πόρος σοι τῆς ὁδοῦ γενήσεται;
125 ναῦς μὲν γὰρ οὐκ ἄξει σε ταύτην τὴν ὁδόν.

ΤΡΥΓΑΙΟΣ

πτηνὸς πορεύσει πῶλος· οὐ ναυσθλώσομαι.

ΠΑΙΔΙΟΝ

τίς δ᾽ ἡπίνοιά σούστὶν ὥστε κάνθαρον
ζεύξαντ᾽ ἐλαύνειν εἰς θεούς, ὦ παππία;

ΤΡΥΓΑΙΟΣ

ἐν τοῖσιν Αἰσώπου λόγοις ἐξηυρέθη
130 μόνος πετηνῶν εἰς θεοὺς ἀφιγμένος.

ΠΑΙΔΙΟΝ

ἄπιστον εἶπας μῦθον, ὦ πάτερ πάτερ,
ὅπως κάκοσμον ζῷον ἦλθεν εἰς θεούς.

ΤΡΥΓΑΙΟΣ

ἦλθεν κατ᾽ ἔχθραν αἰετοῦ πάλαι ποτέ,
ᾧ᾽ ἐκκυλίνδων κἀντιτιμωρούμενος.

ΠΑΙΔΙΟΝ

135 οὐκοῦν ἐχρῆν σε Πηγάσου ζεῦξαι πτερόν,
ὅπως ἐφαίνου τοῖς θεοῖς τραγικώτερος.

PEACE

TRYGAEUS

You may guess, girls, but if truth be told, you annoy me
whenever you ask me for bread and call me dear daddy
when in our house there's nary a droplet of silver at all.
But if I return with success, you'll very soon be enjoying
a great big bun, topped off with a nice knuckle sandwich.

DAUGHTER

And what's to be your way of getting there? A ship certainly
won't take you on this voyage.

TRYGAEUS

A winged colt will take me; I don't intend to ply the sea.

DAUGHTER

But what's your point in harnessing a beetle and riding it
to heaven, daddy?

TRYGAEUS

In Aesop's fables[8] it's the only winged thing I could find
that ever reached the gods.

DAUGHTER

Ah father, father, incredible is your story, that a noisome
creature could ever have reached the gods!

TRYGAEUS

It went there, once upon a time, bearing a grudge against
the eagle, and got revenge by rolling eggs from its nest.

DAUGHTER

Well, you should have harnessed the wings of Pegasus, to
make a more tragic impression on the gods!

[8] See *Wasps* 1448.

ΤΡΤΓΑΙΟΣ

ἀλλ᾽, ὦ μέλ᾽, ἄν μοι σιτίων διπλῶν ἔδει·
νῦν δ᾽ ἅττ᾽ ἂν αὐτὸς καταφάγω τὰ σιτία,
τούτοισι τοῖς αὐτοῖσι τοῦτον χορτάσω.

ΠΑΙΔΙΟΝ

140 τί δ᾽, ἢν ἐς ὑγρὸν πόντιον πέσῃ βάθος;
πῶς ἐξολισθεῖν πτηνὸς ὢν δυνήσεται;

ΤΡΤΓΑΙΟΣ

ἐπίτηδες εἶχον πηδάλιον, ᾧ χρήσομαι·
τὸ δὲ πλοῖον ἔσται Ναξιουργὴς κάνθαρος.

ΠΑΙΔΙΟΝ

λιμὴν δὲ τίς σε δέξεται φορούμενον;

ΤΡΤΓΑΙΟΣ

145 ἐν Πειραιεῖ δήπου ᾽στὶ Κανθάρου λιμήν.

ΠΑΙΔΙΟΝ

ἐκεῖνο τήρει, μὴ σφαλεὶς καταρρυῇς
ἐντεῦθεν, εἶτα χωλὸς ὢν Εὐριπίδῃ
λόγον παράσχῃς καὶ τραγῳδία γένῃ.

ΤΡΤΓΑΙΟΣ

ἐμοὶ μελήσει ταῦτά γ᾽. ἀλλὰ χαίρετε.
150 ὑμεῖς δέ γ᾽, ὑπὲρ ὧν τοὺς πόνους ἐγὼ πονῶ,
μὴ βδεῖτε μηδὲ χέζεθ᾽ ἡμερῶν τριῶν·
ὡς εἰ μετέωρος οὗτος ὢν ὀσφρήσεται,
κατωκάρα ῥίψας με βουκολήσεται.

PEACE

TRYGAEUS

But then, my girl, I'd have needed feed for two; this way, whatever the food I eat myself, I'll reuse to fodder *him*.

DAUGHTER

But what if he falls into the damp depths of the deep? How could he wriggle out, winged though he is?

TRYGAEUS

(*indicating his phallus*) I brought along an oar for use in that event; and my vessel shall be a Naxian-built beetle-ship!

DAUGHTER

But what harbor will receive you when you're adrift?

TRYGAEUS

There's Beetle Bay at Piraeus, of course!

DAUGHTER

Watch out that you don't slip and fall off that thing,[9] and then be lamed and furnish Euripides with a plot, and become a tragedy.

TRYGAEUS

That I'll bear in mind. Now farewell!

DAUGHTERS and SECOND SLAVE go inside.

(*to the spectators*) As for all of you, for whose sake I'm performing these labors, stop farting and shitting for a period of three days; because if this thing picks up the scent while airborne, he'll toss me off head first, and go off to pasture.

---

[9] Like Bellerophon in Euripides' play.

ἀλλ' ἄγε, Πήγασε, χώρει χαίρων,
155 χρυσοχάλινον πάταγον ψαλίων
διακινήσας φαιδροῖς ὠσίν.
τί ποιεῖς, τί ποιεῖς; ποῖ παρακλίνεις
τοὺς μυκτῆρας; πρὸς τὰς λαύρας;
ἵει σαυτὸν θαρρῶν ἀπὸ γῆς,
160 κᾆτα δρομαίαν πτέρυγ' ἐκτείνων
ὀρθὸς χώρει Διὸς εἰς αὐλάς,
ἀπὸ μὲν κάκκης τὴν ῥῖν' ἀπέχων,
ἀπό θ' ἡμερίων σίτων πάντων.
ἄνθρωπε, τί δρᾷς, οὗτος ὁ χέζων
165 ἐν Πειραιεῖ παρὰ ταῖς πόρναις;
ἀπολεῖς μ', ἀπολεῖς. οὐ κατορύξεις
κἀπιφορήσεις τῆς γῆς πολλήν,
κἀπιφυτεύσεις ἕρπυλλον ἄνω
καὶ μύρον ἐπιχεῖς; ὡς ἤν τι πεσὼν
170 ἐνθένδε πάθω, τοὐμοῦ θανάτου
πέντε τάλανθ' ἡ πόλις ἡ Χίων
διὰ τὸν σὸν πρωκτὸν ὀφλήσει.

οἴμ' ὡς δέδοικα, κοὐκέτι σκώπτων λέγω.
ὦ μηχανοποιέ, πρόσεχε τὸν νοῦν, ὡς ἐμὲ
175 ἤδη στρέφει τι πνεῦμα περὶ τὸν ὀμφαλόν,
κεἰ μὴ φυλάξεις, χορτάσω τὸν κάνθαρον.
ἀτὰρ ἐγγὺς εἶναι τῶν θεῶν ἐμοὶ δοκῶ·
καὶ δὴ καθορῶ τὴν οἰκίαν τὴν τοῦ Διός.
τίς ἐν Διὸς θύραισιν; οὐκ ἀνοίξετε;

PEACE

Now giddyup, Pegasus, and bon voyage;
strike up the rattle of curb chains
on your golden bit, with ears laid back.
What are you doing, what are you doing? Where
are you pointing those nostrils? Toward the alleyways?
Hurl yourself bravely away from the ground,
then spread your racing pinions
and head straight to the halls of Zeus,
averting your nose from poop
and from all mortal feeds.
Man! Man in Piraeus, the one shitting
in the whores' quarter: what are you doing?
You'll get me killed, killed! Do cover it up,
pile plenty of dirt on top,
and plant thyme over it,
and pour on perfume! Because if I fall
from here and suffer any harm, for my death
the Chian state will be fined five talents,[10]
all because of your arsehole!

Uh oh, I'm really scared, and I'm not joking now! Stage
mechanic, pay attention, because some wind's already
churning around my navel, and if you aren't careful I'll be
foddering the beetle. (*the beetle descends*) But I think I'm
near the gods now. And yes, I see the house of Zeus down
there. (*lands at Zeus' door, dismounts, and knocks*) Who is
Zeus' doorman? Please open up.

[10] This fine, levied on any allied city in which an Athenian
citizen was killed, had perhaps been recently exacted from the
Chians in questionable circumstances.

ΕΡΜΗΣ

180 πόθεν βροτοῦ με προσέβαλ'— ὦναξ Ἡράκλεις,
τουτὶ τί ἐστι τὸ κακόν;

ΤΡΥΓΑΙΟΣ
ἱπποκάνθαρος.

ΕΡΜΗΣ

ὦ βδελυρὲ καὶ τόλμηρε κἀναίσχυντε σὺ
καὶ μιαρὲ καὶ παμμίαρε καὶ μιαρώτατε,
πῶς δεῦρ' ἀνῆλθες, ὦ μιαρῶν μιαρώτατε;
185 τί σοί ποτ' ἔστ' ὄνομ'; οὐκ ἐρεῖς;

ΤΡΥΓΑΙΟΣ
Μιαρώτατος.

ΕΡΜΗΣ

ποδαπὸς τὸ γένος δ' εἶ; φράζε μοι.

ΤΡΥΓΑΙΟΣ
Μιαρώτατος.

ΕΡΜΗΣ

πατὴρ δέ σοι τίς ἐστιν;

ΤΡΥΓΑΙΟΣ
ἐμοί; Μιαρώτατος.

ΕΡΜΗΣ

οὔτοι μὰ τὴν Γῆν ἔσθ' ὅπως οὐκ ἀποθανεῖ,
εἰ μὴ κατερεῖς μοι τοὔνομ' ὅ τι ποτ' ἐστί σοι.

ΤΡΥΓΑΙΟΣ

190 Τρυγαῖος Ἀθμονεύς, ἀμπελουργὸς δεξιός,
οὐ συκοφάντης οὐδ' ἐραστὴς πραγμάτων.

448

PEACE

HERMES

(*appearing in the doorway*) Whence impinges on me a mortal's—Lord Heracles, what the hell is this?

TRYGAEUS

A horsefly.

HERMES

You loathsome insolent shameless scum, you utter scum, you scum of the earth! How did you get up here, you arch-scum? Have you got a name? Well, speak up!

TRYGAEUS

Arch Scum.

HERMES

What's your race of origin? Tell me.

TRYGAEUS

Arch Scum.

HERMES

And who's your father?

TRYGAEUS

Mine? Arch Scum.

HERMES

So help me Earth, you're as good as dead if you don't declare to me just what your name is.

TRYGAEUS

Trygaeus of Athmonum, an accomplished vintager, no informer and no lover of litigation.

ARISTOPHANES

ΕΡΜΗΣ

ἥκεις δὲ κατὰ τί;

ΤΡΥΓΑΙΟΣ

τὰ κρέα ταυτί σοι φέρων.

ΕΡΜΗΣ

ὦ δειλακρίων, πῶς ἦλθες;

ΤΡΥΓΑΙΟΣ

ὦ γλίσχρων, ὁρᾷς
ὡς οὐκέτ᾽ εἶναί σοι δοκῶ μιαρώτατος;
195 ἴθι νυν κάλεσόν μοι τὸν Δί᾽.

ΕΡΜΗΣ

ἰηῦ ἰηῦ ἰηῦ,
ὅτ᾽ οὐδὲ μέλλεις ἐγγὺς εἶναι τῶν θεῶν·
φροῦδοι γάρ· ἐχθές εἰσιν ἐξῳκισμένοι.

ΤΡΥΓΑΙΟΣ

ποῖ γῆς;

ΕΡΜΗΣ

ἰδοὺ γῆς.

ΤΡΥΓΑΙΟΣ

ἀλλὰ ποῖ;

ΕΡΜΗΣ

πόρρω πάνυ,
ὑπ᾽ αὐτὸν ἀτεχνῶς τοὐρανοῦ τὸν κύτταρον.

ΤΡΥΓΑΙΟΣ

200 πῶς οὖν σὺ δῆτ᾽ ἐνταῦθα κατελείφθης μόνος;

PEACE

HERMES

And here on what errand?

TRYGAEUS

To offer you this meat.

HERMES

Welcome, my poor fellow!

TRYGAEUS

See, old sticky fingers, you don't think I'm arch-scum after all. Now go and call Zeus for me.

HERMES

Haw haw haw! You aren't even going to get near the gods. They're gone; they moved out yesterday.

TRYGAEUS

Where on earth to?

HERMES

"Earth"?

TRYGAEUS

All right, where?

HERMES

Far, far away, right under the very verge of heaven.

TRYGAEUS

Then how come you were left alone here?

---

195 ἰηῦ ἰηῦ ἰηῦ Π1: ἰὴ ἰὴ ἰὴ z

ΕΡΜΗΣ

τὰ λοιπὰ τηρῶ σκευάρια τὰ τῶν θεῶν,
χυτρίδια καὶ σανίδια κἀμφορείδια.

ΤΡΥΓΑΙΟΣ

ἐξῳκίσαντο δ᾽ οἱ θεοὶ τίνος οὕνεκα;

ΕΡΜΗΣ

Ἕλλησιν ὀργισθέντες. εἶτ᾽ ἐνταῦθα μὲν
205 ἵν᾽ ἦσαν αὐτοὶ τὸν Πόλεμον κατῴκισαν,
ὑμᾶς παραδόντες δρᾶν ἀτεχνῶς ὅ τι βούλεται·
αὐτοὶ δ᾽ ἀνῳκίσανθ᾽ ὅπως ἀνωτάτω,
ἵνα μὴ βλέποιεν μαχομένους ὑμᾶς ἔτι
μηδ᾽ ἀντιβολούντων μηδὲν αἰσθανοίατο.

ΤΡΥΓΑΙΟΣ

210 τοῦ δ᾽ οὕνεχ᾽ ἡμᾶς ταῦτ᾽ ἔδρασαν; εἰπέ μοι.

ΕΡΜΗΣ

ὁτιὴ πολεμεῖν ἡρεῖσθ᾽ ἐκείνων πολλάκις
σπονδὰς ποιούντων· κεἰ μὲν οἱ Λακωνικοὶ
ὑπερβάλοιντο μικρόν, ἔλεγον ἂν ταδί·
"ναὶ τὼ σιώ, νῦν ἁττικίων δωσεῖ δίκαν."
215 εἰ δ᾽ αὖ τι πράξαιτ᾽ ἀγαθόν ἀττικωνικοὶ
κἄλθοιεν οἱ Λάκωνες εἰρήνης πέρι,
ἐλέγετ᾽ ἂν ὑμεῖς εὐθύς· "ἐξαπατώμεθα,
νὴ τὴν Ἀθηνᾶν. — νὴ Δί᾽, οὐχὶ πειστέον. —
ἥξουσι καὖθις, ἢν ἔχωμεν τὴν Πύλον."

219 Πύλον pt: πόλιν RV, cf. ΣRV

PEACE

HERMES

I'm looking after the stuff the gods left—utensils, furniture, containers.

TRYGAEUS

And what was their reason for moving out?

HERMES

They grew angry with the Greeks. That's why they've ensconced War here, where they used to live, turning you over to him to treat exactly as he pleases, while they themselves have set up house as far above it all as they could get; that way they won't see any more of your fighting or hear any more of your prayers.

TRYGAEUS

But what was their reason for treating us that way? Do tell.

HERMES

Because you all kept choosing war, though they often tried to arrange a truce. If the Laconians achieved a small advantage, they'd say, "By the Twain Gods,[11] now Johnny Attic is going to pay the piper!" And if you Atticonians[12] achieved some success of your own and the Laconians came asking for peace, at once you'd say, "It's a trick, by Athena!" "Yes, by Zeus! We mustn't listen to them." "They'll be back, if we hold on to Pylos."[13]

---

[11] The Dioscuri ("sons of Zeus"), Castor and Pollux, were Sparta's special protectors.

[12] A name coined to emphasize that the Athenians were just as culpable as the Spartans.

[13] See *Clouds* 186 n.

ΤΡΥΓΑΙΟΣ

220 ὁ γοῦν χαρακτὴρ ἡμεδαπὸς τῶν ῥημάτων.

ΕΡΜΗΣ

ὧν οὕνεκ᾽ οὐκ οἶδ᾽ εἴ ποτ᾽ Εἰρήνην ἔτι
τὸ λοιπὸν ὄψεσθ᾽.

ΤΡΥΓΑΙΟΣ

ἀλλὰ ποῖ γὰρ οἴχεται;

ΕΡΜΗΣ

ὁ Πόλεμος αὐτὴν ἐνέβαλ᾽ εἰς ἄντρον βαθύ.

ΤΡΥΓΑΙΟΣ

εἰς ποῖον;

ΕΡΜΗΣ

εἰς τουτὶ τὸ κάτω. κἄπειθ᾽ ὁρᾷς
225 ὅσους ἄνωθεν ἐπεφόρησε τῶν λίθων,
ἵνα μὴ λάβητε μηδέποτ᾽ αὐτήν.

ΤΡΥΓΑΙΟΣ

εἰπέ μοι,
ἡμᾶς δὲ δὴ τί δρᾶν παρασκευάζεται;

ΕΡΜΗΣ

οὐκ οἶδα πλὴν ἕν, ὅτι θυείαν ἑσπέρας
ὑπερφυᾶ τὸ μέγεθος εἰσηνέγκατο.

ΤΡΥΓΑΙΟΣ

230 τί δῆτα ταύτῃ τῇ θυείᾳ χρήσεται;

ΕΡΜΗΣ

τρίβειν ἐν αὐτῇ τὰς πόλεις βουλεύεται.

TRYGAEUS

That's certainly our trademark way of talking.

HERMES

That's why I don't know whether in the future you'll ever see Peace again.

TRYGAEUS

Why? Where has she gone, then?

HERMES

War has thrown her into a deep cavern.

TRYGAEUS

What cavern?

HERMES

Into that one down there. And do you see how many stones he's piled on top, so that you'll never ever get your hands on her?

TRYGAEUS

Tell me, what's he getting ready to do to *us*?

HERMES

All I know is, he brought a kingsized mortar home last night.

TRYGAEUS

So what's he going to do with this mortar?

HERMES

He wants to pound up the cities in it. Well, I'm going. And

ἀλλ' εἶμι· καὶ γὰρ ἐξιέναι, γνώμην ἐμήν,
μέλλει· θορυβεῖ γοῦν ἔνδον.

ΤΡΥΓΑΙΟΣ
                              οἴμοι δείλαιος.
φέρ' αὐτὸν ἀποδρῶ· καὶ γὰρ ὥσπερ ἠσθόμην
235 καὐτὸς θυείας φθέγμα πολεμιστηρίας.

ΠΟΛΕΜΟΣ
ἰὼ βροτοὶ βροτοὶ βροτοὶ πολυτλήμονες,
ὡς αὐτίκα μάλα τὰς γνάθους ἀλγήσετε.

ΤΡΥΓΑΙΟΣ
ὦναξ Ἄπολλον, τῆς θυείας τοῦ πλάτους·
ὅσον κακὸν καὶ τοῦ Πολέμου τοῦ βλέμματος.
240 ἆρ' οὗτός ἐστ' ἐκεῖνος ὃν καὶ φεύγομεν,
ὁ δεινός, ὁ ταλαύρινος, ὁ κατὰ τοῖν σκελοῖν;

ΠΟΛΕΜΟΣ
ἰὼ Πρασιαὶ τρισάθλιαι καὶ πεντάκις
καὶ πολλοδεκάκις, ὡς ἀπολεῖσθε τήμερον.

ΤΡΥΓΑΙΟΣ
τουτὶ μέν, ἄνδρες, οὐδὲν ἡμῖν πρᾶγμά πω·
245 τὸ γὰρ κακὸν τοῦτ' ἐστὶ τῆς Λακωνικῆς.

ΠΟΛΕΜΟΣ
ἰὼ Μέγαρ', ὡς ξυνεπιτετρίψεσθ' αὐτίκα
ἀπαξάπαντα καταμεμυττωτευμένα.

---

246 ἰὼ pt: ὦ cett.   Μέγαρ', ὡς ξυνεπι- Sommerstein,
CQ 36 (1986) 353-58: Μέγαρα, Μέγαρ' ὡς ἐπι- z
-τετρίψεσθ' Elmsley: -τρίψεσθ' z

in my opinion, *he's* on his way out here, to judge from the racket he's making in there.

HERMES goes inside.

TRYGAEUS

Oh my, what a fix! I've got to run out of his way; I myself sort of caught the sound of a martial mortar. (*conceals himself*)

Enter WAR, with mortar and food basket.

WAR

Oho, mortals, mortals, much-suffering mortals, what sore chops you're going to have, and very soon!

TRYGAEUS

Lord Apollo, the size of that mortar! How nasty is the mere look of War! Is this the actual god that we flee, the awful one, the tough as leather, the one that runs down our legs?

WAR

(*throwing leeks into the mortar*) Oho, Prasiae,[14] thrice wretched, five times wretched, tens of times wretched, how you'll be smashed today!

TRYGAEUS

(*aside to the spectators*) This, gentlemen, isn't *our* problem yet; this trouble is Laconia's.

WAR

(*adding garlic*) Oho, Megara, how you'll be crushed up soon, every last bit, and tumbled into tossed salad!

[14] A Laconian town whose name puns on leeks (*prasa*); War makes a salad containing ingredients associated with the cities he names.

457

ΤΡΥΓΑΙΟΣ

βαβαὶ βαβαιάξ, ὡς μεγάλα καὶ δριμέα
τοῖσι Μεγαρεῦσιν ἐνέβαλεν τὰ κλαύματα.

ΠΟΛΕΜΟΣ

250 ἰὼ Σικελία, καὶ σὺ δ᾽ ὡς ἀπόλλυσαι.

ΤΡΥΓΑΙΟΣ

οἵα πόλις τάλαινα διακναισθήσεται.

ΠΟΛΕΜΟΣ

φέρ᾽ ἐπιχέω καὶ τὸ μέλι τουτὶ τἀττικόν.

ΤΡΥΓΑΙΟΣ

οὗτος, παραινῶ σοι μέλιτι χρῆσθαι ᾿τέρῳ.
τετρώβολον τοῦτ᾽ ἐστί· φείδου τἀττικοῦ.

ΠΟΛΕΜΟΣ

255 παῖ παῖ Κυδοιμέ.

ΚΥΔΟΙΜΟΣ

τί με καλεῖς;

ΠΟΛΕΜΟΣ

κλαύσει μακρά.
ἕστηκας ἀργός; οὑτοσί σοι κόνδυλος.

ΚΥΔΟΙΜΟΣ

ὡς δριμύς. οἴμοι μοι τάλας, ὦ δέσποτα.

ΤΡΥΓΑΙΟΣ

μῶν τῶν σκορόδων ἐνέβαλεν εἰς τὸν κόνδυλον;

ΠΟΛΕΜΟΣ

οἴσεις ἀλετρίβανον τρέχων;

TRYGAEUS

(*aside*) Good gracious, what loud and pungent sobbing he's thrown in for the Megarians!

WAR

(*adding cheese*) Oho, Sicily, how you're to be ruined too!

TRYGAEUS

(*aside*) What a fine state will be haplessly grated up!

WAR

(*adding honey*) Here, let's pour in this Attic honey too.

TRYGAEUS

(*aside*) Hey, I suggest you use another kind of honey; go easy on the Attic, it costs four obols!

WAR

Boy! Boy! Hubbub!

HUBBUB comes out of the house.

HUBBUB

You called?

WAR

You'll really catch it, standing there idle! Have some of these knuckles! (*beats Hubbub*)

HUBBUB

That one stung! Ouch, oh my! Master!

TRYGAEUS

(*aside*) Are you sure you didn't throw some of the garlic into that punch?

WAR

Run and fetch a pestle, will you?

ΚΤΔΟΙΜΟΣ

ἀλλ᾽, ὦ μέλε,
260 οὐκ ἔστιν ἡμῖν· ἐχθὲς εἰσῳκίσμεθα.

ΠΟΛΕΜΟΣ

οὔκουν παρ᾽ Ἀθηναίων μεταθρέξει ταχὺ ‹πάνυ›;

ΚΤΔΟΙΜΟΣ

ἔγωγε νὴ Δί᾽· εἰ δὲ μή γε, κλαύσομαι.

ΤΡΥΓΑΙΟΣ

ἄγε δή, τί δρῶμεν, ὦ πόνηρ᾽ ἀνθρώπια;
ὁρᾶτε τὸν κίνδυνον ἡμῖν ὡς μέγας·
265 εἴπερ γὰρ ἥξει τὸν ἀλετρίβανον φέρων,
τούτῳ ταράξει τὰς πόλεις καθήμενος.
ἀλλ᾽ ὦ Διόνυσ᾽, ἀπόλοιτο καὶ μὴ ᾽λθοι φέρων.

ΚΤΔΟΙΜΟΣ

οὗτος.

ΠΟΛΕΜΟΣ

τί ἐστιν; οὐ φέρεις;

ΚΤΔΟΙΜΟΣ

τὸ δεῖνα γάρ,
ἀπόλωλ᾽ Ἀθηναίοισιν ἀλετρίβανος,
270 ὁ βυρσοπώλης, ὃς ἐκύκα τὴν Ἑλλάδα.

ΤΡΥΓΑΙΟΣ

εὖ γ᾽, ὦ πότνια δέσποιν᾽ Ἀθηναία, ποιῶν
ἀπόλωλ᾽ ἐκεῖνος κἀν δέοντι τῇ πόλει,

PEACE

HUBBUB
But sir, we haven't got one; we only moved in yesterday.

WAR
So why not run and get one from Athens, and quickly?

HUBBUB
I sure will. (*aside*) If I don't, I'll catch it.

HUBBUB runs off.

TRYGAEUS
(*to the spectators*) All right, you sorry little people, what do we do now? You see what serious danger we face: if Hubbub does come back with that pestle, War's going to sit down and mash the cities with it! Please, Dionysus, may he perish before he brings it back![15]

HUBBUB returns.

HUBBUB
Ahem.

WAR
Well? Don't you have it?

HUBBUB
Well, the thing is, the Athenians have lost their pestle: the leather seller who used to churn up Greece.[16]

TRYGAEUS
Lady Mistress Athena, it's a good thing he's lost, and just

[15] Addressed to Dionysus' cult image, which sat in the first row of the theater.
[16] I.e. Cleon; cf. 47-8 n.

461

εἰ πρίν γε τὸν μυττωτὸν ἡμῖν ἐγχέαι.

ΠΟΛΕΜΟΣ
οὔκουν ἕτερον δῆτ' ἐκ Λακεδαίμονος μέτει
275 ἀνύσας τι;

ΚΤΔΟΙΜΟΣ
ταῦτ', ὦ δέσποθ'.

ΠΟΛΕΜΟΣ
ἧκέ νυν ταχύ.

ΤΡΥΓΑΙΟΣ
ὦνδρες, τι πεισόμεσθα; νῦν ἀγὼν μέγας.
ἀλλ' εἴ τις ὑμῶν ἐν Σαμοθρᾴκῃ τυγχάνει
μεμυημένος, νῦν ἐστιν εὔξασθαι καλὸν
ἀποστραφῆναι τοῦ μετιόντος τὼ πόδε.

ΚΤΔΟΙΜΟΣ
280 οἴμοι τάλας, οἴμοι γε κᾆτ' οἴμοι μάλα.

ΠΟΛΕΜΟΣ
τί ἐστι; μῶν οὐκ αὖ φέρεις;

ΚΤΔΟΙΜΟΣ
ἀπόλωλε γὰρ
καὶ τοῖς Λακεδαιμονίοισιν ἀλετρίβανος.

ΠΟΛΕΜΟΣ
πῶς, ὦ πανοῦργ';

273 del. Dindorf

462

in the nick of time for the city, if he was about to pour the pesto on us.

WAR

Then why don't you go fetch one from Sparta, and hurry!

HUBBUB

Yes sir.

HUBBUB runs off.

WAR

Come back quickly, now!

TRYGAEUS

(*to the spectators*) Gentlemen, what's to become of us? Now is our great test. And if by chance there's anyone out there who's been initiated at Samothrace,[17] now's a good time to pray that our fetcher sprains both ankles!

HUBBUB returns.

HUBBUB

Oh me oh my! Oh me oh my again!

WAR

What is it? Don't tell me you still don't have it!

HUBBUB

I don't, because the Spartans have lost their pestle too!

WAR

What do you mean, you rascal?

[17] Initiates of the mysteries there were guaranteed a favorable response to their prayers, especially when traveling.

ΚΥΔΟΙΜΟΣ

εἰς τἀπὶ Θράκης χωρία
χρήσαντες ἑτέροις αὐτὸν εἶτ' ἀπώλεσαν.

ΤΡΥΓΑΙΟΣ

285   εὖ γ', εὖ γε ποιήσαντες, ὦ Διοσκόρω.
ἴσως ἂν εὖ γένοιτο· θαρρεῖτ', ὦ βροτοί.

ΠΟΛΕΜΟΣ

ἀπόφερε τὰ σκεύη λαβὼν ταυτὶ πάλιν·
ἐγὼ δὲ δοίδυκ' εἰσιὼν ποιήσομαι.

ΤΡΥΓΑΙΟΣ

νῦν, τοῦτ' ἐκεῖν', ἥκει τὸ Δάτιδος μέλος.
290   ὃ δεφόμενός ποτ' ᾖδε τῆς μεσημβρίας·
"ὡς ἥδομαι καὶ χαίρομαι κεὐφραίνομαι."
νῦν ἐστιν ἡμῖν, ὦνδρες Ἕλληνες, καλὸν
ἀπαλλαγεῖσι πραγμάτων τε καὶ μαχῶν
ἐξελκύσαι τὴν πᾶσιν Εἰρήνην φίλην,
295   πρὶν ἕτερον αὖ δοίδυκα κωλῦσαί τινα.
ἀλλ', ὦ γεωργοὶ κἄμποροι καὶ τέκτονες
καὶ δημιουργοὶ καὶ μέτοικοι καὶ ξένοι
καὶ νησιῶται, δεῦρ' ἴτ', ὦ πάντες λεῴ,
ὡς τάχιστ' ἅμας λαβόντες καὶ μοχλοὺς καὶ σχοινία·

292 ἡμῖν t: ὑμῖν cett.

---

[18] Brasidas, sent north at the request of King Perdiccas of
Macedon (Thucydides 4.79), like Cleon died the previous sum-
mer at Amphipolis (5.16).

HUBBUB

They lent it to some people to use at the Thracian front, and lost it.[18]

TRYGAEUS

(*aside*) Good! Good for them, you Dioscuri![19] Things just may turn out all right. Take heart, mortals!

WAR

Pick up this equipment and carry it back inside. I'll go in and make a pestle myself.

WAR and HUBBUB go inside.

TRYGAEUS

(*emerging from concealment*) That's that, now! Here comes the song of Datis, which once upon a time he used to sing while masturbating of an afternoon: "How happy, how pleasured, how bubbly I feel!"[20] Now is a good time, men of Greece, to rid ourselves of troubles and battles by excavating Peace, the friend of us all, before some other pestle foils us again. You farmers and merchants and carpenters and craftsmen and immigrants and foreigners and islanders, come here, all you people, as quick as you can; bring shovels and crowbars and ropes;[21] now is our chance

[19] See 214 n.

[20] Datis the Mede jointly commanded the force that the Athenians defeated at Marathon in 490. The origin of the song is unknown; the scholia refer it to one of Carcinus' sons (see *Wasps* 1500 n.), who they say was nicknamed Datis.

[21] This summons recalls the scene in Aeschylus' satyr drama *Netfishers* (fr. 46a Radt) where the chest containing Danae and Perseus is hauled from the sea.

300 νῦν γὰρ ἡμῖν ἑλκύσαι πάρεστιν ἀγαθοῦ δαίμονος.

ΚΟΡΥΦΑΙΟΣ

δεῦρο πᾶς χώρει προθύμως εὐθὺ τῆς σωτηρίας.
ὦ Πανέλληνες, βοηθήσωμεν, εἴπερ πώποτε,
τάξεων ἀπαλλαγέντες καὶ καλῶν φοινικίδων·
ἡμέρα γὰρ ἐξέλαμψεν ἥδε μισολάμαχος.

305 πρὸς τάδ᾿ ἡμῖν, εἴ τι χρὴ δρᾶν, φράζε κἀρχιτεκ-
        τόνει·
οὐ γὰρ ἔσθ᾿ ὅπως ἀπειπεῖν ἂν δοκῶ μοι τήμερον,
πρὶν μοχλοῖς καὶ μηχαναῖσιν εἰς τὸ φῶς ἀνελκύσαι
τὴν θεῶν πασῶν μεγίστην καὶ φιλαμπελωτάτην.

ΤΡΥΓΑΙΟΣ

οὐ σιωπήσεσθ᾿, ὅπως μὴ περιχαρεῖς τῷ πράγματι
310 τὸν Πόλεμον ἐκζωπυρήσετ᾿ ἔνδοθεν κεκραγότες;

ΚΟΡΥΦΑΙΟΣ

ἀλλ᾿ ἀκούσαντες τοιούτου χαίρομεν κηρύγματος·
οὐ γὰρ ἦν ἔχοντας ἥκειν σιτί᾿ ἡμερῶν τριῶν.

ΤΡΥΓΑΙΟΣ

εὐλαβεῖσθέ νυν ἐκεῖνον τὸν κάτωθεν Κέρβερον,
μὴ παφλάζων καὶ κεκραγὼς ὥσπερ ἡνίκ᾿ ἐνθάδ᾿ ἦν,
315 ἐμποδὼν ἡμῖν γένηται τὴν θεὸν μὴ 'ξελκύσαι.

---

300 ἑλκύσαι Blaydes: ἁρπάσαι z
303 καλῶν Sommerstein: κακῶν z

---

[22] The spirit embodying sympotic fellowship, to whom the first libation after a meal was poured neat.

[23] Such as officers both Athenian and Spartan wore.

to hoist one for the Good Spirit![22]

Enter the CHORUS, carrying excavating tools.

CHORUS LEADER

Everyone come this way in high spirits, straight for salvation! All you Greeks, let's lend a hand, now if ever before, and rid ourselves of musters and fine red uniforms;[23] for this is the shining dawn of a Lamachus-loathing day![24] (*to Trygaeus*) So tell us what needs doing here, and be our foreman; I can't imagine myself calling it quits today, till with crowbars and cranes we've hoisted up to the light the greatest of all goddesses, and the one most friendly to vines.

TRYGAEUS

Won't you be quiet? Don't be so overjoyful about our business that you fire up War in there with your shouting.

CHORUS LEADER

But this is the kind of proclamation we're overjoyed to hear; it wasn't "Come with three days' rations."

TRYGAEUS

Now beware of that Cerberus[25] below ground; he might start spluttering and bellowing, as he did when he was up here, and become an obstacle to our excavating the goddess.

[24] The general who had typified bellicosity in *Acharnians* (his name means "Great Battler"), but who would be a signatory to the peace of 421 (Thucydides 5.19).

[25] Aristophanes had compared Cleon, self-styled "watchdog" of the people (*Wasps* 894-994), with Cerberus (Hound of Hades) even before his death (*Knights* 1030).

ARISTOPHANES

ΚΟΡΤΦΑΙΟΣ

οὐδ᾽ ἐκείνων ἔστιν αὐτὴν ὅστις ἐξαιρήσεται,
ἢν ἅπαξ εἰς χεῖρας ἔλθῃ τὰς ἐμάς. ἰοὺ ἰού.

ΤΡΤΓΑΙΟΣ

ἐξολεῖτέ μ᾽, ὦνδρες, εἰ μὴ τῆς βοῆς ἀνήσετε·
ἐκδραμὼν γὰρ πάντα ταυτὶ συνταράξει τοῖν ποδοῖν.

ΚΟΡΤΦΑΙΟΣ

320 ὡς κυκάτω καὶ πατείτω πάντα καὶ ταραττέτω·
οὐ γὰρ ἂν χαίροντες ἡμεῖς τήμερον παυσαίμεθ᾽ ἄν.

ΤΡΤΓΑΙΟΣ

τί τὸ κακόν; τί πάσχετ᾽, ὦνδρες; μηδαμῶς, πρὸς
    τῶν θεῶν,
πρᾶγμα κάλλιστον διαφθείρητε διὰ τὰ σχήματα.

ΚΟΡΤΦΑΙΟΣ

ἀλλ᾽ ἔγωγ᾽ οὐ σχηματίζειν βούλομ᾽, ἀλλ᾽ ὑφ᾽
    ἡδονῆς
325 οὐκ ἐμοῦ κινοῦντος αὐτὼ τὼ σκέλει χορεύετον.

ΤΡΤΓΑΙΟΣ

μή τί μοι νυνί γ᾽ ἔτ᾽, ἀλλὰ παῦε παῦ᾽ ὀρχούμενος.

ΚΟΡΤΦΑΙΟΣ

ἢν ἰδού, καὶ δὴ πέπαυμαι.

ΤΡΤΓΑΙΟΣ

                    φῄς γε, παύει δ᾽ οὐδέπω.

ΚΟΡΤΦΑΙΟΣ

ἓν μὲν οὖν τουτί μ᾽ ἔασον ἑλκύσαι, καὶ μηκέτι.

CHORUS LEADER

Not even one of *them* will be able to snatch her away if once she comes into our hands.[26] Hurrah, hurrah!

TRYGAEUS

You'll be my undoing, men, if you don't abate your shouting. He'll rush out and trample everything underfoot.

CHORUS LEADER

I say let him confound and trample everything and mess it all up; today we're not about to stop rejoicing! (*the Chorus begin to dance*)

TRYGAEUS

Damn it, men, what's the matter with you? Stop it, in heaven's name, don't spoil a marvelous opportunity by cutting capers!

CHORUS LEADER

It's not that I want to cut capers, and I'm not moving my legs, but from sheer joy they're dancing on their own.

TRYGAEUS

Well, no more for now, please. Stop, stop dancing!

CHORUS LEADER

There, then; look, I *have* stopped.

TRYGAEUS

That's what you say, but still you haven't stopped.

CHORUS LEADER

Just let me take one more spin, then that's it.

---

[26] Adapted from Euripides, *Children of Heracles* 976-7.

---

316 οὐδ' ἐκείνων Sharpley: οὔτι καὶ νῦν z

ΤΡΤΓΑΙΟΣ

τοῦτό νυν, καὶ μηκέτ᾿ ἄλλο· μηδὲν ὀρχήσεσθέ τι.

ΚΟΡΤΦΑΙΟΣ

330 οὐκ ἂν ὀρχησαίμεθ᾿, εἴπερ ὠφελήσαιμέν τί σε.

ΤΡΤΓΑΙΟΣ

ἀλλ᾿, ὁρᾶτ᾿, οὔπω πέπαυσθε.

ΚΟΡΤΦΑΙΟΣ

                              τουτογὶ νὴ τὸν Δία
τὸ σκέλος ῥίψαντες ἤδη λήγομεν τὸ δεξιόν.

ΤΡΤΓΑΙΟΣ

ἐπιδίδωμι τοῦτό γ᾿ ὑμῖν, ὥστε μὴ λυπεῖν ἔτι.

ΚΟΡΤΦΑΙΟΣ

ἀλλὰ καὶ τἀριστερόν τοί μ᾿ ἔστ᾿ ἀναγκαίως ἔχον.
335 ἥδομαι γὰρ καὶ γέγηθα καὶ πέπορδα καὶ γελῶ
μᾶλλον ἢ τὸ γῆρας ἐκδὺς ἐκφυγὼν τὴν ἀσπίδα.

ΤΡΤΓΑΙΟΣ

μή τί μοι νυνί γε χαίρετ᾿· οὐ γὰρ ἴστε πω σαφῶς·
ἀλλ᾿ ὅταν λάβωμεν αὐτήν, τηνικαῦτα χαίρετε
καὶ βοᾶτε καὶ γελᾶτ᾿· ἤ-
340   δη γὰρ ἐξέσται τόθ᾿ ὑμῖν
    πλεῖν, μένειν, κινεῖν, καθεύδειν,
    εἰς πανηγύρεις θεωρεῖν,
    ἑστιᾶσθαι, κοτταβίζειν,
    συβαριάζειν,
345   ἰοὺ ἰοὺ κεκραγέναι.

PEACE

TRYGAEUS
That's it then, and no more. I said no more dancing!

CHORUS LEADER
Then we won't dance, if it'll do you any good.

TRYGAEUS
But look, you still haven't stopped!

CHORUS LEADER
We'll flip this right leg here, then I swear we're done.

TRYGAEUS
Have that one on me, so you'll stop being a pain.

CHORUS LEADER
But you know what, the left leg can't help doing it too! Oh
I'm glad, I'm happy, I fart and I laugh about getting free
of my shield, more than if I'd shed my old age!

TRYGAEUS
Please don't rejoice just now; you can't be certain yet. But
when we've got her, then you may rejoice and yell and
laugh, for then at last you'll be free to travel, stay home,
screw, sleep in, attend big festivals, feast, roll dice, live it
up, and yell "hey hey!"

ARISTOPHANES

(στρ) εἴθε μοι γένοιτ᾽ ἰδεῖν τὴν ἡμέραν ταύτην ποτέ.
πολλὰ γὰρ ἀνεσχόμην
πράγματά τε καὶ στιβάδας
ἃς ἔλαχε Φορμίων·
κοὐκέτ᾽ ἄν μ᾽ εὕροις δικαστὴν δριμὺν οὐδὲ δύσκολον
350 οὐδὲ τοὺς τρόπους γε δήπου σκληρὸν ὥσπερ καὶ
πρὸ τοῦ,
ἀλλ᾽ ἀπαλὸν ἄν μ᾽ ἴδοις
καὶ πολὺ νεώτερον ἀπ-
αλλαγέντα πραγμάτων.
καὶ γὰρ ἱκανὸν χρόνον ἀπ-
ολλύμεθα καὶ κατατε-
355 τρίμμεθα πλανώμενοι
εἰς Λύκειον κἀκ Λυκείου σὺν δορὶ ξὺν ἀσπίδι.
ἀλλ᾽ ὅ τι μάλιστα χαρι-
ούμεθα ποιοῦντες, ἄγε,
φράζε· σὲ γὰρ αὐτοκράτορ᾽
360 εἵλετ᾽ ἀγαθή τις ἡμῖν τύχη.

ΤΡΥΓΑΙΟΣ

φέρε δὴ κατίδω πῇ τοὺς λίθους ἀφέλξομεν.

ΕΡΜΗΣ

ὦ μιαρὲ καὶ τόλμηρε, τί ποιεῖν διανοεῖ;

---

27 A famously hardy commander, who probably died in 429/8
(Thucydides 3.7).

PEACE

CHORUS

I hope I've the chance to see that day!
For I've put up with many troubles
and many of those sleeping bags
that Phormio gets issued.[27]
And you'll no longer find me a severe and colicky
    juror,
nor such a hard case as I guess I was before;
no, a gentle me you'll see
and far more youthful,
with trouble off my back.
For long enough we've been
destroying ourselves, and we're
worn out with trudging
to the Lyceum and from the Lyceum[28] "with spear
    and shield."
But whatever we can do
to please you, come
tell us; for a stroke of good luck
has chosen you as our commander.

TRYGAEUS

Very well then, let's see how we're going to clear away these
stones.

HERMES approaches.

HERMES

You brazen skunk! What do you think you're doing?

---

[28] A military drill and mustering ground just east of the city
walls.

ΤΡΥΓΑΙΟΣ

οὐδὲν πονηρόν, ἀλλ᾽ ὅπερ καὶ Κιλλικῶν.

ΕΡΜΗΣ

ἀπόλωλας, ὦ κακόδαιμον.

ΤΡΥΓΑΙΟΣ

οὐκοῦν, ἢν λάχω·

365 Ἑρμῆς γὰρ ὢν κλήρῳ ποιήσεις οἶδ᾽ ὅτι.

ΕΡΜΗΣ

ἀπόλωλας, ἐξόλωλας.

ΤΡΥΓΑΙΟΣ

εἰς τίν᾽ ἡμέραν;

ΕΡΜΗΣ

εἰς αὐτίκα μάλ᾽.

ΤΡΥΓΑΙΟΣ

ἀλλ᾽ οὐδὲν ἠμπόληκά πω,
οὔτ᾽ ἄλφιτ᾽ οὔτε τυρόν, ὡς ἀπολούμενος.

ΕΡΜΗΣ

καὶ μὴν ἐπιτέτριψαί γε.

ΤΡΥΓΑΙΟΣ

κᾆτα τῷ τρόπῳ
370 οὐκ ᾐσθόμην ἀγαθὸν τοσουτονὶ λαβών;

ΕΡΜΗΣ

ἆρ᾽ οἶσθα θάνατον ὅτι προεῖφ᾽ ὁ Ζεὺς ὃς ἂν
ταύτην ἀνορύττων εὑρεθῇ;

PEACE

TRYGAEUS
Nothing wrong, the same as Cillicon.[29]

HERMES
You're done for, you miserable loser!

TRYGAEUS
I guess so, if my number comes up. Being Hermes, I know you'll do it by lots.

HERMES
You're doomed! Utterly doomed!

TRYGAEUS
When is my doom scheduled?

HERMES
This very minute!

TRYGAEUS
But I haven't done the shopping for my last meal yet, no groats or cheese.

HERMES
I mean you're obliterated!

TRYGAEUS
Then how come I didn't notice I'd got such good luck?

HERMES
You do realize that Zeus has ordained death for anyone caught digging her up?

[29] A legendary traitor, who when caught claimed to be doing "only good."

---

365 del. van Leeuwen

ΤΡΥΓΑΙΟΣ

νῦν ἆρά με
ἅπασ᾽ ἀνάγκη 'στ᾽ ἀποθανεῖν;

ΕΡΜΗΣ

εὖ ἴσθ᾽ ὅτι.

ΤΡΥΓΑΙΟΣ

εἰς χοιρίδιόν μοί νυν δάνεισον τρεῖς δραχμάς·
375 δεῖ γὰρ μυηθῆναί με πρὶν τεθνηκέναι.

ΕΡΜΗΣ

ὦ Ζεῦ κεραυνοβρόντα—

ΤΡΥΓΑΙΟΣ

μή, πρὸς τῶν θεῶν,
ἡμῶν κατείπῃς, ἀντιβολῶ σ᾽, ὦ δέσποτα.

ΕΡΜΗΣ

οὐκ ἂν σιωπήσαιμι.

ΤΡΥΓΑΙΟΣ

ναί, πρὸς τῶν κρεῶν,
ἁγὼ προθύμως σοι φέρων ἀφικόμην.

ΕΡΜΗΣ

380 ἀλλ᾽, ὦ μέλ᾽, ὑπὸ τοῦ Διὸς ἀμαλδυνθήσομαι,
εἰ μὴ τετορήσω ταῦτα καὶ λακήσομαι.

ΤΡΥΓΑΙΟΣ

μή νυν λακήσῃς, λίσσομαί σ᾽, ὦρμῄδιον.
εἰπέ μοι, τί πάσχετ᾽, ὦνδρες; ἕστατ᾽ ἐκπεπληγμένοι.
ὦ πόνηροι, μὴ σιωπᾶτ᾽· εἰ δὲ μή, λακήσεται.

PEACE

TRYGAEUS

Then it's absolutely necessary that I die now?

HERMES

That's right.

TRYGAEUS

Then lend me three drachmas for a piglet; I've got to get initiated before I die.[30]

HERMES

(*looking skyward*) O Zeus, Thundercrasher—

TRYGAEUS

Please don't turn us in, by the gods I beg you, my lord!

HERMES

I'll not cover this up!

TRYGAEUS

Please do, by the meat that I eagerly came here to bring you!

HERMES

But my good man, Zeus will demolish me if I don't screech and boom this news abroad!

TRYGAEUS

Don't boom, I pray you, my darling Hermes! (*to the Chorus*) Say there, what's the matter with you, men? You stand there dumbfounded. You rascals, don't hold your tongues; or else he'll start booming!

[30] Into the Eleusinian Mysteries, which promised initiates happiness after death.

ARISTOPHANES

ΧΟΡΟΣ

(ἀντ α’) μηδαμῶς, ὦ δέσποθ’ Ἑρμῆ, μηδαμῶς, μή, μηδαμῶς,
386 εἴ τι κεχαρισμένον
χοιρίδιον οἶσθα παρ’ ἐ-
μοῦ γε κατεδηδοκώς,
τοῦτο μὴ φαῦλον νόμιζ’ ἐν τῷδε τῷ πράγματι.

ΤΡΥΓΑΙΟΣ
οὐκ ἀκούεις οἷα θωπεύουσί σ’, ὦναξ δέσποτα;

ΧΟΡΟΣ
390 μὴ γένῃ παλίγκοτος
σ’ ἀντιάζουσιν ἡμῖν,
ὥστε τήνδε μὴ λαβεῖν·
ἀλλὰ χάρισ’, ὦ φιλαν-
θρωπότατε καὶ μεγαλο-
δωρότατε δαιμόνων,
395 εἴ τι Πεισάνδρου βδελύττει τοὺς λόφους καὶ τὰς
ὀφρῦς.
καί σε θυσίαισιν ἱε-
ραῖσι προσόδοις τε μεγά-
λαισι διὰ παντός, ὦ
δέσποτ’, ἀγαλοῦμεν ἡμεῖς ἀεί.

ΤΡΥΓΑΙΟΣ
400 ἴθ’, ἀντιβολῶ σ’, ἐλέησον αὐτῶν τὴν ὄπα,
ἐπεί σε καὶ τιμῶσι μᾶλλον ἢ πρὸ τοῦ.

391 σ’ ἀντιάζουσιν White: ἀντιβολοῦσιν z

PEACE

CHORUS

Don't, Lord Hermes, don't, no don't!
If you remember ever receiving,
with my compliments, a piglet
for your delectation,
don't despise that gesture at a time like this!

TRYGAEUS

Don't you hear how they flatter you, sovereign lord?

CHORUS

Don't be so hostile
to our entreaties
as to prevent our getting her;
but be gracious, most
philanthropic of divinities
and most bountiful,
if you feel any loathing for Pisander's crests and
    brows,[31]
and we will always, Lord,
pay you homage continually
with holy sacrifices
and great processions.

TRYGAEUS

Come, I beg you, take pity on their cry, since they honor
you even more than ever.

---

[31] A pro-war politician criticized elsewhere in comedy as a
glutton and a coward.

ΕΡΜΗΣ

κλέπται γάρ εἰσι νῦν γε μᾶλλον ἢ πρὸ τοῦ.

ΤΡΥΓΑΙΟΣ

καί σοι φράσω τι πρᾶγμα δεινὸν καὶ μέγα,
ὃ τοῖς θεοῖς ἅπασιν ἐπιβουλεύεται.

ΕΡΜΗΣ

405 ἴθι δή, κάτειπ'· ἴσως γὰρ ἂν πείσαις ἐμέ.

ΤΡΥΓΑΙΟΣ

ἡ γὰρ Σελήνη χὠ πανοῦργος Ἥλιος
ὑμῖν ἐπιβουλεύοντε πολὺν ἤδη χρόνον
τοῖς βαρβάροισι προδίδοτον τὴν Ἑλλάδα.

ΕΡΜΗΣ

ἵνα δὴ τί τοῦτο δρᾶτον;

ΤΡΥΓΑΙΟΣ

         ὁτιὴ νὴ Δία

410 ἡμεῖς μὲν ὑμῖν θύομεν, τούτοισι δὲ
οἱ βάρβαροι θύουσι, διὰ τοῦτ' εἰκότως
βούλοιντ' ἂν ἡμᾶς πάντας ἐξολωλέναι,
ἵνα τὰς τελετὰς λάβοιεν αὐτοὶ τῶν θεῶν.

ΕΡΜΗΣ

ταῦτ' ἄρα πάλαι τῶν ἡμερῶν παρεκλέπτετον
415 καὶ τοῦ κύκλου παρέτρωγον ὑφ' ἁμαρτωλίας.

ΤΡΥΓΑΙΟΣ

ναὶ μὰ Δία. πρὸς ταῦτ', ὦ φίλ' Ἑρμῆ, ξύλλαβε
ἡμῖν προθύμως τήνδε τε ξυνανέλκυσον.
καί σοι τὰ μεγάλ' ἡμεῖς Παναθήnαι' ἄξομεν

HERMES

Because now they're bigger thieves than ever!

TRYGAEUS

And I'm going to tell you something terribly important, something that's being plotted against all the gods.

HERMES

By all means, speak up; perhaps you'll convince me.

TRYGAEUS

Well, the Moon and that nefarious Sun have been plotting against you for some time now and mean to betray Greece to the barbarians.

HERMES

What do they hope to accomplish by that?

TRYGAEUS

Simple: we sacrifice to you and the barbarians sacrifice to them; so naturally they'd want us all annihilated, so they could take over the rites of the gods themselves.

HERMES

So that's why they've long been clipping days and taking bites out of the year: pure chicanery.[32]

TRYGAEUS

Absolutely. And so, my dear Hermes, lend us an eager hand, and help us pull her out, and in your honor we'll celebrate the Great Panathenaea and all the other rites of

---

[32] In *Clouds* 615-26 the moon blames such calendar tampering on the Athenians.

πάσας τε τὰς ἄλλας τελετὰς τὰς τῶν θεῶν,
420 Μυστήρι᾽ Ἑρμῇ, Διπολίει᾽, Ἀδώνια·
ἄλλαι τέ σοι πόλεις πεπαυμέναι κακῶν
Ἀλεξικάκῳ θύσουσιν Ἑρμῇ πανταχοῦ.
χἄτερ᾽ ἔτι πόλλ᾽ ἕξεις ἀγαθά. πρῶτον δέ σοι
δῶρον δίδωμι τήνδ᾽, ἵνα σπένδειν ἔχῃς.

ΕΡΜΗΣ
425 οἴμ᾽ ὡς ἐλεήμων εἴμ᾽ ἀεὶ τῶν χρυσίδων.

ΤΡΥΓΑΙΟΣ
ὑμέτερον ἐντεῦθεν ἔργον, ὦνδρες. ἀλλὰ ταῖς ἅμαις
εἰσιόντες ὡς τάχιστα τοὺς λίθους ἀφέλκετε.

ΚΟΡΥΦΑΙΟΣ
ταῦτα δράσομεν· σὺ δ᾽ ἡμῖν, ὦ θεῶν σοφώτατε,
ἄττα χρὴ ποιεῖν ἐφεστὼς φράζε δημιουργικῶς·
430 τἄλλα δ᾽ εὑρήσεις ὑπουργεῖν ὄντας ἡμᾶς οὐ κακούς.

ΤΡΥΓΑΙΟΣ
ἄγε δή, σὺ ταχέως ὕπεχε τὴν φιάλην, ὅπως
ἔργῳ 'φιαλοῦμεν εὐξάμενοι τοῖσιν θεοῖς.

ΕΡΜΗΣ
σπονδὴ σπονδή·
εὐφημεῖτε εὐφημεῖτε.
435 σπένδοντες εὐχώμεσθα τὴν νῦν ἡμέραν
Ἕλλησιν ἄρξαι πᾶσι πολλῶν κἀγαθῶν,
χὤστις προθύμως ξυλλάβοι τῶν σχοινίων,
τοῦτον τὸν ἄνδρα μὴ λαβεῖν ποτ᾽ ἀσπίδα.

the gods—the Mysteries, the Dipolieia, the Adonia, all for Hermes; and when the other cities are rid of their troubles, they'll sacrifice to you everywhere as Hermes Averter of Trouble. And you'll get other benefits too; to begin with, I'm giving you this as a gift (*gives him a golden bowl*), to use for libations.

HERMES

Uh oh, I've always had such a soft spot for gold plate!

TRYGAEUS

(*to the Chorus*) From here on it's up to you, men. Now get inside there with your shovels and clear away those stones as quick as you can.

CHORUS LEADER

That we'll do. And you, smartest of gods, take charge, and in craftsmanly fashion tell us what needs doing; you'll find us no mean hands at doing the rest of the job.

TRYGAEUS

(*to Hermes*) All right then, hurry up and present that pitcher, so we can pray to the gods and pitch in on the job.

HERMES

Libation, libation! Auspicious tongues, everyone. With this libation let us pray that today is the harbinger of rich blessings for all the Greeks,[33] and that every man who heartily helps with the ropes need never again lift a shield.

---

[33] Reversing the Spartan Melesippus' prediction, made at the war's outset, of "great evils for the Greeks" (Thucydides 2.12).

ARISTOPHANES

ΤΡΥΓΑΙΟΣ

μὰ Δί, ἀλλ᾽ ἐν εἰρήνῃ διαπλέκειν τὸν βίον,
440 ἔχονθ᾽ ἑταίραν καὶ σκαλεύοντ᾽ ἄνθρακας.

ΕΡΜΗΣ

ὅστις δὲ πόλεμον μᾶλλον εἶναι βούλεται—

ΤΡΥΓΑΙΟΣ

μηδέποτε παύσασθ᾽ αὐτόν, ὦ Διόνυσ᾽ ἄναξ,
ἐκ τῶν ὀλεκράνων ἀκίδας ἐξαιρούμενον.

ΕΡΜΗΣ

κεἴ τις ἐπιθυμῶν ταξιαρχεῖν σοὶ φθονεῖ
445 εἰς φῶς ἀνελθεῖν, ὦ πότνι᾽, ἐν ταῖσιν μάχαις—

ΤΡΥΓΑΙΟΣ

πάσχοι γε τοιαῦθ᾽ οἷάπερ Κλεώνυμος.

ΕΡΜΗΣ

κεἴ τις δορυξὸς ἢ κάπηλος ἀσπίδων,
ἵν᾽ ἐμπολᾷ βέλτιον, ἐπιθυμεῖ μαχῶν,—

ΤΡΥΓΑΙΟΣ

ληφθείς ⟨γ᾽⟩ ὑπὸ λῃστῶν ἐσθίοι κριθὰς μόνας.

ΕΡΜΗΣ

450 κεἴ τις στρατηγεῖν βουλόμενος μὴ ξυλλάβῃ
ἢ δοῦλος αὐτομολεῖν παρεσκευασμένος,—

ΤΡΥΓΑΙΟΣ

ἐπὶ τοῦ τροχοῦ γ᾽ ἕλκοιτο μαστιγούμενος.

ΕΡΜΗΣ

ἡμῖν δ᾽ ἀγαθὰ γένοιτ᾽. ἰὴ παιών, ἰή.

TRYGAEUS

God, no; rather may he spend his life in peace, holding a girl and poking her coals!

HERMES

And whoever would rather have war—

TRYGAEUS

—Lord Dionysus, may he never stop pulling arrowheads from his funny-bones!

HERMES

And if anyone ambitious for a command hates to see you come to light again, my Lady, in his battles—

TRYGAEUS

—let him suffer the same fate as Cleonymus!

HERMES

And if any spear maker or shield monger wants battles, to better his business—

TRYGAEUS

—let him be captured by bandits and eat only barley!

HERMES

And if anyone refuses to help because he wants to be a general, or is a slave getting ready to run away—

TRYGAEUS

—let him be stretched on the rack and flogged!

HERMES

And on us let blessings flow. Strike up the Paeon: hip hip—

---

439 διαπλέκειν Carey: διάγειν z

ΤΡΥΓΑΙΟΣ

ἄφελε τὸ παίειν, ἀλλ' ἰὴ μόνον λέγε.

ΕΡΜΗΣ

455 ἰὴ ἰὴ τοίνυν, ἰὴ μόνον λέγω.

ΤΡΥΓΑΙΟΣ

Ἑρμῇ, Χάρισιν, Ὥραισιν, Ἀφροδίτῃ, Πόθῳ.

ΕΡΜΗΣ

Ἄρει δὲ μή.

ΤΡΥΓΑΙΟΣ

μή.

ΕΡΜΗΣ

μηδ' Ἐνυαλίῳ γε.

ΤΡΥΓΑΙΟΣ

μή.

ΕΡΜΗΣ

ὑπότεινε δὴ πᾶς καὶ κάταγε τοῖσιν κάλῳς.

ΚΟΡΥΦΑΙΟΣ

ὢ εἶα.

ΧΟΡΟΣ

460 εἶα μάλα.

ΚΟΡΥΦΑΙΟΣ

ὢ εἶα.

ΧΟΡΟΣ

εἶα ἔτι μάλα.

TRYGAEUS
Omit the striking; just say hooray!

HERMES
Hooray, hooray then, I'll only cry hooray!

TRYGAEUS
(*toasting*) Here's to Hermes; to the Graces; to the Seasons;
to Aphrodite; to Desire.

HERMES
But not to Ares!

TRYGAEUS
No!

HERMES
Nor to Enyalius![34]

TRYGAEUS
No!

HERMES
(*to the Chorus*) Now at my signal, everyone, start hauling,
and pull on those ropes!

CHORUS LEADER
Heave ho!

CHORUS
Heave!

CHORUS LEADER
Heave ho!

CHORUS
Heave again!

[34] A war god sometimes identified with Ares.

ARISTOPHANES

ΚΟΡΥΦΑΙΟΣ

(στρ) ὦ εἶα, ὦ εἶα.

ΤΡΥΓΑΙΟΣ

ἀλλ᾿ οὐχ ἕλκουσ᾿ ἄνδρες ὁμοίως.
465 οὐ ξυλλήψεσθ᾿; οἳ᾿ ὀγκύλλεσθ᾿·
οἰμώξεσθ᾿, οἱ Βοιωτοί.

ΚΟΡΥΦΑΙΟΣ

εἶά νυν.

ΧΟΡΟΣ

εἶα ὤ.

ΚΟΡΥΦΑΙΟΣ

ἄγετε ξυνανέλκετε καὶ σφώ.

ΤΡΥΓΑΙΟΣ

470 οὔκουν ἕλκω κἀξαρτῶμαι
κἀπεμπίπτω καὶ σπουδάζω;

ΚΟΡΥΦΑΙΟΣ

πῶς οὖν οὐ χωρεῖ τοὔργον;

ΤΡΥΓΑΙΟΣ

ὦ Λάμαχ᾿, ἀδικεῖς ἐμποδὼν καθήμενος.
οὐδὲν δεόμεθ᾿, ὦνθρωπε, τῆς σῆς μορμόνος.
475 οὐδ᾿ οἵδε γ᾿ εἷλκον οὐδὲν Ἀργεῖοι πάλαι
ἀλλ᾿ ἢ κατεγέλων τῶν ταλαιπωρουμένων,
καὶ ταῦτα διχόθεν μισθοφοροῦντες ἄλφιτα.

---

[35] The Boeotians disliked the terms of the Peace of Nicias

CHORUS LEADER

Heave ho! Heave ho!

TRYGAEUS

Hey, these men aren't pulling equally! Pitch in, there! How puffed up can you get? You'll be sorry for this, you Boeotians![35]

CHORUS LEADER

Heave ho!

CHORUS

Heave!

CHORUS LEADER

(*to Hermes and Trygaeus*) Come on you two, help us pull!

TRYGAEUS

(*taking hold of a rope*) Aren't I pulling then, and hanging on, and falling to, and doing my best?

CHORUS LEADER

Then why is our work going nowhere?

TRYGAEUS

Lamachus, you've no right to stand in our way! We want none of your bogy-blazon, sir![36] And these Argives have been no help either for quite some time; they just laugh at the hardships of others, while they get their daily bread by taking pay from both sides.[37]

(Thucydides 5.17-18) and in the end did not subscribe to it, instead arranging a more limited truce with Athens (5.26, 32).

[36] For Lamachus' Gorgon blazon see *Acharnians* 572 ff.

[37] The Argives had profited by their neutrality (Thucydides 5.28), and the imminent expiration of their own 30-year treaty with Sparta made a general peace unattractive to them.

ΕΡΜΗΣ

ἀλλ' οἱ Λάκωνες, ὦγάθ', ἕλκουσ' ἀνδρικῶς.

ΤΡΥΓΑΙΟΣ

ἆρ' οἶσθ'; ὅσοι γ' αὐτῶν ἐνέχονται τῷ ξύλῳ
480 μόνοι προθυμοῦντ'· ἀλλ' ὁ χαλκεὺς οὐκ ἐᾷ.

ΕΡΜΗΣ

οὐδ' οἱ Μεγαρῆς δρῶσ' οὐδέν· ἕλκουσιν δ' ὅμως
γλισχρότατα σαρκάζοντες ὥσπερ κυνίδια—

ΤΡΥΓΑΙΟΣ

ὑπὸ τοῦ γε λιμοῦ νὴ Δί' ἐξολωλότες.

ΚΟΡΥΦΑΙΟΣ

οὐδὲν ποιοῦμεν, ὦνδρες. ἀλλ' ὁμοθυμαδὸν
485 ἅπασιν ἡμῖν αὖθις ἀντιληπτέον.
ὦ εἶα.

ΧΟΡΟΣ

εἶα μάλα.

ΚΟΡΥΦΑΙΟΣ

ὦ εἶα.

ΧΟΡΟΣ

εἶα, νὴ Δία.

ΚΟΡΥΦΑΙΟΣ

(ἀντ) μικρόν γε κινοῦμεν.

ΤΡΥΓΑΙΟΣ

491 οὔκουν δεινὸν ⟨κᾆτοπον, ὑμῶν⟩

490

PEACE

HERMES

But the Spartans, friend, are pulling manfully.

TRYGAEUS

Do you know what? It's only the ones held in the stocks[38]
who are eager to help, but the fetterer won't let them.

HERMES

And the Megarians aren't accomplishing anything either;[39]
still, they're pulling hard, gnawing like puppies—

TRYGAEUS

on the point of sheer starvation, that is!

CHORUS LEADER

We're getting nowhere, men. Come on, we've got to take
hold and all pull together. Heave ho!

CHORUS

Heave!

CHORUS LEADER

Heave ho!

CHORUS

Yes, heave!

CHORUS LEADER

We're moving it only a little.

TRYGAEUS

Well, isn't it awfully absurd that some of you are going all

[38] See *Clouds* 186 n.
[39] The Megarians, like the Boeotians, rejected the peace
(Thucydides 5.17).

---

491 ⟨κάτοπον, ὑμῶν⟩ Merry, cf. SV

τοὺς μὲν τείνειν, τοὺς δ' ἀντισπᾶν·
πληγὰς λήψεσθ', ἀργεῖοι.

ΚΟΡΥΦΑΙΟΣ
εἶά νυν.

ΧΟΡΟΣ
495 εἶα ὤ.

ΚΟΡΥΦΑΙΟΣ
κακόνοι τινές εἰσιν ἐν ἡμῖν.

ΤΡΥΓΑΙΟΣ
ὑμεῖς μὲν γοῦν οἱ κιττῶντες
τῆς εἰρήνης σπᾶτ' ἀνδρείως.

ΚΟΡΥΦΑΙΟΣ
ἀλλ' εἴσ' οἳ κωλύουσιν.

ΕΡΜΗΣ
500 ἄνδρες Μεγαρῆς, οὐκ ἐς κόρακας ἐρρήσετε;
μισεῖ γὰρ ὑμᾶς ἡ θεὸς μεμνημένη·
πρῶτοι γὰρ αὐτὴν τοῖς σκορόδοις ἠλείψατε.
καὶ τοῖς Ἀθηναίοισι παύσασθαι λέγω
ἐντεῦθεν ἐχομένοις ὅθεν νῦν ἕλκετε·
505 οὐδὲν γὰρ ἄλλο δρᾶτε πλὴν δικάζετε.
ἀλλ' εἴπερ ἐπιθυμεῖτε τήνδ' ἐξελκύσαι,
πρὸς τὴν θάλατταν ὀλίγον ὑποχωρήσατε.

ΤΡΥΓΑΙΟΣ
ἄγ', ὦνδρες, αὐτοὶ δὴ μόνοι λαβώμεθ' οἱ γεωργοί.

496 ἡμῖν Σ: ὑμῖν z

out, while others are pulling the opposite way? You're look-
ing to get whacked, you Argives!

CHORUS LEADER

Heave ho!

CHORUS

Heave!

CHORUS LEADER

We've got some malcontents here.

TRYGAEUS

Those of you who itch for peace, at least you're hauling
bravely.

CHORUS LEADER

There still are some who hinder us.

HERMES

Men of Megara, why don't you go to hell? The goddess
remembers you with hatred, for you were the first to daub
her with your garlic. And to the Athenians I say: stop hang-
ing on to where you're now pulling from; you're accom-
plishing nothing but litigation. If you really want to pull
this goddess free, retreat a little seaward.[40]

TRYGAEUS

Come on, men, let us farmers take hold, all by ourselves.

[40] I.e. give up your ambition for a land empire.

ΕΡΜΗΣ

χωρεῖ γέ τοι τὸ πρᾶγμα πολλῷ μᾶλλον, ὦνδρες,
   ὑμῖν.

ΤΡΥΓΑΙΟΣ

510 χωρεῖν τὸ πρᾶγμά φησιν· ἀλλὰ πᾶς ἀνὴρ προθυμοῦ.

ΕΡΜΗΣ

οἵ τοι γεωργοὶ τοὔργον ἐξέλκουσι, κἄλλος οὐδείς.

ΚΟΡΥΦΑΙΟΣ

ἄγε νυν, ἄγε πᾶς.

ΕΡΜΗΣ

   καὶ μὴν ὁμοῦ 'στιν ἤδη.

ΚΟΡΥΦΑΙΟΣ

μή νυν ἀνῶμεν, ἀλλ' ἐπεν-
515   τείνωμεν ἀνδρικώτερον.

ΕΡΜΗΣ

   ἤδη 'στὶ τοῦτ' ἐκεῖνο.

ΧΟΡΟΣ

ὦ εἶά νυν, ὦ εἶα πᾶς.
   ὦ εἶα εἶα εἶά νυν.
   ὦ εἶα εἶα εἶα πᾶς.

ΤΡΥΓΑΙΟΣ

520 ὦ πότνια βοτρυόδωρε, τί προσείπω σ' ἔπος;
πόθεν ἂν λάβοιμι ῥῆμα μυριάμφορον
ὅτῳ προσείπω σ'; οὐ γὰρ εἶχον οἴκοθεν.
ὦ χαῖρ', Ὀπώρα, καὶ σὺ δ', ὦ Θεωρία·

PEACE

HERMES

Look, men, you've got the job moving along much better.

TRYGAEUS

He says the job's moving along! Now everyone put your heart into it!

HERMES

Look, the farmers are pulling it off, and nobody else.

CHORUS LEADER

Come on now, come on, everyone!

HERMES

Yes, we're nearly there now!

CHORUS LEADER

Now let's not slacken, let's instead
exert ourselves more manfully still!

HERMES

There she comes!

The eccyclema gradually emerges through the central door, bearing the statue of Peace and her attendants, Cornucopia and Holiday.

CHORUS

Heave now, heave, all!
Heave, heave, heave now!
Heave, heave, heave all!

TRYGAEUS

My Lady, Bestower of Grapes, how shall I express my greeting? Where can I get a ten-thousand-liter word to greet you with? I've got nothing that large of my own. Greetings, Holiday, and you too, Cornucopia. What a

495

οἷον δ᾽ ἔχεις τὸ πρόσωπον, ὦ φίλη θεός·
525 οἷον δὲ πνεῖς, ὡς ἡδὺ κατὰ τῆς καρδίας,
γλυκύτατον, ὥσπερ ἀστρατείας καὶ μύρου.

ΕΡΜΗΣ

μῶν οὖν ὅμοιον καὶ γυλιοῦ στρατιωτικοῦ;

ΤΡΥΓΑΙΟΣ

ἀπέπτυσ᾽ ἐχθροῦ φωτὸς ἔχθιστον πλέκος.
τοῦ μὲν γὰρ ὄζει κρομμυοξυρεγμίας,
530 ταύτης δ᾽ ὀπώρας, ὑποδοχῆς, Διονυσίων,
αὐλῶν, τραγῳδῶν, Σοφοκλέους μελῶν, κιχλῶν,
ἐπυλλίων Εὐριπίδου—

ΕΡΜΗΣ

κλαύσάρα σὺ
ταύτης καταψευδόμενος· οὐ γὰρ ἥδεται
αὕτη ποιητῇ ῥηματίων δικανικῶν.

ΤΡΥΓΑΙΟΣ

535 κιττοῦ, τρυγοίπου, προβατίων βληχωμένων,
κόλπου γυναικῶν διατρεχουσῶν εἰς ἀγρόν,
δούλης μεθυούσης, ἀνατετραμμένου χοῶς,
ἄλλων τε πολλῶν κἀγαθῶν.

ΕΡΜΗΣ

ἴθι νυν, ἄθρει
οἷον πρὸς ἀλλήλας λαλοῦσιν αἱ πόλεις
540 διαλλαγεῖσαι καὶ γελῶσιν ἄσμεναι—

ΤΡΥΓΑΙΟΣ

καὶ ταῦτα δαιμονίως ὑπωπιασμέναι
ἁπαξάπασαι καὶ κυάθους προσκείμεναι.

countenance you've got, dear goddess! And what an aroma,
how delightful to my heart, utterly luscious, with its hints
of demobilization and perfume!

HERMES

Not the same as you get from a soldier's knapsack, I take it?

TRYGAEUS

"I spit away an odious man's most odious bag!"[41] It smells
of oniony vinegar belches, while she smells of harvest time,
parties, festivals for Dionysus, pipes, tragedians, songs by
Sophocles, thrush meat, Euripides' *bons mots*—

HERMES

You'll regret telling that lie about her: she doesn't enjoy a
composer of forensic phraselets.

TRYGAEUS

—ivy, a wine strainer, bleating flocks, the bosoms of
women scampering to the fields, a drunken slave girl, an
upturned jug, and a host of other fine things!

HERMES

Look there, how the reconciled cities chat with one an-
other and laugh happily—

TRYGAEUS

Even though they've all of them got ungodly black eyes,
with eye cups attached.

---

[41] Euripides, *Telephus* fr. 727, substituting "bag" for "child."

---

524 ὦ φίλη θεός Blaydes: ὦ Θεωρία z

ARISTOPHANES

ΕΡΜΗΣ

καὶ τῶνδε τοίνυν τῶν θεωμένων σκόπει
τὰ πρόσωφ᾽, ἵνα γνῷς τὰς τέχνας.

ΤΡΥΓΑΙΟΣ

αἰβοῖ τάλας.

ΕΡΜΗΣ

545 ἐκεινονὶ γοῦν τὸν λοφοποιὸν οὐχ ὁρᾷς
τίλλονθ᾽ ἑαυτόν;

ΤΡΥΓΑΙΟΣ

ὁ δέ γε τὰς σμινύας ποιῶν
κατέπαρδεν ἄρτι τοῦ ξιφουργοῦ ᾽κεινουί.

ΕΡΜΗΣ

ὁ δὲ δρεπανουργὸς οὐχ ὁρᾷς ὡς ἥδεται;

ΤΡΥΓΑΙΟΣ

καὶ τὸν δορυξὸν ⟨γ᾽⟩ οἷον ἐσκιμάλισεν.

ΕΡΜΗΣ

550 ἴθι νυν, ἄνειπε τοὺς γεωργοὺς ἀπιέναι.

ΤΡΥΓΑΙΟΣ

ἀκούετε λεῴ· τοὺς γεωργοὺς ἀπιέναι
τὰ γεωργικὰ σκεύη λαβόντας εἰς ἀγρὸν
ὡς τάχιστ᾽ ἄνευ δορατίου καὶ ξίφους κἀκοντίου·
ὡς ἅπαντ᾽ ἤδη ᾽στὶ μεστὰ τἀνθάδ᾽ εἰρήνης σαπρᾶς.
555 ἀλλὰ πᾶς χώρει πρὸς ἔργον εἰς ἀγρὸν παιωνίσας.

ΚΟΡΥΦΑΙΟΣ

ὦ ποθεινὴ τοῖς δικαίοις καὶ γεωργοῖς ἡμέρα,
ἄσμενός σ᾽ ἰδὼν προσειπεῖν βούλομαι τὰς ἀμπέλους,

HERMES
—and then survey the faces of the spectators here; see if you can recognize their occupations.

TRYGAEUS
Ugh, spare me!

HERMES
Don't you at least see that crest maker, tearing his hair?

TRYGAEUS
Ah yes. And the hoe maker just farted at that swordsmith!

HERMES
And don't you see the sickle maker's happiness?

TRYGAEUS
And how he gave the spear maker the finger?

HERMES
Now then, give notice that the farmers may go home.

TRYGAEUS
Attention, people: the farmers may take their farm tools and go home to the country as soon as they like, without spear, sword, and javelin, since our whole world now brims with late-vintage peace. Now everyone raise the paeon, and be off to your work in the fields!

CHORUS LEADER
Ah, day long craved by farmers and righteous people, I'm glad to see you, and ready to greet my vines; and it is my

---

549 ⟨γ'⟩ Sommerstein

τάς τε συκᾶς ἃς ἐγὼ 'φύτευον ὢν νεώτερος
ἀσπάσασθαι θυμὸς ἡμῖν ἐστι πολλοστῷ χρόνῳ.

ΤΡΥΓΑΙΟΣ

560 νῦν μὲν οὖν, ὦνδρες, προσευξώμεσθα πρῶτον τῇ θεῷ,
ἥπερ ἡμῶν τοὺς λόφους ἀφεῖλε καὶ τὰς Γοργόνας·
εἶθ' ὅπως λιταργιοῦμεν οἴκαδ' εἰς τὰ χωρία,
ἐμπολήσαντές τι χρηστὸν εἰς ἀγρὸν ταρίχιον.

ΕΡΜΗΣ

ὦ Πόσειδον, ὡς καλὸν τὸ στῖφος αὐτῶν φαίνεται
565 καὶ πυκνὸν καὶ γοργόν, ὥσπερ μᾶζα καὶ πανδαισία.

ΤΡΥΓΑΙΟΣ

νὴ Δί', ἡ γοῦν σφῦρα λαμπρὸν ἦν ἄρ' ἐξωπλισμένη,
αἵ τε θρίνακες διαστίλβουσι πρὸς τὸν ἥλιον.
ἦ καλῶς αὐτῶν ἀπαλλάξειεν ἂν μετόρχιον.
ὥστ' ἔγωγ' ἤδη 'πιθυμῶ καὐτὸς ἐλθεῖν εἰς ἀγρὸν
570 καὶ τριαινοῦν τῇ δικέλλῃ διὰ χρόνου τὸ γῄδιον.
ἀλλ' ἀναμνησθέντες, ὦνδρες,
τῆς διαίτης τῆς παλαιᾶς,
ἣν παρεῖχ' αὕτη ποθ' ἡμῖν,
τῶν τε παλασίων ἐκείνων
575 τῶν τε σύκων, τῶν τε μύρτων,
τῆς τρυγός τε τῆς γλυκείας
τῆς ἰωνιᾶς τε τῆς πρὸς
τῷ φρέατι, τῶν τ' ἐλαῶν,
ὧν ποθοῦμεν,
580 ἀντὶ τούτων τήνδε νυνὶ
τὴν θεὸν προσείπατε.

heart's desire, after many a long season, to embrace the fig trees that I planted myself when I was young.

TRYGAEUS

(*as farm equipment is distributed to the Chorus*) Now then, gentlemen, let's address our first prayers to the goddess who has rid us of crests and Gorgon blazons; then let's dash off home to our lands, after we've bought a bit of good salt fish for the farm. (*the Chorus form ranks like soldiers*)

HERMES

Poseidon, what a good-looking troop they make, compact and lustrous, like cakes at a full-scale feast!

TRYGAEUS

Yes indeed, that clod-buster really is a splendid thing when it's ready for action, and the pitchforks glitter in the sun. They'll certainly leave a vineyard row in fine shape. So now I'm anxious to get back to the country myself, and at long last to start hoeing my own spot of earth. (*to the Chorus*) Now, gentlemen, recall the old way of life this goddess once afforded us—those pressed figs and fresh figs, the myrtle berries, the sweet new wine, the bed of violets by the well, the olive trees that we long for—and for these now voice your thanks to this goddess.

ΧΟΡΟΣ

(ἀντ β') χαῖρε, χαῖρ᾽, ὡς ἦλθες ἡμῖν ἀσμένοις, ὦ φιλτάτη·
σῷ γὰρ ἐδάμην πόθῳ,

585 δαιμόνια βουλόμενος
εἰς ἀγρὸν ἀνερπύσαι.

<

ἦσθα γὰρ μέγιστον ἡμῖν κέρδος, ὦ ποθουμένη,
πᾶσιν ὁπόσοι γεωρ-

590 γὸν βίον ἐτρίβομεν·
καὶ μόνη γὰρ ὠφέλεις.

πολλὰ γὰρ ἐπάσχομεν
πρίν ποτ᾽ ἐπὶ σοῦ γλυκέα
κἀδάπανα καὶ φίλα.

595 τοῖς ἀγροίκοισιν γὰρ ἦσθα χῖδρα καὶ σωτηρία.
ὥστε σὲ τά τ᾽ ἀμπέλια
καὶ τὰ νέα συκίδια
τἄλλα θ᾽ ὁπόσ᾽ ἐστὶ φυτὰ

600 προσγελάσεται λαβόντ᾽ ἄσμενα.

ΚΟΡΥΦΑΙΟΣ

ἀλλὰ ποῦ ποτ᾽ ἦν ἀφ᾽ ἡμῶν τὸν πολὺν τοῦτον χρόνον
ἥδε; τοῦθ᾽ ἡμᾶς δίδαξον, ὦ θεῶν εὐνούστατε.

ΕΡΜΗΣ

ὦ λιπερνῆτες γεωργοί, τἀμὰ δὴ ξυνίετε
ῥήματ᾽, εἰ βούλεσθ᾽ ἀκοῦσαι τήνδ᾽ ὅπως ἀπώλετο.

[591] καὶ μόνη γὰρ Dover: μόνη γὰρ ἡμᾶς z
[603] λιπερνῆτες Diod. Sic. 12.40.6, Aristodem. *FGrH* 104 F 16:
σοφώτατοι z

PEACE

CHORUS

Welcome, welcome! We're so happy, most beloved,
    that you've come home to us.
I'm overcome with longing for you
in my amazing desire
to head back to the country.
‹
For you were the greatest boon, desired one,
for all of us who led
life on the land, for
you alone would help us.
Yes, our benefits were many
in your day long ago—sweet,
freely given, and precious—
for you were the country folk's chowder and shelter.
And so the vines
and the young fig trees
and all the other plants together
will receive you with joyful smiles.

CHORUS LEADER

But wherever can this goddess have been, away from us all
this time? Tell us that, most benevolent of gods.

HERMES

"Ye forlorn farmers, hearken to my words,"[42] if you would
hear how she disappeared.[43] First of all Phidias had at her,

---

[42] Archilochus fr. 109, substituting "farmers" for "citizens."

[43] The hero Dicaeopolis' account of the war's origins in
Acharnians 509-39 is different, save for the assertion that Pericles
proposed the Megarian decree from personal motives.

605 πρῶτα μέν γὰρ ἧψατ᾽ αὐτῆς Φειδίας πράξας κακῶς.
εἶτα Περικλέης φοβηθεὶς μὴ μετάσχοι τῆς τύχης,
τὰς φύσεις ὑμῶν δεδοικὼς καὶ τὸν αὐτοδὰξ τρόπον,
πρὶν παθεῖν τι δεινὸν αὐτός, ἐξέφλεξε τὴν πόλιν
ἐμβαλὼν σπινθῆρα μικρὸν Μεγαρικοῦ ψηφίσματος·
610 κἀξεφύσησεν τοσοῦτον πόλεμον ὥστε τῷ καπνῷ
πάντας Ἕλληνας δακρῦσαι, τούς τ᾽ ἐκεῖ τούς τ᾽
ἐνθάδε.
ὡς δ᾽ ἅπαξ τὸ πρῶτον ἄκουσ᾽ ἐψόφησεν ἄμπελος
καὶ πίθος πληγεὶς ὑπ᾽ ὀργῆς ἀντελάκτισεν πίθῳ,
οὐκέτ᾽ ἦν οὐδεὶς ὁ παύσων, ἥδε δ᾽ ἠφανίζετο.

ΤΡΥΓΑΙΟΣ

615 ταῦτα τοίνυν μὰ τὸν Ἀπόλλω 'γὼ 'πεπύσμην
οὐδενός,
οὐδ᾽ ὅπως αὐτῇ προσήκοι Φειδίας ἠκηκόη.

ΚΟΡΥΦΑΙΟΣ

οὐδ᾽ ἔγωγε, πλήν γε νυνί. ταῦτ᾽ ἄρ᾽ εὐπρόσωπος ἦν,
οὖσα συγγενὴς ἐκείνου. πολλά γ᾽ ἡμᾶς λανθάνει.

ΕΡΜΗΣ

κᾆτ᾽ ἐπειδὴ 'γνωσαν ὑμᾶς αἱ πόλεις ὧν ἤρχετε
620 ἠγριωμένους ἐπ᾽ ἀλλήλοισι καὶ σεσηρότας,
πάντ᾽ ἐμηχανῶντ᾽ ἐφ᾽ ὑμῖν τοὺς φόρους φοβούμεναι,

605 ἧψατ᾽ αὐτῆς Herington: αὐτῆς ἦρξε z: αὐτῆς ἦρχε Diod.
Sic.: ἦρξατ᾽ αὐτῆς Aristodem.

when he'd gotten into trouble.[44] Then Pericles got frightened that he'd share Phidias' bad luck, dreading your inherently mordant behavior, so before he had to face anything terrible himself, he torched the city by tossing in a small spark of a Megarian decree,[45] and blew up so great a war that the smoke brought tears to the eyes of all Greeks, here and elsewhere; and as soon as the first unwilling vine began to crackle, and the first smitten jug kicked back in anger at another jug, there was no one left to call a halt, and this goddess began to disappear.

TRYGAEUS

Well, by Apollo, no one ever told me that, nor had I heard how Phidias was related to the goddess.

CHORUS LEADER

Nor I, until just now. So that's why her face is so lovely, being related to him! There's lots we don't know about.

HERMES

And then the cities subject to your rule, seeing you enraged and snarling at one another, started to form plots against you in anxiety about their tribute, and tried to win over the

---

[44] Phidias, the sculptor and friend of Pericles, was accused of embezzling funds for the building of Athena's chryselephantine statue in the Parthenon and fled before trial; cf. Ephorus in Diodorus Siculus 12.39.1-2, Plutarch, *Pericles* 31.2-5, and Philochorus *FGrH* 328 F 121. These sources do not give us a reliable date, but the sale of surplus gold and ivory listed in the Parthenon accounts of 434 (*IG* i³ 449.389-94) may give a *terminus post quem,* if the sale indicates that the statue was completed in that year.

[45] For this decree of 432 see Thucydides 1.39, 67, 144.

κἀνέπειθον τῶν Λακώνων τοὺς μεγίστους χρήμασιν.
οἱ δ' ἅτ' ὄντες αἰσχροκερδεῖς καὶ διειρωνόξενοι
τήνδ' ἀπορρίψαντες αἰσχρῶς τὸν Πόλεμον ἀνήρ-
πασαν·
625 κᾆτα τἀκείνων γε κέρδη τοῖς γεωργοῖς ἦν κακά·
αἱ γὰρ ἐνθένδ' αὖ τριήρεις ἀντιτιμωρούμεναι
οὐδὲν αἰτίων ἂν ἀνδρῶν τὰς κράδας κατήσθιον.

ΤΡΥΓΑΙΟΣ

ἐν δίκῃ μὲν οὖν, ἐπεί τοι τὴν κορώνεών γέ μου
ἐξέκοψαν, ἣν ἐγὼ 'φύτευσα κἀξεθρεψάμην.

ΚΟΡΥΦΑΙΟΣ

630 νὴ Δί', ὦ μέλ', ἐν δίκῃ ⟨γε⟩ δῆτ', ἐπεὶ κἀμοῦ λίθον
ἐμβαλόντες ἐξμέδιμνον κυψέλην ἀπώλεσαν.

ΕΡΜΗΣ

κἀνθάδ' ὡς ἐκ τῶν ἀγρῶν ξυνῆλθεν οὑργάτης λεώς,
τὸν τρόπον πωλούμενος τὸν αὐτὸν οὐκ ἐμάνθανεν,
ἀλλ' ἅτ' ὢν ἄνευ γιγάρτων καὶ φιλῶν τὰς ἰσχάδας
635 ἔβλεπεν πρὸς τοὺς λέγοντας· οἱ δὲ γιγνώσκοντες εὖ
τοὺς πένητας ἀσθενοῦντας κἀποροῦντας ἀλφίτων,
τήνδε μὲν δικροῖς ἐώθουν τὴν θεὸν κεκράγμασιν,
πολλάκις φανεῖσαν αὐτὴν τῆσδε τῆς χώρας πόθῳ,
τῶν δὲ συμμάχων ἔσειον τοὺς παχεῖς καὶ πλουσίους,
640 αἰτίας ἂν προστιθέντες ὡς "φρονεῖ τὰ Βρασίδου."

632 κἀνθάδ' Dobree: κᾆτα δ' z

---

46 I.e., an attack on Athens would facilitate a revolt; but in the

most powerful of the Spartans with money.[46] And they, being greedy for gain and quite unreliable in dealing with outsiders, tossed this goddess out disgracefully and seized on War.[47] And their gain became the farmers' loss, for the warships despatched from here to retaliate would consume the figs on trees belonging to wholly blameless men.

TRYGAEUS

No, they deserved it! You see, they cut down that black fig tree of mine, which I'd planted and nurtured.[48]

CHORUS LEADER

Quite right, sir, they did deserve it, for they ruined my six-bushel grain bin as well, by staving it in with a stone.

HERMES

And as for this place, when the working folk arrived from the countryside, they didn't understand that they were being sold out in the very same way, but because they lacked raisins and were fond of their figs, they looked to the orators for help. The orators, fully aware that the poor were weak and needed bread, took to driving this goddess away with double-pronged bellowings, though many times she appeared of her own accord out of longing for this land, and they started to harass the rich and substantial among the allies, pinning on them charges of "siding with Brasi-

---

period at issue only Potidaea is recorded as having made such a request (Thucydides 1.58).

[47] For the Spartans' avarice cf. Euripides, *Andromache* 451, and for their periodic expulsion of foreigners see *Birds* 1012-13, Thucydides 1.144.

[48] Euripides, *Medea* 1349 (Jason, of his children), substituting "planted" for "begot."

εἶτ᾽ ἂν ὑμεῖς τοῦτον ὥσπερ κυνίδι᾽ ἐσπαράττετε·
ἡ πόλις γὰρ ὠχριῶσα κἂν φόβῳ καθημένη,
ἅττα διαβάλοι τις αὐτῇ, ταῦτ᾽ ἂν ἥδιστ᾽ ἤσθιεν.
οἱ δὲ τὰς πληγὰς ὁρῶντες ἃς ἐτύπτονθ᾽, οἱ ξένοι,
645   χρυσίῳ τῶν ταῦτα ποιούντων ἐβύνουν τὸ στόμα,
ὥστ᾽ ἐκείνους μὲν ποιῆσαι πλουσίους, ἡ δ᾽ Ἑλλὰς ἂν
ἐξερημωθεῖσ᾽ ἂν ὑμᾶς ἔλαθε. ταῦτα δ᾽ ἦν ὁ δρῶν
βυρσοπώλης—

ΤΡΥΓΑΙΟΣ

παῦε παῦ᾽, ὦ δέσποθ᾽ Ἑρμῆ, μὴ λέγε,
ἀλλ᾽ ἔα τὸν ἄνδρ᾽ ἐκεῖνον οὗπέρ ἐστ᾽ εἶναι κάτω·
650   οὐ γὰρ ἡμέτερος ἔτ᾽ ἔστ᾽ ἐκεῖνος ἀνήρ, ἀλλὰ σός.
ἅττ᾽ ἂν οὖν λέγῃς ἐκεῖνον,
κεἰ πανοῦργος ἦν, ὅτ᾽ ἔζη,
καὶ λάλος καὶ συκοφάντης
καὶ κύκηθρον καὶ τάρακτρον,
655   ταῦθ᾽ ἁπαξάπαντα νυνὶ
τοὺς σεαυτοῦ λοιδορεῖς.
ἀλλ᾽ ὅ τι σιωπᾷς, ὦ πότνια, κάτειπέ μοι.

ΕΡΜΗΣ

ἀλλ᾽ οὐκ ἂν εἴποι πρός γε τοὺς θεωμένους·
ὀργὴν γὰρ αὐτοῖς ὧν ἔπαθε πολλὴν ἔχει.

ΤΡΥΓΑΙΟΣ

660   ἢ δ᾽ ἀλλὰ πρὸς σὲ μικρὸν εἰπάτω μόνον.

ΕΡΜΗΣ

εἴφ᾽ ὅ τι νοεῖς αὐτοῖσι πρὸς ἔμ᾽, ὦ φιλτάτη.
ἴθ᾽ ὦ γυναικῶν μισοπορπακιστάτη.

das." Then you'd mangle the man like a pack of puppies, because the city, pale and crouching in fear, was quite happy to swallow whatever slanders anyone tossed its way. And when the allies saw the blows being struck at them, they began to stuff gold into the mouths of those who were doing it, making them rich, while you wouldn't have noticed if Greece had been left destitute. And the one who did this was a leather seller[49]—

TRYGAEUS

Stop, stop, Lord Hermes, say no more! Just let that man stay right where he is, down below. That man's no longer ours, he's yours.[50] So whatever you say about him—even if he was a scoundrel while he lived, and a bigmouth and a frame-up artist and an agitator and a troublemaker—all these names you'll now be calling one of your own. (*to Peace*) But tell me, Lady, why do you keep silent?

HERMES

Ah, she won't say anything in front of *this* audience; she's still very angry with them about the treatment she got.

TRYGAEUS

Then let her whisper to you privately.

HERMES

(*moves close to Peace*) Tell *me* what you think about them, my dear. Go ahead, most shield-averse of females. Ah. I

---

[49] I.e. Cleon; cf. 47–8n.
[50] Hermes conducted souls to the underworld.

εἶέν· ἀκούω. ταῦτ᾽ ἐπικαλεῖς; μανθάνω.
ἀκούσαθ᾽ ὑμεῖς ὧν ἕνεκα μομφὴν ἔχει.
665 ἐλθοῦσά φησιν αὐτομάτη μετὰ τὰν Πύλῳ
σπονδῶν φέρουσα τῇ πόλει κίστην πλέαν
ἀποχειροτονηθῆναι τρὶς ἐν τἠκκλησίᾳ.

ΤΡΥΓΑΙΟΣ

ἡμάρτομεν ταῦτ᾽· ἀλλὰ συγγνώμην ἔχε·
ὁ νοῦς γὰρ ἡμῶν ἦν τότ᾽ ἐν τοῖς σκύτεσιν.

ΕΡΜΗΣ

670 ἴθι νυν, ἄκουσον οἷον ἄρτι μ᾽ ἤρετο·
ὅστις κακόνους αὐτῇ μάλιστ᾽ ἦν ἐνθάδε,
χὤστις φίλος κἄσπευδεν εἶναι μὴ μάχας.

ΤΡΥΓΑΙΟΣ

εὐνούστατος μὲν ἦν μακρῷ Κλεώνυμος.

ΕΡΜΗΣ

ποῖός τις οὖν εἶναι ᾽δόκει τὰ πολεμικὰ
675 ὁ Κλεώνυμος;

ΤΡΥΓΑΙΟΣ

ψυχήν γ᾽ ἄριστος, πλήν γ᾽ ὅτι
οὐκ ἦν ἄρ᾽ οὗπέρ φησιν εἶναι τοῦ πατρός.
εἰ γάρ ποτ᾽ ἐξέλθοι στρατιώτης, εὐθέως
ἀποβολιμαῖος τῶν ὅπλων ἐγίγνετο.

ΕΡΜΗΣ

ἔτι νυν ἄκουσον οἷον ἄρτι μ᾽ ἤρετο·
680 ὅστις κρατεῖ νῦν τοῦ λίθου τοῦ ᾽ν τῇ πυκνί.

hear you. That's your complaint? I understand. (*to the spectators*) Listen, all of you, to her grounds for blame. She says that after the events at Pylos she came here of her own accord, offering the city a basketful of treaties, and was voted down three times in the Assembly. [51]

TRYGAEUS

Our mistake, but do pardon us: at that time our brains were in our shoe leather.

HERMES

Now then, here's a question she just asked me: who was her principal detractor here, and who was her friend and worked hard to keep battles from happening?

TRYGAEUS

Well, her principal partisan by far was Cleonymus.

HERMES

So what was this Cleonymus like as regards warfare?

TRYGAEUS

Outstanding in spirit, except that he wasn't after all the son of the father he claimed was his. You see, whenever he went out with the troops, he'd treat his weapons like a castaway!

HERMES

Now here's another question she just asked me: who's the current master of the rock on Pnyx Hill?[52]

---

[51] For Pylos see 219 n.; for the Spartan offers of peace see Thucydides 4.41.

[52] The speakers' platform in meetings of the Athenian Assembly.

ARISTOPHANES

ΤΡΥΓΑΙΟΣ

Ὑπέρβολος νῦν τοῦτ᾽ ἔχει τὸ χωρίον.
αὕτη, τί ποιεῖς; τὴν κεφαλὴν ποῖ περιάγεις;

ΕΡΜΗΣ

ἀποστρέφεται τὸν δῆμον ἀχθεσθεῖσ᾽ ὅτι
οὕτω πονηρὸν προστάτην ἐπεγράψατο.

ΤΡΥΓΑΙΟΣ

685 ἀλλ᾽ οὐκέτ᾽ αὐτῷ χρησόμεθ᾽ οὐδέν, ἀλλὰ νῦν
ἀπορῶν ὁ δῆμος ἐπιτρόπου καὶ γυμνὸς ὢν
τοῦτον τέως τὸν ἄνδρα περιεζώσατο.

ΕΡΜΗΣ

πῶς οὖν ξυνοίσει ταῦτ᾽ ἐρωτᾷ τῇ πόλει.

ΤΡΥΓΑΙΟΣ

εὐβουλότεροι γενησόμεθα.

ΕΡΜΗΣ

τρόπῳ τίνι;

ΤΡΥΓΑΙΟΣ

690 ὅτι τυγχάνει λυχνοποιὸς ὤν. πρὸ τοῦ μὲν οὖν
ἐψηλαφῶμεν ἐν σκότῳ τὰ πράγματα,
νυνὶ δ᾽ ἅπαντα πρὸς λύχνον βουλεύσομεν.

ΕΡΜΗΣ

ὢ ὤ,
οἷά μ᾽ ἐκέλευσεν ἀναπυθέσθαι σου.

ΤΡΥΓΑΙΟΣ

τὸ τί;

TRYGAEUS

Hyperbolus currently holds that position. (*to Peace*) Here now, what are you doing? Why do you turn your head away?

HERMES

She's turning away from the people because she's cross at them for choosing such a sleazy champion.

TRYGAEUS

Actually, we're not going to rely on him any more, but at present the people need a guardian and are unclothed, so he's the man they're wearing for the moment.

HERMES

She wants to know how this will benefit the city.

TRYGAEUS

We'll become better deliberators.

HERMES

How so?

TRYGAEUS

Because he happens to be a lamp maker. So, whereas previously we groped in the dark at our problems, now we'll be planning everything by lamplight!

HERMES

Uh oh, the things she's told me to find out from you!

TRYGAEUS

What things?

513

ΕΡΜΗΣ

πάμπολλα, καὶ τἀρχαῖ ἃ κατέλιπεν τότε·
695 πρῶτον δ' ὅ τι πράττει Σοφοκλέης ἀνήρετο.

ΤΡΥΓΑΙΟΣ

εὐδαιμονεῖ· πάσχει δὲ θαυμαστόν.

ΕΡΜΗΣ

τὸ τί;

ΤΡΥΓΑΙΟΣ

ἐκ τοῦ Σοφοκλέους γίγνεται Σιμωνίδης.

ΕΡΜΗΣ

Σιμωνίδης; πῶς;

ΤΡΥΓΑΙΟΣ

ὅτι γέρων ὢν καὶ σαπρὸς
κέρδους ἕκατι κἂν ἐπὶ ῥιπὸς πλέοι.

ΕΡΜΗΣ

700 τί δαὶ Κρατῖνος ὁ σοφός; ἔστιν;

ΤΡΥΓΑΙΟΣ

ἀπέθανεν,
ὅθ' οἱ Λάκωνες ἐνέβαλον.

ΕΡΜΗΣ

τί παθών;

---

53 The point of the following joke is quite obscure.
54 Simonides, reputedly the first poet to compose for a fee, had an ancient reputation for avarice; see testimonia 22-3 Campbell.

HERMES

All kinds, especially the old-time things she left behind when she left. First she asked how Sophocles is doing.[53]

TRYGAEUS

He's thriving, but something amazing is happening to him.

HERMES

Namely?

TRYGAEUS

He's turning from Sophocles into Simonides.[54]

HERMES

Simonides? How so?

TRYGAEUS

Because even though he's a decrepit old man, "to make a profit he would go to sea on a wicker mat."[55]

HERMES

And what about the masterly Cratinus?[56] Is he alive?

TRYGAEUS

He died when the Spartans invaded.[57]

HERMES

Died of what?

---

[55] The two halves of this line are found separately in Euripides (frs. 397 and 566.2), but the verse may have been proverbial.

[56] The leading comic poet of the generation before Aristophanes, and thus suitably paired with Sophocles (cf. *Frogs* 357, where he is aligned with Aeschylus); his last known competition was at the Dionysia of 423, when his *Wine Flask* won first prize. Aristophanes had ridiculed him as a washed-up drunk in *Acharnians* (848-53, 1173) and *Knights* (400, 526-36).   [57] Not literally true, since the last Spartan invasion had been in 425.

ΤΡΥΓΑΙΟΣ

ὅ τι;

ὠρακιάσας· οὐ γὰρ ἐξηνέσχετο
ἰδὼν πίθον καταγνύμενον οἴνου πλέων.
χἄτερα πόσ᾽ ἄττ᾽ οἴει γεγενῆσθ᾽ ἐν τῇ πόλει;
705 ὥστ᾽ οὐδέποτ᾽, ὦ δέσποιν᾽, ἀφησόμεσθά σου.

ΕΡΜΗΣ

ἴθι νυν, ἐπὶ τούτοις τὴν Ὀπώραν λάμβανε
γυναῖκα σαυτῷ τήνδε· κᾆτ᾽ ἐν τοῖς ἀγροῖς
ταύτῃ ξυνοικῶν ἐκποιοῦ σαυτῷ βότρυς.

ΤΡΥΓΑΙΟΣ

ὦ φιλτάτη, δεῦρ᾽ ἐλθὲ καὶ δός μοι κύσαι.
710 ἆρ᾽ ἂν βλαβῆναι διὰ χρόνου τί σοι δοκῶ,
ὦ δέσποθ᾽ Ἑρμῆ, τῆς Ὀπώρας κατελάσας;

ΕΡΜΗΣ

οὔκ, εἴ γε κυκεῶν᾽ ἐπιπίοις βληχωνίαν.
ἀλλ᾽ ὡς τάχιστα τήνδε τὴν Θεωρίαν
ἀπάγαγε τῇ βουλῇ λαβών, ἧσπέρ ποτ᾽ ἦν.

ΤΡΥΓΑΙΟΣ

715 ὦ μακαρία βουλὴ σὺ τῆς Θεωρίας,
ὅσον ῥοφήσει ζωμὸν ἡμερῶν τριῶν,
ὅσας δὲ κατέδει χόλικας ἑφθὰς καὶ κρέα.
ἀλλ᾽, ὦ φίλ᾽ Ἑρμῆ, χαῖρε πολλά.

ΕΡΜΗΣ

καὶ σύ γε,
ὦνθρωπε, χαίρων ἄπιθι καὶ μέμνησό μου.

TRYGAEUS

Actually, he just keeled over; he couldn't abide the sight of a full wine jar being smashed. And you can't imagine how many other such things have happened in the city. That's why, my Lady, we'll never let go of you again.

HERMES

Very well then, on these terms you may take Cornucopia here for your own wife; then set up house with her in the countryside and beget yourself a brood of grapes.

TRYGAEUS

Dear girl, come here and let me kiss you! Lord Hermes, after such a long abstinence do you think it would do me any harm to tuck into this Cornucopia?

HERMES

Not if you washed it down with pennyroyal.[58] But now take Holiday here, and give her to the Council right away;[59] she used to belong to them.

TRYGAEUS

Lucky Council, to get this Holiday! You'll be slurping quite a lot of broth in the next three days, and bolting quite a lot of hot links and tenderloin. And now, Hermes my friend, a warm farewell to you!

HERMES

And to you, dear mortal! Go in peace, and remember me.

[58] A remedy for indigestion.
[59] The 500 members of the Council enjoyed reserved seating in the theater.

ΤΡΥΓΑΙΟΣ

720 ὦ κάνθαρ᾽, οἴκαδ᾽ οἴκαδ᾽ ἀποπετώμεθα.

ΕΡΜΗΣ

οὐκ ἐνθάδ᾽, ὦ τᾶν, ἐστι.

ΤΡΥΓΑΙΟΣ

ποῖ γὰρ οἴχεται;

ΕΡΜΗΣ

ὑφ᾽ ἅρματ᾽ ἐλθὼν Ζηνὸς ἀστραπηφορεῖ.

ΤΡΥΓΑΙΟΣ

πόθεν οὖν ὁ τλήμων ἐνθάδ᾽ ἕξει σιτία;

ΕΡΜΗΣ

τὴν τοῦ Γανυμήδους ἀμβροσίαν σιτήσεται.

ΤΡΥΓΑΙΟΣ

725 πῶς δῆτ᾽ ἐγὼ καταβήσομαι;

ΕΡΜΗΣ

θάρρει, καλῶς·
τῃδὶ παρ᾽ αὐτὴν τὴν θεόν.

ΤΡΥΓΑΙΟΣ

δεῦρ᾽, ὦ κόραι,
ἔπεσθον ἅμ᾽ ἐμοὶ θᾶττον, ὡς πολλοὶ πάνυ
ποθοῦντες ὑμᾶς ἀναμένουσ᾽ ἐστυκότες.

PEACE

TRYGAEUS

Beetle! Let's fly home now, home!

HERMES

Your beetle's not here, my friend.

TRYGAEUS

Why, where's he gone?

HERMES

"Yoked to Zeus' car, he bears the lightning."[60]

TRYGAEUS

But where's the poor thing going to get his feed up here?

HERMES

He'll feed on Ganymede's ambrosia![61]

TRYGAEUS

Then how will I get back down?

HERMES

Don't worry, you'll be fine; this way, right past the goddess.

TRYGAEUS

(*following Hermes to the central door*) This way, girls, follow me, and quickly: a great many horny men await you with hard-ons.

HERMES, TRYGAEUS, Holiday, and Cornucopia exit into the stage building.

[60] Euripides, *Bellerophon* fr. 312 (of Pegasus).
[61] The handsome Trojan prince Ganymede was seized by Zeus to be his cupbearer and "catamite" (a word derived from his name).

ΚΟΡΥΦΑΙΟΣ

ἀλλ᾽ ἴθι χαίρων· ἡμεῖς δὲ τέως τάδε τὰ σκεύη παρα-
δόντες

730 τοῖς ἀκολούθοις δῶμεν σῴζειν, ὡς εἰώθασι μάλιστα
περὶ τὰς σκηνὰς πλεῖστοι κλέπται κυπτάζειν καὶ
κακοποιεῖν.

ἀλλὰ φυλάττετε ταῦτ᾽ ἀνδρείως· ἡμεῖς δ᾽ αὖ τοῖσι
θεαταῖς

ἣν ἔχομεν ὁδὸν λόγων εἴπωμεν ὅσα τε νοῦς ἔχει.

χρῆν μὲν τύπτειν τοὺς ῥαβδούχους, εἴ τις κωμῳδο-
ποιητὴς

735 αὐτὸν ἐπῄνει πρὸς τὸ θέατρον παραβὰς ἐν τοῖς ἀνα-
παίστοις.

εἰ δ᾽ οὖν εἰκός τινα τιμῆσαι, θύγατερ Διός, ὅστις
ἄριστος

κωμῳδοδιδάσκαλος ἀνθρώπων καὶ κλεινότατος
γεγένηται,

ἄξιος εἶναί φησ᾽ εὐλογίας μεγάλης ὁ διδάσκαλος
ἡμῶν.

πρῶτον μὲν γὰρ τοὺς ἀντιπάλους μόνος ἀνθρώπων
κατέπαυσεν

740 εἰς τὰ ῥάκια σκώπτοντας ἀεὶ καὶ τοῖς φθειρσὶν
πολεμοῦντας·

741 τούς θ᾽ Ἡρακλέας τοὺς μάττοντας καὶ τοὺς πεινῶν-
τας ἐκείνους

743 ἐξήλασ᾽ ἀτιμώσας πρῶτος, καὶ τοὺς δούλους
παρέλυσεν

CHORUS LEADER

Go, and good luck to you. Meanwhile, let's surrender this
equipment to our attendants for safekeeping, because a
great many thieves routinely lurk around stage buildings
and make mischief. Now guard these bravely, and we'll tell
the spectators the path our words are taking and what's on
our mind. The ushers should beat any comic poet who
praises himself before the audience in the anapests of a
parabasis, but if after all it's fitting, daughter of Zeus,[62] to
honor one who has been and still is the world's best and
most renowned comic producer, then our producer says
that he's worthy of high praise. In the first place, he was
the only man on earth to stop his rivals from making jokes
about rags and waging war on lice; and he was the first to
outlaw and banish from the stage those Heracleses who
knead bread and go hungry, and to cashier those slaves who

---

[62] I.e. the Muse.

742–3 transp. Bergk

ARISTOPHANES

742 τοὺς φεύγοντας κἀξαπατῶντας καὶ τυπτομένους
ἐπίτηδες,
744 [οὓς ἐξῆγον κλάοντας ἀεί, καὶ τούτους οὕνεκα τουδί,]
745 ἵν᾽ ὁ σύνδουλος σκώψας αὐτοῦ τὰς πληγὰς εἶτ᾽
ἀνέροιτο·
"ὦ κακόδαιμον, τί τὸ δέρμ᾽ ἔπαθες; μῶν ὑστριχὶς
εἰσέβαλέν σοι
εἰς τὰς πλευρὰς πολλῇ στρατιᾷ κἀδενδροτόμησε τὸ
νῶτον;"
τοιαῦτ᾽ ἀφελὼν κακὰ καὶ φόρτον καὶ
βωμολοχεύματ᾽ ἀγεννῆ
ἐποίησε τέχνην μεγάλην ἡμῖν κἀπύργωσ᾽ οἰκοδο-
μήσας
750 ἔπεσιν μεγάλοις καὶ διανοίαις καὶ σκώμμασιν οὐκ
ἀγοραίοις,
οὐκ ἰδιώτας ἀνθρωπίσκους κωμῳδῶν οὐδὲ γυναῖκας,
ἀλλ᾽ Ἡρακλέους ὀργήν τιν᾽ ἔχων τοῖσι μεγίστοις
ἐπεχείρει,
διαβὰς βυρσῶν ὀσμὰς δεινὰς κἀπειλὰς βορβοροθύ-
μους.
καὶ πρῶτον μὲν μάχομαι πάντων αὐτῷ τῷ καρχα-
ρόδοντι,
755 οὗ δεινόταται μὲν ἀπ᾽ ὀφθαλμῶν Κύννης ἀκτῖνες
ἔλαμπον,
ἑκατὸν δὲ κύκλῳ κεφαλαὶ κολάκων οἰμωξομένων
ἐλιχμῶντο
περὶ τὴν κεφαλήν, φωνὴν δ᾽ εἶχεν χαράδρας ὄλε-
θρον τετοκυίας,

522

run away or pull hoaxes or get a beating, just so a fellow
slave can jeer at his partner's injuries and ask, "Hey, sad
sack, what happened to your hide? Could it be that the lash
has stormed your flanks in great strength and defoliated
your rear?" By getting rid of such poor, lowbrow buffoon-
ery, he's made our art great and built it up to towering size
with impressive verses, conceptions, and uncommon jokes.
He didn't satirize ordinary little men and women, [63] but in
the very spirit of Heracles he came to grips with the great-
est monsters, braving terrible smells of raw leather and
mudslinging threats. First of all I battled old Jagged Teeth
himself, whose eyes like the bitch Cynna's flashed terrible
beams, and all around his pate licked a hundred heads of
damned flatterers, and he had the voice of a death-dealing

[63] The following boasts refer to the poet's attacks on Cleon,
and incorporates almost verbatim *Wasps* 1030-37.

---

744 auctoris fort. versum cum v. 742 variantem del. Bergk

φώκης δ᾽ ὀσμήν, Λαμίας δ᾽ ὄρχεις ἀπλύτους,
   πρωκτὸν δὲ καμήλου.
τοιοῦτον ἰδὼν τέρας οὐ κατέδεισ᾽, ἀλλ᾽ ὑπὲρ ὑμῶν
   πολεμίζων
760 ἀντεῖχον ἀεὶ καὶ τῶν ἄλλων νήσων. ὧν εἵνεκα νυνὶ
ἀποδοῦναί μοι τὴν χάριν ὑμᾶς εἰκὸς καὶ μνήμονας
   εἶναι.
καὶ γὰρ πρότερον πράξας κατὰ νοῦν οὐχὶ παλαί-
   στρας περινοστῶν
παῖδας ἐπείρων, ἀλλ᾽ ἀράμενος τὴν σκευὴν εὐθὺς
   ἐχώρουν,
παῦρ᾽ ἀνιάσας, πόλλ᾽ εὐφράνας, πάντα παρασχὼν
   τὰ δέοντα.
765 πρὸς ταῦτα χρεὼν εἶναι μετ᾽ ἐμοῦ
καὶ τοὺς ἄνδρας καὶ τοὺς παῖδας.
καὶ τοῖς φαλακροῖσι παραινοῦμεν
ξυσπουδάζειν περὶ τῆς νίκης·
πᾶς γάρ τις ἐρεῖ νικῶντος ἐμοῦ
770 κἀπὶ τραπέζῃ καὶ ξυμποσίοις·
"φέρε τῷ φαλακρῷ, δὸς τῷ φαλακρῷ
τῶν τρωγαλίων, καὶ μὴ 'φαίρει
γενναιοτάτου τῶν ποιητῶν
774 ἀνδρὸς τὸ μέτωπον ἔχοντος".

ΧΟΡΟΣ

(στρ) μοῦσα, σὺ μὲν πολέμους ἀπωσαμένη μετ᾽ ἐμοῦ
   τοῦ φίλου χόρευσον,

torrent, the smell of a seal, the unwashed balls of a Lamia,
and the arsehole of a camel. On seeing this dreadful appa-
rition, I didn't get cold feet, but always stood my ground
and fought for you and for the islands. It's therefore fitting
that you should here and now return the favor and remem-
ber it. For even after my earlier successes, I didn't tour the
wrestling schools and make passes at boys, but immedi-
ately packed up my traps and departed, after giving little
pain and much pleasure, and providing all that was wanted.

> And so the men and the boys alike
> should be on my side.
> And we advise all bald men
> to join me in vying for victory,
> for if I win, at every
> feast and party they'll say,
> "Here's to the baldy," "Give the baldy
> some dessert," and "Don't hold out
> on a man with the brow
> of the noblest of poets."

CHORUS[64]

Muse, reject the theme of war and join me,
your friend, in the dance,

[64] The scholiast identifies the openings of this song's strophe
and antistrophe as adaptations of Stesichorus' *Oresteia* (cf. frs.
210-12 Campbell).

κλείουσα θεῶν τε γάμους
ἀνδρῶν τε δαῖτας καὶ θαλίας μακάρων·
780 σοὶ γὰρ τάδ᾽ ἐξ ἀρχῆς μέλει.
ἢν δέ σε Καρκίνος ἐλθὼν
ἀντιβολῇ μετὰ τῶν παίδων χορεῦσαι,
785 μήθ᾽ ὑπάκουε μήτ᾽ ἔλ-
θῃς συνέριθος αὐτοῖς,
ἀλλὰ νόμιζε πάντας
ὄρτυγας οἰκογενεῖς, γυλιαύχενας ὀρχηστὰς
790 νανοφυεῖς, σφυράδων ἀποκνίσματα, μηχανοδίφας.
καὶ γὰρ ἔφασχ᾽ ὁ πατὴρ ὃ παρ᾽ ἐλπίδας
795 εἶχε τὸ δρᾶμα γαλῆν τῆς
ἑσπέρας ἀπάγξαι.

(ἀντ)

τοιάδε χρὴ Χαρίτων δαμώματα καλλικόμων
τὸν σοφὸν ποιητὴν
ὑμνεῖν, ὅταν ἠρινὰ μὲν
800 φωνῇ χελιδὼν ἡδομένη κελαδῇ,
χορὸν δὲ μὴ 'χῃ Μόρσιμος
μηδὲ Μελάνθιος, οὗ δὴ
805 πικροτάτην ὄπα γηρύσαντος ἤκουσ᾽,
ἡνίκα τῶν τραγῳδῶν
τὸν χορὸν εἶχον ἀδελ-
φός τε καὶ αὐτός, ἄμφω
810 Γοργόνες ὀψοφάγοι, βατιδοσκόποι Ἅρπυιαι,
γραοσόβαι μιαροί, τραγομάσχαλοι ἰχθυολῦμαι·

811 ἡδομένη Bergk: ἑζομένη z

526

celebrating the weddings of gods,
the banquets of men, and the festivities of the blest,
for these are your original themes.
And should Carcinus come
and beg you to dance with his sons,
don't listen, don't go
as their hired hand,
but consider them all
home-bred quails, hump-necked dancers
of dwarfish build, demi-dungballs, caper-chasers.
For their father once insisted that the play
he'd unexpectedly got booked
was throttled one night by the cat.

Such public songs of the Graces with lovely hair
must the masterly poet
sing, when the swallow sounds
spring songs with her tuneful voice,
and when Morsimus[65] gets no chorus,
nor does Melanthius,[66] the one whose
very shrill voice I heard vocalizing
when for the tragedies
he and his brother
were granted a chorus, a pair of
gourmet Gorgons, skate-ogling Harpies,
foul crone-swatters, fish-molestors with rank armpits.

[65] Son of the tragic poet Philocles and great-nephew of
Aeschylus.
[66] Another tragic poet, frequently criticized in comedy both as
a bad artist and as a dissolute person.

527

815 ὧν καταχρεμψαμένη μέγα καὶ πλατύ,
μοῦσα θεά, μετ' ἐμοῦ ξύμ-
παιζε τὴν ἑορτήν.

ΤΡΥΓΑΙΟΣ
ὡς χαλεπὸν ἐλθεῖν ἦν ἄρ' εὐθὺ τῶν θεῶν.
820 ἔγωγέ τοι πεπόνηκα κομιδῇ τὼ σκέλει.
μικροὶ δ' ὁρᾶν ἄνωθεν ἦστ'. ἔμοιγέ τοι
ἀπὸ τοὐρανοῦ 'φαίνεσθε κακοήθεις πάνυ,
ἐντευθενὶ δὲ πολύ τι κακοηθέστεροι.

ΟΙΚΕΤΗΣ
ὦ δέσποθ', ἥκεις;

ΤΡΥΓΑΙΟΣ
ὥς γ' ἐγὼ 'πυθόμην τινός.

ΟΙΚΕΤΗΣ
825 τί δ' ἔπαθες;

ΤΡΥΓΑΙΟΣ
ἤλγουν τὼ σκέλει μακρὰν ὁδὸν
διεληλυθώς.

ΟΙΚΕΤΗΣ
ἴθι νυν, κάτειπέ μοι—

ΤΡΥΓΑΙΟΣ
τὸ τί;

ΟΙΚΕΤΗΣ
ἄλλον τιν' εἶδες ἄνδρα κατὰ τὸν ἀέρα
πλανώμενον πλὴν σαυτόν;

528

On them spit a big fat one,
Muse divine, and come play with me
in this festival.

Enter TRYGAEUS *with Cornucopia and Holiday.*

TRYGAEUS
(*to the spectators*) It really was quite a job, going all the
way to the gods. I know I've got a pair of very sore legs.
You looked small from up there. From my heavenly van-
tage you seemed a very bad lot, but from down here you
seem a far sight worse!

A SLAVE *comes out of* TRYGAEUS' *house.*

SLAVE
Master, you're really back?

TRYGAEUS
Well, that's what I hear!

SLAVE
What happened to you?

TRYGAEUS
I got sore legs on the long trip back.

SLAVE
Well now, tell me—

TRYGAEUS
Yes?

SLAVE
—did you see anyone else wandering through the air, other
than yourself?

529

ΤΡΥΓΑΙΟΣ

οὔκ, εἰ μή γέ που
ψυχὰς δύ᾽ ἢ τρεῖς διθυραμβοδιδασκάλων.

ΟΙΚΕΤΗΣ

830 τί δ᾽ ἔδρων;

ΤΡΥΓΑΙΟΣ

ξυνελέγοντ᾽ ἀναβολὰς ποτώμεναι
τὰς ἐνδιαεριαυρονηχέτους τινάς.

ΟΙΚΕΤΗΣ

οὐκ ἦν ἄρ᾽ οὐδ᾽ ἃ λέγουσι, κατὰ τὸν ἀέρα
ὡς ἀστέρες γιγνόμεθ᾽, ὅταν τις ἀποθάνῃ;

ΤΡΥΓΑΙΟΣ

μάλιστα.

ΟΙΚΕΤΗΣ

καὶ τίς ἐστιν ἀστὴρ νῦν ἐκεῖ;

ΤΡΥΓΑΙΟΣ

835 Ἴων ὁ Χῖος, ὅσπερ ἐποίησεν πάλαι
ἐνθάδε τὸν Ἀοῖόν ποθ᾽· ὡς δ᾽ ἦλθ᾽, εὐθέως
Ἀοῖον αὐτὸν πάντες ἐκάλουν ἀστέρα.

ΟΙΚΕΤΗΣ

τίνες γάρ εἰσ᾽ οἱ διατρέχοντες ἀστέρες,
οἳ καόμενοι θέουσιν;

ΤΡΥΓΑΙΟΣ

ἀπὸ δείπνου τινὲς
840 τῶν πλουσίων οὗτοι βαδίζουσ᾽ ἀστέρων
ἰπνοὺς ἔχοντες, ἐν δὲ τοῖς ἰπνοῖσι πῦρ.

TRYGAEUS

No, unless you'd include two or three souls of dithyrambic composers.[67]

SLAVE

What were they doing?

TRYGAEUS

Winging about, collecting overtures of the aerial breeze-cruising sort.

SLAVE

That also means the legend isn't true, that when we die we turn into stars in the sky.

TRYGAEUS

Oh yes it is!

SLAVE

So who's a star there now?

TRYGAEUS

Ion of Chios,[68] who some years ago on earth composed *The Dawn Star*.[69] When he arrived up there, everybody dubbed him Dawn Star right away!

SLAVE

And who are the shooting stars that blaze on their course?

TRYGAEUS

They're some of the rich stars walking home from dinner with lanterns in hand, and fire in the lanterns. (*presenting*

[67] See *Clouds* 333-39.

[68] Born *c.* 480, a prolific writer of poetry, drama, and prose, and for many years a frequent visitor to Athens.

[69] A dithyramb; cf. fr. 745 Campbell.

ἀλλ' εἴσαγ' ὡς τάχιστα ταυτηνὶ λαβών,
καὶ τὴν πύελον κατάκλυζε καὶ θέρμαιν' ὕδωρ,
στόρνυ τ' ἐμοὶ καὶ τῇδε κουρίδιον λέχος.
845 καὶ ταῦτα δράσας ἧκε δεῦρ' αὖθις πάλιν·
ἐγὼ δ' ἀποδώσω τήνδε τῇ βουλῇ τέως.

OIKETHΣ

πόθεν δ' ἔλαβες ταύτας σύ;

TPYΓAIOΣ

πόθεν; ἐκ τοὐρανοῦ.

OIKETHΣ

οὐκ ἂν ἔτι δοίην τῶν θεῶν τριώβολον,
εἰ πορνοβοσκοῦσ' ὥσπερ ἡμεῖς οἱ βροτοί.

TPYΓAIOΣ

850 οὔκ, ἀλλὰ κἀκεῖ ζῶσιν ἀπὸ τούτων τινές.

OIKETHΣ

ἄγε νυν ἴωμεν. εἰπέ μοι, δῶ καταφαγεῖν
ταύτῃ τι;

TPYΓAIOΣ

μηδέν· οὐ γὰρ ἐθελήσει φαγεῖν
οὔτ' ἄρτον οὔτε μᾶζαν, εἰωθυῖ' ἀεὶ
παρὰ τοῖς θεοῖσιν ἀμβροσίαν λείχειν ἄνω.

OIKETHΣ

855 λείχειν ἄρ' αὐτῇ κἀνθάδε σκευαστέον.

XOPOΣ

(στρ) εὐδαιμονικῶς γ' ὁ πρε-
σβύτης, ὅσα γ' ὧδ' ἰδεῖν,

Cornucopia) But right now, take this girl inside, rinse the bathtub, heat water, and make up a marriage bed for her and me. When that's done, come back here again. Meanwhile I'll give this other girl back to the Council.

SLAVE

Where did you get these girls?

TRYGAEUS

Why, from heaven.

SLAVE

I wouldn't give two bits for the gods if they pimp girls as we mortals do!

TRYGAEUS

You've got it wrong, though even up there some live off girls like her.

SLAVE

(*to Cornucopia*) Come on then, in we go. (*to Trygaeus*) Say, should I give her something to eat?

TRYGAEUS

Nothing. She'll not want to eat bread or cake, when up there with the gods her tongue's been used to ambrosia.

SLAVE

Then we'll have to get something ready for her to put her tongue on down here too!

SLAVE takes Cornucopia inside.

CHORUS

Lucky indeed,
to judge from what I see,

τὰ νῦν τάδε πράττει.

ΤΡΥΓΑΙΟΣ

τί δῆτ᾽, ἐπειδὰν νυμφίον μ᾽ ὁρᾶτε λαμπρὸν ὄντα;

ΧΟΡΟΣ

860 ζηλωτὸς ἔσει, γέρων
αὖθις νέος ὢν πάλιν,
μύρῳ κατάλειπτος.

ΤΡΥΓΑΙΟΣ

οἶμαι. τί δῆθ᾽, ὅταν ξυνὼν τῶν τιτθίων ἔχωμαι;

ΚΟΡΥΦΑΙΟΣ

εὐδαιμονέστερος φανεῖ τῶν Καρκίνου στροβίλων.

ΤΡΥΓΑΙΟΣ

865 οὔκουν δικαίως; ὅστις εἰς
ὄχημα κανθάρου 'πιβὰς
ἔσωσα τοὺς Ἕλληνας, ὥστ᾽
ἐν τοῖς ἀγροῖσιν αὐτοὺς
ἅπαντας ὄντας ἀσφαλῶς
κινεῖν τε καὶ καθεύδειν.

ΟΙΚΕΤΗΣ

ἡ παῖς λέλουται καὶ τὰ τῆς πυγῆς καλά·
ὁ πλακοῦς πέπεπται, σησαμῆ ξυμπλάττεται,
870 καὶ τἄλλ᾽ ἁπαξάπαντα· τοῦ πέους δὲ δεῖ.

860 γέρων B: γέρον cett.
866 ἀγροῖσιν αὐτοὺς t: ἀγροῖς cett.

is the old man's situation now.

TRYGAEUS
Just wait till you see me as a splendid bridegroom!

CHORUS
You'll be enviable, a codger
become a young man once again,
anointed with scent.

TRYGAEUS
I imagine so. Just wait till we're together and I've got those
tits in my hands!

CHORUS
You'll seem luckier than Carcinus' whirligigs!

TRYGAEUS
And rightly, no? For I alone
rode on beetle-back
and saved the Greeks, who now
can all live safely
in the countryside,
screwing and snoozing.

SLAVE comes out of the house.

SLAVE
The girl's had a bath, and all's well with her bottom. The
cake's baked, the sesame rolls are being shaped, and every-
thing else is done. All we need is the prick!

ΤΡΥΓΑΙΟΣ

ἴθι νυν ἀποδῶμεν τήνδε τὴν Θεωρίαν
ἀνύσαντε τῇ βουλῇ.

ΟΙΚΕΤΗΣ

τίς αὑτηί; τί φῄς;
αὑτὴ Θεωρία 'στίν, ἣν ἡμεῖς ποτε
ἐπαίομεν Βραυρωνάδ᾽ ὑποπεπωκότες;

ΤΡΥΓΑΙΟΣ

875 σάφ᾽ ἴσθι, κἀλήφθη γε μόλις.

ΟΙΚΕΤΗΣ

ὦ δέσποτα,
ὅσην ἔχει τὴν πρωκτοπεντετηρίδα.

ΤΡΥΓΑΙΟΣ

εἶέν· τίς ἐσθ᾽ ὑμῶν δίκαιος; τίς ποτε;
τίς διαφυλάξει τήνδε τῇ βουλῇ λαβών;
οὗτος, τί περιγράφεις;

ΟΙΚΕΤΗΣ

τὸ δεῖν᾽, εἰς Ἴσθμια
880 σκηνὴν ἐμαυτοῦ τῷ πέει καταλαμβάνω.

ΤΡΥΓΑΙΟΣ

οὔπω λέγεθ᾽ ὑμεῖς τίς ὁ φυλάξων; δεῦρο σύ·
καταθήσομαι γὰρ αὐτὸς εἰς μέσους ⟨σ᾽⟩ ἄγων.

TRYGAEUS

Then come on, let's hurry up and give Holiday here to the Council.

SLAVE

What, this girl here? Do you mean to say this is the Holiday we used to have when we'd had a few drinks and banged our way to Brauron?[70]

TRYGAEUS

That's right, and it was quite a job getting hold of her.

SLAVE

Oh Master, look at her arse: it's positively quadrennial!

TRYGAEUS

(*presenting Holiday to the spectators*) Well now, who among you is honest? Anyone at all? Who will take this girl and safeguard her for the Council? (*to the Slave*) Hey there, why are you tracing her outlines?

SLAVE

Er, well, it's for the Isthmian Games:[71] I'm reserving accommodations for my prick!

TRYGAEUS

(*to the spectators*) You still won't nominate a guardian? (*leading Holiday to the Councillors' seats*) Come this way; I'm going to escort you personally and put you down right in their midst.

---

[70] A sanctuary in east Attica where an initiation festival for maidens was held every four years.

[71] An international contest held biennially at the Isthmus of Corinth; "isthmus" was sexual slang ("the place connecting two legs").

ΟΙΚΕΤΗΣ

ἐκεινοσὶ νεύει.

ΤΡΥΓΑΙΟΣ

τίς;

ΟΙΚΕΤΗΣ

ὅστις; Ἀριφράδης,

ἄγειν παρ' αὐτὸν ἀντιβολῶν.

ΤΡΥΓΑΙΟΣ

ἀλλ', ὦ μέλε,

885   τὸν ζωμὸν αὐτῆς προσπεσὼν ἐκλάψεται.
ἄγε δὴ σὺ κατάθου πρῶτα τὴν σκευὴν χαμαί.
βουλή, πρυτάνεις, ὁρᾶτε τὴν Θεωρίαν.
σκέψασθ' ὅσ' ὑμῖν ἀγαθὰ παραδώσω φέρων,
ὥστ' εὐθέως ἄραντας ὑμᾶς τὼ σκέλει
890   ταύτης μετεώρω κᾆτ' ἀγαγεῖν ἀνάρρυσιν.
τουτὶ δ' ὁρᾶτε τοὐπτάνιον.

ΟΙΚΕΤΗΣ

οἴμ' ὡς καλόν.

διὰ ταῦτα καὶ κεκάπνικεν ἄρ'· ἐνταῦθα γὰρ
πρὸ τοῦ πολέμου τὰ λάσανα τῇ βουλῇ ποτ' ἦν.

ΤΡΥΓΑΙΟΣ

ἔπειτ' ἀγῶνά γ' εὐθὺς ἐξέσται ποιεῖν
895   ταύτην ἔχουσιν αὔριον καλὸν πάνυ,
896a   ἐπὶ γῆς παλαίειν, τετραποδηδὸν ἱστάναι,
896b   [πλαγίαν καταβάλλειν, εἰς γόνατα κυβδ' ἱστάναι,]
897   καὶ παγκράτιόν γ' ὑπαλειψαμένοις νεανικῶς

538

SLAVE

There's someone signalling!

TRYGAEUS

Who?

SLAVE

Why, it's Ariphrades, begging you to take her to him.

TRYGAEUS

But my boy, he'll kneel down and lap up her broth! (*to Holiday*) Come on, first lay your things on the ground. (*Holiday disrobes*) Councillors, Chairmen, behold Holiday! Look what good times I've brought to give you; you can lift her legs in the air right away and have a Liberation Feast![72] Just look at this cooker of hers!

SLAVE

My, she's a fine thing! Now I see why she's scorched: before the war she used to be the Council's trivet!

TRYGAEUS

Now that you have her, you're free to hold a fine sporting competition first thing tomorrow. You can wrestle her to the ground, stand her on all fours, oil up for the pancration, and like young lads bang and gouge with fist and prick

[72] *Anarrhysis*, the second day of the Apaturia festival.

---

886 τὴν σκευὴν Meineke: τὰ σκεύη z
896b auctoris fort. versum cum 896a variantem exhibet R: om. Vy: del. Rogers

παίειν, ὀρύττειν, πὺξ ὁμοῦ καὶ τῷ πέει·
τρίτῃ δὲ μετὰ ταῦθ' ἱπποδρομίαν ἄξετε,
900 ἵνα δὴ κέλης κέλητα παρακελητιεῖ,
ἅρματα δ' ἐπ' ἀλλήλοισιν ἀνατετραμμένα
φυσῶντα καὶ πνέοντα προσκινήσεται·
ἕτεροι δὲ κείσονταί γ' ἀπεψωλημένοι
περὶ ταῖσι καμπαῖς ἡνίοχοι πεπτωκότες.
905 ἀλλ', ὦ πρυτάνεις, δέχεσθε τὴν Θεωρίαν.
θέασ' ὡς προθύμως ὁ πρύτανις παρεδέξατο.
ἀλλ' οὐκ ἄν, εἴ τι προῖκα προσαγαγεῖν σ' ἔδει,
ἀλλ' ηὗρον ἄν σ' ὑπέχοντα τὴν ἐκεχειρίαν.

ΧΟΡΟΣ

(ἀντ) ἦ χρηστὸς ἀνὴρ πολί-
910 ταις ἐστὶν ἅπασιν ὅσ-
τις γ' ἐστὶ τοιοῦτος.

ΤΡΥΓΑΙΟΣ

ὅταν τρυγᾶτ', εἴσεσθε πολλῷ μᾶλλον οἷός εἰμι.

ΧΟΡΟΣ

καὶ νῦν σύ γε δῆλος εἶ·
σωτὴρ γὰρ ἅπασιν ἀν-
915 θρώποις γεγένησαι.

ΤΡΥΓΑΙΟΣ

φήσεις ‹γ'›, ἐπειδὰν ἐκπίῃς οἴνου νέου λεπαστήν.

ΚΟΡΥΦΑΙΟΣ

καὶ πλήν γε τῶν θεῶν ἀεί σ' ἡγησόμεσθα πρῶτον.

alike! Then on the second day you'll hold the equestrian events, where jockey will outjockey jockey, and chariots will tumble over each other and match thrusts, puffing and panting, and other drivers will lie with cocks unfurled, collapsed at the goal line. Now, Chairmen, you're welcome to Holiday! (*giving Holiday to the Councillors*) Look how heartily this Chairman took her from me! You wouldn't have been so hearty if you'd had to move some business gratis; no, I'd have found you offering to "take ten."

CHORUS

Yes, a man
like this one is good
for all the citizenry.

TRYGAEUS

When you gather in your vintage, you'll realize much better what a man I am.

CHORUS

Even now we plainly see,
for you've become a savior
for all mankind.

TRYGAEUS

That's what you'll say when you drink off a cup of new wine!

CHORUS LEADER

Yes, and that, next to the gods, we'll always consider you the best.

---

910 πολίταις Hermann: πολίτης z

ΤΡΤΓΑΙΟΣ

πολλῶν γὰρ ὑμῖν ἄξιος
  Τρυγαῖος ἀθμονεὺς ἐγώ,
  δεινῶν ἀπαλλάξας πόνων
920 τὸν δημότην ὅμιλον
  καὶ τὸν γεωργικὸν λεὼν
  Ὑπέρβολόν τε παύσας.

ΟΙΚΕΤΗΣ

ἄγε δή, τί νῶν ἐντευθενὶ ποιητέον;

ΤΡΤΓΑΙΟΣ

τί δ' ἄλλο γ' ἢ ταύτην χύτραις ἱδρυτέον;

ΟΙΚΕΤΗΣ

χύτραισιν, ὥσπερ μεμφόμενον Ἑρμήδιον;

ΤΡΤΓΑΙΟΣ

925 τί δαὶ δοκεῖ; βούλεσθε λαρινῷ βοΐ;

ΟΙΚΕΤΗΣ

βοΐ; μηδαμῶς, ἵνα μὴ βοηθεῖν ποι δέῃ.

ΤΡΤΓΑΙΟΣ

ἀλλ' ὑὶ παχείᾳ καὶ μεγάλῃ;

ΟΙΚΕΤΗΣ

μὴ μή.

ΤΡΤΓΑΙΟΣ

τιή;

928 Θεο- Dindorf: Θεα- z

542

TRYGAEUS

You do owe me a lot,
Trygaeus of Athmonum,
for freeing the commons
and the country folk
from terrible hardships,
and putting a stop to Hyperbolus.

SLAVE

Well now, what's next on our agenda?

TRYGAEUS

To install this goddess with pots, what else?[73]

SLAVE

With pots, like a contemptible little herm?[74]

TRYGAEUS

Then what's your suggestion? Do you prefer a fatted bull?

SLAVE

A bull? Absolutely not, or we might have to man the bulwarks somewhere!

TRYGAEUS

Then how about a big fat pig?

SLAVE

No, no!

TRYGAEUS

Why not?

[73] I.e. pots of bloodless offerings, as would be appropriate for Peace.
[74] See *Clouds* 1478 n.

ΟΙΚΕΤΗΣ

ἵνα μὴ γένηται Θεογένους ὑηνία.

ΤΡΥΓΑΙΟΣ

τῷ δαὶ δοκεῖ σοι δῆτα τῶν λοιπῶν;

ΟΙΚΕΤΗΣ

οἴ.

ΤΡΥΓΑΙΟΣ

930 οἴ;

ΟΙΚΕΤΗΣ

ναὶ μὰ Δί'.

ΤΡΥΓΑΙΟΣ

ἀλλὰ τοῦτό γ' ἔστ' Ἰωνικὸν

τὸ ῥῆμ'.

ΟΙΚΕΤΗΣ

ἐπίτηδές γ', ἵν' <ὅταν> ἐν τἠκκλησίᾳ

ὡς χρὴ πολεμεῖν λέγῃ τις, οἱ καθήμενοι

ὑπὸ τοῦ δέους λέγωσ' Ἰωνικῶς οἰ—

ΤΡΥΓΑΙΟΣ

εὖ τοι λέγεις.

ΟΙΚΕΤΗΣ

καὶ τἄλλα γ' ὦσιν ἤπιοι.

935 ὥστ' ἐσόμεθ' ἀλλήλοισιν ἀμνοὶ τοὺς τρόπους

καὶ τοῖσι συμμάχοισι πραότεροι πολύ.

ΤΡΥΓΑΙΟΣ

ἴθι νυν, ἄγ' ὡς τάχιστα τὸ πρόβατον λαβών·

ἐγὼ δὲ ποριῶ βωμὸν ἐφ' ὅτου θύσομεν.

SLAVE

So we don't turn piggish like Theogenes!

TRYGAEUS

Then which of the remaining options appeals to you?

SLAVE

A boo lamb.

TRYGAEUS

Boo lamb?

SLAVE

That's right.

TRYGAEUS

But that's an Ionic pronunciation.

SLAVE

I used it on purpose, so that whenever anyone in Assembly says we've got to go to war, the assemblymen will be frightened and say in Ionic, "Boo!"—

TRYGAEUS

Good idea!

SLAVE

—and be gentle otherwise, so that we'll be like lambs in the way we treat one another, and much milder toward our allies.

TRYGAEUS

Then go fetch the victim as quick as you can, and I'll provide us an altar for the sacrifice.

SLAVE goes into the house.

ARISTOPHANES

(στρ) ὡς πάνθ᾽ ὅσ᾽ ἂν θεὸς θέλῃ χἠ τύχη κατορθοῖ
940 χωρεῖ κατὰ νοῦν, ἕτερον δ᾽ ἑτέρῳ
τούτων κατὰ καιρὸν ἀπαντᾷ.

ΤΡΥΓΑΙΟΣ

ὡς ταῦτα δῆλά γ᾽ ἔσθ᾽· ὁ γὰρ βωμὸς θύρασι καὶ
δή.

ΧΟΡΟΣ

⟨ἄγ᾽⟩ ἐπείγετέ νυν ἐν ὅσῳ σοβαρὰ
θεόθεν κατέχει πολέμου μετάτροπος
945   αὔρα· νῦν γὰρ δαίμων φανερῶς
εἰς ἀγαθὰ μεταβιβάζει.

ΟΙΚΕΤΗΣ

τὸ κανοῦν πάρεστ᾽ ὀλὰς ἔχον καὶ στέμμα καὶ
μάχαιραν,
καὶ πῦρ γε τουτί, κοὐδὲν ἴσχει πλὴν τὸ πρόβατον
ὑμᾶς.

ΧΟΡΟΣ

950 οὔκουν ἁμιλλήσεσθον; ὡς
ἢν Χαῖρις ὑμᾶς ἴδῃ,
πρόσεισιν αὐλήσων ἄκλη-
τος, κᾆτα τοῦτ᾽ εὖ οἶδ᾽ ὅτι
φυσῶντι καὶ πονουμένῳ
955   προσδώσετε δήπου.

PEACE

CHORUS
Surely all that God wills and fortune favors
goes forward according to plan, with one success
leading to another at just the right time.

TRYGAEUS
How evident that is (*pointing to the stage altar*), because
here's an altar right in front of the door.

CHORUS
Come then, make haste while the blustery breeze
with God's help holds its course
away from war; yes, the divinity clearly
is changing our course to the good.

SLAVE returns with sacrificial paraphernalia.

SLAVE
Here's the basket, with barley meal, a garland, and a knife,
and here's kindling, and nothing's holding us up except the
victim!

SLAVE fetches the lamb while TRYGAEUS lights the fire.

CHORUS
Hadn't you better race each other? For
if Chaeris[75] spots you,
he'll show up uninvited to play
his pipes, until—mark my words—
for his tooting and toiling
you'll end up tipping him.

[75] A piper and lyre player frequently ridiculed in comedy for
ineptitude.

ΤΡΥΓΑΙΟΣ

ἄγε δή, τὸ κανοῦν λαβὼν σὺ καὶ τὴν χέρνιβα
περίιθι τὸν βωμὸν ταχέως ἐπιδέξια.

ΟΙΚΕΤΗΣ

ἰδού. λέγοις ἂν ἄλλο· περιελήλυθα.

ΤΡΥΓΑΙΟΣ

φέρε δή, τὸ δαλίον τόδ᾽ ἐμβάψω λαβών.
960 σείου σὺ ταχέως· σὺ δὲ πρότεινε τῶν ὀλῶν,
καὐτός γε χερνίπτου παραδοὺς ταύτην ἐμοί,
καὶ τοῖς θεαταῖς ῥῖπτε τῶν κριθῶν.

ΟΙΚΕΤΗΣ

ἰδού.

ΤΡΥΓΑΙΟΣ

ἔδωκας ἤδη;

ΟΙΚΕΤΗΣ

νὴ τὸν Ἑρμῆν, ὥστε γε
τούτων ὅσοιπέρ εἰσι τῶν θεωμένων
965 οὐκ ἔστιν οὐδεὶς ὅστις οὐ κριθὴν ἔχει.

ΤΡΥΓΑΙΟΣ

οὐχ αἱ γυναῖκές γ᾽ ἔλαβον.

ΟΙΚΕΤΗΣ

ἀλλ᾽ εἰς ἑσπέραν
δώσουσιν αὐταῖς ἄνδρες.

ΤΡΥΓΑΙΟΣ

ἀλλ᾽ εὐχώμεθα.
τίς τῇδε; ποῦ ποτ᾽ εἰσὶ πολλοὶ κἀγαθοί;

SLAVE returns with the lamb.

TRYGAEUS

Now then, you take the basket and the lustral water, and make a quick circuit of the altar, left to right.

SLAVE

There you are. I've done the circuit, what now?

TRYGAEUS

Here, I'll take this brand and dip it. (*to the lamb, as he sprinkles its head*) Hurry up, move your head! (*to the Slave*) Hand me some barley meal; give me the basin after you dip your own hands; and throw the spectators some of the barley pips.

SLAVE

(*tossing pips*) There.

TRYGAEUS

You've tossed them already?

SLAVE

By Hermes I have; there isn't a one of these spectators who hasn't got a pip.

TRYGAEUS

The women haven't got any.

SLAVE

Well, their husbands will give it to them tonight!

TRYGAEUS

Now let us pray. Who is here?[76] (*silence from the spectators*) Where might the good men aplenty be?

---

[76] A ritual question to which a sacrificial congregation was expected to reply, "good men aplenty."

ARISTOPHANES

ΟΙΚΕΤΗΣ

τοισδὶ φέρε δῶ· πολλοὶ γάρ εἰσι κἀγαθοί.

ΤΡΥΓΑΙΟΣ

970 τούτους ἀγαθοὺς ἐνόμισας;

ΟΙΚΕΤΗΣ

οὐ γάρ, οἵτινες
ἡμῶν καταχεόντων ὕδωρ τοσουτονὶ
εἰς ταὐτὸ τοῦθ᾽ ἑστᾶσ᾽ ἰόντες χωρίον;

ΤΡΥΓΑΙΟΣ

ἀλλ᾽ ὡς τάχιστ᾽ εὐχώμεθ᾽.

ΟΙΚΕΤΗΣ

εὐχώμεσθα δή.

ΤΡΥΓΑΙΟΣ

ὦ σεμνοτάτη βασίλεια θεά,
975 πότνι᾽ Εἰρήνη,
δέσποινα χορῶν, δέσποινα γάμων,
δέξαι θυσίαν τὴν ἡμετέραν.

ΟΙΚΕΤΗΣ

δέξαι δῆτ᾽, ὦ πολυτιμήτη,
νὴ Δία, καὶ μὴ ποίει γ᾽ ἅπερ αἱ
980 μοιχευόμεναι δρῶσι γυναῖκες.
καὶ γὰρ ἐκεῖναι παρακλίνασαι
τῆς αὐλείας παρακύπτουσιν·
κἄν τις προσέχῃ τὸν νοῦν αὐταῖς
ἀναχωροῦσιν·
985 κᾆτ᾽ ἢν ἀπίῃ, παρακύπτουσ᾽ αὖ.
τούτων σὺ ποίει μηδὲν ἔθ᾽ ἡμᾶς.

550

PEACE

SLAVE

(*sprinkling lustral water at the Chorus*) Here, let me give it to these here: they're good men aplenty. (*the Chorus dodges the water*)

TRYGAEUS

You considered them good men?

SLAVE

Why not? After I sprinkled them with all that water they came right back to the same place they were standing before.

TRYGAEUS

Now let's get right to the prayer.

SLAVE

Yes, let us pray.

TRYGAEUS

Most august sovereign goddess,
Lady Peace,
mistress of choruses, mistress of weddings,
accept this our sacrifice.

SLAVE

Yes, do accept it, greatly revered one,
in Zeus' name, and don't act as
adulterous wives do.
They open the door
a crack, and peep out,
and if anyone heeds them,
they draw back inside,
and when he's gone, they peep out again.
Don't treat us like that any more!

ΤΡΥΓΑΙΟΣ

μὰ Δί', ἀλλ' ἀπόφηνον ὅλην σαυτὴν
γενναιοπρεπῶς τοῖσιν ἐρασταῖς
ἡμῖν, οἵ σου τρυχόμεθ' ἤδη
990 τρία καὶ δέκ' ἔτη·
λῦσον δὲ μάχας καὶ κορκορυγάς,
ἵνα Λυσιμάχην σε καλῶμεν·
παῦσον δ' ἡμῶν τὰς ὑπονοίας
τὰς περικόμψους,
995 αἷς στωμυλλόμεθ' εἰς ἀλλήλους·
μεῖξον δ' ἡμᾶς τοὺς Ἕλληνας πάλιν ἐξ ἀρχῆς
φιλίας χυλῷ καὶ συγγνώμῃ
τινὶ πραοτέρᾳ κέρασον τὸν νοῦν·
καὶ τὴν ἀγορὰν ἡμῖν ἀγαθῶν
1000 ἐμπλησθῆναι, 'κ Μεγάρων σκορόδων,
σικύων πρῴων, μήλων, ῥοιῶν,
δούλοισι χλανισκιδίων μικρῶν·
κἀκ Βοιωτῶν γε φέροντας ἰδεῖν
χῆνας, νήττας, φάττας, τροχίλους·
1005 καὶ Κωπάδων ἐλθεῖν σπυρίδας,
καὶ περὶ ταύτας ἡμᾶς ἀθρόους
ὀψωνοῦντας τυρβάζεσθαι
Μορύχῳ, Τελέᾳ, Γλαυκέτῃ, ἄλλοις
τένθαις πολλοῖς· κᾆτα Μελάνθιον

1000 'κ Μεγάρων Hamaker cl. Σⱽ: μεγάλων RV

77 "Thirteen years" (instead of the actual ten since the out-

TRYGAEUS

God no! Rather show all of yourself
steadfastly to us your lovers,
who have been pining for you now
these thirteen years.[77]
Release us from battles and tumults,
so we may call you Lysimache.[78]
Rid us of those suspicions,
oh so savvy,
that make claptrap of our parleys;
and blend us Greeks, starting afresh,
with the juice of friendship, and imbue
our thinking with a more obliging fellowship.
Have our market fill up
with bounties: from Megara garlic,
early cucumbers, apples, pomegranates,
little wool jackets for our slaves;
and from Boeotia men seen bearing
geese, ducks, pigeons, wrens,
and Copaic eels coming by the basketful;
and amid this may all of us together
go shopping, jostling
Morychus, Teleas,[79] Glaucetes,[80] and
many another glutton; and may Melanthius

break of the war) is used as an indefinite round number with
unlucky connotations.

[78] The name, which means "Releaser from Battles," was in fact
borne by the incumbent priestess of Athena Polias, who may have
inspired Aristophanes in creating the heroine of *Lysistrata*.

[79] A minor politician.

[80] Possibly the father of the prominent politician Pisander.

1010 ἥκειν ὕστερον εἰς τὴν ἀγοράν,
τὰς δὲ πεπρᾶσθαι, τὸν δ᾽ ὀτοτύζειν,
εἶτα μονῳδεῖν ἐκ Μηδείας·
"ὀλόμαν, ὀλόμαν ἀποχηρωθεὶς
τᾶς ἐν τεύτλοισι λοχευομένας·"
1015 τοὺς δ᾽ ἀνθρώπους ἐπιχαίρειν.

ταῦτ᾽, ὦ πολυτίμητ᾽, εὐχομένοις ἡμῖν δίδου.
λαβὲ τὴν μάχαιραν· εἶθ᾽ ὅπως μαγειρικῶς
σφάξεις τὸν οἶν.

ΟΙΚΕΤΗΣ
ἀλλ᾽ οὐ θέμις.

ΤΡΥΓΑΙΟΣ
τιὴ τί δή;

ΟΙΚΕΤΗΣ
οὐχ ἥδεται δήπουθεν Εἰρήνη σφαγαῖς,
1020 οὐδ᾽ αἱματοῦται βωμός.

ΤΡΥΓΑΙΟΣ
ἀλλ᾽ εἴσω φέρων
θύσας τὰ μηρί᾽ ἐξελὼν δεῦρ᾽ ἔκφερε,
χοὔτω τὸ πρόβατον τῷ χορηγῷ σῴζεται.

ΧΟΡΟΣ
(ἀντ) σέ τοι θύρασι †χρὴ μένοντα τοίνυν†
σχίζας δευρὶ τιθέναι ταχέως
1025 τά τε πρόσφορα πάντ᾽ ἐπὶ τούτοις.

554

get to the market late,
when everything's sold, and shriek in despair,
then sing an ode from *Medea*,[81]
"I'm done for, done for, and bereft
of her that lay in amid beets!"[82]
and may the people rejoice at his grief.

All this, greatly revered goddess, give us in answer to our prayers. (*to the Slave*) Take the knife, and be sure to slaughter the lamb like a master chef.

SLAVE

But that's not proper.

TRYGAEUS

And why not?

SLAVE

Surely Peace takes no pleasure in slaughter, nor is her altar bloodied.

TRYGAEUS

All right, take it inside and sacrifice it, then remove the thigh pieces and bring them out here; that way our producer gets to keep his lamb!

SLAVE goes inside.

CHORUS

Meanwhile you've got to stay outdoors
and quickly arrange the kindling here
and everything that properly goes atop it.

[81] Not the play by Euripides, but probably one of Melanthius' own plays; cf. 804 n.   [82] I.e., a Copaic eel.

555

ARISTOPHANES

ΤΡΥΓΑΙΟΣ

οὔκουν δοκῶ σοι μαντικῶς τὸ φρύγανον τίθεσθαι;

ΧΟΡΟΣ

πῶς δ᾽ οὐχί; τί γάρ σε πέφευγ᾽ ὅσα χρὴ
σοφὸν ἄνδρα; τί δ᾽ οὐ σὺ φρονεῖς ὁπόσα χρε-
ὼν ἐστιν τόν γε σοφῇ δόκιμον
1030 φρενὶ πορίμῳ τε τόλμῃ;

ΤΡΥΓΑΙΟΣ

ἡ σχίζα γοῦν ἐνημμένη τὸν Στιλβίδην πιέζει.
καὶ τὴν τράπεζαν οἴσομαι, καὶ παιδὸς οὐ δεήσει.

ΧΟΡΟΣ

τίς οὖν ἂν οὐκ ἐπαινέσει-
εν ἄνδρα τοιοῦτον, ὅσ-
1035 τις πόλλ᾽ ἀνατλὰς ἔσω-
σε τὴν ἱερὰν πόλιν;
ὥστ᾽ οὐχὶ μὴ παύσει ποτ᾽ ὢν
ζηλωτὸς ἅπασιν.

ΟΙΚΕΤΗΣ

ταυτὶ δέδραται. τίθεσο τὼ μηρὼ λαβών·
1040 ἐγὼ δ᾽ ἐπὶ σπλάγχν᾽ εἶμι καὶ θυλήματα.

ΤΡΥΓΑΙΟΣ

ἐμοὶ μελήσει ταῦτά γ᾽· ἀλλ᾽ ἥκειν ἐχρῆν.

---

83 The renowned seer who would accompany Nicias to Sicily
in 415 (Plutarch, *Nicias* 23.7).

TRYGAEUS

Wouldn't you say that I'm arranging the firewood in seerly style?

CHORUS

How could I not? What have you missed
that makes for a wise man? What don't you know
that makes a man notable for a wise
mind and resourceful daring?

TRYGAEUS

In any case, the kindling's alight, and it's putting pressure on Stilbides![83] I'll fetch the table myself; a slave's not needed.

TRYGAEUS goes inside.

CHORUS

Now who wouldn't extol
such a man as this, who
by braving many hardships
has rescued our sacred city?
And so you'll never stop being
the envy of everyone.

Enter TRYGAEUS *with a table,* SLAVE *with the thighs.*

SLAVE

That job is done. Take the thighs and put them on; I'll go for the innards and offerings.

SLAVE goes inside.

TRYGAEUS

I'll see to this. (*calling into the house*) You should have been back by now!

557

ARISTOPHANES

ΟΙΚΕΤΗΣ

ἰδού, πάρειμι. μῶν ἐπισχεῖν σοι δοκῶ;

ΤΡΥΓΑΙΟΣ

ὄπτα καλῶς νυν αὐτά· καὶ γὰρ οὑτοσὶ
προσέρχεται δάφνῃ τις ἐστεφανωμένος.

ΟΙΚΕΤΗΣ

1045 τίς ἄρα ποτ᾽ ἐστίν; ὡς ἀλαζὼν φαίνεται.
μάντις τίς ἐστιν;

ΤΡΥΓΑΙΟΣ

οὐ μὰ Δί᾽, ἀλλ᾽ Ἱεροκλέης
οὗτός γέ πού 'σθ᾽ ὁ χρησμολόγος οὑξ Ὠρεοῦ.

ΟΙΚΕΤΗΣ

τί ποτ᾽ ἄρα λέξει;

ΤΡΥΓΑΙΟΣ

δῆλός ἐσθ᾽ οὗτός γ᾽ ὅτι
ἐναντιώσεταί τι ταῖς διαλλαγαῖς.

ΟΙΚΕΤΗΣ

1050 οὔκ, ἀλλὰ κατὰ τὴν κνῖσαν εἰσελήλυθεν.

ΤΡΥΓΑΙΟΣ

μή νυν ὁρᾶν δοκῶμεν αὐτόν.

ΟΙΚΕΤΗΣ

εὖ λέγεις.

---

[84] An oracular expert who had served the Athenians in an official capacity in 446 (*IG* I³ 40.64-7) and had been granted a

558

SLAVE comes out with spitted innards and offerings.

SLAVE
Look, here I am. You don't think I was taking my time,
do you?

TRYGAEUS
Now roast these nicely, because here comes somebody
wearing a laurel crown.

SLAVE
Now who in the world is that? Looks like a charlatan. Is he
a seer?

TRYGAEUS
Certainly no seer, but evidently Hierocles, the oracle mon-
ger from Oreus.[84]

SLAVE
What's he got to tell us?

TRYGAEUS
Obviously, he means to make some objection to the treaty.

SLAVE
No, he's drawn by this aroma.

TRYGAEUS
Well, let's pretend we don't see him.

SLAVE
Good idea.

Enter HIEROCLES.

settlement in Oreus, on land confiscated in 445 (Thucydides
1.114).

ARISTOPHANES

ΙΕΡΟΚΛΗΣ
τίς ἡ θυσία ποθ' αὑτηὶ καὶ τῷ θεῶν;

ΤΡΥΓΑΙΟΣ
ὅπτα σὺ σιγῇ κἄπαγ' ἀπὸ τῆς ὀσφύος.

ΙΕΡΟΚΛΗΣ
ὅτῳ δὲ θύετ' οὐ φράσεθ';

ΤΡΥΓΑΙΟΣ
ἡ κέρκος ποιεῖ
1055 καλῶς.

ΟΙΚΕΤΗΣ
καλῶς δῆτ', ὦ πότνι' Εἰρήνη φίλη.

ΙΕΡΟΚΛΗΣ
ἄγε νυν ἀπάρχου κᾆτα δὸς τἀπάργματα.

ΤΡΥΓΑΙΟΣ
ὀπτᾶν ἄμεινον πρῶτον.

ΙΕΡΟΚΛΗΣ
ἀλλὰ ταυταγὶ
ἤδη 'στὶν ὀπτά.

ΤΡΥΓΑΙΟΣ
πολλὰ πράττεις, ὅστις εἶ.
κατάτεμνε.

ΟΙΚΕΤΗΣ
ποῦ τράπεζα;

ΤΡΥΓΑΙΟΣ
τὴν σπονδὴν φέρε.

HIEROCLES
What sacrifice might this be, and to which god?

TRYGAEUS
(*to the Slave*) Be quiet while you roast, and steer clear of the rump.

HIEROCLES
Won't you tell me who you're sacrificing to?

TRYGAEUS
The tail is doing nicely.

SLAVE
Nicely indeed. Dear Lady Peace!

HIEROCLES
Come on then, cut the firstlings and give them to me.

TRYGAEUS
It's better to do the roasting first.

HIEROCLES
But these here are already done.

TRYGAEUS
You're pretty nosy, whoever you are. (*to the Slave*) Start carving.

SLAVE
Where's a table?

TRYGAEUS
Bring the libation.

ΙΕΡΟΚΛΗΣ

1060 ἡ γλῶττα χωρὶς τέμνεται.

ΤΡΥΓΑΙΟΣ
            μεμνήμεθα.

ἀλλ᾽ οἶσθ᾽ ὃ δρᾶσον;

ΙΕΡΟΚΛΗΣ
            ἢν φράσῃς.

ΤΡΥΓΑΙΟΣ
                        μὴ διαλέγου
νῷν μηδέν· Εἰρήνῃ γὰρ ἱερὰ θύομεν.

ΙΕΡΟΚΛΗΣ
ὦ μέλεοι θνητοὶ καὶ νήπιοι—

ΤΡΥΓΑΙΟΣ
            εἰς κεφαλὴν σοί.

ΙΕΡΟΚΛΗΣ
οἵτινες ἀφραδίῃσι θεῶν νόον οὐκ ἀίοντες
1065 συνθήκας πεποίησθ᾽ ἄνδρες χαροποῖσι πιθήκοις—

ΤΡΥΓΑΙΟΣ
αἰβοιβοῖ.

ΙΕΡΟΚΛΗΣ
      τί γελᾷς;

ΤΡΥΓΑΙΟΣ
            ἥσθην χαροποῖσι πιθήκοις.

ΙΕΡΟΚΛΗΣ
καὶ κέπφοι τρήρωνες ἀλωπεκιδεῦσι πέπεισθε,

HIEROCLES

The tongue gets cut separately.

TRYGAEUS

We know. But do you know what you should do?

HIEROCLES

Please say.

TRYGAEUS

Don't talk to us at all. You see, this is a sacrifice to Peace.[85]

HIEROCLES

"O mortals pitiful and foolish—"

TRYGAEUS

The same to you!

HIEROCLES

"—men who in senselessness know not the mind of
the gods,
you have struck a pact with glaring-eyed monkeys—"

TRYGAEUS

Ha ha ha!

HIEROCLES

What's so funny?

TRYGAEUS

"Glaring-eyed monkeys" is a good one!

HIEROCLES

"—and like tremulous pigeons give credence to fox
cubs,

[85] The following dialogue (to line 1114) is conducted in vatic
hexameters.

ὧν δόλιαι ψυχαί, δόλιαι φρένες.

ΤΡΥΓΑΙΟΣ

εἴθε σου εἶναι
ὤφελεν, ὦλαζών, οὑτωσὶ θερμὸς ὁ πλεύμων.

ΙΕΡΟΚΛΗΣ

1070   εἰ γὰρ μὴ νύμφαι γε θεαὶ Βάκιν ἐξαπάτασκον,
μηδὲ Βάκις θνητούς, μηδ᾽ αὖ νύμφαι Βάκιν αὐτὸν—

ΤΡΥΓΑΙΟΣ

ἐξώλης ἀπόλοι᾽, εἰ μὴ παύσαιο βακίζων.

ΙΕΡΟΚΛΗΣ

οὔπω θέσφατον ἦν Εἰρήνης δέσμ᾽ ἀναλῦσαι,
ἀλλὰ τόδε πρότερον—

ΤΡΥΓΑΙΟΣ

τοῖς ἁλσί γε παστέα ταυτί.

ΙΕΡΟΚΛΗΣ

1075   οὐ γάρ πω τοῦτ᾽ ἐστὶ φίλον μακάρεσσι θεοῖσιν,
1076a φυλόπιδος λῆξαι, πρίν κεν λύκος οἶν ὑμεναιοῖ.

ΤΡΥΓΑΙΟΣ

1076b καὶ πῶς, ὦ κατάρατε, λύκος ποτ᾽ ἂν οἶν ὑμεναιοῖ;

ΙΕΡΟΚΛΗΣ

1077   ἕως ἡ σφονδύλη φεύγουσα πονηρότατον βδεῖ,

---

86 A Boeotian prophet credited with success in predicting
events of the Persian wars (Herodotus 8.20, 77, 96, 9.43); oracles

whose hearts are wily, and wily their minds."

TRYGAEUS

You charlatan, I hope your lungs are as hot as this
  meat!

HIEROCLES

"If the Nymphs divine did not play Bacis[86] false,
nor Bacis mortals, nor yet the Nymphs Bacis
  himself—"

TRYGAEUS

Damn and blast you, if you don't stop Bacizing!

HIEROCLES

"—'twere yet not ordained that the fetters of Peace
  be loosened,
for this must first happen—"

TRYGAEUS

(*to the Slave*)   First we must season these pieces.

HIEROCLES

"—for this is not yet agreeable to the blessed gods,
to leave off the din of battle ere the wolf beds down
  with the lamb."

TRYGAEUS

You pariah, how could a wolf ever bed down with a
  lamb?

HIEROCLES

"So long as the bombardier beetle in flight farts most
  foully,

attributed to him were widely read and discussed during the
Peloponnesian War; cf. *Knights* 123-4, 1003-4.

κῴδων ἀκαλανθὶς ἐπειγομένη τυφλὰ τίκτει,
τουτάκις οὔπω χρῆν τὴν εἰρήνην πεποιῆσθαι.

ΤΡΥΓΑΙΟΣ

1080 ἀλλὰ τί χρῆν ἡμᾶς; οὐ παύσασθαι πολεμοῦντας;
ἢ διακαννιάσαι πότεροι κλαυσούμεθα μεῖζον,
ἐξὸν σπεισαμένοις κοινῇ τῆς Ἑλλάδος ἄρχειν;

ΙΕΡΟΚΛΗΣ

οὔποτε ποιήσεις τὸν καρκίνον ὀρθὰ βαδίζειν.

ΤΡΥΓΑΙΟΣ

οὔποτε δειπνήσεις ἔτι τοῦ λοιποῦ ’ν πρυτανείῳ,
1085 οὐδ’ ἐπὶ τῷ πραχθέντι ποιήσεις ὕστερον οὐδέν.

ΙΕΡΟΚΛΗΣ

οὐδέποτ’ ἂν θείης λεῖον τὸν τρηχὺν ἐχῖνον.

ΤΡΥΓΑΙΟΣ

ἆρα φενακίζων ποτ’ Ἀθηναίους ἔτι παύσει;

ΙΕΡΟΚΛΗΣ

ποῖον γὰρ κατὰ χρησμὸν ἐκαύσατε μῆρα θεοῖσιν;

ΤΡΥΓΑΙΟΣ

ὅνπερ κάλλιστον δήπου πεποίηκεν Ὅμηρος·

1078 κῴδων Agar: χή κώδων z

---

87 In the Prytaneum, which housed the sacred hearth of Athens, foreign dignitaries and Athenian officials were entertained at public expense; extraordinary benefactors (like Cleon after Pylos) could be awarded privileges there for life.

and the bitch too eager for labor brings forth blind
  pups,
so long were it not yet meet for peace to be
  sanctioned."

TRYGAEUS

What should we have done instead? Ceaselessly wage
  war?
Or draw lots for which side would suffer more,
when we could make a treaty and rule Greece
  together?

HIEROCLES

"Never shall you manage to make the crab walk
  straight."

TRYGAEUS

Nevermore shall you be dining in the Prytaneum[87] in
  future,
nor fashion any more prophecies after the event.

HIEROCLES

"Never shall you manage to smooth the spines of the
  hedgehog."

TRYGAEUS

And will *you* ever stop bamboozling the people of
  Athens?

HIEROCLES

Say, what oracle authorized you to burn thighs for the
  gods?

TRYGAEUS

The very fine one that Homer composed, of course:[88]

---

[88] Trygaeus' oracle is a pastiche of Homeric phrases.

1090 "ὡς οἱ μὲν νέφος ἐχθρὸν ἀπωσάμενοι πολέμοιο
Εἰρήνην εἵλοντο καὶ ἱδρύσανθ᾽ ἱερείῳ.
αὐτὰρ ἐπεὶ κατὰ μῆρ᾽ ἐκάη καὶ σπλάγχν᾽ ἐπάσαντο,
ἔσπενδον δεπάεσσιν, ἐγὼ δ᾽ ὁδὸν ἡγεμόνευον·"
χρησμολόγῳ δ᾽ οὐδεὶς ἐδίδου κώθωνα φαεινόν.

ΙΕΡΟΚΛΗΣ

1095 οὐ μετέχω τούτων· οὐ γὰρ ταῦτ᾽ εἶπε Σίβυλλα.

ΤΡΥΓΑΙΟΣ

ἀλλ᾽ ὁ σοφός τοι νὴ Δί᾽ Ὅμηρος δεξιὸν εἶπεν·
"ἀφρήτωρ, ἀθέμιστος, ἀνέστιός ἐστιν ἐκεῖνος,
ὃς πολέμου ἔραται ἐπιδημίου ὀκρυόεντος."

ΙΕΡΟΚΛΗΣ

φράζεο δή, μή πώς σε δόλῳ φρένας ἐξαπατήσας
1100 ἰκτῖνος μάρψῃ—

ΤΡΥΓΑΙΟΣ

τουτὶ μέντοι σὺ φυλάττου,
ὡς οὗτος φοβερὸς τοῖς σπλάγχνοις ἐστὶν ὁ
χρησμός.
ἔγχει δὴ σπονδὴν καὶ τῶν σπλάγχνων φέρε δευρί.

ΙΕΡΟΚΛΗΣ

ἀλλ᾽ εἰ ταῦτα δοκεῖ, κἀγὼ 'μαυτῷ βαλανεύσω.

ΤΡΥΓΑΙΟΣ

σπονδὴ σπονδή.

---

[89] An early ecstatic prophetess; oracles attributed to her were popular in this period (cf. *Knights* 61).

"Thus casting away the detestable vapor of warfare,
they opted for Peace and with a victim established her.
And when the thighs were burnt and the innards
 devoured,
they poured libation from cups, and I led the way"—
but to the oracle monger no one passed a gleaming
 goblet!

HIEROCLES

That's nothing to me; Sibyl[89] did not say it.

TRYGAEUS

But here's something the sage Homer said that, by
 god, is well put:[90]
"Clanless, lawless, hearthless is that man
who lusts for the horror of warfare among his own
 people."

HIEROCLES

"Take heed, lest a kite somehow beguile your wits by
 deception
and snatch up—"

TRYGAEUS

(*to the Slave*)   Do keep an eye out for just that;
for this oracle means menace to the innards.
Now pour in the libation, and bring me here some
 innards.

HIEROCLES

If that is your plan, I too will be my own bathman.[91]

TRYGAEUS

Libation! Libation!

---

[90] See *Iliad* 9.63-4.   [91] I.e., not wait to be served.

ΙΕΡΟΚΛΗΣ

1105 ἔγχει δὴ κἀμοὶ καὶ σπλάγχνων μοῖραν ὄρεξον.

ΤΡΥΓΑΙΟΣ

ἀλλ᾽ οὔπω τοῦτ᾽ ἐστὶ φίλον μακάρεσσι θεοῖσιν·
ἀλλὰ τόδε πρότερον, σπένδειν ἡμᾶς, σὲ δ᾽ ἀπελθεῖν.
ὦ πότνι᾽ Εἰρήνη, παράμεινον τὸν βίον ἡμῖν.

ΙΕΡΟΚΛΗΣ

πρόσφερε τὴν γλῶτταν.

ΤΡΥΓΑΙΟΣ

σὺ δὲ τὴν σαυτοῦ γ᾽ ἀπένεγκε.
1110 σπονδή. καὶ ταυτὶ μετὰ τῆς σπονδῆς λαβὲ θᾶττον.

ΙΕΡΟΚΛΗΣ

οὐδεὶς προσδώσει μοι σπλάγχνων;

ΤΡΥΓΑΙΟΣ

οὐ γὰρ οἷόν τε
ἡμῖν προσδιδόναι, πρίν κεν λύκος οἶν ὑμεναιοῖ.

ΙΕΡΟΚΛΗΣ

ναί, πρὸς τῶν γονάτων.

ΤΡΥΓΑΙΟΣ

ἄλλως, ὦ τᾶν, ἱκετεύεις·
οὐ γὰρ ποιήσεις λεῖον τὸν τρηχὺν ἐχῖνον.
1115 ἄγε δή, θεαταί, δεῦρο συσπλαγχνεύετε
μετὰ νῶν.

ΙΕΡΟΚΛΗΣ

τί δαὶ ᾽γώ;

570

HIEROCLES

Pour me some too, and pass me a portion of innards.

TRYGAEUS

But this is not yet agreeable to the blessed gods,
for this must first happen: we make libation, you hit
   the road.
Lady Peace, remain with us throughout our lives.

HIEROCLES

Please give me the tongue.

TRYGAEUS

               And you take yours away!
Libation! (*to the Slave*) And take these with the
   libation, quickly.

HIEROCLES

Will no one give me some innards?

TRYGAEUS

                  No, it's impossible
for us to give any, ere the wolf beds down with the
   lamb.

HIEROCLES

Do, I implore you!

TRYGAEUS

            In vain, sir, do you beseech me,
for never shall you manage to smooth the spines of
   the hedgehog.
Here now, spectators, come and share the innards with us!

HIEROCLES

And what about me?

ΤΡΥΓΑΙΟΣ

τὴν Σίβυλλαν ἔσθιε.

ΙΕΡΟΚΛΗΣ

οὔτοι μὰ τὴν Γῆν ταῦτα κατέδεσθον μόνω,
ἀλλ᾽ ἁρπάσομαι σφῷν αὐτά· κεῖται δ᾽ ἐν μέσῳ.

ΤΡΥΓΑΙΟΣ

ὦ παῖε παῖε τὸν Βάκιν.

ΙΕΡΟΚΛΗΣ

μαρτύρομαι.

ΤΡΥΓΑΙΟΣ

1120   κἄγωγ᾽, ὅτι τένθης εἶ σὺ κἀλαζὼν ἀνήρ.
παῖ᾽ αὐτὸν ἐπέχων τῷ ξύλῳ, τὸν ἀλαζόνα.

ΙΕΡΟΚΛΗΣ

σὺ μὲν οὖν· ἐγὼ δὲ τουτονὶ τῶν κῳδίων,
ἀλάμβαν᾽ αὐτὸς ἐξαπατῶν, ἐκβολβιῶ.
οὐ καταβαλεῖς τὰ κῴδι᾽, ὦ θυηπόλε;

ΤΡΥΓΑΙΟΣ

1125   ἤκουσας; ὁ κόραξ οἷος ἦλθ᾽ ἐξ Ὠρεοῦ.
οὐκ ἀποπετήσει θᾶττον εἰς Ἐλύμνιον;

ΧΟΡΟΣ

(στρ)   ἥδομαί γ᾽ ἥδομαι
κράνους ἀπηλλαγμένος
τυροῦ τε καὶ κρομμύων.

TRYGAEUS

Go eat your Sibyl!

HIEROCLES

No, by Earth, you two shan't eat all this by yourselves; I'll snatch it away from you; it's all up for grabs!

TRYGAEUS

(*striking Hierocles*) Here, beat him! Beat this Bacis!

HIEROCLES

I summon witnesses!

TRYGAEUS

So do I: that you're a glutton and a charlatan. (*to the Slave*) Keep beating him with that stick, the charlatan!

SLAVE

No, you do the beating; I'm going to peel these sheepskins off him, that he's been getting by bamboozlement. Off with those sheepskins, sacrificer!

TRYGAEUS

Did you hear?

HIEROCLES drops the skins and runs away.

There goes the buzzard, just as he came from Oreus.[92] (*calling after him*) Fly off now, and quick, to Elymnium![93]

CHORUS

I'm delighted, yes delighted,
to be rid of helmets
and cheese and onions.

[92] I.e. without the skins.
[93] A Euboean sanctuary near Oreus.

1130 οὐ γὰρ φιληδῶ μάχαις,
  ἀλλὰ πρὸς πῦρ διέλ-
   κων μετ᾽ ἀνδρῶν ἑταί-
   ρων φίλων ἐκκέας
   τῶν ξύλων ἅττ᾽ ἂν ᾖ
   δανότατα τοῦ θέρους
1135 ἐκπεπρεμνισμένα,
  κἀνθρακίζων τοὐρεβίνθου
  τήν τε φηγὸν ἐμπυρεύων,
  χἄμα τὴν Θρᾷτταν κυνῶν
  τῆς γυναικὸς λουμένης.

1140 οὐ γὰρ ἔσθ᾽ ἥδιον ἢ τυχεῖν μὲν ἤδη 'σπαρμένα,
  τὸν θεὸν δ᾽ ἐπιψακάζειν, καί τιν᾽ εἰπεῖν γείτονα·
  "εἰπέ μοι, τί τηνικαῦτα δρῶμεν, ὦ Κωμαρχίδη;"
  "ἐμπιεῖν ἔμοιγ᾽ ἀρέσκει τοῦ θεοῦ δρῶντος καλῶς.
  ἀλλ᾽ ἄφαυε τῶν φασήλων, ὦ γύναι, τρεῖς χοίνικας,
1145 τῶν τε πυρῶν μεῖξον αὐτοῖς, τῶν τε σύκων ἔξελε,
  τόν τε Μανῆν ἡ Σύρα βωστρησάτω 'κ τοῦ χωρίου.
  οὐ γὰρ οἷόν τ᾽ ἐστὶ πάντως οἰναρίζειν τήμερον
  οὐδὲ τυντλάζειν, ἐπειδὴ παρδακὸν τὸ χωρίον."
  "κἀξ ἐμοῦ δ᾽ ἐνεγκάτω τις τὴν κίχλην καὶ τὼ σπίνω·
1150 ἦν δὲ καὶ πυός τις ἔνδον καὶ λαγῷα τέτταρα,
  εἴ τι μὴ 'ξήνεγκεν αὐτῶν ἡ γαλῆ τῆς ἑσπέρας·
  ἐψόφει γοῦν ἔνδον οὐκ οἶδ᾽ ἄττα κἀκυδοιδόπα·

1135 ἐκπεπρεμνισμένα Bergk: ἐκπεπρισμένα RV: ἐκπεπιεσμένα t: om. p

For I take no pleasure in battles,
but in bending an elbow
by the fire with good
friends, setting ablaze
the logs that were
stubbed up last summer
and are nice and dry,
and toasting the pease,
and roasting some acorn,
and kissing the Thracian maid
while the wife's in the bath.

CHORUS LEADER

Yes, nothing's more delightful than having the seed in the
ground, the god pattering it with rain, and a neighbor say-
ing, "Say, Comarchides,[94] how shall we pass the time?"
"I fancy heavy drinking, since the god's so well disposed.
Wife, start parching three quarts of the kidney beans, and
mix in some of the barley, and break out some of the figs;
and have Syra call Manes in from the vineyard.[95] It's no use
at all trying to prune vines today, or turn the soil; the
ground's muddy." "And someone from my house fetch the
thrush and the two chaffinches; there should be some
beestings there too, and four rabbit fillets, unless the cat
took some of them off last night; it sure was making an
astonishing racket and hubbub in there. Bring us three of

[94] "Master of Revels" or "Village Chief."
[95] Typical slave names.

ὧν ἔνεγκ᾽, ὦ παῖ, τρί᾽ ἡμῖν, ἓν δὲ δοῦναι τῷ πατρί·
μυρρίνας τ᾽ αἴτησον ἐξ παρ᾽ Αἰσχίνου τῶν καρπίμων·
1155 χἄμα τῆς αὐτῆς ὁδοῦ Χαρινάδην τις βωσάτω,
ὡς ἂν ἐμπίῃ μεθ᾽ ἡμῶν,
εὖ ποιοῦντος κὠφελοῦντος
τοῦ θεοῦ τἀρώματα."

ΧΟΡΟΣ

(ἀντ) ἡνίκ᾽ ἂν δ᾽ ἀχέτας
1160 ᾄδῃ τὸν ἡδὺν νόμον,
διασκοπῶν ἥδομαι
τὰς Λημνίας ἀμπέλους,
εἰ πεπαίνουσιν ἤ-
δη—τὸ γὰρ φῖτυ πρῶ-
1165 ον φύσει—τόν τε φή-
ληχ᾽ ὁρῶν οἰδάνοντ᾽·
εἶθ᾽ ὁπόταν ᾖ πέπων,
ἐσθίω κἀπέχω
χἄμα φήμ᾽· "Ὧραι φίλαι" καὶ
τοῦ θύμου τρίβων κυκῶμαι·
1170 κᾆτα γίγνομαι παχὺς
τηνικαῦτα τοῦ θέρους—

ΚΟΡΥΦΑΙΟΣ

μᾶλλον ἢ θεοῖσιν ἐχθρὸν ταξίαρχον προσβλέπων
τρεῖς λόφους ἔχοντα καὶ φοινικίδ᾽ ὀξεῖαν πάνυ,
ἣν ἐκεῖνός φησιν εἶναι βάμμα Σαρδιανικόν·

1154 ἐξ παρ᾽ Αἰσχίνου van Leeuwen: ἐξ Αἰσχινάδου z

them, boy, and give one to my father. And ask at Aeschines'
house for six myrtle branches with berries on them;[96] and
as you're going that way, someone give Charinades a shout,

so he can drink with us,
since the god's tending
and helping the crops."

CHORUS

And when the cicada
sings his sweet tune,
I enjoy inspecting
my Lemnian vines,
to see if they're ripening yet
(they're naturally
early ones), and to see
the wild fig swelling;
and when it's ready,
I eat and keep eating,
saying the while "dear Seasons!" and
pounding thyme for a cordial;
and then I grow plump
in the high summer—

CHORUS LEADER

—more so than by standing at attention before a godfor-
saken commander, with his triple plumes and very glittery
crimson uniform, whose dye according to him is genuine

[96] Aeschines (for the MSS' unmetrical Aeschinades) was a
typical name; myrtle branches were used at banquets to make
wreaths and to hold while singing drinking songs.

1175 ἢν δέ που δέῃ μάχεσθ᾽ ἔχοντα τὴν φοινικίδα,
τηνικαῦτ᾽ αὐτὸς βέβαπται βάμμα Κυζικηνικόν·
κᾆτα φεύγει πρῶτος ὥσπερ ξουθὸς ἱππαλεκτρυὼν
τοὺς λόφους σείων· ἐγὼ δ᾽ ἕστηκα λινοπτώμενος.
ἡνίκ᾽ ἂν δ᾽ οἴκοι γένωνται, δρῶσιν οὐκ ἀνασχετά,

1180 τοὺς μὲν ἐγγράφοντες ἡμῶν, τοὺς δ᾽ ἄνω τε καὶ κάτω
ἐξαλείφοντες δὶς ἢ τρίς. αὔριον δ᾽ ἔσθ᾽ ἤξοδος,
τῷ δὲ σιτί᾽ οὐκ ἐώνητ᾽· οὐ γὰρ ᾔδειν ἐξιών·
εἶτα προσστὰς πρὸς τὸν ἀνδριάντα τὸν Πανδίονος
εἶδεν αὑτόν, κἀπορῶν θεῖ τῷ κακῷ βλέπων ὀπόν.

1185 ταῦτα δ᾽ ἡμᾶς τοὺς ἀγροίκους δρῶσι, τοὺς δ᾽ ἐξ
     ἄστεως
ἧττον, οἱ θεοῖσιν οὗτοι κἀνδράσιν ῥιψάσπιδες.
ὧν ἔτ᾽ εὐθύνας ἐμοὶ δώσουσιν, ἢν θεὸς θέλῃ.
πολλὰ γὰρ δή μ᾽ ἠδίκησαν,
    ὄντες οἴκοι μὲν λέοντες,

1190   ἐν μάχῃ δ᾽ ἀλώπεκες.

ΤΡΥΓΑΙΟΣ

ἰοὺ ἰού.
ὅσον τὸ χρῆμ᾽ ἐπὶ δεῖπνον ἦλθ᾽ εἰς τοὺς γάμους.
ἔχ᾽, ἀποκάθαιρε τὰς τραπέζας ταυτηί·
πάντως γὰρ οὐδὲν ὄφελός ἐστ᾽ αὐτῆς ἔτι.

1195 ἔπειτ᾽ ἐπιφόρει τοὺς ἀμύλους καὶ τὰς κίχλας
καὶ τῶν λαγῴων πολλὰ καὶ τοὺς κολλάβους.

Sardian; though I think if he ever has to fight in that uniform, that's when he dyes it himself—a genuine Brownsville! Then he's the first to take to his heels, fluttering his plumes like a zooming horsecock, while I hold my position like the snare-guard in a rabbit hunt. And when they get stationed at home, their behavior's intolerable: they enter some of us on the roster and strike others, haphazardly, two or three times. We move out tomorrow, but he's bought no provisions, being unaware that he was going; then he stops at Pandion's statue[97] and sees his name, and rushes off in a tizzy, his expression curdled by this misfortune. That's how they treat the country folk, less so the city folk, casting in the face of gods and men their—shields! For all this, god willing, they'll settle accounts with me yet,

for they've done me much wrong,
acting like lions on the home front,
like foxes in the fight!

TRYGAEUS and SLAVE come out of the house.

TRYGAEUS

My, my! What a lot of people have come for the wedding feast! (*handing him a helmet crest*) Here, use this to wipe the table; there's no further use for it anyway. Then pile on the cookies and thrushes, and lots of the rabbit, and the rolls.

SLAVE goes inside; enter a SICKLE MAKER and a Potter with wares and wedding gifts.

---

[97] One of the ten eponymous tribal heroes whose statues stood in the Agora; notices relevant to a tribe's members were posted there. Aristophanes belonged to the tribe Pandionis.

ARISTOPHANES

ΔΡΕΠΑΝΟΤΡΓΟΣ

ποῦ ποῦ Τρυγαῖός ἐστιν;

ΤΡΥΓΑΙΟΣ

ἀναβράττω κίχλας.

ΔΡΕΠΑΝΟΤΡΓΟΣ

ὦ φίλτατ᾽, ὦ Τρυγαῖ᾽, ὅσ᾽ ἡμᾶς τἀγαθὰ
δέδρακας εἰρήνην ποιήσας· ὡς πρὸ τοῦ
1200 οὐδεὶς ἐπρίατ᾽ ἂν δρέπανον οὐδὲ κολλύβου,
νυνὶ δὲ πεντήκοντα δραχμῶν ἐμπολῶ,
ὁδὶ δὲ τριδράχμους τοὺς κάδους εἰς τοὺς ἀγρούς.
ἀλλ᾽, ὦ Τρυγαῖε, τῶν δρεπάνων τε λάμβανε
καὶ τῶνδ᾽ ὅ τι βούλει προῖκα· καὶ ταυτὶ δέχου·
1205 ἀφ᾽ ὧν γὰρ ἀπεδόμεσθα κἀκερδάναμεν
τὰ δῶρα ταυτί σοι φέρομεν εἰς τοὺς γάμους.

ΤΡΥΓΑΙΟΣ

ἴθι νυν, καταθέμενοι παρ᾽ ἐμοὶ ταῦτ᾽ εἴσιτε
ἐπὶ δεῖπνον ὡς τάχιστα· καὶ γὰρ οὑτοσὶ
ὅπλων κάπηλος ἀχθόμενος προσέρχεται.

ΟΠΛΩΝ ΚΑΠΗΛΟΣ

1210 οἴμ᾽ ὡς προθέλυμνόν μ᾽, ὦ Τρυγαῖ᾽, ἀπώλεσας.

ΤΡΥΓΑΙΟΣ

τί δ᾽ ἐστίν, ὦ κακόδαιμον; οὔ τί που λοφᾷς;

ΟΠΛΩΝ ΚΑΠΗΛΟΣ

ἀπώλεσάς μου τὴν τέχνην καὶ τὸν βίον,
καὶ τουτουὶ καὶ τοῦ δορυξοῦ ᾽κεινουί.

PEACE

SICKLE MAKER
Where's Trygaeus, where's Trygaeus?

TRYGAEUS
I'm stewing thrushes.

SICKLE MAKER
My dear friend Trygaeus, what great blessings you've brought us by making peace! Until today no one would pay a penny for a sickle, but now I'm selling them for fifty drachmas, and this man gets three drachmas for his country crocks. So, Trygaeus, take any of these sickles and crocks that you like, at no charge. (*offering wedding gifts*) And accept these too; out of our sales and profits we're bringing you these wedding gifts.

TRYGAEUS
Well now, put them down next to me, and hurry on inside for dinner. Because here comes an arms dealer, looking irritated.

Enter an ARMS DEALER, *a Helmet Maker, and a Spear Maker with their wares.*

ARMS DEALER
Damn it, Trygaeus, you've destroyed me root and branch!

TRYGAEUS
What's the matter, poor fellow? Come down with a touch of plume-onia?

ARMS DEALER
You've destroyed my business and my livelihood, and this man's, and this spear maker's too.

581

ΤΡΥΓΑΙΟΣ

τί δῆτα τουτοινὶ καταθῶ σοι τοῖν λόφοιν;

ΟΠΛΩΝ ΚΑΠΗΛΟΣ

1215 αὐτὸς σὺ τί δίδως;

ΤΡΥΓΑΙΟΣ

ὅ τι δίδωμ'; αἰσχύνομαι.
ὅμως δ' ὅτι τὸ σφήκωμ' ἔχει πόνον πολύν,
δοίην ἂν αὐτοῖν ἰσχάδων τρεῖς χοίνικας.
[ἵν' ἀποκαθαίρω τὴν τράπεζαν τουτῳί.]

ΟΠΛΩΝ ΚΑΠΗΛΟΣ

ἔνεγκε τοίνυν εἰσιὼν τὰς ἰσχάδας·
1220 κρεῖττον γάρ, ὦ τᾶν, ἐστιν ἢ μηδὲν λαβεῖν.

ΤΡΥΓΑΙΟΣ

ἀπόφερ' ἀπόφερ' ἐς κόρακας ἀπὸ τῆς οἰκίας.
τριχορρυεῖτον, οὐδέν ἐστον τὼ λόφω.
οὐκ ἂν πριαίμην οὐδ' ἂν ἰσχάδος μιᾶς.

ΟΠΛΩΝ ΚΑΠΗΛΟΣ

τί δαὶ δεκάμνῳ τῷδε θώρακος κύτει
1225 ἐνημμένῳ κάλλιστα χρήσομαι τάλας;

ΤΡΥΓΑΙΟΣ

οὗτος μὲν οὐ μή σοι ποιήσει ζημίαν.
ἀλλ' αἶρέ μοι τοῦτόν γε τῆς ἰσωνίας·
ἐναποπατεῖν γάρ ἐστ' ἐπιτήδειος πάνυ—

ΟΠΛΩΝ ΚΑΠΗΛΟΣ

παῦσαι 'νυβρίζων τοῖς ἐμοῖσι χρήμασιν.

1218 del. Hamaker

TRYGAEUS

All right, what will you take for this pair of crests?

ARMS DEALER

What's your offer?

TRYGAEUS

My offer? I'm embarrassed to say, but considering the workmanship of the fastening, I'd offer three quarts of dried figs for the pair.

ARMS DEALER

Done; go in and fetch the figs.

TRYGAEUS goes inside.

(*to a companion*) It's better than nothing, my friend.

TRYGAEUS comes out.

TRYGAEUS

Get these the hell out of here, get them away from my house! They're losing their hair, they're worthless. I wouldn't even pay a single fig for them.

ARMS DEALER

And what am I to do with this "corslet round," a beautiful fit and worth ten minas, damn it?

TRYGAEUS

Well, that one won't be a loss for you; give it to me at cost. (*taking the corslet*) Look, this will make a handy crapper—

ARMS DEALER

Stop outraging my wares!

ΤΡΥΓΑΙΟΣ

1230 ὡδί, παραθέντι τρεῖς λίθους. οὐ δεξιῶς;

ΟΠΛΩΝ ΚΑΠΗΛΟΣ

ποίᾳ δ᾽ ἀποψήσει ποτ᾽, ὠμαθέστατε;

ΤΡΥΓΑΙΟΣ

τῃδί, διεὶς τὴν χεῖρα διὰ τῆς θαλαμιᾶς
καὶ τῇδ᾽.

ΟΠΛΩΝ ΚΑΠΗΛΟΣ

ἅμ᾽ ἀμφοῖν δῆτ᾽;

ΤΡΥΓΑΙΟΣ

ἔγωγε νὴ Δία,
ἵνα μή γ᾽ ἁλῶ τρύπημα κλέπτων τῆς νεώς.

ΟΠΛΩΝ ΚΑΠΗΛΟΣ

1235 ἔπειτ᾽ ἐπὶ δεκάμνῳ χεσεῖ καθήμενος;

ΤΡΥΓΑΙΟΣ

ἔγωγε νὴ Δί᾽, ὠπίτριπτ᾽. οἴει γὰρ ἂν
τὸν πρωκτὸν ἀποδόσθαι με χιλιῶν δραχμῶν;

ΟΠΛΩΝ ΚΑΠΗΛΟΣ

ἴθι δή, 'ξένεγκε τἀργύριον.

ΤΡΥΓΑΙΟΣ

ἀλλ᾽, ὦγαθέ,
θλίβει τὸν ὄρρον. ἀπόφερ᾽, οὐκ ὠνήσομαι.

ΟΠΛΩΝ ΚΑΠΗΛΟΣ

1240 τί δ᾽ ἆρα τῇ σάλπιγγι τῇδε χρήσομαι,
ἣν ἐπριάμην δραχμῶν ποθ᾽ ἑξήκοντ᾽ ἐγώ;

584

PEACE

TRYGAEUS

—this way, if I prop it up with three stones. Neat, eh?

ARMS DEALER

But how will you ever wipe yourself, you utter ignoramus?

TRYGAEUS

This way, with my hand through the oarport, and this way
with the other hand.

ARMS DEALER

You use both hands?

TRYGAEUS

I certainly do: I don't want to be caught padding my bottom
line with an unmanned oarport!

ARMS DEALER

So you intend to sit on a ten-mina corslet and shit?

TRYGAEUS

I certainly do, you damned scoundrel! Do you think I'd sell
my arsehole for a thousand drachmas?

ARMS DEALER

All right then, fetch the money.

TRYGAEUS

On second thought, dear fellow, it irritates my bottom.
Take it away; I won't buy it.

ARMS DEALER

And what will I do with this bugle, then, that one time I
bought for sixty drachmas?

ΤΡΥΓΑΙΟΣ

μόλυβδον εἰς τουτὶ τὸ κοῖλον ἐγχέας
ἔπειτ᾽ ἄνωθεν ῥάβδον ἐνθεὶς ὑπόμακρον,
γενήσεταί σοι τῶν κατακτῶν κοττάβων.

ΟΠΛΩΝ ΚΑΠΗΛΟΣ

1245 οἴμοι καταγελᾷς.

ΤΡΥΓΑΙΟΣ

    ἀλλ᾽ ἕτερον παραινέσω·
τὸν μὲν μόλυβδον, ὥσπερ εἶπον, ἔγχεον,
ἐντευθενὶ δὲ σπαρτίοις ἠρτημένην
πλάστιγγα πρόσθες, καὐτό σοι γενήσεται
τὰ σῦκ᾽ ἐν ἀγρῷ τοῖς οἰκέταισιν ἱστάναι.

ΟΠΛΩΝ ΚΑΠΗΛΟΣ

1250 ὦ δυσκάθαρτε δαῖμον, ὥς μ᾽ ἀπώλεσας,
ὅτ᾽ ἀντέδωκα κἀντὶ τῶνδε μνᾶν ποτέ.
καὶ νῦν τί δράσω; τίς γὰρ αὔτ᾽ ὠνήσεται;

ΤΡΥΓΑΙΟΣ

πώλει βαδίζων αὐτὰ τοῖς Αἰγυπτίοις·
ἔστιν γὰρ ἐπιτήδεια συρμαίαν μετρεῖν.

ΟΠΛΩΝ ΚΑΠΗΛΟΣ

1255 οἴμ᾽, ὦ κρανοποί, ὡς ἀθλίως πεπράγαμεν.

ΤΡΥΓΑΙΟΣ

οὗτος μὲν οὐ πέπονθεν οὐδέν.

ΟΠΛΩΝ ΚΑΠΗΛΟΣ

      ἀλλὰ τί
ἔτ᾽ ἐστὶ τοῖσι κράνεσιν ὅ τι τις χρήσεται;

TRYGAEUS

Pour lead into its bell here, then into the mouthpiece stick
a longish rod, and you'll have yourself a target for cottabus
tosses.[98]

ARMS DEALER

Damn it, you're making fun of me!

TRYGAEUS

Then here's another idea: pour in the lead, as I said, and
from this end attach a scale pan hung with cords, and you'll
have just the thing for weighing out figs for your farm-
hands.

ARMS DEALER

O unappeasable spirit, how thou hast ruined me! (*holding
up two helmets*) Because these too once cost me a mina.
And now what am I going to do? Who'll buy them?

TRYGAEUS

Go sell them to the Egyptians; they'll do for measuring out
laxative.

ARMS DEALER

Damn it, helmet maker, we've really fallen on hard times.

TRYGAEUS

Nothing bad has happened to *him*.

ARMS DEALER

But what use will anyone have for helmets any more?

[98] Cottabus was a drinking game whose object was to hit vari-
ous targets with wine dregs tossed from the cups.

ΤΡΥΓΑΙΟΣ

ἐὰν τοιαυτασὶ μάθῃ λαβὰς ποιεῖν,
ἄμεινον ἢ νῦν αὔτ' ἀποδώσεται πολύ.

ΟΠΛΩΝ ΚΑΠΗΛΟΣ

1260 ἀπίωμεν, ὦ δορυξέ.

ΤΡΥΓΑΙΟΣ

μηδαμῶς γ', ἐπεὶ
τούτῳ γ' ἐγὼ τὰ δόρατα ταῦτ' ὠνήσομαι.

ΟΠΛΩΝ ΚΑΠΗΛΟΣ

πόσον δίδως δῆτ';

ΤΡΥΓΑΙΟΣ

εἰ διαπρισθείη δίχα,
λάβοιμ' ἂν αὔτ' εἰς χάρακας ἑκατὸν τῆς δραχμῆς.

ΟΠΛΩΝ ΚΑΠΗΛΟΣ

ὑβριζόμεθα. χωρῶμεν, ὦ τᾶν, ἐκποδών.

ΤΡΥΓΑΙΟΣ

1265 νὴ τὸν Δί', ὡς τὰ παιδί' ἤδη 'ξέρχεται
οὐρησόμενα τὰ τῶν ἐπικλήτων δεῦρ', ἵνα
ἅττ' ᾄσεται προαναβάλητ', ἐμοὶ δοκεῖ.
ἀλλ' ὅ τι περ ᾄδειν ἐπινοεῖς, ὦ παιδίον,
αὐτοῦ παρ' ἐμὲ στὰν πρότερον ἀναβαλοῦ 'νθαδί.

ΠΑΙΔΙΟΝ Α'

1270 νῦν αὖθ' ὁπλοτέρων ἀνδρῶν ἀρχώμεθα—

---

99 The opening of the cyclic epic *Epigoni*, which told of the
attack on Thebes by the sons of the original Seven. As in the scene

TRYGAEUS

(*pointing to the helmet maker's ears*) If he learns to make handles like these, he'll make a much higher profit on them than he does now.

ARMS DEALER

Let's be off, spear maker.

TRYGAEUS

No, don't go; I'm going to buy those spears from him.

ARMS DEALER

All right, for how much?

TRYGAEUS

If they're sawn in two, I'll take them for vine poles, a hundred for a drachma.

ARMS DEALER

That's an insult! Let's get out of here, my friend.

ARMS DEALER and his associates depart.

TRYGAEUS

(*calling after them*) A very good idea, because the guests' children are already coming out here to piss—so they can rehearse the preludes they're going to sing, is my guess.

Two BOYS come out of the house.

Whatever you've got in mind to sing, my boy, stand right here beside me and preview the prelude.

FIRST BOY

"Now let us begin a song of younger blood—"[99]

with Hierocles earlier, Trygaeus responds in kind to the boys' hexameters.

ARISTOPHANES

ΤΡΥΓΑΙΟΣ

παῦσαι

ὁπλοτέρους ᾄδων, καὶ ταῦτ᾽, ὦ τρισκακόδαιμον,
εἰρήνης οὔσης· ἀμαθές γ᾽ εἶ καὶ κατάρατον.

ΠΑΙΔΙΟΝ Α΄

οἱ δ᾽ ὅτε δὴ σχεδὸν ἦσαν ἐπ᾽ ἀλλήλοισιν ἰόντες,
σύν ῥ᾽ ἔβαλον ῥινούς τε καὶ ἀσπίδας ὀμφαλοέσσας.

ΤΡΥΓΑΙΟΣ

1275 ἀσπίδας; οὐ παύσει μεμνημένος ἀσπίδος ἡμῖν;

ΠΑΙΔΙΟΝ Α΄

ἔνθα δ᾽ ἅμ᾽ οἰμωγή τε καὶ εὐχωλὴ πέλεν ἀνδρῶν.

ΤΡΥΓΑΙΟΣ

ἀνδρῶν οἰμωγή; κλαύσει, νὴ τὸν Διόνυσον,
οἰμωγὰς ᾄδων, καὶ ταύτας ὀμφαλοέσσας.

ΠΑΙΔΙΟΝ Α΄

ἀλλὰ τί δῆτ᾽ ᾄδω; σὺ γὰρ εἰπέ μοι οἷστισι χαίρεις.

ΤΡΥΓΑΙΟΣ

1280 "ὣς οἱ μὲν δαίνυντο βοῶν κρέα," καὶ τὰ τοιαυτί·
"ἄριστον προτίθεντο καὶ ἅσσ᾽ ἥδιστα πάσασθαι."

ΠΑΙΔΙΟΝ Α΄

"ὣς οἱ μὲν δαίνυντο βοῶν κρέα, καὐχένας ἵππων

---

100 Lines 1273-74, 1276, and 1286-87 are Iliadic centos.

590

PEACE

TRYGAEUS

Stop
singing about blood, you triple jinx, and in peacetime
to boot! You're a dunce and a damned brat!

FIRST BOY

"And when in their advance they had come together
   at close quarters,
they dashed their bucklers together and their shields
   massive in the middle."[100]

TRYGAEUS

Shields? Do stop reminding us of shields!

FIRST BOY

"Then arose together the groans and the cheers of
   warriors."

TRYGAEUS

The groans of warriors? You'll be the one wailing, by
   Dionysus,
if you sing about groans, and groans massive in the
   middle at that!

FIRST BOY

But what should I sing of instead? You tell me the
   subjects that please you.

TRYGAEUS

"Thus did they feast on the flesh of beeves," and this
   sort of thing:
"Their breakfast was laid out before them, and
   whatever was good to eat."

FIRST BOY

"Thus did they feast on the flesh of beeves, and from
   the harness

591

ἔκλυον ἱδρώοντας, ἐπεὶ πολέμου ἐκόρεσθεν."

ΤΡΤΓΑΙΟΣ
εἶέν· ἐκόρεσθεν τοῦ πολέμου κᾆτ' ἤσθιον.
1285 ταῦτ' ᾆδε, ταῦθ', ὡς ἤσθιον κεκορημένοι.

ΠΑΙΔΙΟΝ Α΄
θωρήσσοντ' ἄρ' ἔπειτα πεπαυμένοι—

ΤΡΤΓΑΙΟΣ
                     ἄσμενοι, οἶμαι.

ΠΑΙΔΙΟΝ Α΄
πύργων δ' ἐξεχέοντο, βοὴ δ' ἄσβεστος ὀρώρει.

ΤΡΤΓΑΙΟΣ
κάκιστ' ἀπόλοιο, παιδάριον, αὐταῖς μάχαις·
οὐδὲν γὰρ ᾄδεις πλὴν πολέμους. τοῦ καί ποτ' εἶ;

ΠΑΙΔΙΟΝ Α΄
1290 ἐγώ;

ΤΡΤΓΑΙΟΣ
   σὺ μέντοι νὴ Δί'.

ΠΑΙΔΙΟΝ Α΄
            υἱὸς Λαμάχου.

ΤΡΤΓΑΙΟΣ
αἰβοῖ.
ἦ γὰρ ἐγὼ θαύμαζον ἀκούων, εἰ σὺ μὴ εἴης
ἀνδρὸς βουλομάχου καὶ κλαυσιμάχου τινὸς υἱός.

---

101 Adapted from the *Contest of Homer and Hesiod*, 107-8.

loosed the reeking necks of their steeds, since they
were sated with warfare." [101]

TRYGAEUS

Good: they were sated with warfare, then they fell to
eating.
That's what to sing, right there, that they fell to
eating when sated!

FIRST BOY

"And when they had finished, they started to pour—"

TRYGAEUS

Happily, I wager!

FIRST BOY

"—forth from the battlements, and a clamor
unquenchable rose up."

TRYGAEUS

Damn and blast you, little boy, and your battles too! You
sing of nothing but wars. Whose son are you, anyway?

FIRST BOY

Me?

TRYGAEUS

Of course you!

FIRST BOY

I'm the son of Lamachus.

TRYGAEUS

Yuk!
Truly amazed had I been as I listened, were you not
the scion
of some champion spoiling for battles and tearful
thereafter.

ἄπερρε καὶ τοῖς λογχοφόροισιν ᾆδ' ἰών.

1295 ποῦ μοι τὸ τοῦ Κλεωνύμου 'στὶ παιδίον;
ᾆσον πρὶν εἰσιέναι τι· σὺ γὰρ εὖ οἶδ' ὅτι
οὐ πράγματ' ᾄσει· σώφρονος γὰρ εἶ πατρός.

ΠΑΙΔΙΟΝ Β΄

ἀσπίδι μὲν Σαΐων τις ἀγάλλεται, ἣν παρὰ θάμνῳ
ἔντος ἀμώμητον κάλλιπον οὐκ ἐθέλων—

ΤΡΥΓΑΙΟΣ

1300 εἰπέ μοι, ὦ πόσθων, εἰς τὸν σαυτοῦ πατέρ' ᾄδεις;

ΠΑΙΔΙΟΝ Β΄

ψυχὴν δ' ἐξεσάωσα—

ΤΡΥΓΑΙΟΣ

κατῄσχυνας δὲ τοκῆας.

ἀλλ' εἰσίωμεν· εὖ γὰρ οἶδ' ἐγὼ σαφῶς
ὅτι ταῦθ' ὅσ' ᾖσας ἄρτι περὶ τῆς ἀσπίδος
1304 οὐ μὴ 'πιλάθῃ ποτ' ὢν ἐκείνου τοῦ πατρός.

(στρ) ὑμῶν τὸ λοιπὸν ἔργον ἤδη 'νταῦθα τῶν μενόντων
φλᾶν ταῦτα πάντα καὶ σποδεῖν, καὶ μὴ κενὰς
παρέλκειν
ἀλλ' ἀνδρικῶς ἐμβάλλετε
καὶ σμώχετ' ἀμφοῖν τοῖν γνάθοιν· οὐδὲν γάρ, ὦ
πόνηροι,
1310 λευκῶν ὀδόντων ἔργον ἔστ', ἢν μή τι καὶ μασῶνται.

---

[102] Archilochus fr. 5.

Get lost, go sing for the spearsmen.

FIRST BOY goes off.

Now where's the son of Cleonymus got to? (*Second Boy comes forward*) Sing me something before you go in. I'm sure that *you* won't sing about conflicts; you've got a prudent father.

SECOND BOY
"Some Saean now vaunts my shield, a splendid
    weapon
that all unwilling I abandoned by a bush—"[102]

TRYGAEUS
Tell me, little weenie, are you singing about your own
    father?

SECOND BOY
"—but I saved my life—"

TRYGAEUS
                    and disgraced your begetters!
But let's go in. I'm quite sure that you'll never forget what
you were singing about that shield, with a father like yours!

For you who are staying outside here it now remains
to munch and crunch all this food, and not drag your
    oars.
Yes, tuck into it like real men,
and mash it with both jaws, for there's no point, you
    rascals,
in having white teeth, if they don't do any real
    chewing.

ARISTOPHANES

ΚΟΡΤΦΑΙΟΣ

(ἀντ) ἡμῖν μελήσει ταῦτά γ᾽· εὖ ποιεῖς δὲ καὶ σὺ φράζων.
ἀλλ᾽, ὦ πρὸ τοῦ πεινῶντες, ἐμβάλλεσθε τῶν λαγῴων·
ὡς οὐχὶ πᾶσαν ἡμέραν
πλακοῦσιν ἔστιν ἐντυχεῖν πλανωμένοις ἐρήμοις.

1315 πρὸς ταῦτα βρύκετ᾽ ἢ τάχ᾽ ὑμῖν φημι μεταμελήσειν.

ΤΡΥΓΑΙΟΣ

εὐφημεῖν χρὴ καὶ τὴν νύμφην ἔξω τινὰ δεῦρο κομί-
ζειν
δᾷδάς τε φέρειν, καὶ πάντα λεὼν συγχαίρειν
κἀπικελεύειν.
καὶ τὰ σκεύη πάλιν εἰς τὸν ἀγρὸν νυνὶ χρὴ πάντα
κομίζειν
ὀρχησαμένους καὶ σπείσαντας καὶ Ὑπέρβολον
ἐξελάσαντας,

1320 κἀπευξαμένους τοῖσι θεοῖσιν
διδόναι πλοῦτον τοῖς Ἕλλησιν,
κριθάς τε ποιεῖν ἡμᾶς πολλὰς
πάντας ὁμοίως οἶνόν τε πολύν,
συκά τε τρώγειν,

1325 τάς τε γυναῖκας τίκτειν ἡμῖν,
καὶ τἀγαθὰ πάνθ᾽ ὅσ᾽ ἀπωλέσαμεν
συλλέξασθαι πάλιν ἐξ ἀρχῆς,
λῆξαί τ᾽ αἴθωνα σίδηρον.

1317 κἀπικελεύειν] κἀπιχορεύειν V²

596

PEACE

CHORUS LEADER

That we'll take care of, and thank you too for
    reminding us.

TRYGAEUS and SECOND BOY go inside.

You've all been hungry hitherto, so now tuck into the
    rabbit,
for it's not every day
that you run into cakes wandering about unclaimed!
So start gobbling it up, or you'll soon be sorry you
    didn't.

TRYGAEUS comes out of the house dressed as a bridegroom.

TRYGAEUS

Let us speak auspiciously, and escort the bride
    outside here,
and fetch torches, and all the people rejoice with us
    and cheer us on,
and move all our equipment back to the country
    right now,
dancing and pouring libations and driving
    Hyperbolus away,
and making prayers to the gods
that they grant prosperity to the Greeks
and help us produce lots of barley,
all of us alike, and lots of wine,
and figs to nibble,
and that our wives bear us children,
and together we recover all that we lost
just as it was to begin with,
and have done with the shining blade.

δεῦρ᾽, ὦ γύναι, εἰς ἀγρόν,
1330   χὤπως μετ᾽ ἐμοῦ καλὴ
καλῶς κατακείσει.

ΧΟΡΟΣ

Ὑμήν, Ὑμέναι᾽ ὤ.
Ὑμήν, Ὑμέναι᾽ ὤ.

ΚΟΡΤΦΑΙΟΣ

ὦ τρισμάκαρ, ὡς δικαί-
ως τἀγαθὰ νῦν ἔχεις.

ΧΟΡΟΣ

1335   Ὑμήν, Ὑμέναι᾽ ὤ.
Ὑμήν, Ὑμέναι᾽, ὤ.

ΚΟΡΤΦΑΙΟΣ

τί δράσομεν αὐτήν;

ΧΟΡΟΣ

τί δράσομεν αὐτήν;

ΚΟΡΤΦΑΙΟΣ

τρυγήσομεν αὐτήν.

ΧΟΡΟΣ

1340   τρυγήσομεν αὐτήν.

ΚΟΡΤΦΑΙΟΣ

ἀλλ᾽ ἀράμενοι φέρω-

PEACE

Cornucopia, dressed as a bride, is escorted from the house.

Come along, wife, to the countryside,[103]
and with me, my beauty,
lie down beautifully.

CHORUS
Hymen, Hymeneus O!
Hymen, Hymeneus O!

CHORUS LEADER
Happy, happy, happy man,
right worthy of your blessings!

CHORUS
Hymen, Hymeneus O!
Hymen, Hymeneus O!

CHORUS LEADER
What shall we do with the bride?

CHORUS
What shall we do with the bride?

CHORUS LEADER
We'll gather her fruit!

CHORUS
We'll gather her fruit!

CHORUS LEADER
Let's those of us up front

[103] The text of the concluding hymeneal song (lines 1329-end)
is uncertainly transmitted, and its structure is variously arranged
by editors.

μεν οἱ προτεταγμένοι
τὸν νυμφίον, ὦνδρες.

ΧΟΡΟΣ

Ὑμήν, Ὑμέναι᾽, ὤ.
1345 Ὑμήν, Ὑμέναι᾽ ὤ.

ΚΟΡΥΦΑΙΟΣ

οἰκήσετε γοῦν καλῶς
οὐ πράγματ᾽ ἔχοντες, ἀλ-
λὰ συκολογοῦντες.

ΧΟΡΟΣ

Ὑμήν, Ὑμέναι᾽, ὤ.
1350 Ὑμήν, Ὑμέναι᾽, ὤ.

ΚΟΡΥΦΑΙΟΣ

τοῦ μὲν μέγα καὶ παχύ,
τῆς δ᾽ ἡδὺ τὸ σῦκον.

ΤΡΥΓΑΙΟΣ

φήσεις γ᾽ ὅταν ἐσθίῃς
οἶνόν τε πίῃς πολύν.

ΧΟΡΟΣ

1355 Ὑμήν, Ὑμέναι᾽, ὤ.
Ὑμήν, Ὑμέναι᾽, ὤ.

ΤΡΥΓΑΙΟΣ

ὦ χαίρετε χαίρετ᾽ ἄν-
δρες· κἂν ξυνέπησθέ μοι,
πλακοῦντας ἔδεσθε.

hoist the bridegroom aloft
and carry him, lads!

CHORUS

Hymen, Hymeneus O!
Hymen, Hymeneus O!

CHORUS LEADER

You will live happily,
and free of troubles
gather in your figs.

CHORUS

Hymen, Hymeneus O!
Hymen, Hymeneus O!

CHORUS LEADER

His fig is big and ripe,
hers is nice and sweet!

TRYGAEUS

So you'll say when you're feasting
and drinking plenty of wine!

CHORUS

Hymen, Hymeneus O!
Hymen, Hymeneus O!

TRYGAEUS

Good luck and fare ye well,
gentlemen; and if you follow me,
you'll all have cakes to eat!

The CHORUS *follows* TRYGAEUS *and Cornucopia off.*

INDEX OF PERSONAL NAMES

Reference is to play and line number. Italicized references are footnoted in the text.

INDEX

Composed in ZephGreek and ZephText by
Technologies 'N Typography, Merrimac, Massachusetts.
Printed in Great Britain by St Edmundsbury Press Ltd,
Bury St Edmunds, Suffolk, on acid-free paper.
Bound by Hunter & Foulis Ltd, Edinburgh, Scotland.